K.O.!

GOLD FOR GLORY

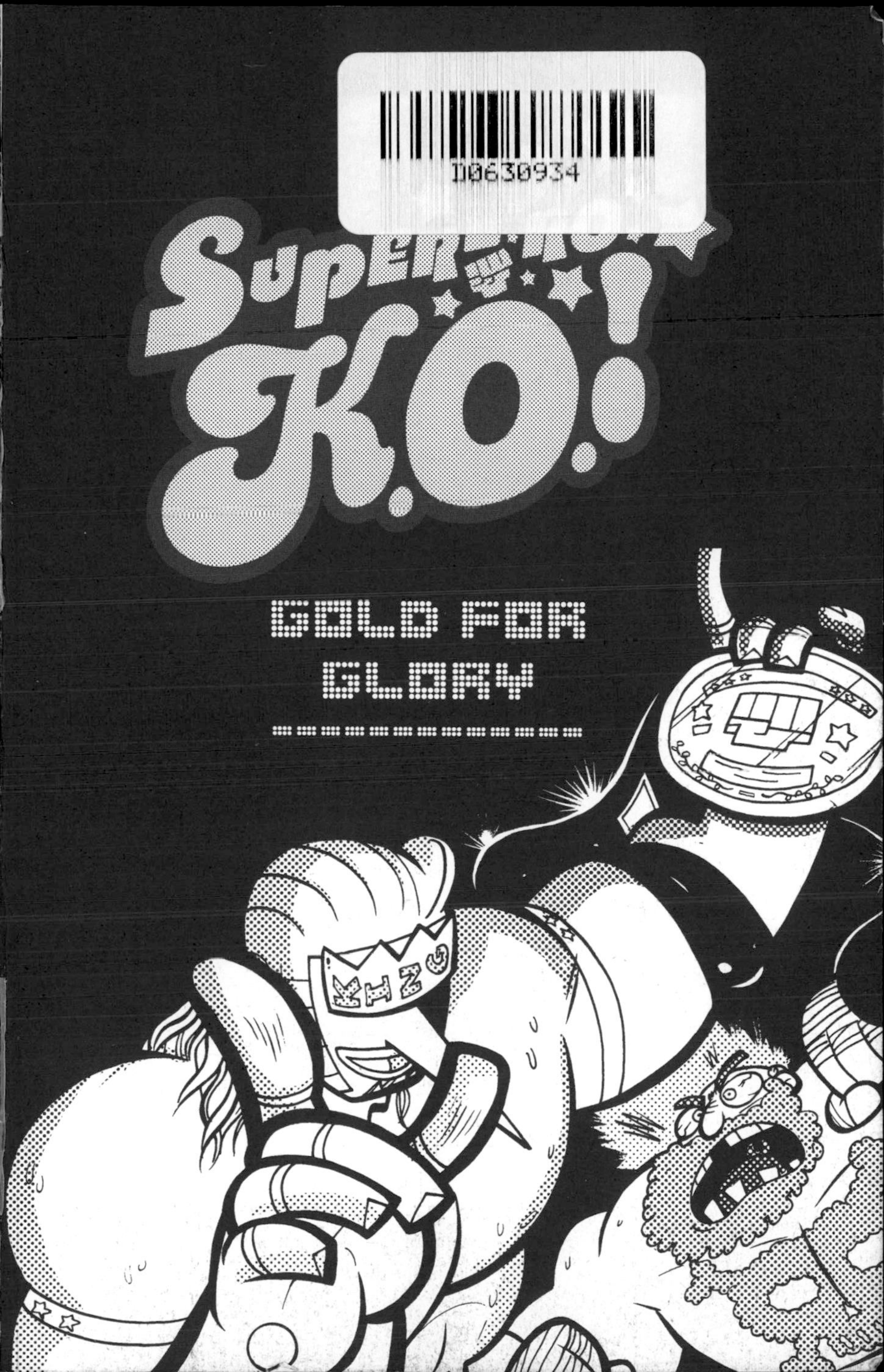

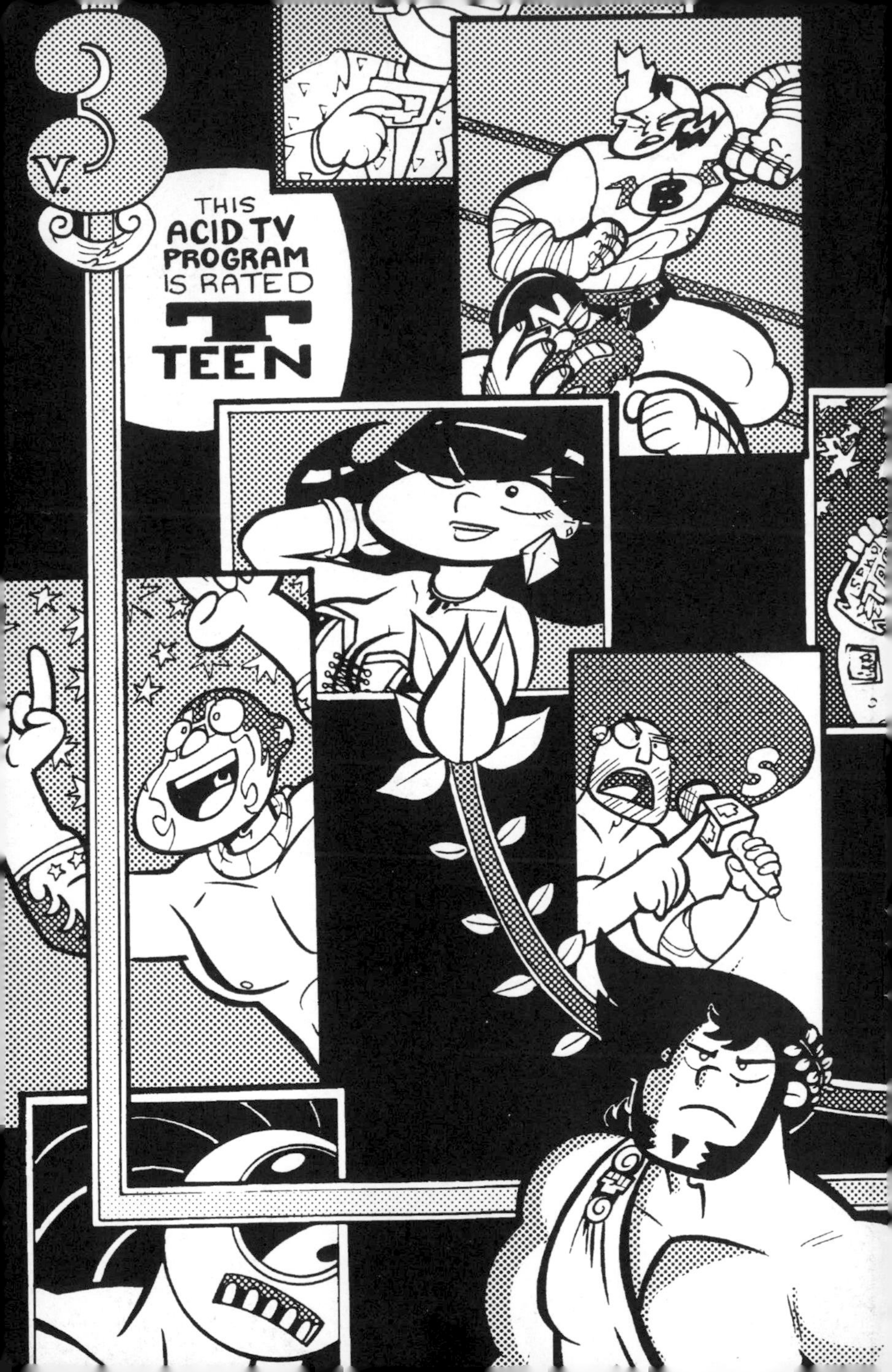
v. 3
THIS ACID TV PROGRAM IS RATED
T
TEEN

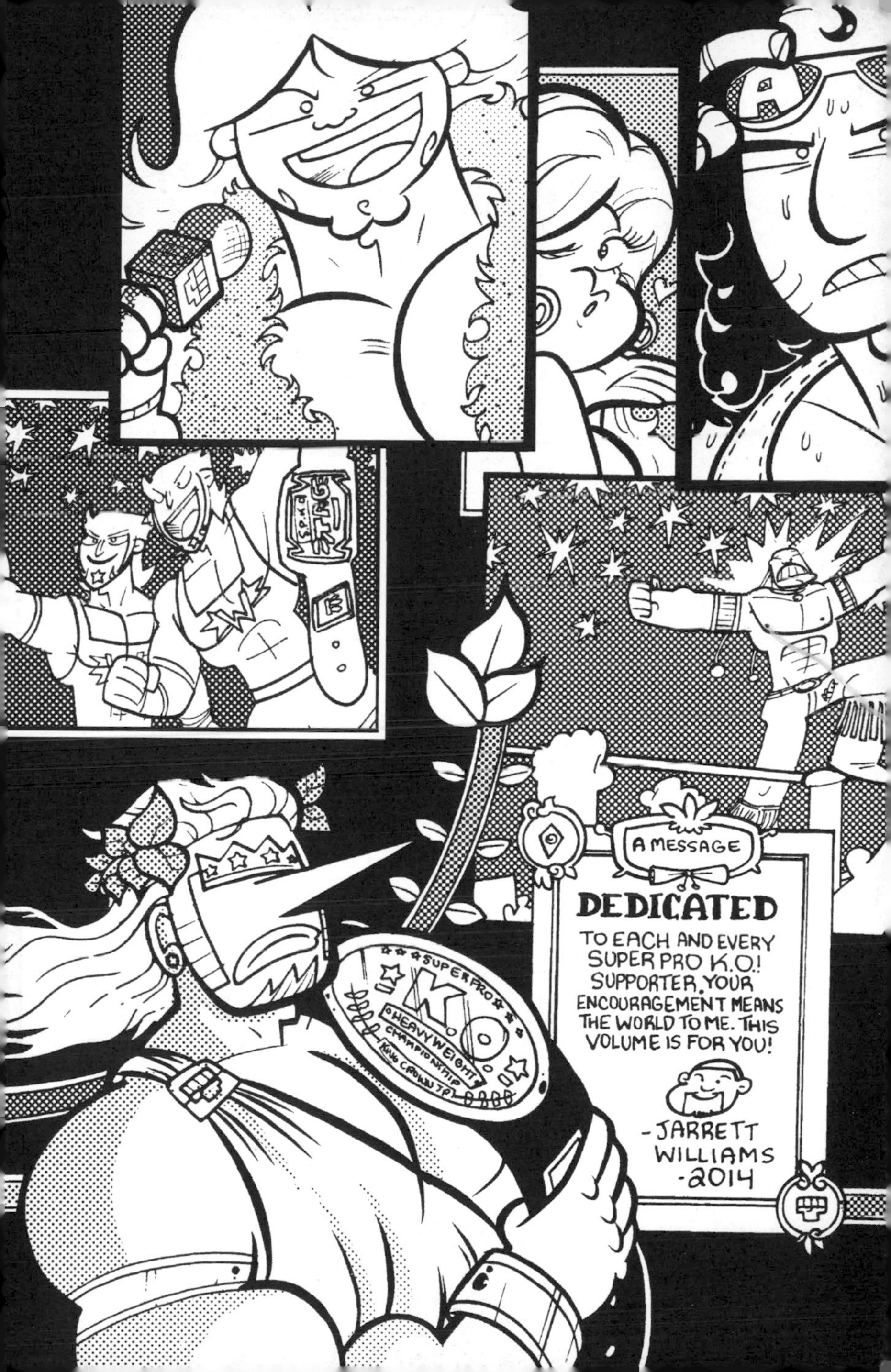
A MESSAGE
DEDICATED
TO EACH AND EVERY SUPER PRO K.O.! SUPPORTER. YOUR ENCOURAGEMENT MEANS THE WORLD TO ME. THIS VOLUME IS FOR YOU!
-JARRETT WILLIAMS -2014
SUPER PRO K.O. HEAVYWEIGHT CHAMPIONSHIP

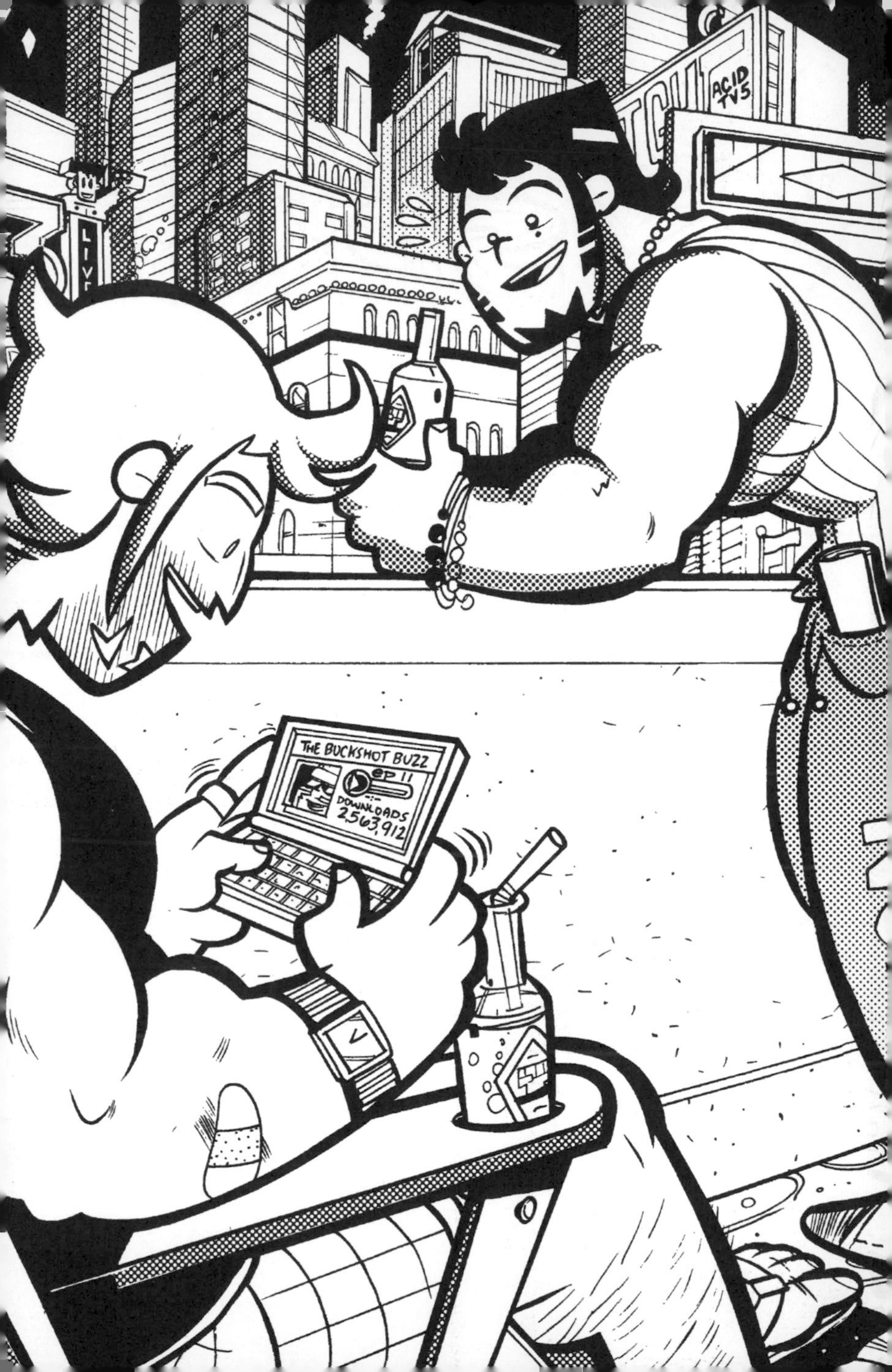
ACID TV5
THE BUCKSHOT BUZZ
EP 11
DOWNLOADS
2,563,912

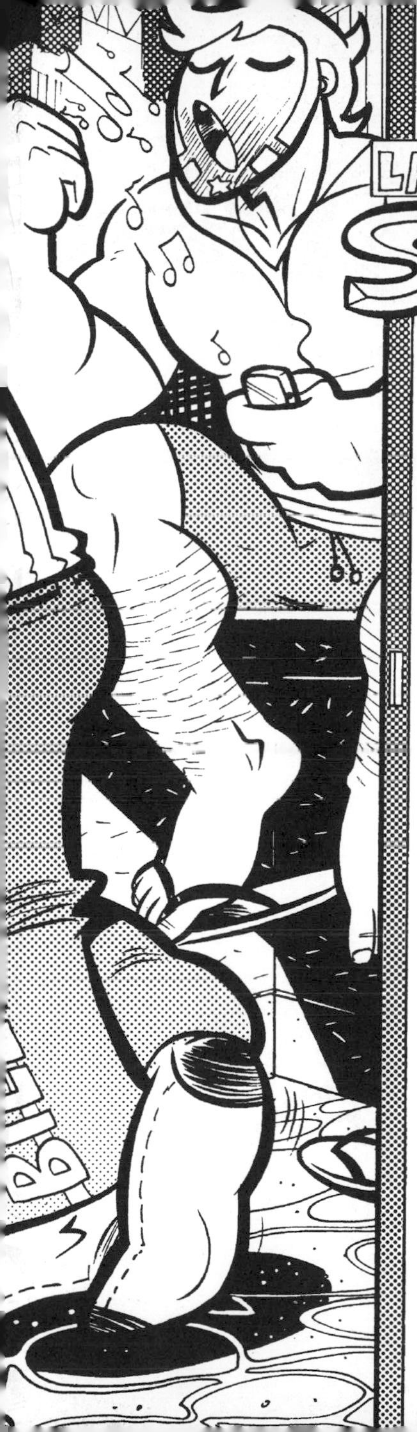

LAST TIME in S.P.K.O!

Super Pro K.O. is the world's greatest pro-wrestling organization, home of the rowdiest and craziest high-flying athletes, all vying for a shot at the S.P.K.O. Heavyweight Championship!

S.P.K.O.'s current champion is **King Crown Jr.**, who is as popular as he is despised for his heel antics inside and outside the ring. Hotshot rookie **Joe Somiano** is the league's rising star, riding high on some great matches in his short career, but he's got a long road ahead of him before he becomes a serious contender for the title belt!

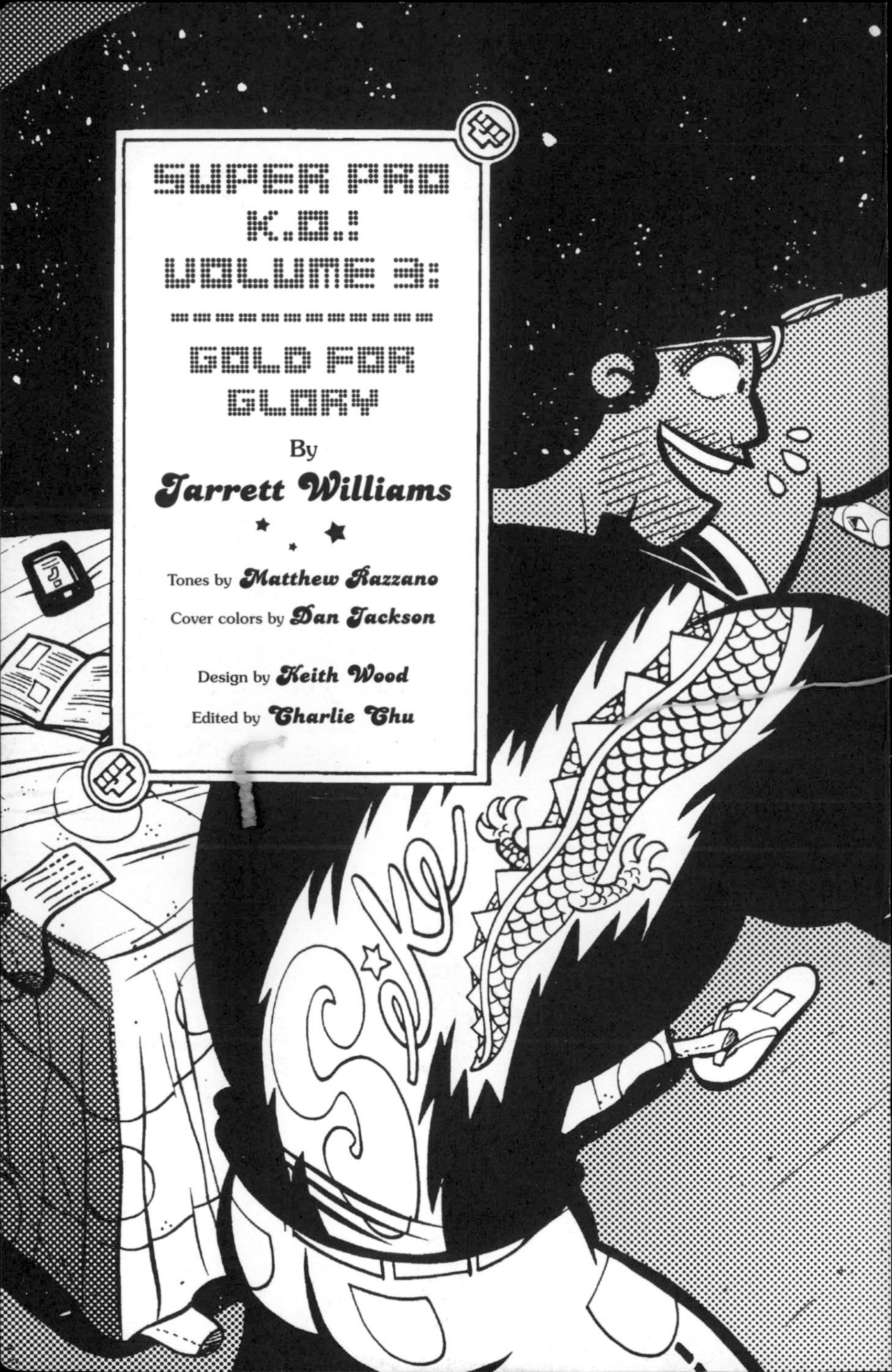

SUPER PRO K.O.! VOLUME 3: GOLD FOR GLORY

By

Jarrett Williams

Tones by *Matthew Razzano*

Cover colors by *Dan Jackson*

Design by *Keith Wood*

Edited by *Charlie Chu*

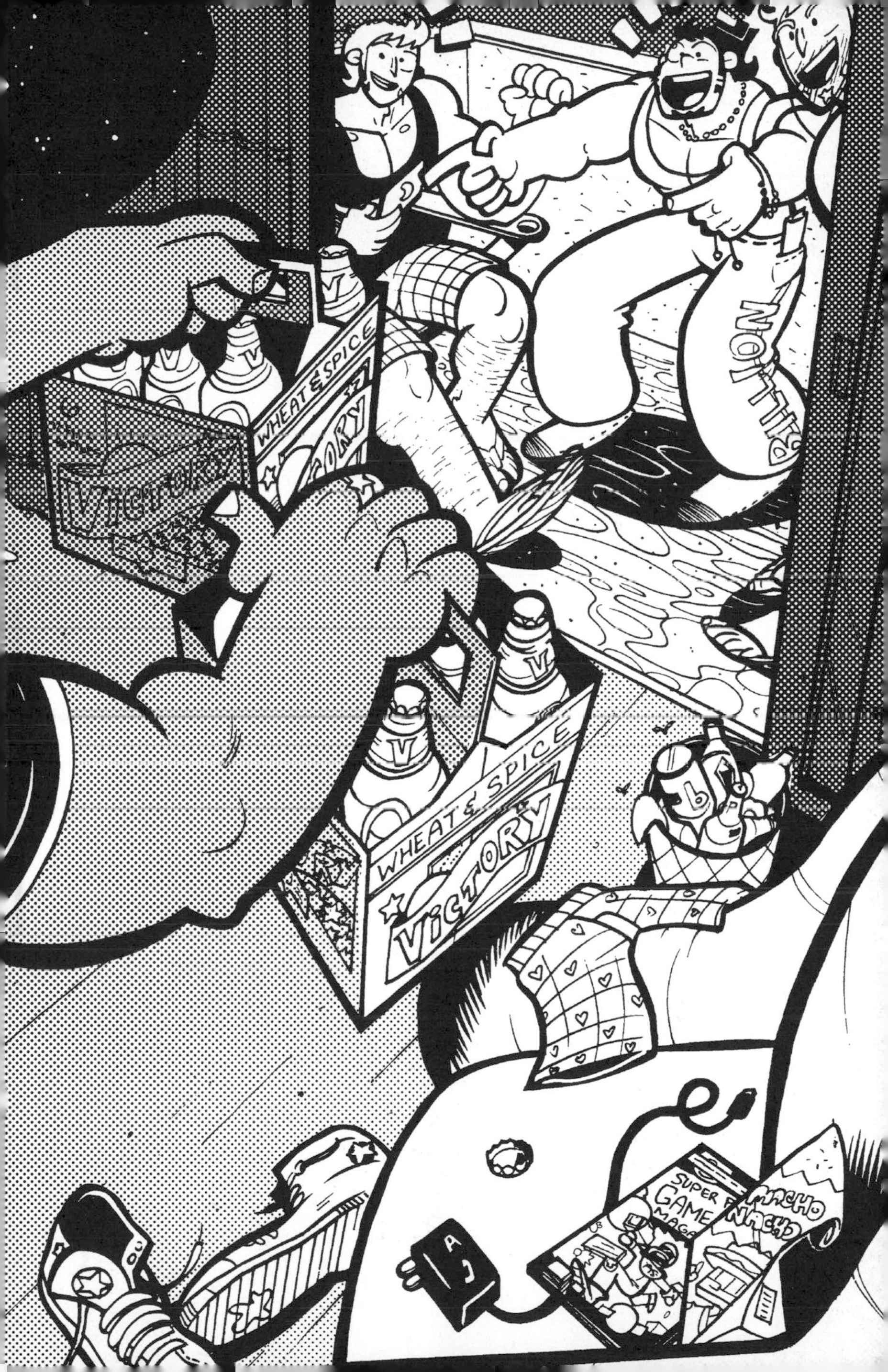
WHEAT & SPICE
VICTORY

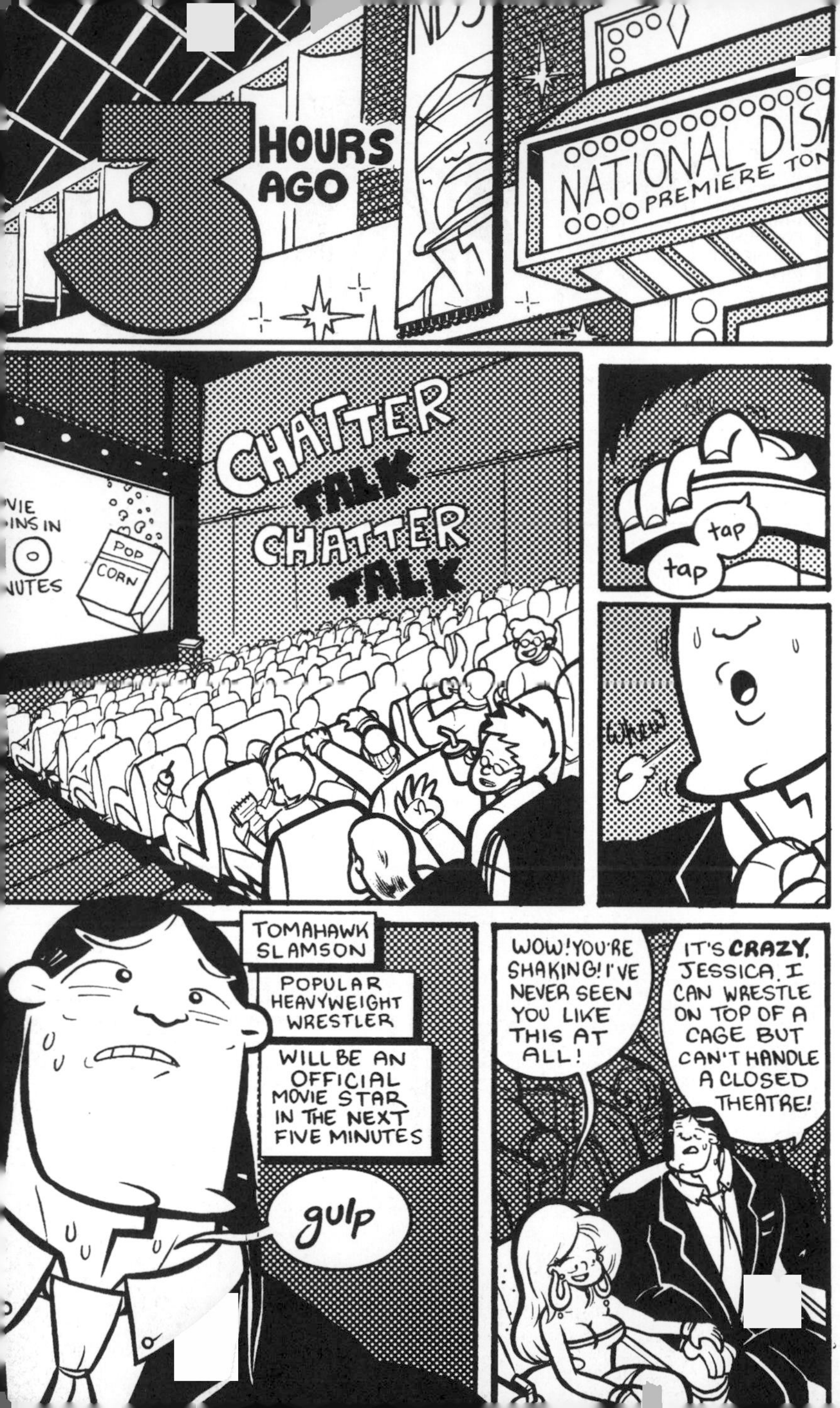

3 HOURS AGO
NATIONAL DIS
PREMIERE TON
CHATTER TALK CHATTER TALK
VIE INS IN 0 NUTES
POP CORN
tap tap
TOMAHAWK SLAMSON
POPULAR HEAVYWEIGHT WRESTLER
WILL BE AN OFFICIAL MOVIE STAR IN THE NEXT FIVE MINUTES
gulp
WOW! YOU'RE SHAKING! I'VE NEVER SEEN YOU LIKE THIS AT ALL!
IT'S CRAZY, JESSICA. I CAN WRESTLE ON TOP OF A CAGE BUT CAN'T HANDLE A CLOSED THEATRE!

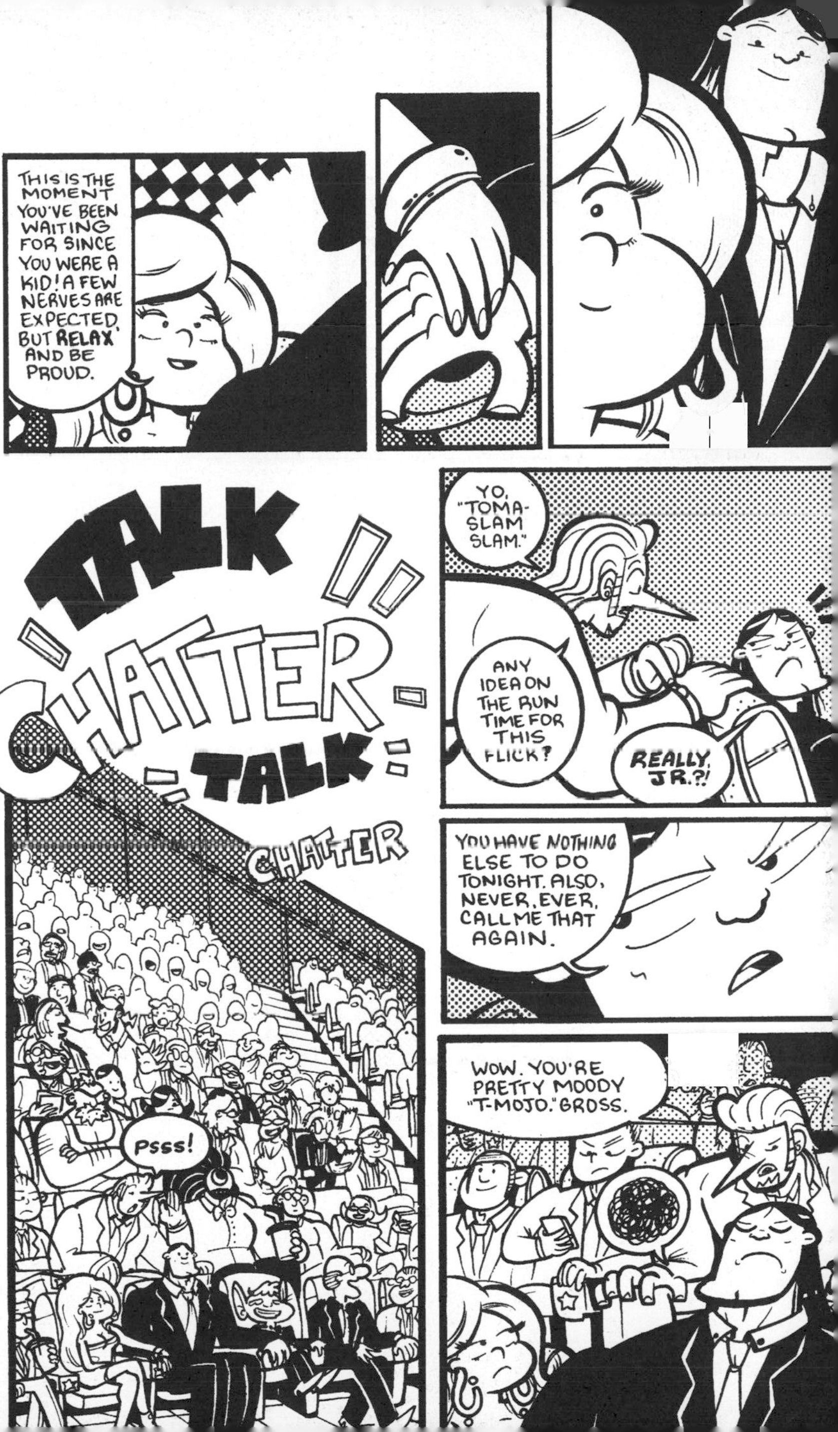
THIS IS THE MOMENT YOU'VE BEEN WAITING FOR SINCE YOU WERE A KID! A FEW NERVES ARE EXPECTED, BUT **RELAX** AND BE PROUD.
TALK
CHATTER
TALK
CHATTER
Psss!
YO, "TOMA-SLAM SLAM."
ANY IDEA ON THE RUN TIME FOR THIS FLICK?
REALLY, JR.?!
YOU HAVE NOTHING ELSE TO DO TONIGHT. ALSO, NEVER, EVER, CALL ME THAT AGAIN.
WOW. YOU'RE PRETTY MOODY "T-MOJO." GROSS.

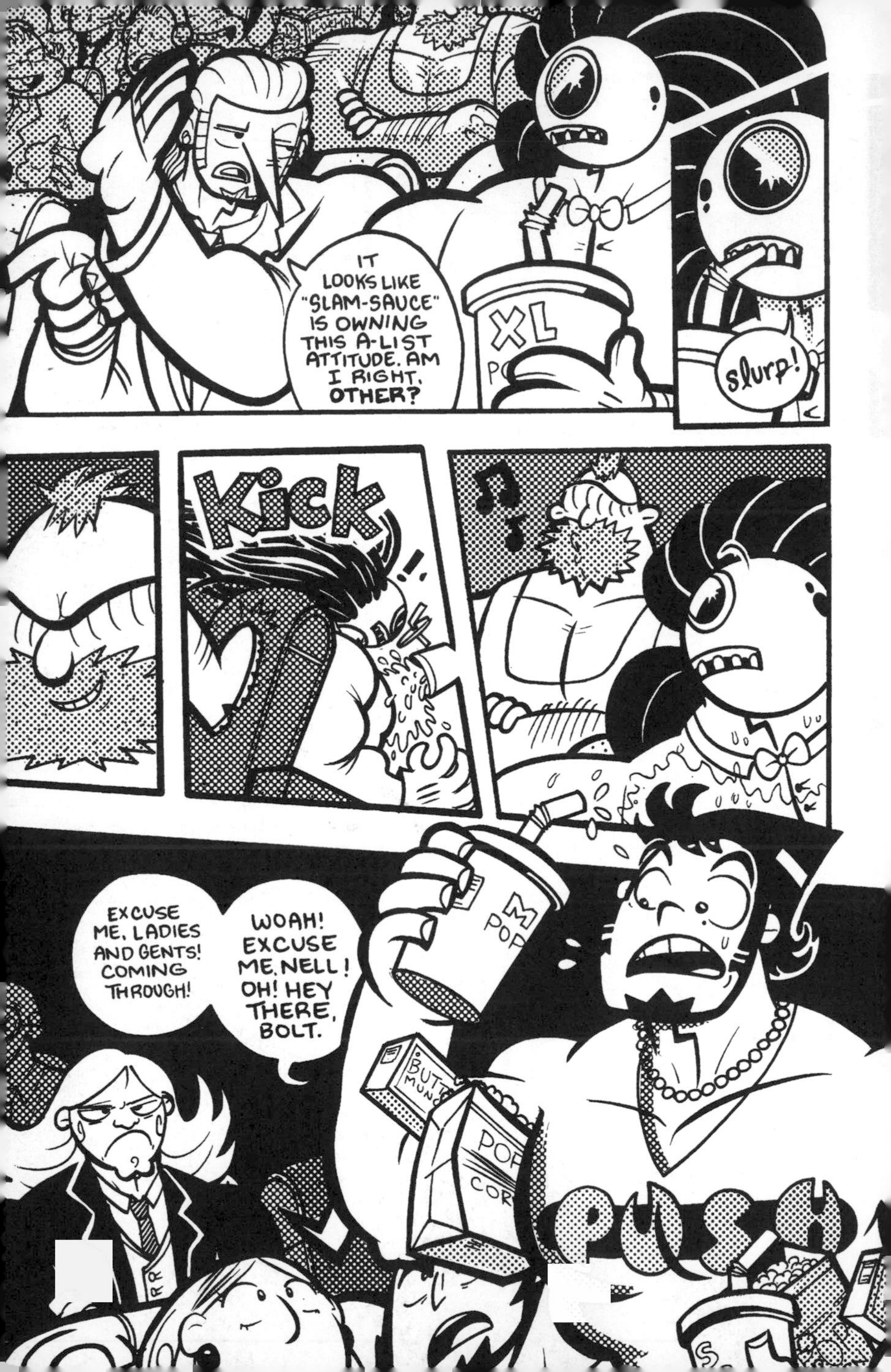
IT LOOKS LIKE "SLAM-SAUCE" IS OWNING THIS A-LIST ATTITUDE. AM I RIGHT, OTHER?
XL
slurp!
KICK
!!
EXCUSE ME, LADIES AND GENTS! COMING THROUGH!
WOAH! EXCUSE ME, NELL! OH! HEY THERE, BOLT.
M POP
POP COR
PUSH

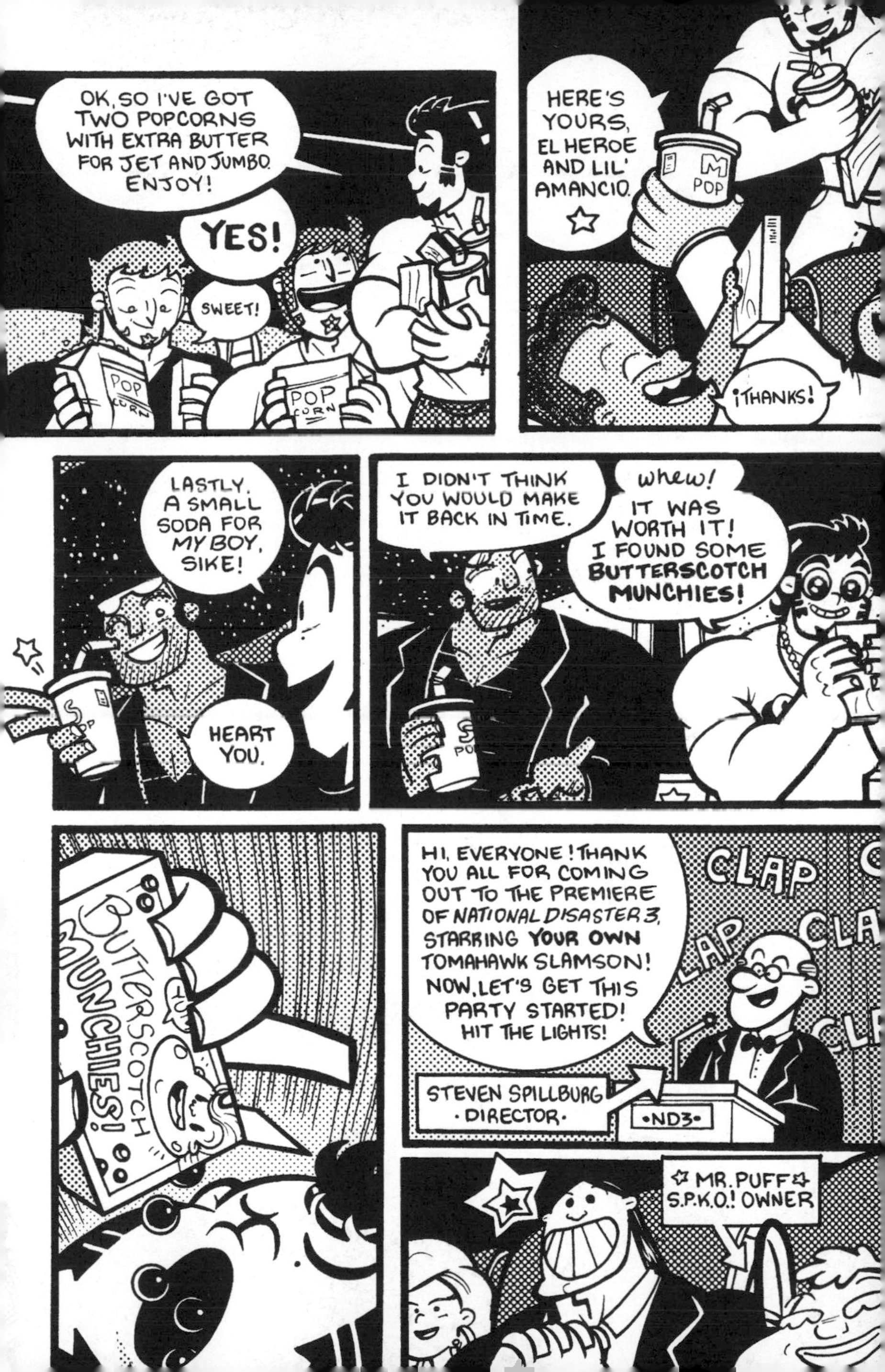

OK, SO I'VE GOT TWO POPCORNS WITH EXTRA BUTTER FOR JET AND JUMBO. ENJOY!
YES!
SWEET!
POP CORN
POP CORN
HERE'S YOURS, EL HEROE AND LIL' AMANCIO.
M POP
¡THANKS!
LASTLY, A SMALL SODA FOR MY BOY, SIKE!
HEART YOU.
I DIDN'T THINK YOU WOULD MAKE IT BACK IN TIME.
whew!
IT WAS WORTH IT! I FOUND SOME BUTTERSCOTCH MUNCHIES!
BUTTERSCOTCH MUNCHIES!
HI, EVERYONE! THANK YOU ALL FOR COMING OUT TO THE PREMIERE OF NATIONAL DISASTER 3, STARRING YOUR OWN TOMAHAWK SLAMSON! NOW, LET'S GET THIS PARTY STARTED! HIT THE LIGHTS!
CLAP
CLAP
CLAP
STEVEN SPILLBURG ·DIRECTOR·
•ND3•
MR. PUFF S.P.K.O.! OWNER

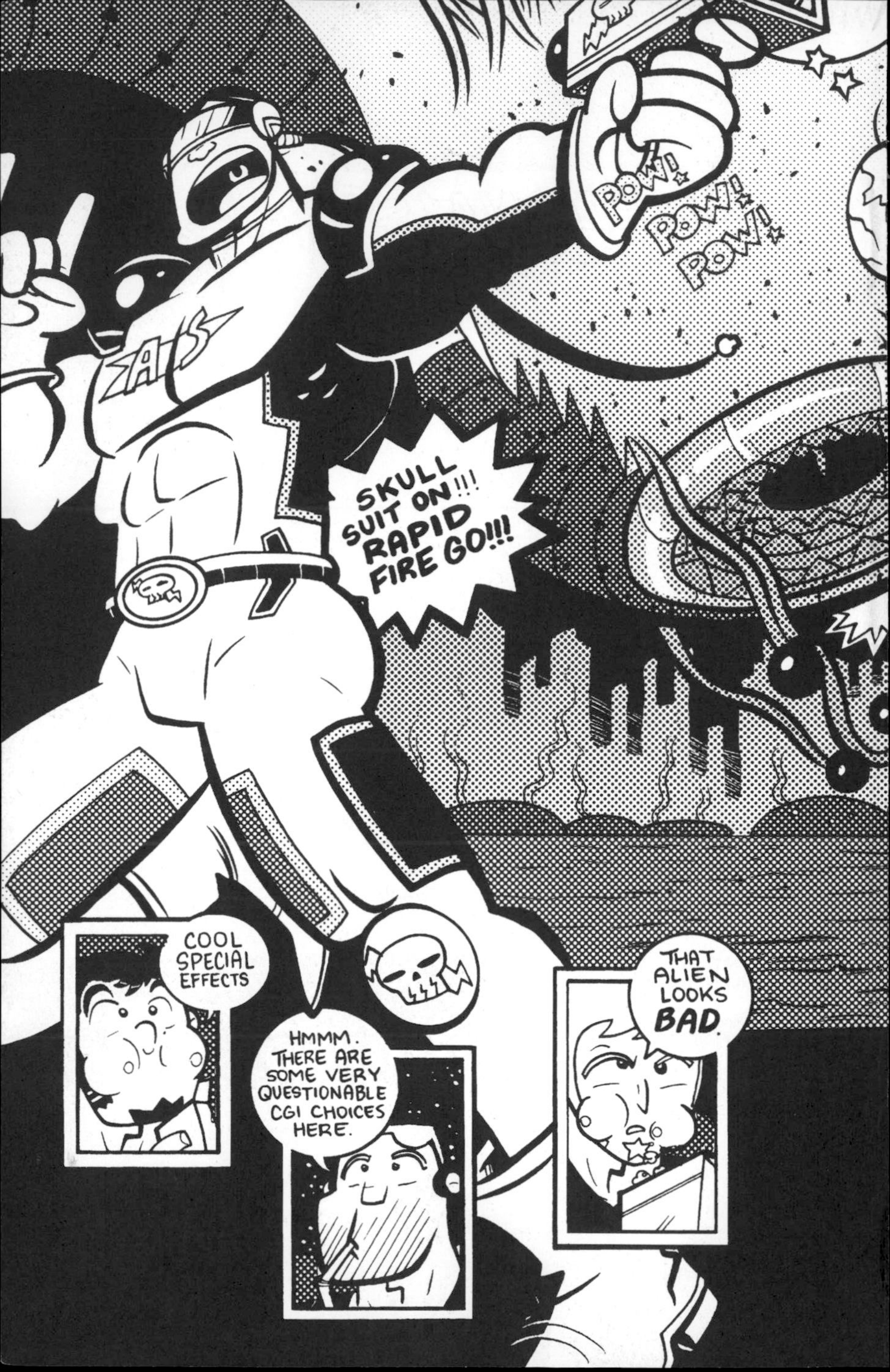
POW! POW! POW!
SKULL SUIT ON!!! RAPID FIRE GO!!!
COOL SPECIAL EFFECTS
HMMM. THERE ARE SOME VERY QUESTIONABLE CGI CHOICES HERE.
THAT ALIEN LOOKS **BAD**.

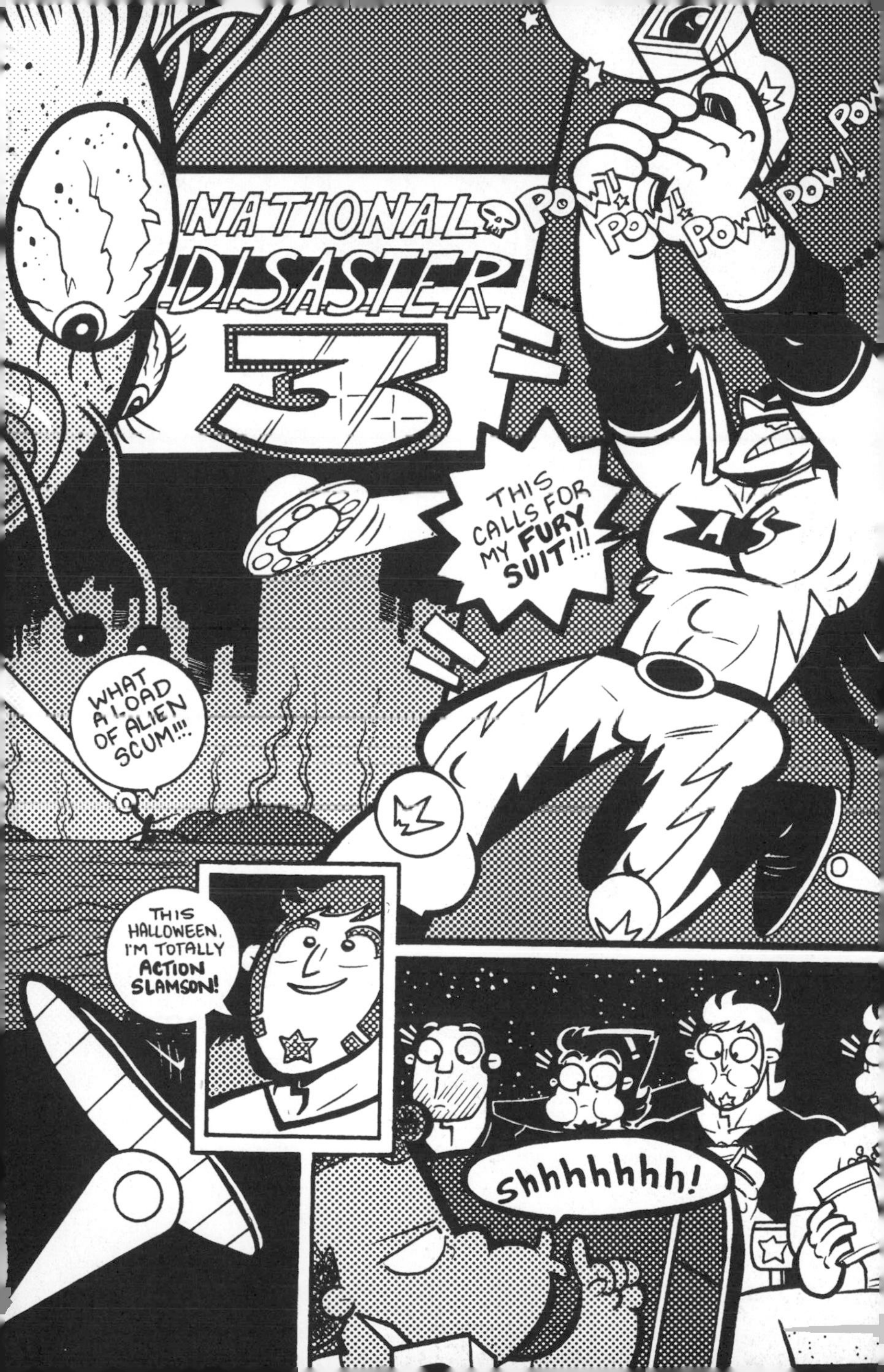

NATIONAL DISASTER 3
POW! POW! POW! POW! POW! POW!
THIS CALLS FOR MY FURY SUIT!!!
WHAT A LOAD OF ALIEN SCUM!!!
THIS HALLOWEEN, I'M TOTALLY ACTION SLAMSON!
shhhhhhh!

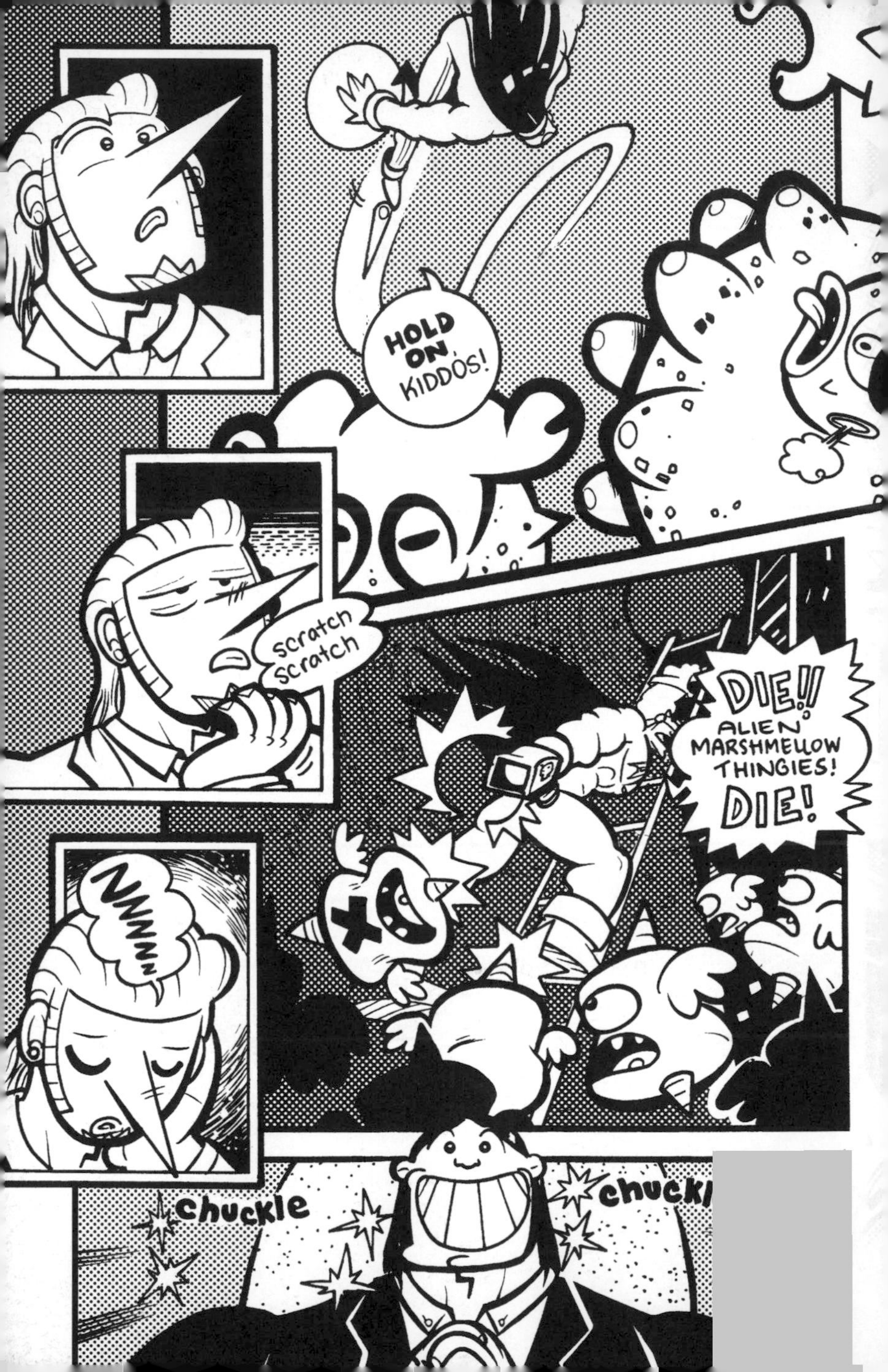
HOLD ON, KIDDOS!
scratch scratch
DIE!! ALIEN MARSHMELLOW THINGIES! DIE!
NNNNN
chuckle
chuckl

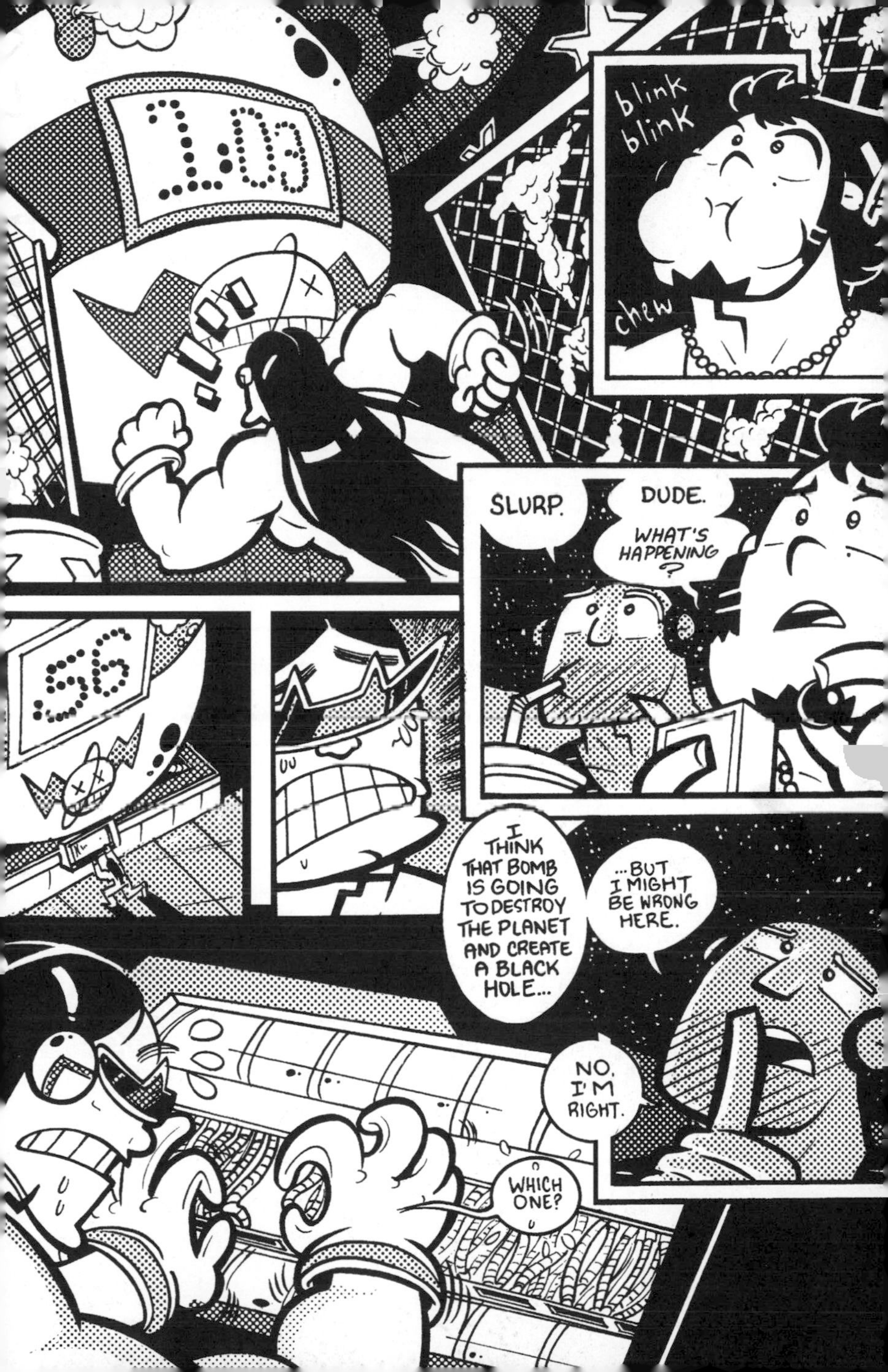
1:03
blink blink
chew
SLURP.
DUDE.
WHAT'S HAPPENING?
.56
I THINK THAT BOMB IS GOING TO DESTROY THE PLANET AND CREATE A BLACK HOLE...
...BUT I MIGHT BE WRONG HERE.
NO, I'M RIGHT.
WHICH ONE?

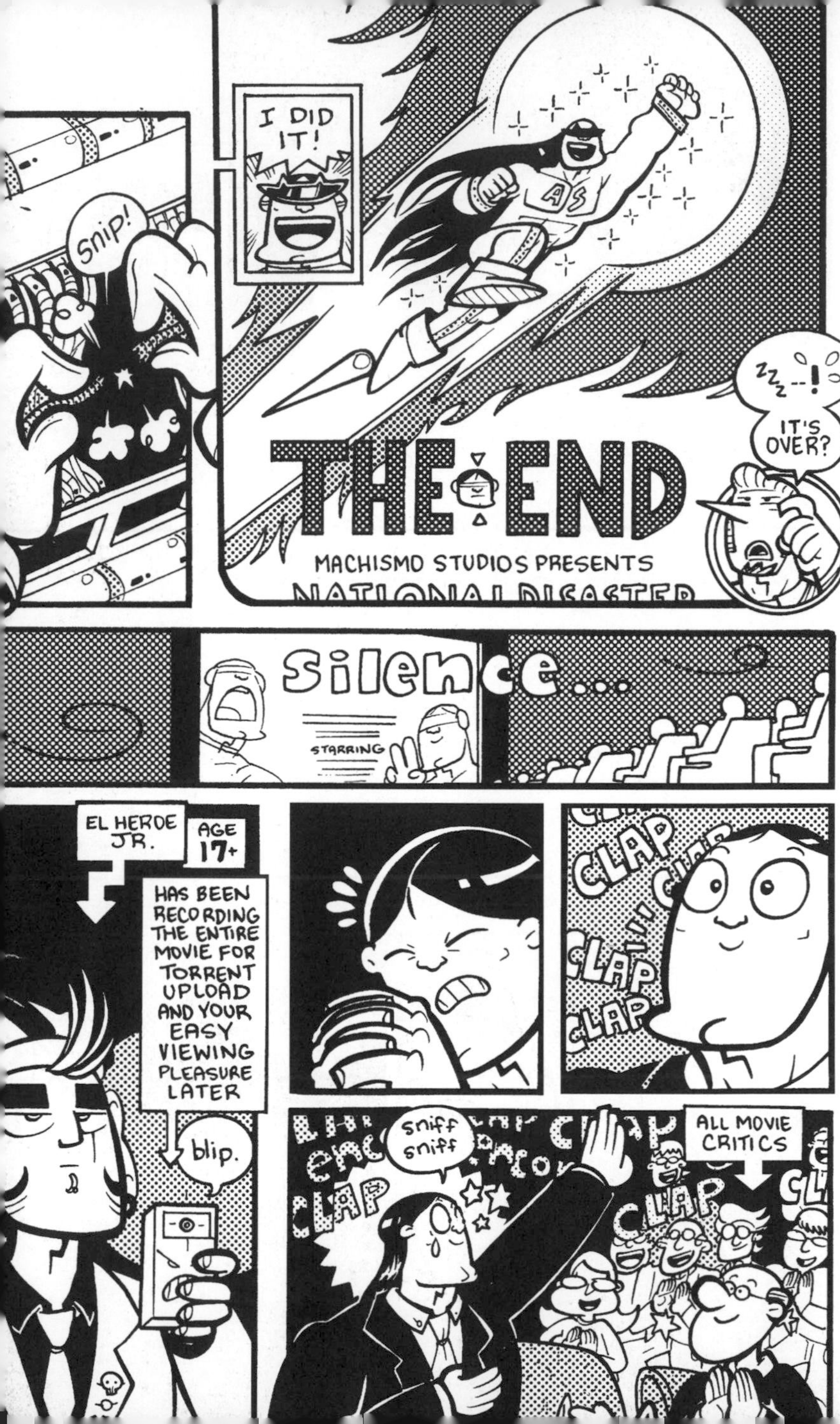
Snip!
I DID IT!
THE END
MACHISMO STUDIOS PRESENTS
zzz--!
IT'S OVER?
silence...
STARRING
EL HEROE JR.
AGE 17+
HAS BEEN RECORDING THE ENTIRE MOVIE FOR TORRENT UPLOAD AND YOUR EASY VIEWING PLEASURE LATER
blip.
CLAP
CLAP
CLAP
CLAP
sniff sniff
CLAP
ALL MOVIE CRITICS
CLAP

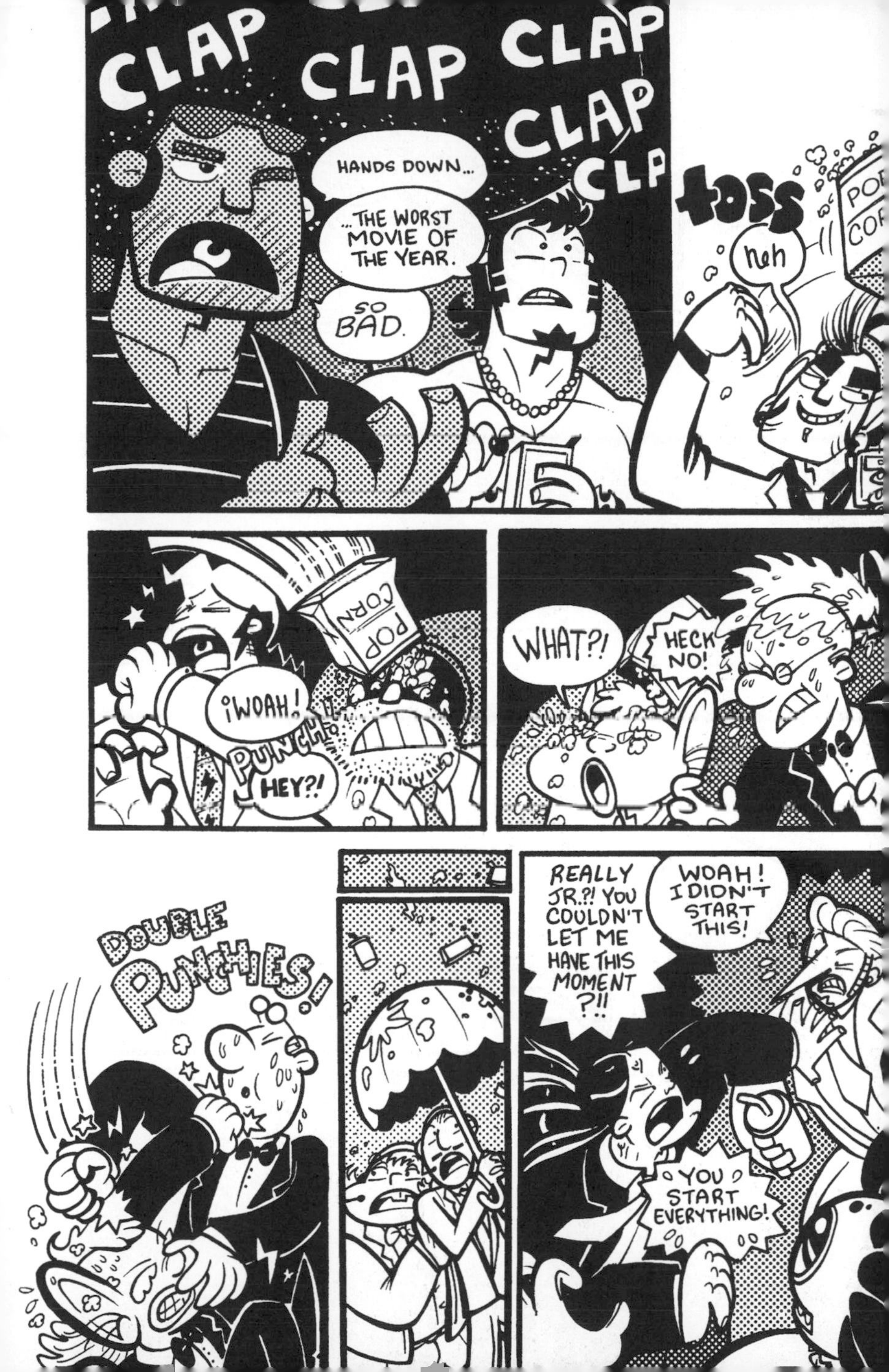
CLAP
CLAP
CLAP
CLAP
CLP
HANDS DOWN...
...THE WORST MOVIE OF THE YEAR.
SO BAD.
TOSS
heh
POP COR
POP CORN
¡WOAH!
PUNCH
HEY?!
WHAT?!
HECK NO!
DOUBLE PUNCHES!
REALLY JR.?! YOU COULDN'T LET ME HAVE THIS MOMENT ?!!
WOAH! I DIDN'T START THIS!
YOU START EVERYTHING!

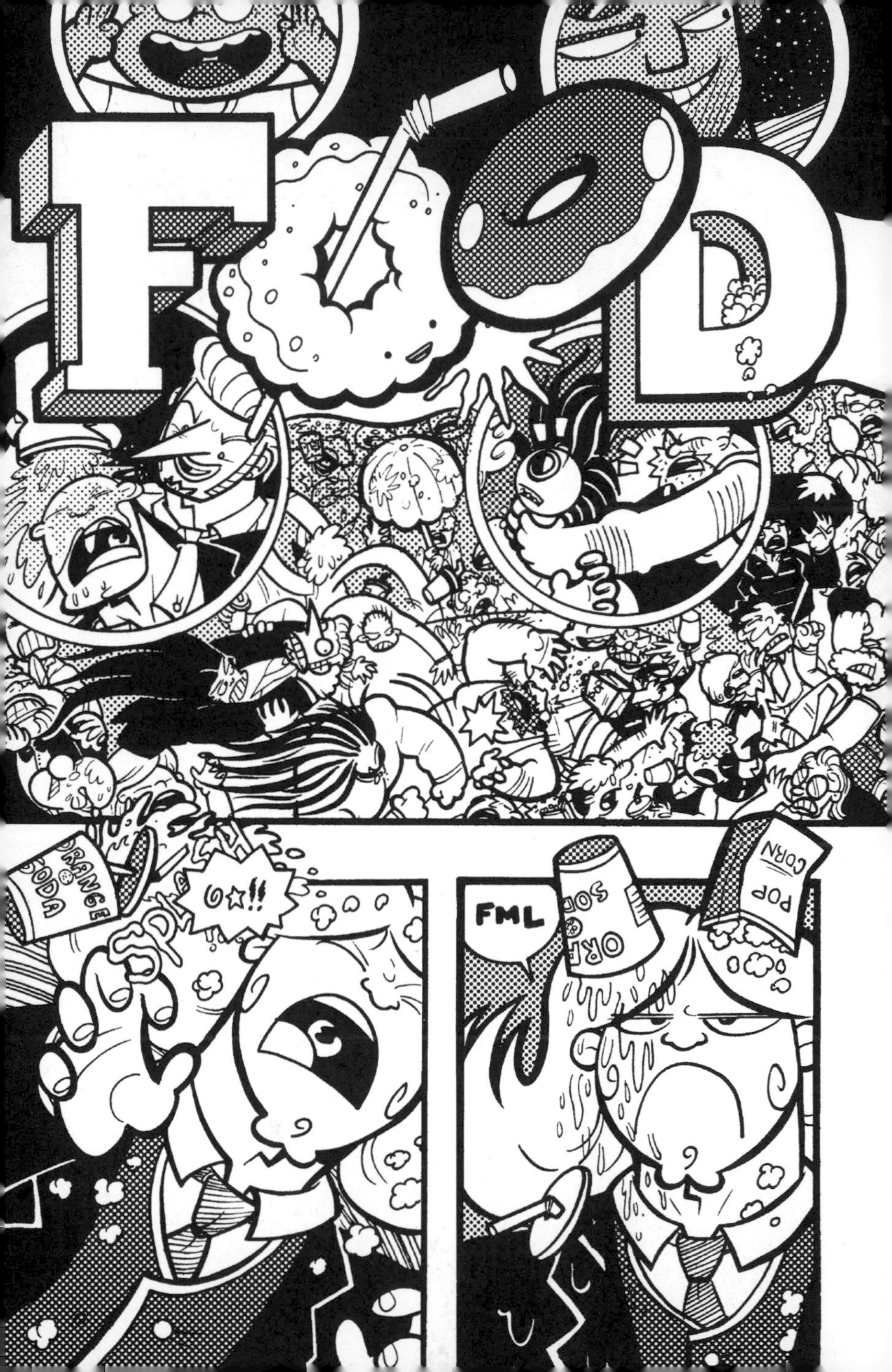
ORANGE SODA
FML
POP CORN

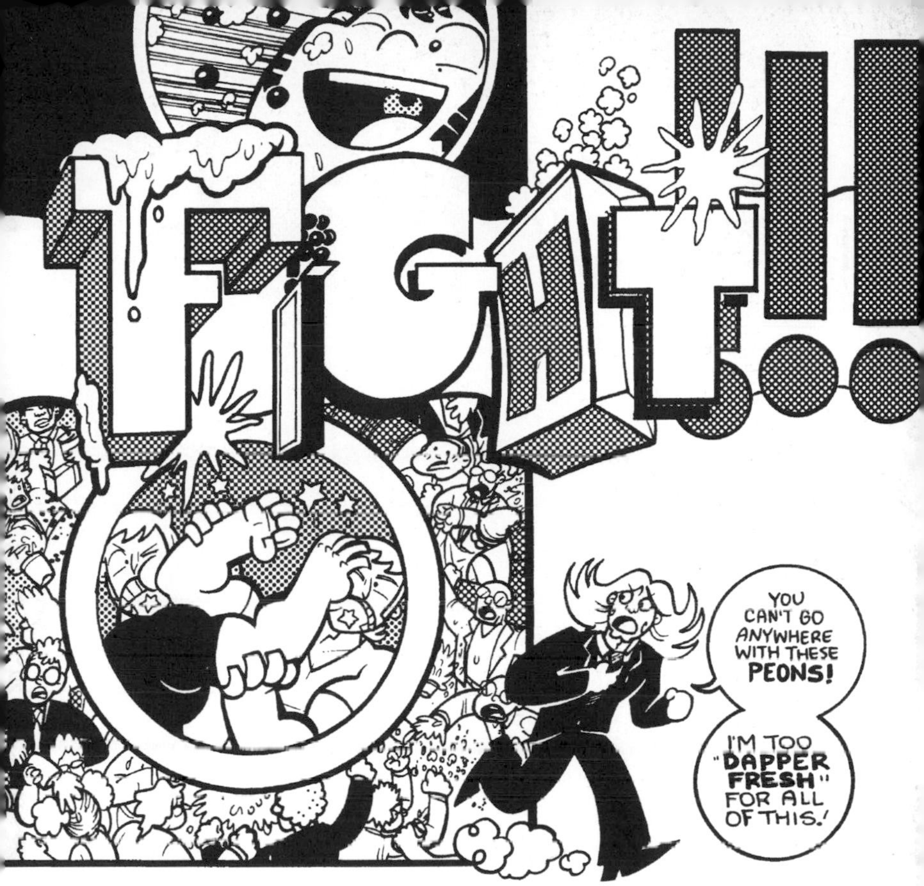
FIGHT!!
YOU CAN'T GO ANYWHERE WITH THESE **PEONS!**
I'M TOO "**DAPPER FRESH**" FOR ALL OF THIS.!

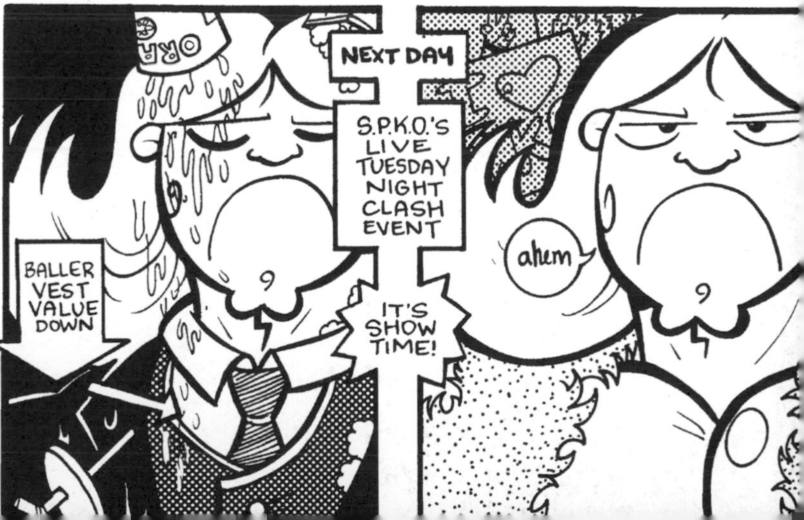
NEXT DAY
S.P.K.O.'S LIVE TUESDAY NIGHT CLASH EVENT
BALLER VEST VALUE DOWN
IT'S SHOW TIME!
ahem

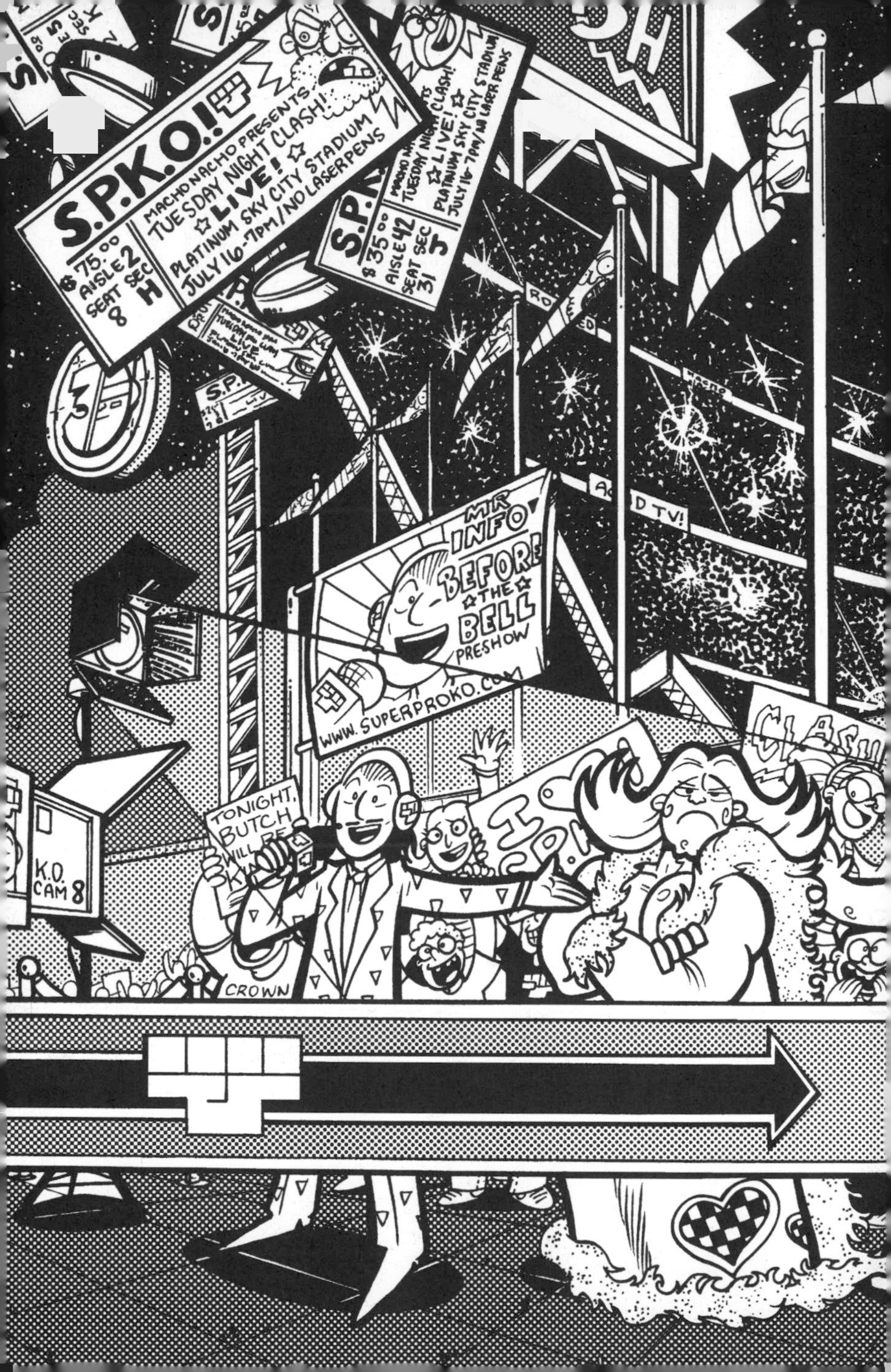
S.P.K.O.!
MACHO NACHO PRESENTS
TUESDAY NIGHT CLASH!
☆ LIVE! ☆
PLATINUM SKY CITY STADIUM
JULY 16 - 7PM / NO LASERPENS
$75.00 AISLE 2 SEAT 8 SEC H
TUESDAY NIGHT CLASH!
☆ LIVE! ☆
PLATINUM SKY CITY STADIUM
JULY 16 - 7PM / NO LASER PENS
$35.00 AISLE 42 SEAT 31 SEC J
MR INFO
BEFORE ☆ THE ☆ BELL
PRESHOW
WWW.SUPERPROKO.COM
TONIGHT, BUTCH WILL BE
K.O. CAM 8
CROWN

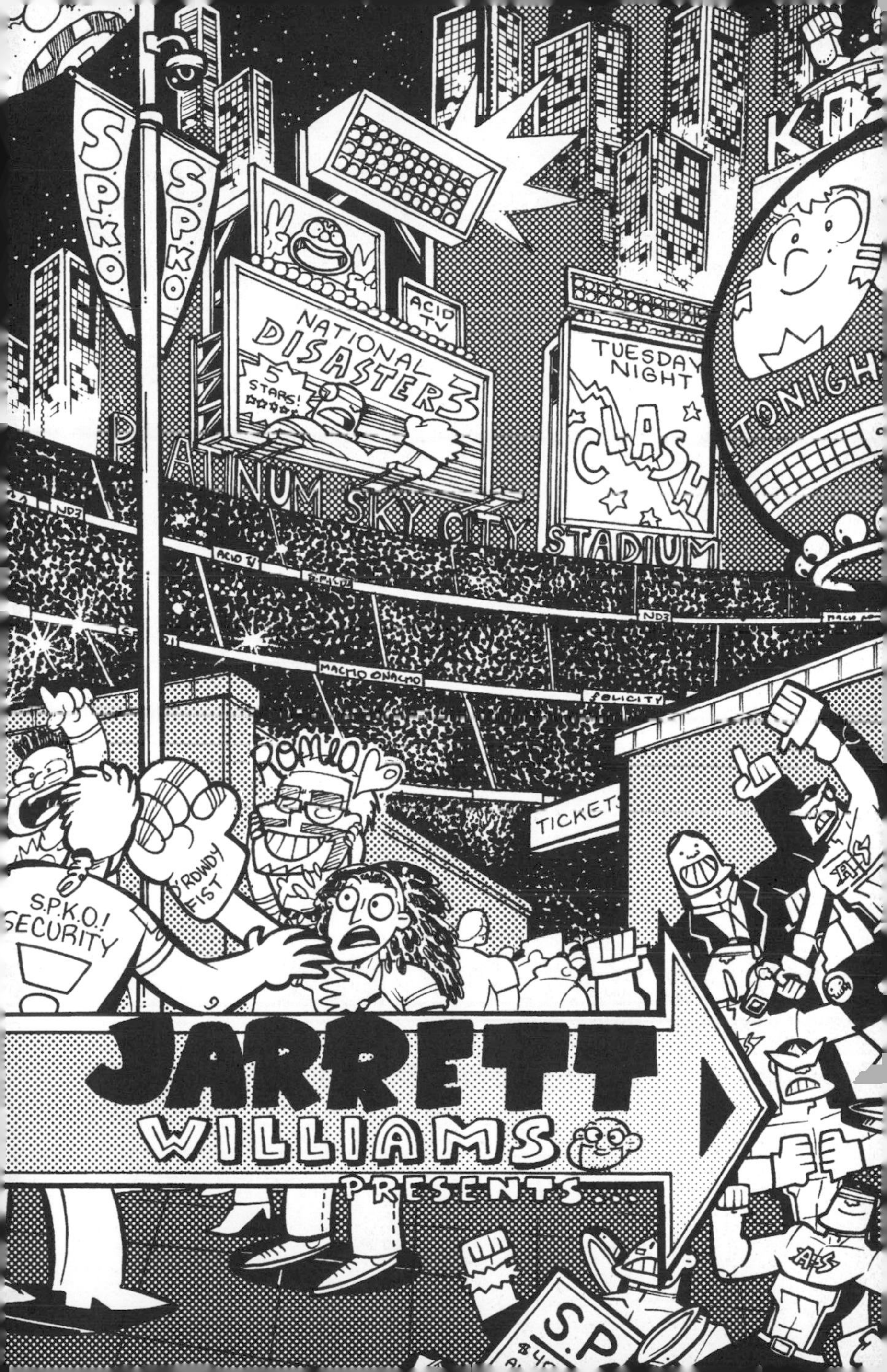
S.P.K.O.
S.P.K.O.
ACID TV
NATIONAL DISASTER 3
5 STARS!
TUESDAY NIGHT CLASH
PLATINUM SKY CITY STADIUM
TONIGH
ND3
ACID TV
MACHO NACHO
FELICITY
TICKETS
ROMEO
S.P.K.O.! SECURITY
ROWDY FIST
JARRETT WILLIAMS PRESENTS...
S.P.

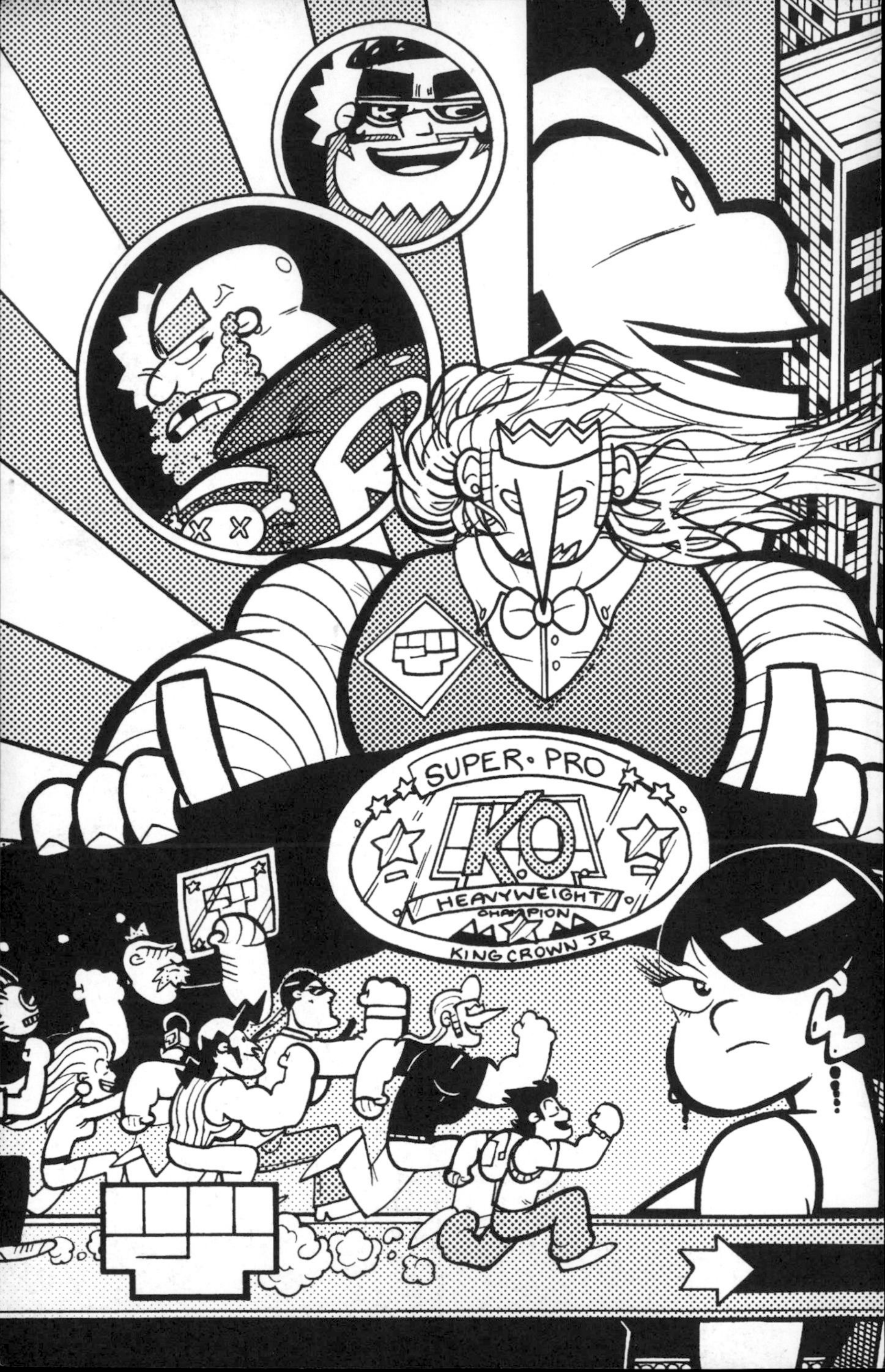
SUPER • PRO
K.O.
HEAVYWEIGHT
CHAMPION
KING CROWN JR

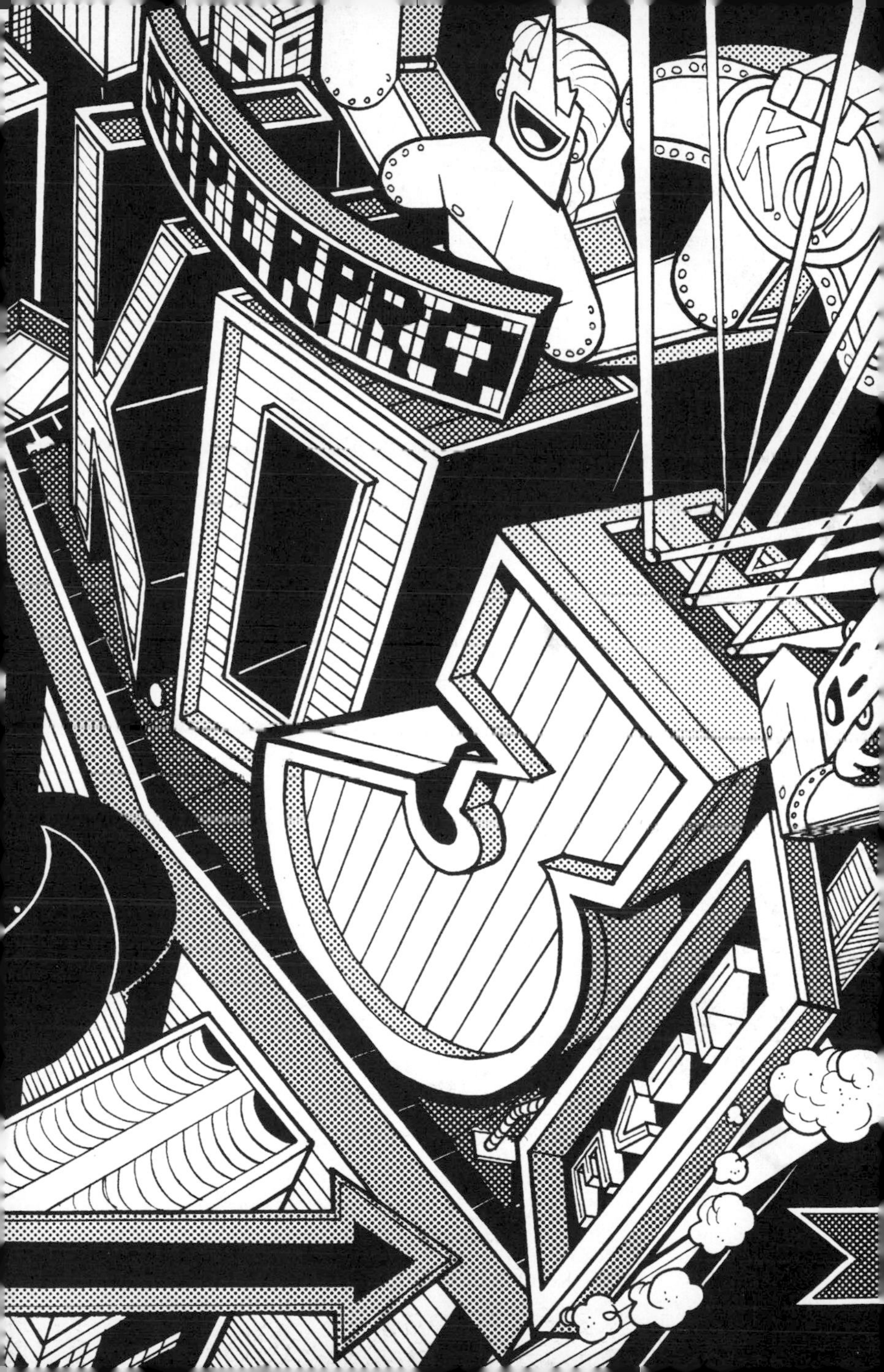

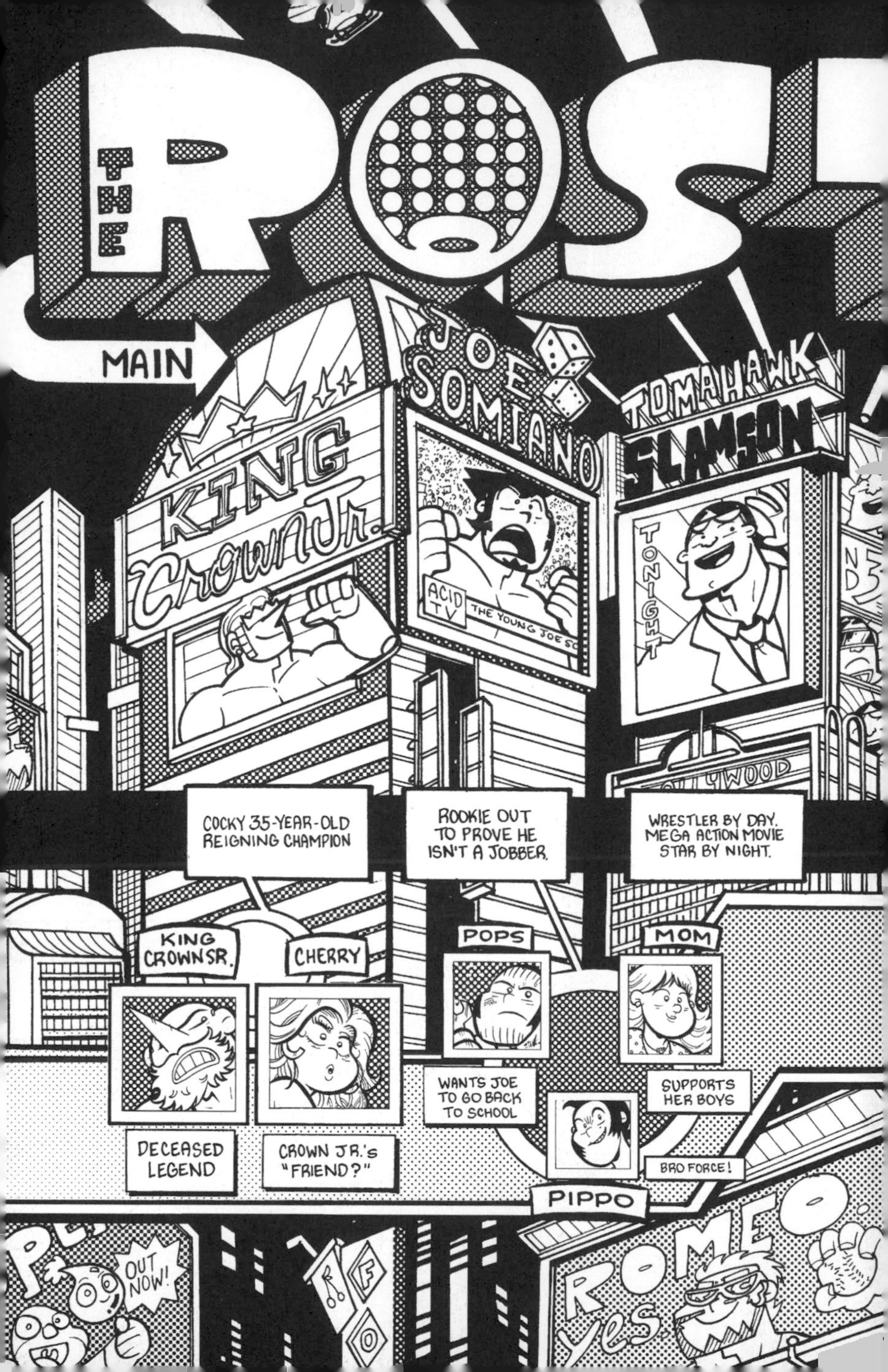
THE ROSTER
MAIN
KING CROWN Jr.
JOE SOMIANO
TOMAHAWK SLAMSON
ACID TV
THE YOUNG JOE SO
TONIGHT
COCKY 35-YEAR-OLD REIGNING CHAMPION
ROOKIE OUT TO PROVE HE ISN'T A JOBBER.
WRESTLER BY DAY. MEGA ACTION MOVIE STAR BY NIGHT.
KING CROWN SR.
CHERRY
POPS
MOM
WANTS JOE TO GO BACK TO SCHOOL
SUPPORTS HER BOYS
DECEASED LEGEND
CROWN JR.'s "FRIEND?"
BRO FORCE!
PIPPO
OUT NOW!
ROMEO
yes.

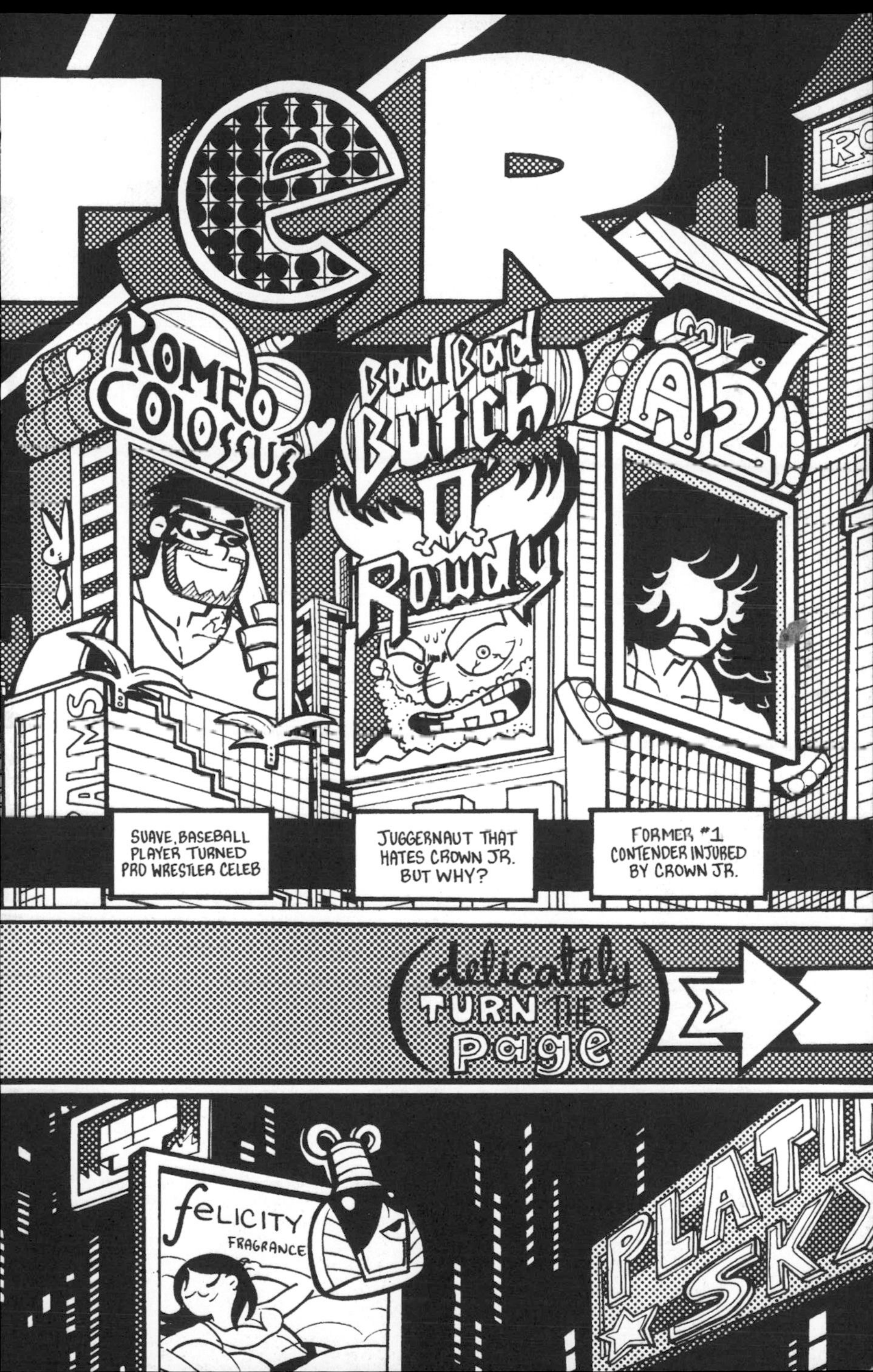
ROMEO COLOSSUS
Bad Bad Butch O' Rowdy
A2
SUAVE, BASEBALL PLAYER TURNED PRO WRESTLER CELEB
JUGGERNAUT THAT HATES CROWN JR. BUT WHY?
FORMER #1 CONTENDER INJURED BY CROWN JR.
(delicately TURN THE page)
felicity FRAGRANCE

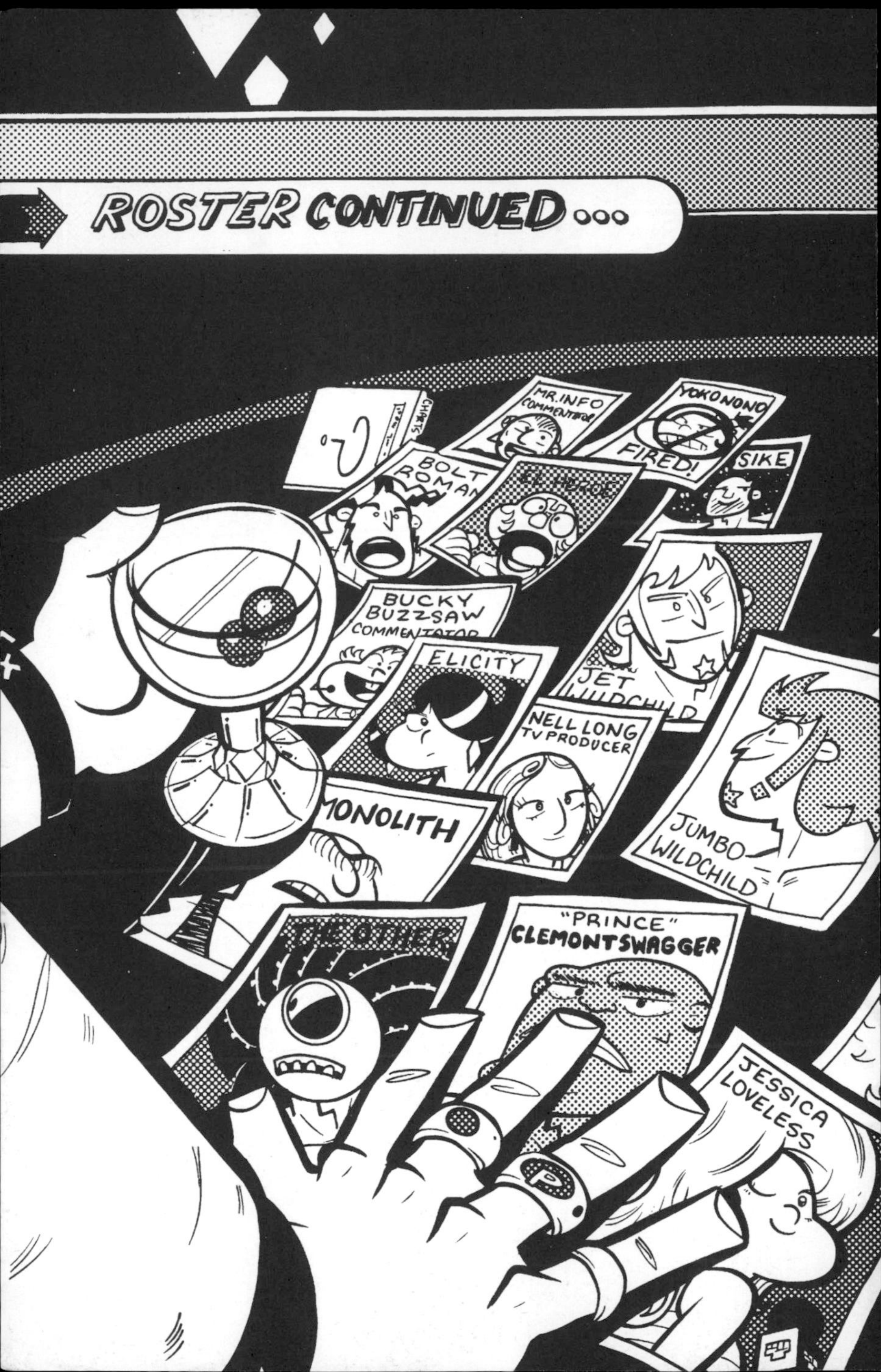
ROSTER CONTINUED...
CHARTS
MR. INFO
COMMENTATOR
YOKO NONO
FIRED!
SIKE
BOLT ROMAN
BUCKY BUZZSAW
COMMENTATOR
ELICITY
JET WILDCHILD
NELL LONG
TV PRODUCER
MONOLITH
JUMBO WILDCHILD
THE OTHER
"PRINCE" CLEMONTSWAGGER
JESSICA LOVELESS

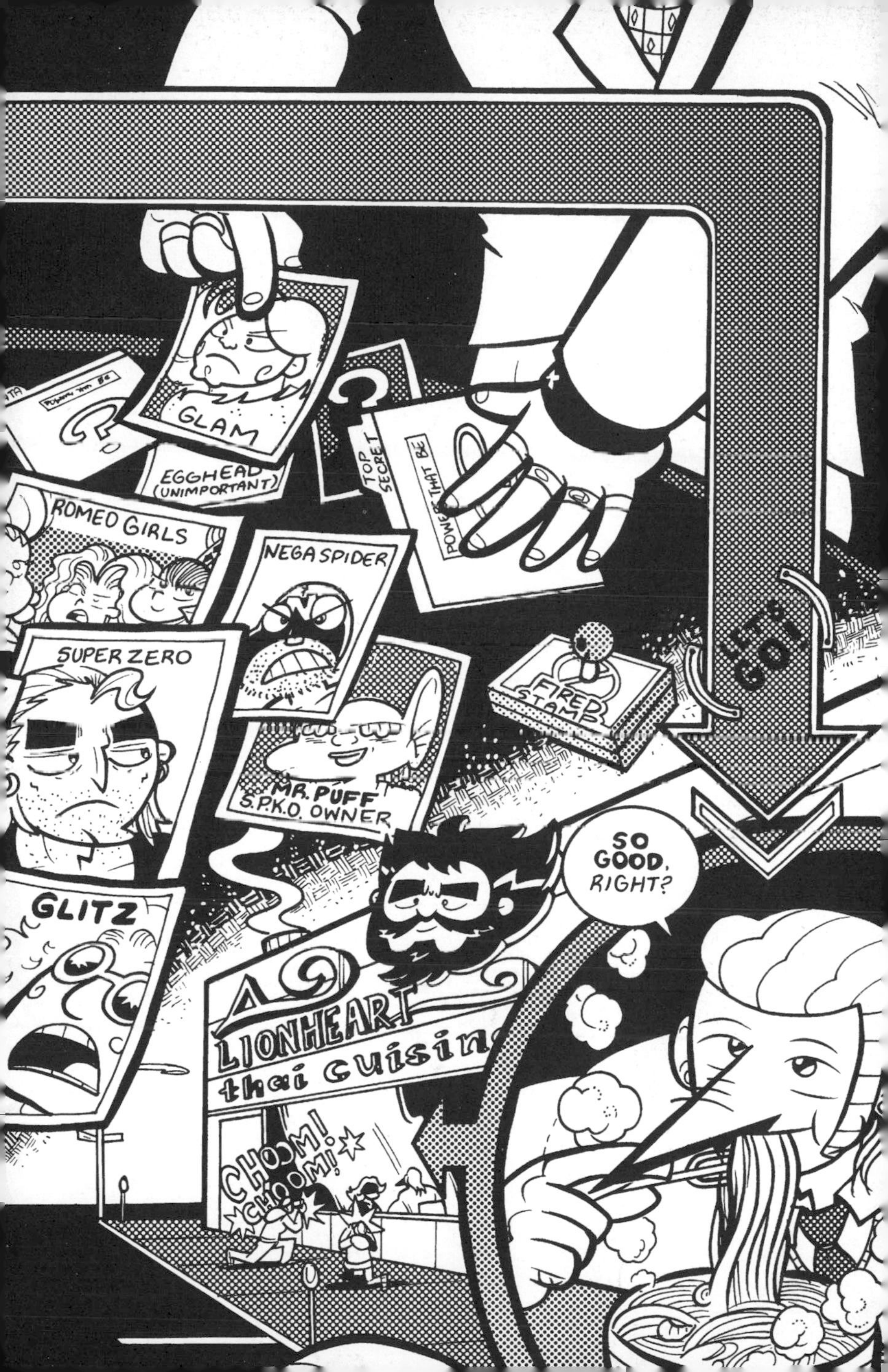
GLAM
EGGHEAD (UNIMPORTANT)
TOP SECRET
POWERS THAT BE
ROMEO GIRLS
NEGA SPIDER
SUPER ZERO
FIRED STAMP
MR. PUFF S.P.K.O. OWNER
SO GOOD, RIGHT?
GLITZ
LIONHEART thai Cuisin
CHOOM! CHOOM!

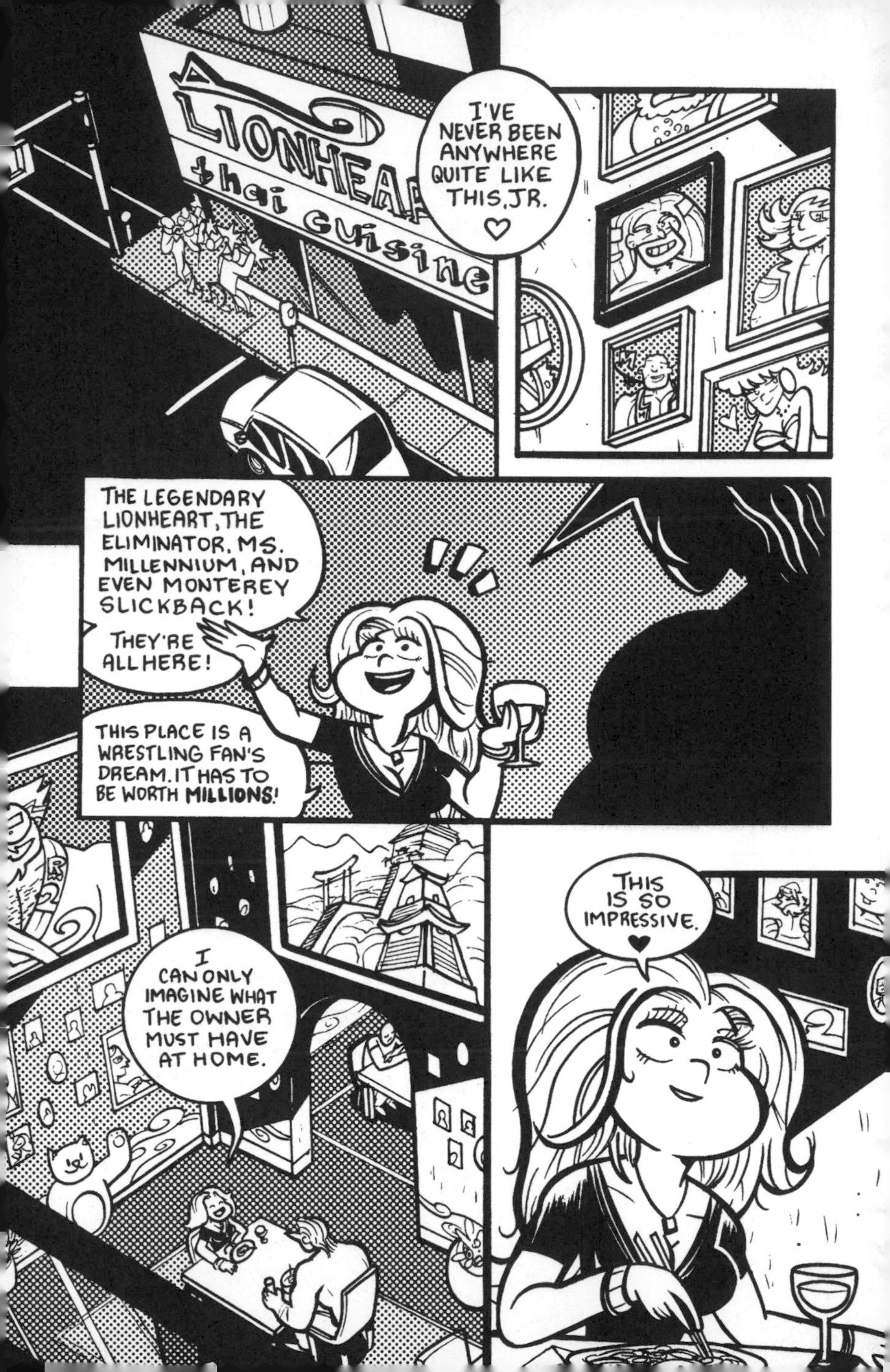
LIONHEAR
thai cuisine
I'VE NEVER BEEN ANYWHERE QUITE LIKE THIS, JR. ♥
THE LEGENDARY LIONHEART, THE ELIMINATOR, MS. MILLENNIUM, AND EVEN MONTEREY SLICKBACK!
THEY'RE ALL HERE!
THIS PLACE IS A WRESTLING FAN'S DREAM. IT HAS TO BE WORTH **MILLIONS**!
I CAN ONLY IMAGINE WHAT THE OWNER MUST HAVE AT HOME.
THIS IS SO IMPRESSIVE. ♥

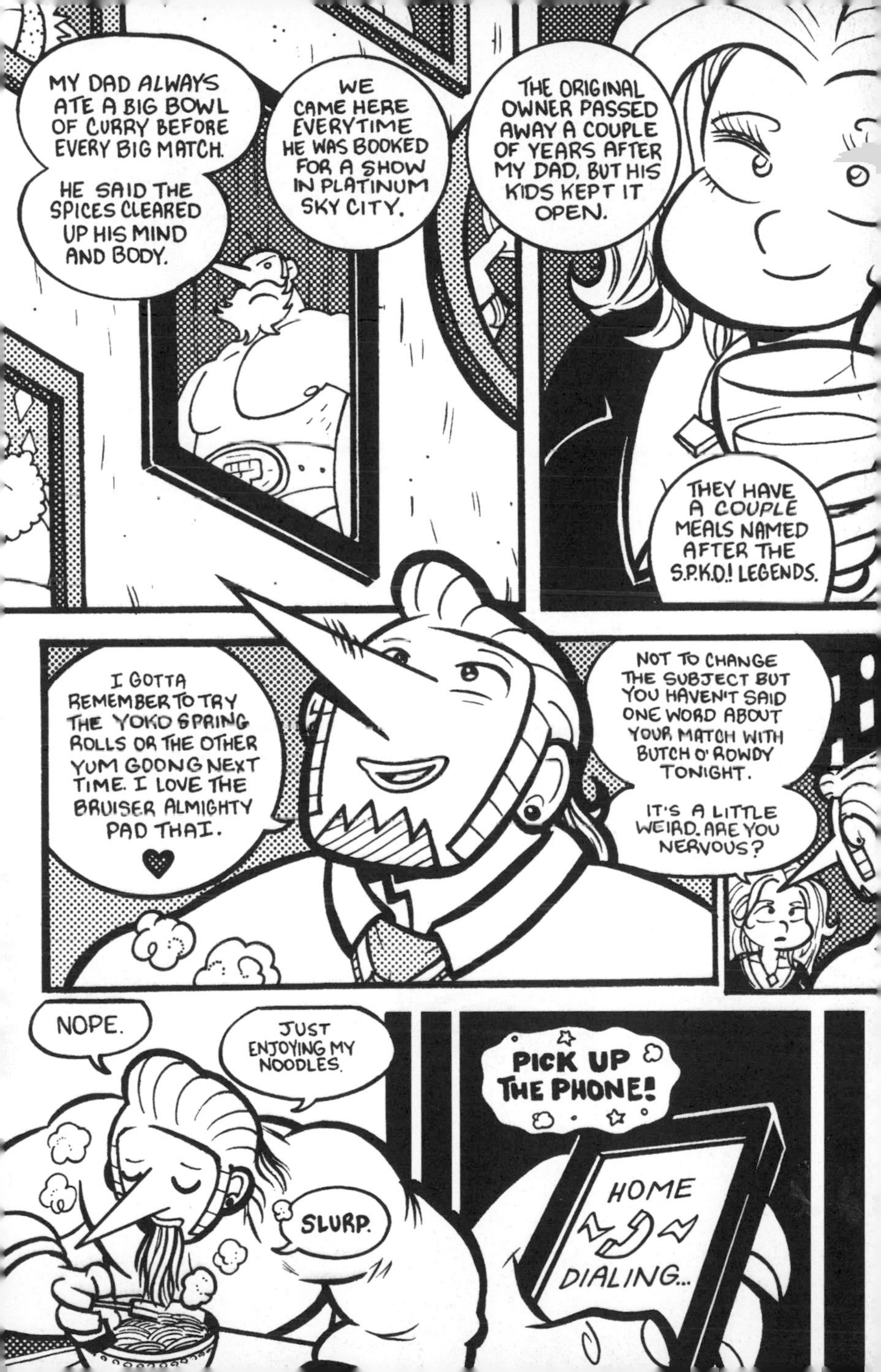

MY DAD ALWAYS ATE A BIG BOWL OF CURRY BEFORE EVERY BIG MATCH.
HE SAID THE SPICES CLEARED UP HIS MIND AND BODY.
WE CAME HERE EVERYTIME HE WAS BOOKED FOR A SHOW IN PLATINUM SKY CITY.
THE ORIGINAL OWNER PASSED AWAY A COUPLE OF YEARS AFTER MY DAD, BUT HIS KIDS KEPT IT OPEN.
THEY HAVE A COUPLE MEALS NAMED AFTER THE S.P.K.D.! LEGENDS.
I GOTTA REMEMBER TO TRY THE YOKO SPRING ROLLS OR THE OTHER YUM GOONG NEXT TIME. I LOVE THE BRUISER ALMIGHTY PAD THAI.
NOT TO CHANGE THE SUBJECT BUT YOU HAVEN'T SAID ONE WORD ABOUT YOUR MATCH WITH BUTCH O' ROWDY TONIGHT.
IT'S A LITTLE WEIRD. ARE YOU NERVOUS?
NOPE.
JUST ENJOYING MY NOODLES.
SLURP.
PICK UP THE PHONE!
HOME
DIALING...

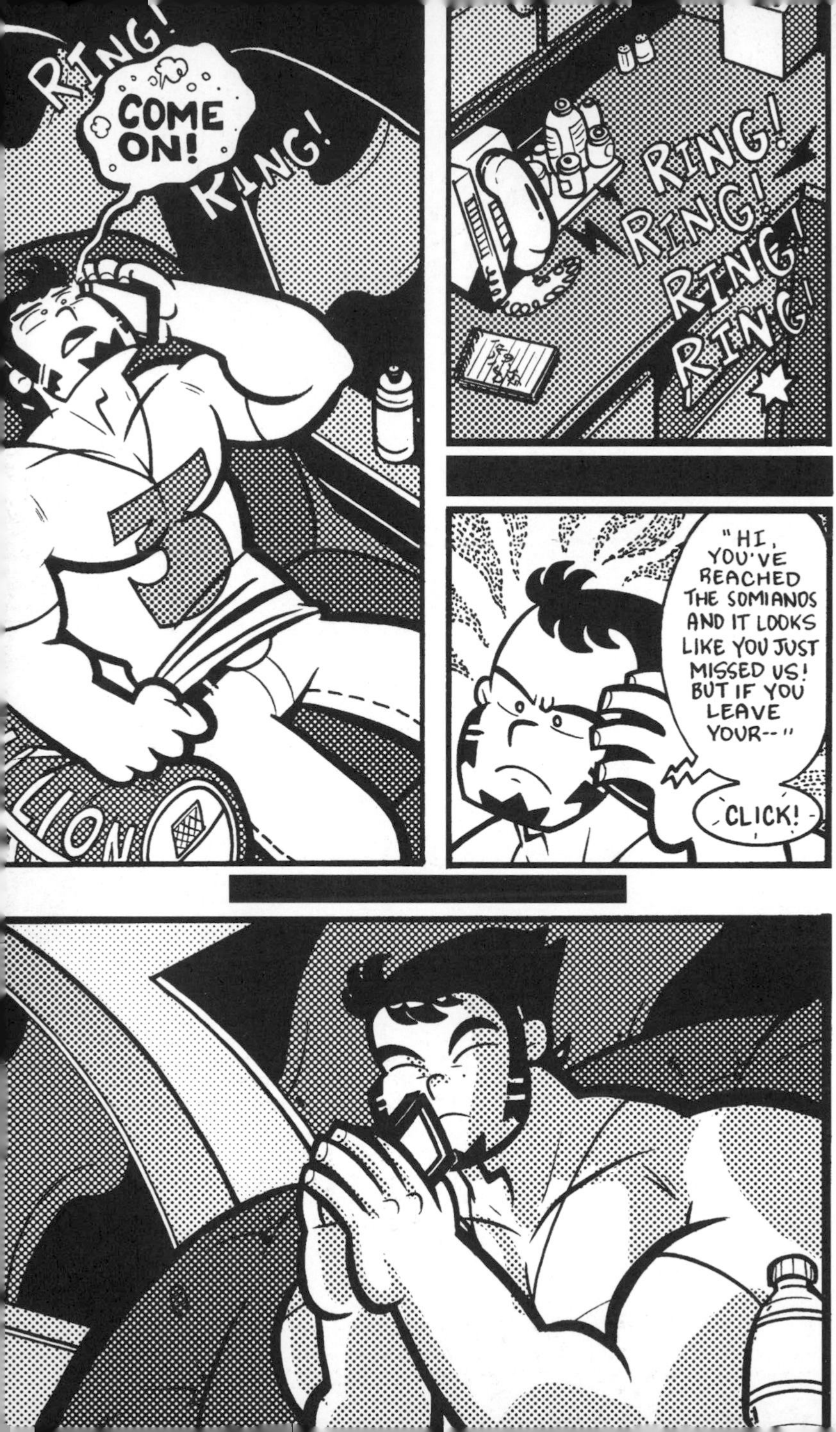
RING!
COME ON!
RING!
RING!
RING!
RING!
RING!
"HI, YOU'VE REACHED THE SOMIANOS AND IT LOOKS LIKE YOU JUST MISSED US! BUT IF YOU LEAVE YOUR--"
CLICK!

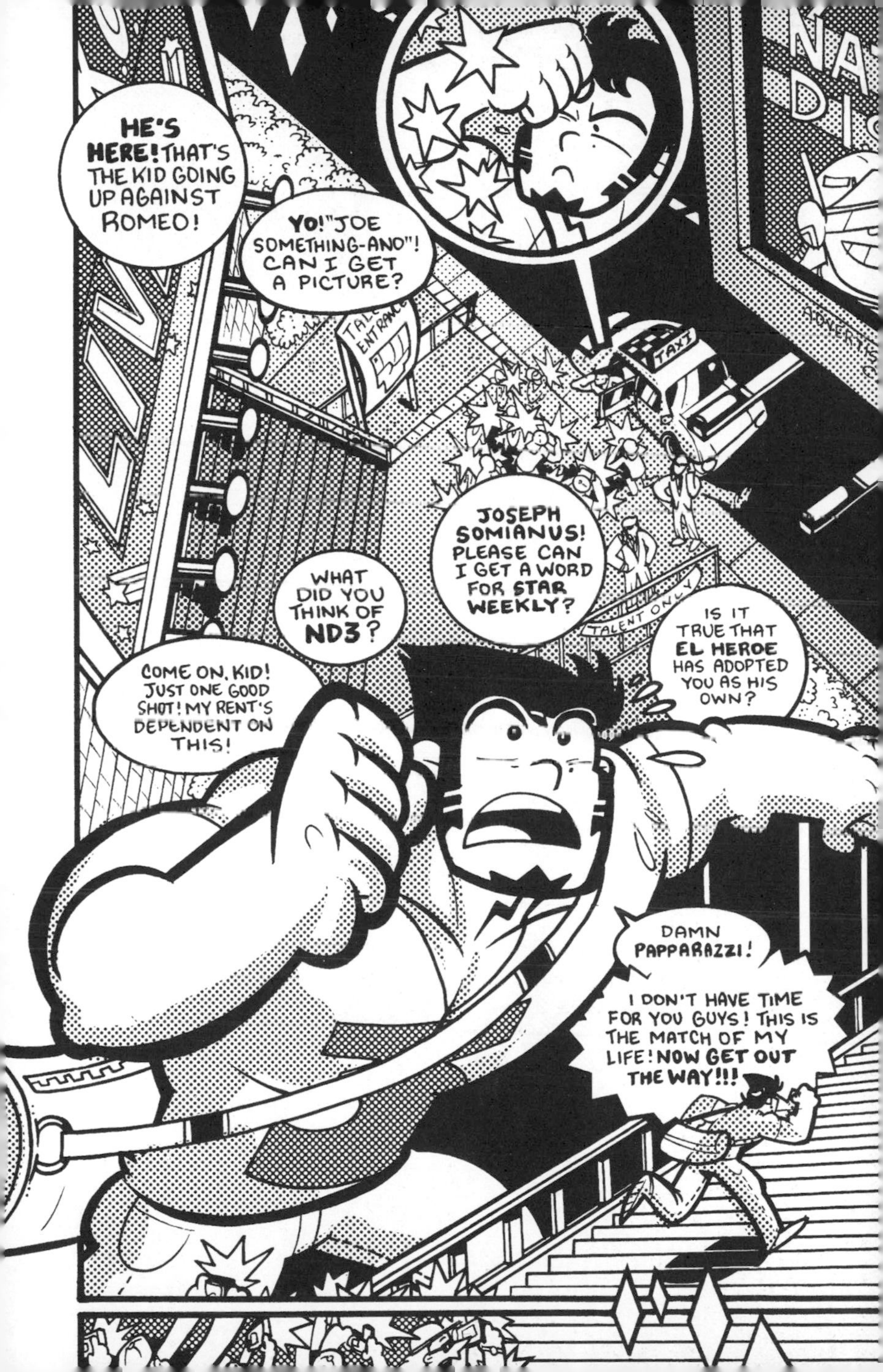
HE'S HERE! THAT'S THE KID GOING UP AGAINST ROMEO!
YO! "JOE SOMETHING-AND"! CAN I GET A PICTURE?
TAXI
JOSEPH SOMIANUS! PLEASE CAN I GET A WORD FOR STAR WEEKLY?
WHAT DID YOU THINK OF ND3?
TALENT ONLY
IS IT TRUE THAT EL HEROE HAS ADOPTED YOU AS HIS OWN?
COME ON, KID! JUST ONE GOOD SHOT! MY RENT'S DEPENDENT ON THIS!
DAMN PAPPARAZZI!
I DON'T HAVE TIME FOR YOU GUYS! THIS IS THE MATCH OF MY LIFE! NOW GET OUT THE WAY!!!

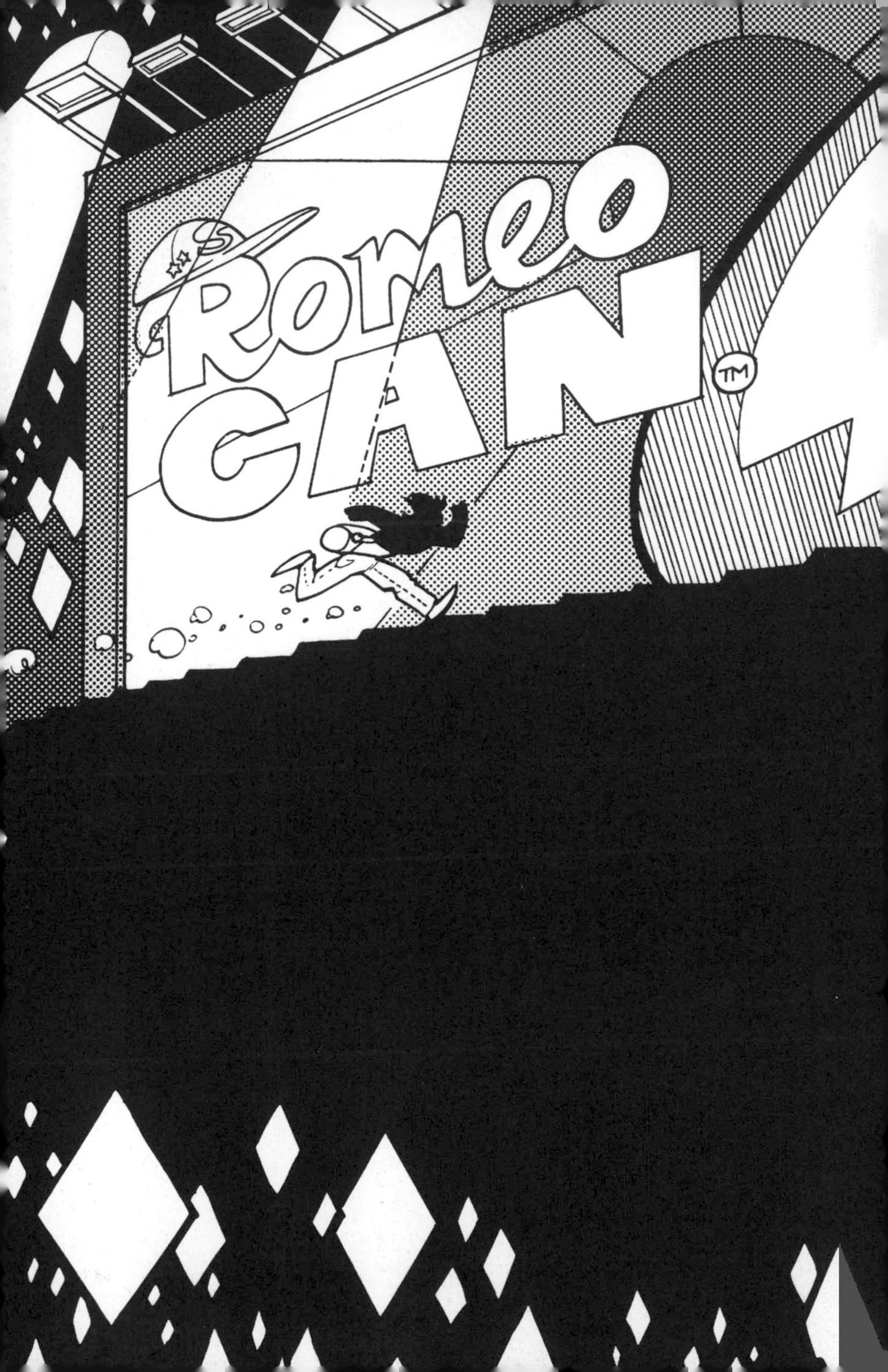
Romeo
CAN™

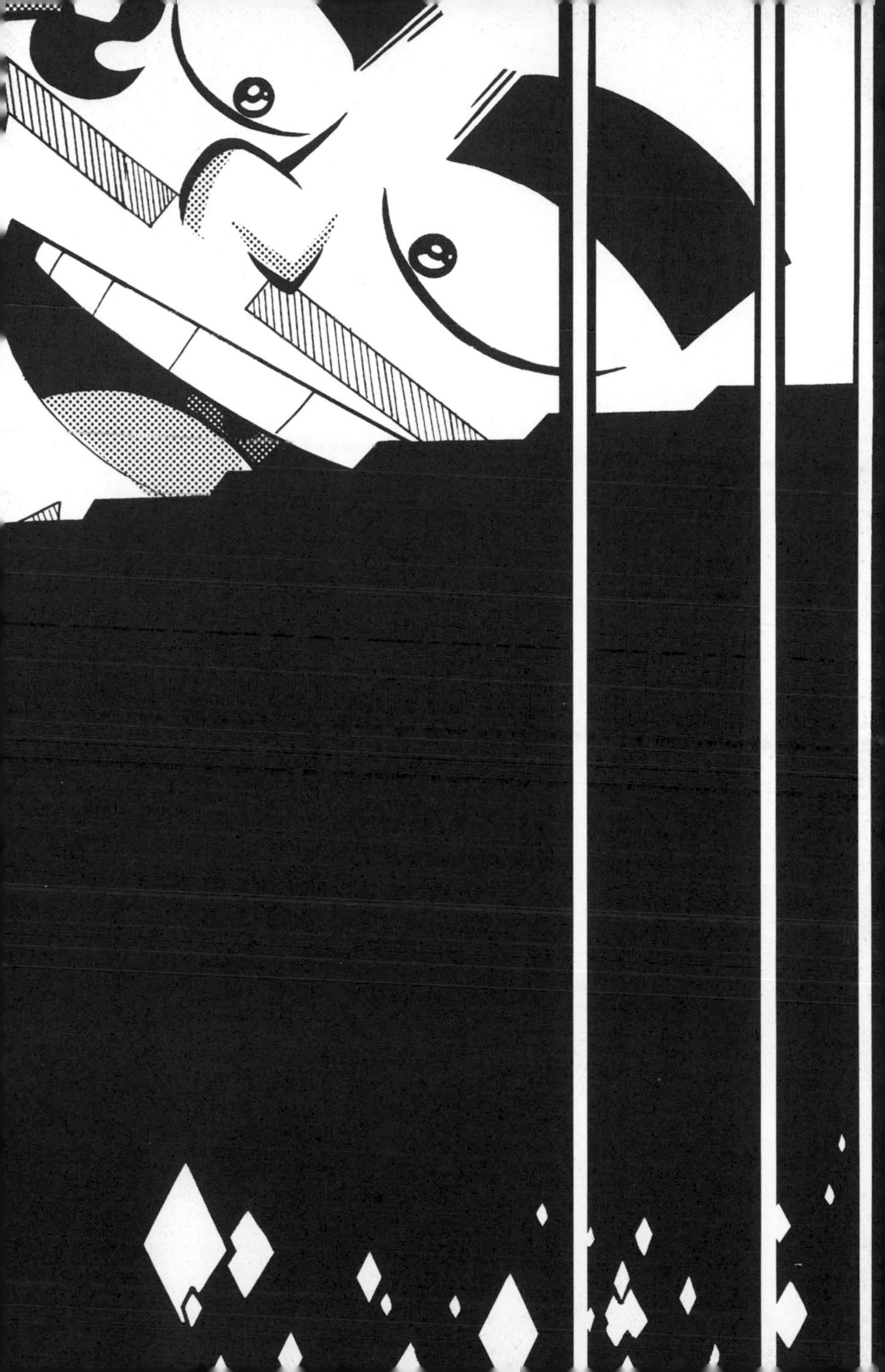

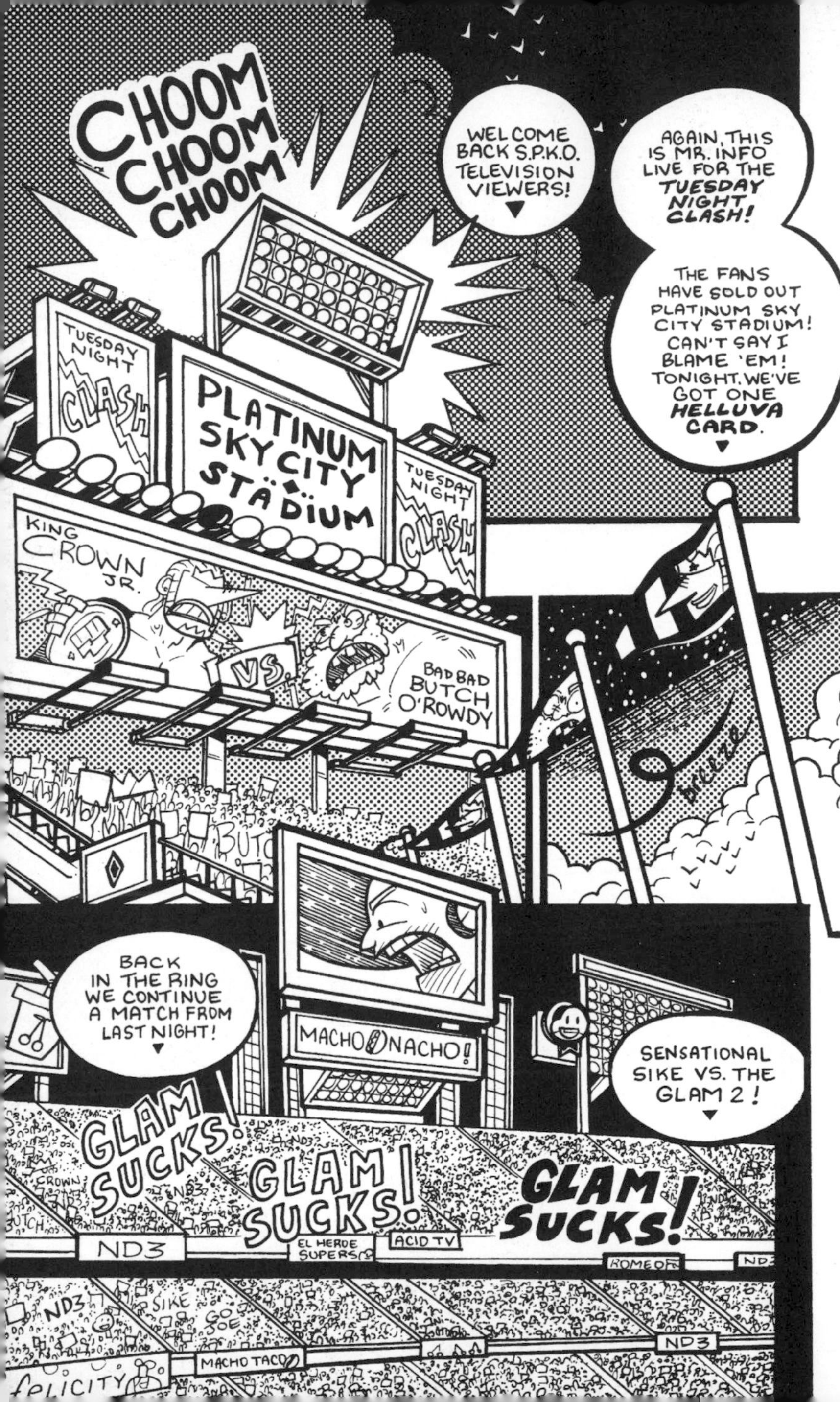
CHOOM CHOOM CHOOM
WELCOME BACK S.P.K.O. TELEVISION VIEWERS!
AGAIN, THIS IS MR. INFO LIVE FOR THE TUESDAY NIGHT CLASH!
THE FANS HAVE SOLD OUT PLATINUM SKY CITY STADIUM! CAN'T SAY I BLAME 'EM! TONIGHT, WE'VE GOT ONE HELLUVA CARD.
TUESDAY NIGHT CLASH
PLATINUM SKY CITY STÄDIUM
TUESDAY NIGHT CLASH
KING CROWN JR.
VS
BAD BAD BUTCH O'ROWDY
breeze
BACK IN THE RING WE CONTINUE A MATCH FROM LAST NIGHT!
MACHO NACHO!
SENSATIONAL SIKE VS. THE GLAM 2!
GLAM SUCKS!
GLAM SUCKS!
GLAM SUCKS!
ND3
EL HEROE SUPERS
ACID TV
ROMEO
ND3
SIKE
GO JOE
MACHO TACO
ND3
felicity

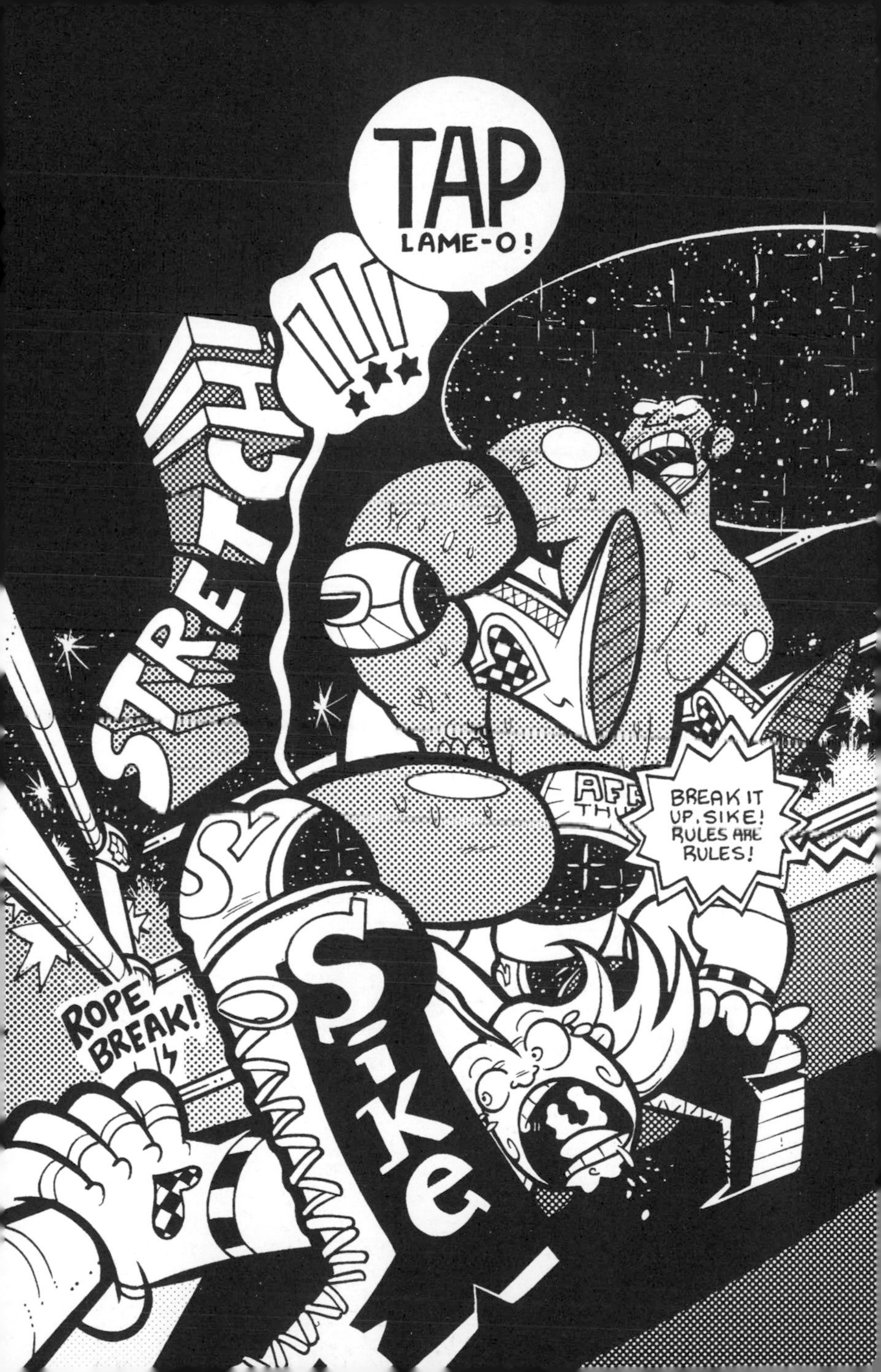
TAP
LAME-O!
STRETCH!!!!
BREAK IT UP, SIKE! RULES ARE RULES!
ROPE BREAK!
SIKE

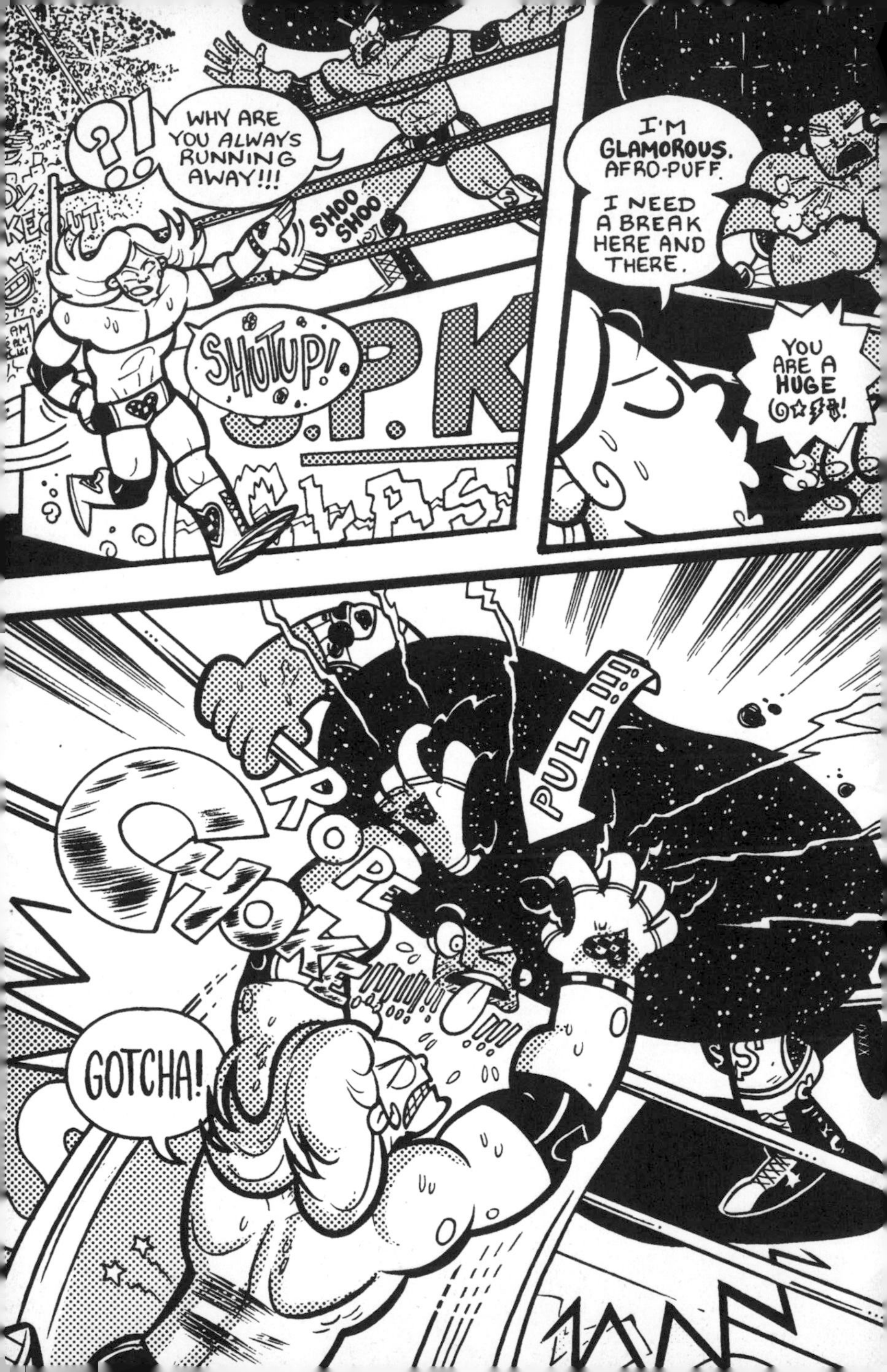
?!
WHY ARE YOU ALWAYS RUNNING AWAY!!!
SHOO SHOO
SHUTUP!
I'M GLAMOROUS. AFRO-PUFF.
I NEED A BREAK HERE AND THERE.
YOU ARE A HUGE @☆⚡#!
PULL!!!
ROPE CHOKE
GOTCHA!

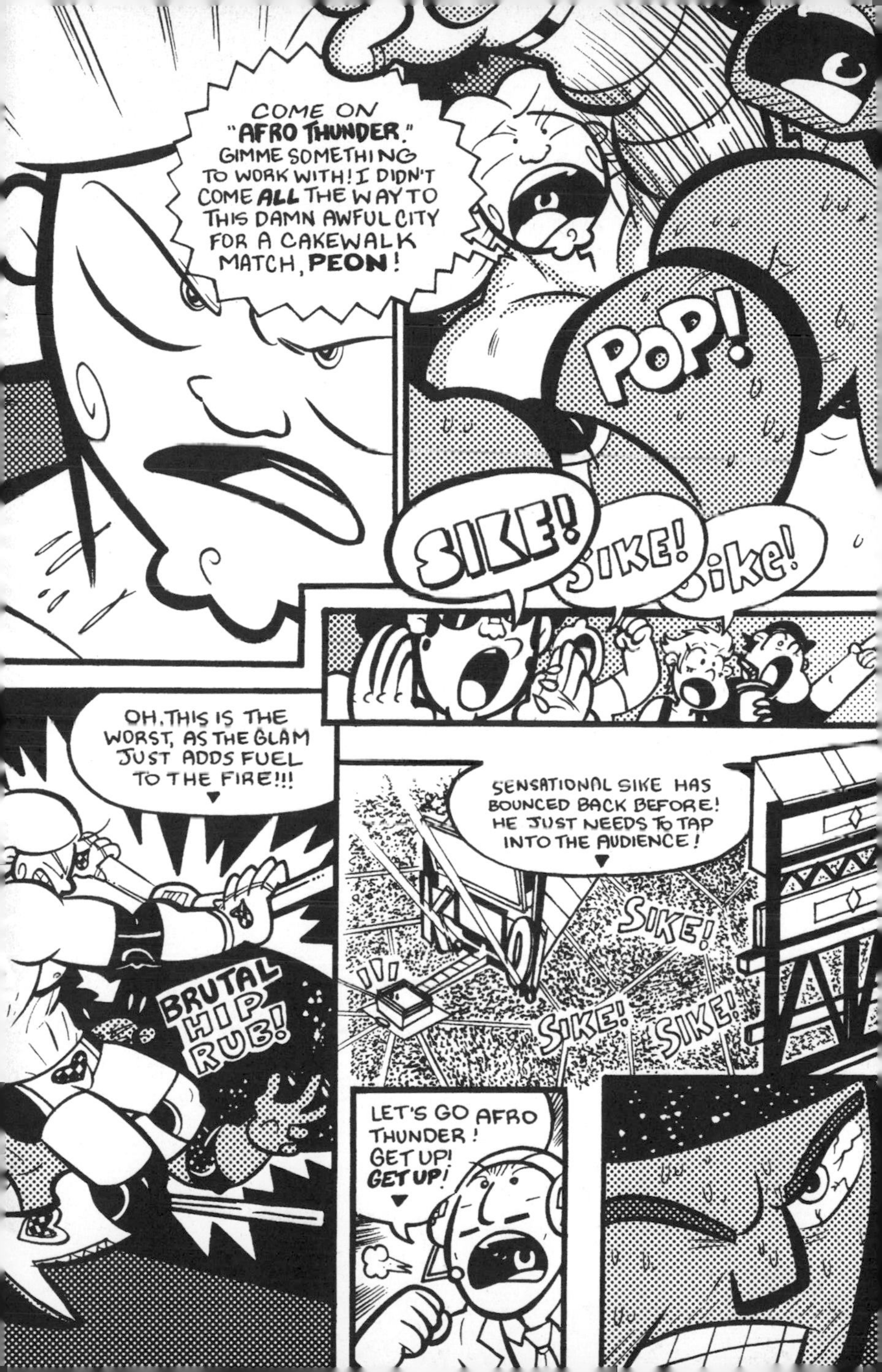
COME ON "AFRO THUNDER." GIMME SOMETHING TO WORK WITH! I DIDN'T COME ALL THE WAY TO THIS DAMN AWFUL CITY FOR A CAKEWALK MATCH, PEON!
POP!
SIKE!
SIKE!
Sike!
OH, THIS IS THE WORST, AS THE GLAM JUST ADDS FUEL TO THE FIRE!!!
BRUTAL HIP RUB!
SENSATIONAL SIKE HAS BOUNCED BACK BEFORE! HE JUST NEEDS TO TAP INTO THE AUDIENCE!
SIKE!
SIKE!
SIKE!
LET'S GO AFRO THUNDER! GET UP! GET UP!

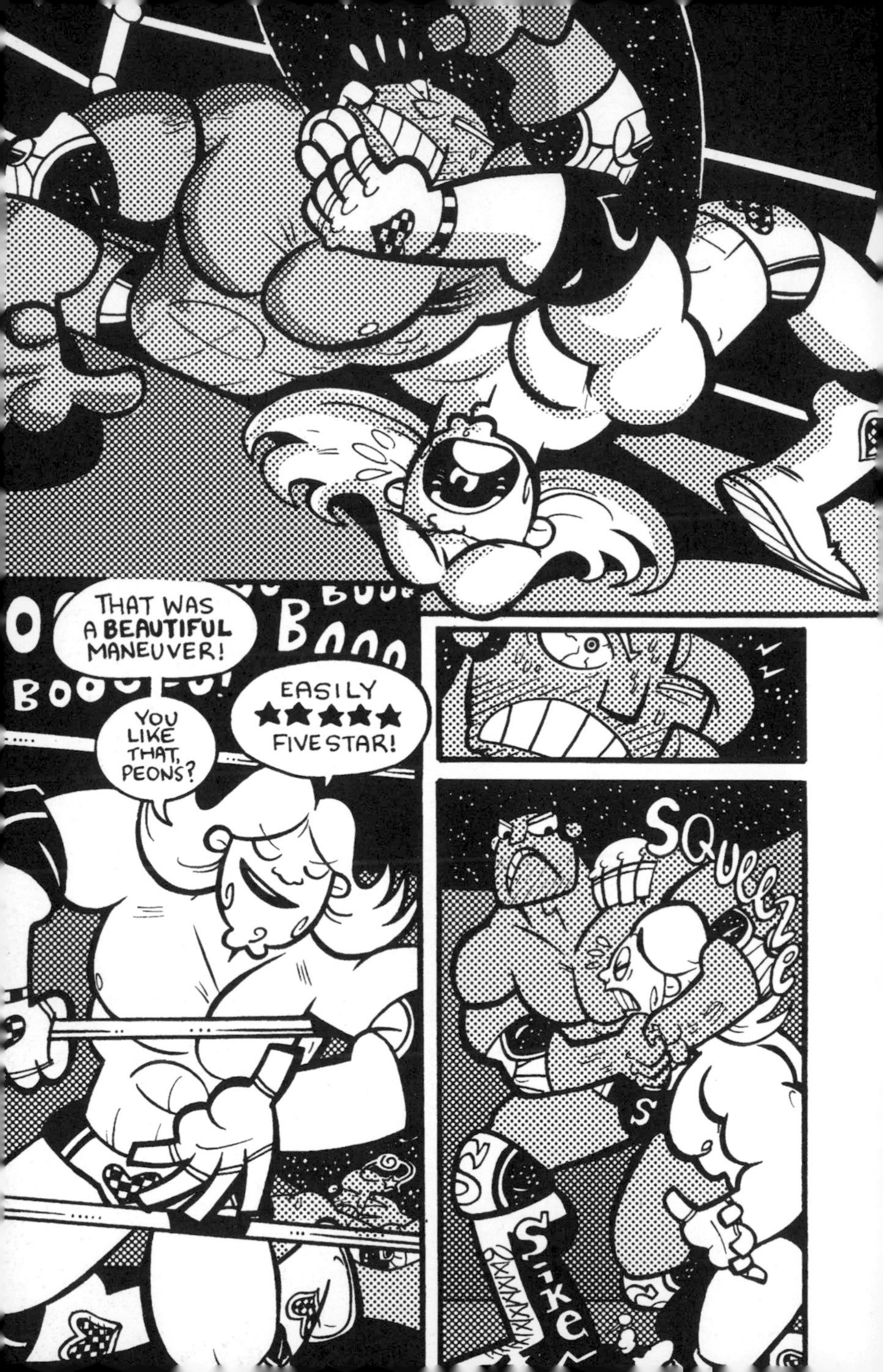
THAT WAS A **BEAUTIFUL** MANEUVER!
YOU LIKE THAT, PEONS?
EASILY ★★★★★ FIVE STAR!
SQUEEZE

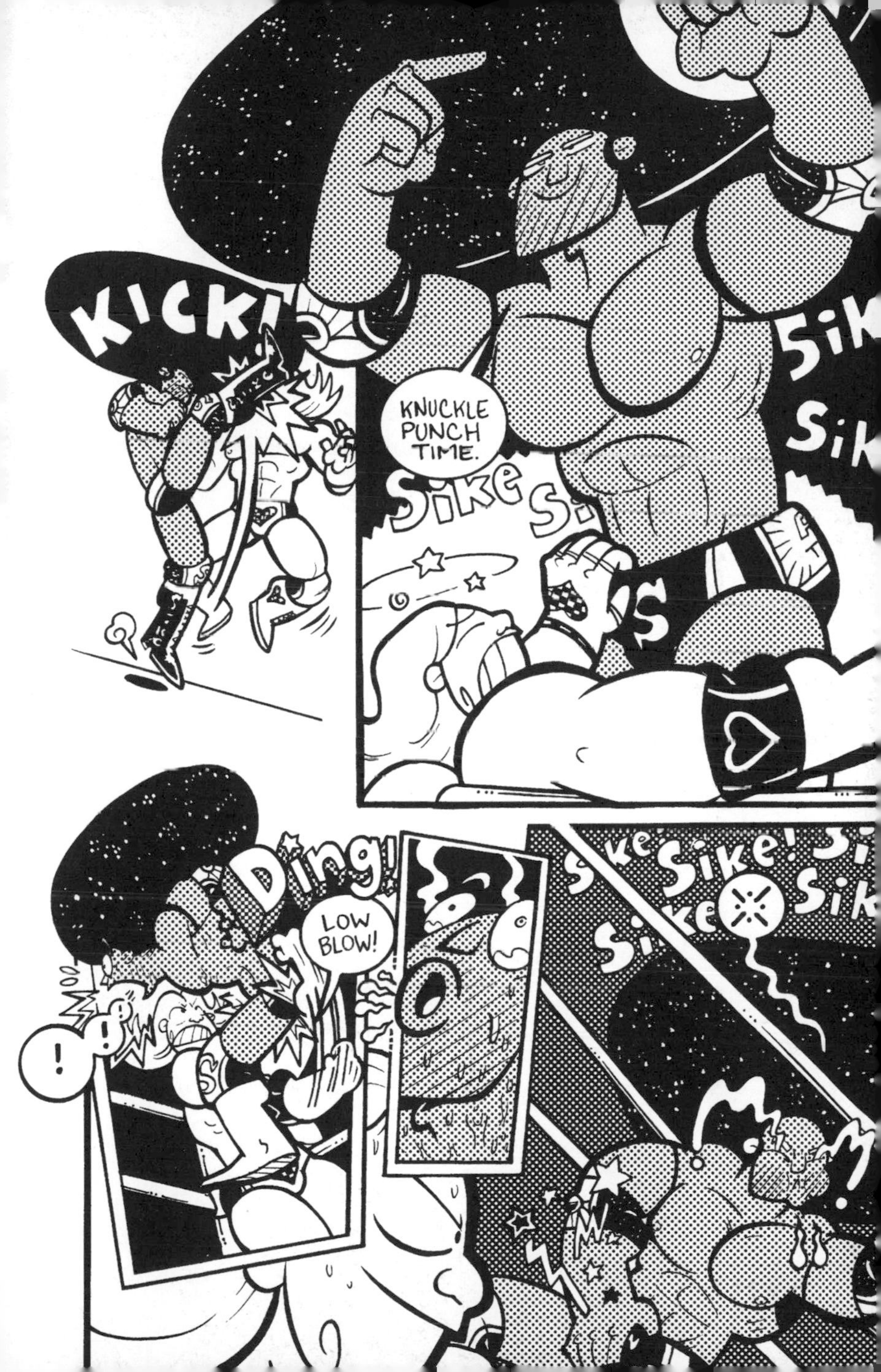
KICK!
KNUCKLE PUNCH TIME.
Sike
Si
Sik
Sik
S
Ding!
LOW BLOW!
!
Sike
Sike!
Sike
Sik

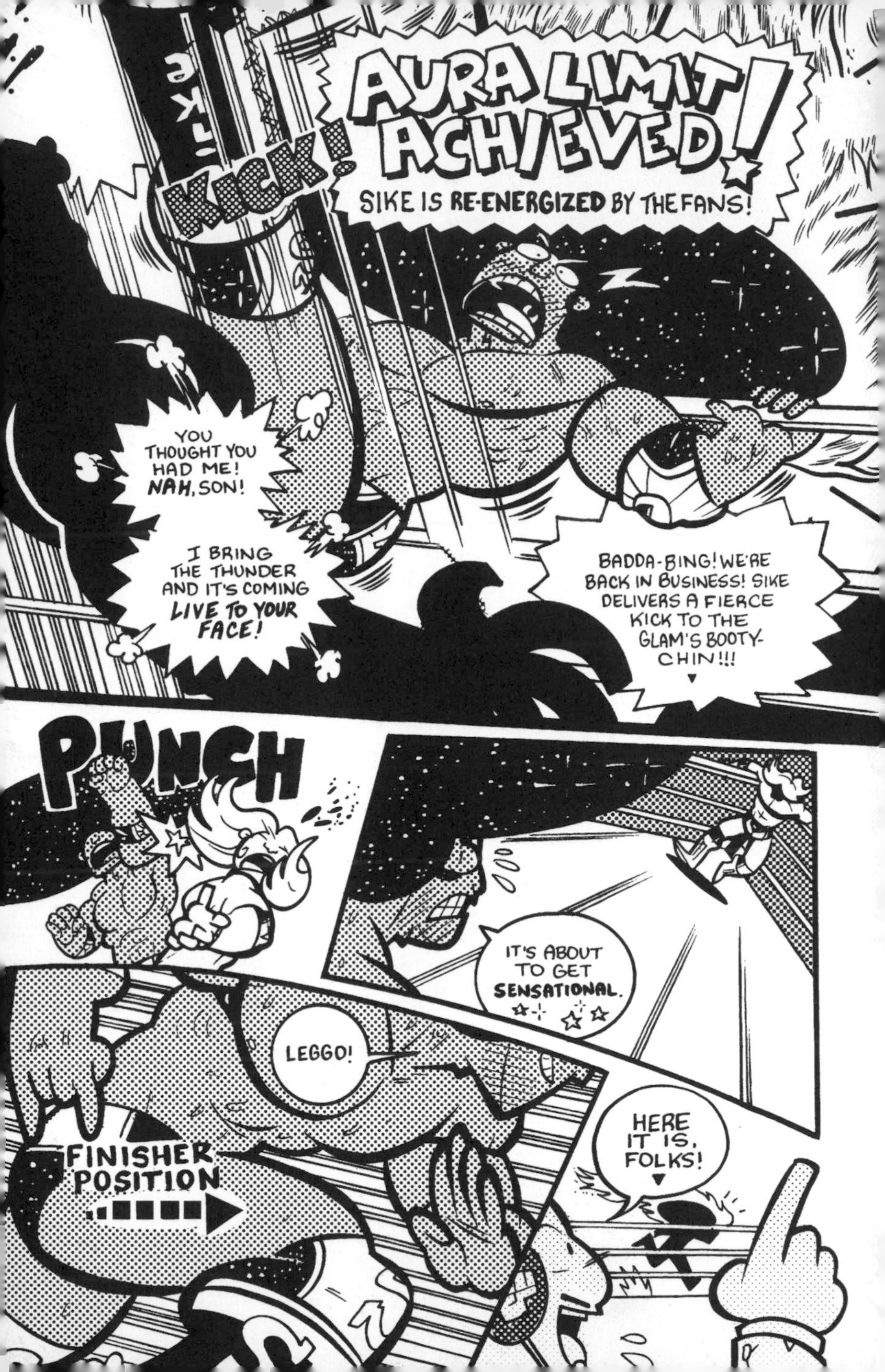
KICK!
AURA LIMIT ACHIEVED!
SIKE IS RE-ENERGIZED BY THE FANS!
YOU THOUGHT YOU HAD ME! NAH, SON!
I BRING THE THUNDER AND IT'S COMING LIVE TO YOUR FACE!
BADDA-BING! WE'RE BACK IN BUSINESS! SIKE DELIVERS A FIERCE KICK TO THE GLAM'S BOOTY-CHIN!!!
PUNCH
IT'S ABOUT TO GET SENSATIONAL.
LEGGO!
FINISHER POSITION
HERE IT IS, FOLKS!

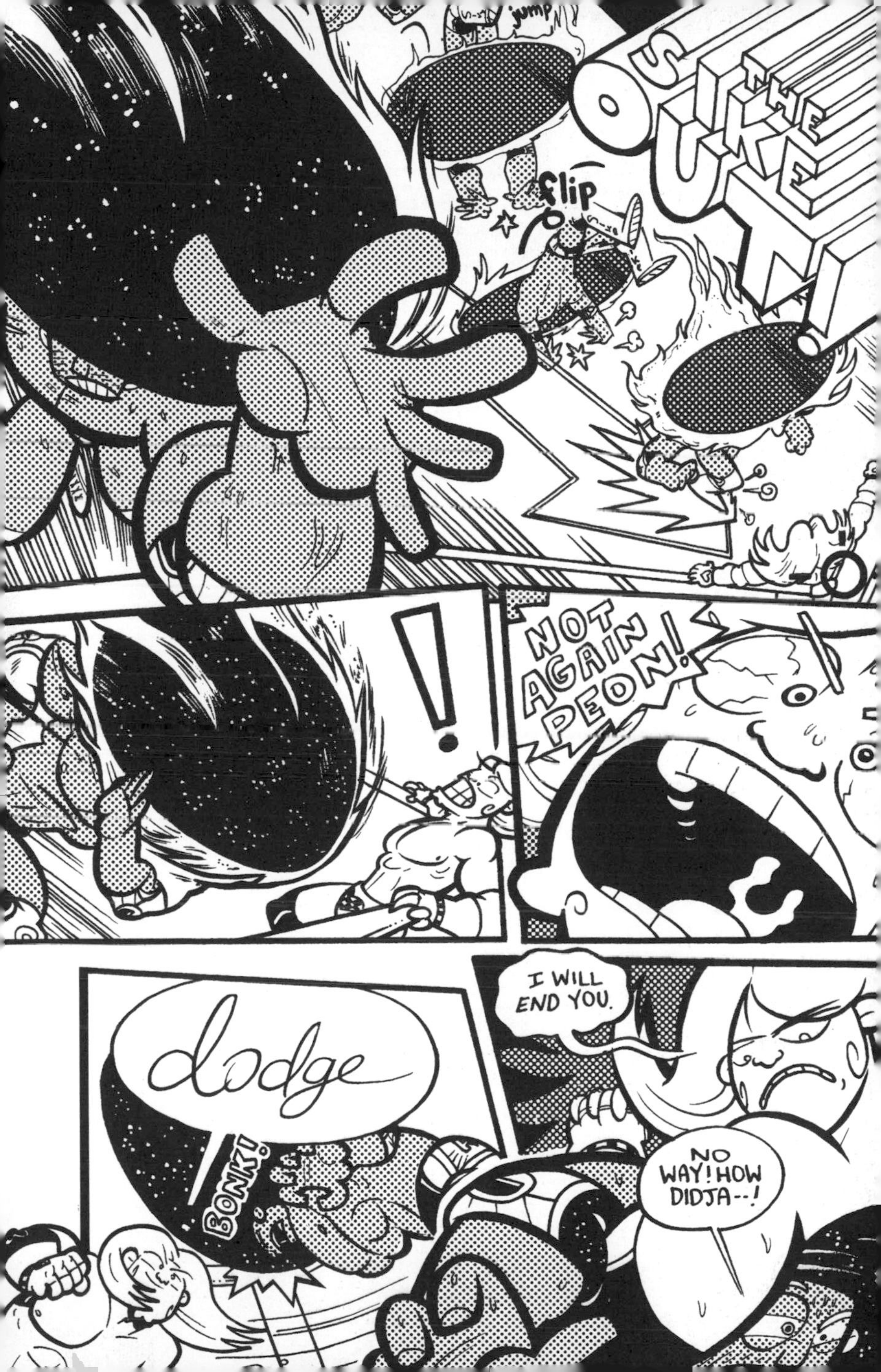
jump
flip
!
NOT AGAIN PEON!
dodge
BONK!
I WILL END YOU.
NO WAY! HOW DIDJA--!

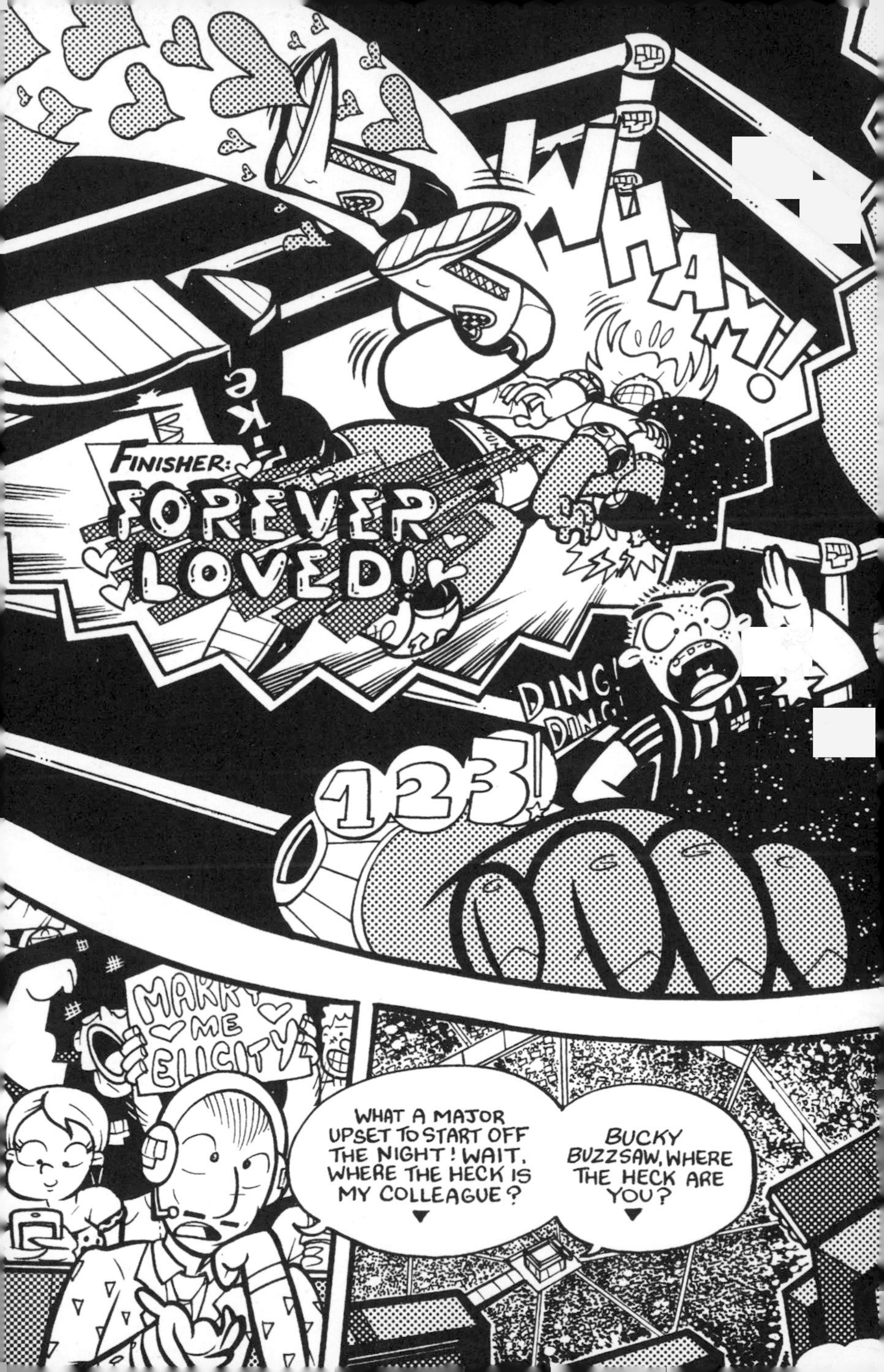
WHAM!
FINISHER: FOREVER LOVED!
DING! DING!
1 2 3
MARRY ME ELICITY
WHAT A MAJOR UPSET TO START OFF THE NIGHT! WAIT. WHERE THE HECK IS MY COLLEAGUE?
BUCKY BUZZSAW, WHERE THE HECK ARE YOU?

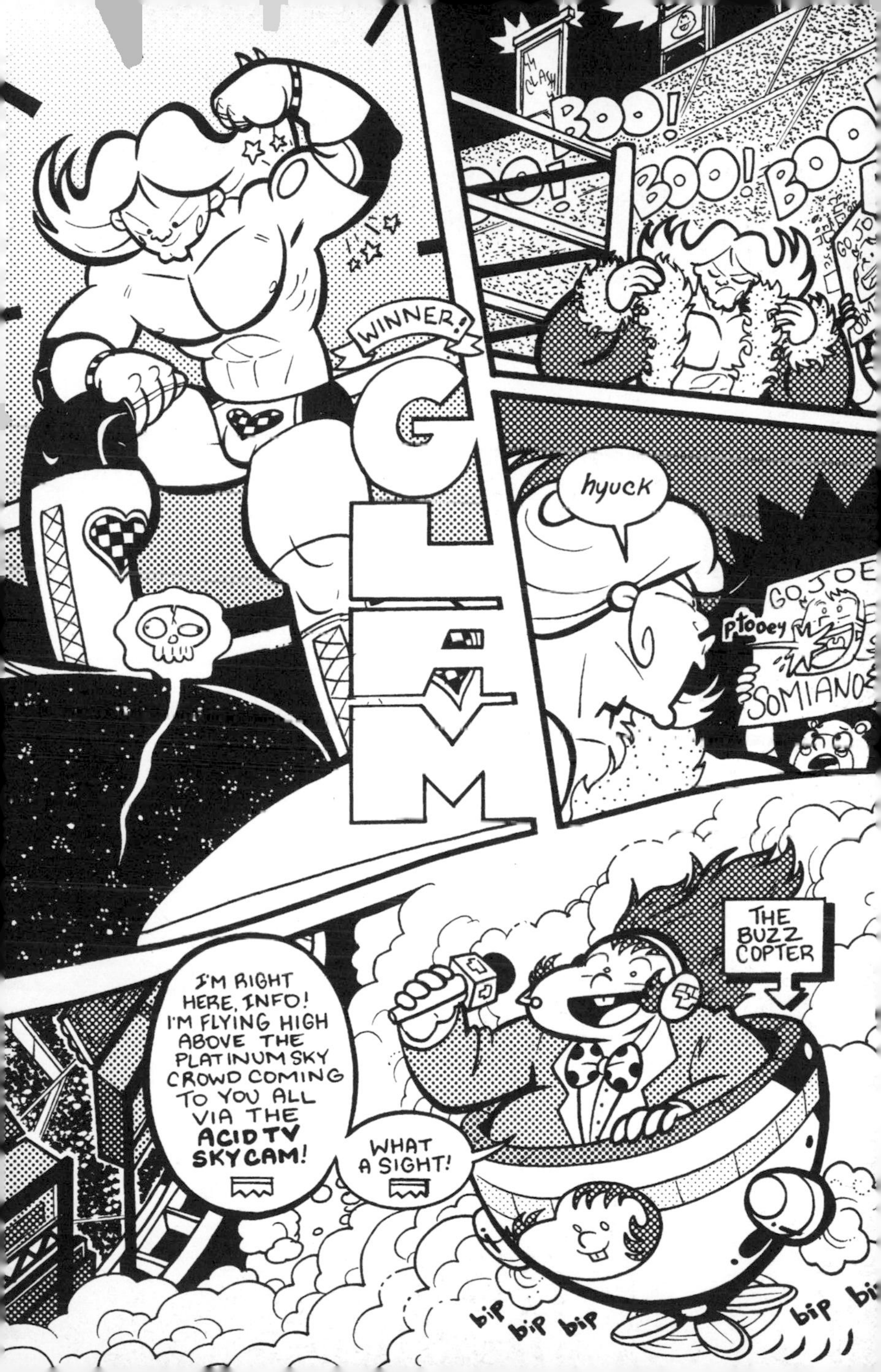
WINNER!
GLAM
BOO!
BOO!
BOO!
hyuck
ptooey
GO JOE
SOMIANO
I'M RIGHT HERE, INFO! I'M FLYING HIGH ABOVE THE PLATINUM SKY CROWD COMING TO YOU ALL VIA THE **ACID TV SKYCAM!**
WHAT A SIGHT!
THE BUZZ COPTER
bip bip bip
bip

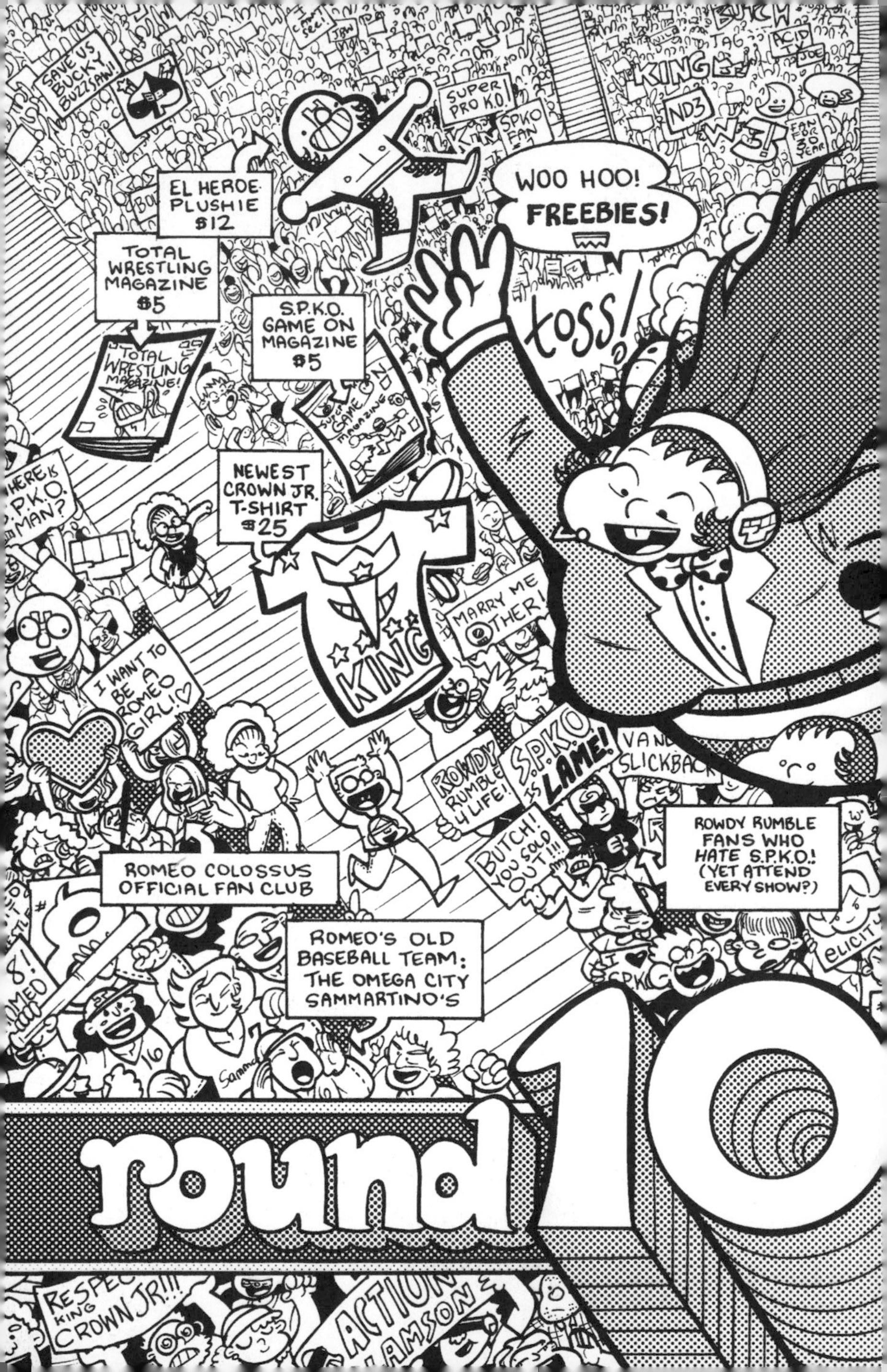
SAVE US BUCKY BUZZSAW!
SUPER PRO K.O.
SPKO FAN
KING
ND3
FAN FOR 30 YEAR
EL HEROE PLUSHIE $12
WOO HOO! FREEBIES!
TOTAL WRESTLING MAGAZINE $5
TOTAL WRESTLING MAGAZINE!
toss!
S.P.K.O. GAME ON MAGAZINE $5
NEWEST CROWN JR. T-SHIRT $25
KING
MARRY ME OTHER!
I WANT TO BE A ROMEO GIRL!♡
ROWDY RUMBLE 4 LIFE!
S.P.K.O. IS LAME!
SLICKBACK
BUTCH! YOU SOLD OUT!!!
ROWDY RUMBLE FANS WHO HATE S.P.K.O.! (YET ATTEND EVERY SHOW?)
ROMEO COLOSSUS OFFICIAL FAN CLUB
ROMEO'S OLD BASEBALL TEAM: THE OMEGA CITY SAMMARTINO'S
round 10
RESPECT KING CROWN JR!!!
ACTION

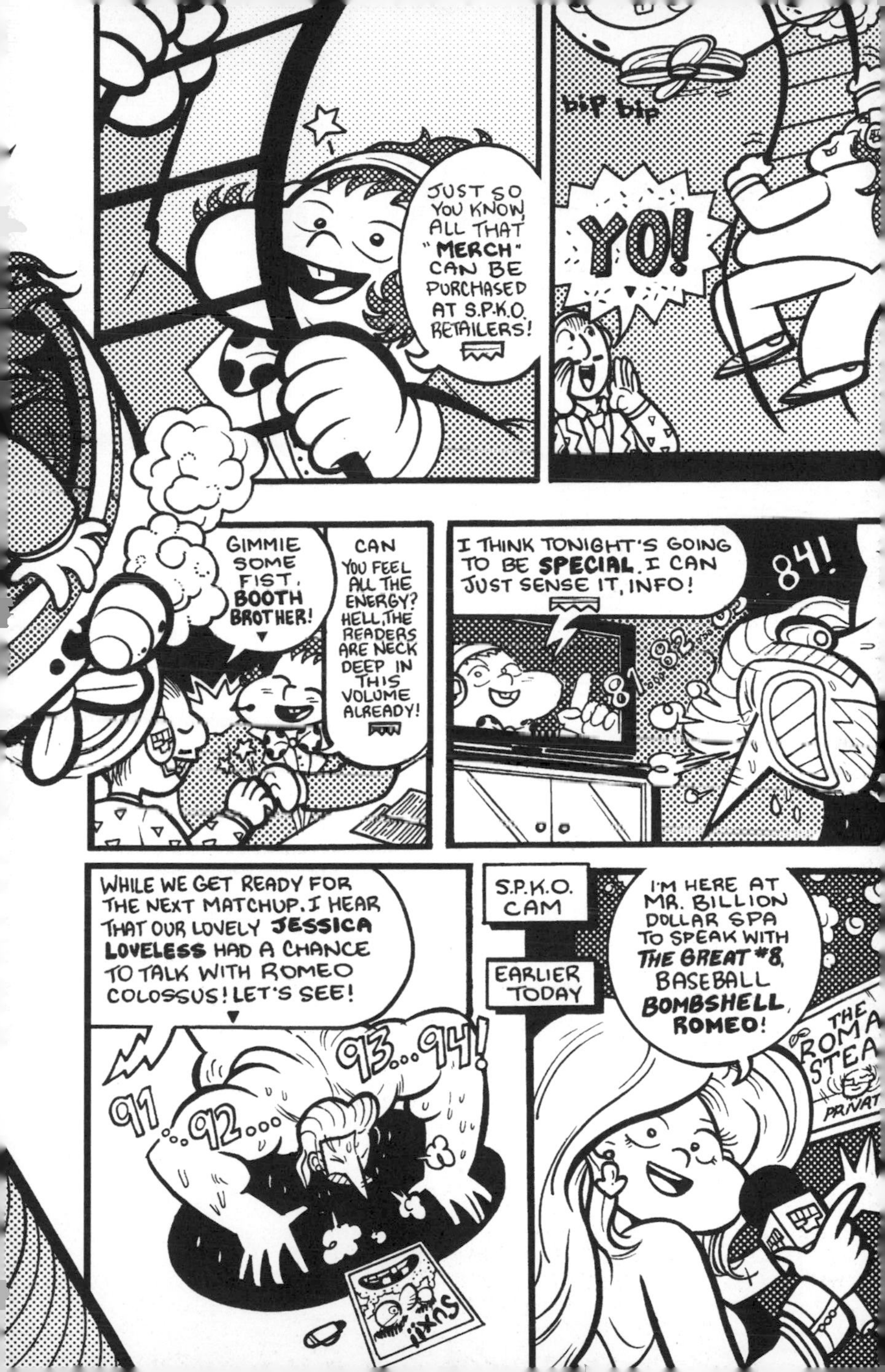
JUST SO YOU KNOW, ALL THAT "MERCH" CAN BE PURCHASED AT S.P.K.O. RETAILERS!
bip bip
YO!
GIMMIE SOME FIST, BOOTH BROTHER!
CAN YOU FEEL ALL THE ENERGY? HELL, THE READERS ARE NECK DEEP IN THIS VOLUME ALREADY!
I THINK TONIGHT'S GOING TO BE SPECIAL. I CAN JUST SENSE IT, INFO!
81...82
84!
WHILE WE GET READY FOR THE NEXT MATCHUP, I HEAR THAT OUR LOVELY JESSICA LOVELESS HAD A CHANCE TO TALK WITH ROMEO COLOSSUS! LET'S SEE!
91...92...
93...94!
SUKI!
S.P.K.O. CAM
EARLIER TODAY
I'M HERE AT MR. BILLION DOLLAR SPA TO SPEAK WITH THE GREAT #8, BASEBALL BOMBSHELL, ROMEO!

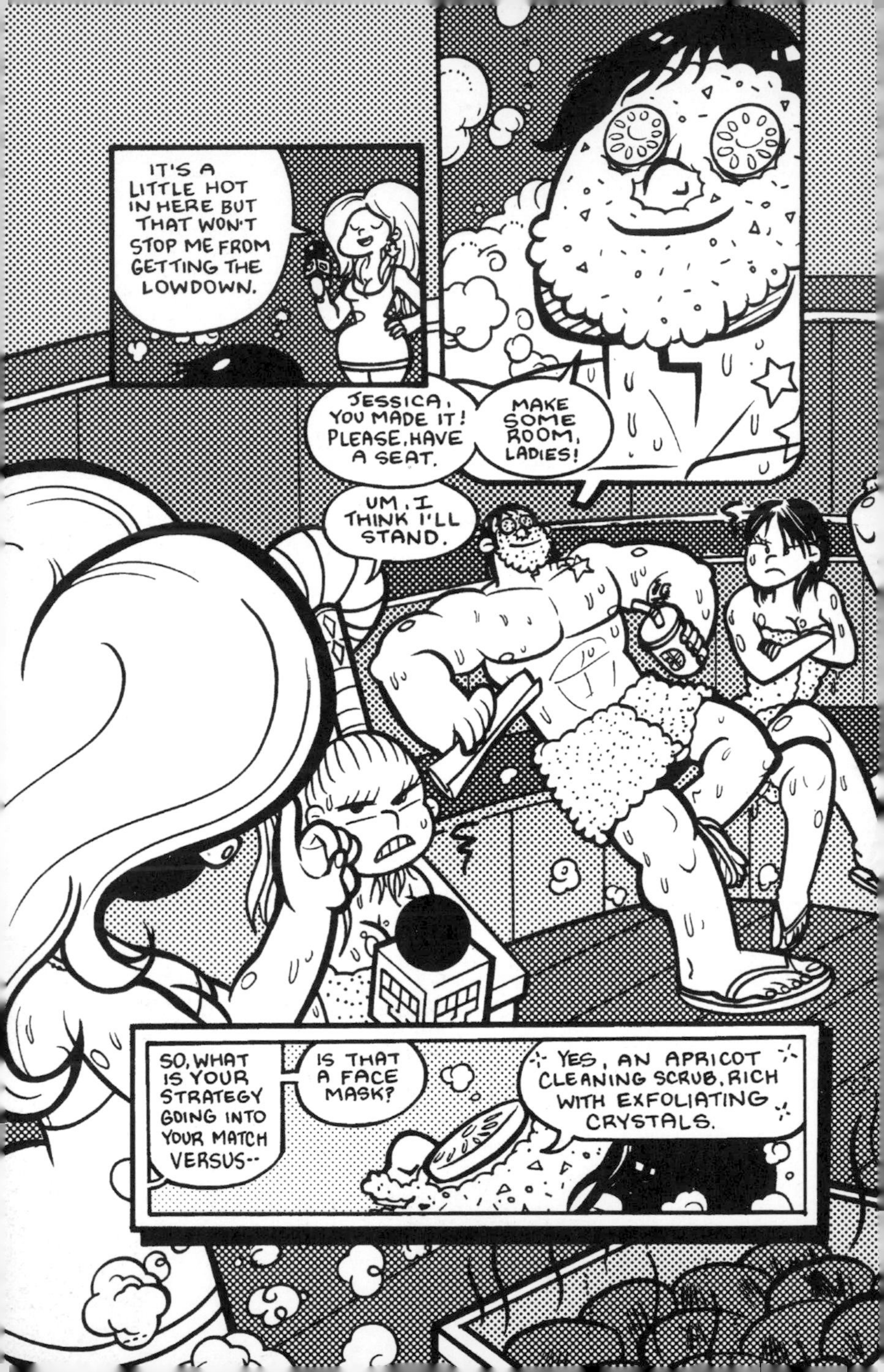
IT'S A LITTLE HOT IN HERE BUT THAT WON'T STOP ME FROM GETTING THE LOWDOWN.
JESSICA, YOU MADE IT! PLEASE, HAVE A SEAT.
MAKE SOME ROOM, LADIES!
UM, I THINK I'LL STAND.
SO, WHAT IS YOUR STRATEGY GOING INTO YOUR MATCH VERSUS--
IS THAT A FACE MASK?
YES, AN APRICOT CLEANING SCRUB, RICH WITH EXFOLIATING CRYSTALS.

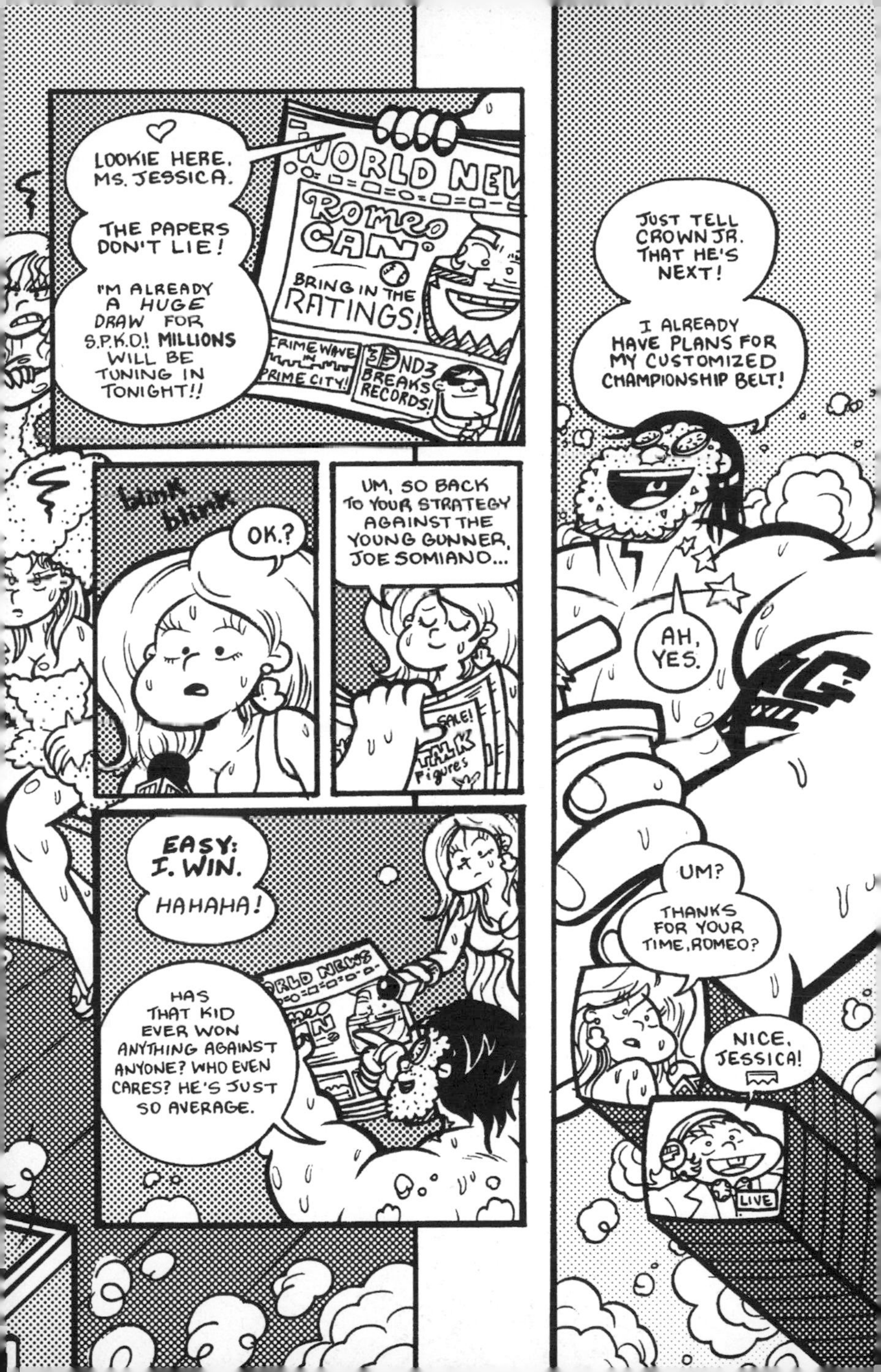
LOOKIE HERE, MS. JESSICA.
THE PAPERS DON'T LIE!
I'M ALREADY A HUGE DRAW FOR S.P.K.D.! MILLIONS WILL BE TUNING IN TONIGHT!!
WORLD NEW
Romeo CAN
BRING IN THE RATINGS!
CRIME WAVE IN PRIME CITY!
BREAKS RECORDS!
blink blink
OK.?
UM, SO BACK TO YOUR STRATEGY AGAINST THE YOUNG GUNNER, JOE SOMIANO...
SALE!
EASY: I. WIN.
HAHAHA!
HAS THAT KID EVER WON ANYTHING AGAINST ANYONE? WHO EVEN CARES? HE'S JUST SO AVERAGE.
JUST TELL CROWN JR. THAT HE'S NEXT!
I ALREADY HAVE PLANS FOR MY CUSTOMIZED CHAMPIONSHIP BELT!
AH, YES.
UM?
THANKS FOR YOUR TIME, ROMEO?
NICE, JESSICA!
LIVE

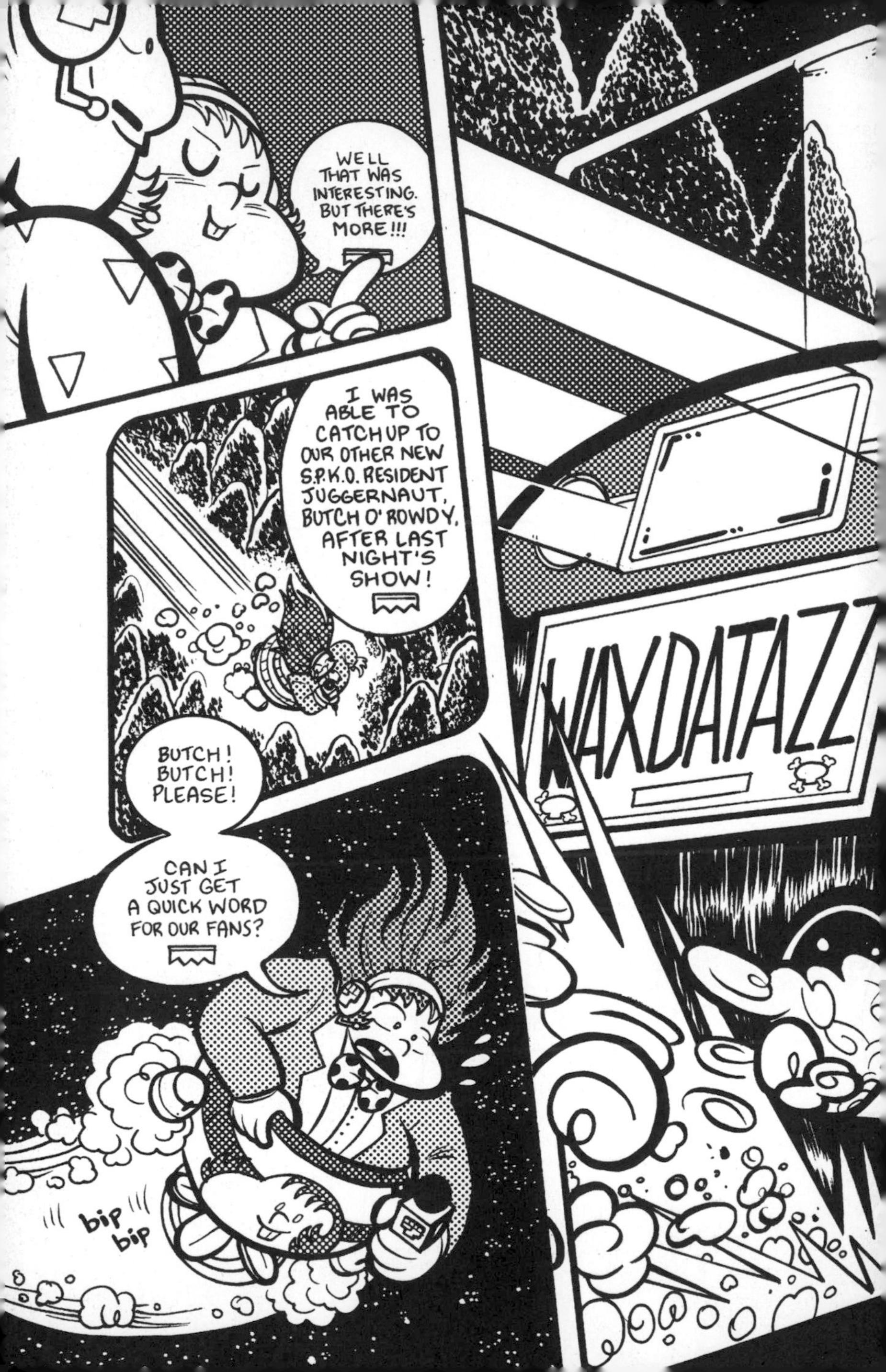
WELL THAT WAS INTERESTING. BUT THERE'S MORE!!!
I WAS ABLE TO CATCH UP TO OUR OTHER NEW S.P.K.O. RESIDENT JUGGERNAUT, BUTCH O' ROWDY, AFTER LAST NIGHT'S SHOW!
WAXDATAZZ
BUTCH! BUTCH! PLEASE!
CAN I JUST GET A QUICK WORD FOR OUR FANS?
bip bip

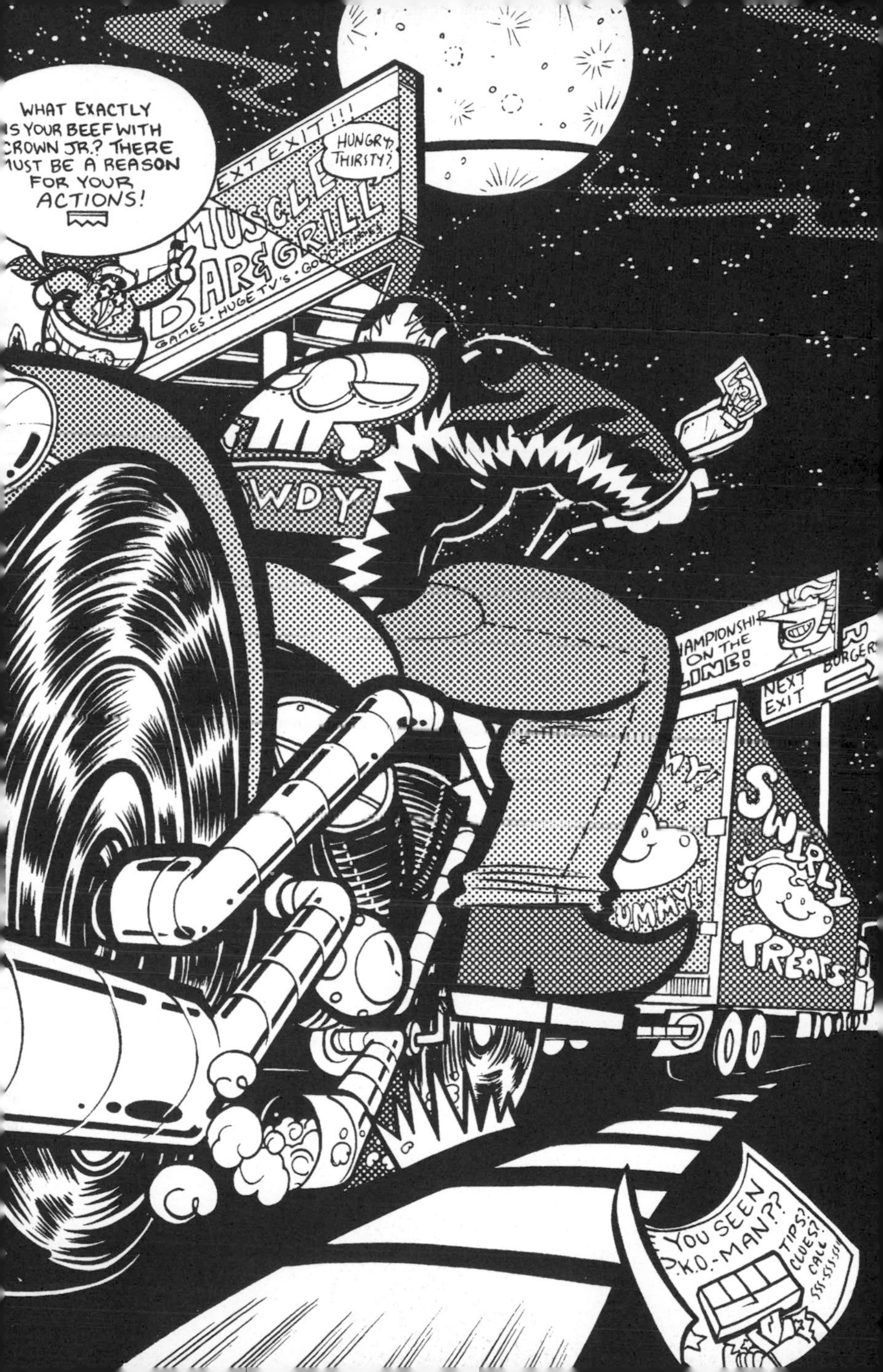
WHAT EXACTLY IS YOUR BEEF WITH CROWN JR.? THERE MUST BE A REASON FOR YOUR ACTIONS!
NEXT EXIT!!!
HUNGRY? THIRSTY?
MUSCLE BAR & GRILL
GAMES · HUGE TV'S · GOOD TIMES
WDY
CHAMPIONSHIP ON THE LINE!
NEXT EXIT
BURGERS
YUMMY!
SWIRLY TREATS
YOU SEEN K.O.-MAN??
TIPS? CLUES? CALL 555-555-55

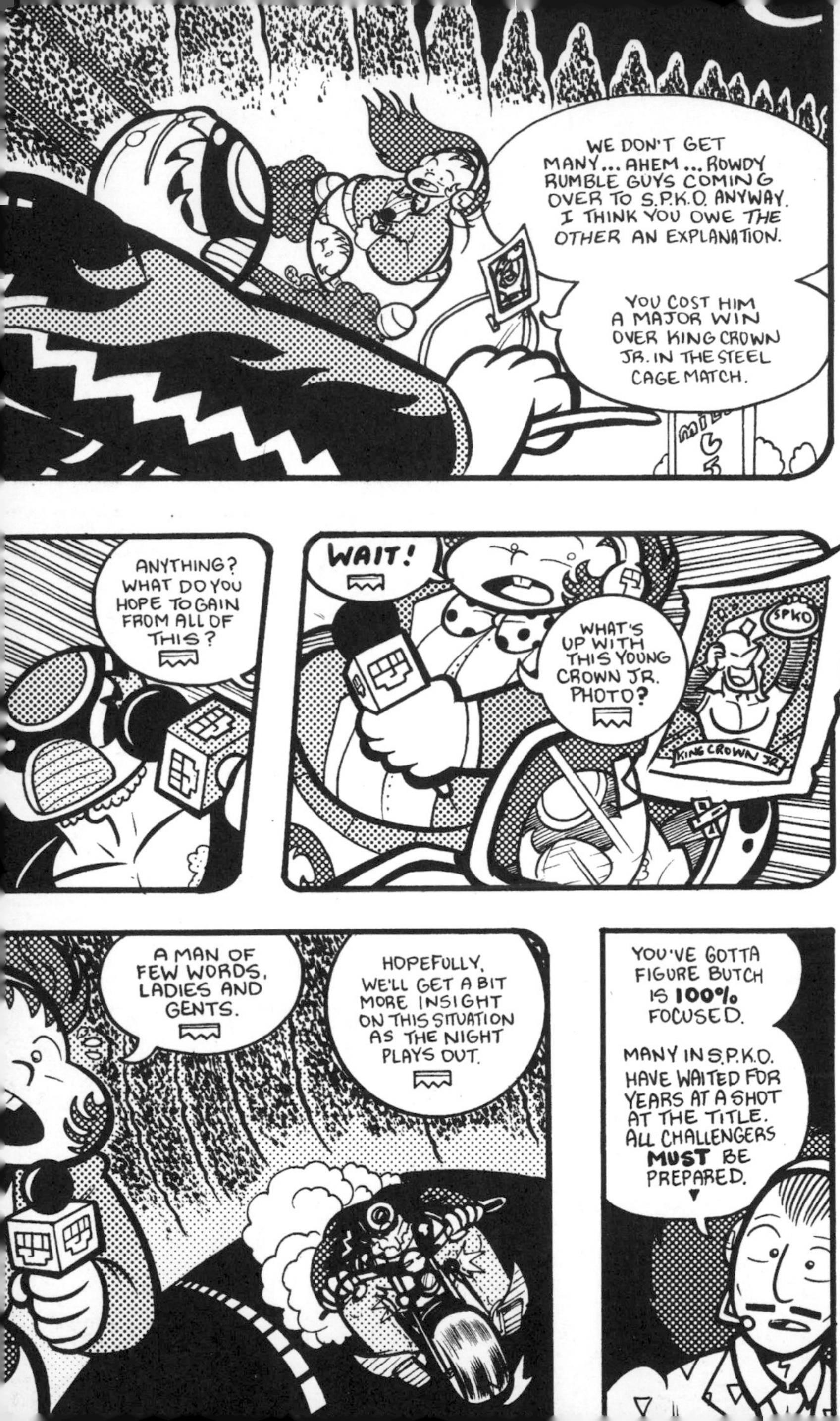
WE DON'T GET MANY... AHEM... ROWDY RUMBLE GUYS COMING OVER TO S.P.K.O. ANYWAY. I THINK YOU OWE *THE OTHER* AN EXPLANATION.
YOU COST HIM A MAJOR WIN OVER KING CROWN JR. IN THE STEEL CAGE MATCH.
ANYTHING? WHAT DO YOU HOPE TO GAIN FROM ALL OF THIS?
WAIT!
WHAT'S UP WITH THIS YOUNG CROWN JR. PHOTO?
SPKO
KING CROWN JR.
A MAN OF FEW WORDS, LADIES AND GENTS.
HOPEFULLY, WE'LL GET A BIT MORE INSIGHT ON THIS SITUATION AS THE NIGHT PLAYS OUT.
YOU'VE GOTTA FIGURE BUTCH IS **100%** FOCUSED.
MANY IN S.P.K.O. HAVE WAITED FOR YEARS AT A SHOT AT THE TITLE. ALL CHALLENGERS **MUST** BE PREPARED.

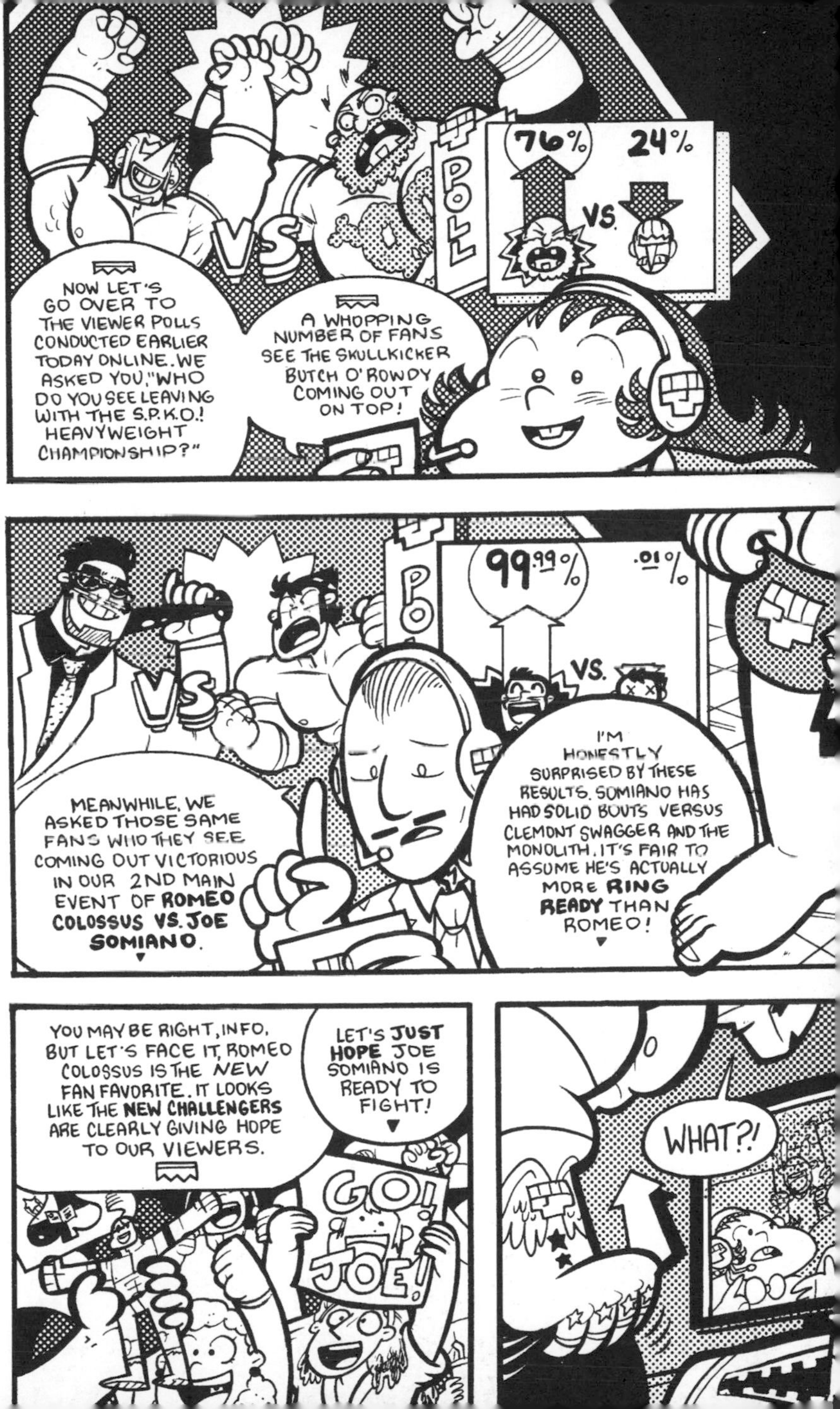
VS
POLL
76%
24%
VS.
NOW LET'S GO OVER TO THE VIEWER POLLS CONDUCTED EARLIER TODAY ONLINE. WE ASKED YOU, "WHO DO YOU SEE LEAVING WITH THE S.P.K.O.! HEAVYWEIGHT CHAMPIONSHIP?"
A WHOPPING NUMBER OF FANS SEE THE SKULLKICKER BUTCH O'ROWDY COMING OUT ON TOP!
VS
99.99%
.01%
VS.
MEANWHILE, WE ASKED THOSE SAME FANS WHO THEY SEE COMING OUT VICTORIOUS IN OUR 2ND MAIN EVENT OF **ROMEO COLOSSUS VS. JOE SOMIANO**.
I'M HONESTLY SURPRISED BY THESE RESULTS. SOMIANO HAS HAD SOLID BOUTS VERSUS CLEMONT SWAGGER AND THE MONOLITH. IT'S FAIR TO ASSUME HE'S ACTUALLY MORE **RING READY** THAN ROMEO!
YOU MAY BE RIGHT, INFO. BUT LET'S FACE IT, ROMEO COLOSSUS IS THE *NEW* FAN FAVORITE. IT LOOKS LIKE THE **NEW CHALLENGERS** ARE CLEARLY GIVING HOPE TO OUR VIEWERS.
LET'S **JUST HOPE** JOE SOMIANO IS READY TO FIGHT!
GO! JOE!
WHAT?!

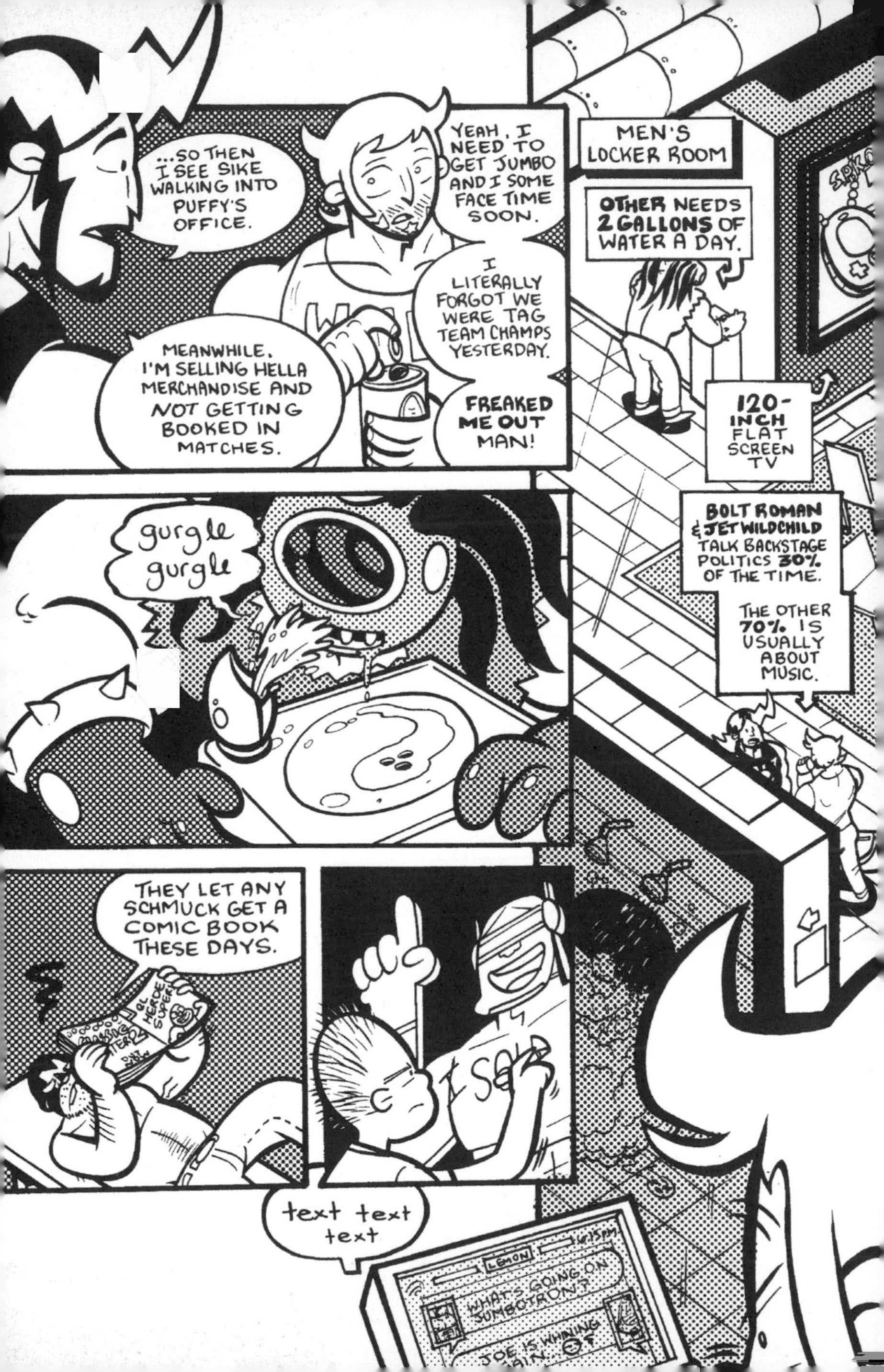
...SO THEN I SEE SIKE WALKING INTO PUFFY'S OFFICE.
YEAH, I NEED TO GET JUMBO AND I SOME FACE TIME SOON.
MEANWHILE, I'M SELLING HELLA MERCHANDISE AND NOT GETTING BOOKED IN MATCHES.
I LITERALLY FORGOT WE WERE TAG TEAM CHAMPS YESTERDAY.
FREAKED ME OUT MAN!
gurgle gurgle
THEY LET ANY SCHMUCK GET A COMIC BOOK THESE DAYS.
I SOLD
text text text
MEN'S LOCKER ROOM
OTHER NEEDS 2 GALLONS OF WATER A DAY.
120-INCH FLAT SCREEN TV
BOLT ROMAN & JET WILDCHILD TALK BACKSTAGE POLITICS 30% OF THE TIME.
THE OTHER 70% IS USUALLY ABOUT MUSIC.
LEMON
WHAT'S GOING ON JUMBOTRON?
JOE IS WHINING AGAIN.

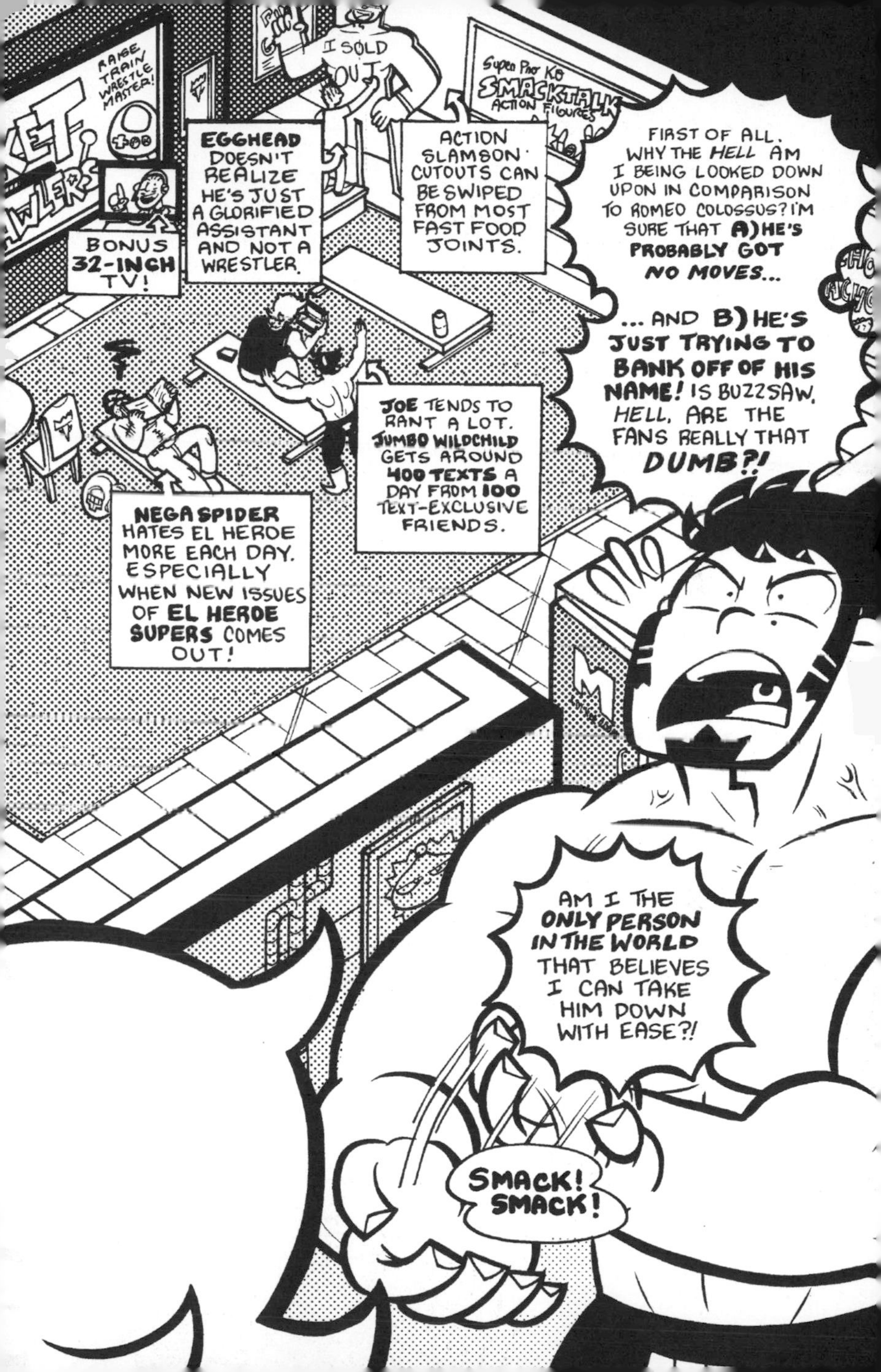

RAISE TRAIN WRESTLE MASTER!
I SOLD OUT
SUPER PRO KO SMACKTALK ACTION FIGURES
EGGHEAD DOESN'T REALIZE HE'S JUST A GLORIFIED ASSISTANT AND NOT A WRESTLER.
ACTION SLAMSON CUTOUTS CAN BE SWIPED FROM MOST FAST FOOD JOINTS.
BONUS 32-INCH TV!
FIRST OF ALL. WHY THE HELL AM I BEING LOOKED DOWN UPON IN COMPARISON TO ROMEO COLOSSUS? I'M SURE THAT A) HE'S PROBABLY GOT NO MOVES...
... AND B) HE'S JUST TRYING TO BANK OFF OF HIS NAME! IS BUZZSAW, HELL, ARE THE FANS REALLY THAT DUMB?!
JOE TENDS TO RANT A LOT. JUMBO WILDCHILD GETS AROUND 400 TEXTS A DAY FROM 100 TEXT-EXCLUSIVE FRIENDS.
NEGA SPIDER HATES EL HEROE MORE EACH DAY. ESPECIALLY WHEN NEW ISSUES OF EL HEROE SUPERS COMES OUT!
AM I THE ONLY PERSON IN THE WORLD THAT BELIEVES I CAN TAKE HIM DOWN WITH EASE?!
SMACK! SMACK!

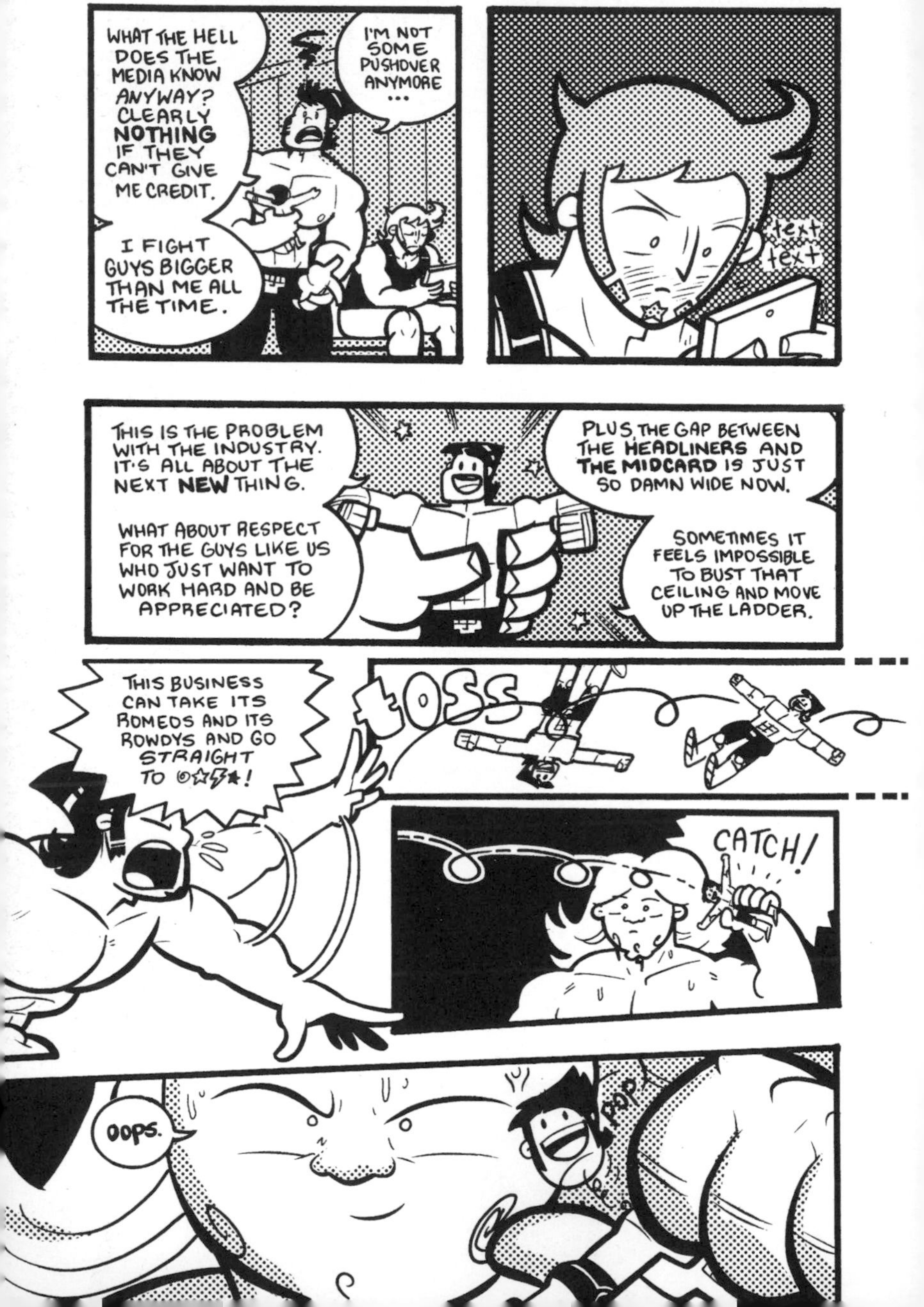
WHAT THE HELL DOES THE MEDIA KNOW ANYWAY? CLEARLY NOTHING IF THEY CAN'T GIVE ME CREDIT.
I FIGHT GUYS BIGGER THAN ME ALL THE TIME.
I'M NOT SOME PUSHOVER ANYMORE ...
text text
THIS IS THE PROBLEM WITH THE INDUSTRY. IT'S ALL ABOUT THE NEXT NEW THING.
WHAT ABOUT RESPECT FOR THE GUYS LIKE US WHO JUST WANT TO WORK HARD AND BE APPRECIATED?
PLUS, THE GAP BETWEEN THE HEADLINERS AND THE MIDCARD IS JUST SO DAMN WIDE NOW.
SOMETIMES IT FEELS IMPOSSIBLE TO BUST THAT CEILING AND MOVE UP THE LADDER.
THIS BUSINESS CAN TAKE ITS ROMEOS AND ITS ROWDYS AND GO STRAIGHT TO @☆ϟ★!
TOSS
CATCH!
OOPS.
POP

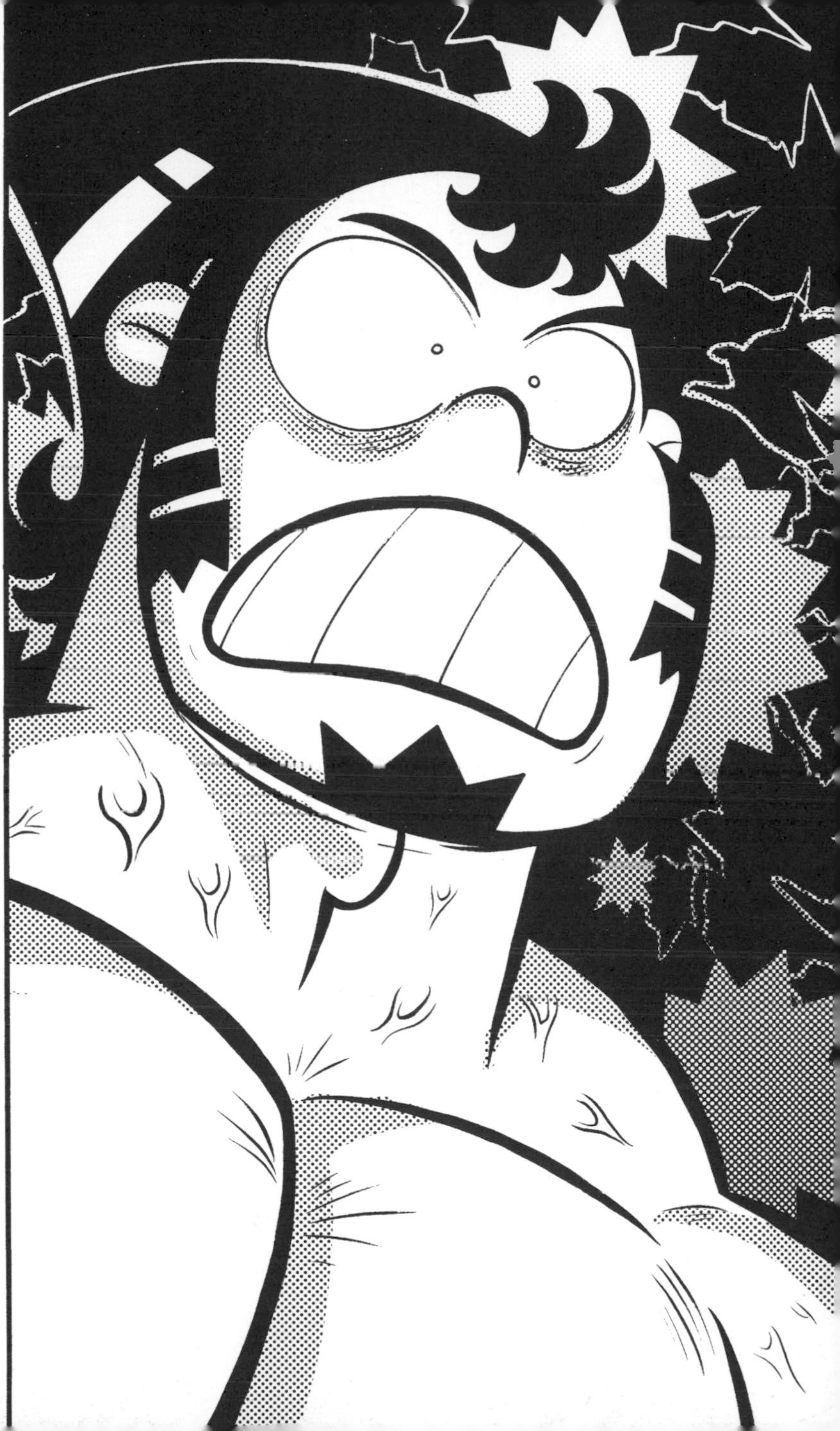

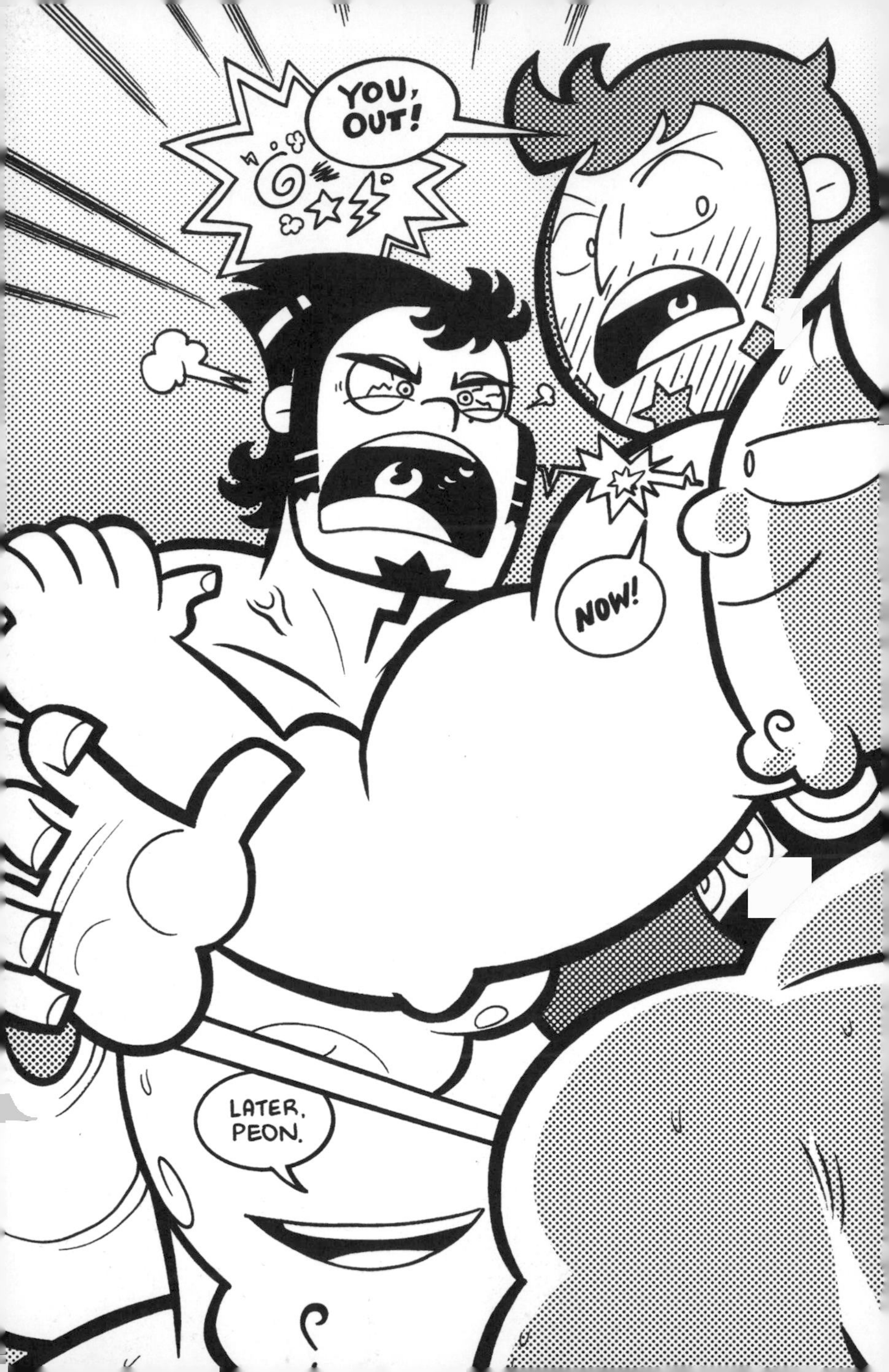
YOU, OUT!
NOW!
LATER, PEON.

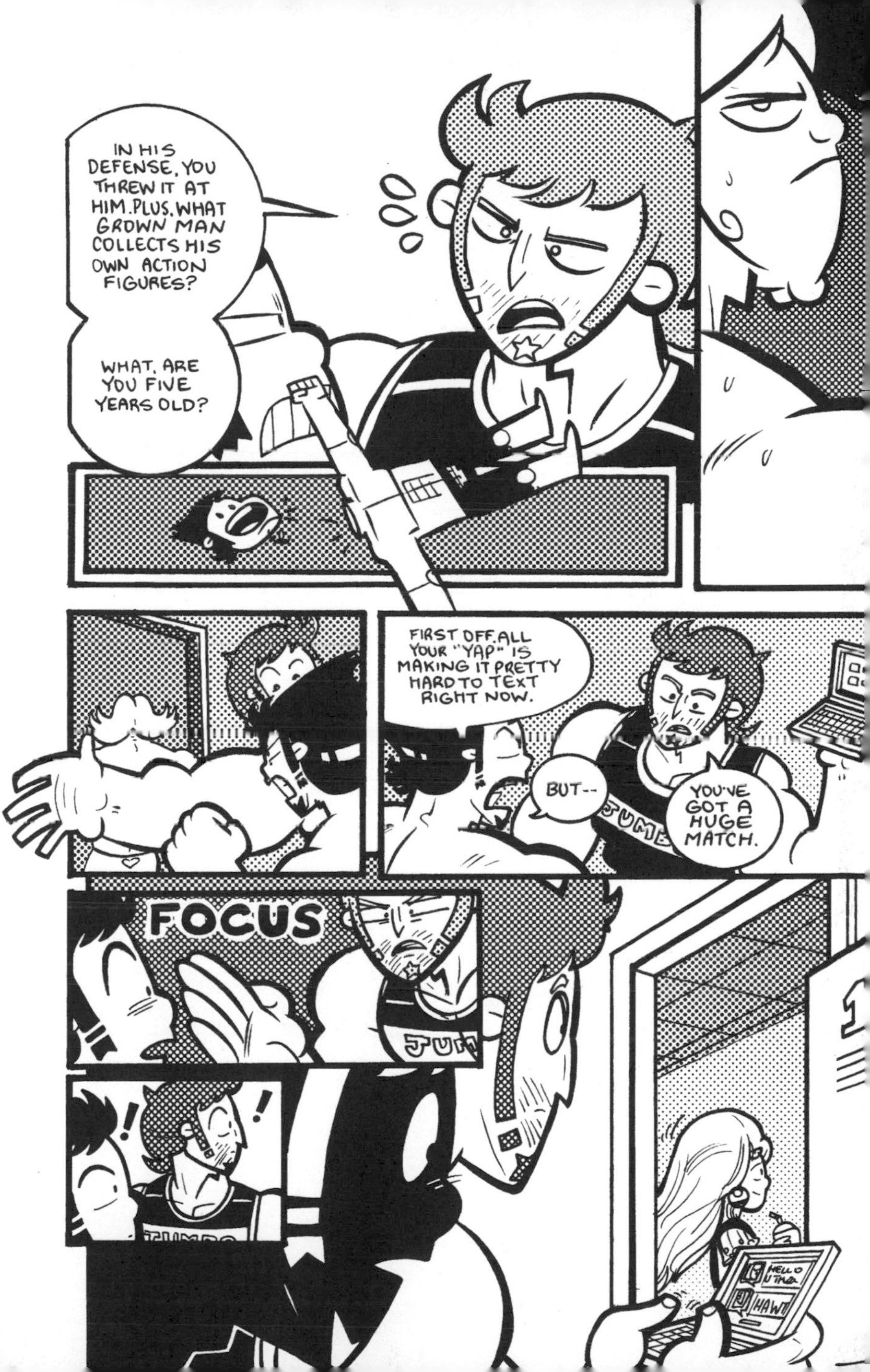
IN HIS DEFENSE, YOU THREW IT AT HIM. PLUS, WHAT GROWN MAN COLLECTS HIS OWN ACTION FIGURES?
WHAT, ARE YOU FIVE YEARS OLD?
FIRST OFF, ALL YOUR "YAP" IS MAKING IT PRETTY HARD TO TEXT RIGHT NOW.
BUT--
YOU'VE GOT A HUGE MATCH.
FOCUS
!
!
HELLO
HAWT

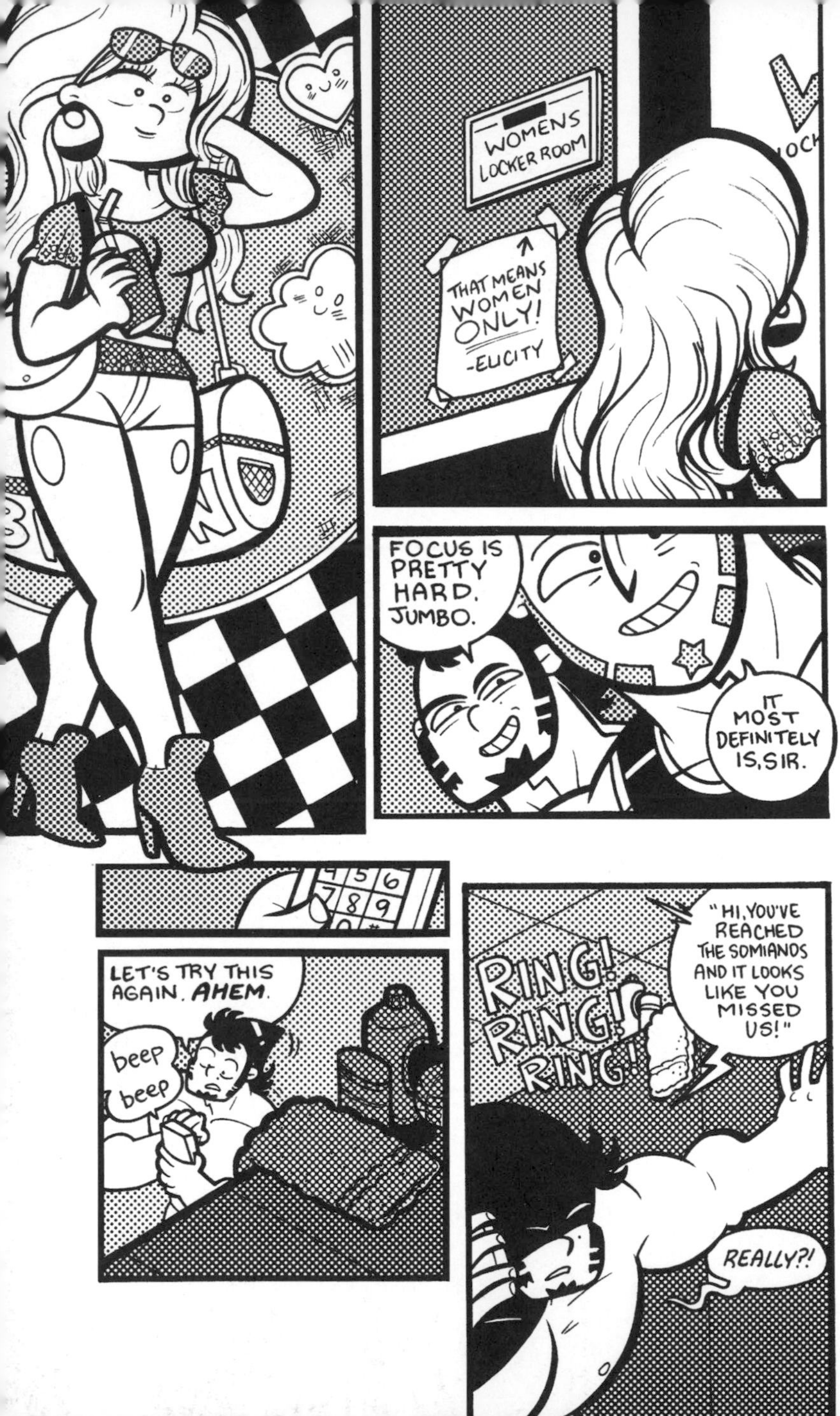

WOMENS LOCKER ROOM
THAT MEANS WOMEN ONLY! -ELICITY
FOCUS IS PRETTY HARD, JUMBO.
IT MOST DEFINITELY IS, SIR.
4 5 6
7 8 9
LET'S TRY THIS AGAIN. AHEM.
beep beep
RING! RING! RING!
"HI, YOU'VE REACHED THE SOMIANDS AND IT LOOKS LIKE YOU MISSED US!"
REALLY?!

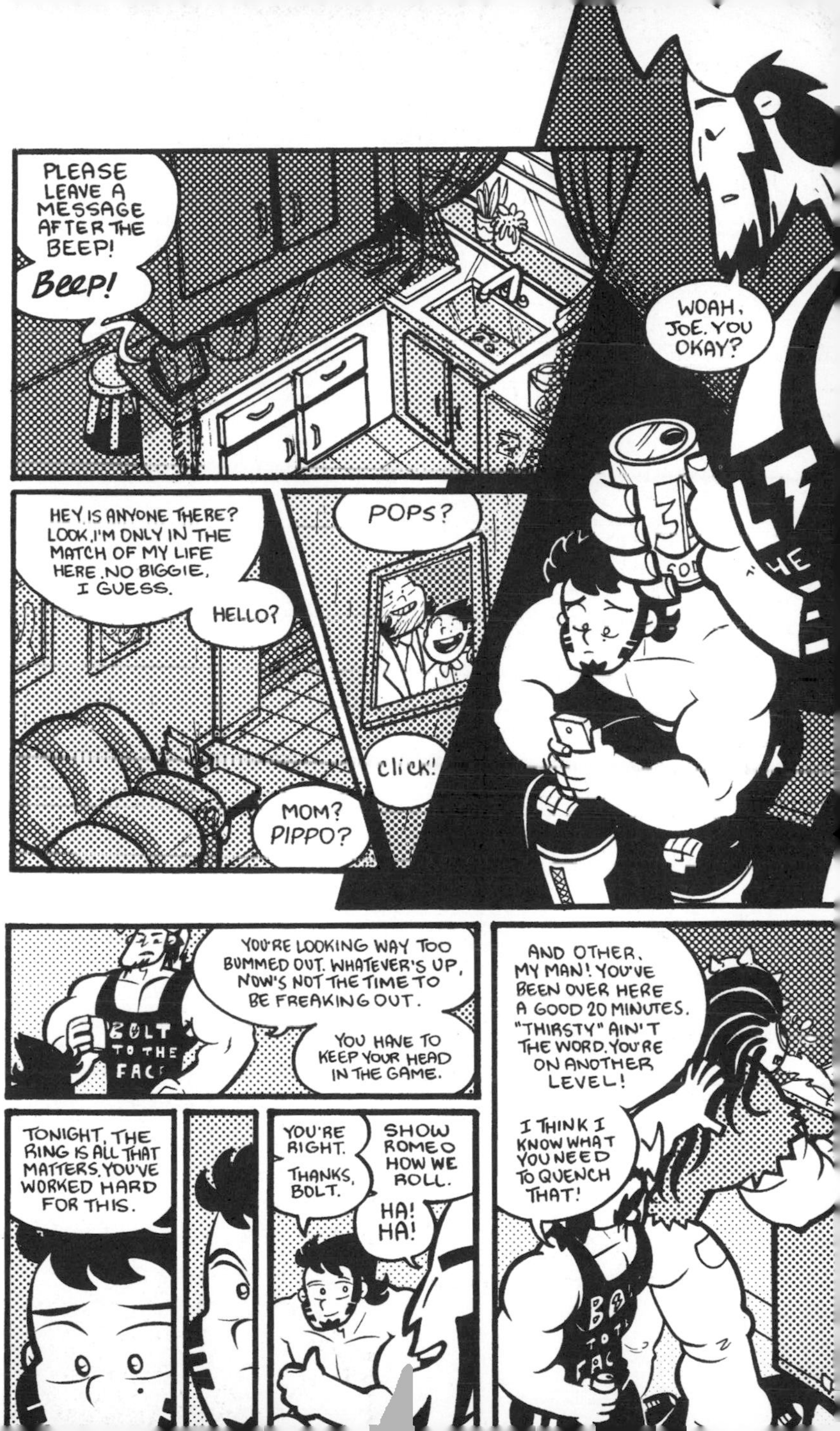
PLEASE LEAVE A MESSAGE AFTER THE BEEP!
Beep!
HEY, IS ANYONE THERE? LOOK, I'M ONLY IN THE MATCH OF MY LIFE HERE. NO BIGGIE, I GUESS.
HELLO?
MOM? PIPPO?
POPS?
Click!
WOAH, JOE. YOU OKAY?
YOU'RE LOOKING WAY TOO BUMMED OUT. WHATEVER'S UP, NOW'S NOT THE TIME TO BE FREAKING OUT.
YOU HAVE TO KEEP YOUR HEAD IN THE GAME.
TONIGHT, THE RING IS ALL THAT MATTERS. YOU'VE WORKED HARD FOR THIS.
YOU'RE RIGHT.
THANKS, BOLT.
SHOW ROMEO HOW WE ROLL.
HA! HA!
AND OTHER, MY MAN! YOU'VE BEEN OVER HERE A GOOD 20 MINUTES. "THIRSTY" AIN'T THE WORD. YOU'RE ON ANOTHER LEVEL!
I THINK I KNOW WHAT YOU NEED TO QUENCH THAT!

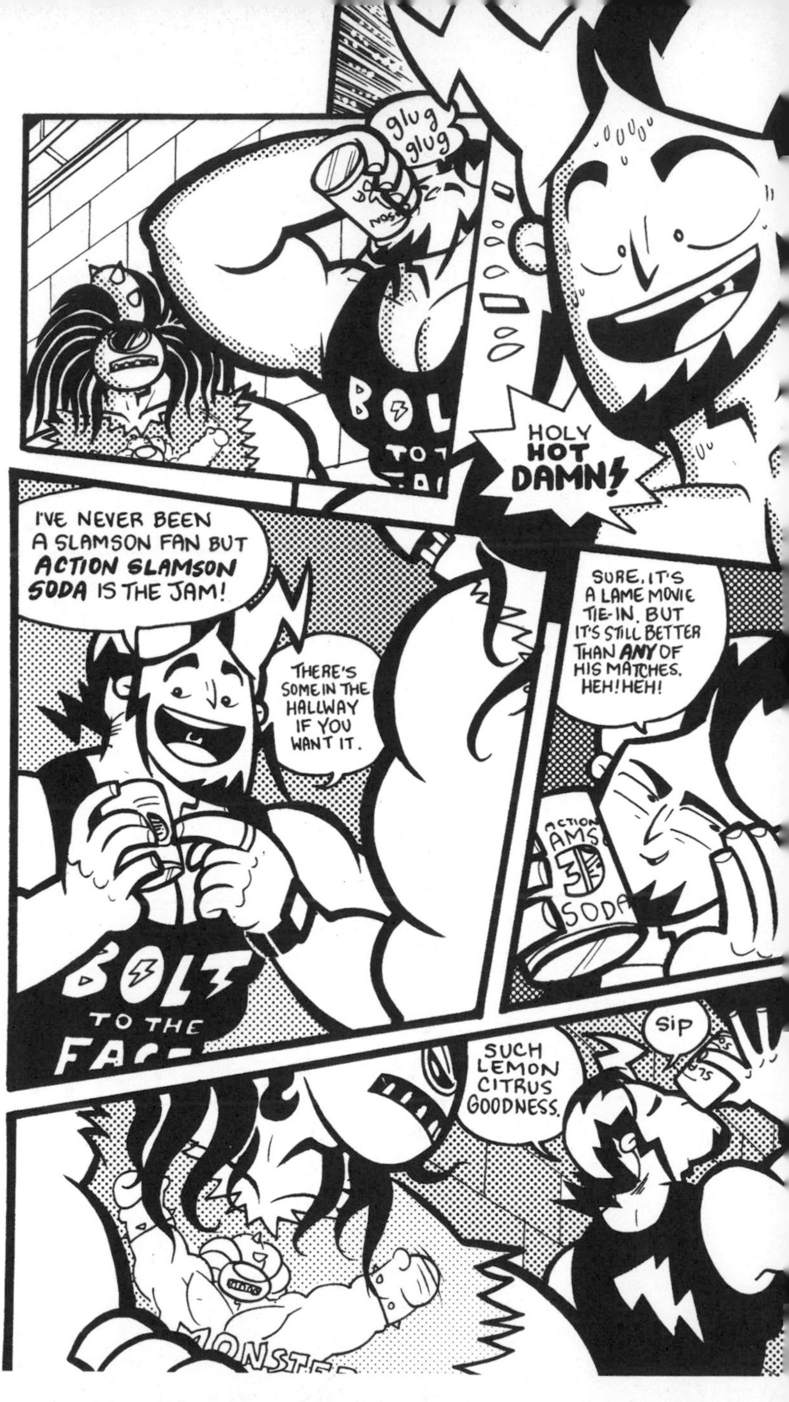
glug glug
HOLY HOT DAMN!
I'VE NEVER BEEN A SLAMSON FAN BUT ACTION SLAMSON SODA IS THE JAM!
BOLT TO THE
THERE'S SOME IN THE HALLWAY IF YOU WANT IT.
SURE, IT'S A LAME MOVIE TIE-IN. BUT IT'S STILL BETTER THAN ANY OF HIS MATCHES. HEH! HEH!
SODA
SUCH LEMON CITRUS GOODNESS.
sip

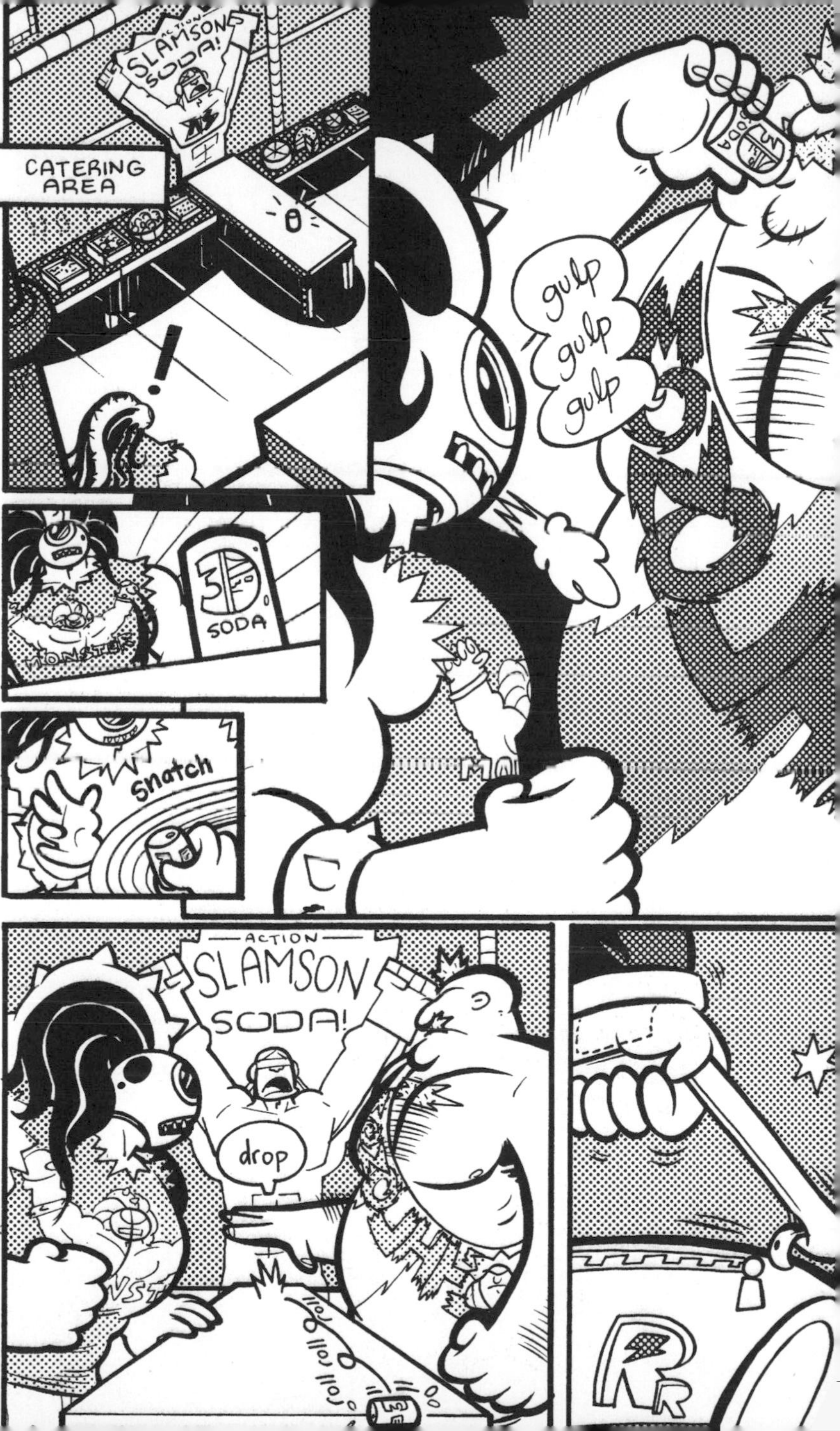
ACTION
SLAMSON SODA!
CATERING AREA
!
SODA
snatch
gulp gulp gulp
ACTION
SLAMSON SODA!
drop
roll roll roll

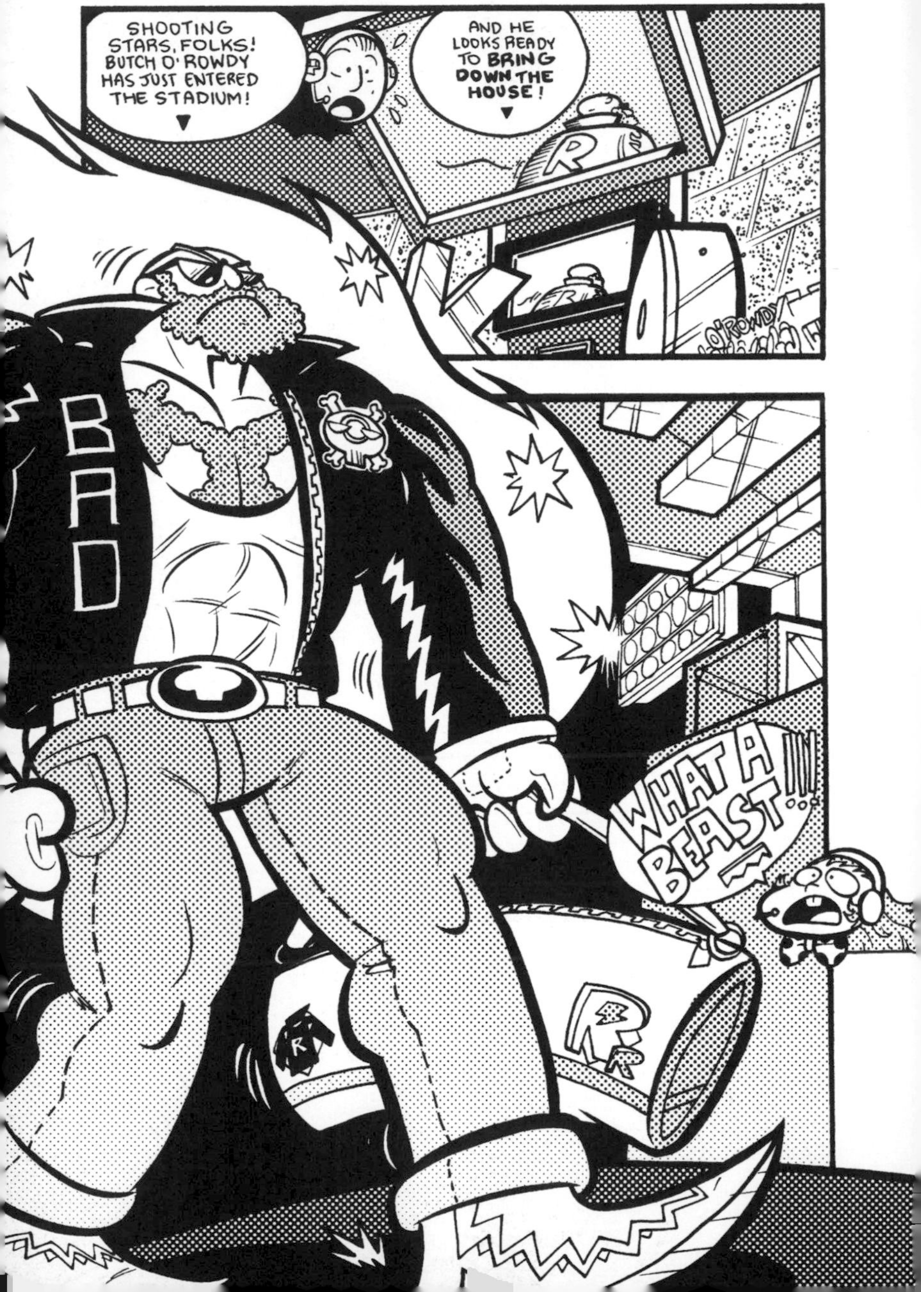
SHOOTING STARS, FOLKS! BUTCH O' ROWDY HAS JUST ENTERED THE STADIUM!
AND HE LOOKS READY TO **BRING DOWN THE HOUSE**!
O'ROWDY
BAD
WHAT A BEAST!!!

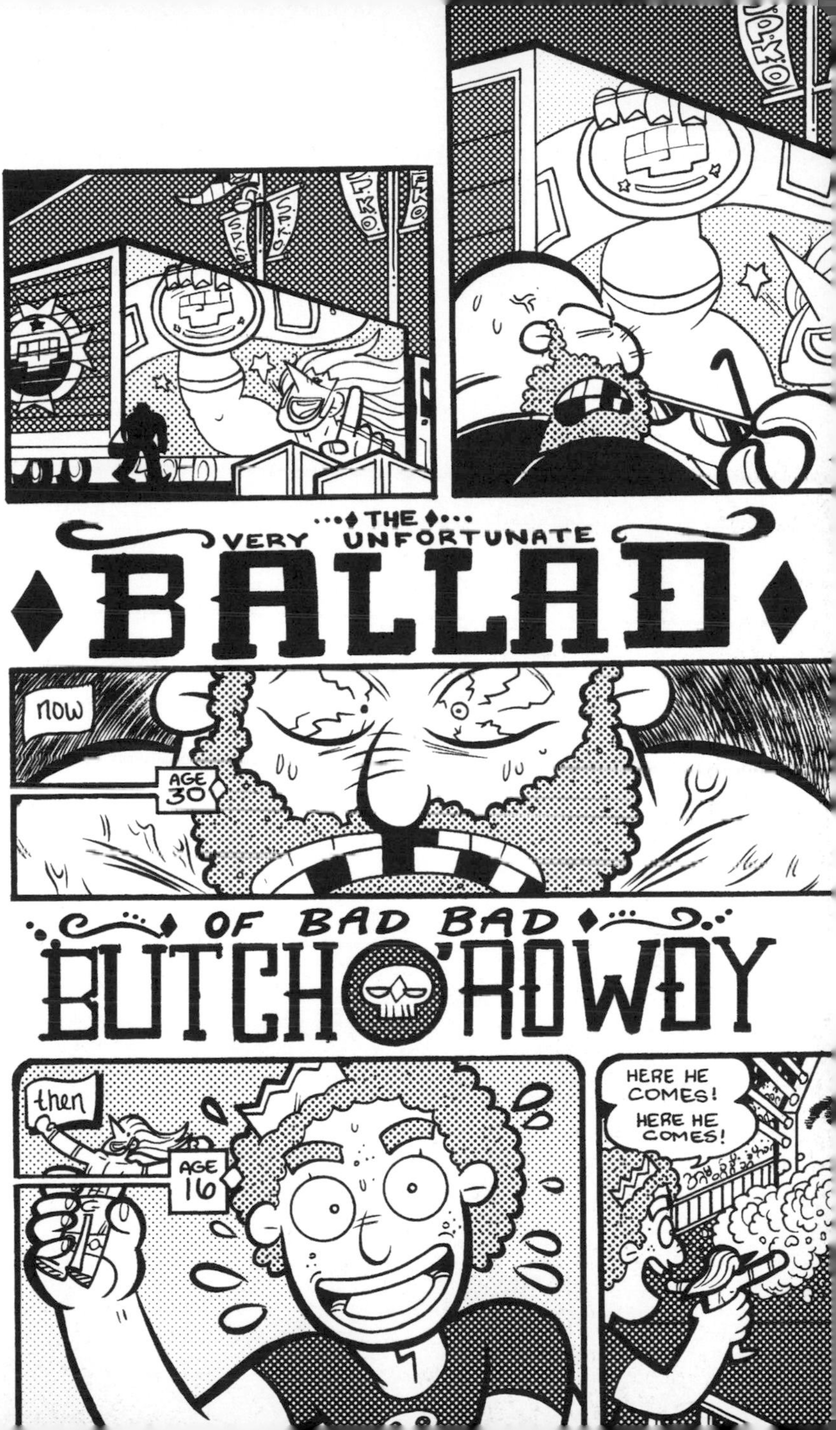
THE VERY UNFORTUNATE
BALLAD
now
AGE 30
OF BAD BAD
BUTCH O'ROWDY
then
AGE 16
HERE HE COMES!
HERE HE COMES!

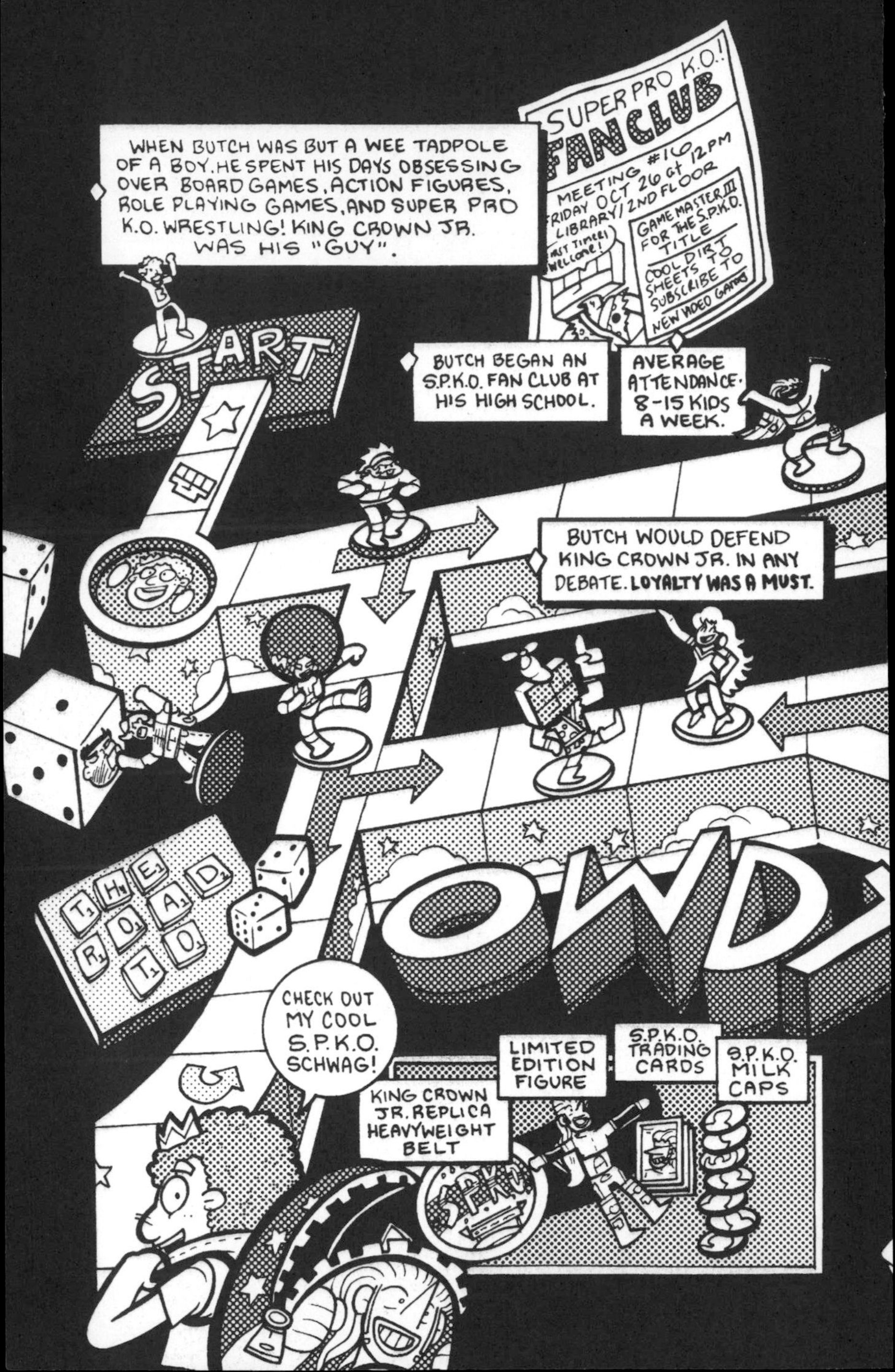

WHEN BUTCH WAS BUT A WEE TADPOLE OF A BOY. HE SPENT HIS DAYS OBSESSING OVER BOARD GAMES, ACTION FIGURES, ROLE PLAYING GAMES, AND SUPER PRO K.O. WRESTLING! KING CROWN JR. WAS HIS "GUY".
SUPER PRO K.O.! FANCLUB
MEETING #16
FRIDAY OCT 26 at 12PM
LIBRARY/ 2ND FLOOR
GAME MASTER III FOR THE S.P.K.O. TITLE
COOL DIRT SHEETS TO SUBSCRIBE TO
NEW VIDEO GAMES
START
BUTCH BEGAN AN S.P.K.O. FAN CLUB AT HIS HIGH SCHOOL.
AVERAGE ATTENDANCE. 8-15 KIDS A WEEK.
BUTCH WOULD DEFEND KING CROWN JR. IN ANY DEBATE. **LOYALTY WAS A MUST.**
THE ROAD TO
OWDY
CHECK OUT MY COOL S.P.K.O. SCHWAG!
LIMITED EDITION FIGURE
S.P.K.O. TRADING CARDS
S.P.K.O. MILK CAPS
KING CROWN JR. REPLICA HEAVYWEIGHT BELT
S.P.K.O.

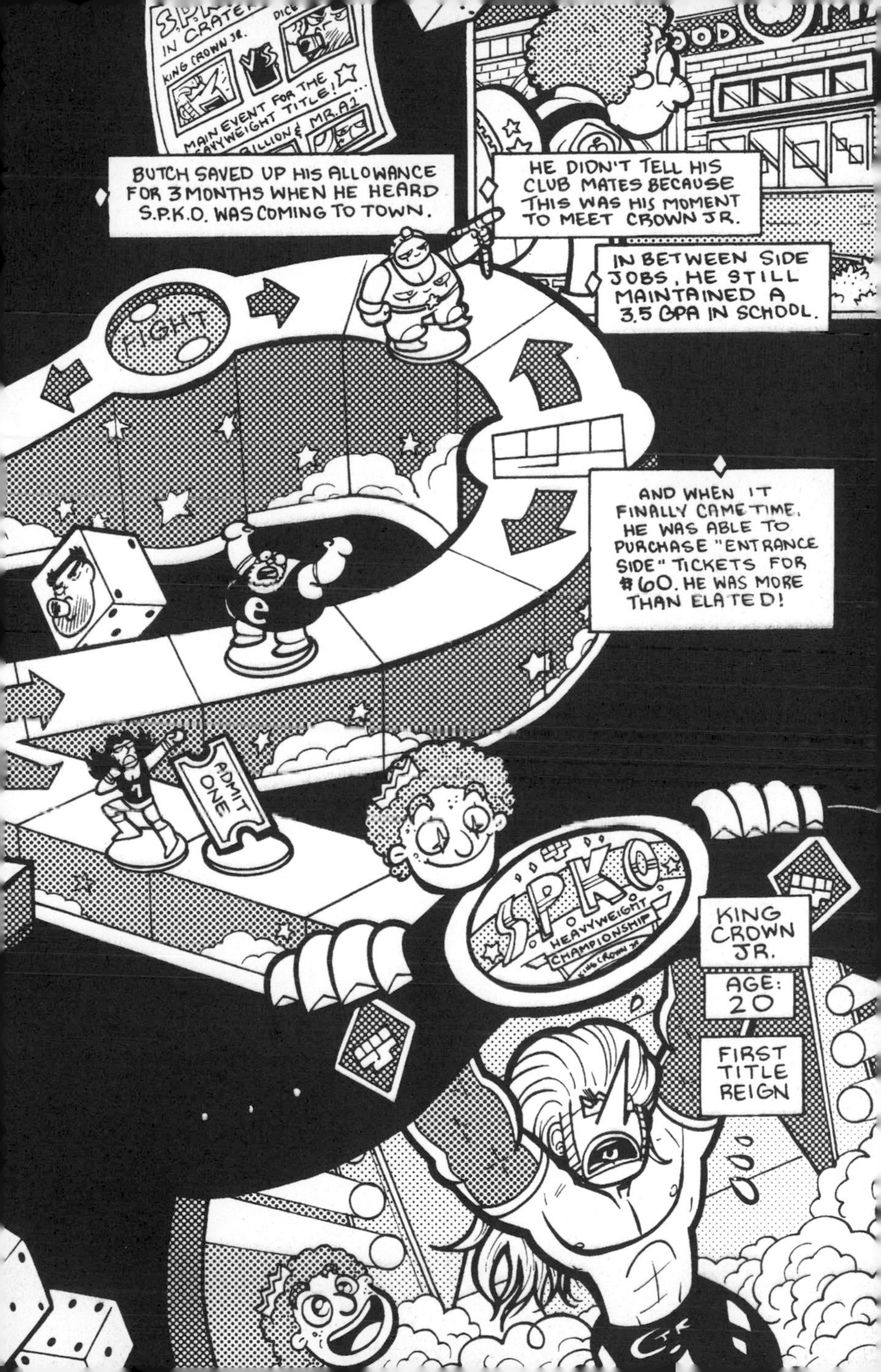

IN CRATE
KING CROWN JR.
VS
MAIN EVENT FOR THE
WEIGHT TITLE!
BUTCH SAVED UP HIS ALLOWANCE FOR 3 MONTHS WHEN HE HEARD S.P.K.O. WAS COMING TO TOWN.
HE DIDN'T TELL HIS CLUB MATES BECAUSE THIS WAS HIS MOMENT TO MEET CROWN JR.
IN BETWEEN SIDE JOBS, HE STILL MAINTAINED A 3.5 GPA IN SCHOOL.
FIGHT
AND WHEN IT FINALLY CAME TIME, HE WAS ABLE TO PURCHASE "ENTRANCE SIDE" TICKETS FOR $60. HE WAS MORE THAN ELATED!
ADMIT ONE
S.P.K.O.
HEAVYWEIGHT CHAMPIONSHIP
KING CROWN JR.
AGE: 20
FIRST TITLE REIGN

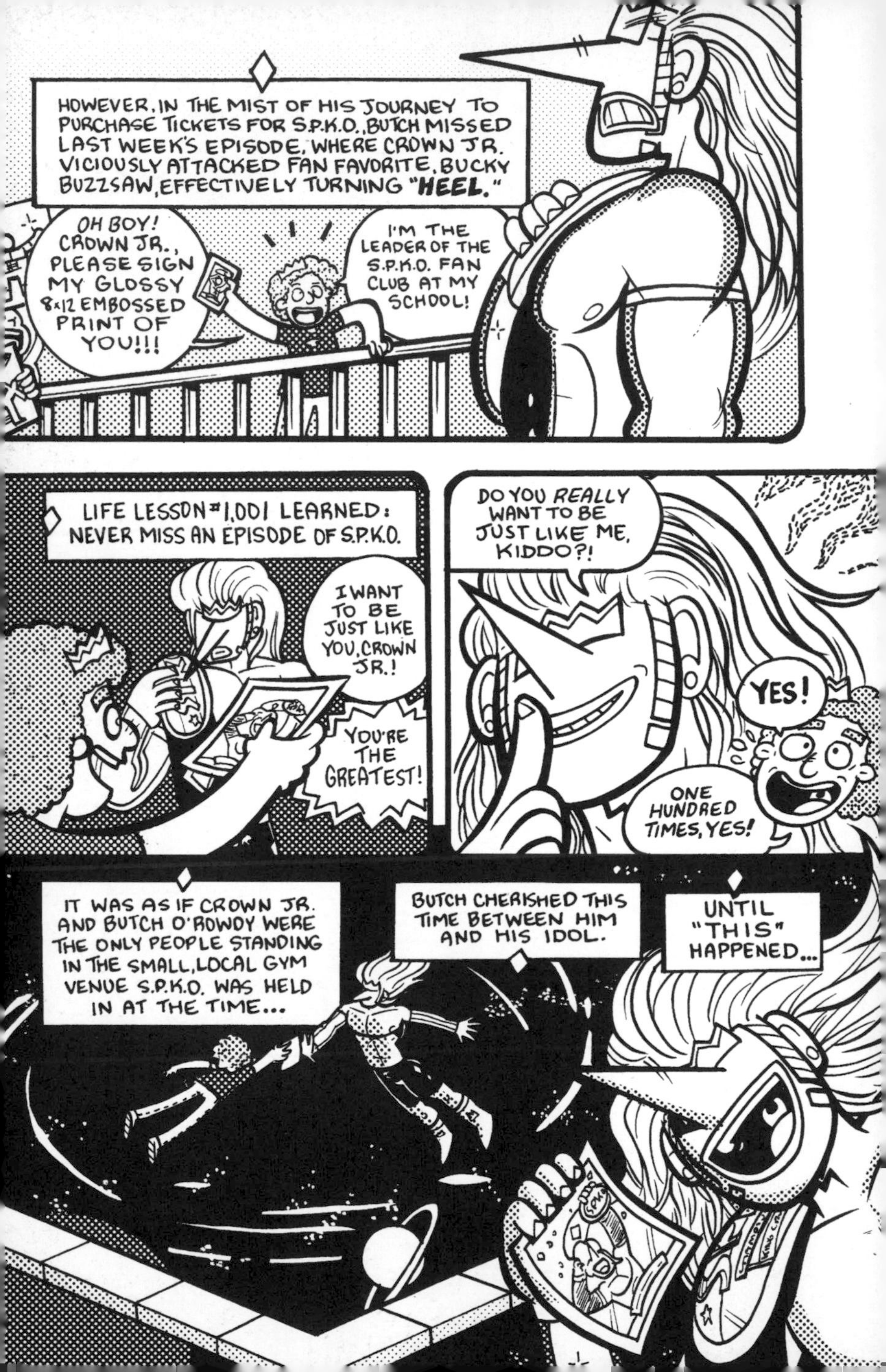
HOWEVER, IN THE MIST OF HIS JOURNEY TO PURCHASE TICKETS FOR S.P.K.O., BUTCH MISSED LAST WEEK'S EPISODE, WHERE CROWN JR. VICIOUSLY ATTACKED FAN FAVORITE, BUCKY BUZZSAW, EFFECTIVELY TURNING "HEEL."
OH BOY! CROWN JR., PLEASE SIGN MY GLOSSY 8x12 EMBOSSED PRINT OF YOU!!!
I'M THE LEADER OF THE S.P.K.O. FAN CLUB AT MY SCHOOL!
LIFE LESSON #1,001 LEARNED: NEVER MISS AN EPISODE OF S.P.K.O.
I WANT TO BE JUST LIKE YOU, CROWN JR.!
YOU'RE THE GREATEST!
DO YOU REALLY WANT TO BE JUST LIKE ME, KIDDO?!
YES!
ONE HUNDRED TIMES, YES!
IT WAS AS IF CROWN JR. AND BUTCH O'ROWDY WERE THE ONLY PEOPLE STANDING IN THE SMALL, LOCAL GYM VENUE S.P.K.O. WAS HELD IN AT THE TIME...
BUTCH CHERISHED THIS TIME BETWEEN HIM AND HIS IDOL.
UNTIL "THIS" HAPPENED...

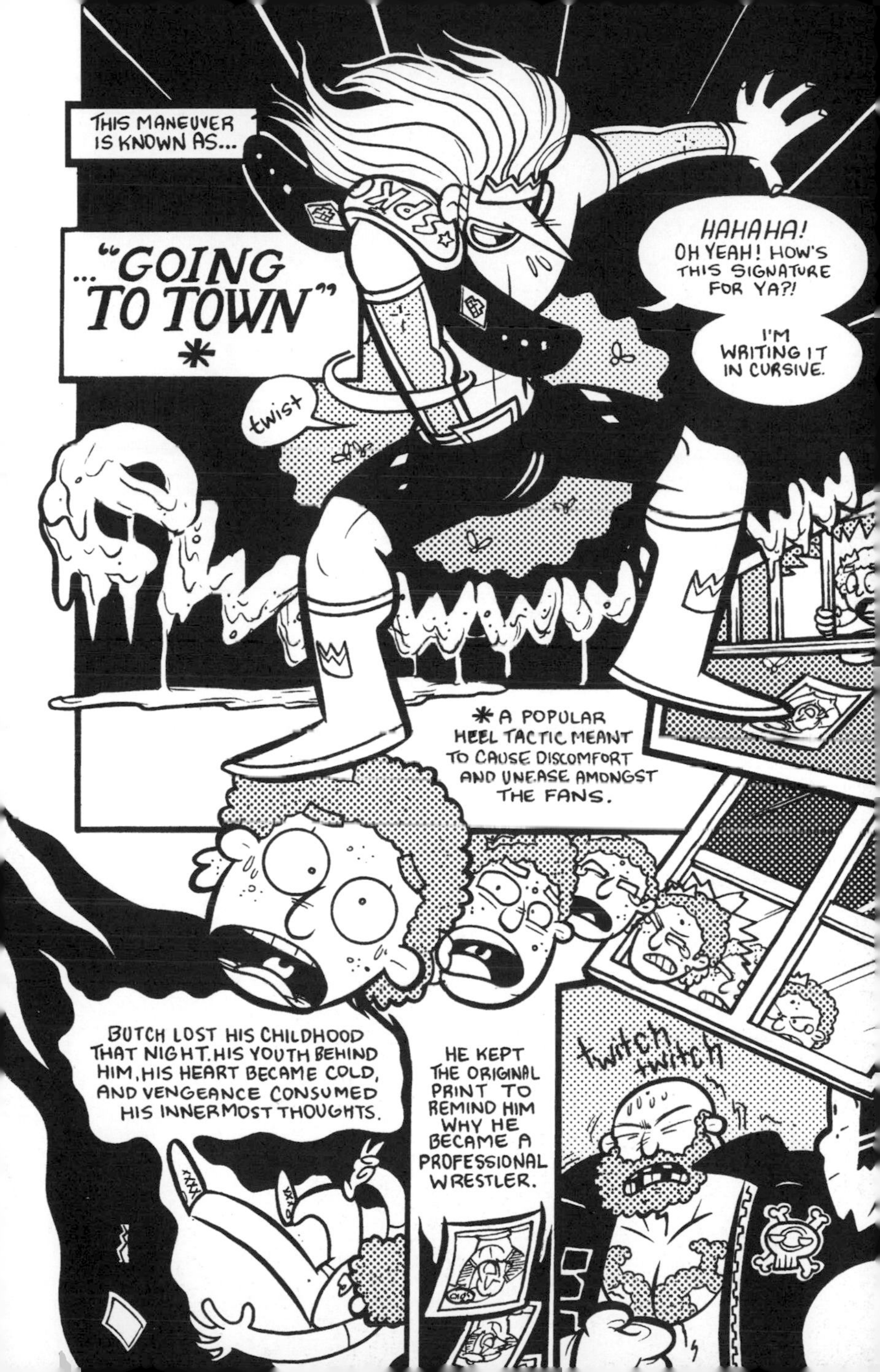
THIS MANEUVER IS KNOWN AS...
..."GOING TO TOWN" *
HAHAHA! OH YEAH! HOW'S THIS SIGNATURE FOR YA?!
I'M WRITING IT IN CURSIVE.
twist
* A POPULAR HEEL TACTIC MEANT TO CAUSE DISCOMFORT AND UNEASE AMONGST THE FANS.
BUTCH LOST HIS CHILDHOOD THAT NIGHT. HIS YOUTH BEHIND HIM, HIS HEART BECAME COLD, AND VENGEANCE CONSUMED HIS INNERMOST THOUGHTS.
HE KEPT THE ORIGINAL PRINT TO REMIND HIM WHY HE BECAME A PROFESSIONAL WRESTLER.
twitch twitch

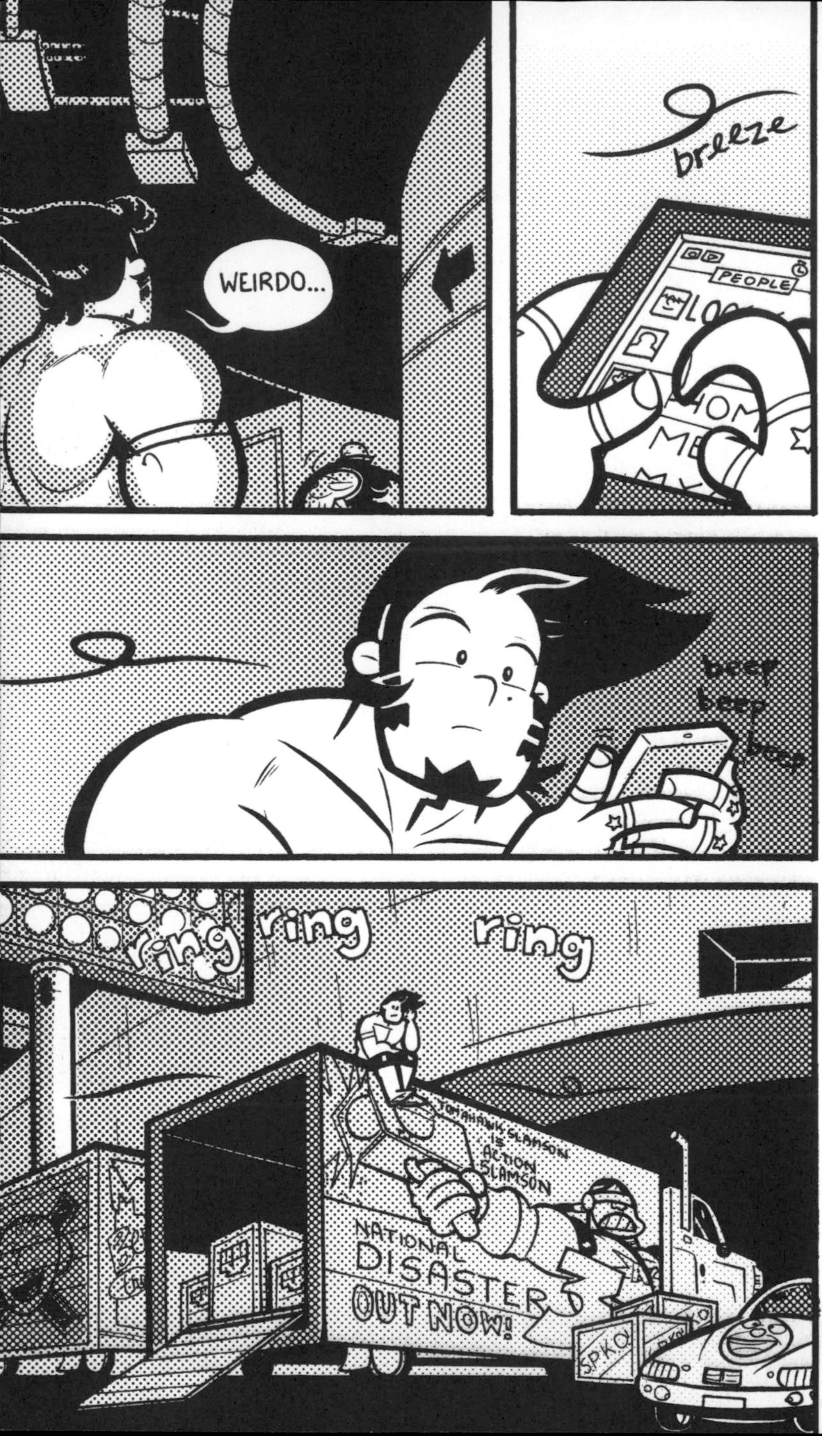
WEIRDO...
breeze
PEOPLE
beep
beep
beep
ring ring ring
TOMAHAWK SLAMSON IS ACTION SLAMSON
NATIONAL DISASTER
OUT NOW!
SPKO

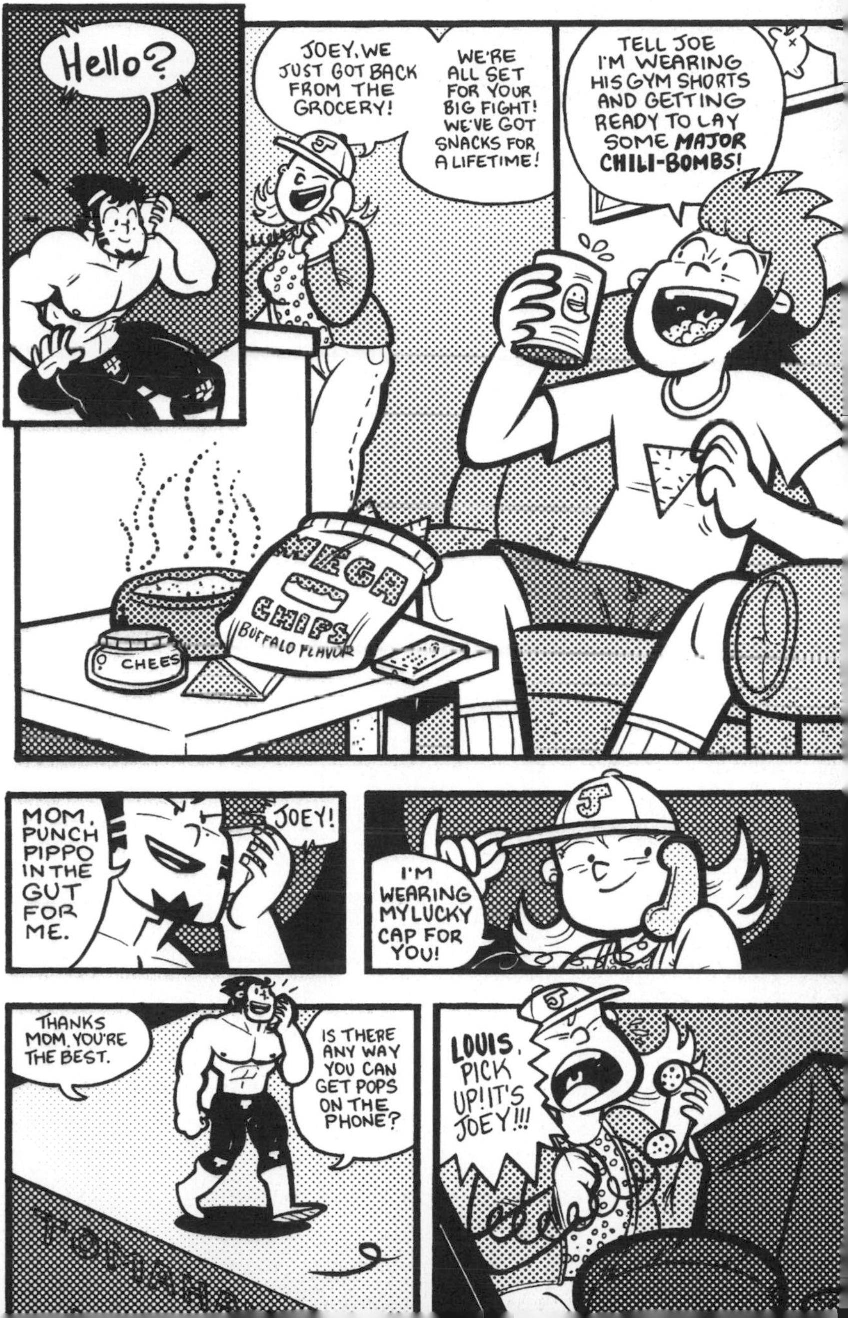
Hello?
JOEY, WE JUST GOT BACK FROM THE GROCERY!
WE'RE ALL SET FOR YOUR BIG FIGHT! WE'VE GOT SNACKS FOR A LIFETIME!
TELL JOE I'M WEARING HIS GYM SHORTS AND GETTING READY TO LAY SOME **MAJOR CHILI-BOMBS!**
CHIPS
BUFFALO FLAVOR
CHEES
MOM, PUNCH PIPPO IN THE GUT FOR ME.
JOEY!
I'M WEARING MY LUCKY CAP FOR YOU!
THANKS MOM, YOU'RE THE BEST.
IS THERE ANY WAY YOU CAN GET POPS ON THE PHONE?
LOUIS, PICK UP! IT'S JOEY!!!

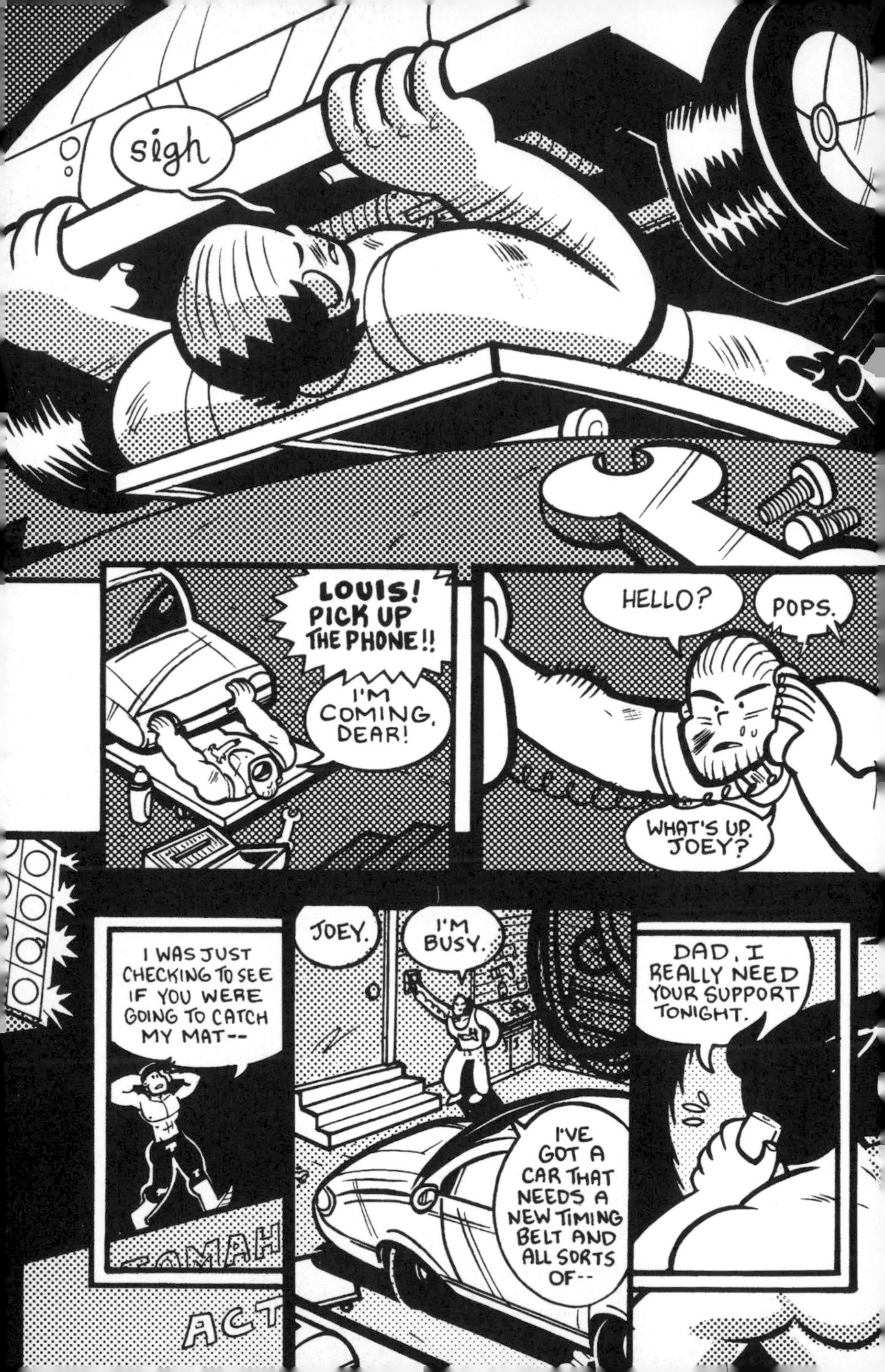
sigh
LOUIS! PICK UP THE PHONE!!
I'M COMING, DEAR!
HELLO?
POPS.
WHAT'S UP, JOEY?
I WAS JUST CHECKING TO SEE IF YOU WERE GOING TO CATCH MY MAT--
JOEY.
I'M BUSY.
I'VE GOT A CAR THAT NEEDS A NEW TIMING BELT AND ALL SORTS OF--
DAD, I REALLY NEED YOUR SUPPORT TONIGHT.
ACT

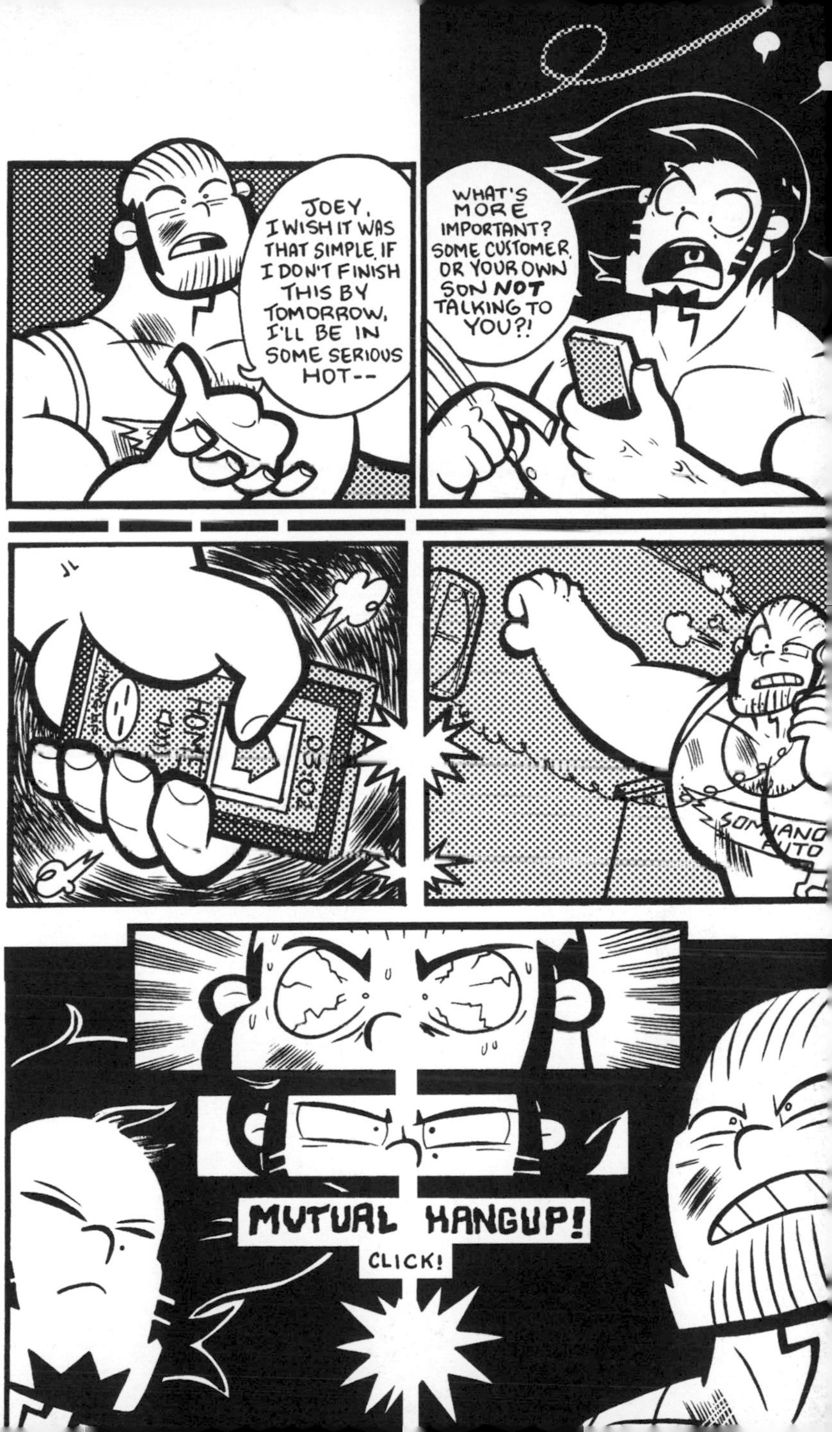
JOEY, I WISH IT WAS THAT SIMPLE. IF I DON'T FINISH THIS BY TOMORROW, I'LL BE IN SOME SERIOUS HOT--
WHAT'S MORE IMPORTANT? SOME CUSTOMER, OR YOUR OWN SON **NOT** TALKING TO YOU?!
MUTUAL HANGUP!
CLICK!

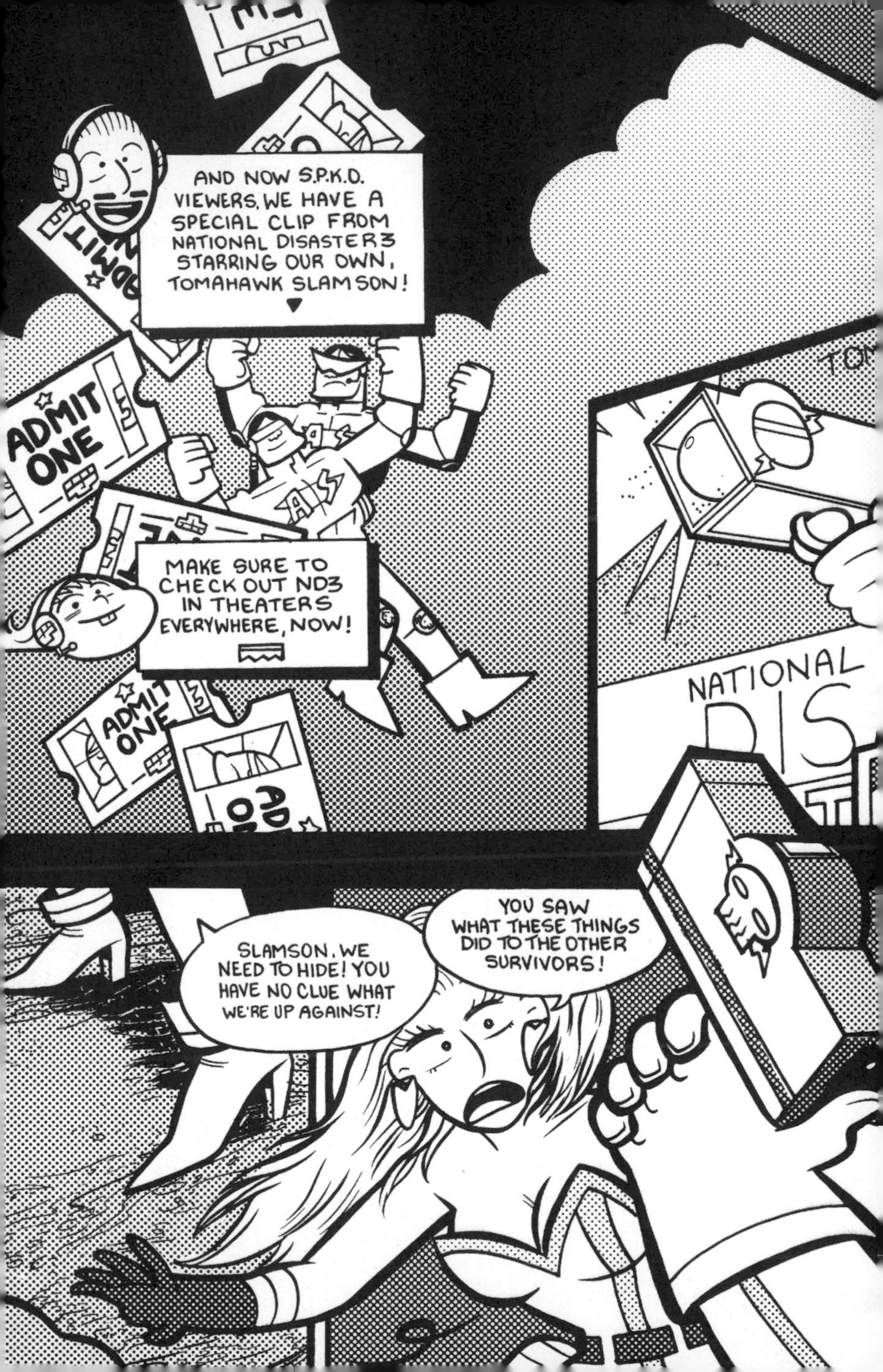
AND NOW S.P.K.D. VIEWERS, WE HAVE A SPECIAL CLIP FROM NATIONAL DISASTER 3 STARRING OUR OWN, TOMAHAWK SLAMSON!
ADMIT ONE
MAKE SURE TO CHECK OUT ND3 IN THEATERS EVERYWHERE, NOW!
ADMIT ONE
NATIONAL
SLAMSON, WE NEED TO HIDE! YOU HAVE NO CLUE WHAT WE'RE UP AGAINST!
YOU SAW WHAT THESE THINGS DID TO THE OTHER SURVIVORS!

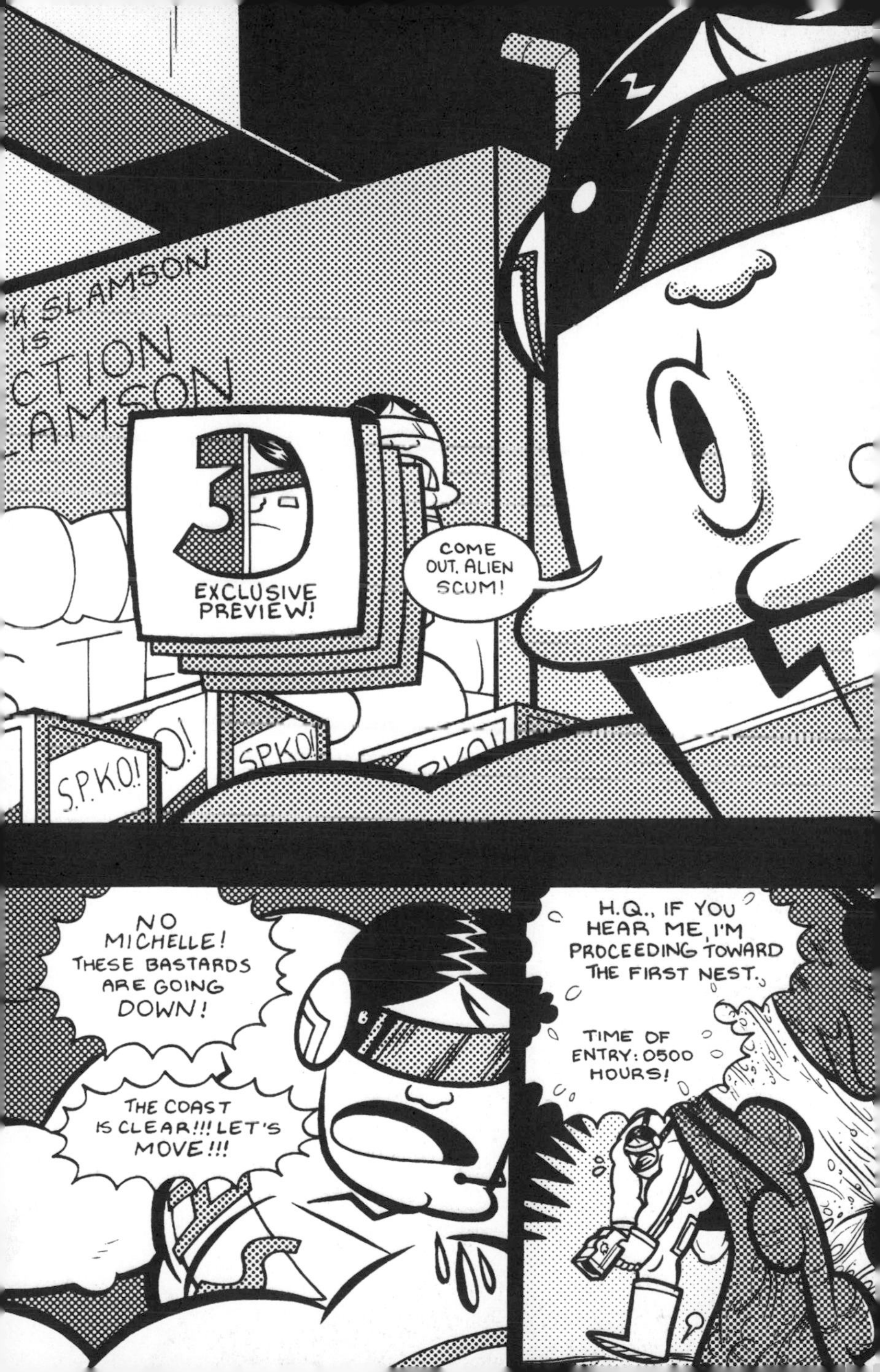
SLAMSON
IS
EXCLUSIVE PREVIEW!
S.P.K.O.!
S.P.K.O.!
COME OUT, ALIEN SCUM!
NO MICHELLE! THESE BASTARDS ARE GOING DOWN!
THE COAST IS CLEAR!!! LET'S MOVE!!!
H.Q., IF YOU HEAR ME, I'M PROCEEDING TOWARD THE FIRST NEST.
TIME OF ENTRY: 0500 HOURS!

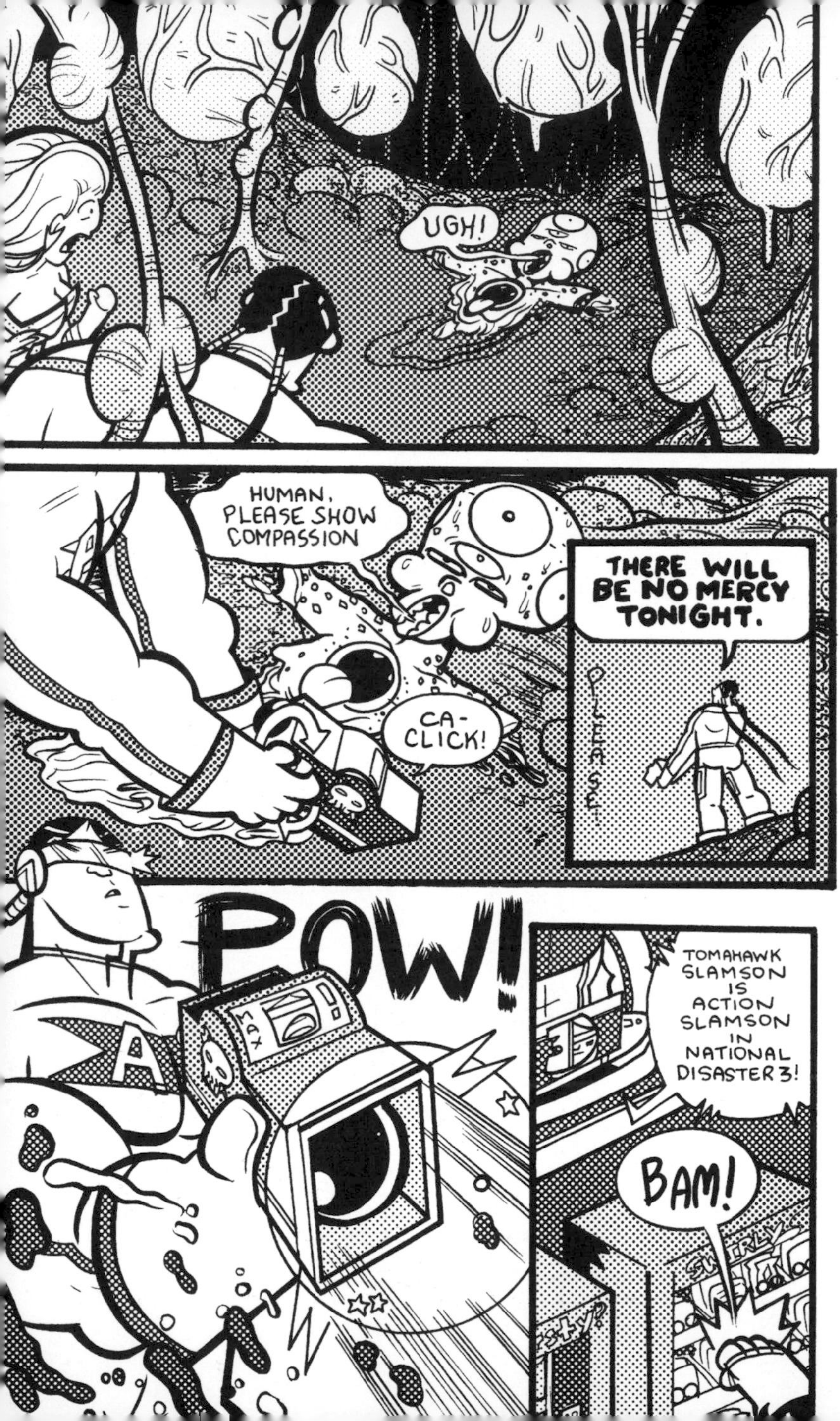
UGH!
HUMAN, PLEASE SHOW COMPASSION
CA-CLICK!
THERE WILL BE NO MERCY TONIGHT.
PLEASE
POW!
MAX
TOMAHAWK SLAMSON IS ACTION SLAMSON IN NATIONAL DISASTER 3!
BAM!

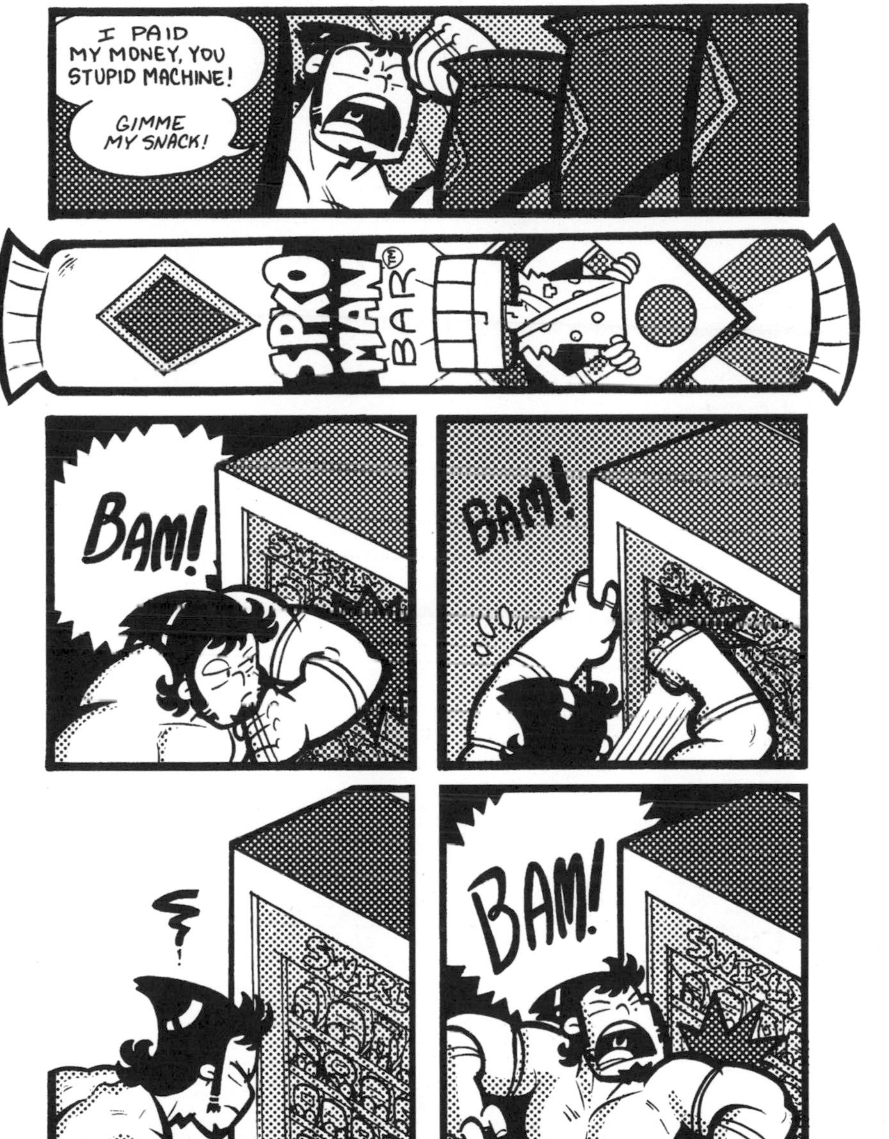
I PAID MY MONEY, YOU STUPID MACHINE!
GIMME MY SNACK!
SPKO MAN BAR™
BAM!
BAM!
BAM!

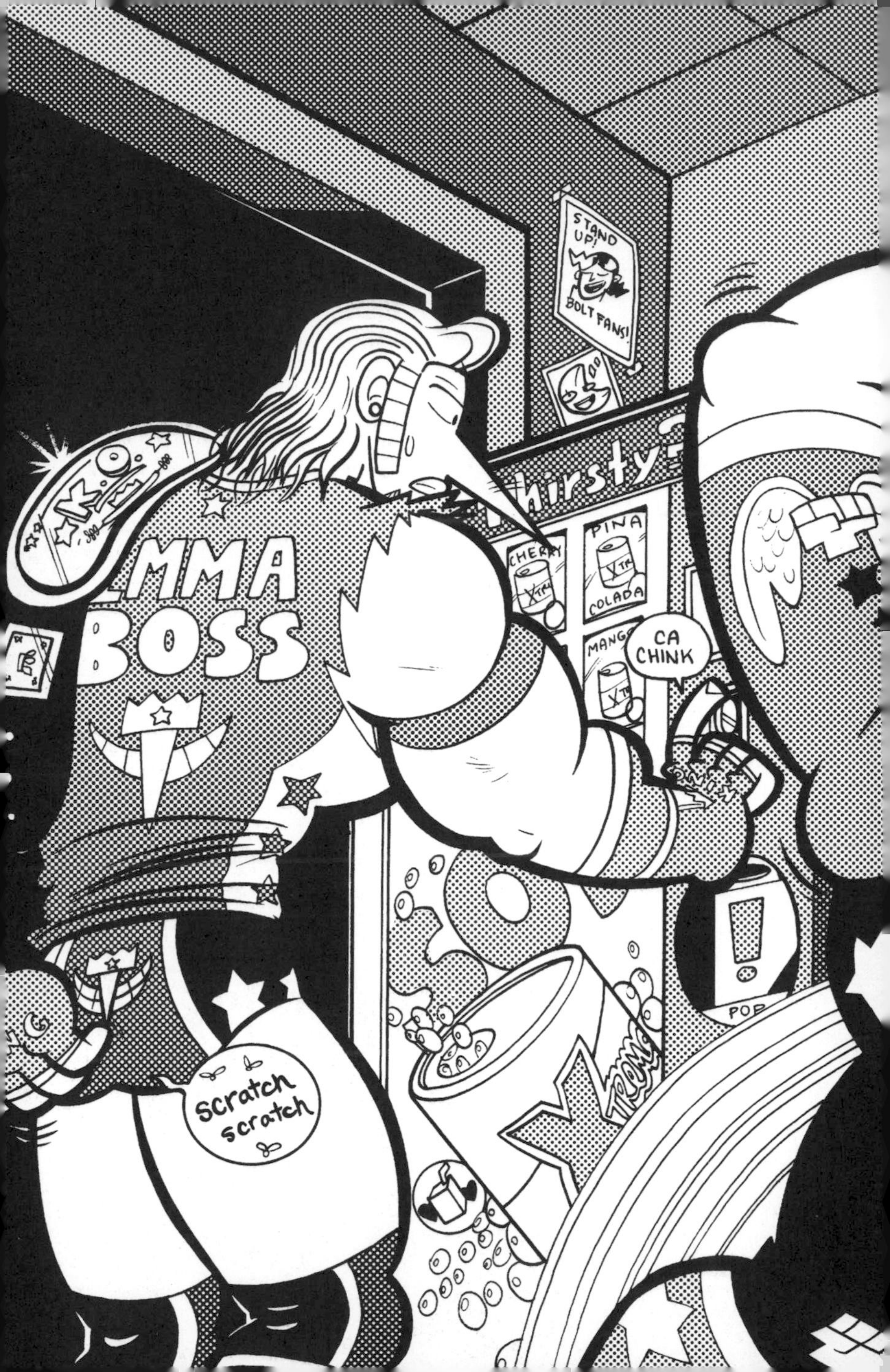
STAND UP, BOLT FANS!
Thirsty?
CHERRY
PINA COLADA
MANGO
CA CHINK
MMA BOSS
POP
scratch scratch

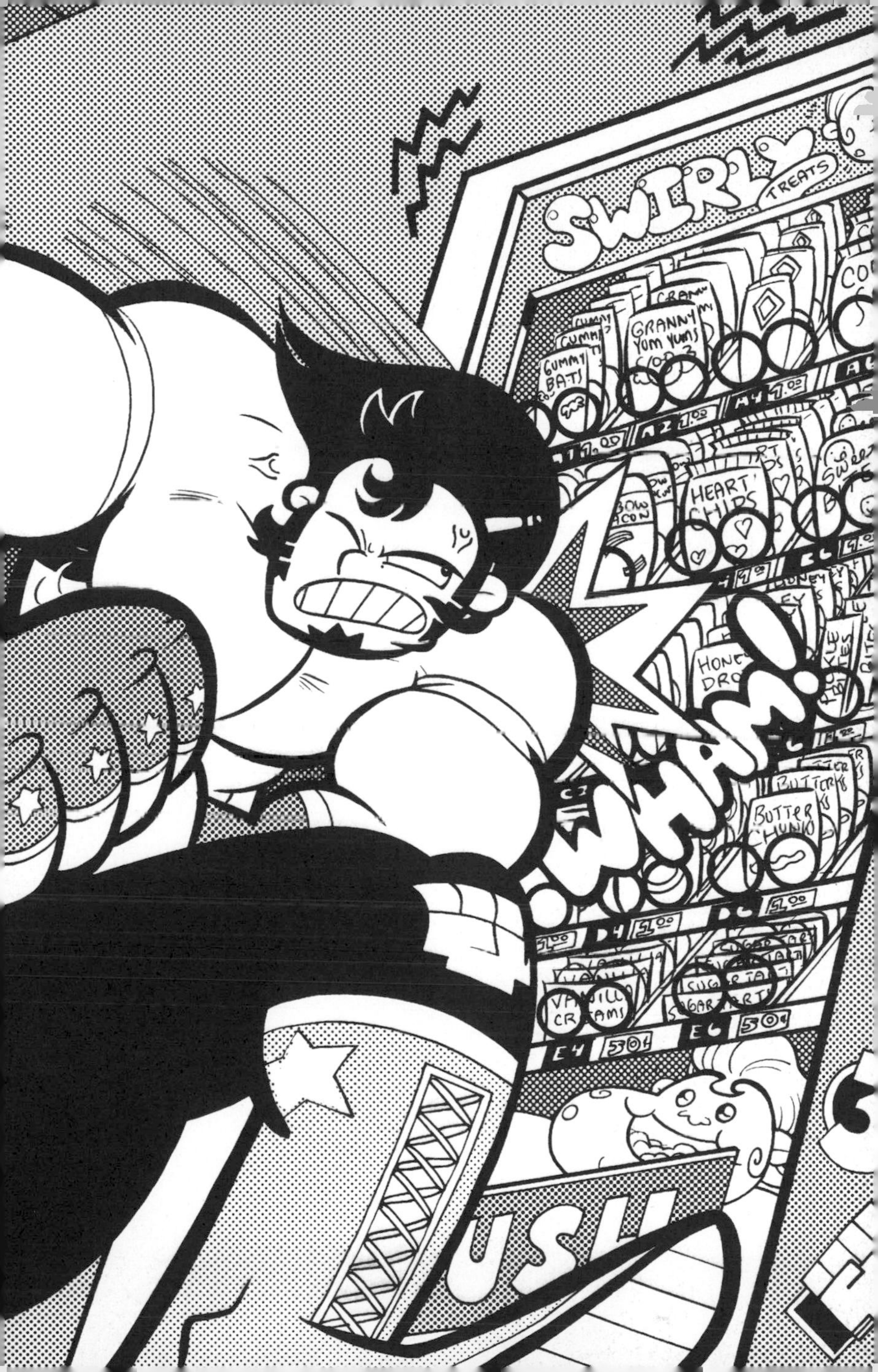
SWIRLY TREATS
GUMMY BATS
GRANNY YUM YUMS
HEART CHIPS
WHAM!

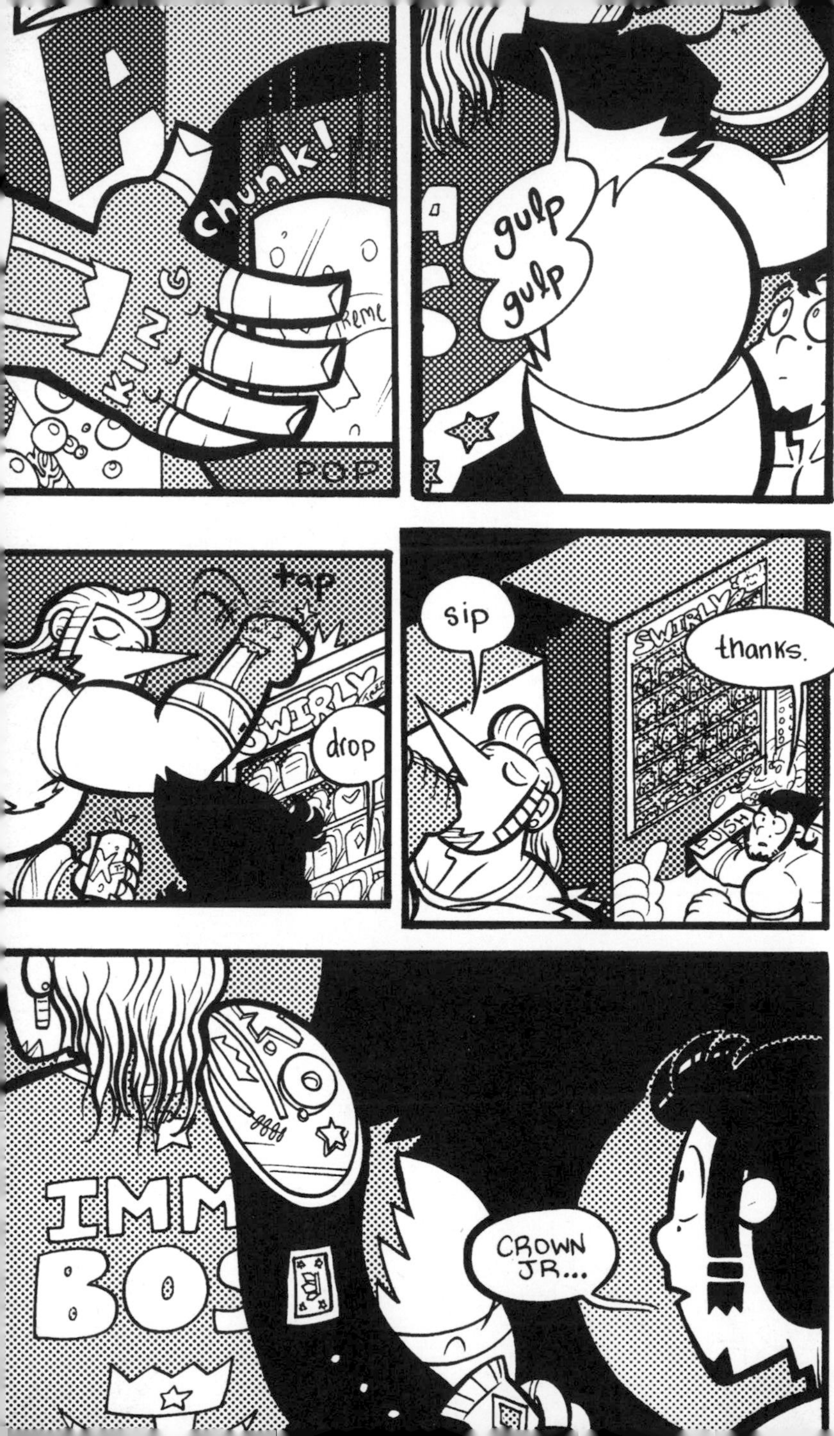
chunk!
REME
POP
gulp
gulp
tap
SWIRLY
drop
sip
SWIRLY
thanks.
PUSH
IMM
BOS
CROWN
JR...

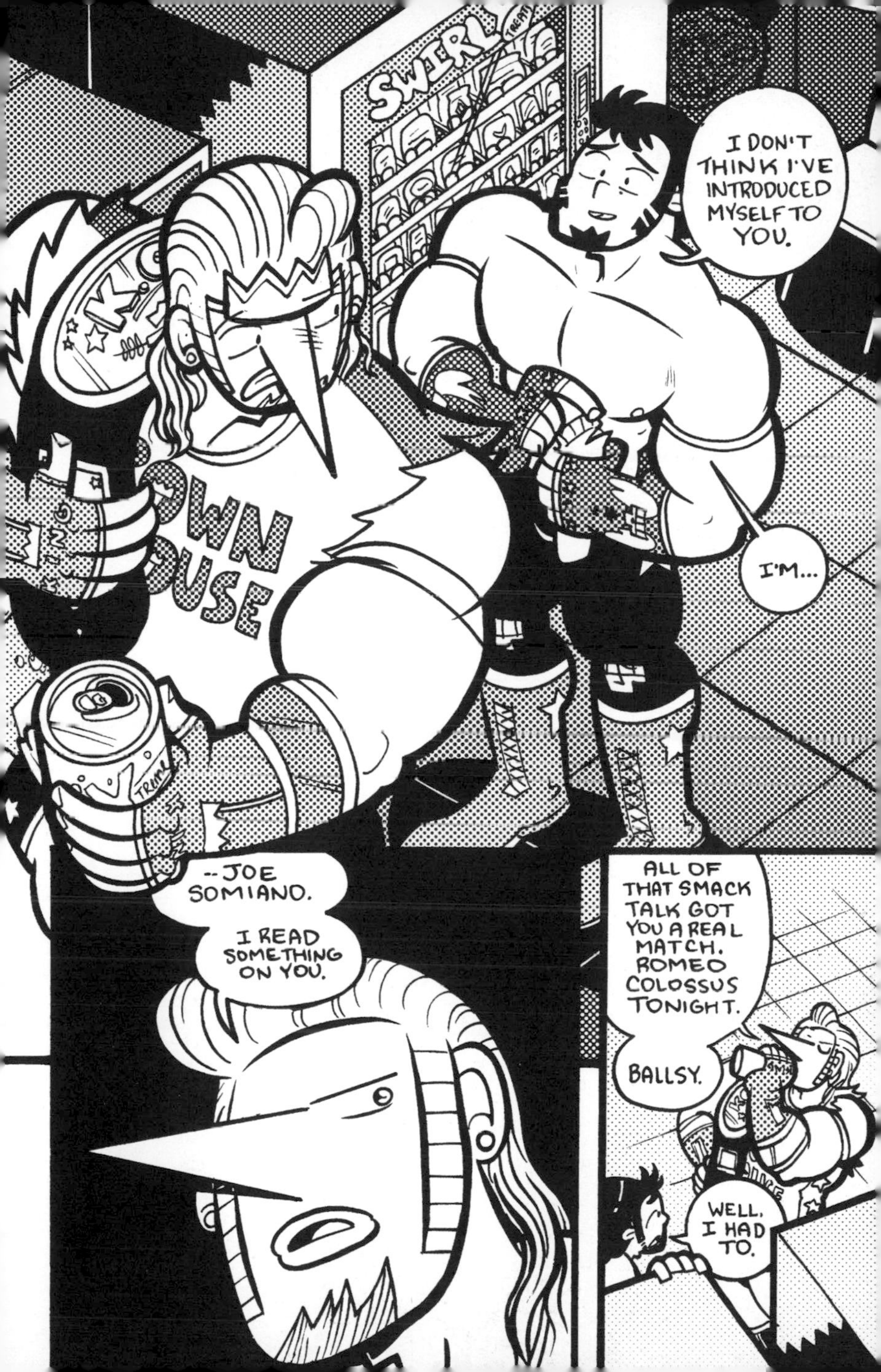
SWIRL
I DON'T THINK I'VE INTRODUCED MYSELF TO YOU.
I'M...
--JOE SOMIANO.
I READ SOMETHING ON YOU.
ALL OF THAT SMACK TALK GOT YOU A REAL MATCH. ROMEO COLOSSUS TONIGHT.
BALLSY.
WELL, I HAD TO.

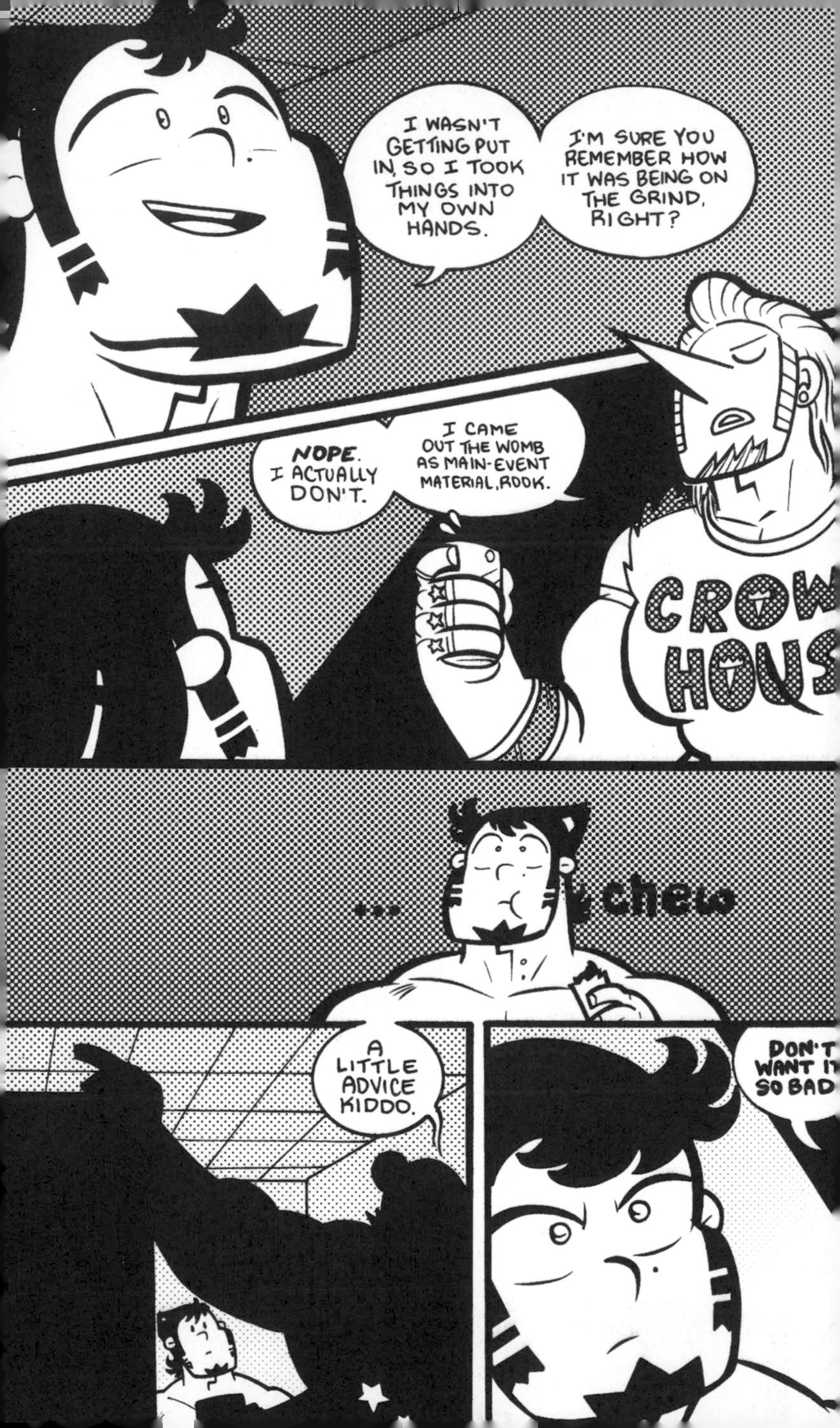
I WASN'T GETTING PUT IN, SO I TOOK THINGS INTO MY OWN HANDS.
I'M SURE YOU REMEMBER HOW IT WAS BEING ON THE GRIND, RIGHT?
NOPE. I ACTUALLY DON'T.
I CAME OUT THE WOMB AS MAIN-EVENT MATERIAL, ROOK.
CROW HOUS
... chew
A LITTLE ADVICE KIDDO.
DON'T WANT IT SO BAD

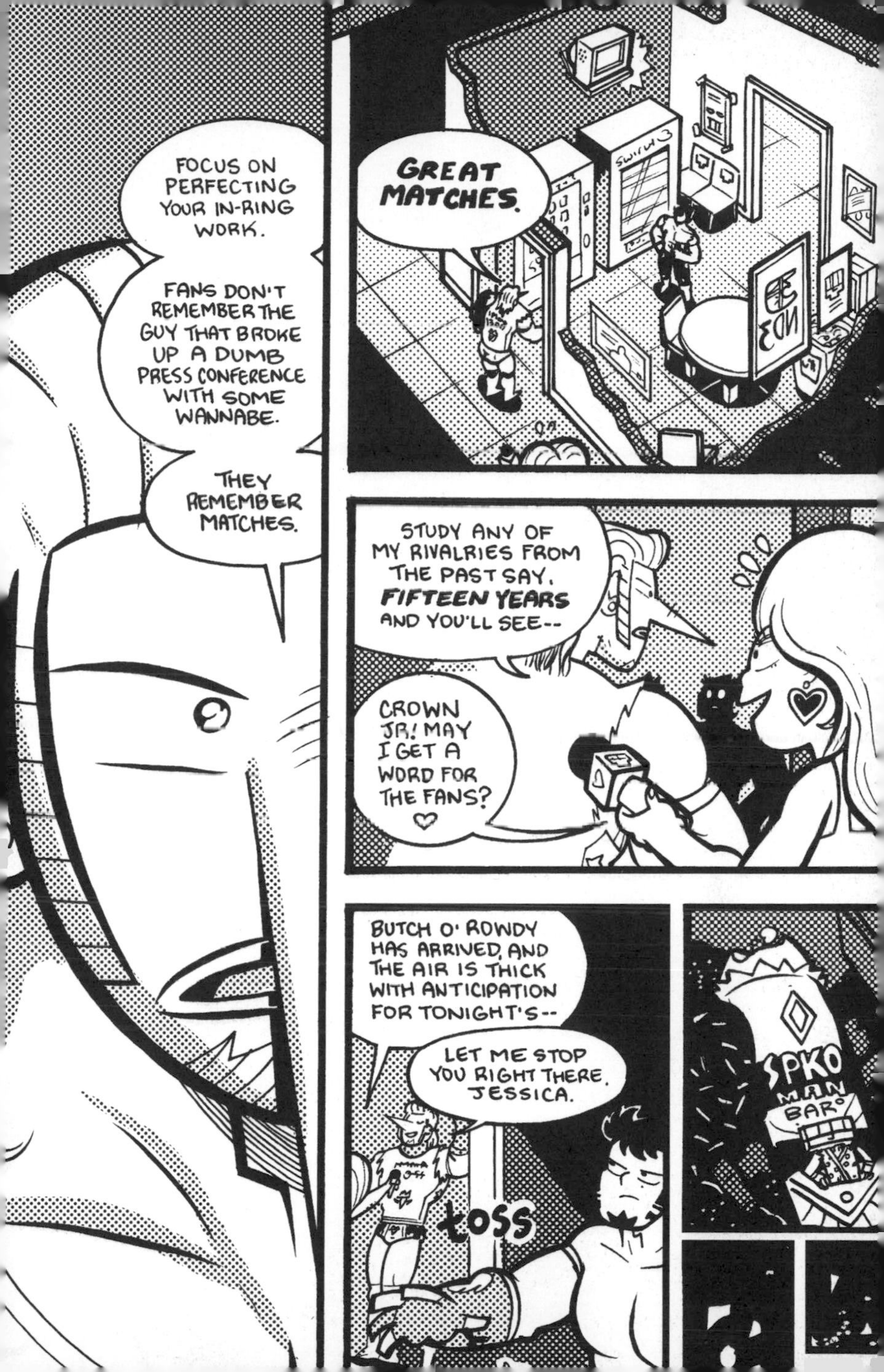
FOCUS ON PERFECTING YOUR IN-RING WORK.
FANS DON'T REMEMBER THE GUY THAT BROKE UP A DUMB PRESS CONFERENCE WITH SOME WANNABE.
THEY REMEMBER MATCHES.
GREAT MATCHES.
STUDY ANY OF MY RIVALRIES FROM THE PAST SAY, FIFTEEN YEARS AND YOU'LL SEE--
CROWN JR! MAY I GET A WORD FOR THE FANS? ♡
BUTCH O' ROWDY HAS ARRIVED, AND THE AIR IS THICK WITH ANTICIPATION FOR TONIGHT'S--
LET ME STOP YOU RIGHT THERE, JESSICA.
toss
SPKO
BAR

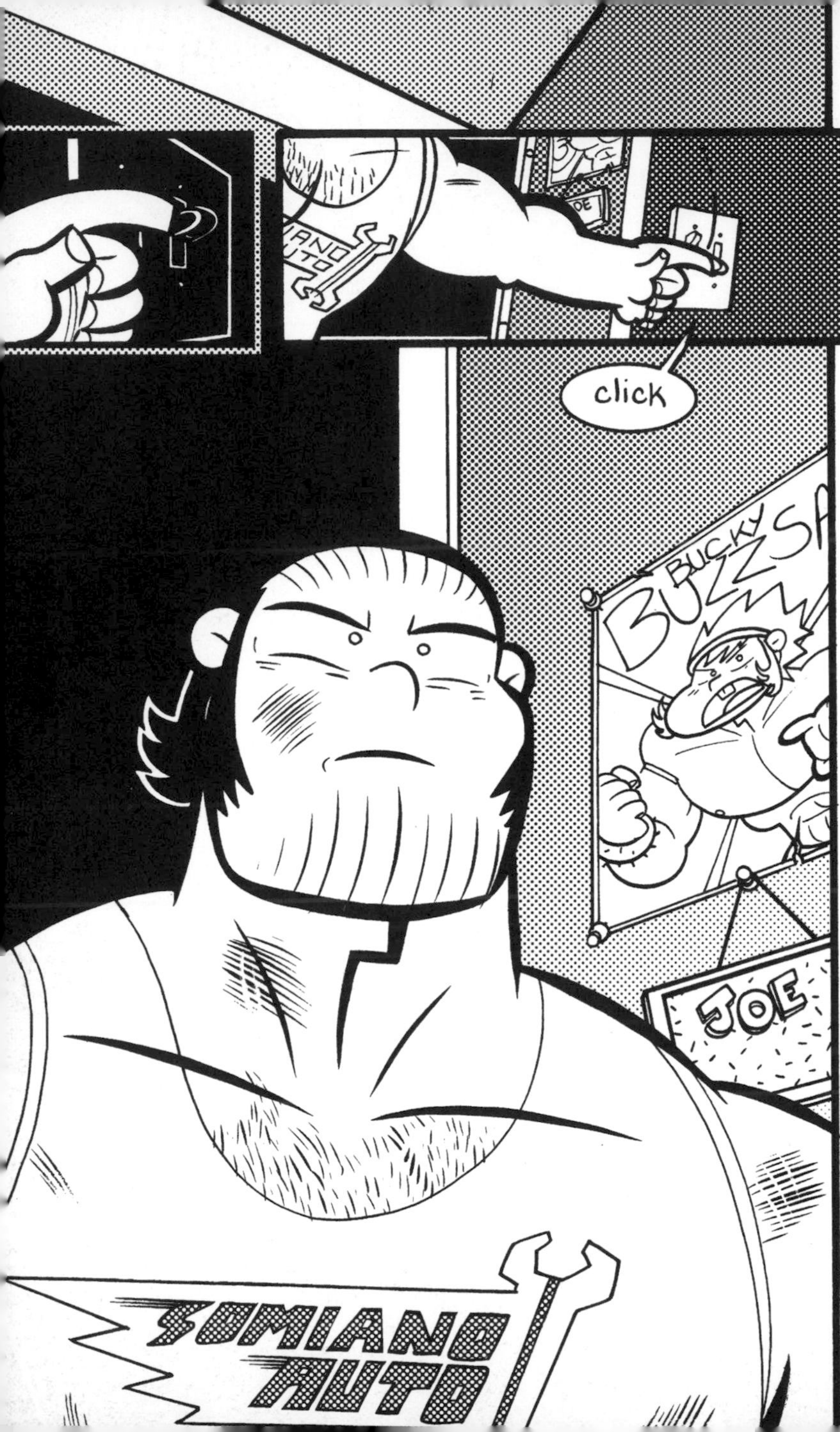
click
BUCKY
BUZZSA
JOE
SOMIANO
AUTO

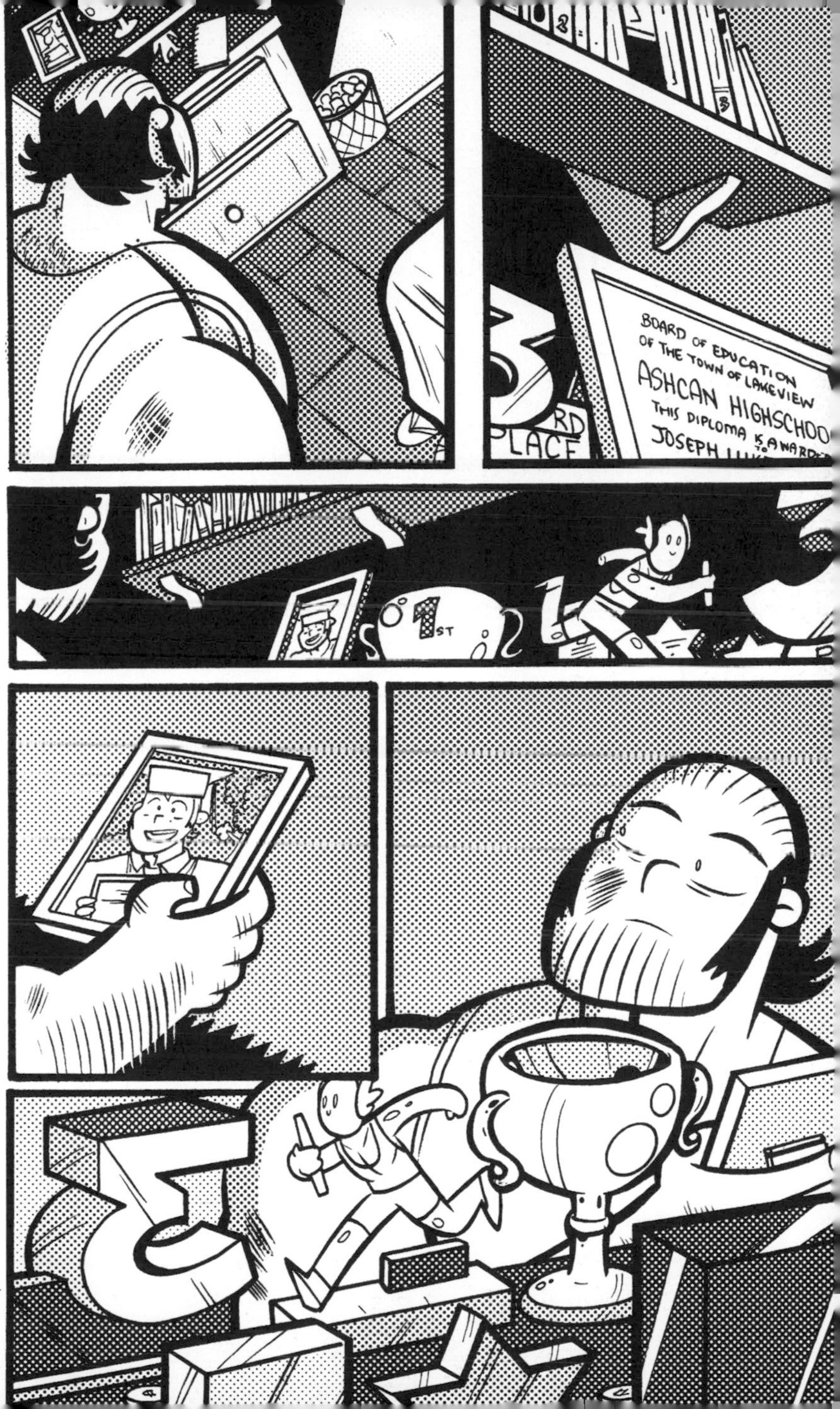
BOARD OF EDUCATION
OF THE TOWN OF LAKEVIEW
ASHCAN HIGHSCHOO
THIS DIPLOMA IS AWARD
TO
JOSEPH
RD
PLACE
1ST

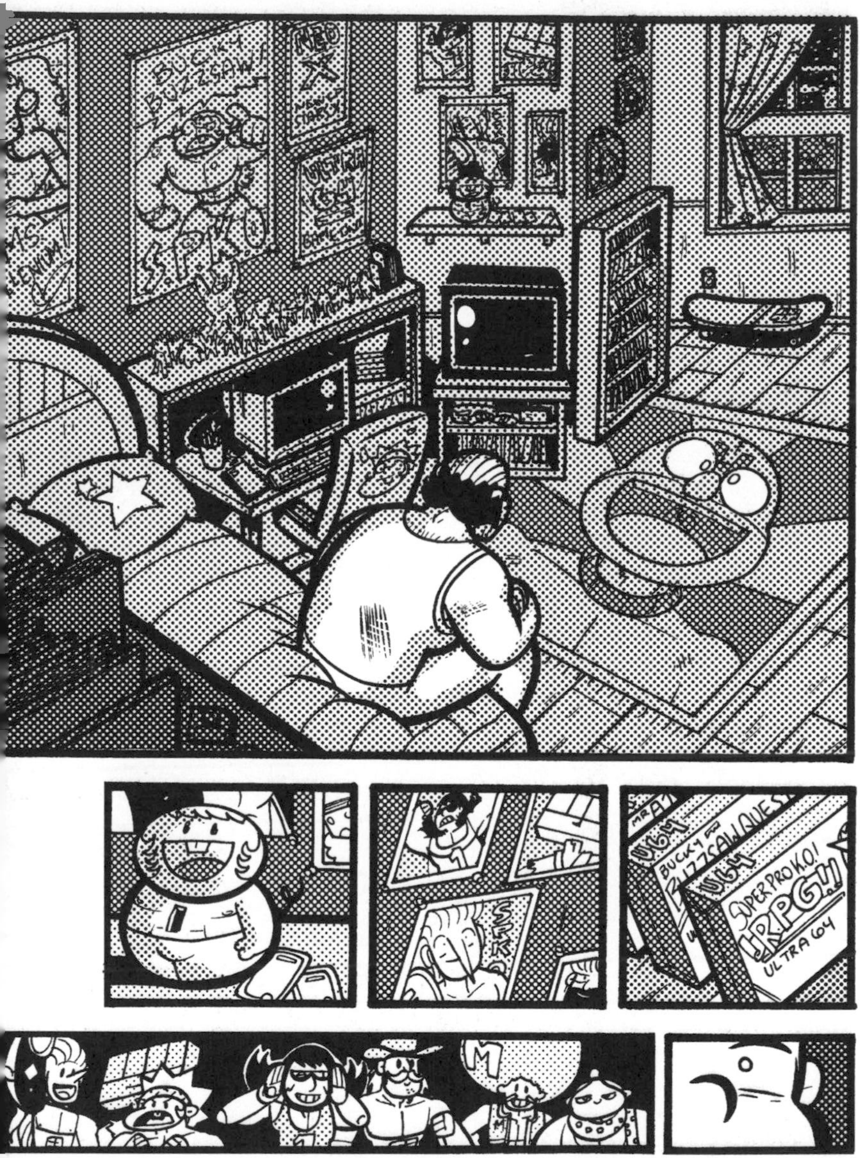
BUCKY BUZZSAW
U64
BUCKY BUZZSAW QUEST
U64
SUPER PRO K.O.!
URPG!!
ULTRA 64

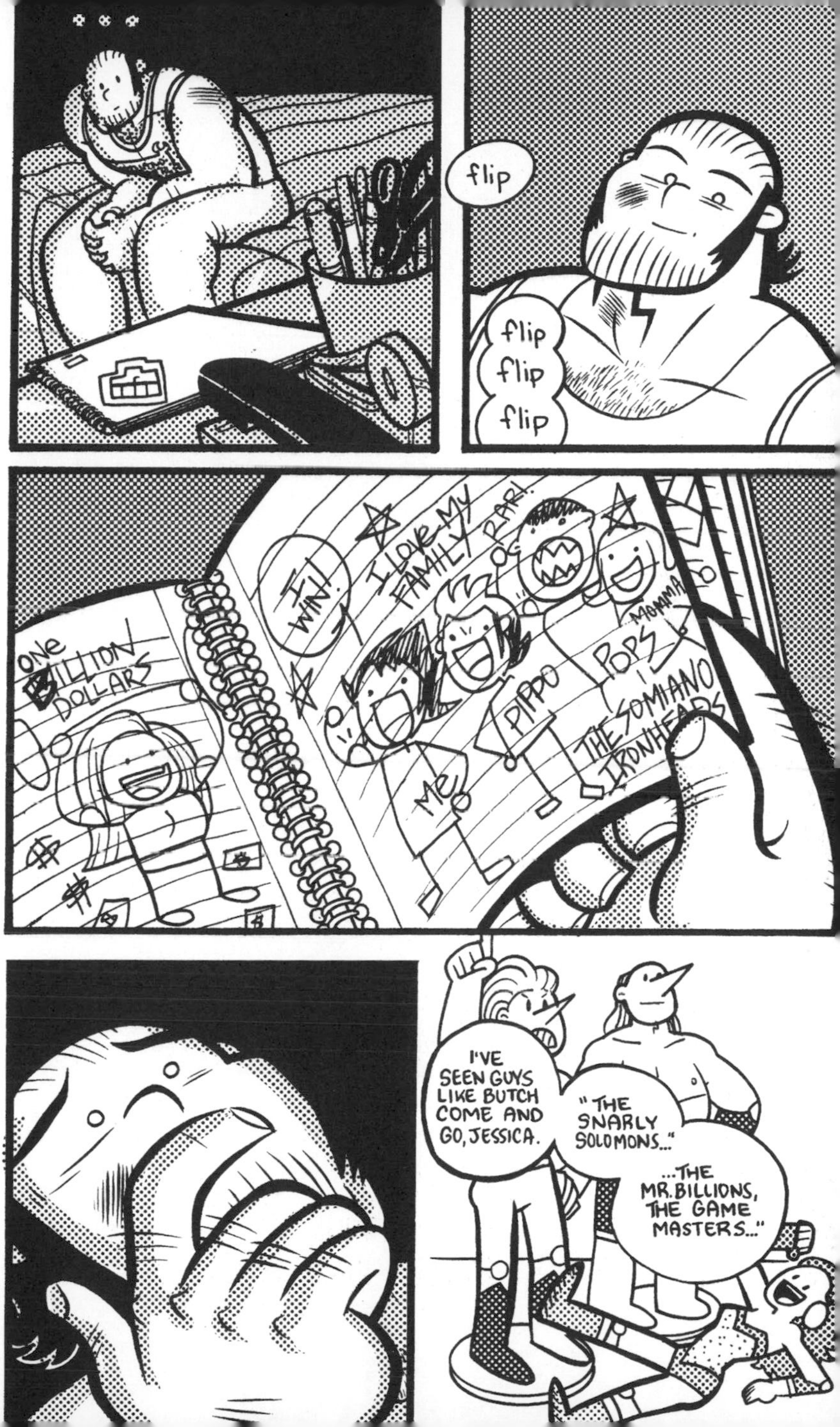
flip
flip
flip
flip
ONE BILLION DOLLARS
I WIN!
I LOVE MY FAMILY RAR!
MOMMA
POPS
PIPPO
ME
THE SOMIANO IRONHEADS
I'VE SEEN GUYS LIKE BUTCH COME AND GO, JESSICA.
"THE SNARLY SOLOMONS..."
...THE MR. BILLIONS, THE GAME MASTERS..."

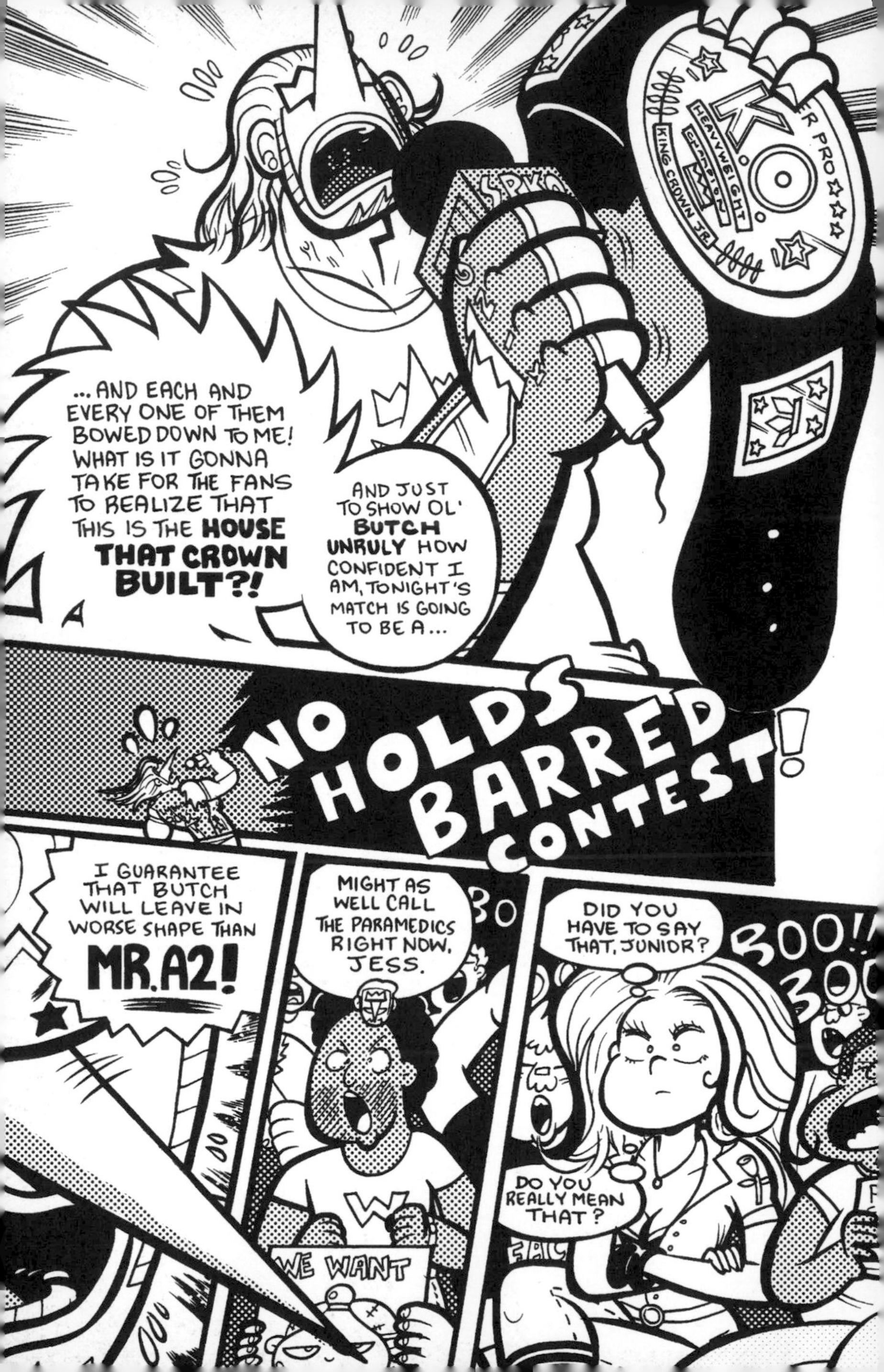
KING CROWN JR.
HEAVYWEIGHT CHAMPION
K.O.
...AND EACH AND EVERY ONE OF THEM BOWED DOWN TO ME! WHAT IS IT GONNA TAKE FOR THE FANS TO REALIZE THAT THIS IS THE **HOUSE THAT CROWN BUILT?!**
AND JUST TO SHOW OL' **BUTCH UNRULY** HOW CONFIDENT I AM, TONIGHT'S MATCH IS GOING TO BE A...
NO HOLDS BARRED CONTEST!
I GUARANTEE THAT BUTCH WILL LEAVE IN WORSE SHAPE THAN **MR.A2!**
MIGHT AS WELL CALL THE PARAMEDICS RIGHT NOW, JESS.
WE WANT
DID YOU HAVE TO SAY THAT, JUNIOR?
BOO!!
DO YOU REALLY MEAN THAT?

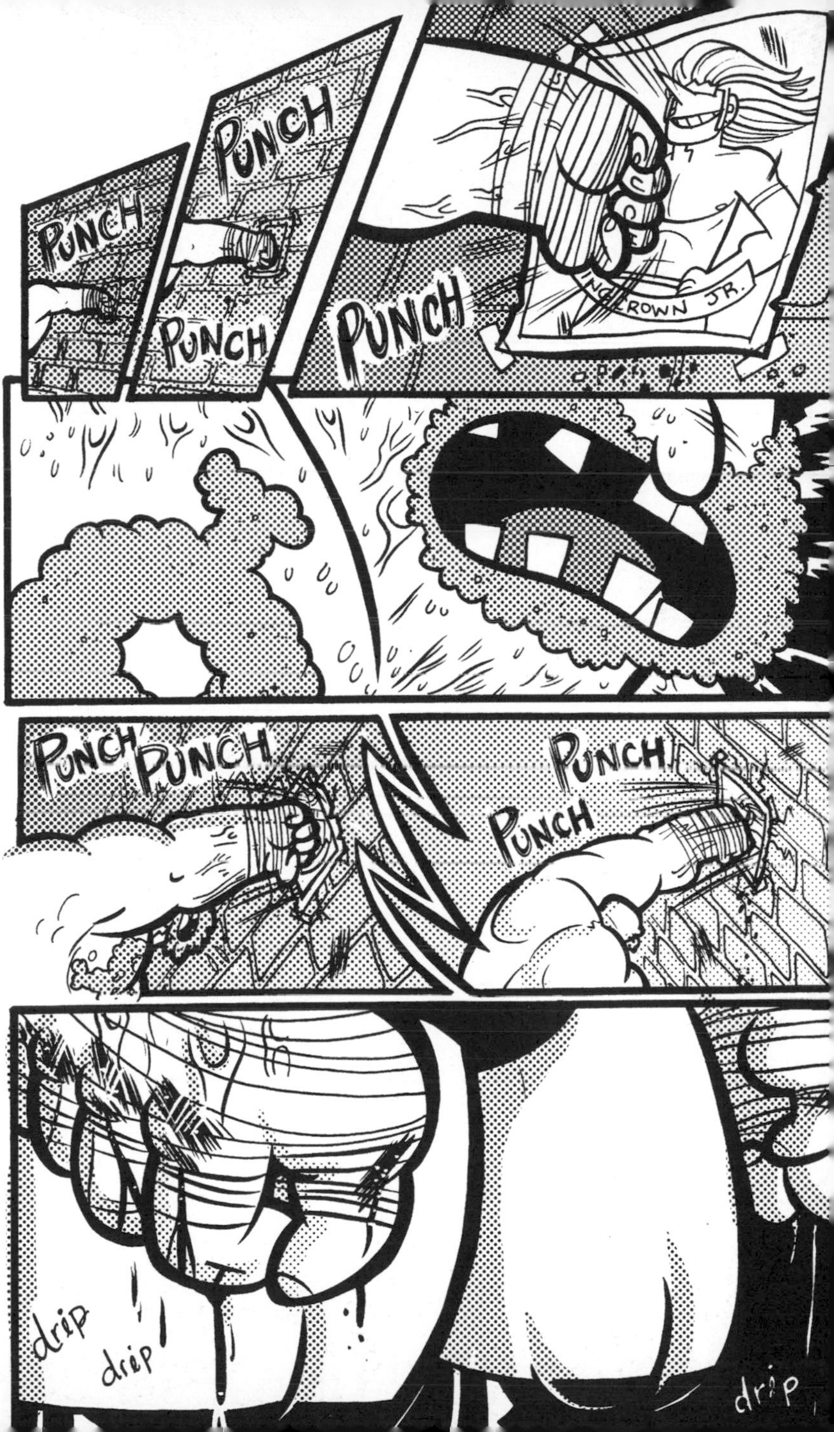
PUNCH
PUNCH
PUNCH
PUNCH
INGROWN JR.
PUNCH
PUNCH
PUNCH
PUNCH
PUNCH
drip
drip
drip

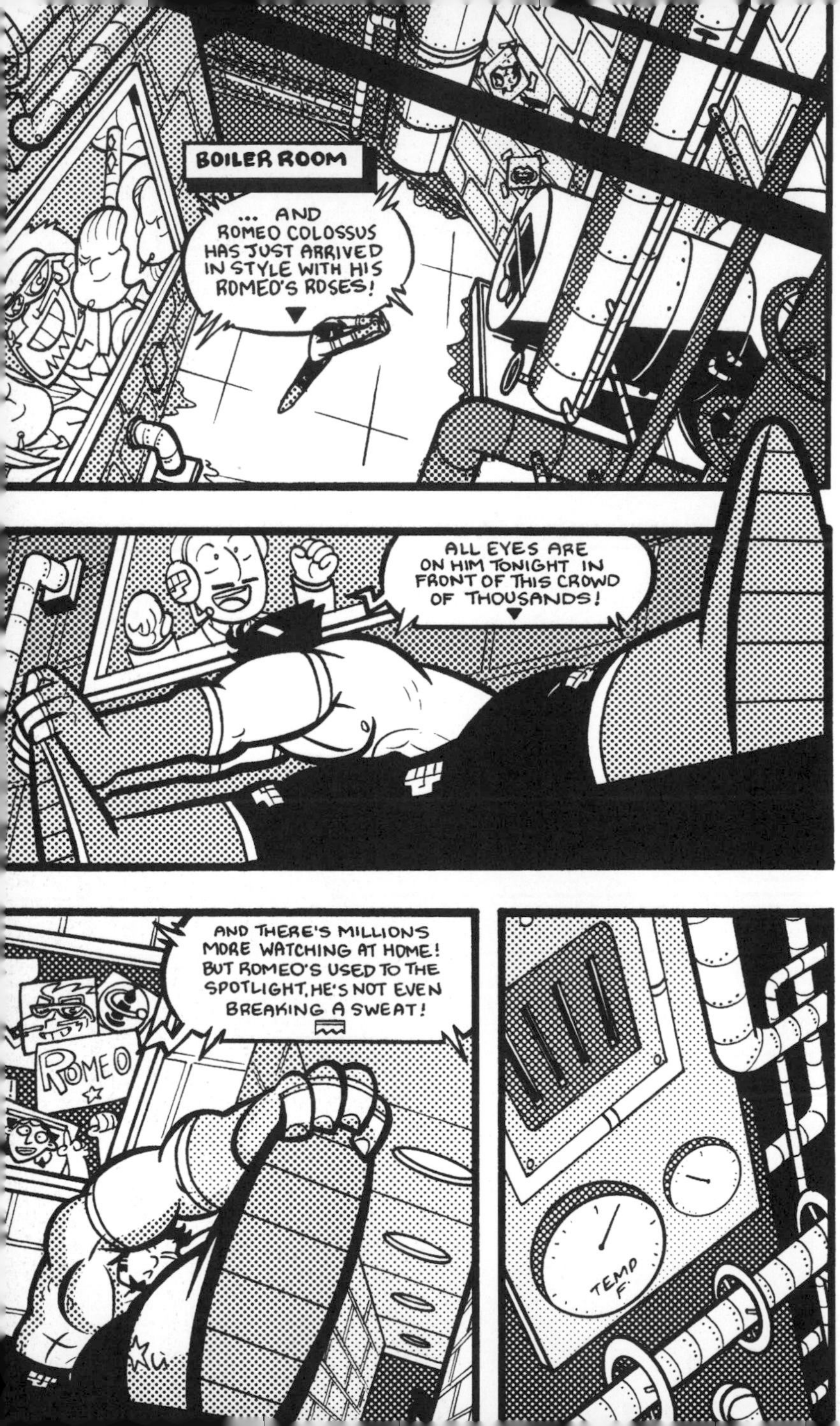
BOILER ROOM
... AND ROMEO COLOSSUS HAS JUST ARRIVED IN STYLE WITH HIS ROMEO'S ROSES!
ALL EYES ARE ON HIM TONIGHT IN FRONT OF THIS CROWD OF THOUSANDS!
AND THERE'S MILLIONS MORE WATCHING AT HOME! BUT ROMEO'S USED TO THE SPOTLIGHT, HE'S NOT EVEN BREAKING A SWEAT!
ROMEO
TEMP F.

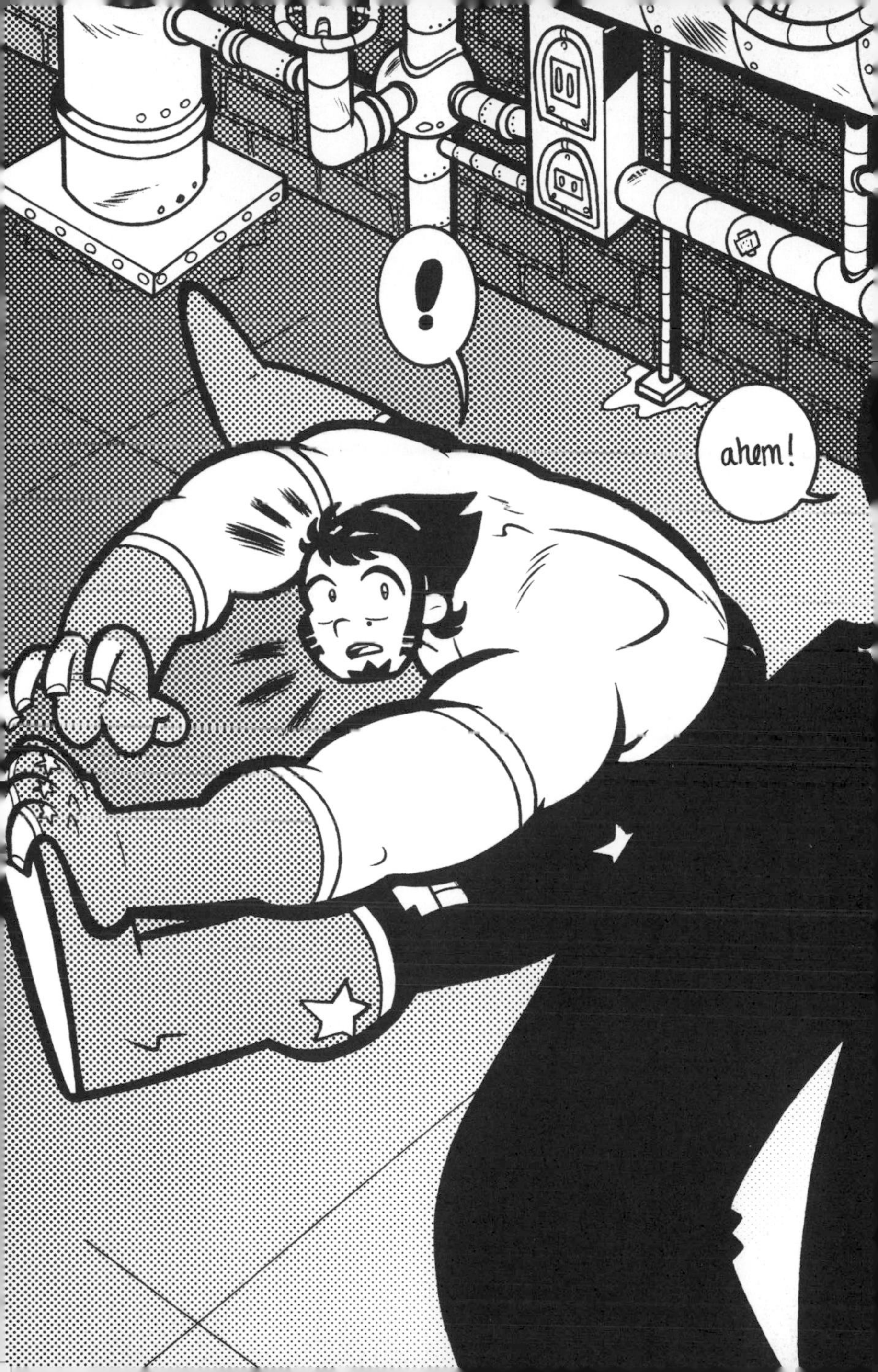
!
ahem!

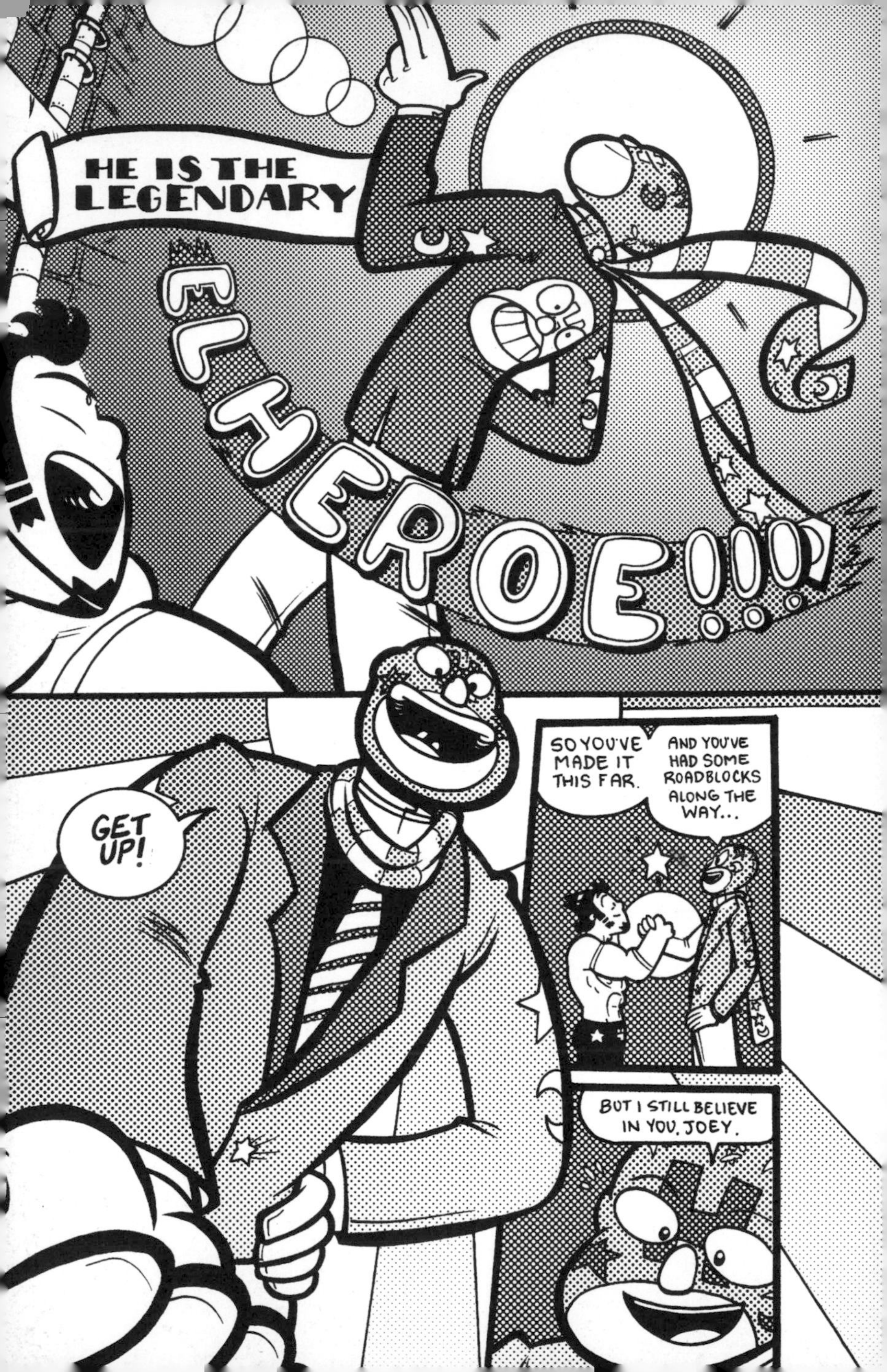
HE IS THE LEGENDARY
EL HEROE!!!
GET UP!
SO YOU'VE MADE IT THIS FAR.
AND YOU'VE HAD SOME ROADBLOCKS ALONG THE WAY...
BUT I STILL BELIEVE IN YOU, JOEY.

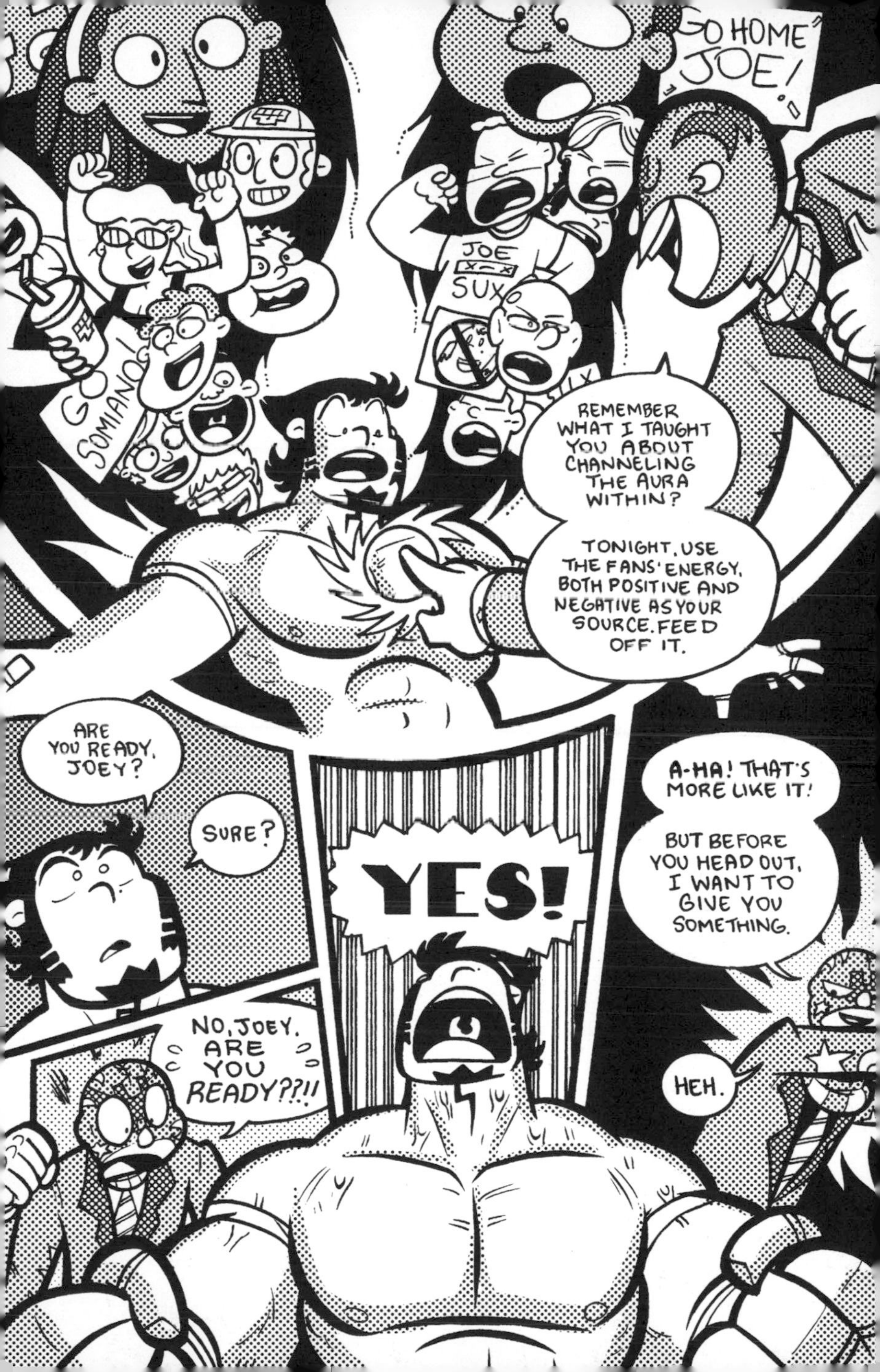
GO SOMIANO!
JOE SUX
GO HOME JOE!
REMEMBER WHAT I TAUGHT YOU ABOUT CHANNELING THE AURA WITHIN?
TONIGHT, USE THE FANS' ENERGY, BOTH POSITIVE AND NEGATIVE AS YOUR SOURCE. FEED OFF IT.
ARE YOU READY, JOEY?
SURE?
NO, JOEY. ARE YOU READY??!!
YES!
A-HA! THAT'S MORE LIKE IT!
BUT BEFORE YOU HEAD OUT, I WANT TO GIVE YOU SOMETHING.
HEH.

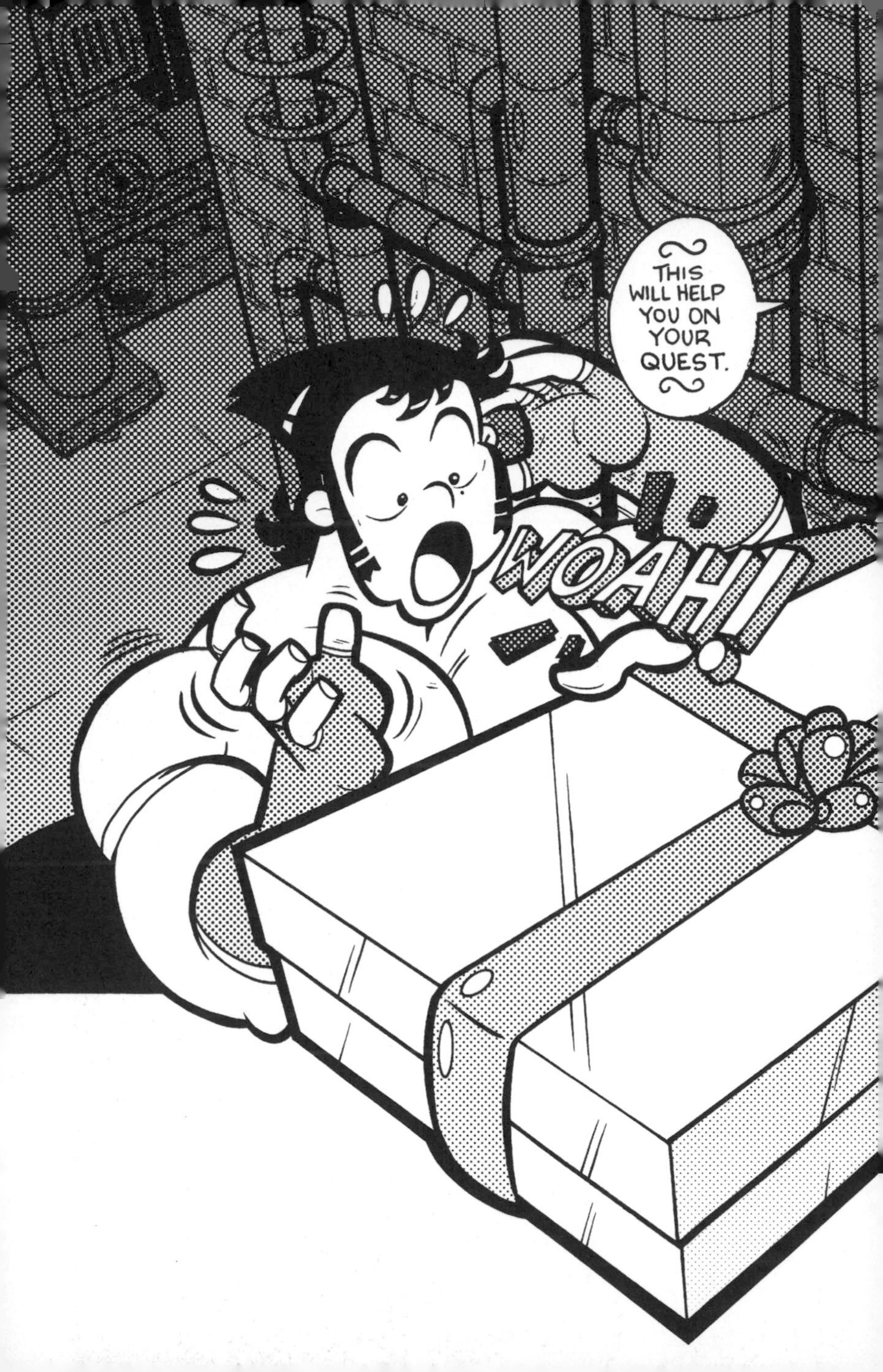
THIS WILL HELP YOU ON YOUR QUEST.
WOAH!

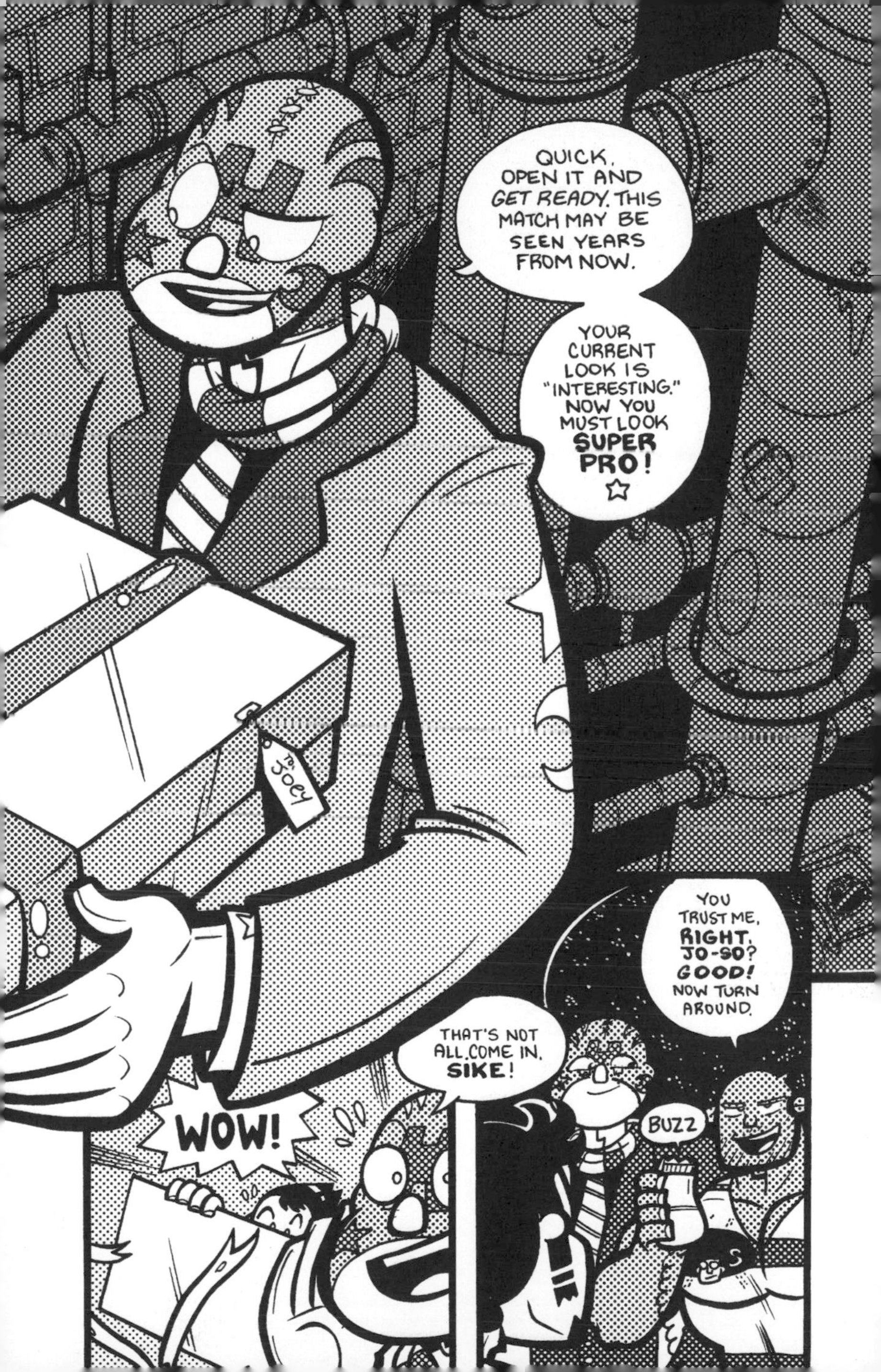
QUICK. OPEN IT AND GET READY. THIS MATCH MAY BE SEEN YEARS FROM NOW.
YOUR CURRENT LOOK IS "INTERESTING." NOW YOU MUST LOOK SUPER PRO! ☆
TO: JOEY
WOW!
THAT'S NOT ALL. COME IN, SIKE!
YOU TRUST ME, RIGHT, JO-SO? GOOD! NOW TURN AROUND.
BUZZ

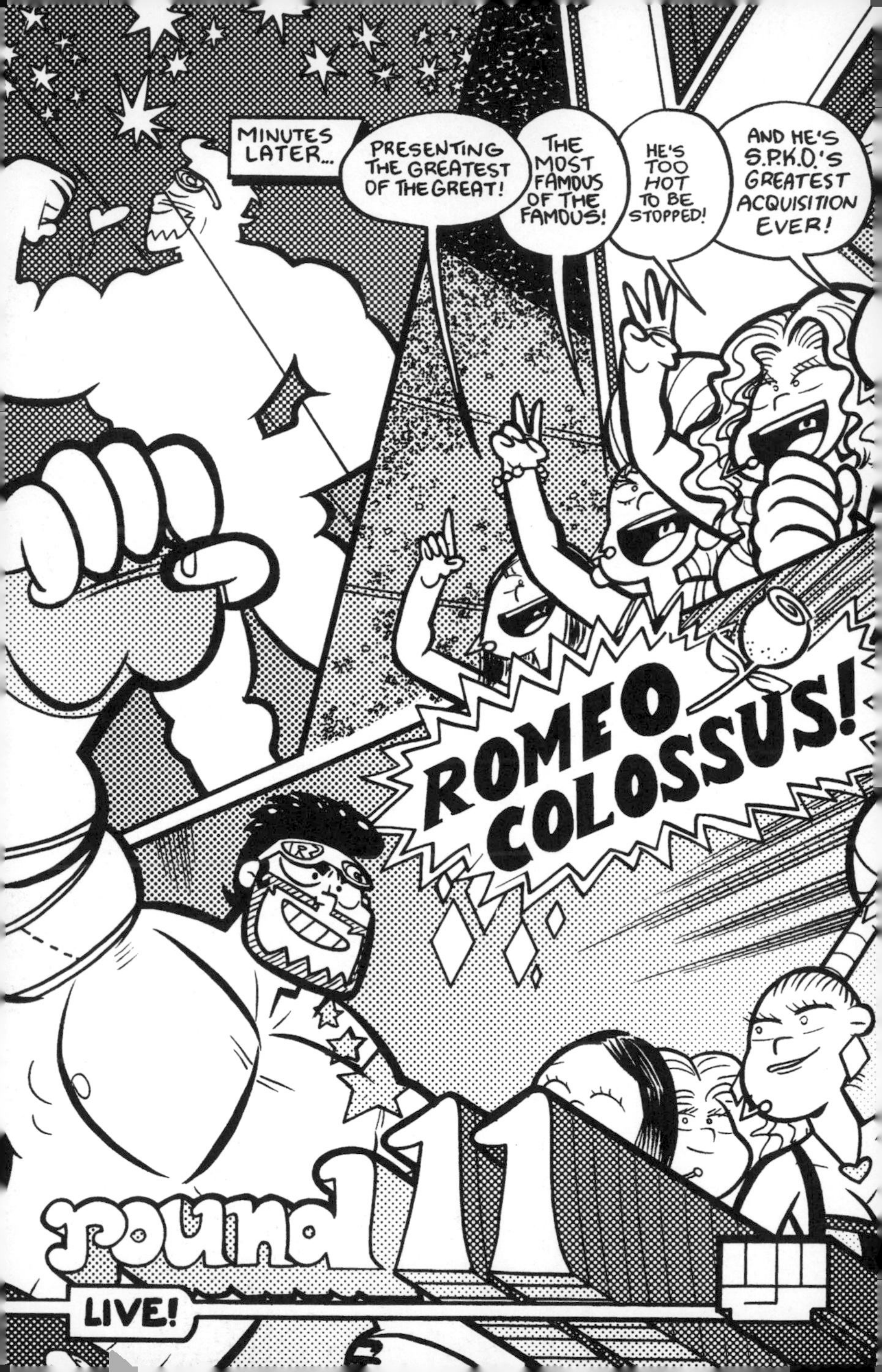
MINUTES LATER...
PRESENTING THE GREATEST OF THE GREAT!
THE MOST FAMOUS OF THE FAMOUS!
HE'S TOO HOT TO BE STOPPED!
AND HE'S S.P.K.O.'S GREATEST ACQUISITION EVER!
ROMEO COLOSSUS!
round 11
LIVE!

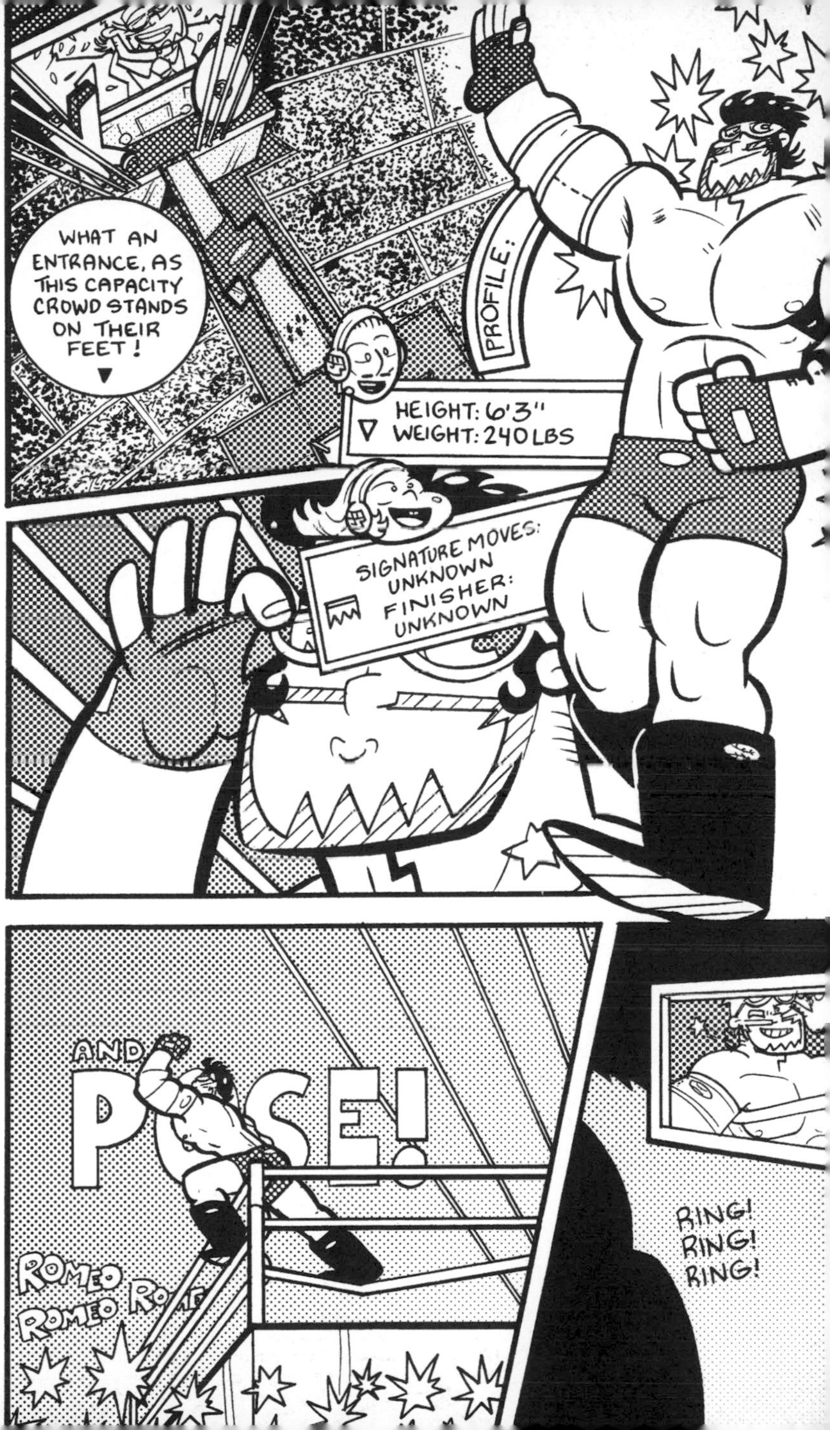
WHAT AN ENTRANCE, AS THIS CAPACITY CROWD STANDS ON THEIR FEET!
PROFILE:
HEIGHT: 6'3"
WEIGHT: 240 LBS
SIGNATURE MOVES: UNKNOWN
FINISHER: UNKNOWN
AND
POSE!
ROMEO
ROMEO
RING!
RING!
RING!

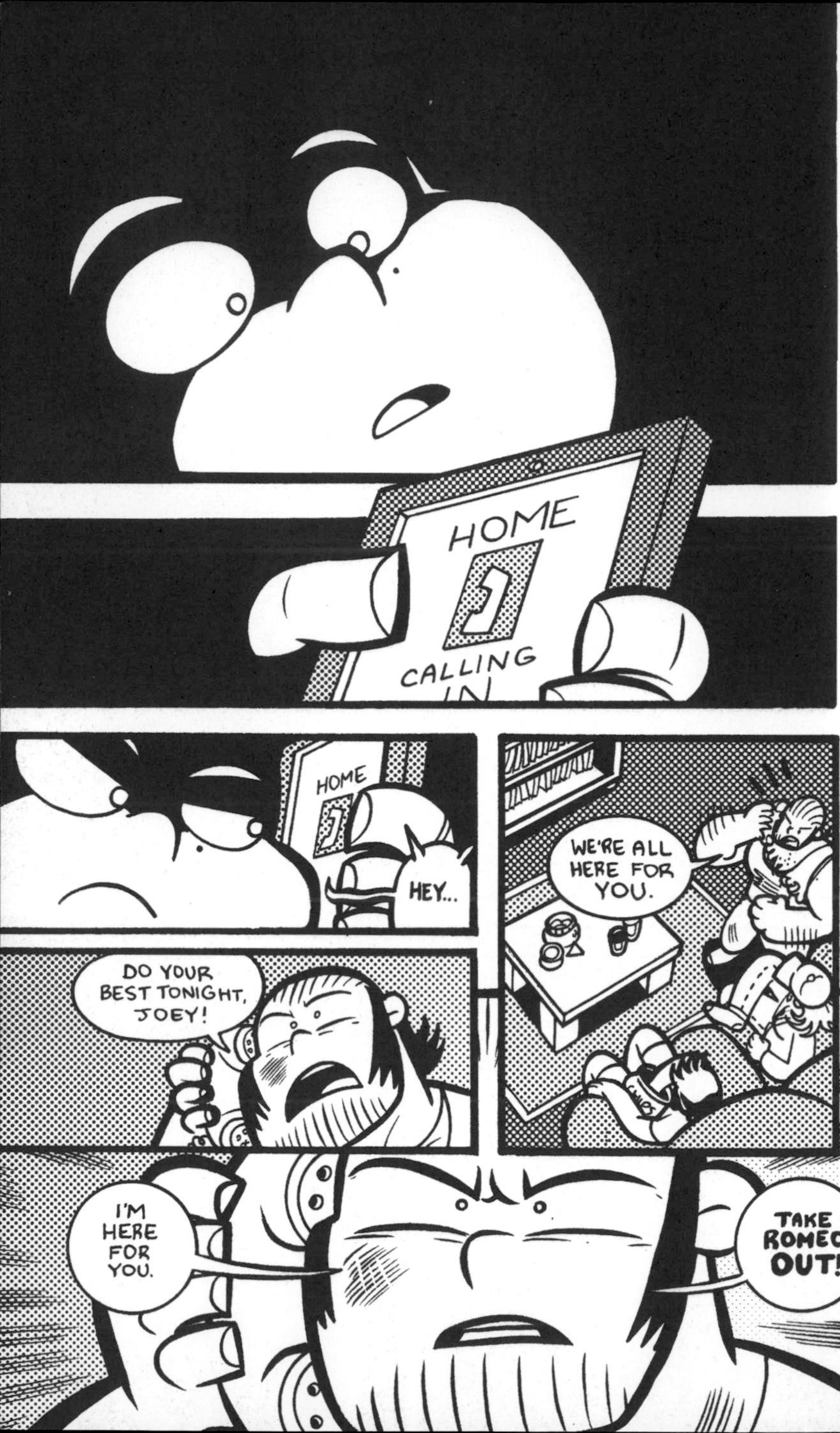
HOME
CALLING IN
HOME
HEY...
WE'RE ALL HERE FOR YOU.
DO YOUR BEST TONIGHT, JOEY!
I'M HERE FOR YOU.
TAKE ROMEO OUT!

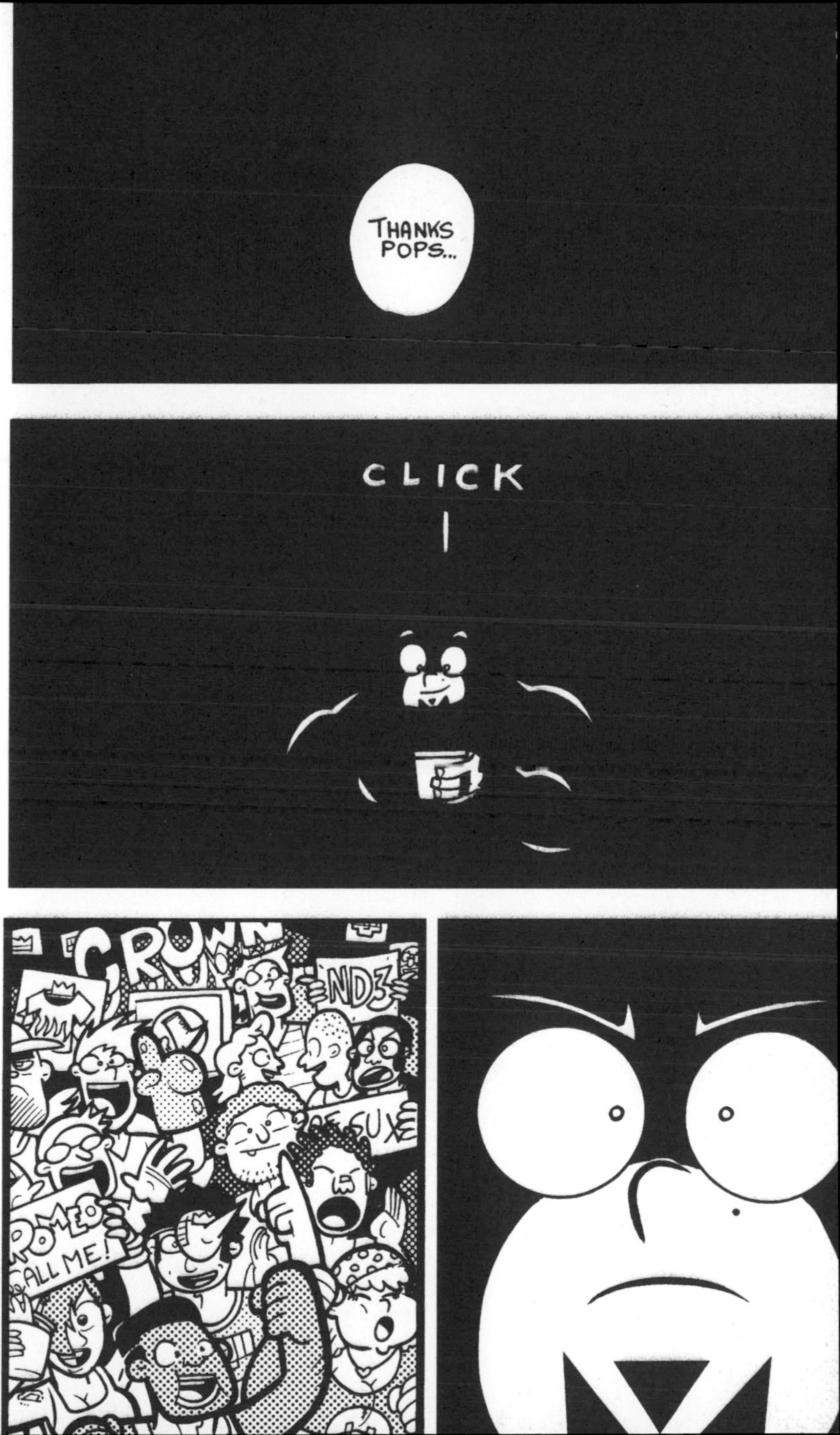
THANKS POPS...
CLICK
ND3
ROMEO
CALL ME!

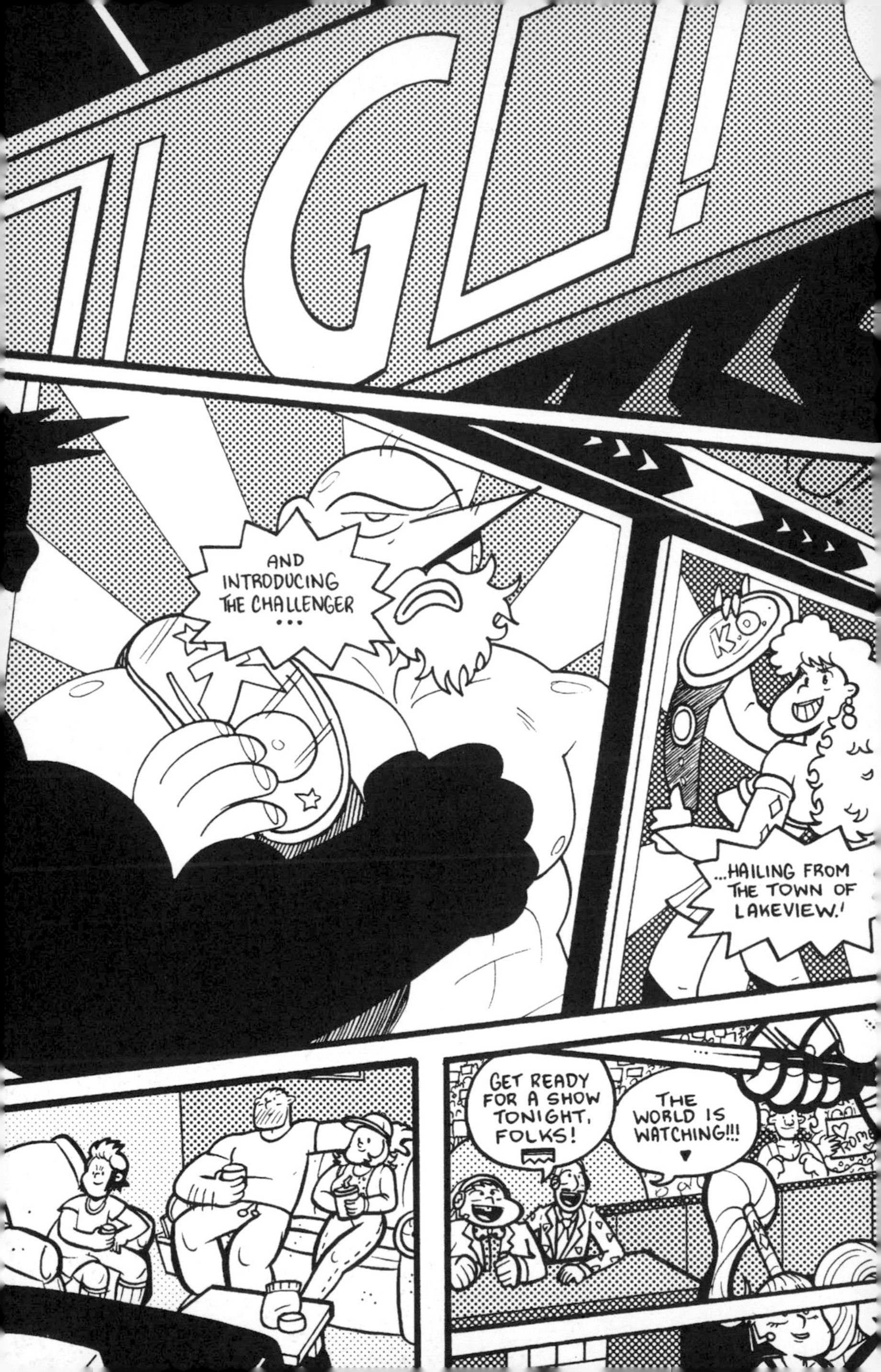
AND INTRODUCING THE CHALLENGER ...
...HAILING FROM THE TOWN OF LAKEVIEW!
GET READY FOR A SHOW TONIGHT, FOLKS!
THE WORLD IS WATCHING!!!

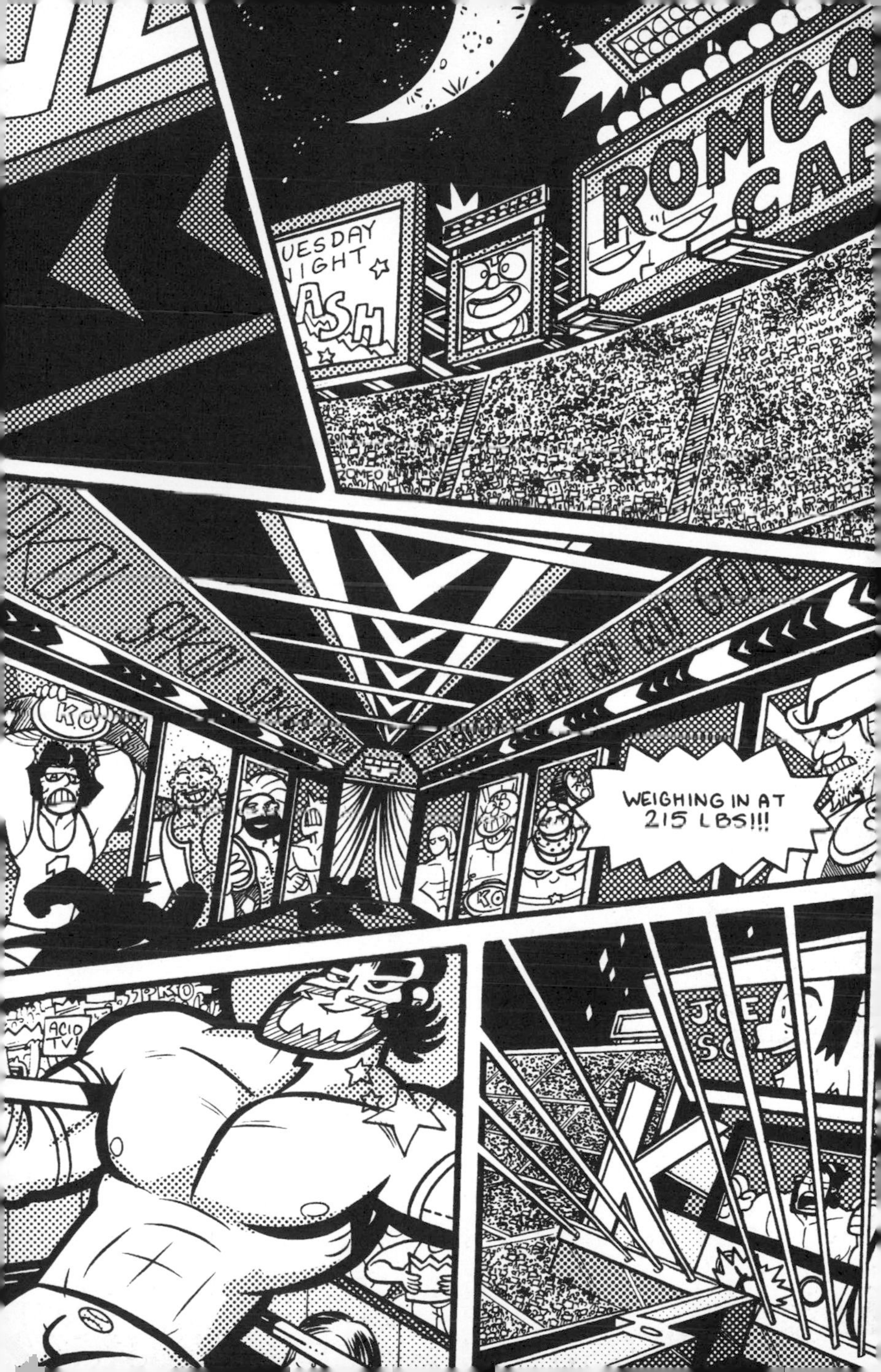

UESDAY
NIGHT
ASH
ROMEO
CA
WEIGHING IN AT
215 LBS!!!
ACID TV!
JOE
SO

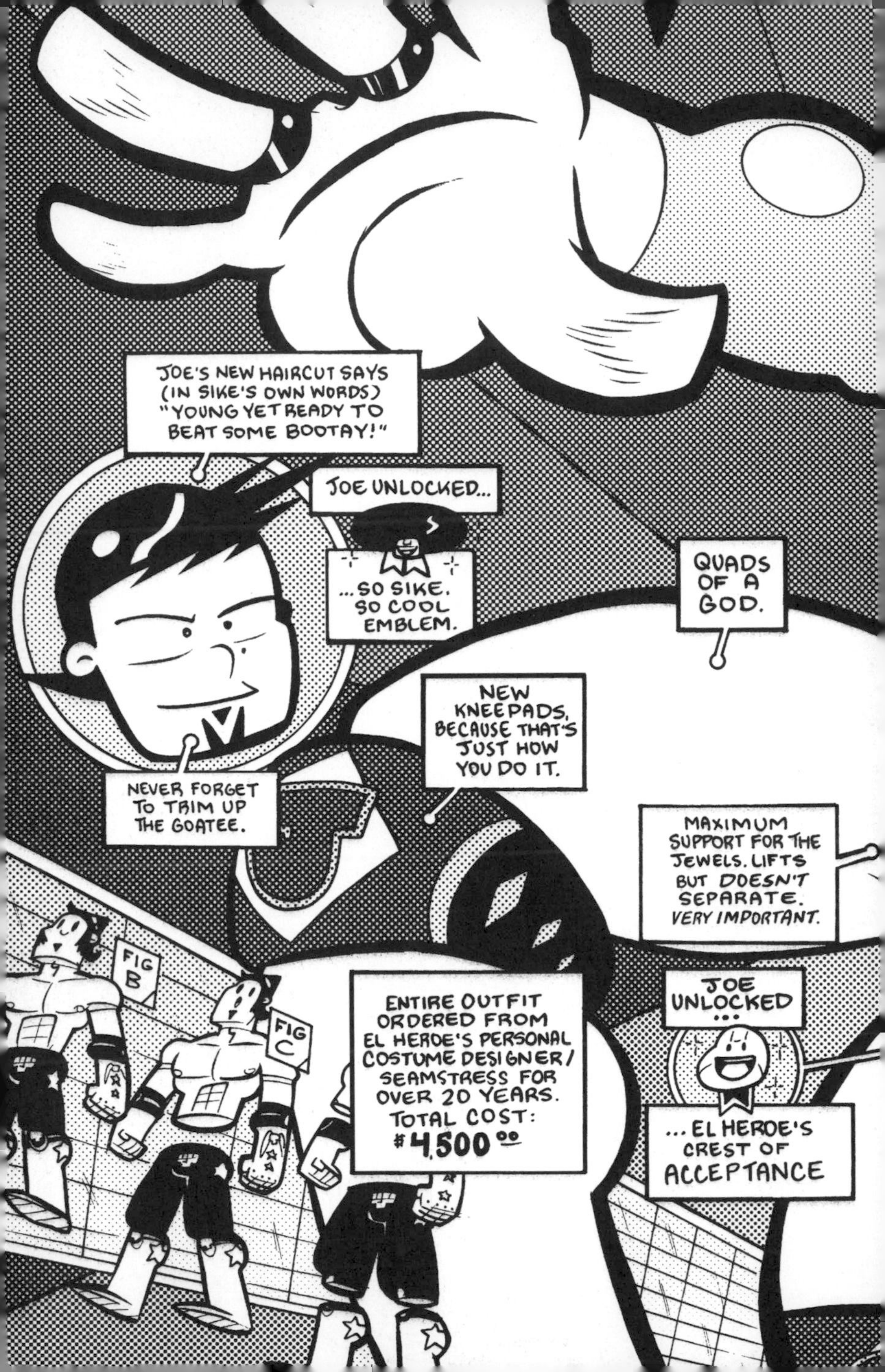

JOE'S NEW HAIRCUT SAYS (IN SIKE'S OWN WORDS) "YOUNG YET READY TO BEAT SOME BOOTAY!"
JOE UNLOCKED...
...SO SIKE. SO COOL EMBLEM.
QUADS OF A GOD.
NEW KNEEPADS, BECAUSE THAT'S JUST HOW YOU DO IT.
NEVER FORGET TO TRIM UP THE GOATEE.
MAXIMUM SUPPORT FOR THE JEWELS. LIFTS BUT DOESN'T SEPARATE. VERY IMPORTANT.
FIG B
FIG C
ENTIRE OUTFIT ORDERED FROM EL HEROE'S PERSONAL COSTUME DESIGNER/ SEAMSTRESS FOR OVER 20 YEARS. TOTAL COST: $4,500.00
JOE UNLOCKED...
...EL HEROE'S CREST OF ACCEPTANCE

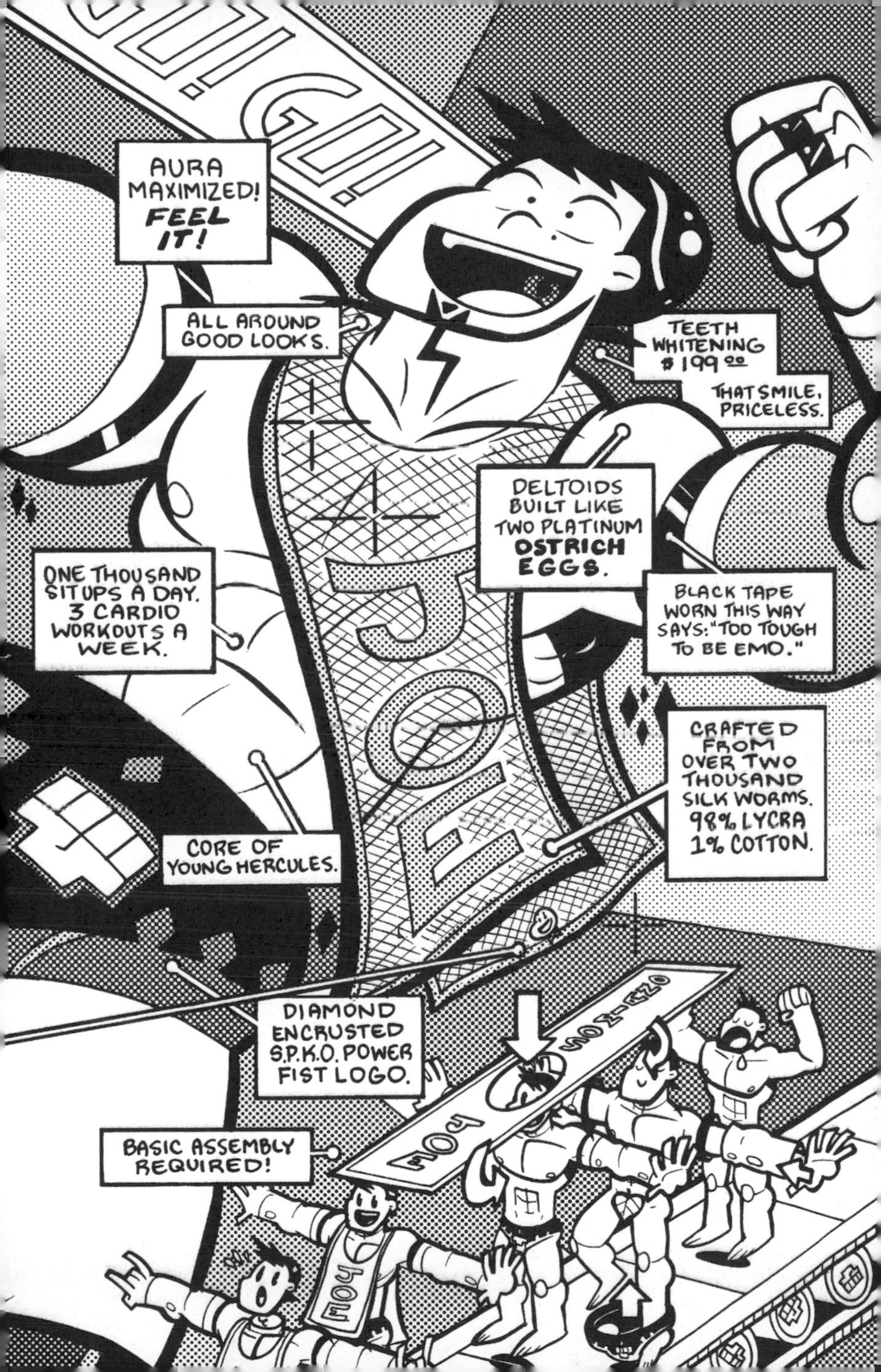
AURA MAXIMIZED! **FEEL IT!**
ALL AROUND GOOD LOOKS.
TEETH WHITENING $199.00
THAT SMILE, PRICELESS.
DELTOIDS BUILT LIKE TWO PLATINUM **OSTRICH EGGS.**
ONE THOUSAND SITUPS A DAY. 3 CARDIO WORKOUTS A WEEK.
BLACK TAPE WORN THIS WAY SAYS: "TOO TOUGH TO BE EMO."
CRAFTED FROM OVER TWO THOUSAND SILK WORMS. 98% LYCRA 1% COTTON.
CORE OF YOUNG HERCULES.
DIAMOND ENCRUSTED S.P.K.O. POWER FIST LOGO.
BASIC ASSEMBLY REQUIRED!

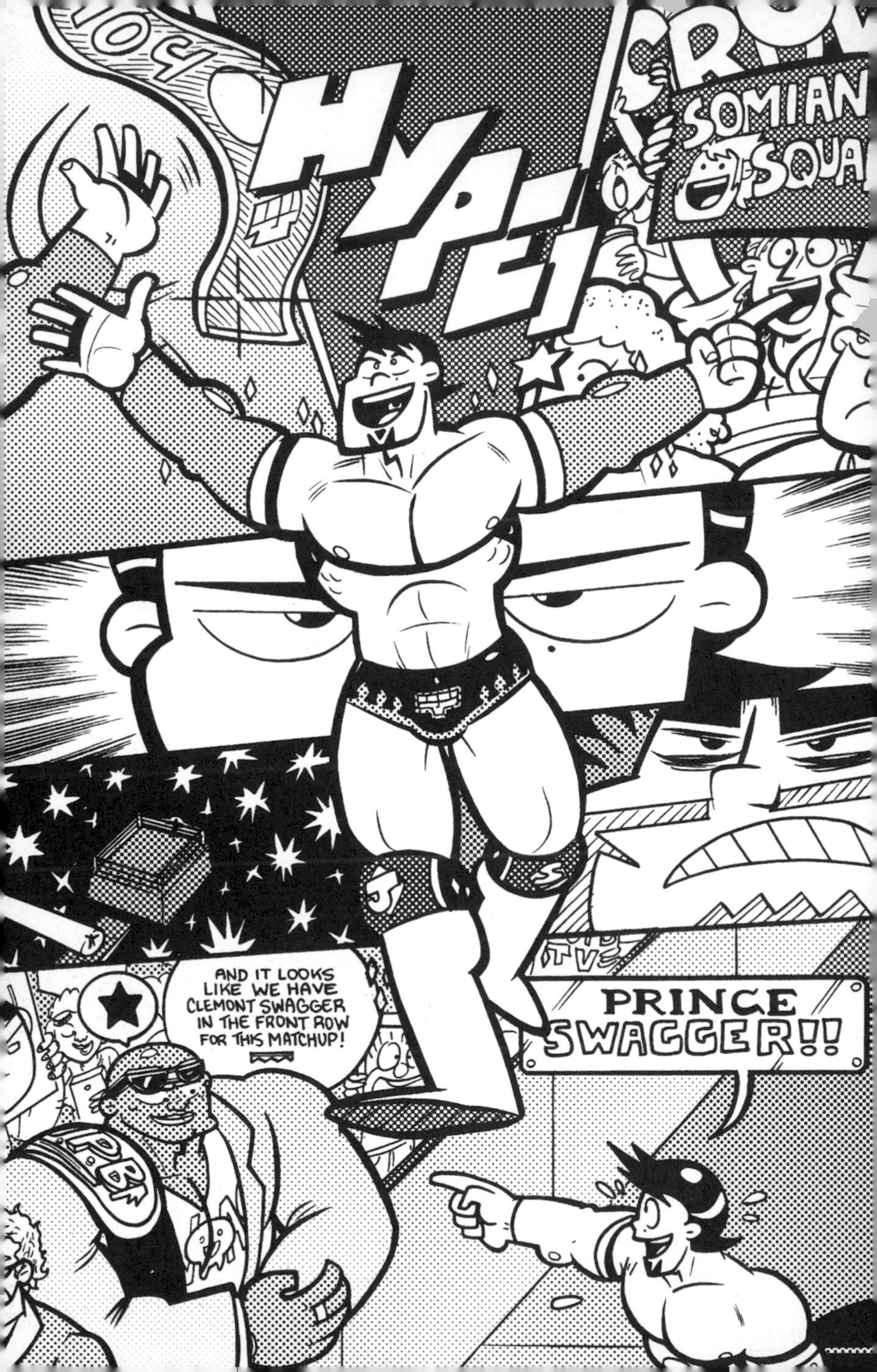
HYPE!
AND IT LOOKS LIKE WE HAVE CLEMONT SWAGGER IN THE FRONT ROW FOR THIS MATCHUP!
PRINCE SWAGGER!!

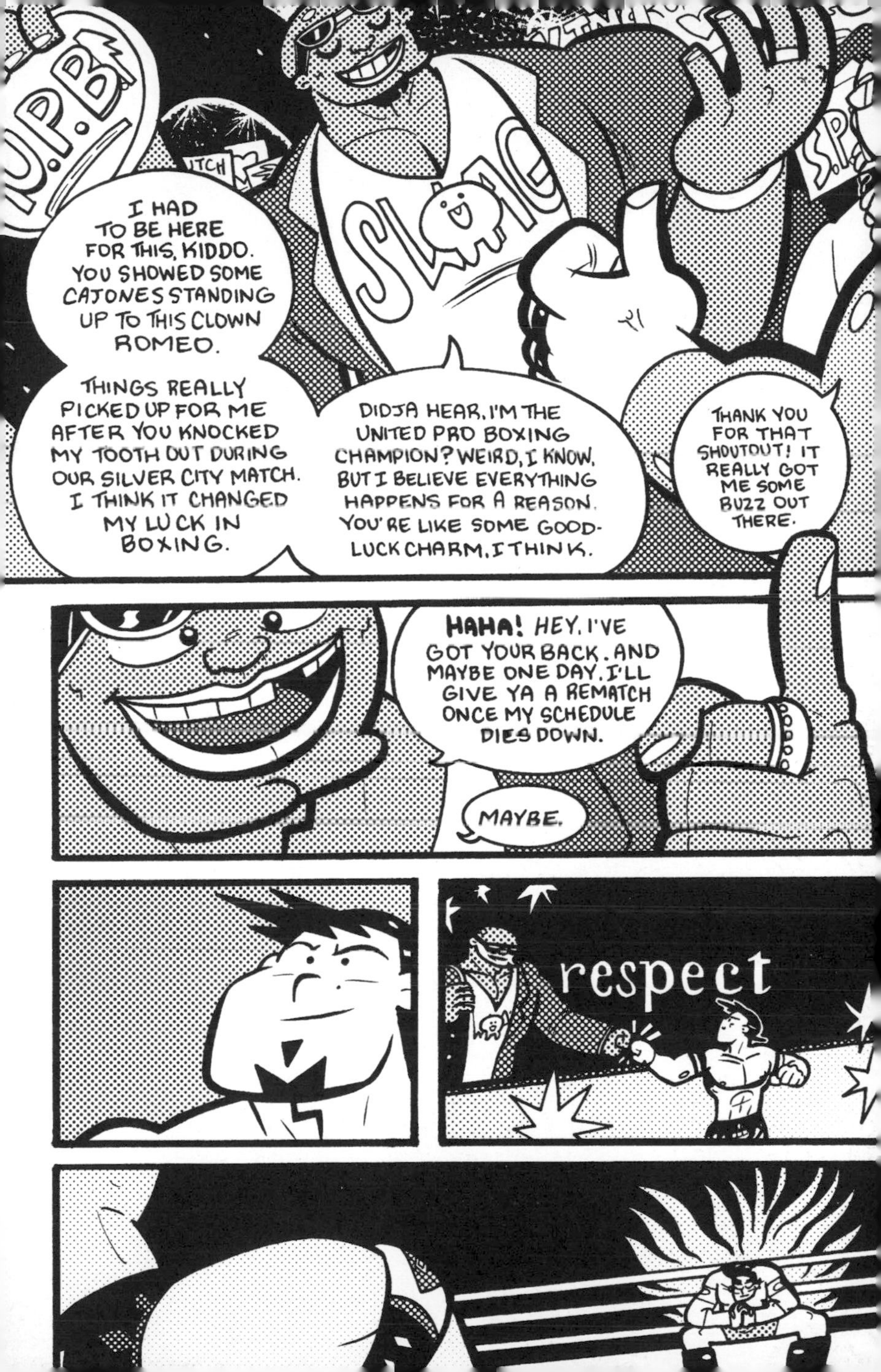
U.P.B.
S.P.
SLOTG
I HAD TO BE HERE FOR THIS, KIDDO. YOU SHOWED SOME CAJONES STANDING UP TO THIS CLOWN ROMEO.
THINGS REALLY PICKED UP FOR ME AFTER YOU KNOCKED MY TOOTH OUT DURING OUR SILVER CITY MATCH. I THINK IT CHANGED MY LUCK IN BOXING.
DIDJA HEAR, I'M THE UNITED PRO BOXING CHAMPION? WEIRD, I KNOW, BUT I BELIEVE EVERYTHING HAPPENS FOR A REASON. YOU'RE LIKE SOME GOOD-LUCK CHARM, I THINK.
THANK YOU FOR THAT SHOUTOUT! IT REALLY GOT ME SOME BUZZ OUT THERE.
HAHA! HEY, I'VE GOT YOUR BACK. AND MAYBE ONE DAY, I'LL GIVE YA A REMATCH ONCE MY SCHEDULE DIES DOWN.
MAYBE.
respect

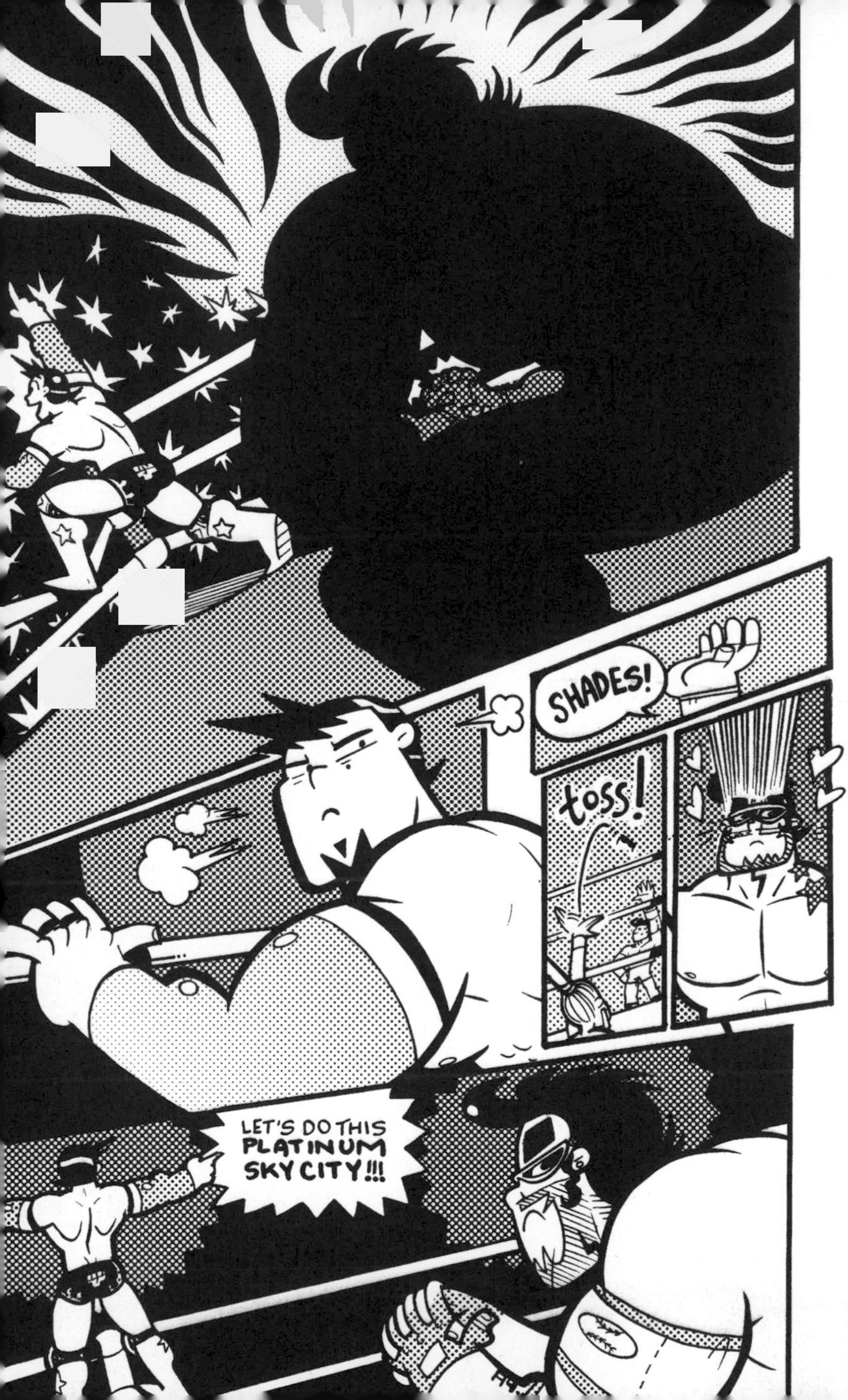
SHADES!
toss!
LET'S DO THIS PLATINUM SKY CITY!!!

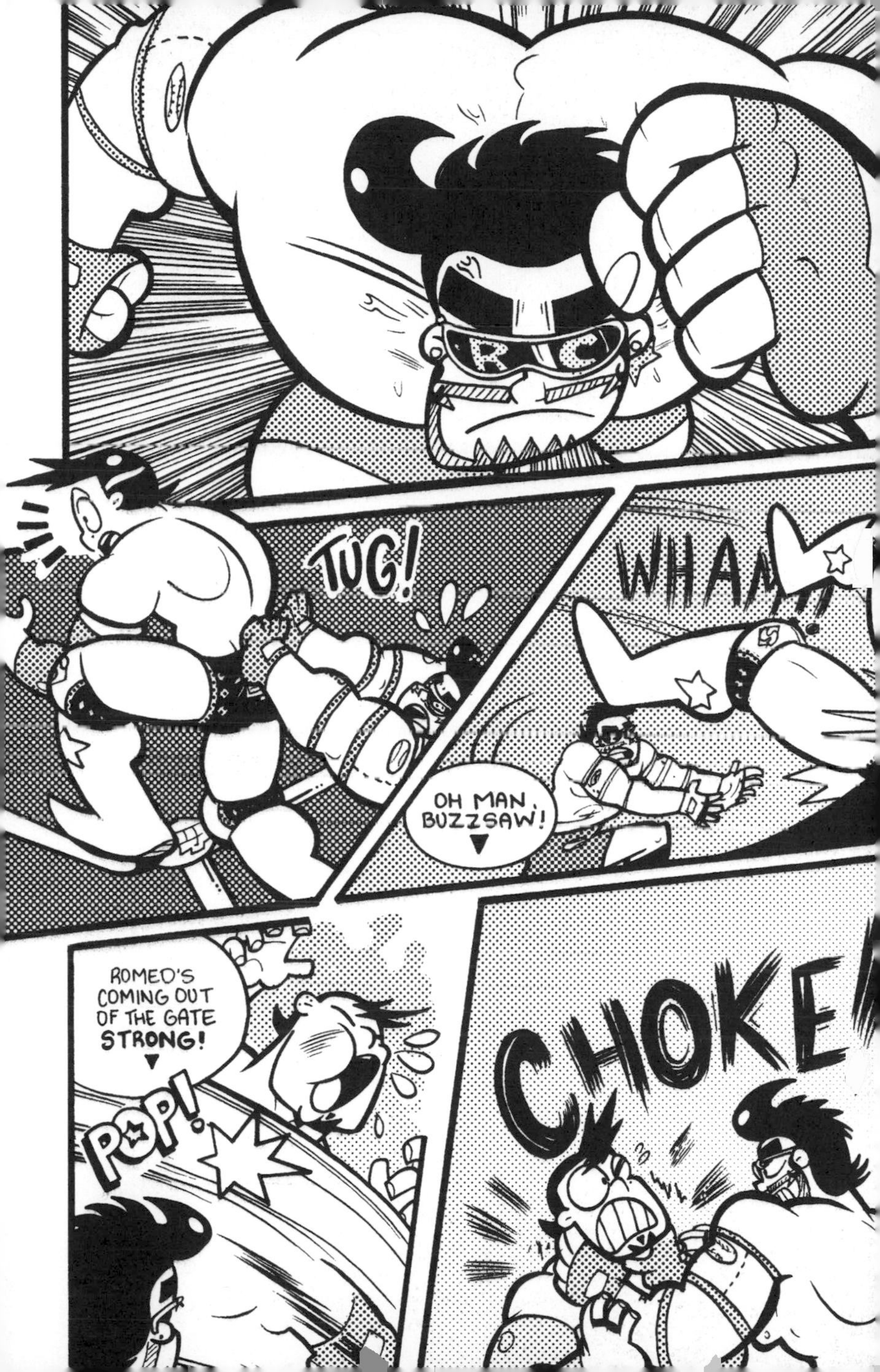
TUG!
WHAM!!
OH MAN, BUZZSAW!
ROMEO'S COMING OUT OF THE GATE **STRONG!**
POP!
CHOKE!

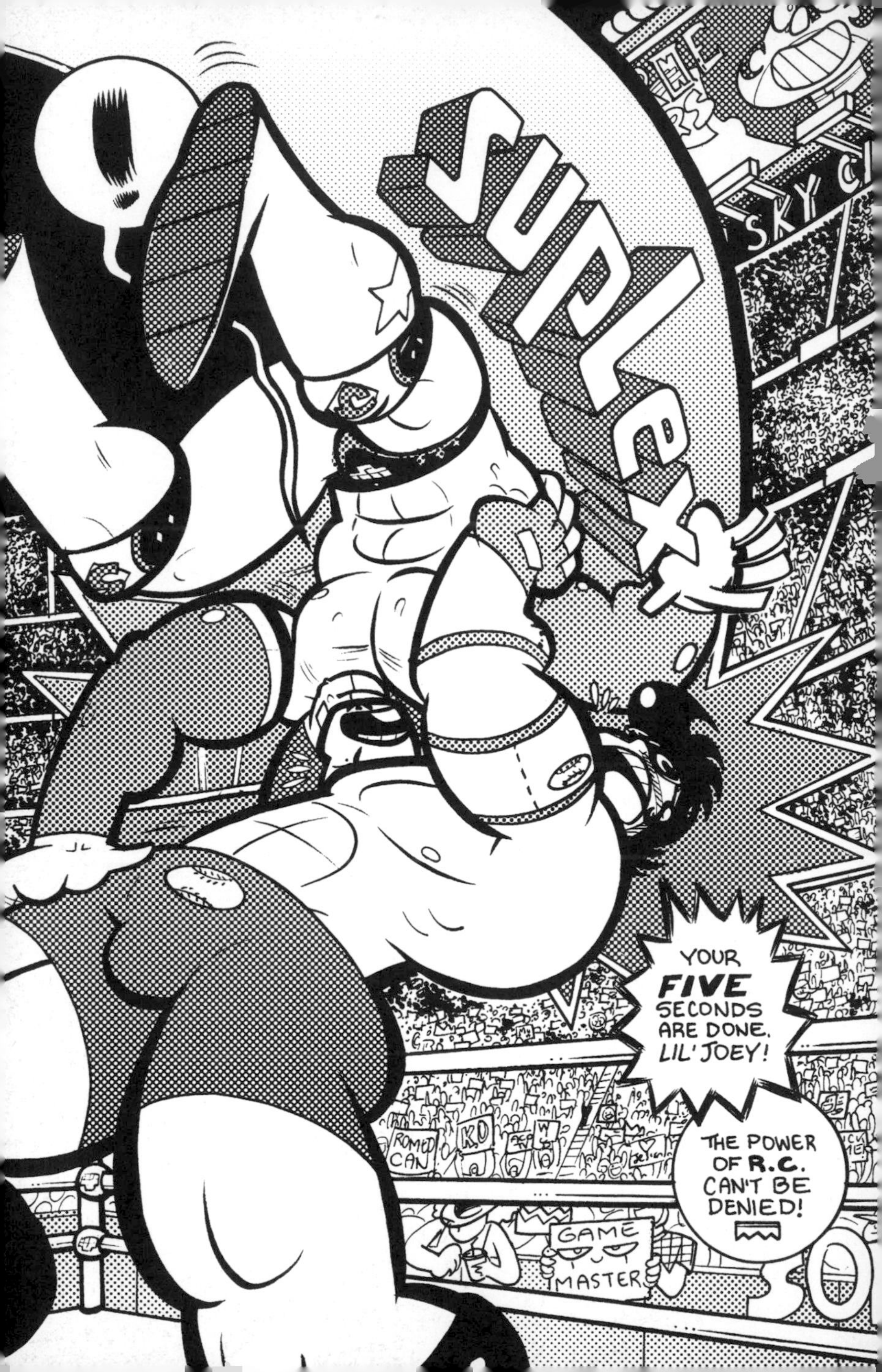
!
SUPLEX
YOUR FIVE SECONDS ARE DONE, LIL' JOEY!
THE POWER OF R.C. CAN'T BE DENIED!
ROMEO CAN
KO
GAME MASTER
SKY

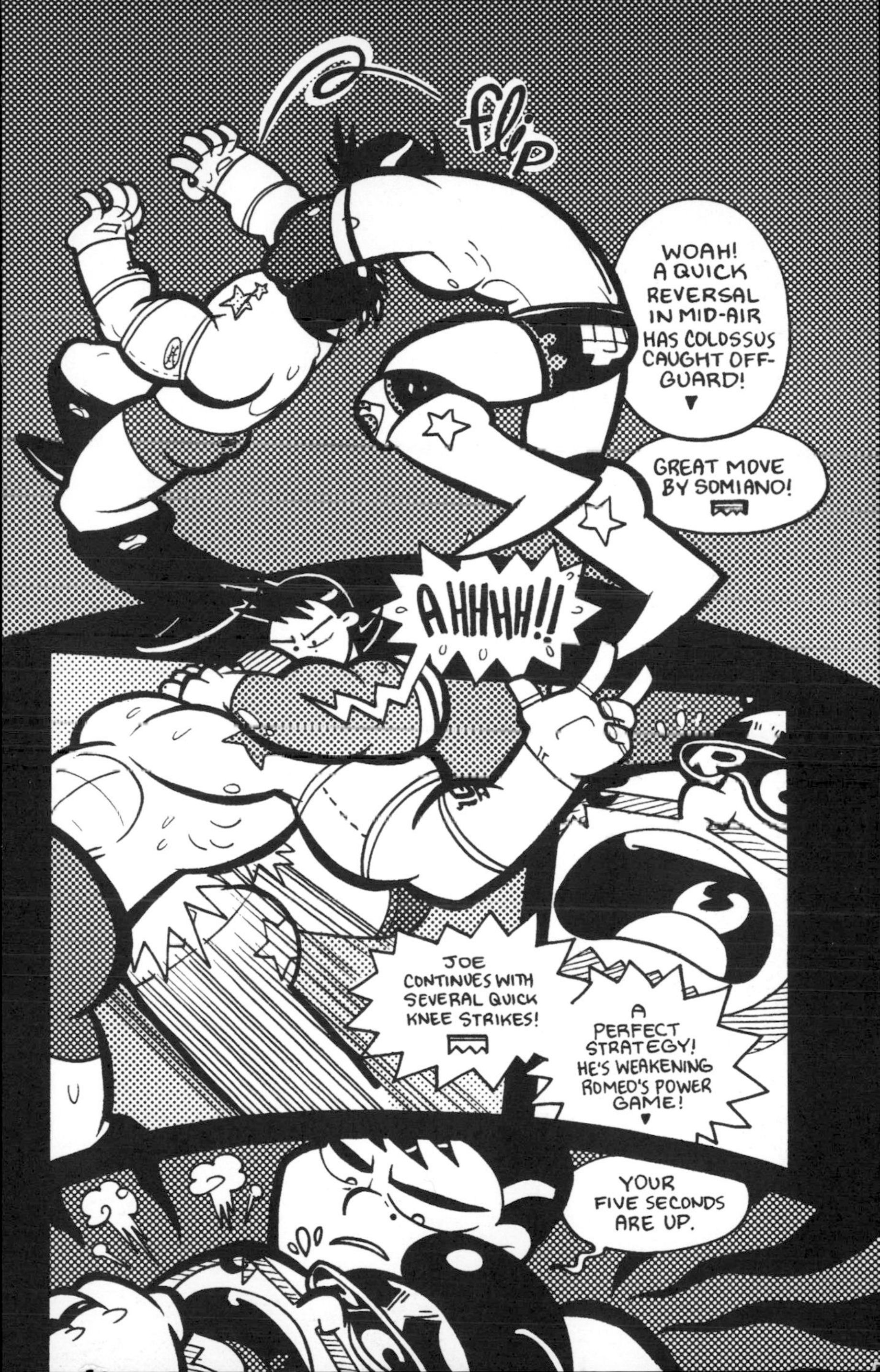
flip
WOAH! A QUICK REVERSAL IN MID-AIR HAS COLOSSUS CAUGHT OFF-GUARD!
GREAT MOVE BY SOMIANO!
AHHHH!!
JOE CONTINUES WITH SEVERAL QUICK KNEE STRIKES!
A PERFECT STRATEGY! HE'S WEAKENING ROMEO'S POWER GAME!
YOUR FIVE SECONDS ARE UP.

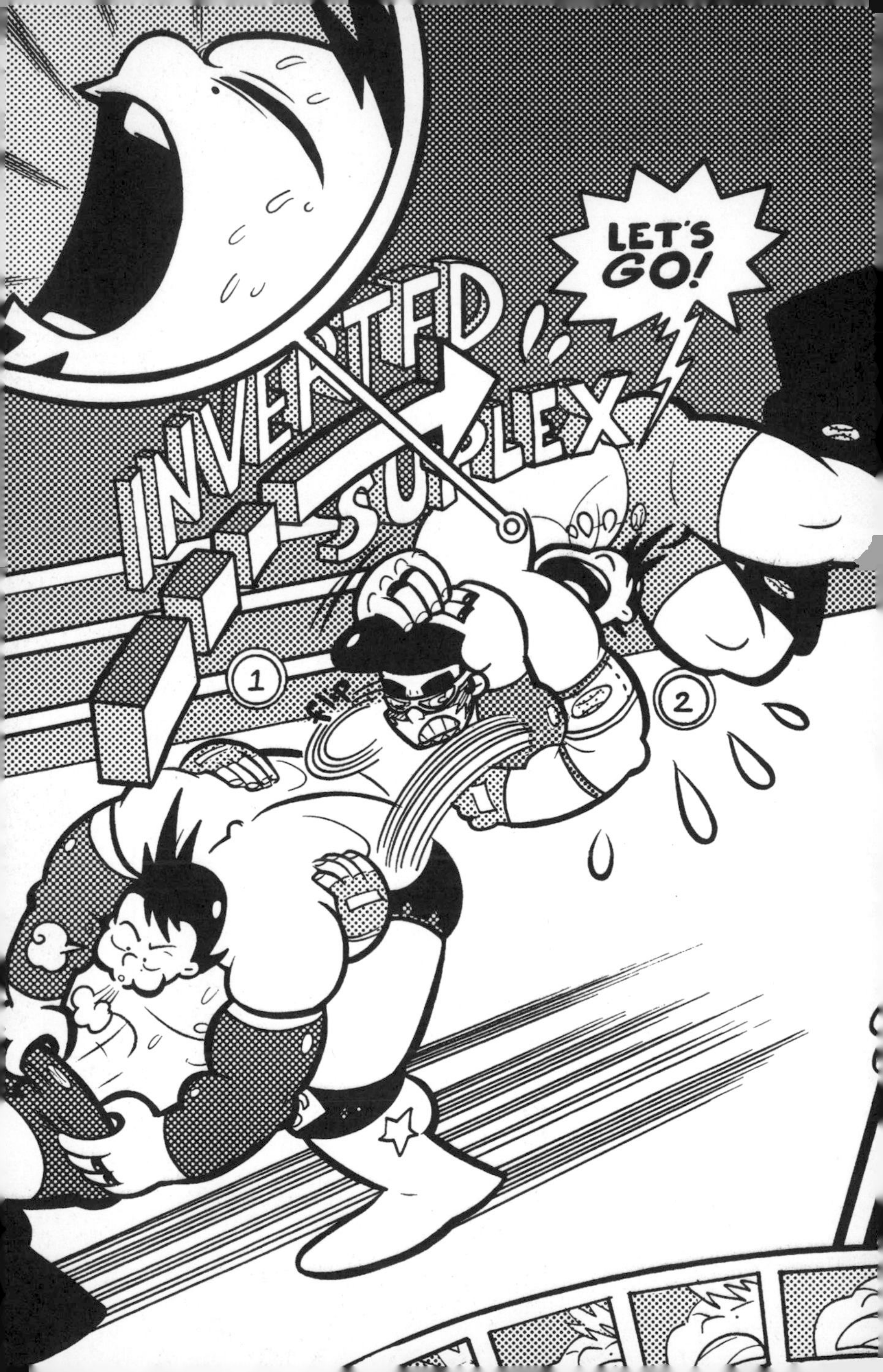
LET'S GO!
INVERTED SUPLEX
FLIP
1
2

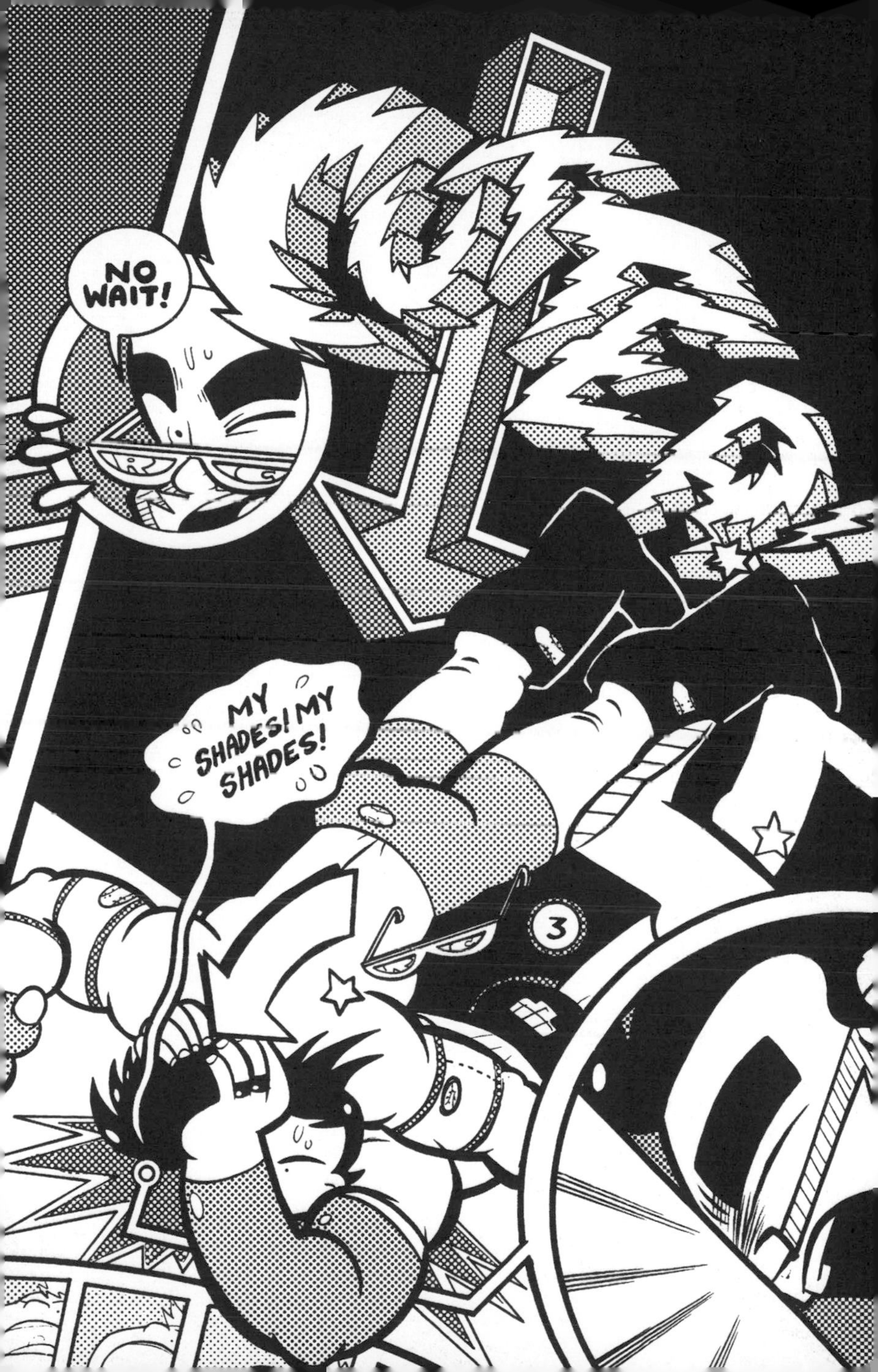
NO WAIT!
MY SHADES! MY SHADES!
3

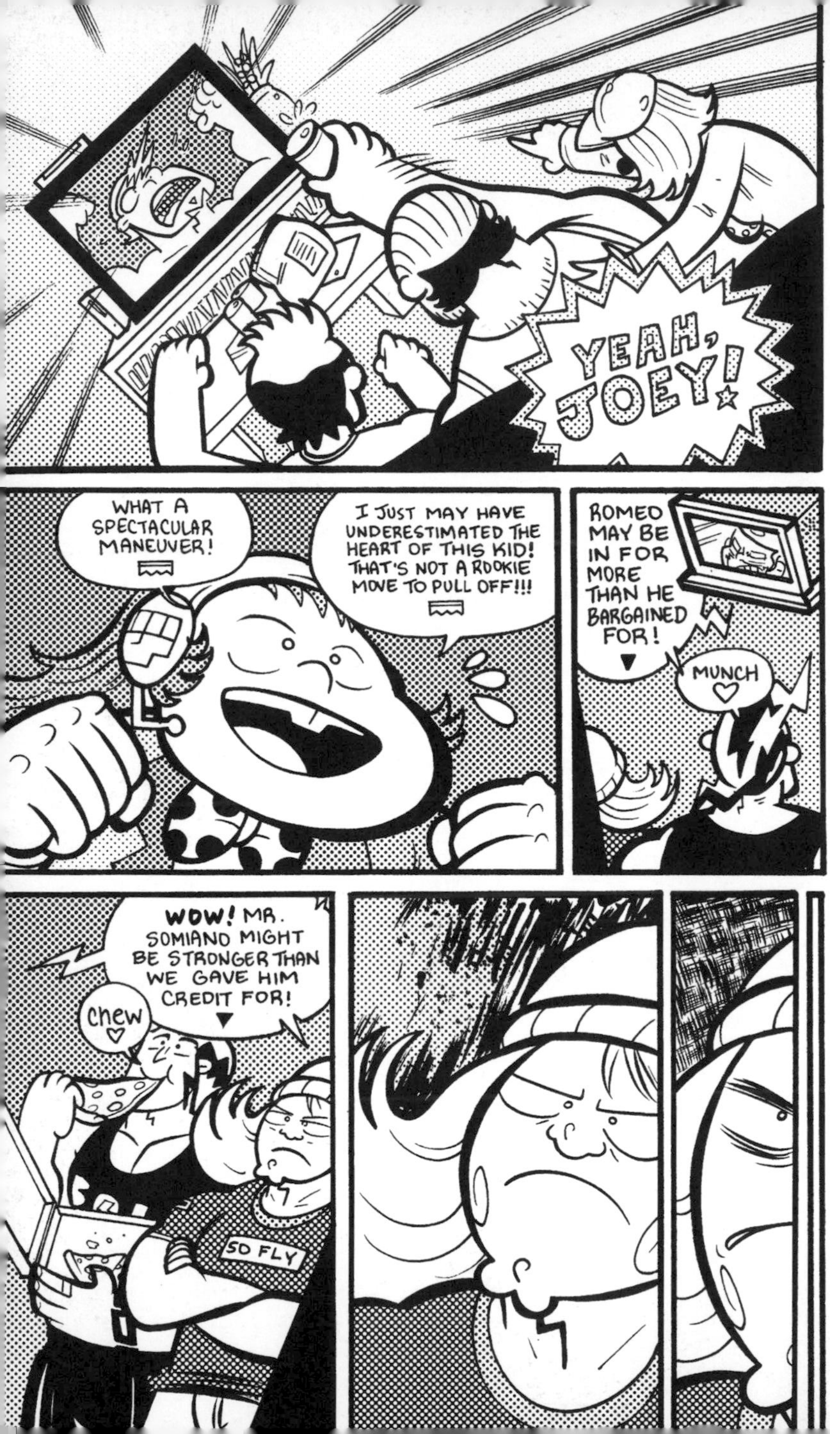
YEAH, JOEY!
WHAT A SPECTACULAR MANEUVER!
I JUST MAY HAVE UNDERESTIMATED THE HEART OF THIS KID! THAT'S NOT A ROOKIE MOVE TO PULL OFF!!!
ROMEO MAY BE IN FOR MORE THAN HE BARGAINED FOR!
MUNCH
WOW! MR. SOMIANO MIGHT BE STRONGER THAN WE GAVE HIM CREDIT FOR!
chew
SO FLY

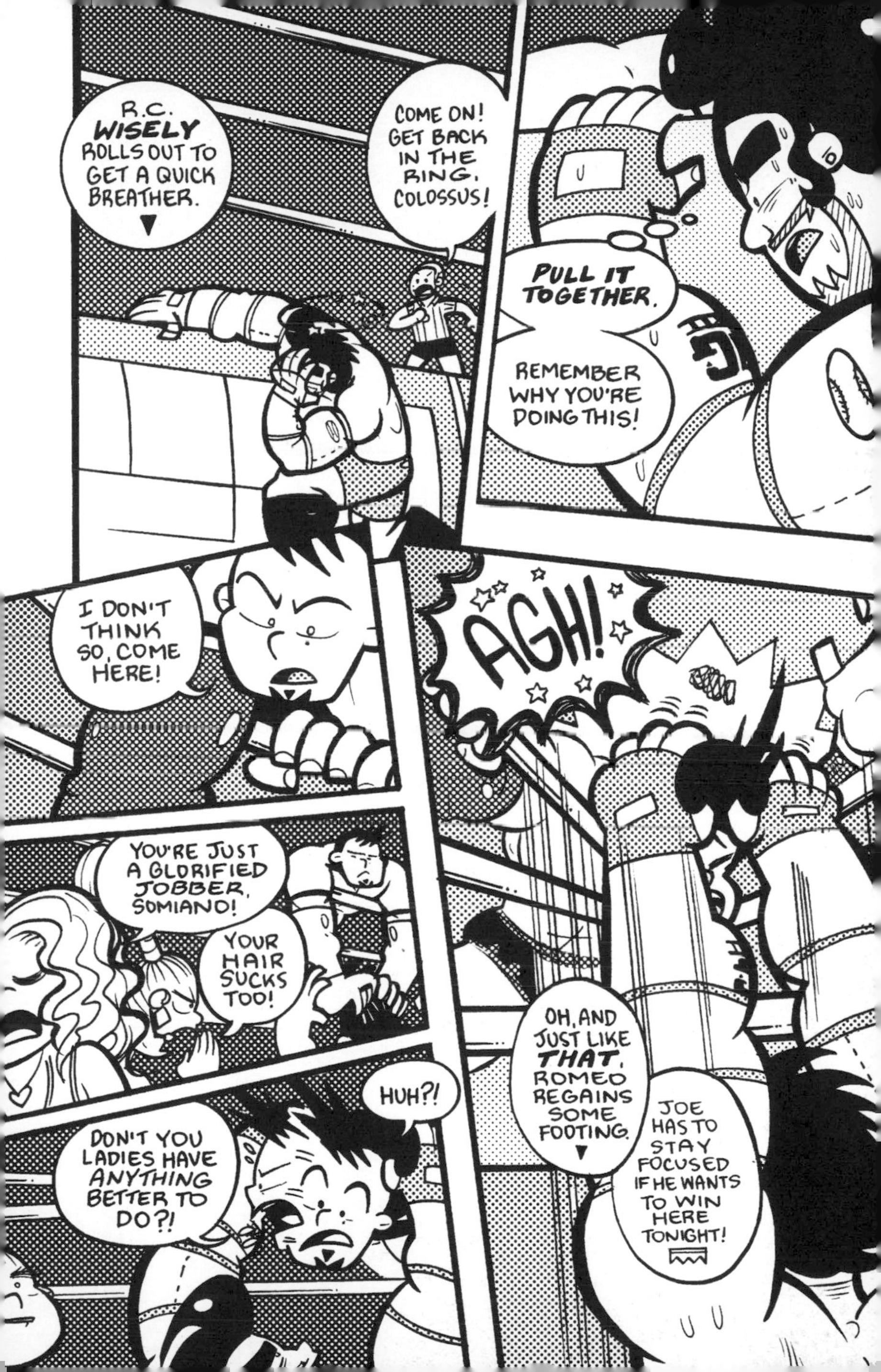
R.C. **WISELY** ROLLS OUT TO GET A QUICK BREATHER.
COME ON! GET BACK IN THE RING, COLOSSUS!
PULL IT TOGETHER.
REMEMBER WHY YOU'RE DOING THIS!
I DON'T THINK SO, COME HERE!
AGH!
YOU'RE JUST A GLORIFIED JOBBER, SOMIANO!
YOUR HAIR SUCKS TOO!
HUH?!
DON'T YOU LADIES HAVE *ANYTHING* BETTER TO DO?!
OH, AND JUST LIKE ***THAT***, ROMEO REGAINS SOME FOOTING.
JOE HAS TO STAY FOCUSED IF HE WANTS TO WIN HERE TONIGHT!

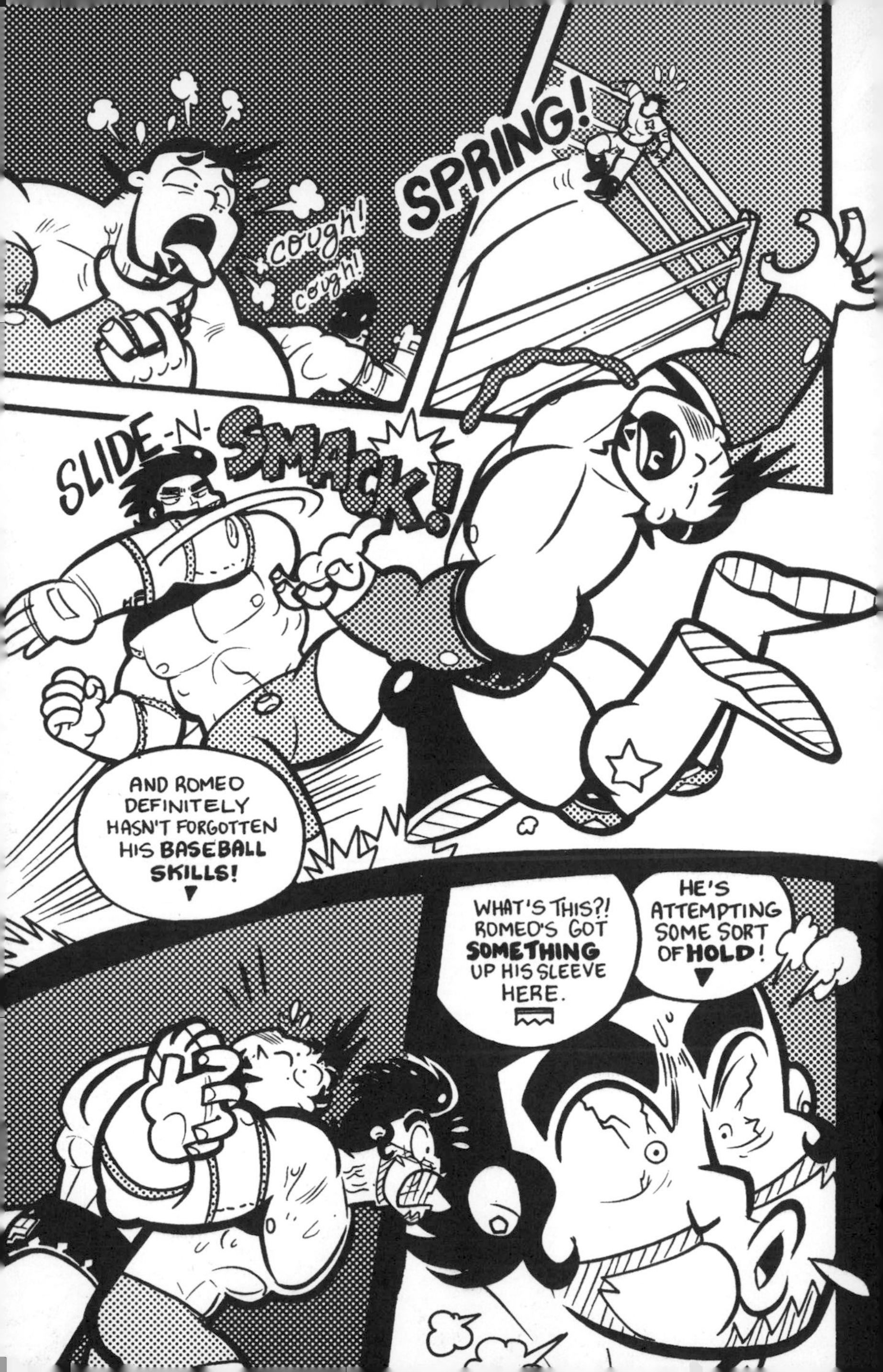
COUGH!
COUGH!
SPRING!
SLIDE-N-SMACK!
AND ROMEO DEFINITELY HASN'T FORGOTTEN HIS **BASEBALL SKILLS!**
WHAT'S THIS?! ROMEO'S GOT **SOMETHING** UP HIS SLEEVE HERE.
HE'S ATTEMPTING SOME SORT OF **HOLD**!

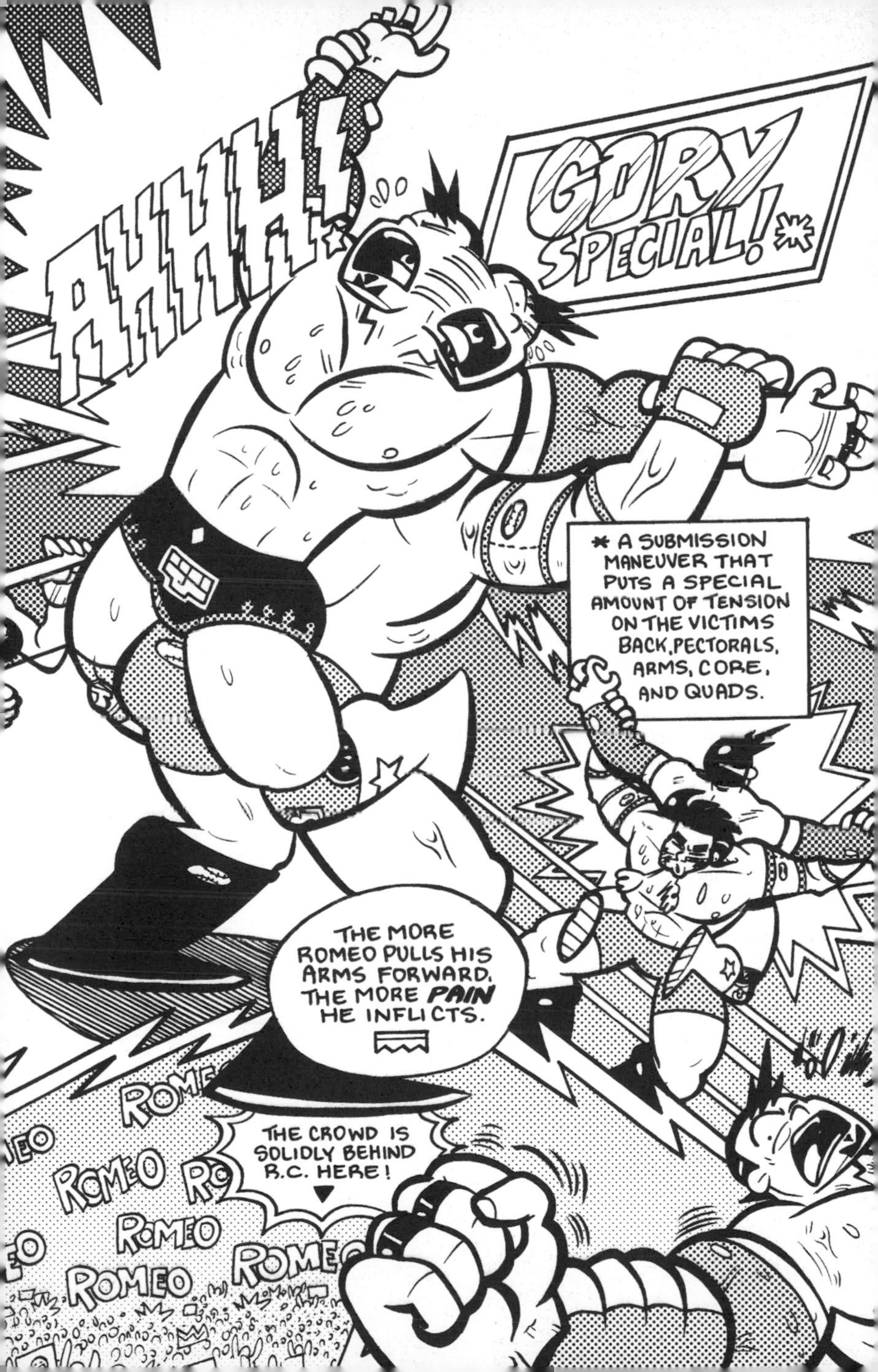
AHHH!
GORY SPECIAL!*
* A SUBMISSION MANEUVER THAT PUTS A SPECIAL AMOUNT OF TENSION ON THE VICTIMS BACK, PECTORALS, ARMS, CORE, AND QUADS.
THE MORE ROMEO PULLS HIS ARMS FORWARD, THE MORE PAIN HE INFLICTS.
ROMEO ROMEO ROMEO ROMEO ROMEO
THE CROWD IS SOLIDLY BEHIND R.C. HERE!

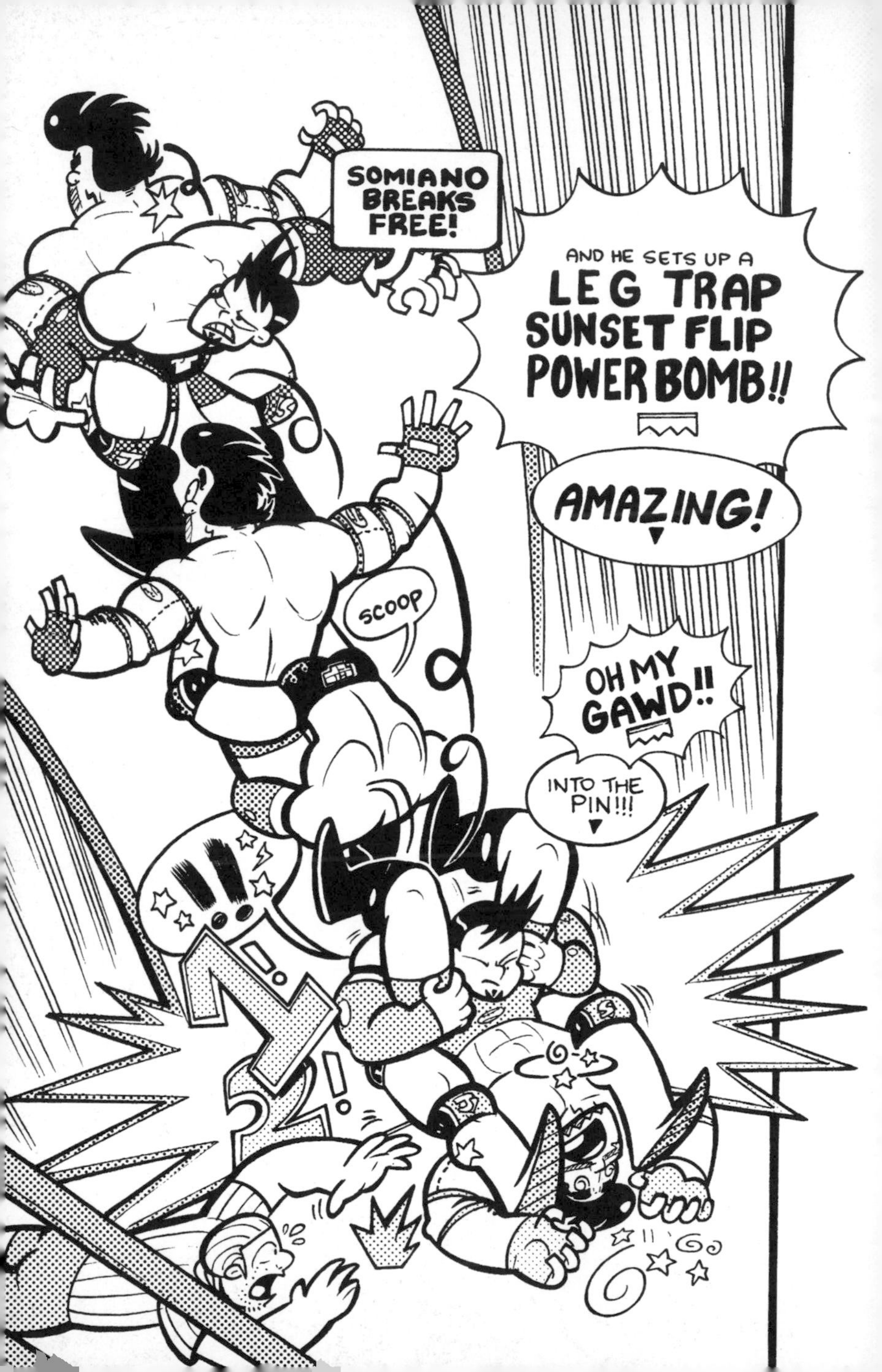
SOMIANO BREAKS FREE!
AND HE SETS UP A LEG TRAP SUNSET FLIP POWER BOMB!!
AMAZING!
scoop
OH MY GAWD!!
INTO THE PIN!!!

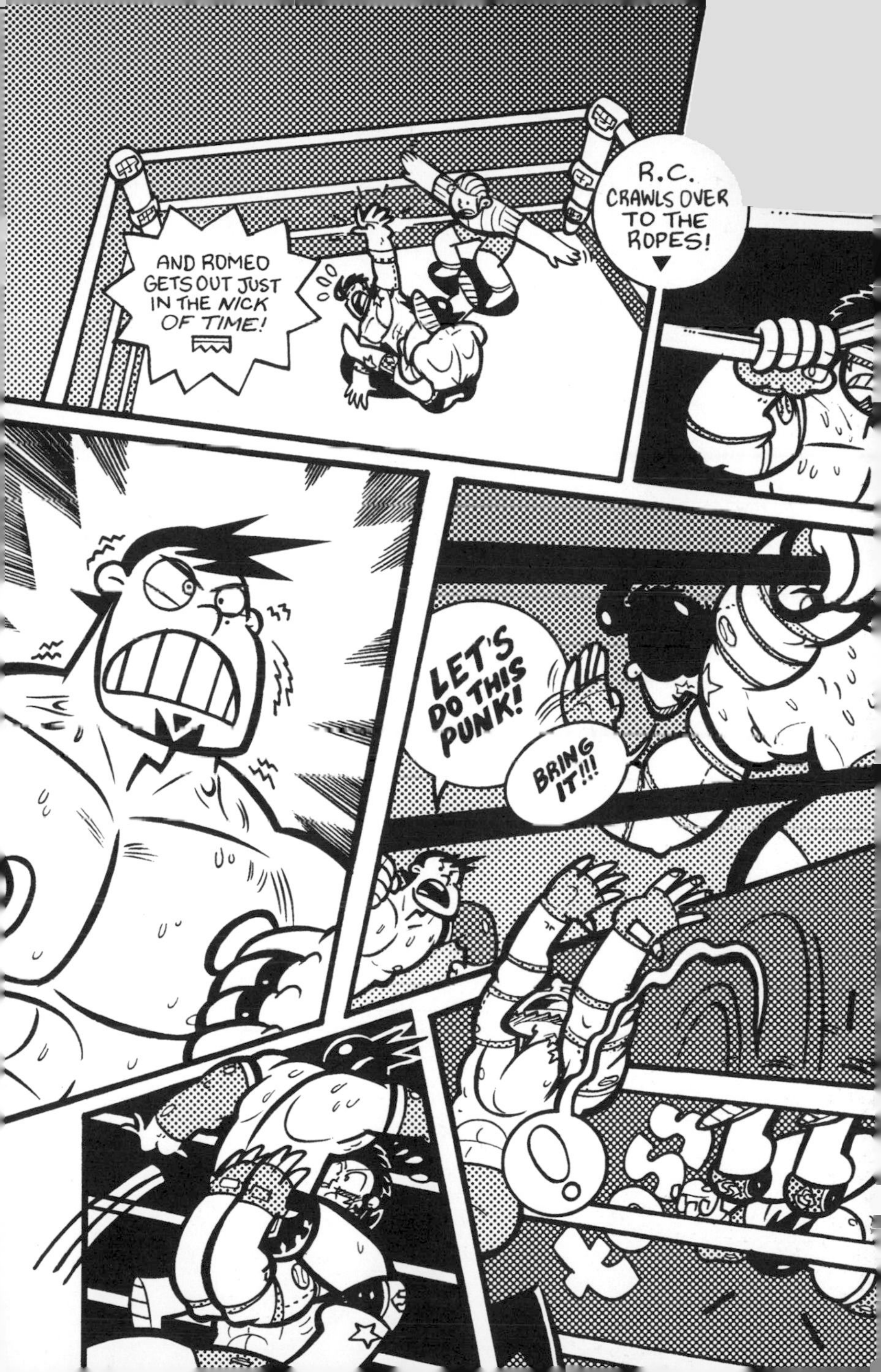
AND ROMEO GETS OUT JUST IN THE NICK OF TIME!
R.C. CRAWLS OVER TO THE ROPES!
LET'S DO THIS PUNK!
BRING IT!!!

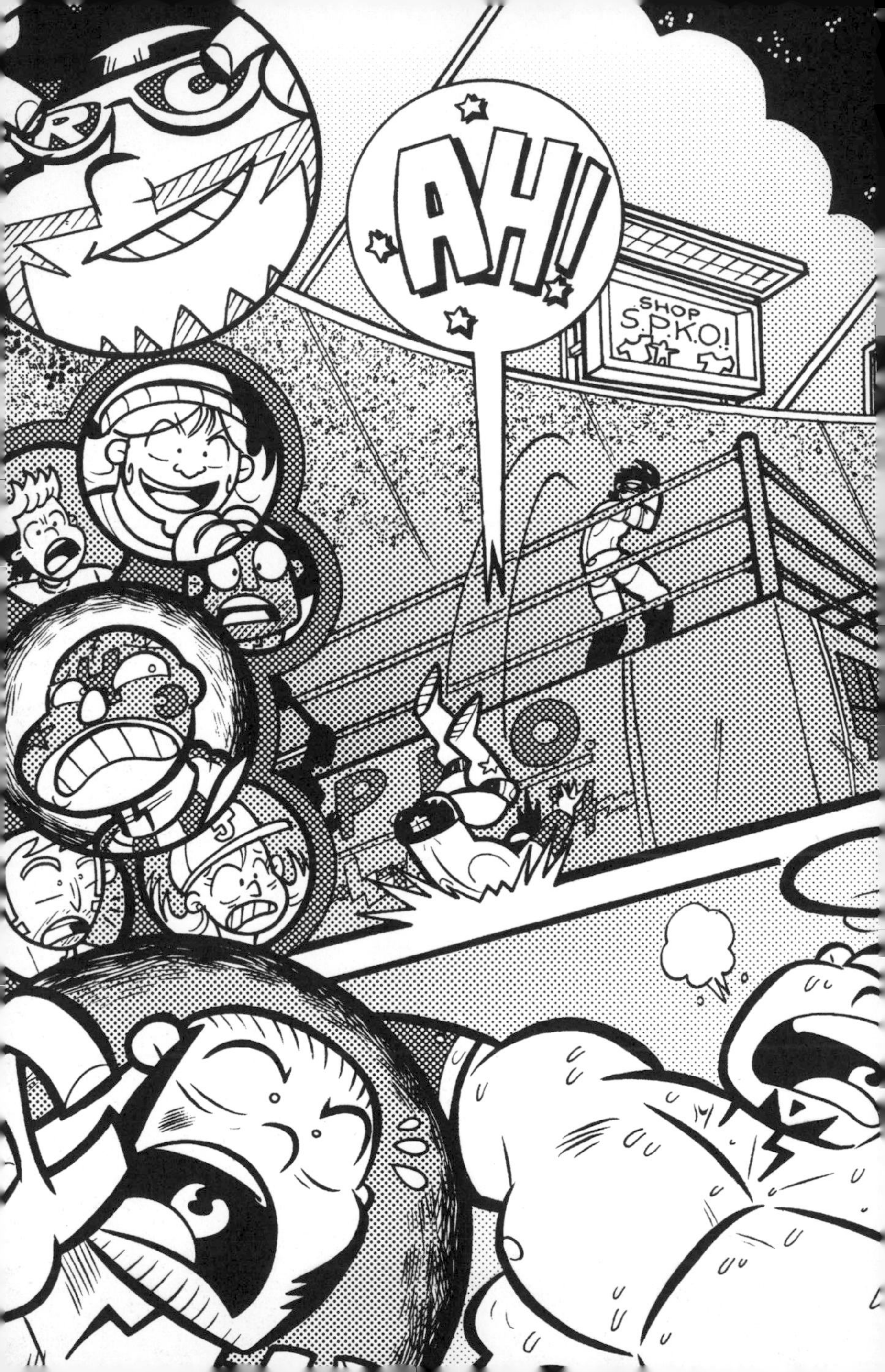
AH!
SHOP
S.P.K.O.!

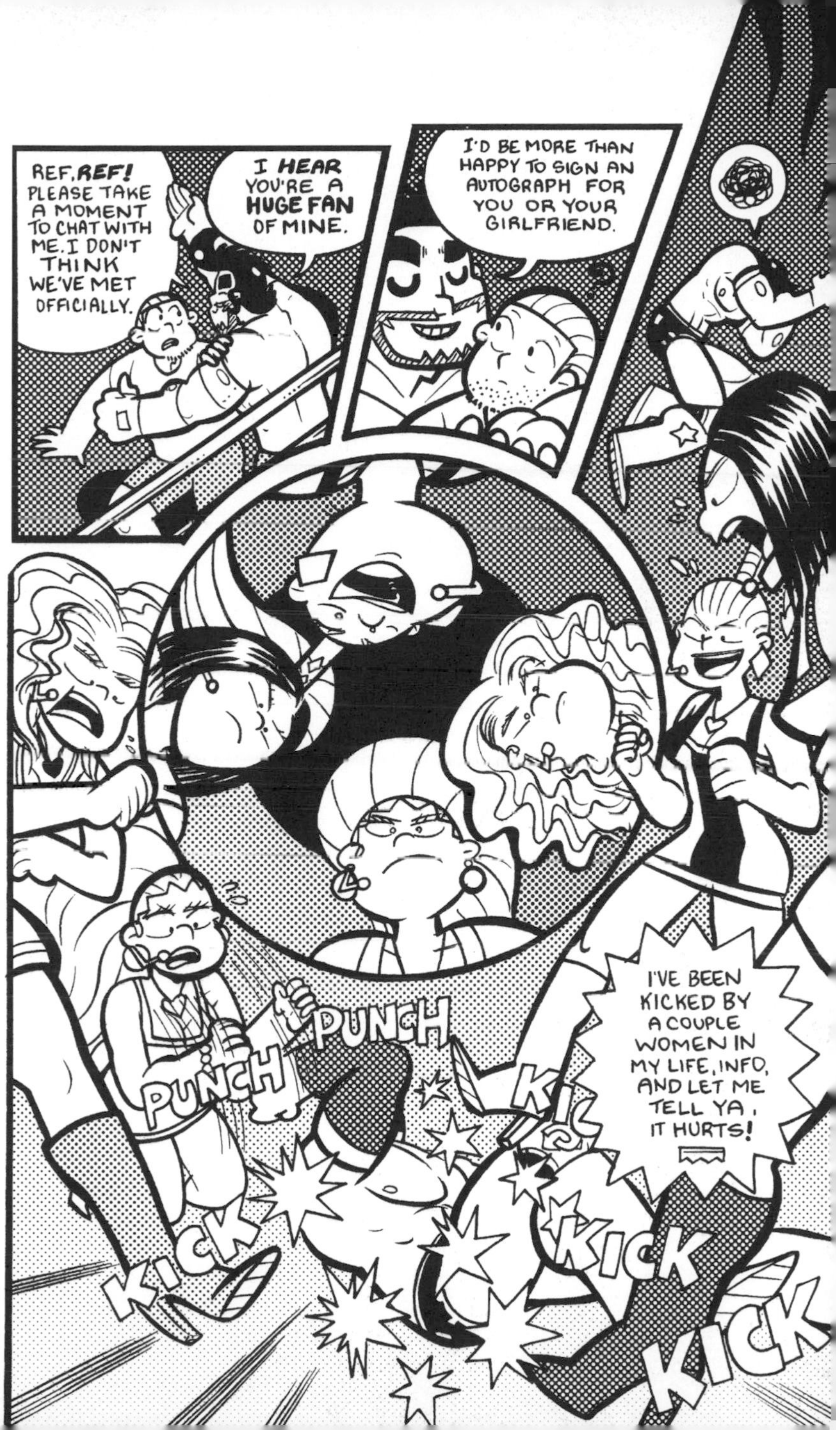
REF, REF! PLEASE TAKE A MOMENT TO CHAT WITH ME. I DON'T THINK WE'VE MET OFFICIALLY.
I HEAR YOU'RE A HUGE FAN OF MINE.
I'D BE MORE THAN HAPPY TO SIGN AN AUTOGRAPH FOR YOU OR YOUR GIRLFRIEND.
PUNCH
PUNCH
I'VE BEEN KICKED BY A COUPLE WOMEN IN MY LIFE, INFO, AND LET ME TELL YA, IT HURTS!
KICK
KICK
KICK

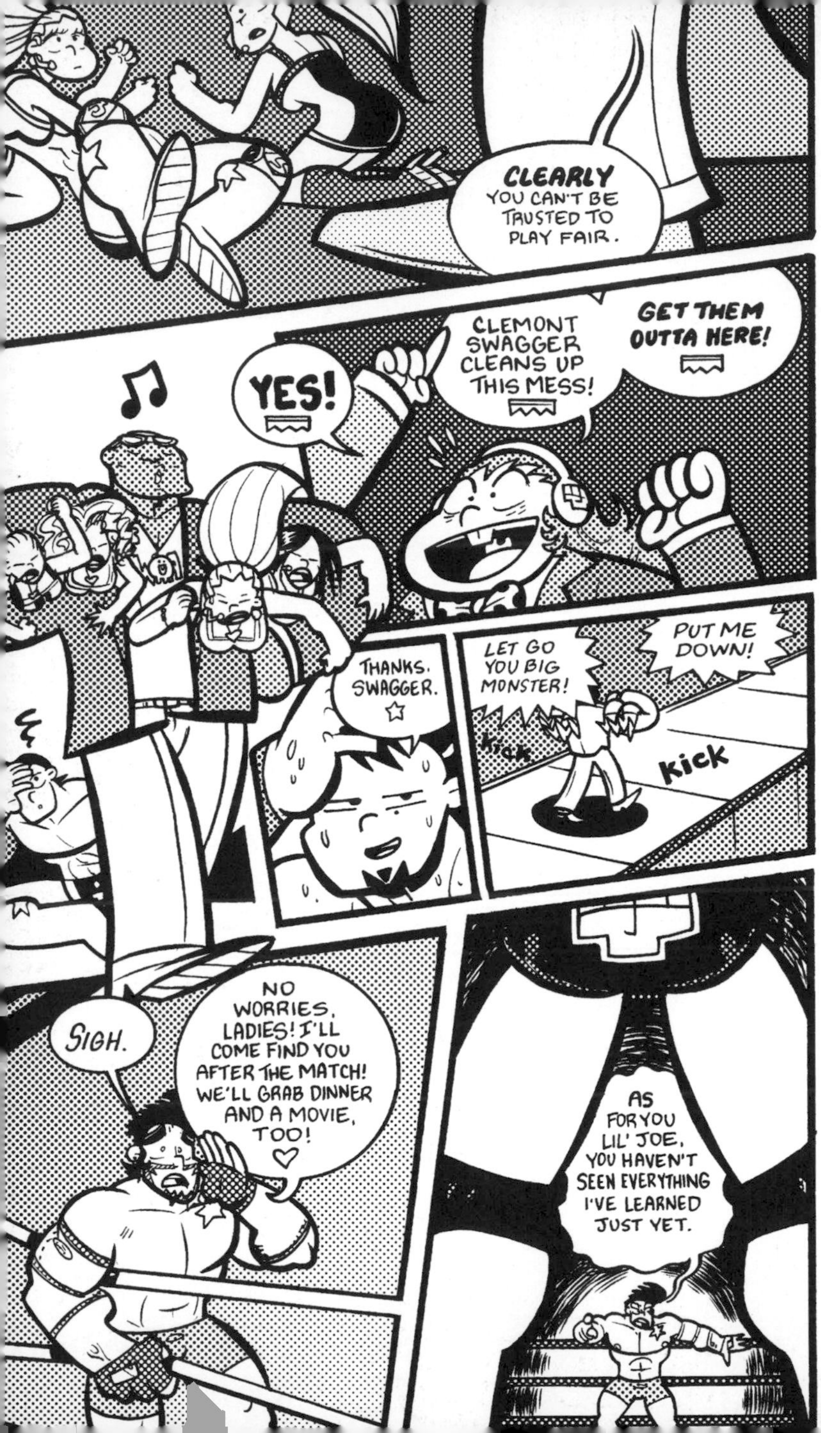
CLEARLY YOU CAN'T BE TRUSTED TO PLAY FAIR.
CLEMONT SWAGGER CLEANS UP THIS MESS!
GET THEM OUTTA HERE!
YES!
THANKS, SWAGGER.
LET GO YOU BIG MONSTER!
PUT ME DOWN!
KICK
KICK
SIGH.
NO WORRIES, LADIES! I'LL COME FIND YOU AFTER THE MATCH! WE'LL GRAB DINNER AND A MOVIE, TOO!
AS FOR YOU LIL' JOE, YOU HAVEN'T SEEN EVERYTHING I'VE LEARNED JUST YET.

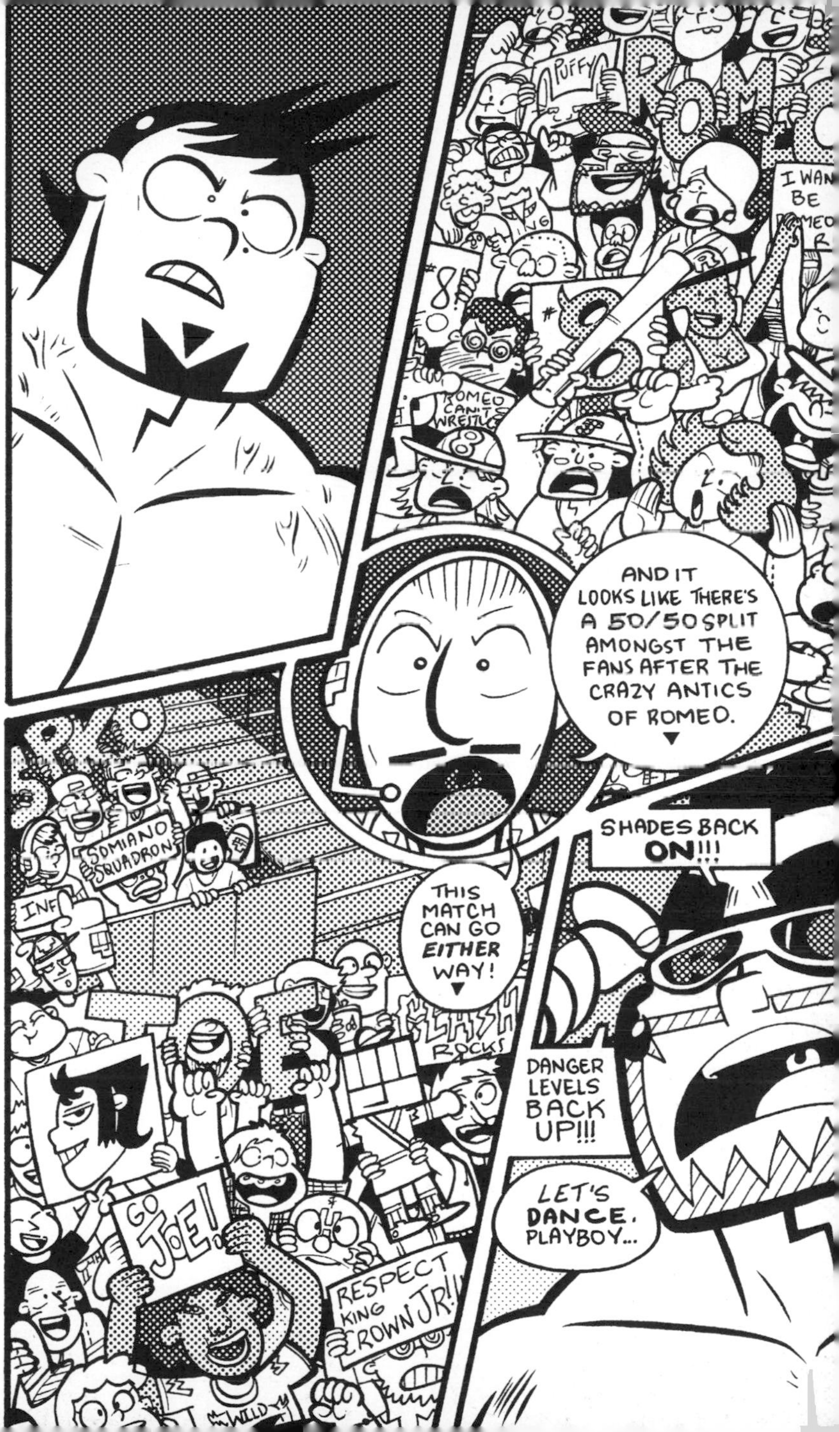
PUFFY
I WAN BE ROMEO
ROMEO CAN'T WRESTLE
AND IT LOOKS LIKE THERE'S A 50/50 SPLIT AMONGST THE FANS AFTER THE CRAZY ANTICS OF ROMEO.
SOMIANO SQUADRON
THIS MATCH CAN GO *EITHER* WAY!
SHADES BACK **ON**!!!
FLASH ROCKS
DANGER LEVELS BACK UP!!!
GO JOE!
LET'S **DANCE**, PLAYBOY...
RESPECT KING CROWN JR!!
WILD

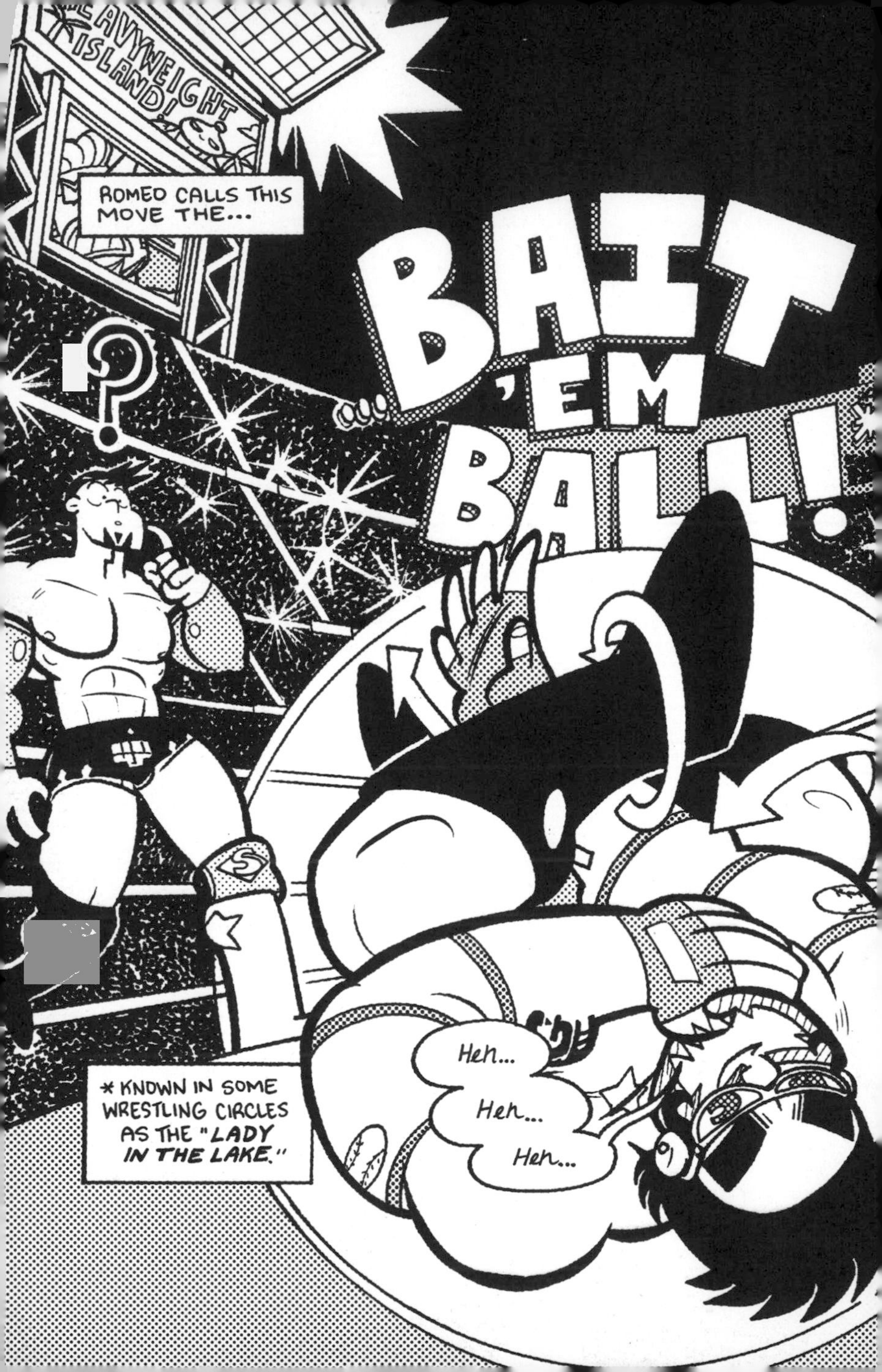
HEAVYWEIGHT ISLAND!
ROMEO CALLS THIS MOVE THE...
BAIT 'EM BALL!
!?
Heh...
Heh...
Heh...
* KNOWN IN SOME WRESTLING CIRCLES AS THE "LADY IN THE LAKE."

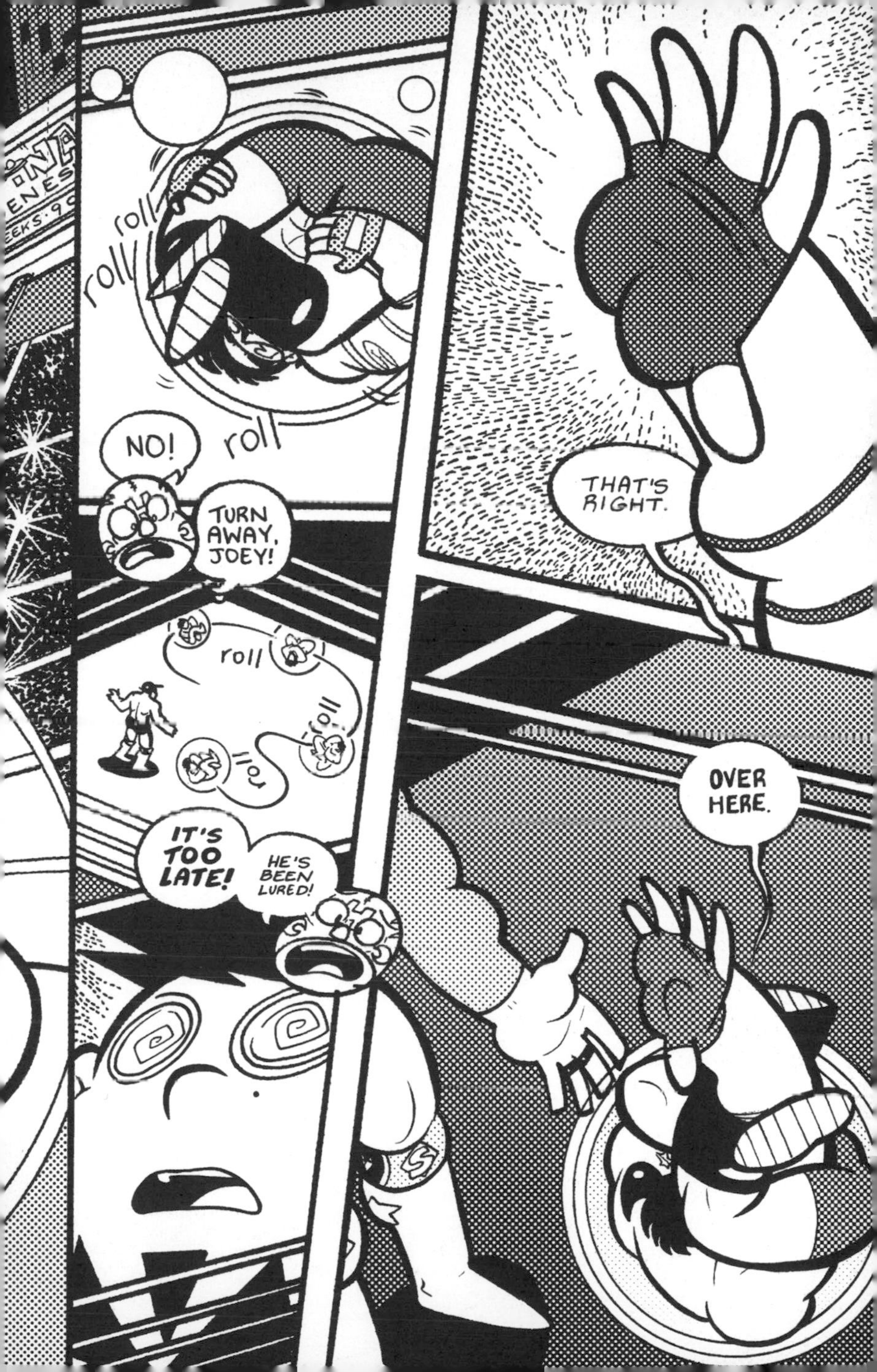

roll
roll
NO!
roll
TURN AWAY, JOEY!
roll
roll
roll
roll
IT'S TOO LATE!
HE'S BEEN LURED!
THAT'S RIGHT.
OVER HERE.

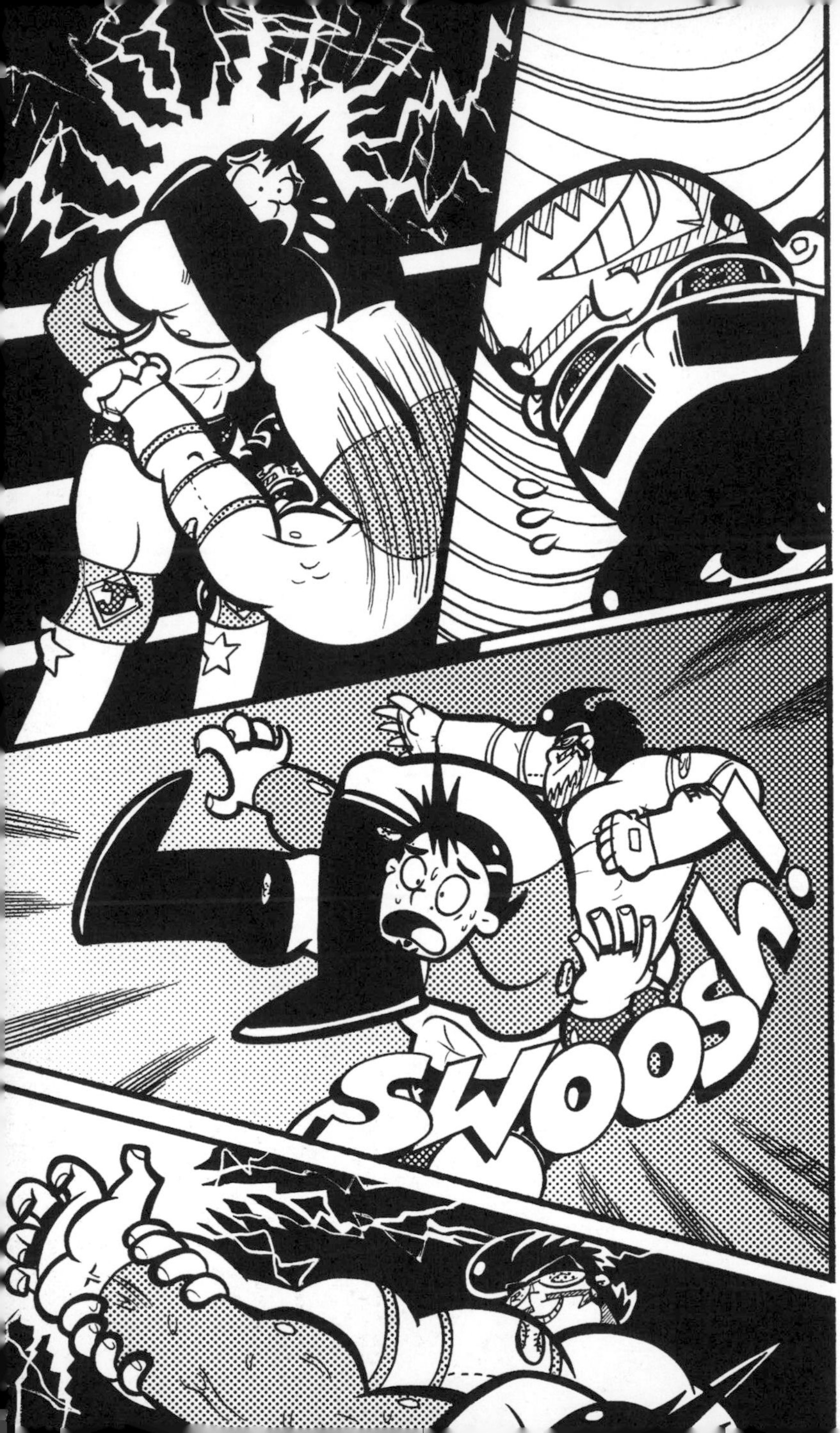
SWOOSH!

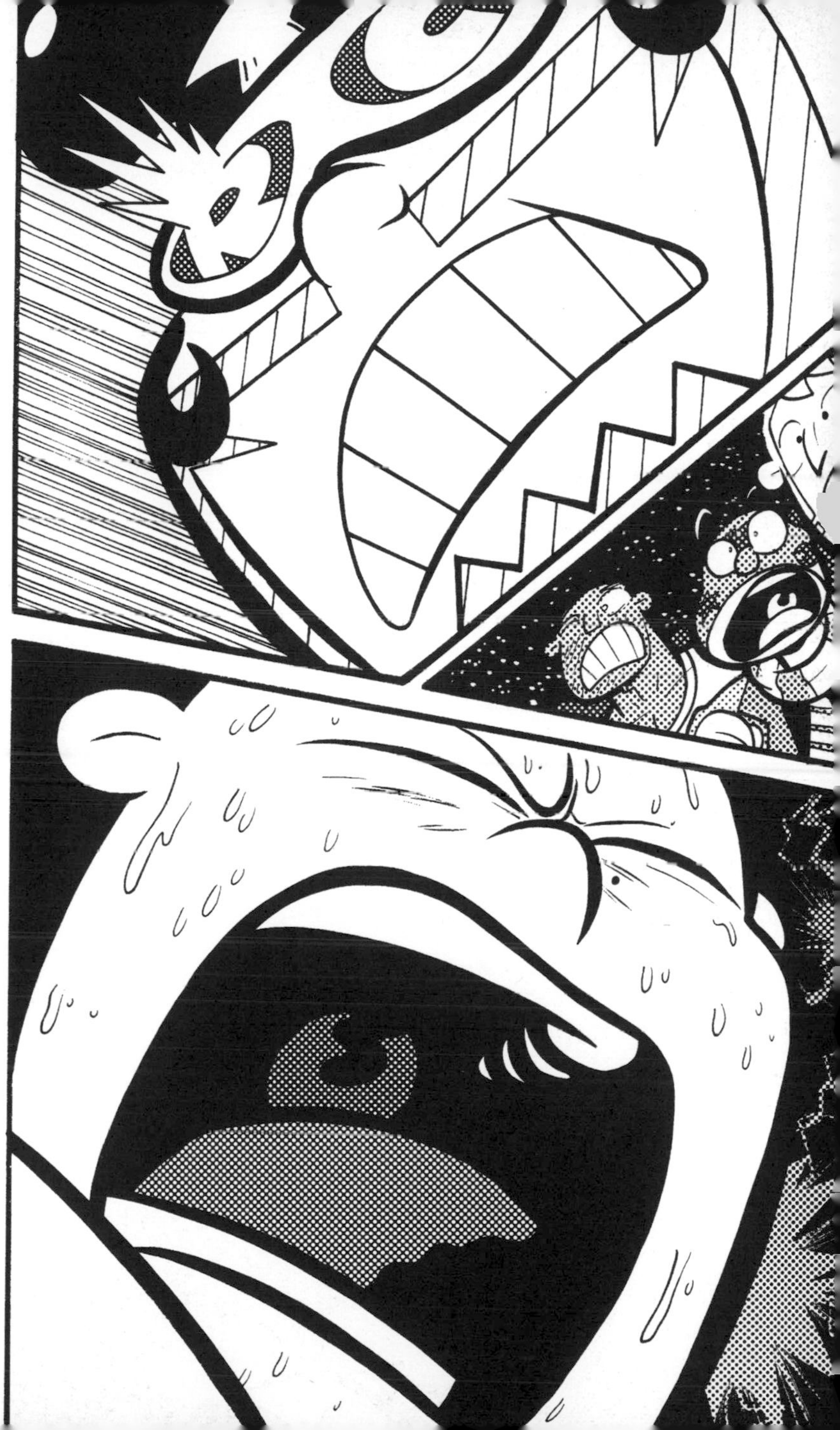

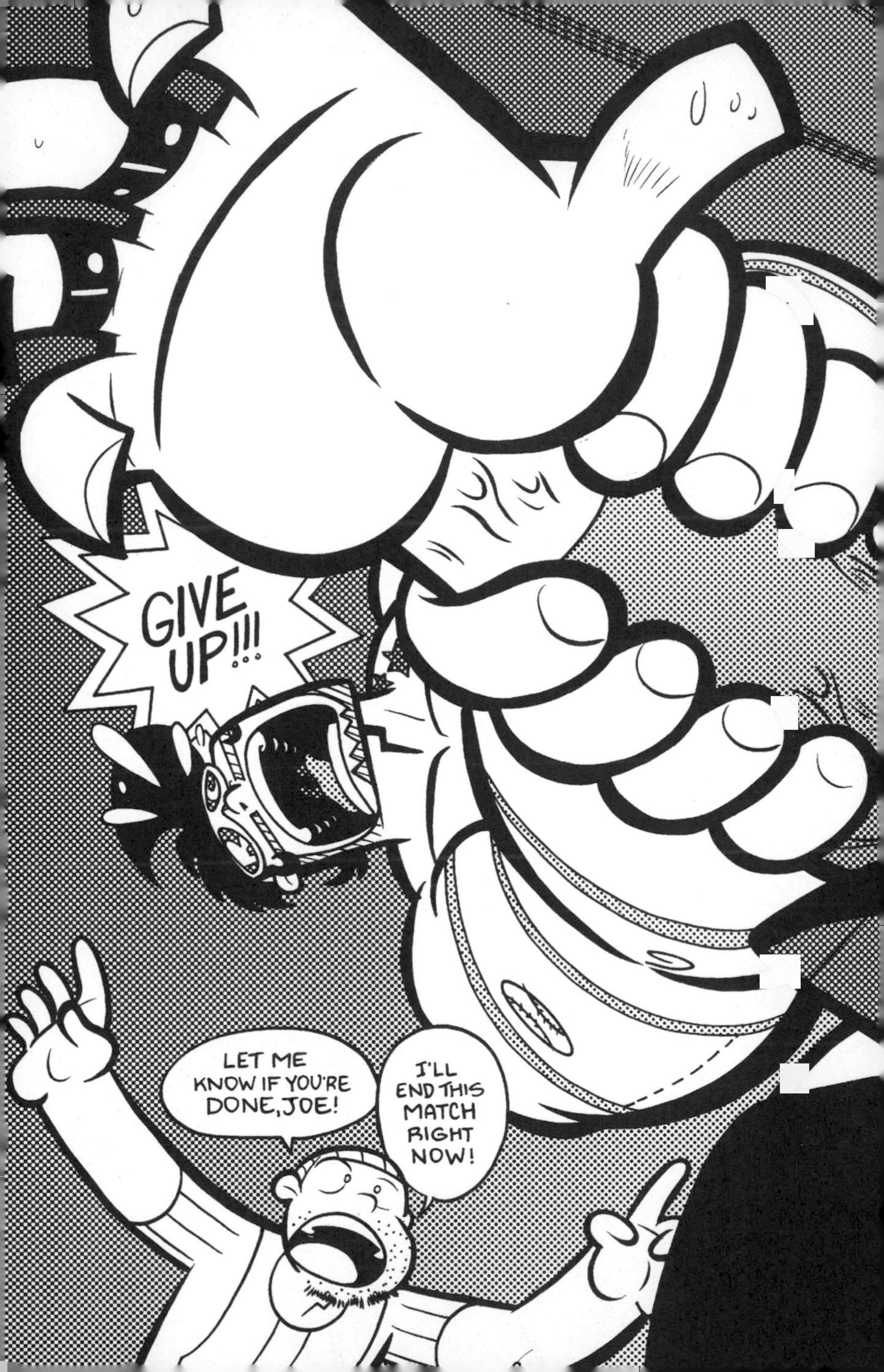
GIVE UP!!!
LET ME KNOW IF YOU'RE DONE, JOE!
I'LL END THIS MATCH RIGHT NOW!

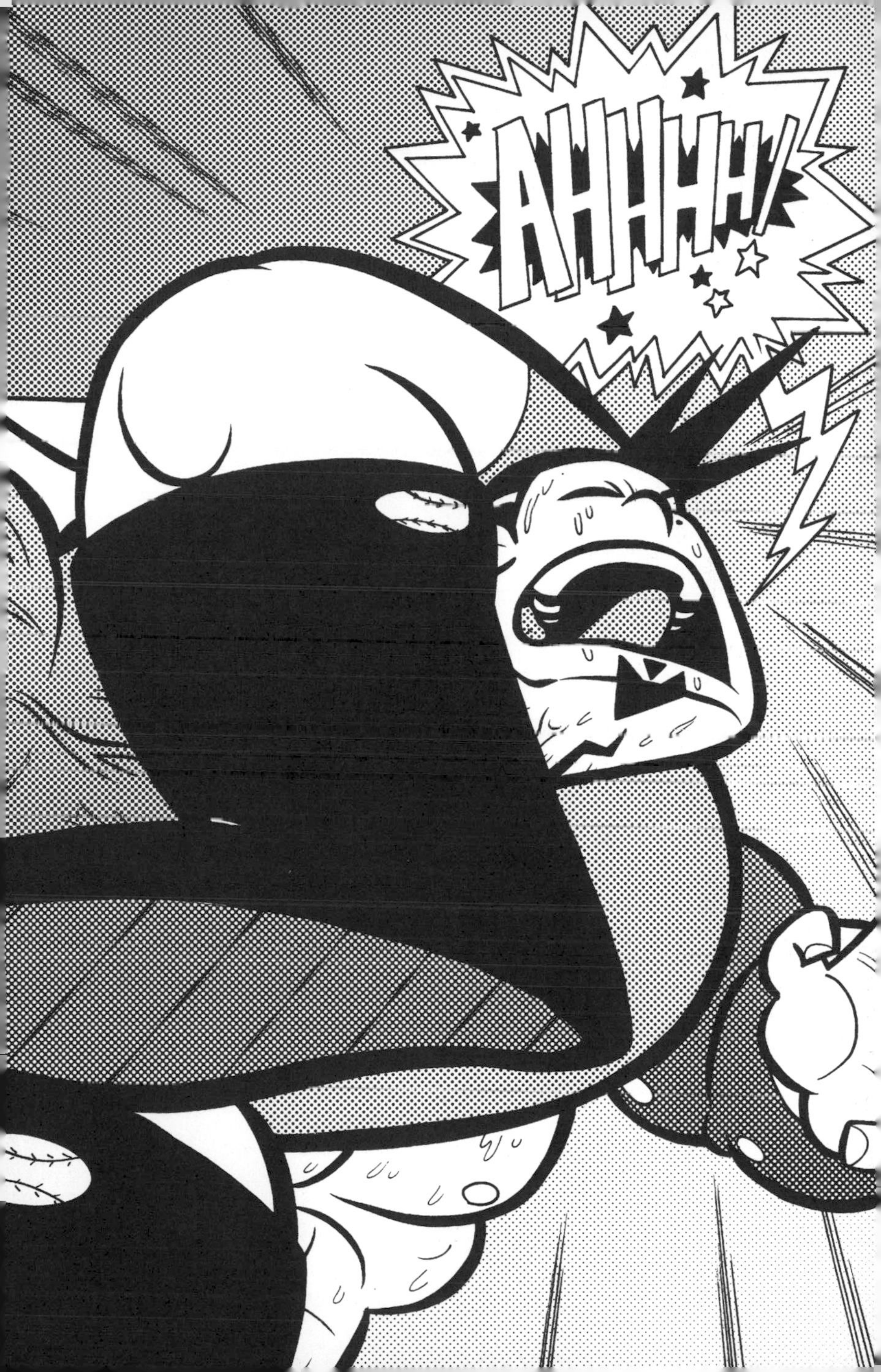
AHHHHH!

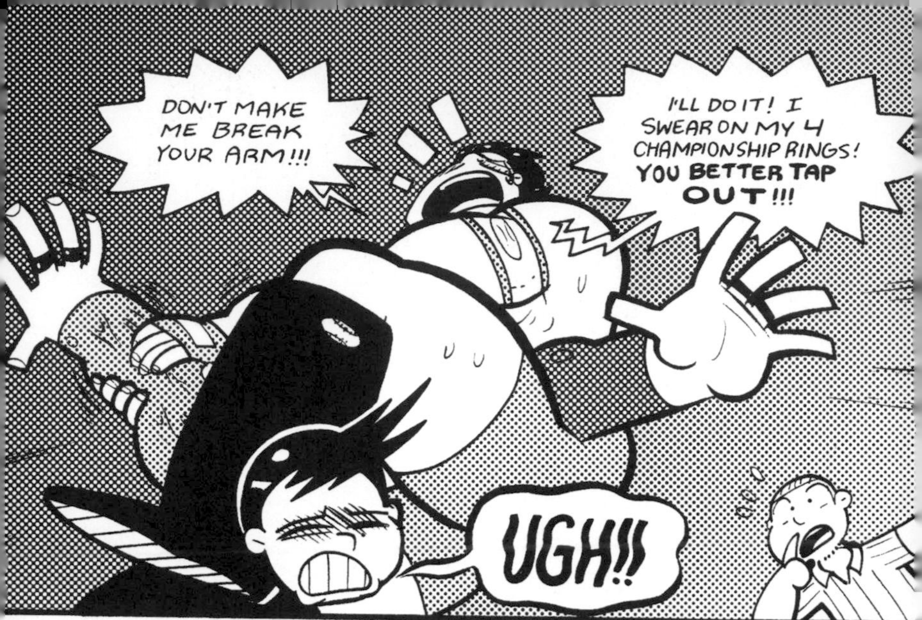
DON'T MAKE ME BREAK YOUR ARM!!!
I'LL DO IT! I SWEAR ON MY 4 CHAMPIONSHIP RINGS! YOU BETTER TAP OUT!!!
UGH!!

...HOWEVER, ROMEO (BEING THE CONNOISSEUR HE IS) CALLS THIS "THE SWEET SPOT"

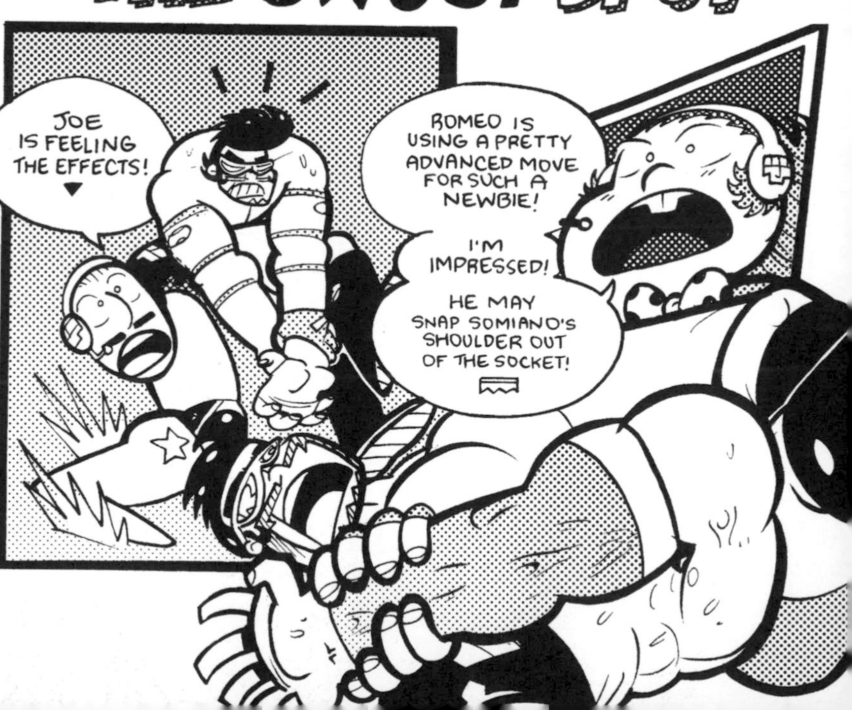
JOE IS FEELING THE EFFECTS!
ROMEO IS USING A PRETTY ADVANCED MOVE FOR SUCH A NEWBIE!
I'M IMPRESSED!
HE MAY SNAP SOMIANO'S SHOULDER OUT OF THE SOCKET!

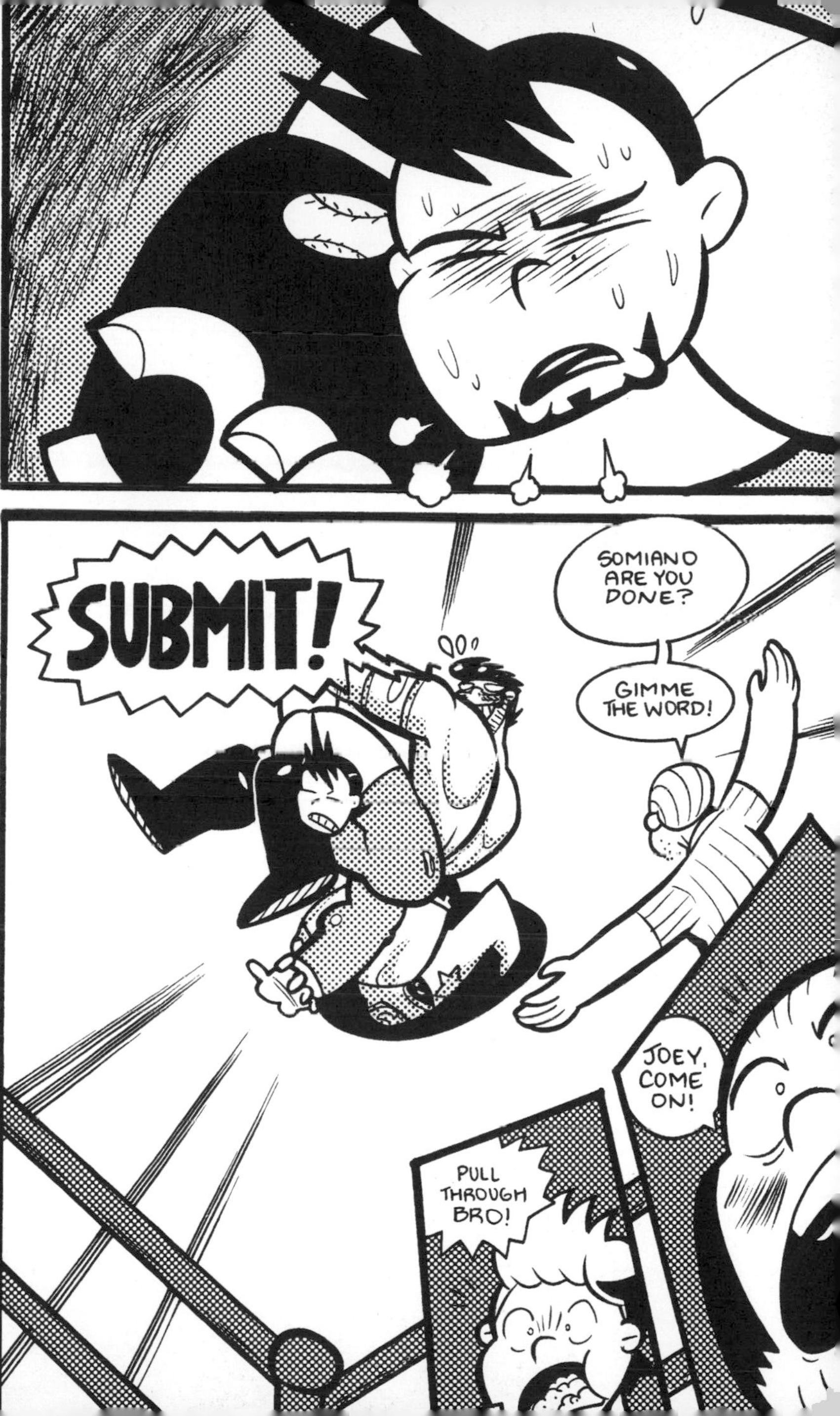
SUBMIT!
SOMIANO ARE YOU DONE?
GIMME THE WORD!
JOEY, COME ON!
PULL THROUGH BRO!

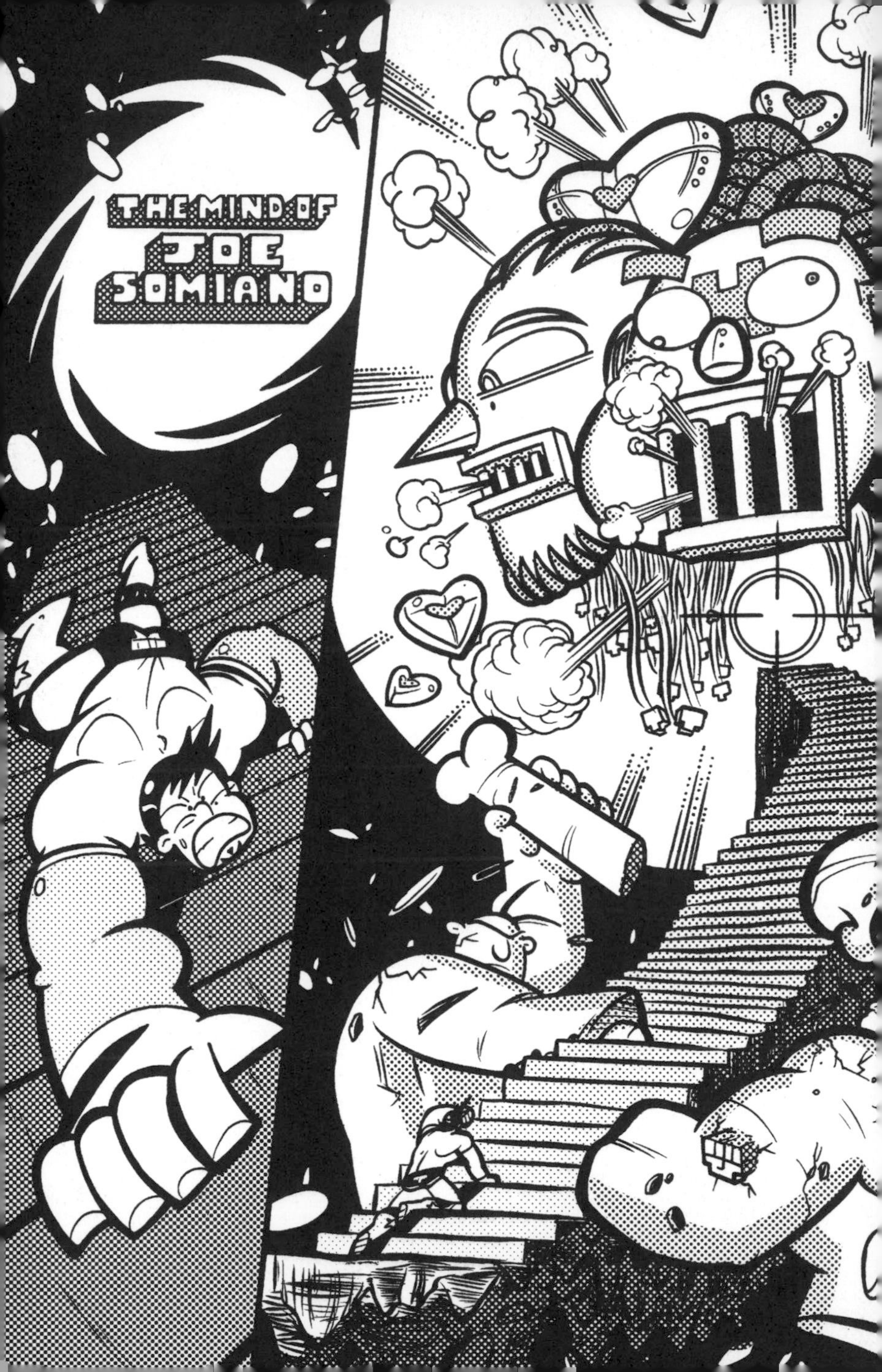
THE MIND OF
JOE
SOMIANO

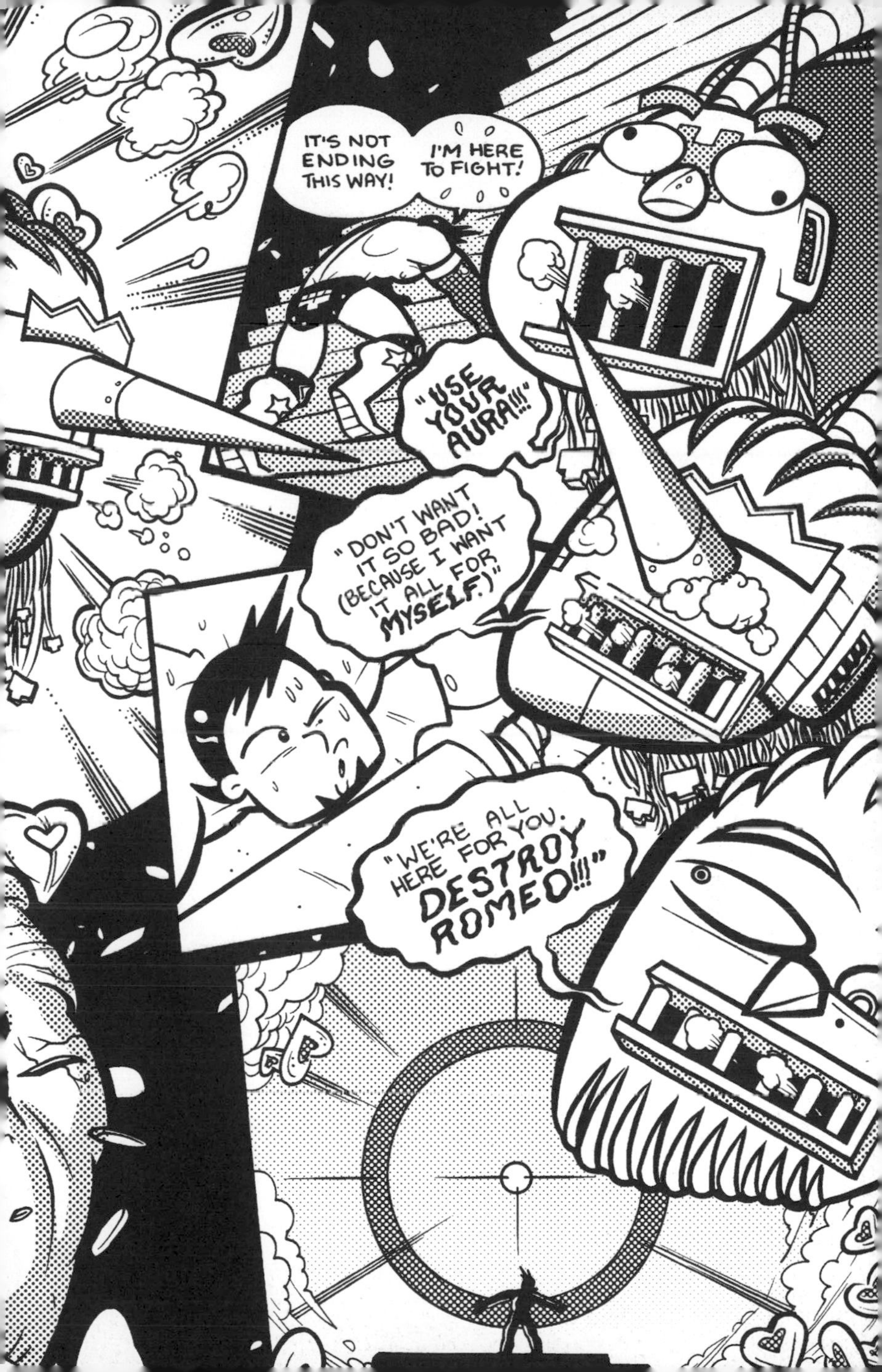

IT'S NOT ENDING THIS WAY!
I'M HERE TO FIGHT!
"USE YOUR AURA!!!"
"DON'T WANT IT SO BAD! (BECAUSE I WANT IT ALL FOR MYSELF.)"
"WE'RE ALL HERE FOR YOU. DESTROY ROMEO!!!"

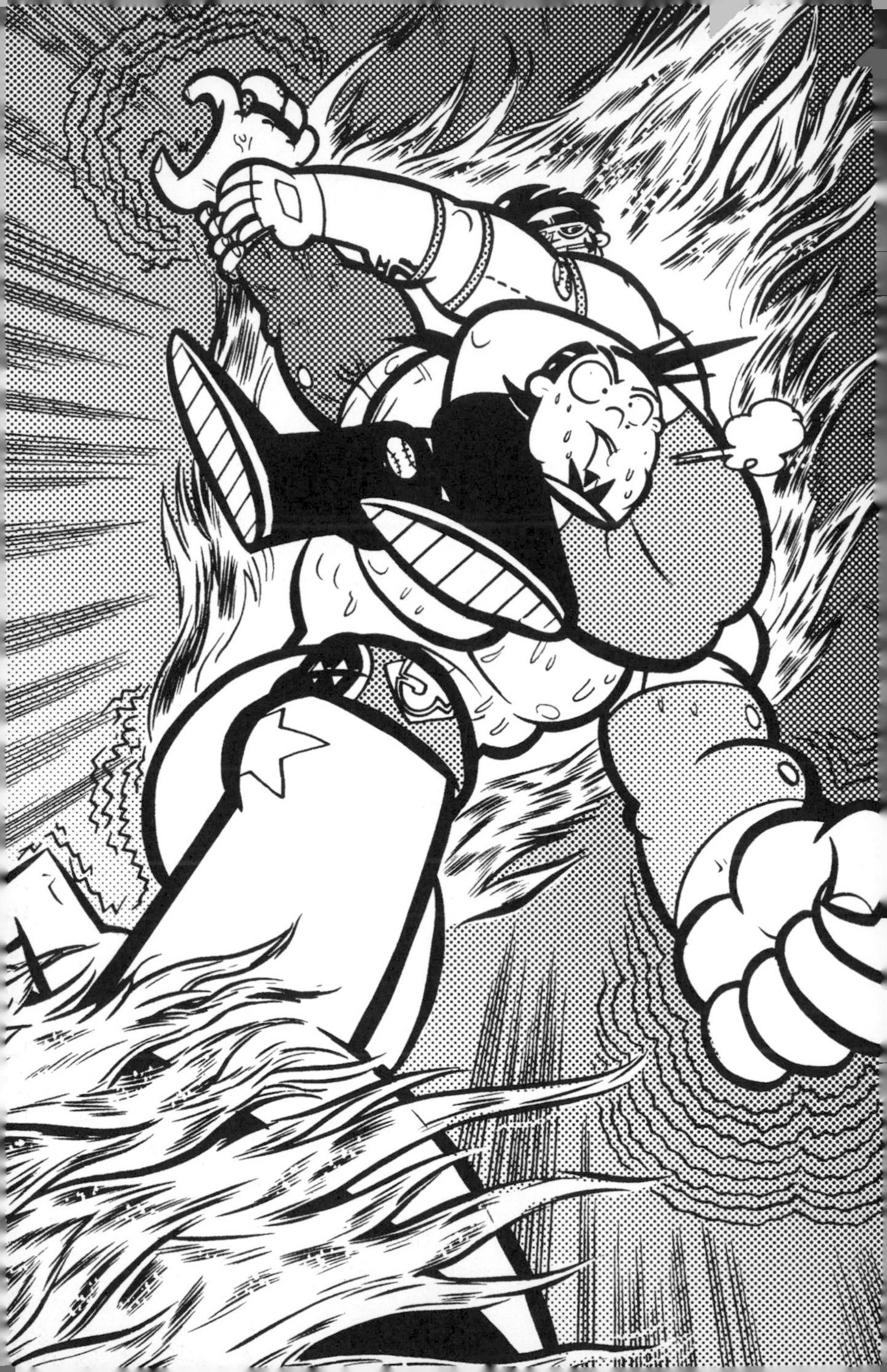

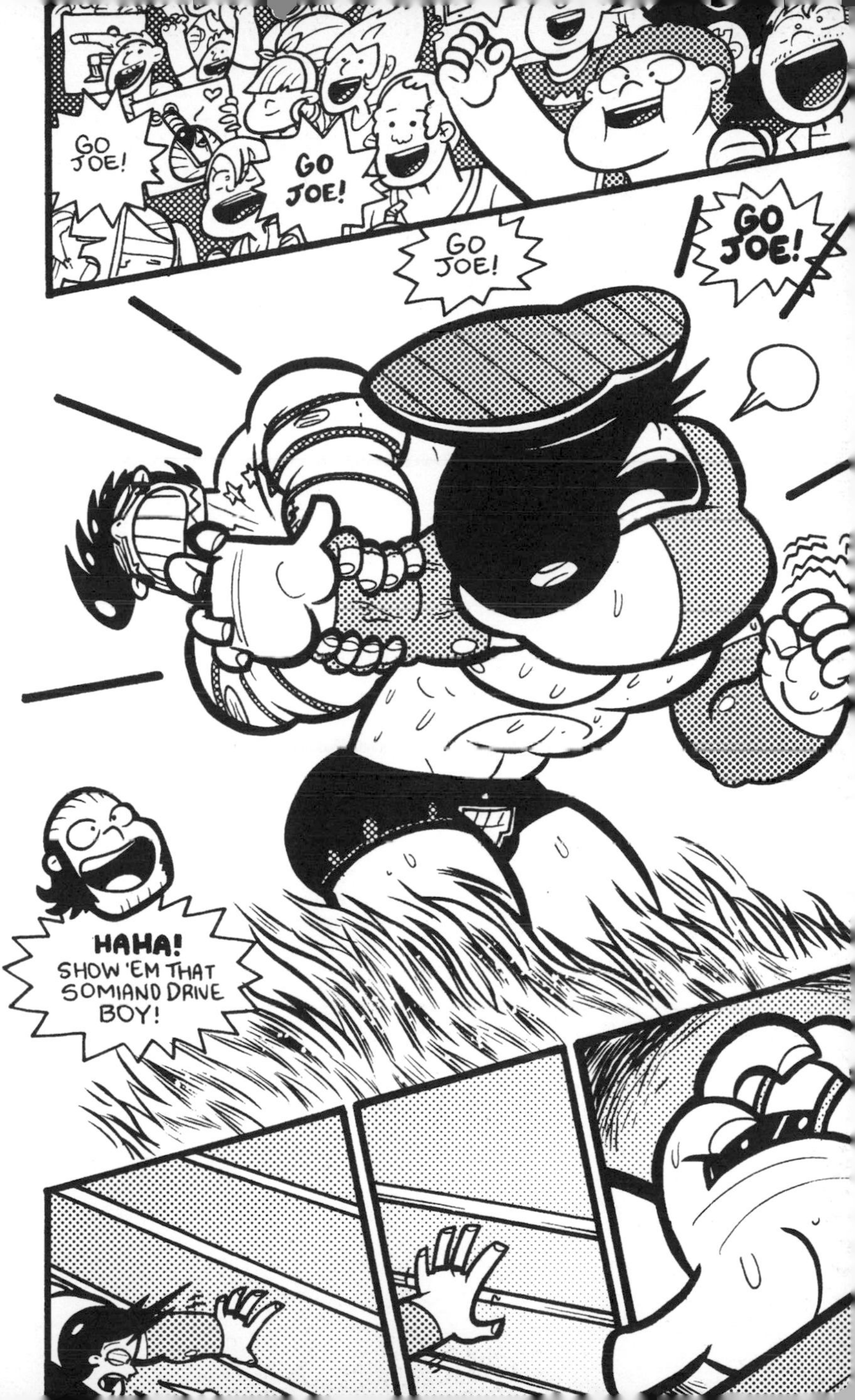
GO JOE!
GO JOE!
GO JOE!
GO JOE!
HAHA! SHOW 'EM THAT SOMIAND DRIVE BOY!

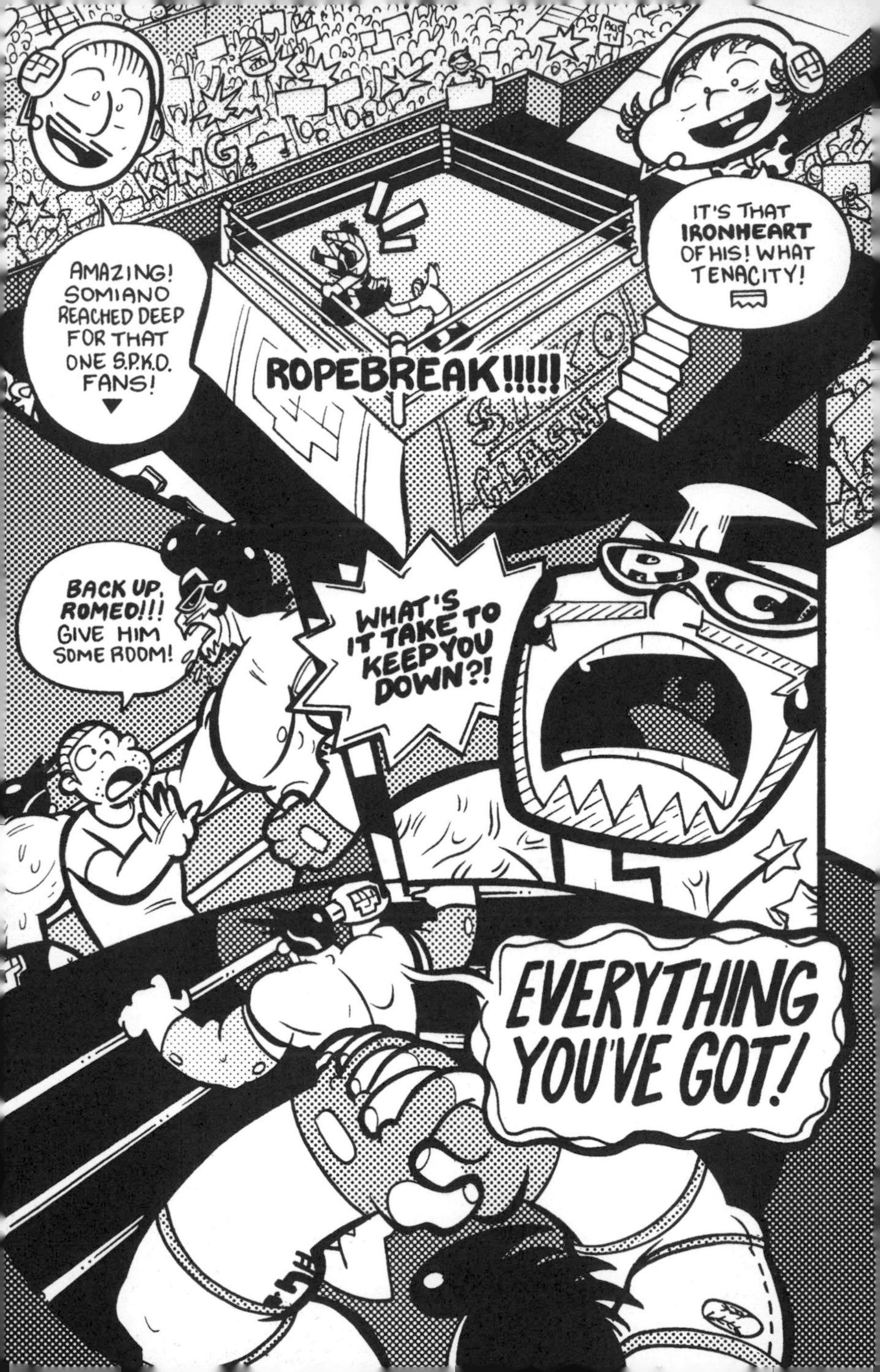

AMAZING! SOMIANO REACHED DEEP FOR THAT ONE S.P.K.O. FANS!
IT'S THAT IRONHEART OF HIS! WHAT TENACITY!
ROPEBREAK!!!!!
BACK UP, ROMEO!!! GIVE HIM SOME ROOM!
WHAT'S IT TAKE TO KEEP YOU DOWN?!
EVERYTHING YOU'VE GOT!

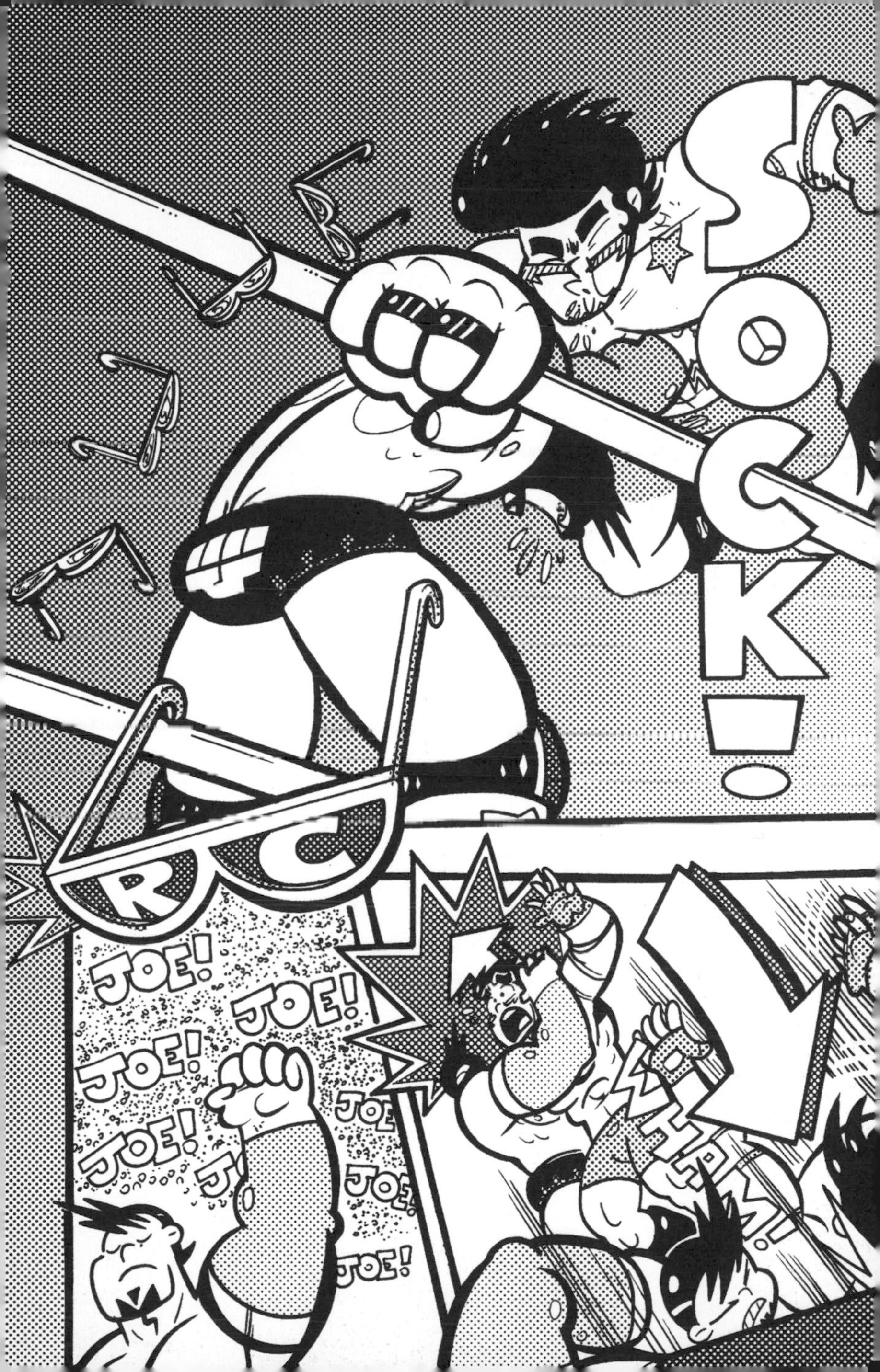
SOCK!
RRC
JOE! JOE! JOE! JOE! JOE! JOE! JOE! JOE!
WHAM!

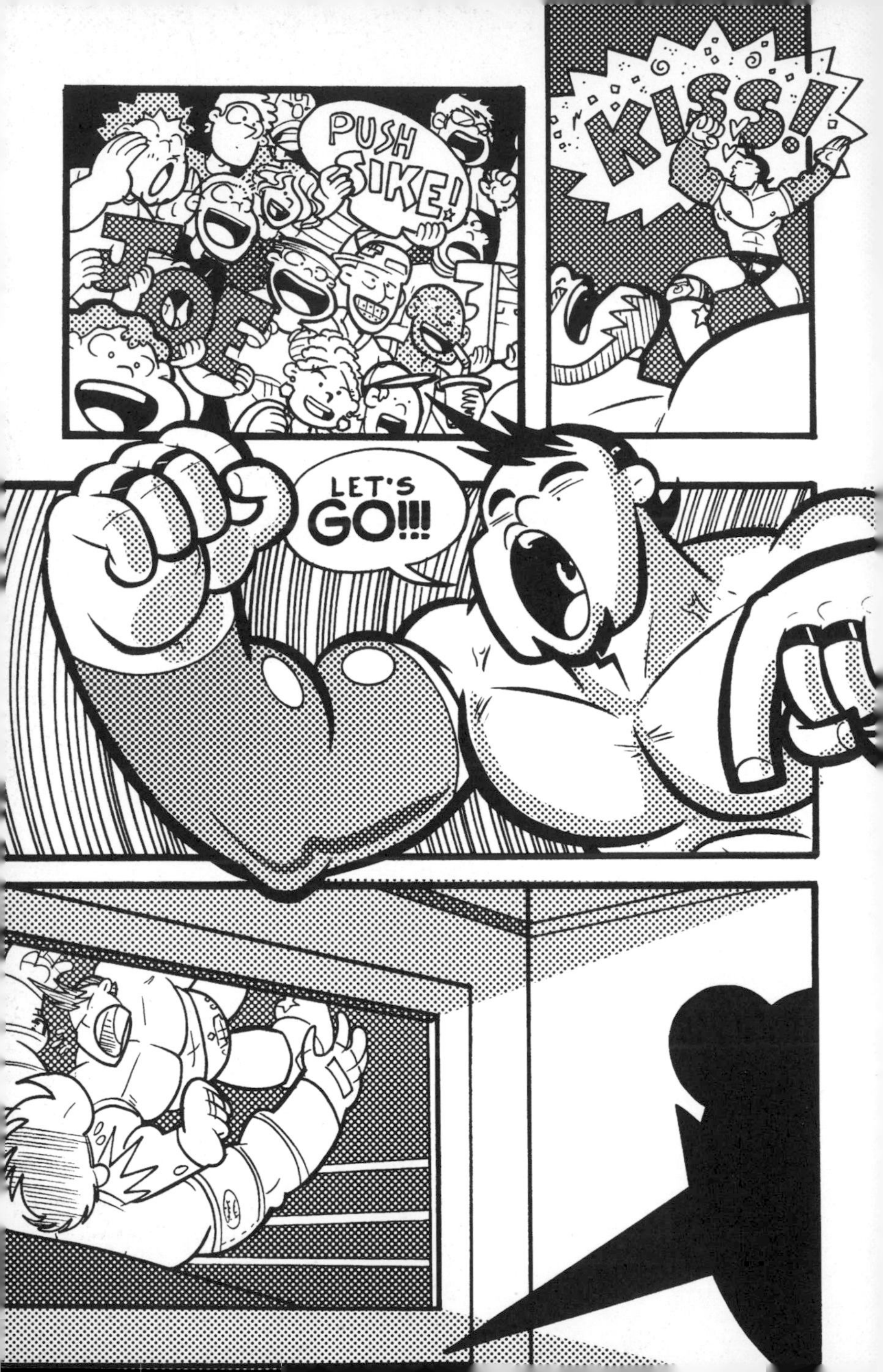
PUSH SIKE!
KISS!
LET'S GO!!!

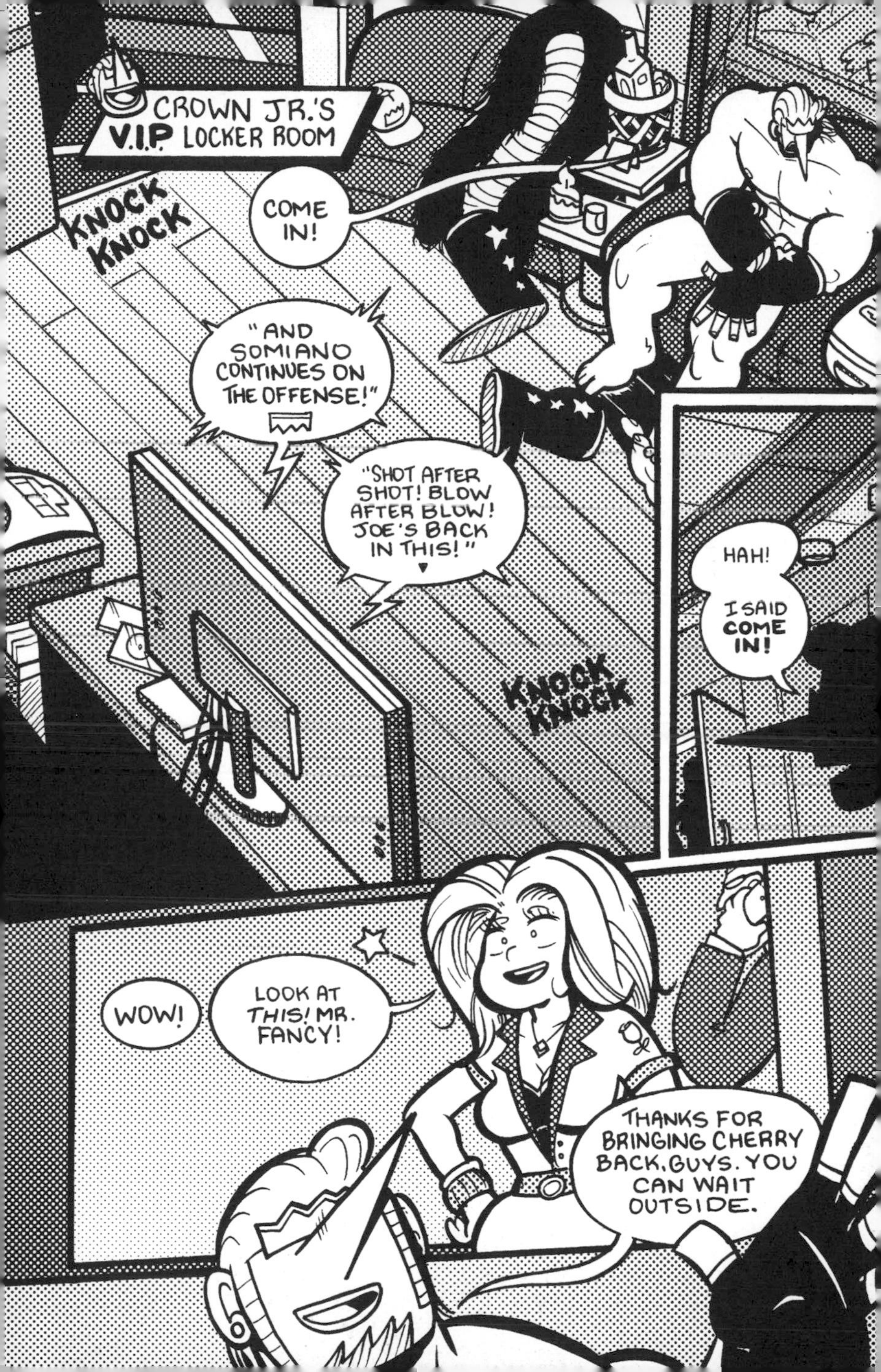
CROWN JR.'S V.I.P. LOCKER ROOM
KNOCK KNOCK
COME IN!
"AND SOMIANO CONTINUES ON THE OFFENSE!"
"SHOT AFTER SHOT! BLOW AFTER BLOW! JOE'S BACK IN THIS!"
KNOCK KNOCK
HAH!
I SAID COME IN!
WOW!
LOOK AT THIS! MR. FANCY!
THANKS FOR BRINGING CHERRY BACK, GUYS. YOU CAN WAIT OUTSIDE.

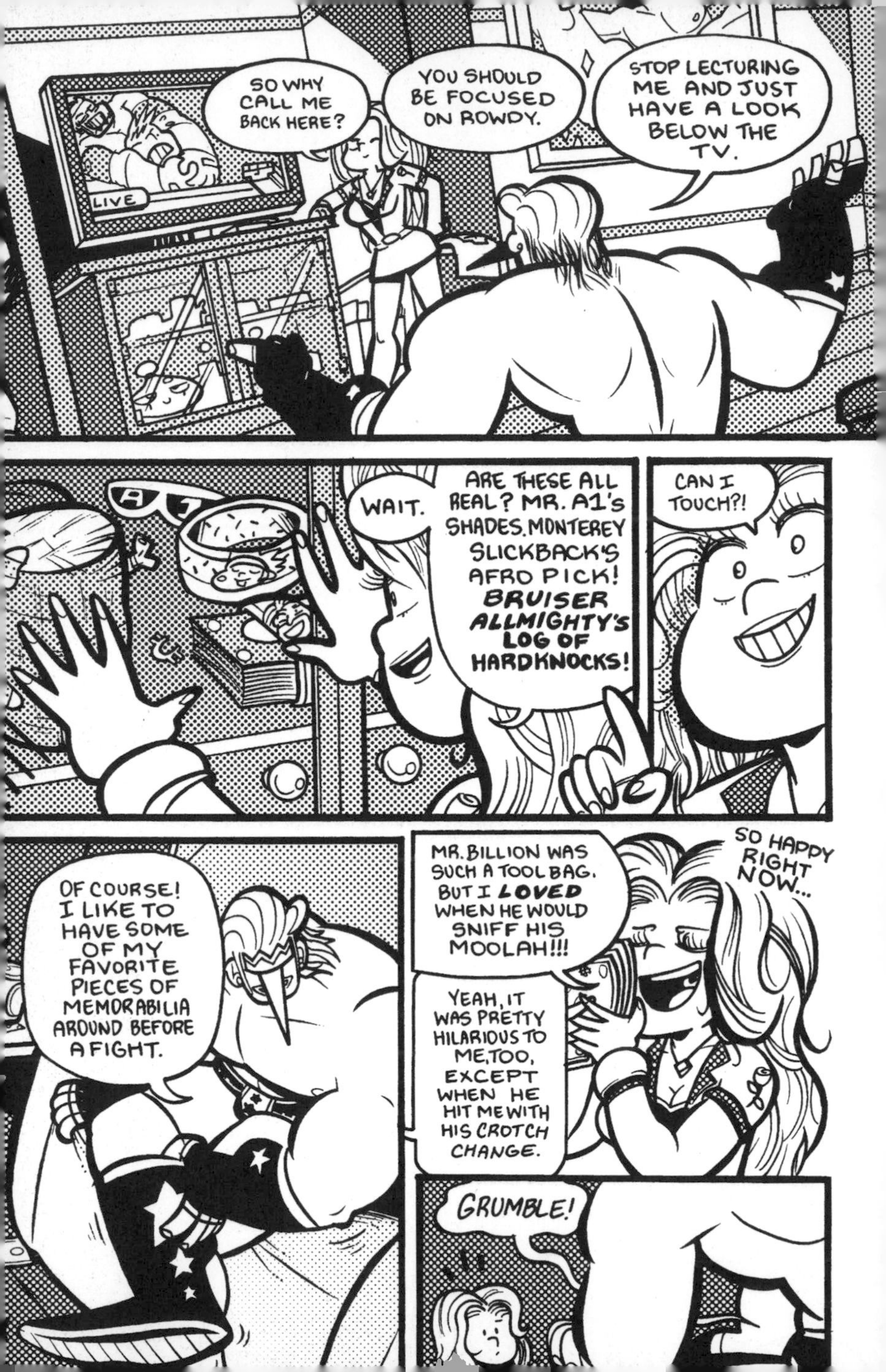

LIVE
SO WHY CALL ME BACK HERE?
YOU SHOULD BE FOCUSED ON ROWDY.
STOP LECTURING ME AND JUST HAVE A LOOK BELOW THE TV.
WAIT.
ARE THESE ALL REAL? MR. A1's SHADES. MONTEREY SLICKBACK'S AFRO PICK! BRUISER ALLMIGHTY'S LOG OF HARDKNOCKS!
CAN I TOUCH?!
OF COURSE! I LIKE TO HAVE SOME OF MY FAVORITE PIECES OF MEMORABILIA AROUND BEFORE A FIGHT.
MR. BILLION WAS SUCH A TOOL BAG. BUT I LOVED WHEN HE WOULD SNIFF HIS MOOLAH!!!
SO HAPPY RIGHT NOW...
YEAH, IT WAS PRETTY HILARIOUS TO ME, TOO, EXCEPT WHEN HE HIT ME WITH HIS CROTCH CHANGE.
GRUMBLE!

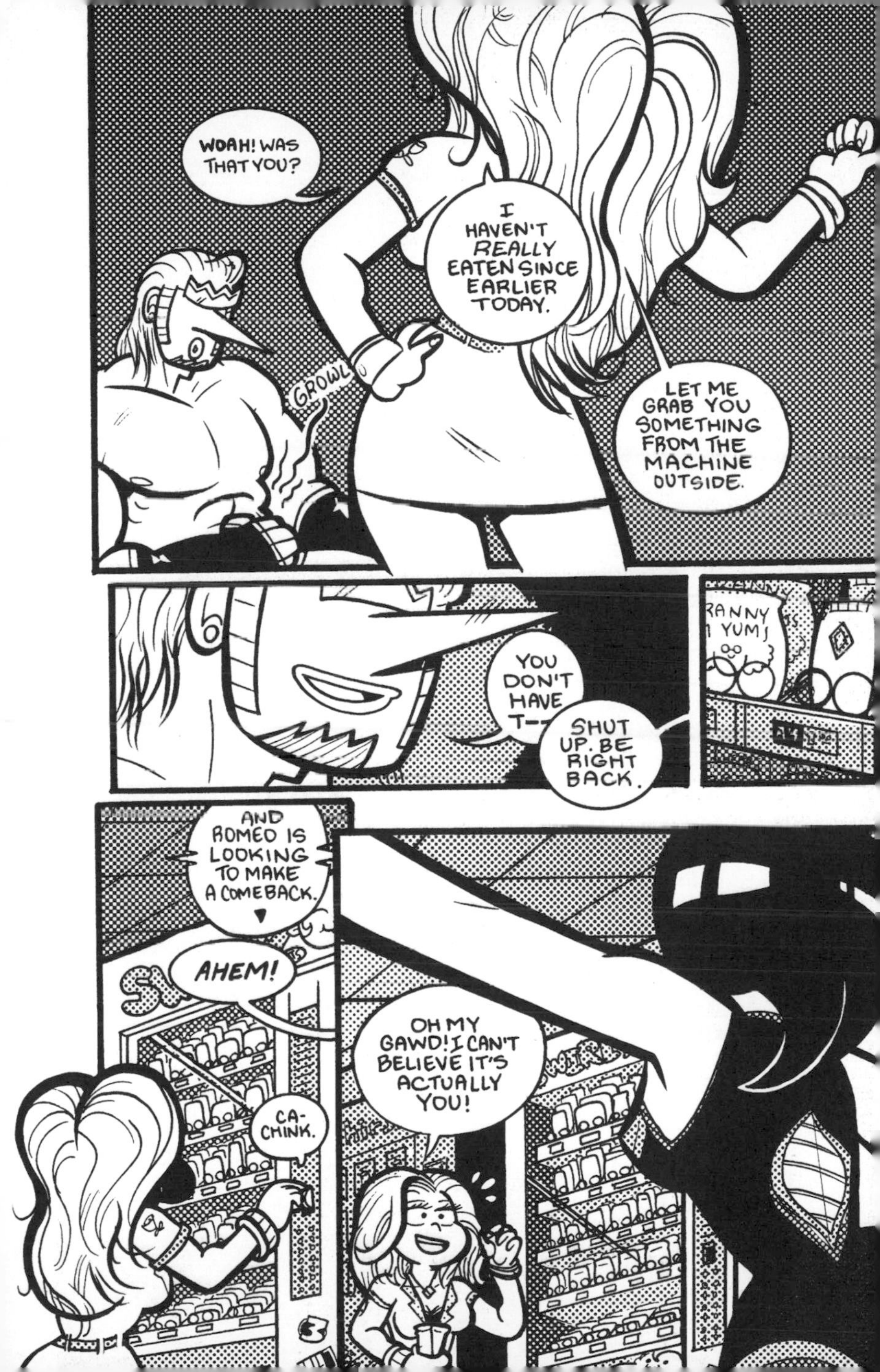
WOAH! WAS THAT YOU?
I HAVEN'T REALLY EATEN SINCE EARLIER TODAY.
GROWL
LET ME GRAB YOU SOMETHING FROM THE MACHINE OUTSIDE.
YOU DON'T HAVE T--
SHUT UP. BE RIGHT BACK.
AND ROMEO IS LOOKING TO MAKE A COMEBACK.
AHEM!
CA-CHINK.
OH MY GAWD! I CAN'T BELIEVE IT'S ACTUALLY YOU!

YOU HAVE NO IDEA HOW HUGE OF A FAN I AM OF--

DON'T.

ELICITY

ONE OF THE MOST RESPECTED WOMEN WRESTLERS IN THE WORLD.

YOU KNOW, YOU TOTALLY PHOTOGRAPH WELL, AND YOU DEFINITELY ARE "HIS" TYPE.

EXCUSE ME.

A LITTLE HOMELY. NOT *TOO* INTIMIDATING. MAKES SENSE.

I THINK YOU'VE GOT IT MIXED UP. ME AND CROWN JR. AREN'T DATING.

THIS IS CALLED A **DIRT SHEET.**

READ IT.

OH YEAH.

ELICITY DATED CROWN JR. ONCE.

OR TWICE.

IT WAS TOO COMPLICATED AND TOO MUCH TO EXPLAIN IN ONE VOLUME OF S.P.K.O.

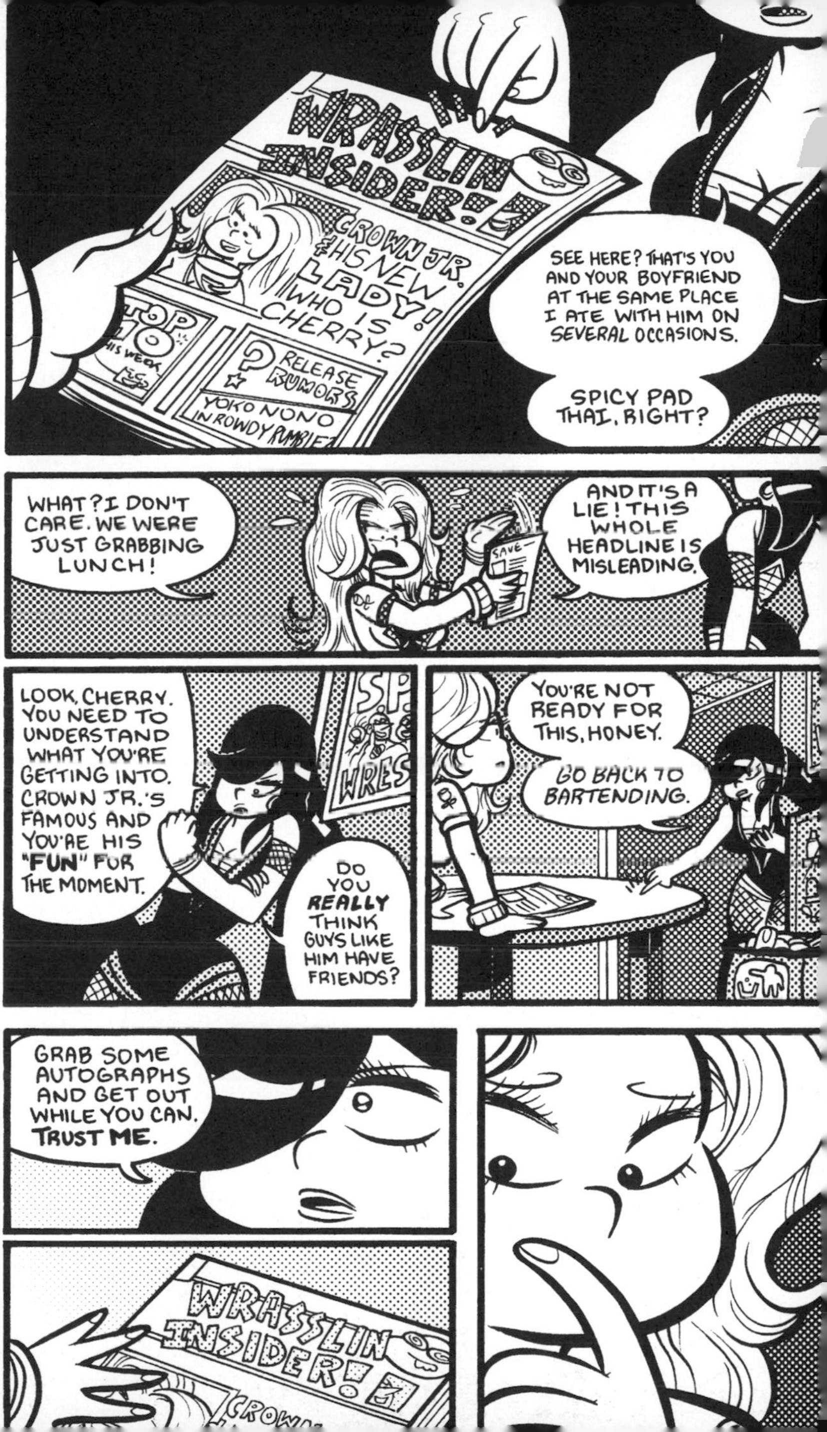
WRASSLIN INSIDER!
CROWN JR. & HIS NEW LADY! WHO IS CHERRY?
TOP 10 THIS WEEK
RELEASE RUMORS
YOKO NONO IN ROWDY RUMBLE
SEE HERE? THAT'S YOU AND YOUR BOYFRIEND AT THE SAME PLACE I ATE WITH HIM ON SEVERAL OCCASIONS.
SPICY PAD THAI, RIGHT?
WHAT? I DON'T CARE. WE WERE JUST GRABBING LUNCH!
SAVE
AND IT'S A LIE! THIS WHOLE HEADLINE IS MISLEADING.
LOOK, CHERRY. YOU NEED TO UNDERSTAND WHAT YOU'RE GETTING INTO. CROWN JR.'S FAMOUS AND YOU'RE HIS "FUN" FOR THE MOMENT.
DO YOU REALLY THINK GUYS LIKE HIM HAVE FRIENDS?
YOU'RE NOT READY FOR THIS, HONEY.
GO BACK TO BARTENDING.
GRAB SOME AUTOGRAPHS AND GET OUT WHILE YOU CAN. TRUST ME.
WRASSLIN INSIDER!

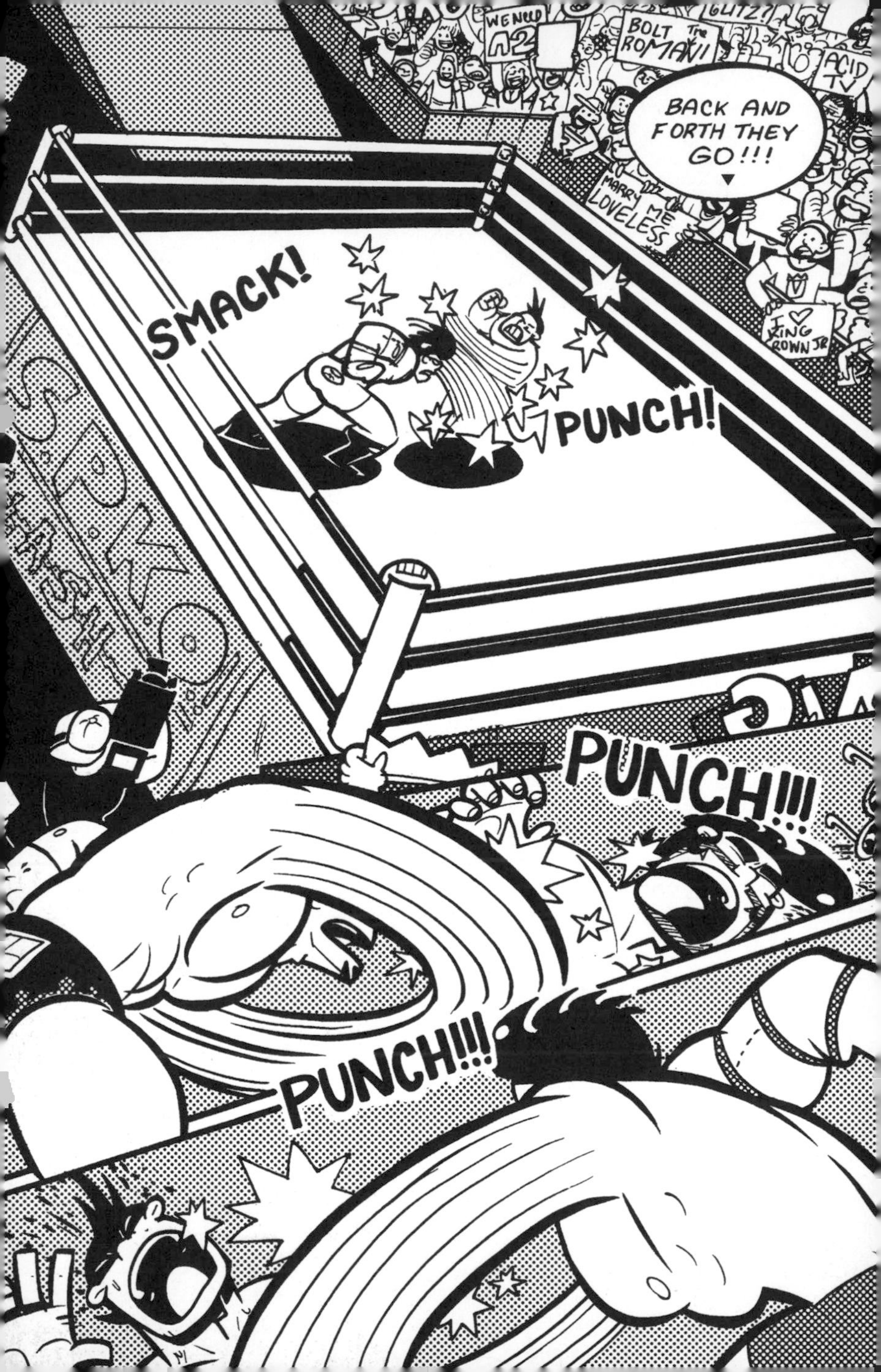

BOLT THE ROMAN!
ACID TV
BACK AND FORTH THEY GO!!!
MARRY ME LOVELESS
SMACK!
PUNCH!
PUNCH!!!
PUNCH!!!

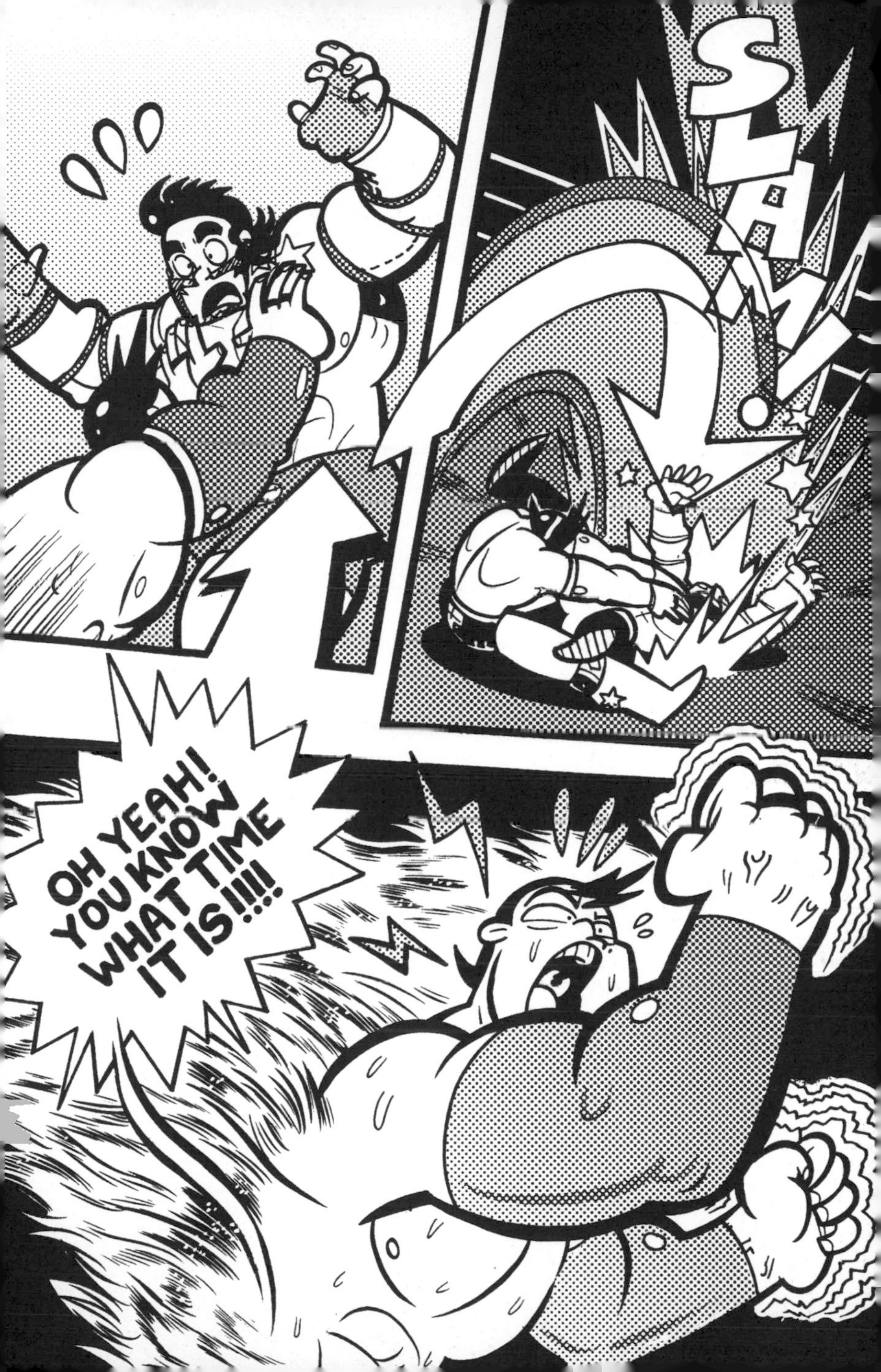
SLAM!
OH YEAH! YOU KNOW WHAT TIME IT IS!!!!

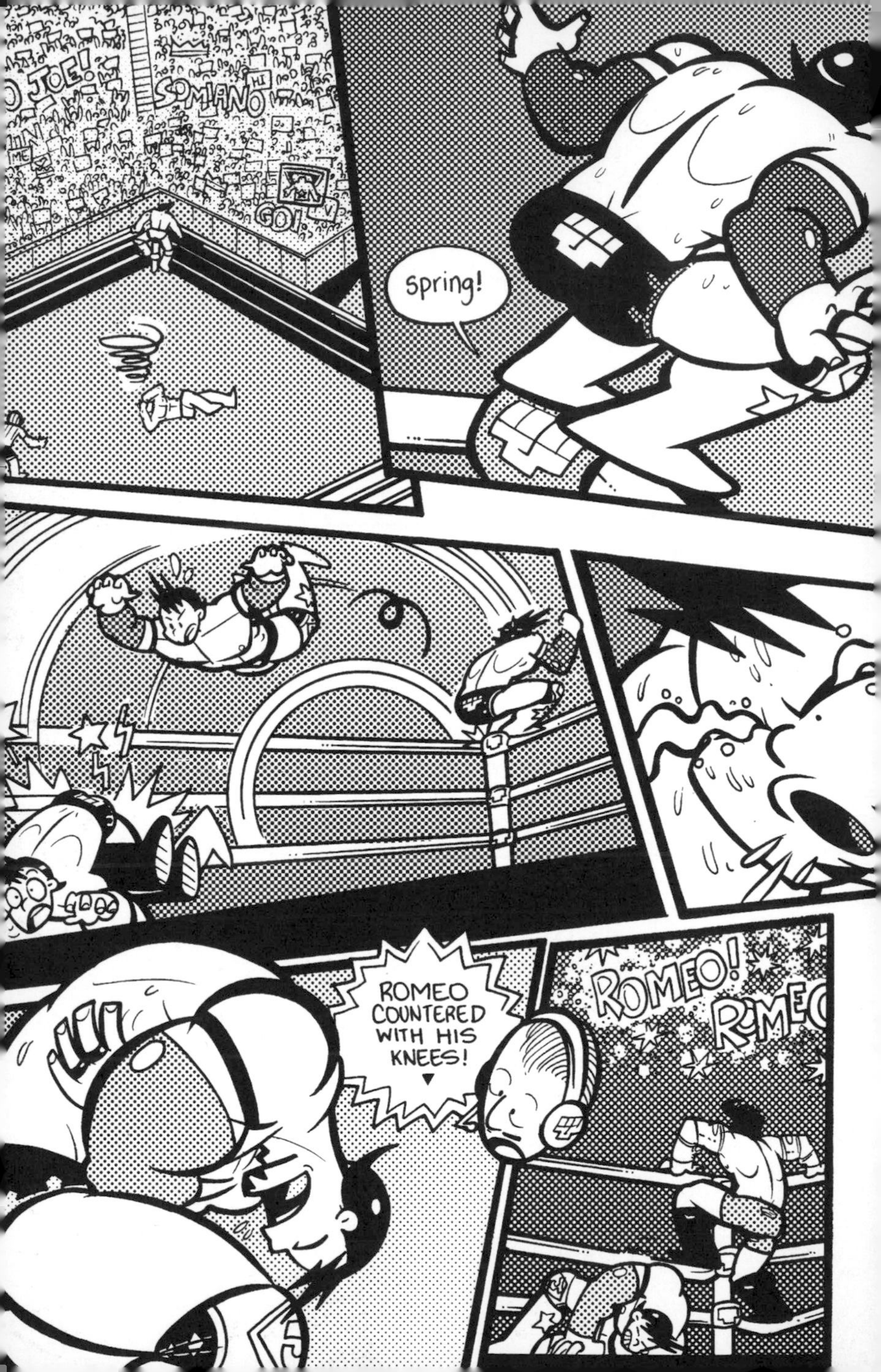
JOE!
SOMIANO
HI
ME
GO!
Spring!
ROMEO COUNTERED WITH HIS KNEES!
ROMEO!
ROMEO

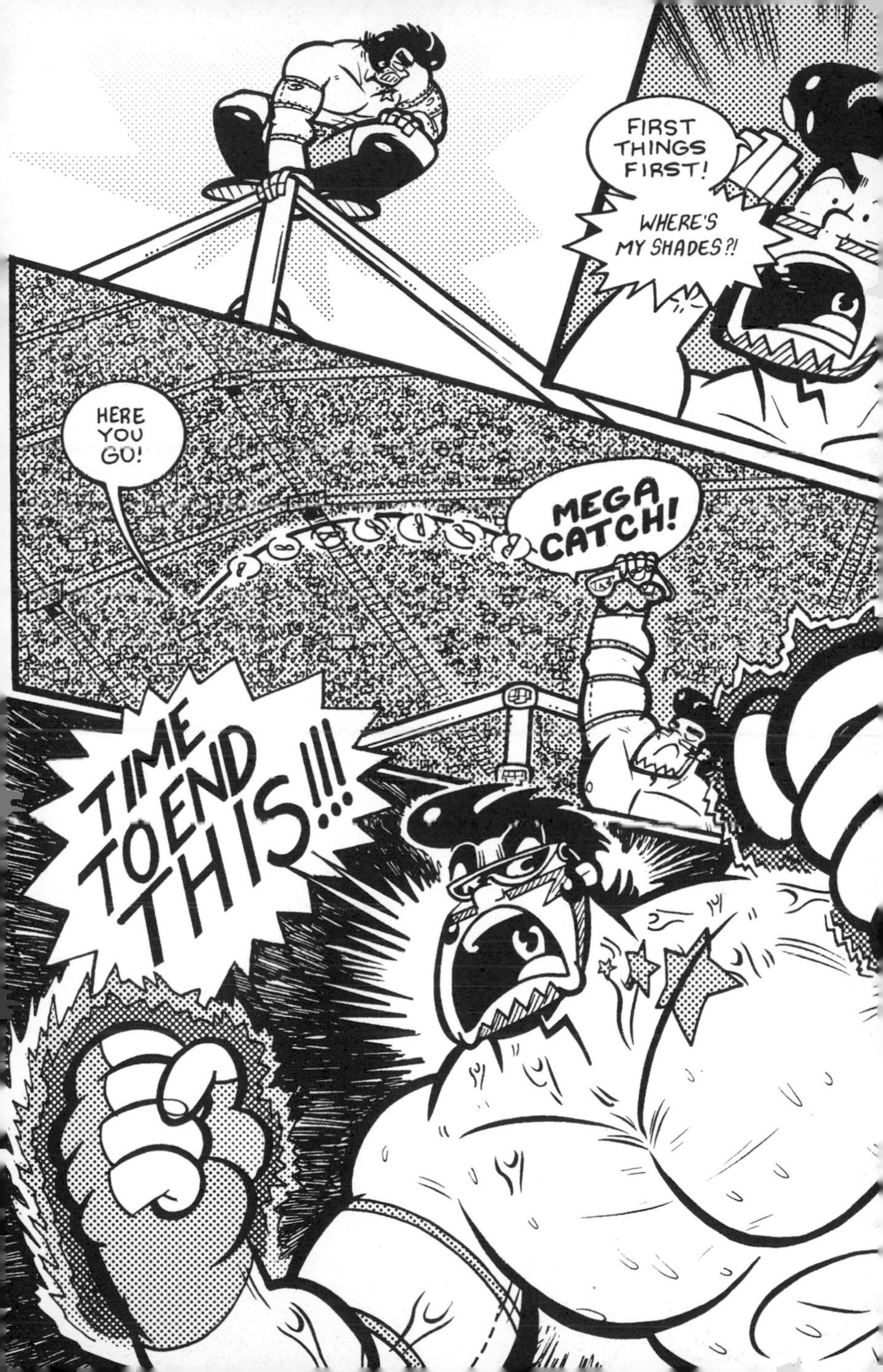
FIRST THINGS FIRST!
WHERE'S MY SHADES?!
HERE YOU GO!
MEGA CATCH!
TIME TO END THIS!!!

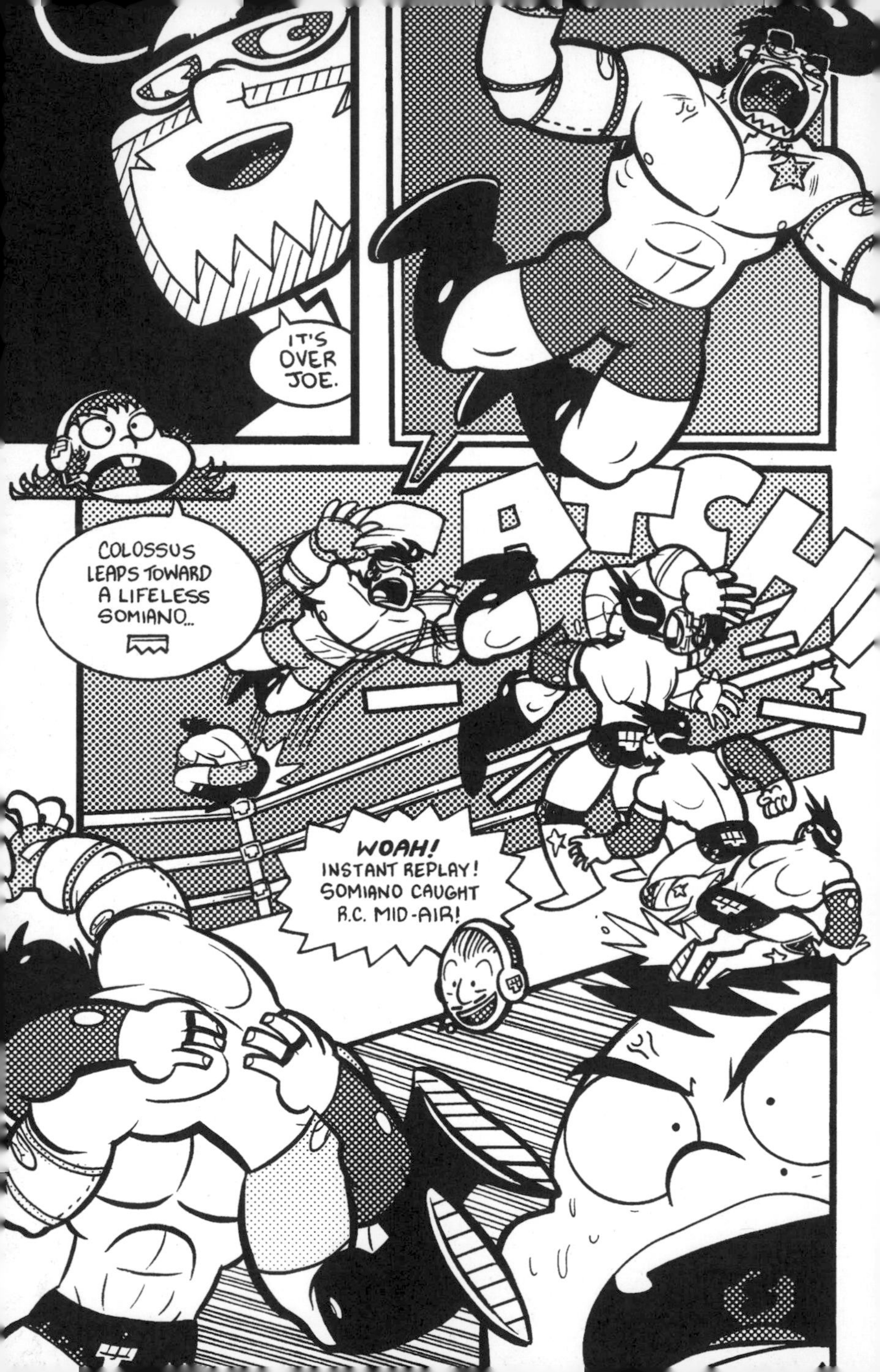
IT'S OVER JOE.
ATCH
COLOSSUS LEAPS TOWARD A LIFELESS SOMIANO...
WOAH! INSTANT REPLAY! SOMIANO CAUGHT R.C. MID-AIR!

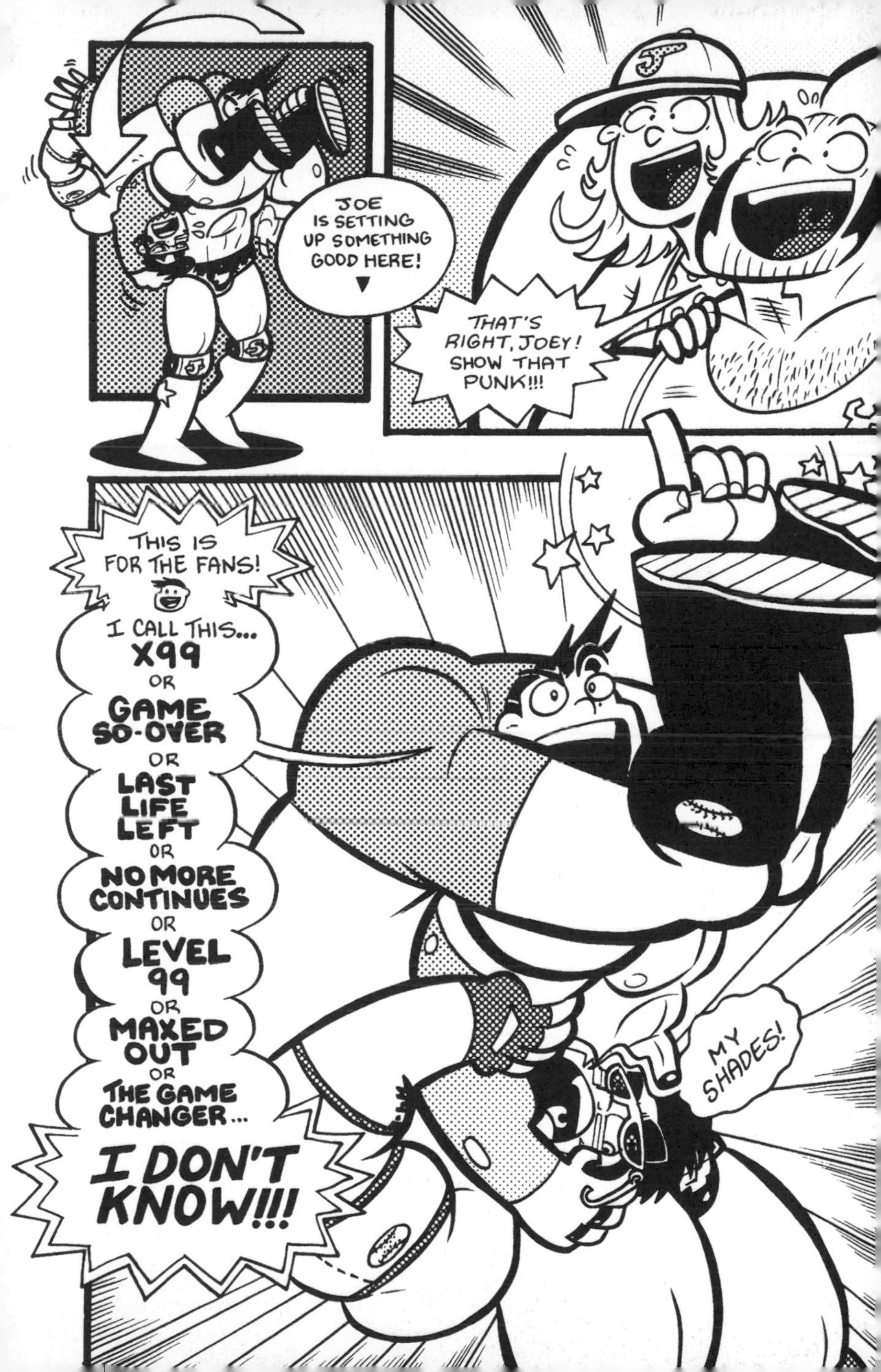

JOE IS SETTING UP SOMETHING GOOD HERE!
THAT'S RIGHT, JOEY! SHOW THAT PUNK!!!
THIS IS FOR THE FANS!
I CALL THIS... X99 OR GAME SO-OVER OR LAST LIFE LEFT OR NO MORE CONTINUES OR LEVEL 99 OR MAXED OUT OR THE GAME CHANGER...
I DON'T KNOW!!!
MY SHADES!

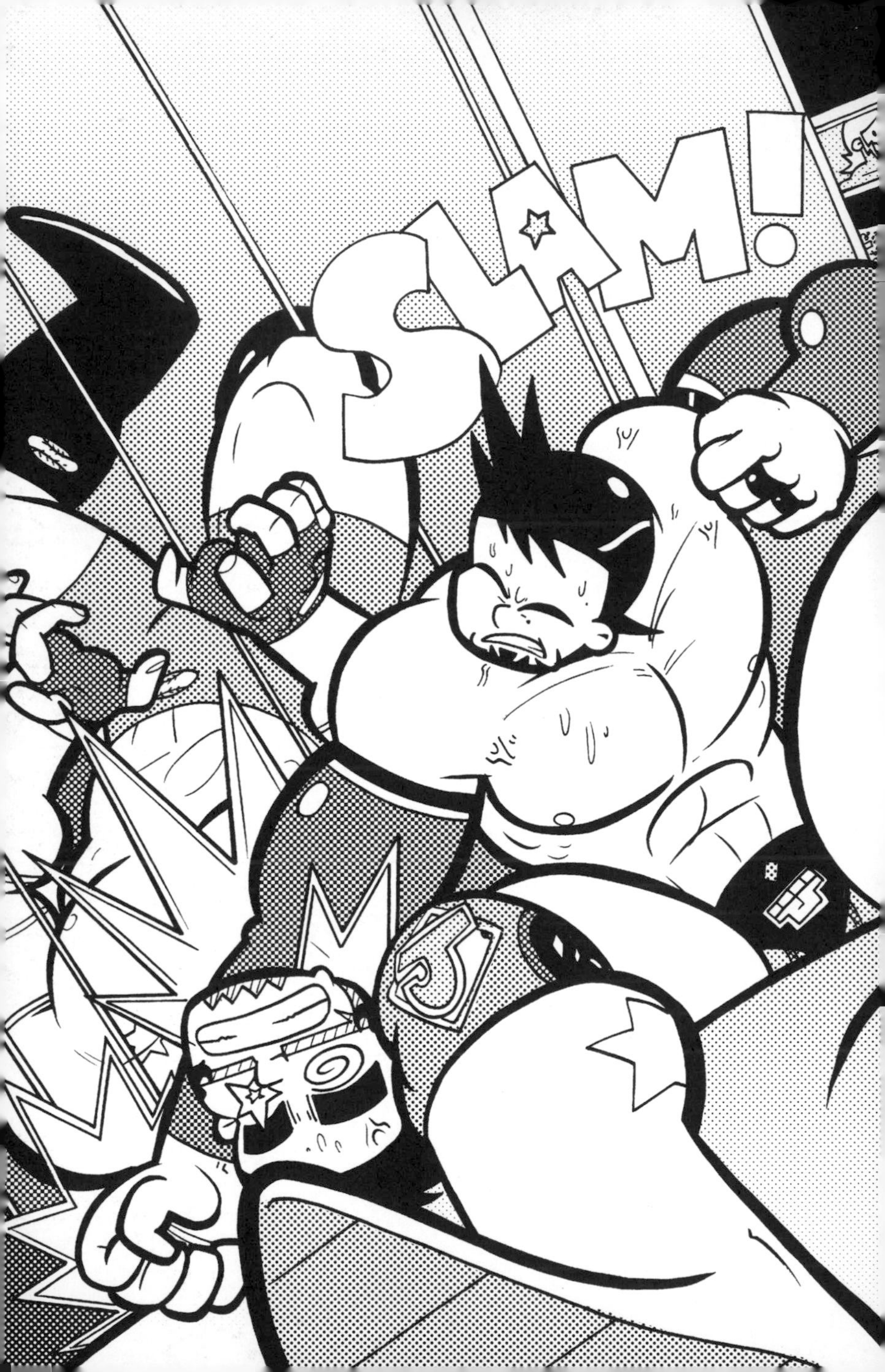
SLAM!

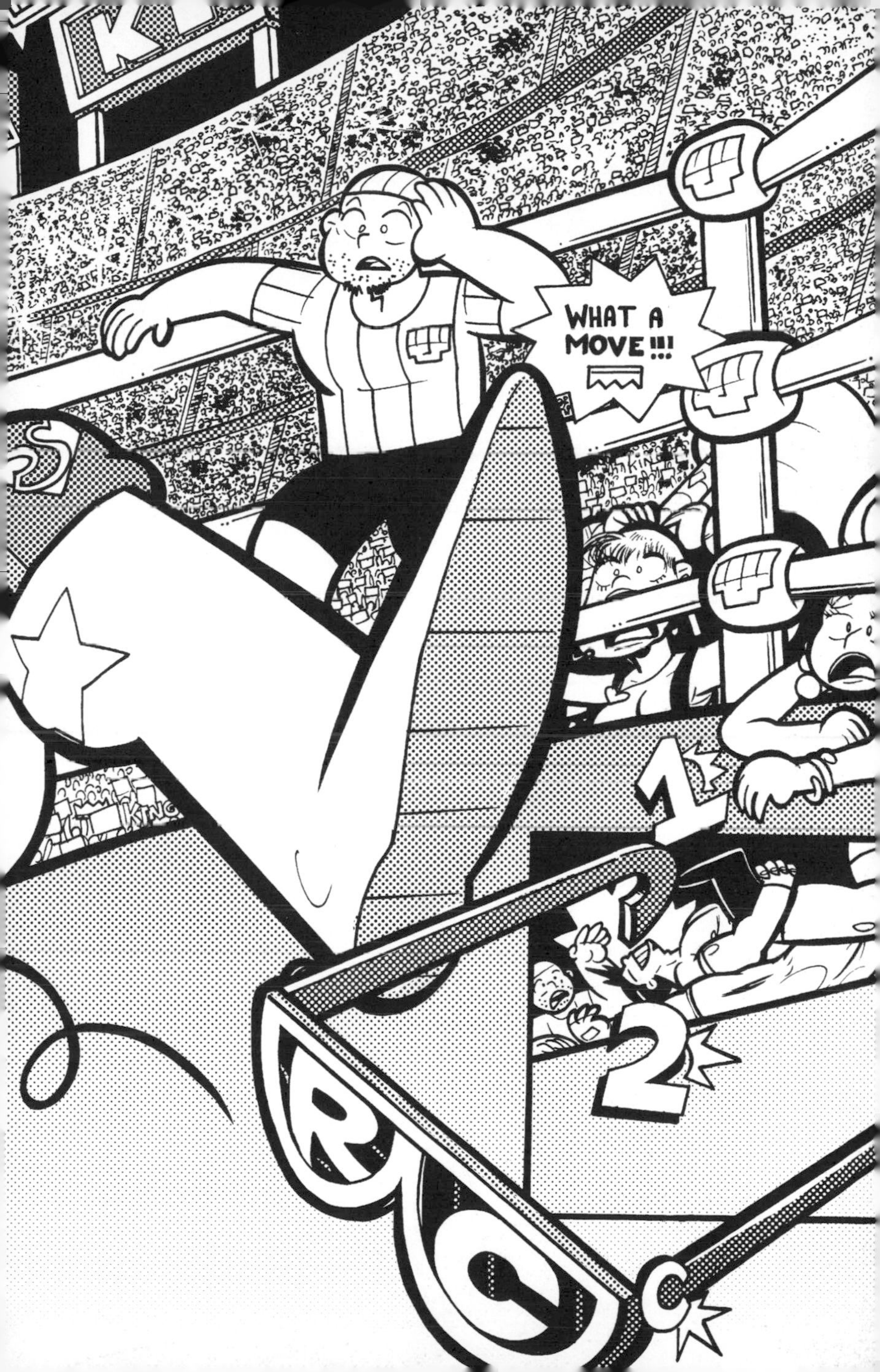
WHAT A MOVE!!!
1
2
R
C

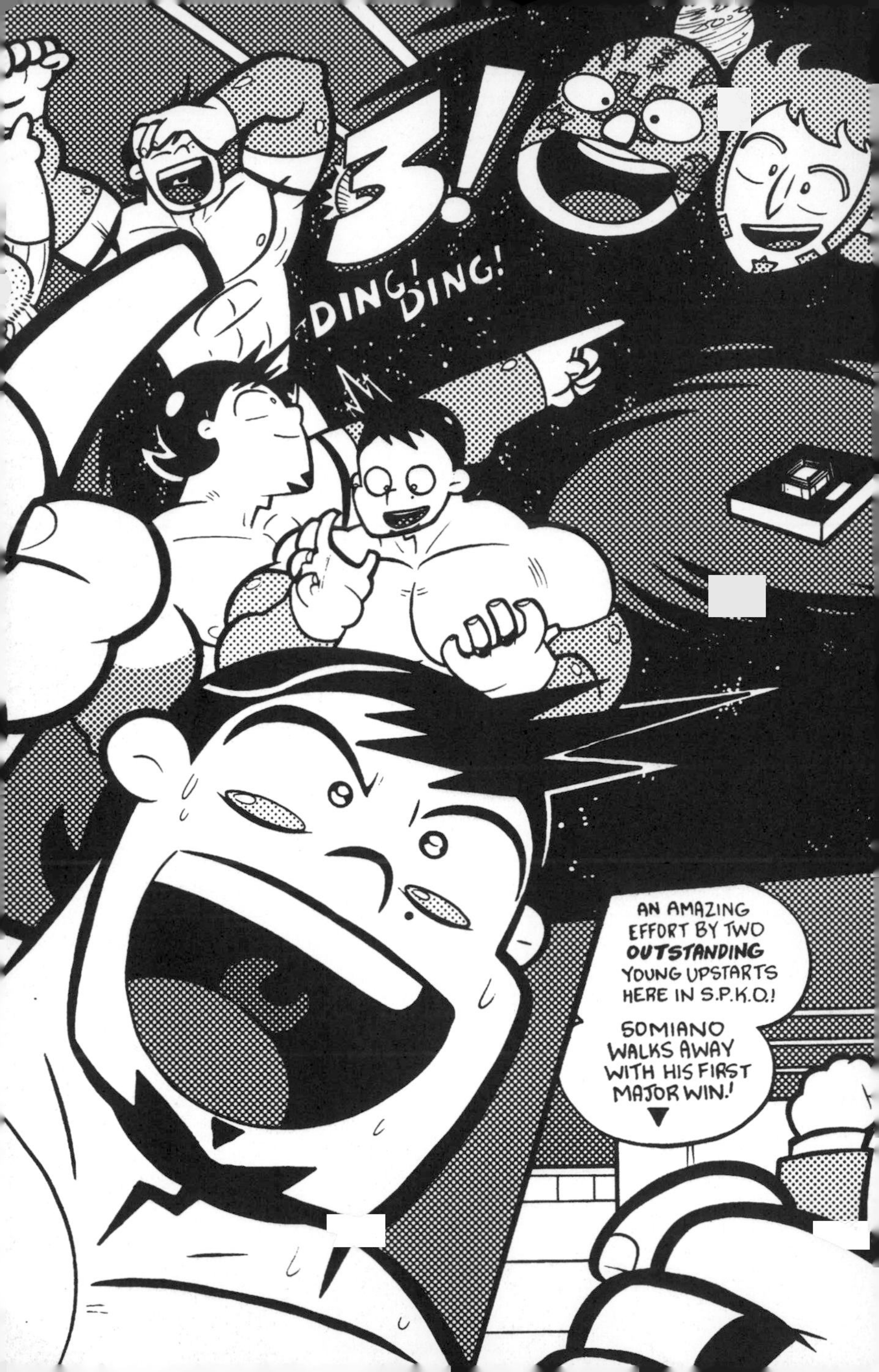
3!
DING! DING!
AN AMAZING EFFORT BY TWO **OUTSTANDING** YOUNG UPSTARTS HERE IN S.P.K.O.!
SOMIANO WALKS AWAY WITH HIS FIRST MAJOR WIN!

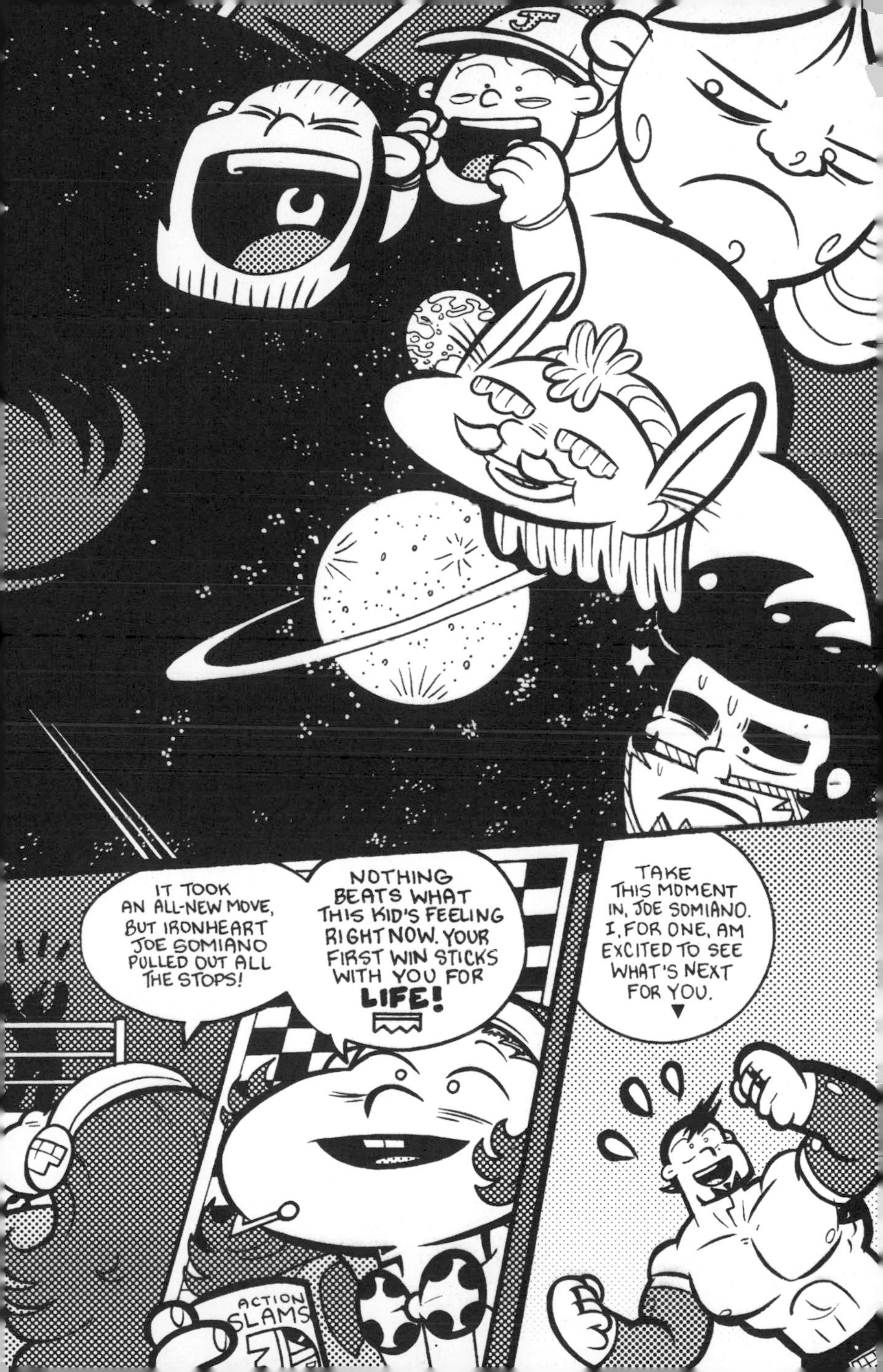
IT TOOK AN ALL-NEW MOVE, BUT IRONHEART JOE SOMIANO PULLED OUT ALL THE STOPS!
NOTHING BEATS WHAT THIS KID'S FEELING RIGHT NOW. YOUR FIRST WIN STICKS WITH YOU FOR LIFE!
TAKE THIS MOMENT IN, JOE SOMIANO. I, FOR ONE, AM EXCITED TO SEE WHAT'S NEXT FOR YOU.
ACTION SLAMS

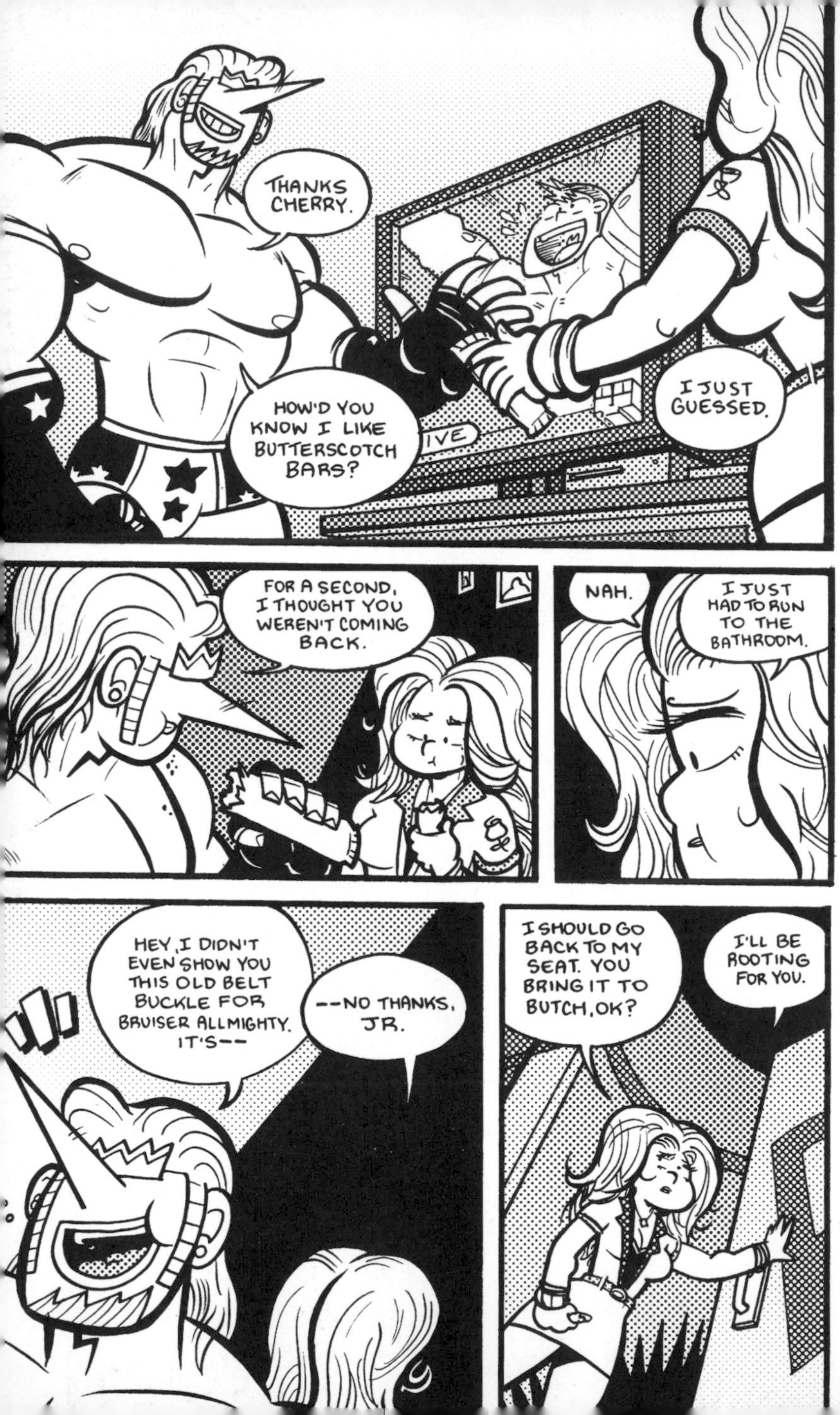
THANKS CHERRY.
HOW'D YOU KNOW I LIKE BUTTERSCOTCH BARS?
IVE
I JUST GUESSED.
FOR A SECOND, I THOUGHT YOU WEREN'T COMING BACK.
NAH.
I JUST HAD TO RUN TO THE BATHROOM.
HEY, I DIDN'T EVEN SHOW YOU THIS OLD BELT BUCKLE FOR BRUISER ALLMIGHTY. IT'S--
--NO THANKS, JR.
I SHOULD GO BACK TO MY SEAT. YOU BRING IT TO BUTCH, OK?
I'LL BE ROOTING FOR YOU.

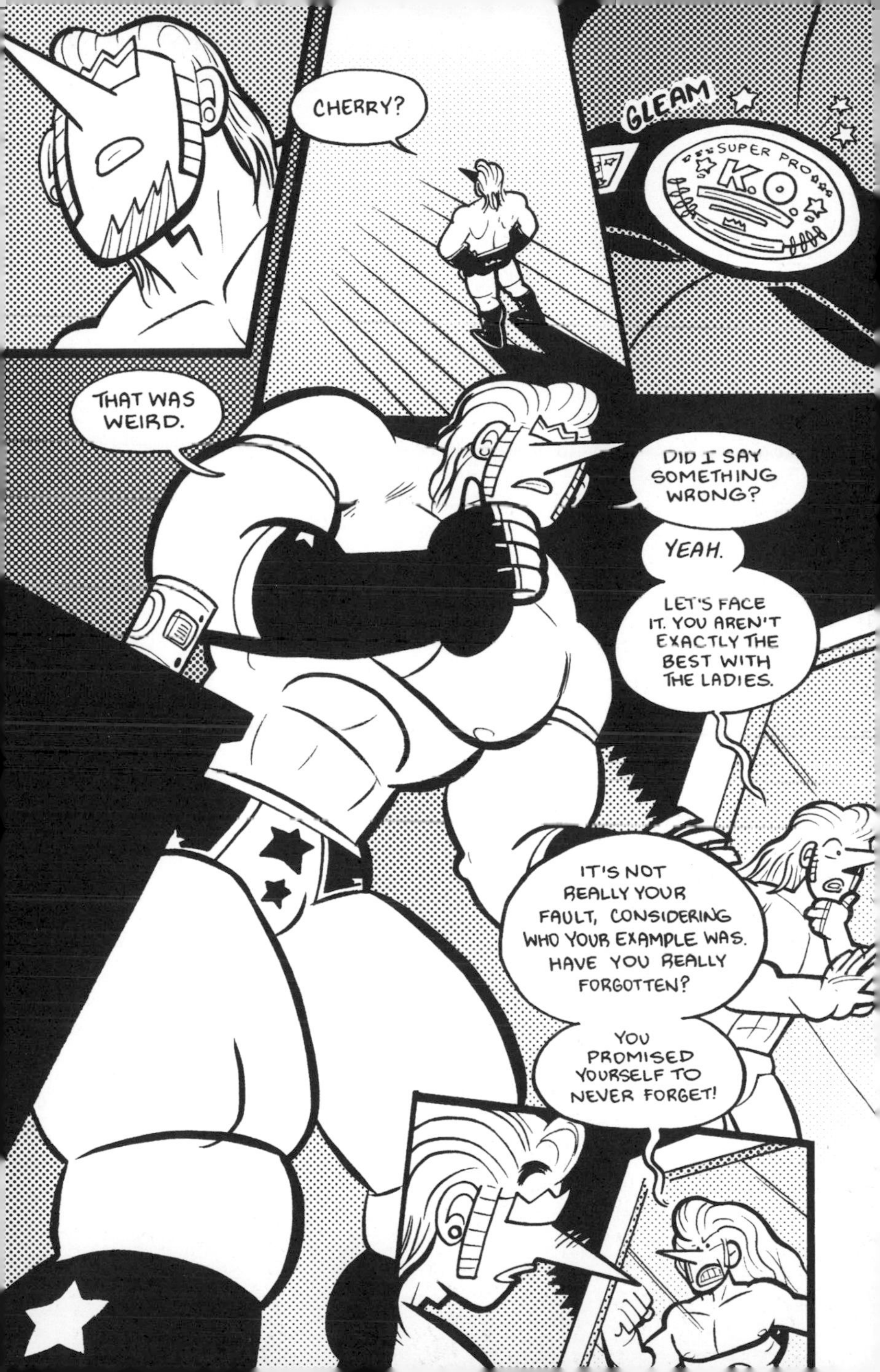
CHERRY?
GLEAM
SUPER PRO K.O.
THAT WAS WEIRD.
DID I SAY SOMETHING WRONG?
YEAH.
LET'S FACE IT. YOU AREN'T EXACTLY THE BEST WITH THE LADIES.
IT'S NOT REALLY YOUR FAULT, CONSIDERING WHO YOUR EXAMPLE WAS. HAVE YOU REALLY FORGOTTEN?
YOU PROMISED YOURSELF TO NEVER FORGET!

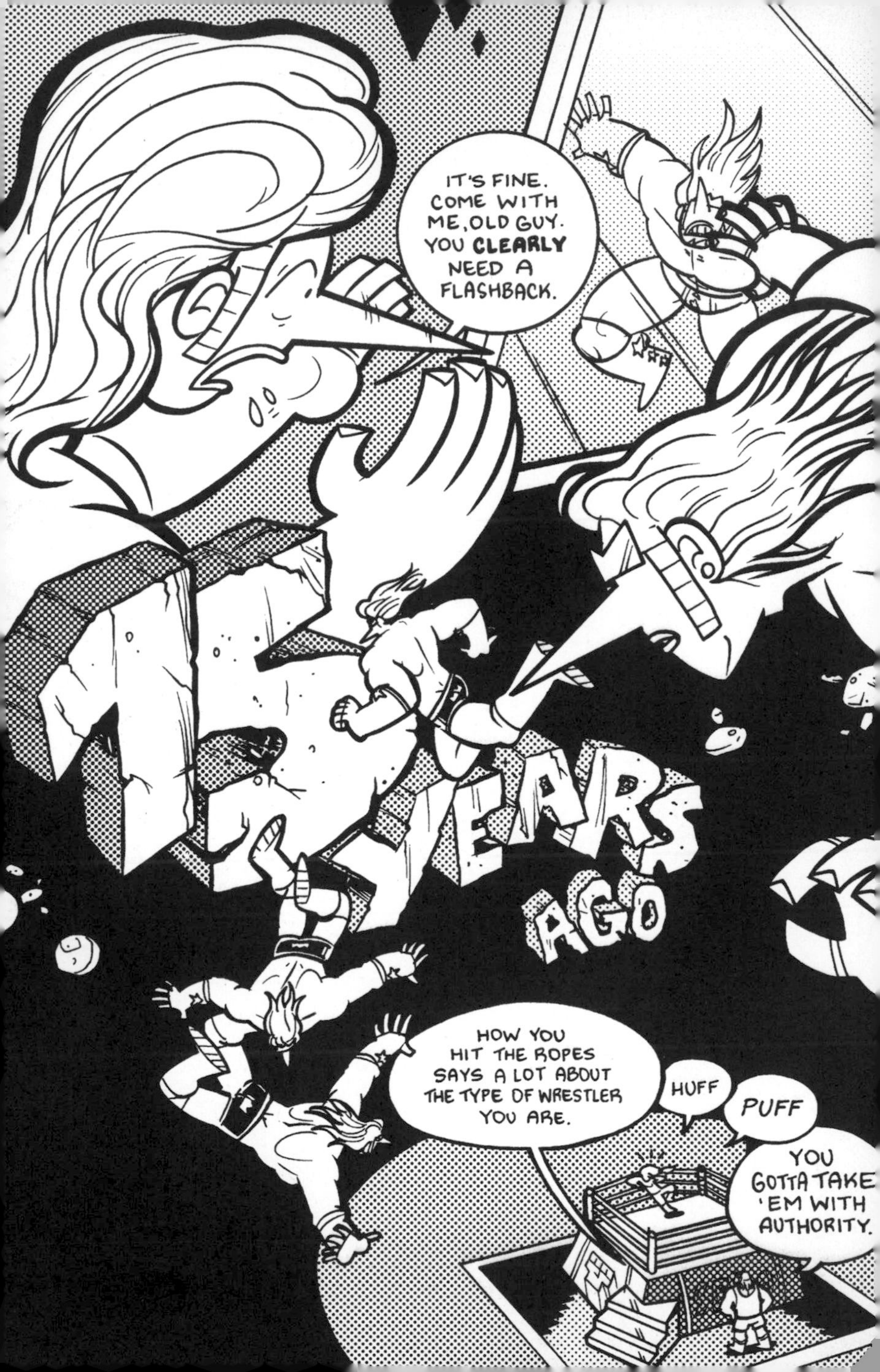
IT'S FINE. COME WITH ME, OLD GUY. YOU **CLEARLY** NEED A FLASHBACK.
YEARS AGO
HOW YOU HIT THE ROPES SAYS A LOT ABOUT THE TYPE OF WRESTLER YOU ARE.
HUFF
PUFF
YOU GOTTA TAKE 'EM WITH AUTHORITY.

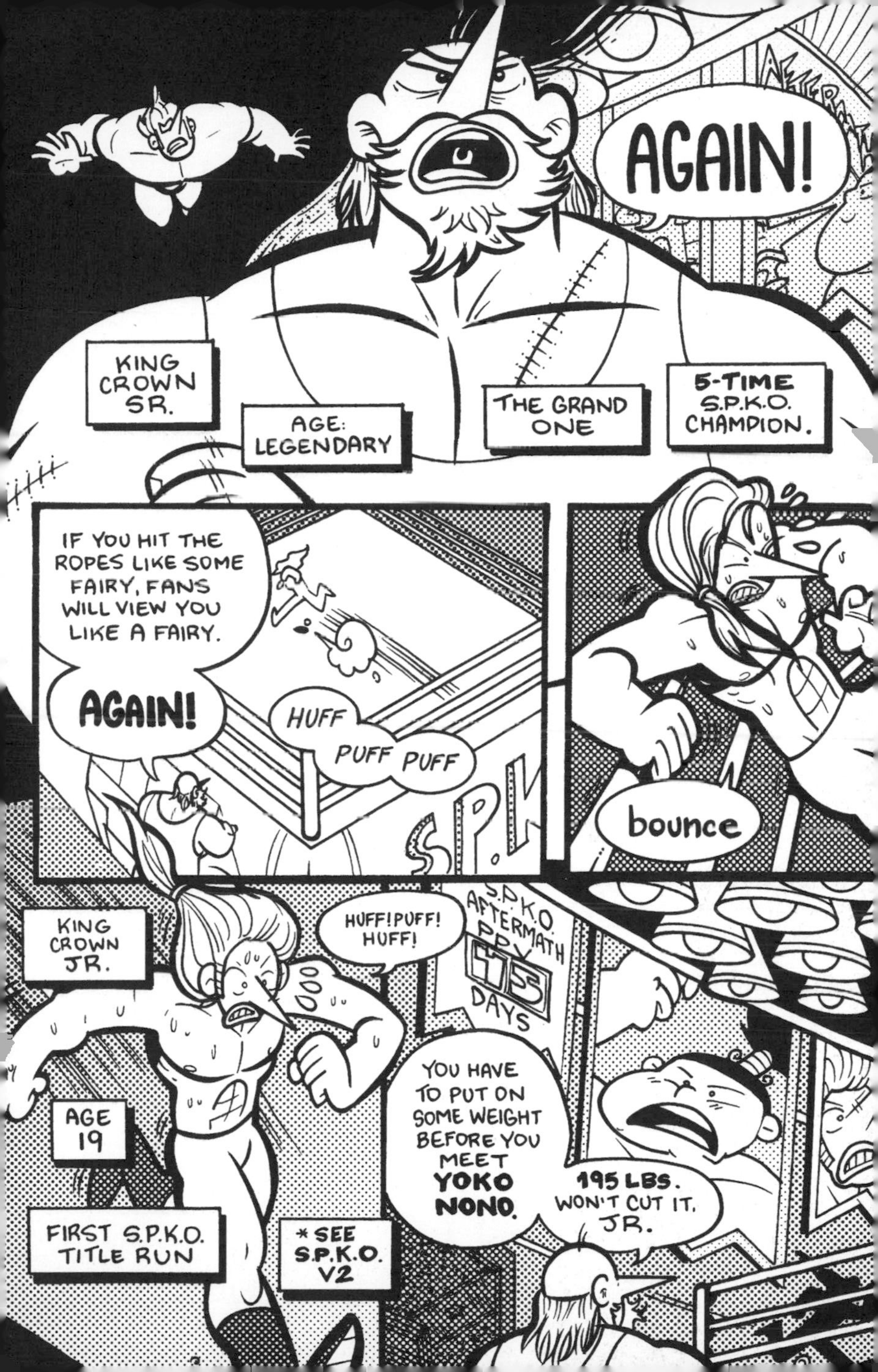
AGAIN!
KING CROWN SR.
AGE: LEGENDARY
THE GRAND ONE
5-TIME S.P.K.O. CHAMPION.
IF YOU HIT THE ROPES LIKE SOME FAIRY, FANS WILL VIEW YOU LIKE A FAIRY.
AGAIN!
HUFF
PUFF PUFF
S.P.K
bounce
KING CROWN JR.
AGE 19
FIRST S.P.K.O. TITLE RUN
HUFF! PUFF! HUFF!
S.P.K.O. AFTERMATH PPV 45 DAYS
*SEE S.P.K.O. V2
YOU HAVE TO PUT ON SOME WEIGHT BEFORE YOU MEET YOKO NONO.
195 LBS. WON'T CUT IT, JR.

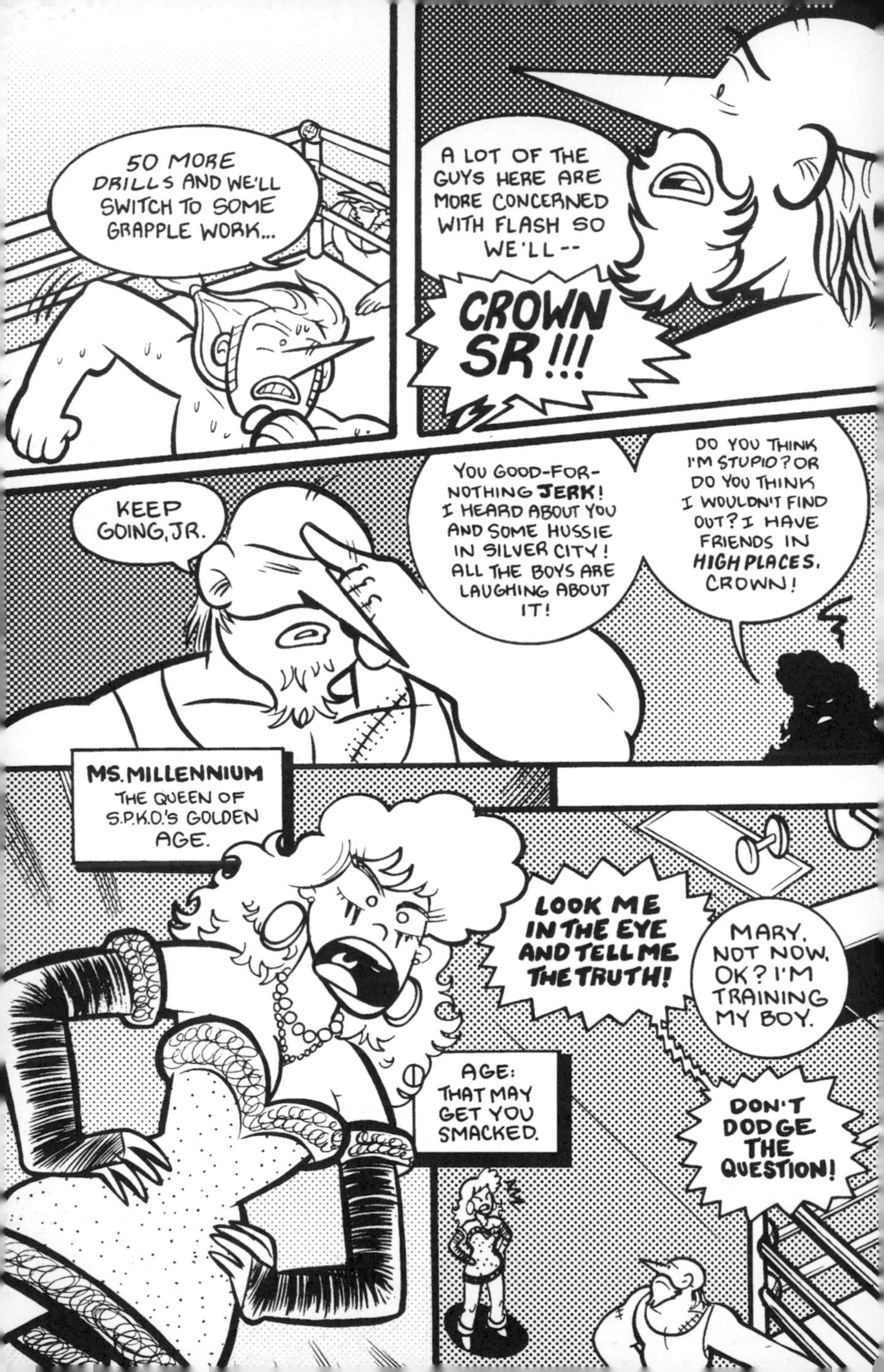
50 MORE DRILLS AND WE'LL SWITCH TO SOME GRAPPLE WORK...
A LOT OF THE GUYS HERE ARE MORE CONCERNED WITH FLASH SO WE'LL --
CROWN SR!!!
KEEP GOING, JR.
YOU GOOD-FOR-NOTHING JERK! I HEARD ABOUT YOU AND SOME HUSSIE IN SILVER CITY! ALL THE BOYS ARE LAUGHING ABOUT IT!
DO YOU THINK I'M STUPID? OR DO YOU THINK I WOULDN'T FIND OUT? I HAVE FRIENDS IN HIGH PLACES, CROWN!
MS. MILLENNIUM THE QUEEN OF S.P.K.O.'S GOLDEN AGE.
LOOK ME IN THE EYE AND TELL ME THE TRUTH!
MARY, NOT NOW, OK? I'M TRAINING MY BOY.
AGE: THAT MAY GET YOU SMACKED.
DON'T DODGE THE QUESTION!

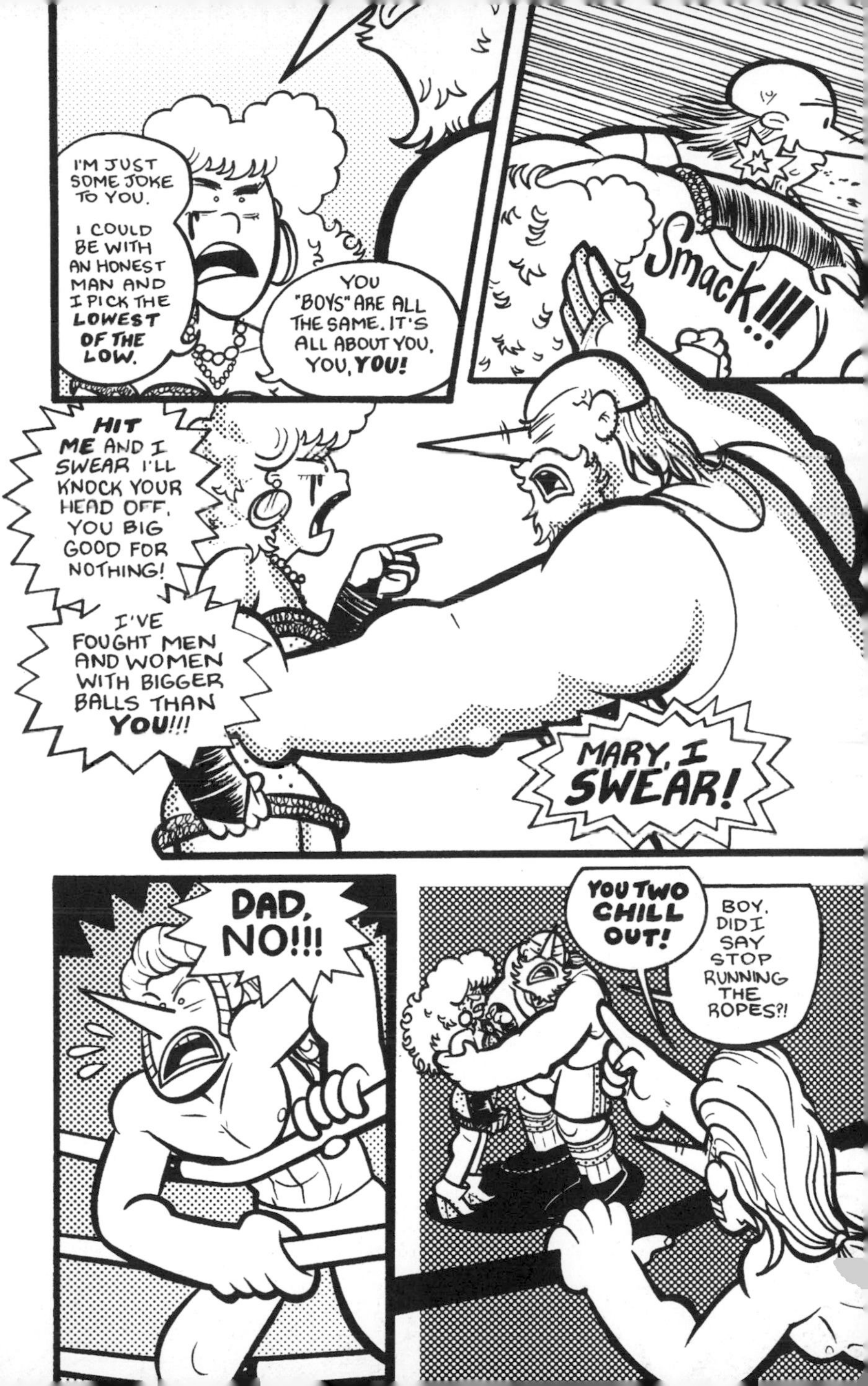
I'M JUST SOME JOKE TO YOU.
I COULD BE WITH AN HONEST MAN AND I PICK THE **LOWEST OF THE LOW.**
YOU "BOYS" ARE ALL THE SAME. IT'S ALL ABOUT YOU. YOU, **YOU!**
Smack!!!
HIT ME AND I **SWEAR** I'LL KNOCK YOUR HEAD OFF, YOU BIG GOOD FOR NOTHING!
I'VE FOUGHT MEN AND WOMEN WITH BIGGER BALLS THAN **YOU**!!!
MARY, I **SWEAR!**
DAD, NO!!!
YOU TWO CHILL OUT!
BOY. DID I SAY STOP RUNNING THE ROPES?!

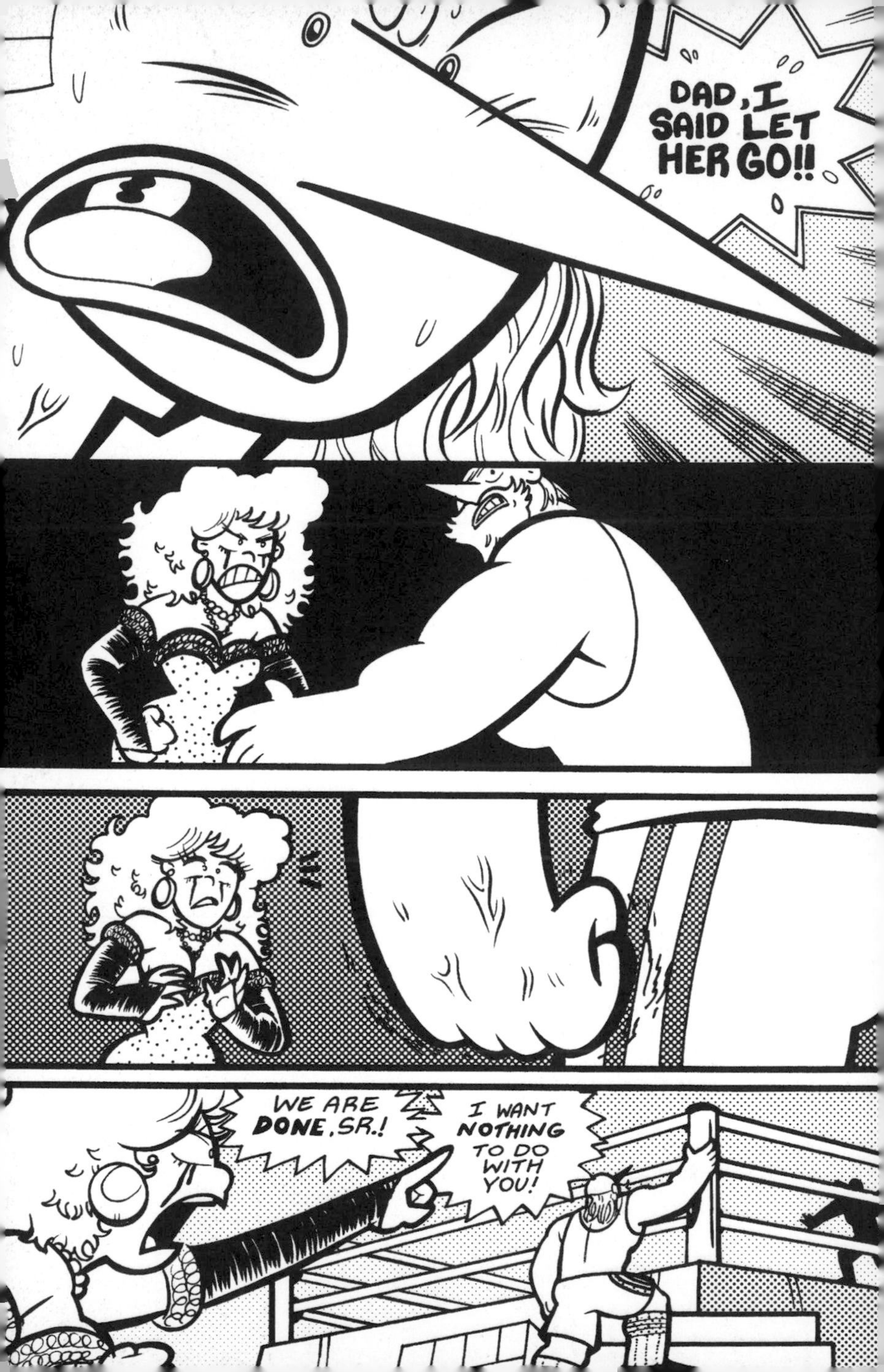
DAD, I SAID LET HER GO!!
WE ARE DONE, SR.!
I WANT NOTHING TO DO WITH YOU!

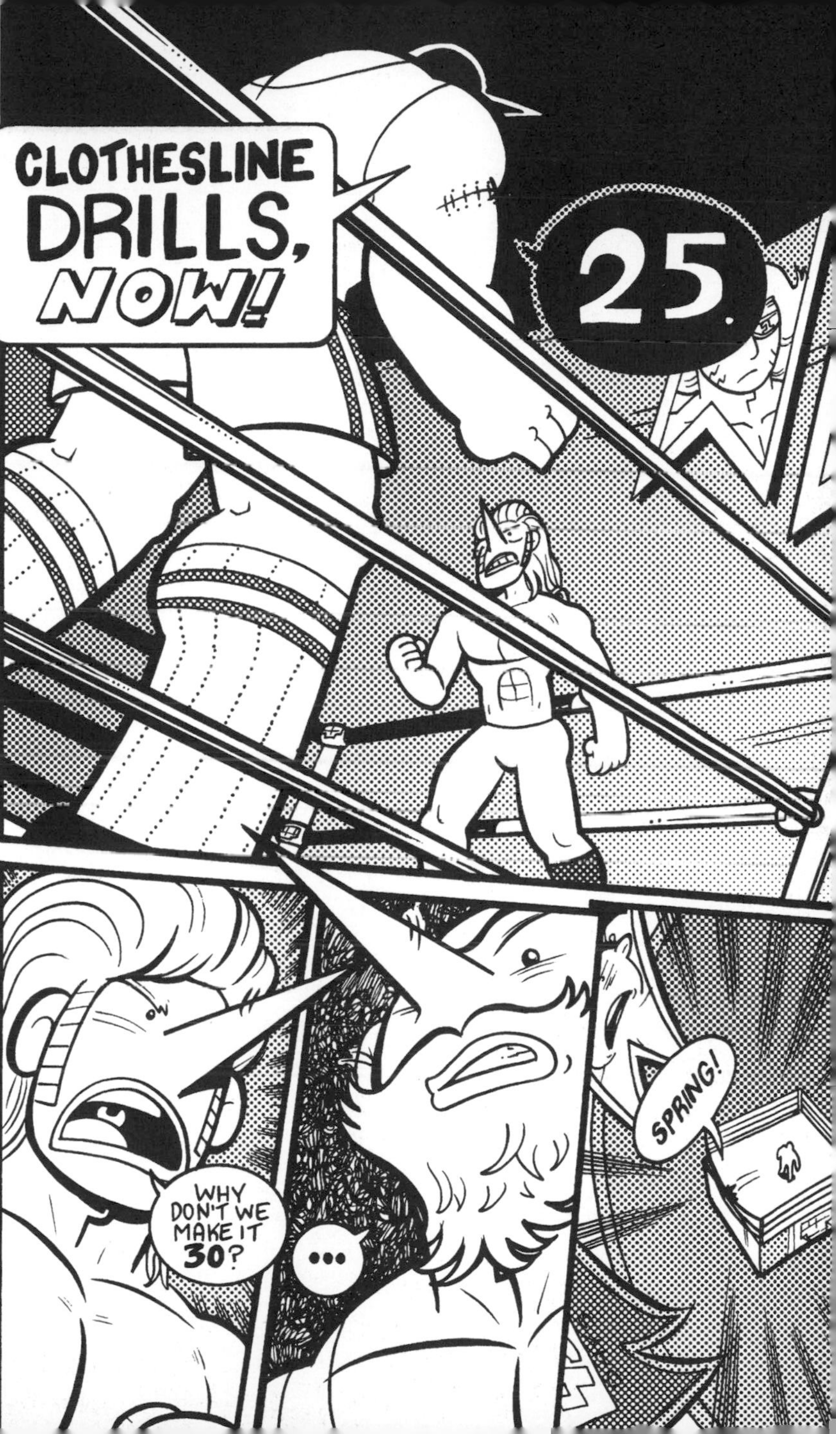
CLOTHESLINE DRILLS, NOW!
25.
WHY DON'T WE MAKE IT 30?
...
SPRING!

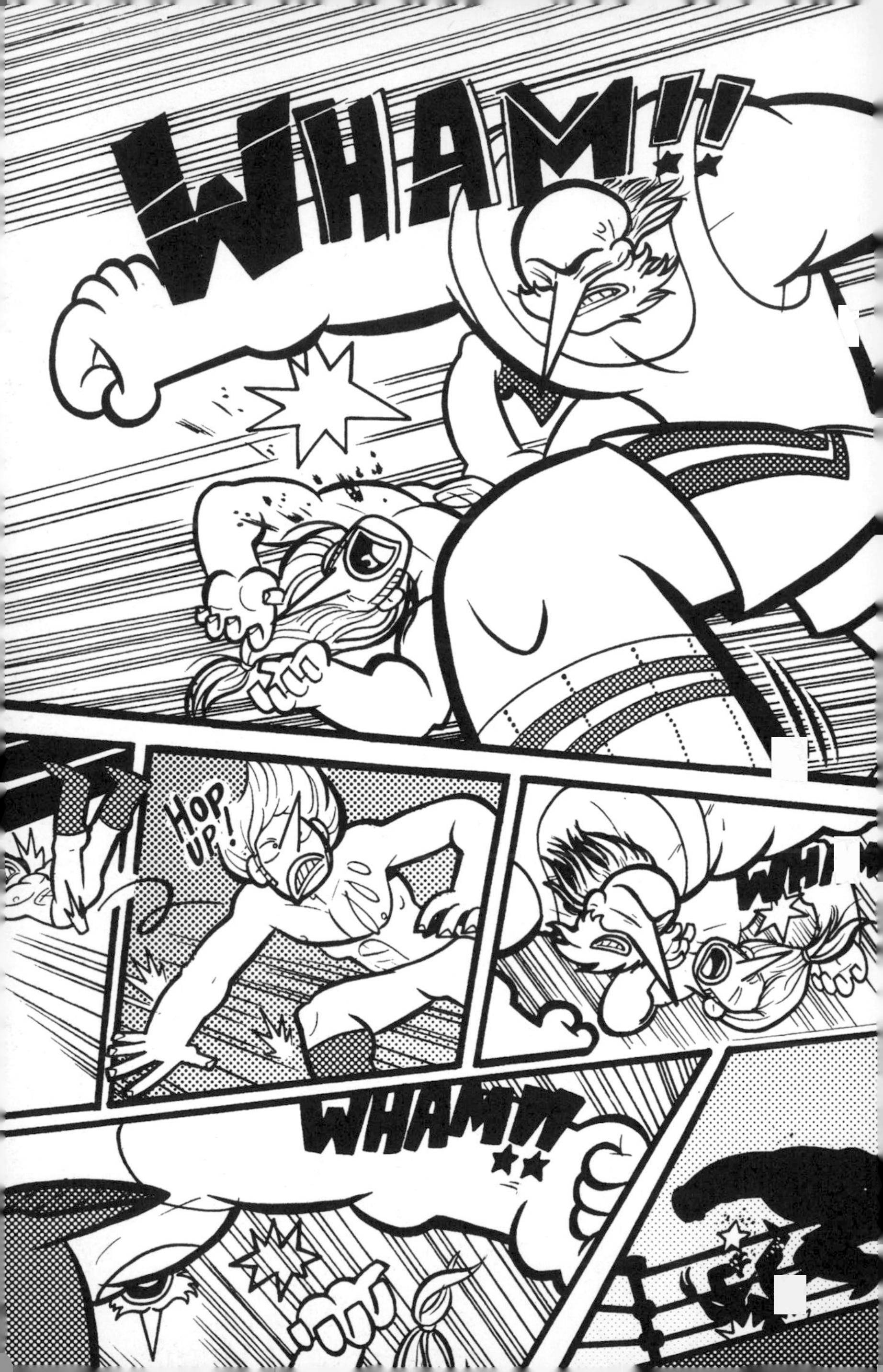
WHAM!!
HOP UP!
WHAM!!

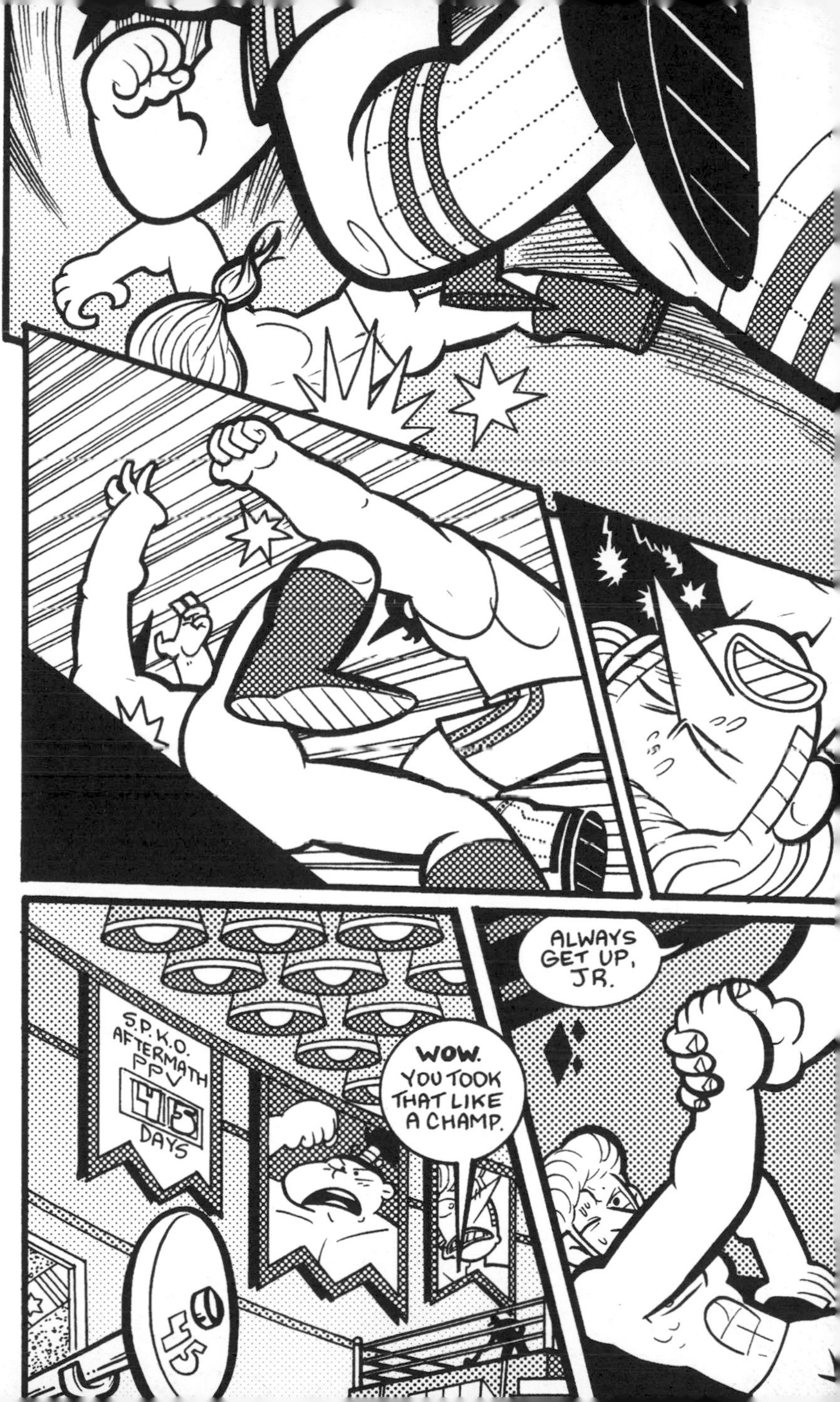
S.P.K.O. AFTERMATH PPV
47 53
DAYS
WOW. YOU TOOK THAT LIKE A CHAMP.
ALWAYS GET UP, JR.

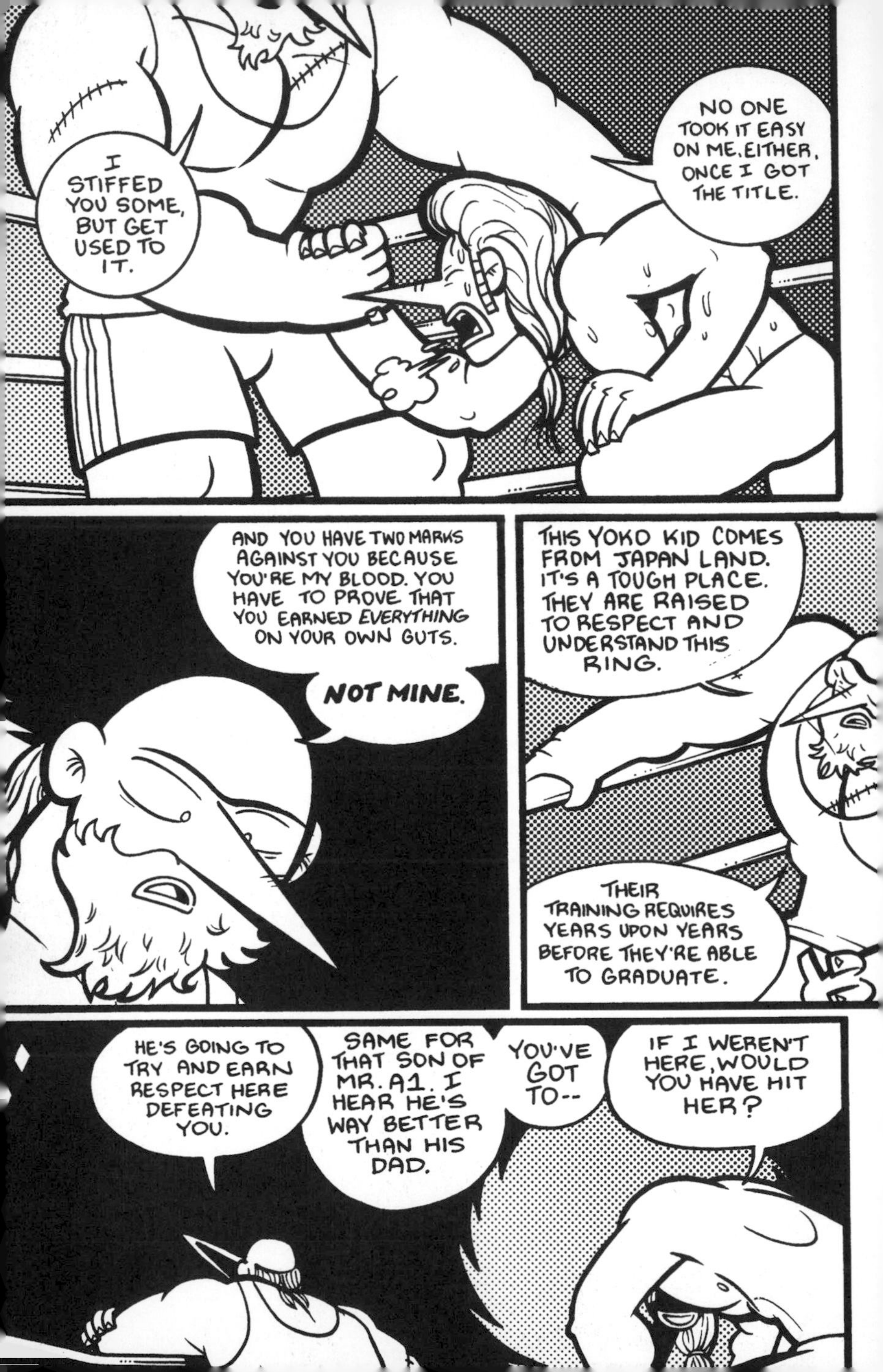
I STIFFED YOU SOME, BUT GET USED TO IT.
NO ONE TOOK IT EASY ON ME, EITHER, ONCE I GOT THE TITLE.
AND YOU HAVE TWO MARKS AGAINST YOU BECAUSE YOU'RE MY BLOOD. YOU HAVE TO PROVE THAT YOU EARNED *EVERYTHING* ON YOUR OWN GUTS.
NOT MINE.
THIS YOKO KID COMES FROM JAPAN LAND. IT'S A TOUGH PLACE. THEY ARE RAISED TO RESPECT AND UNDERSTAND THIS RING.
THEIR TRAINING REQUIRES YEARS UPON YEARS BEFORE THEY'RE ABLE TO GRADUATE.
HE'S GOING TO TRY AND EARN RESPECT HERE DEFEATING YOU.
SAME FOR THAT SON OF MR. A1. I HEAR HE'S WAY BETTER THAN HIS DAD.
YOU'VE GOT TO--
IF I WEREN'T HERE, WOULD YOU HAVE HIT HER?

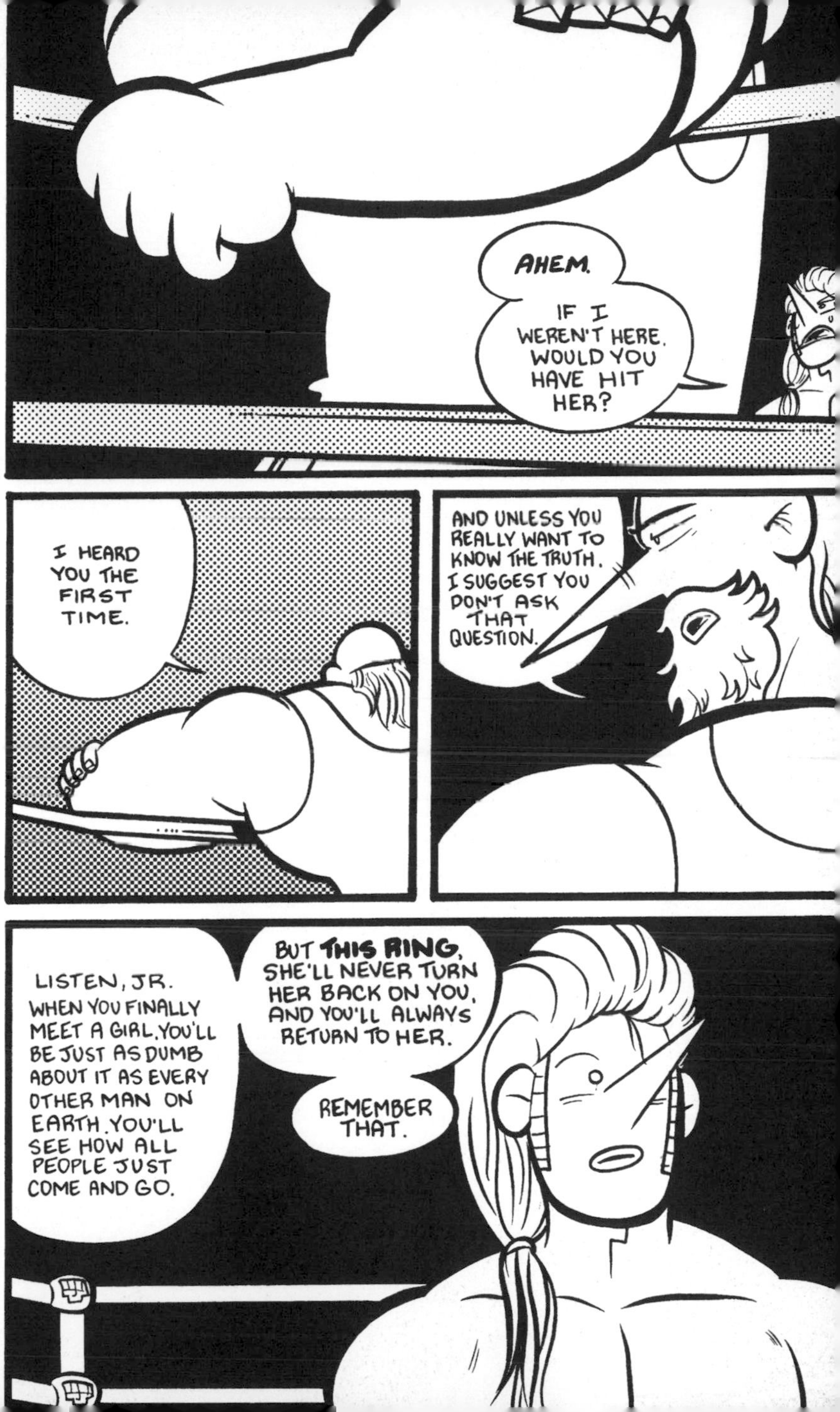
AHEM.
IF I WEREN'T HERE, WOULD YOU HAVE HIT HER?
I HEARD YOU THE FIRST TIME.
AND UNLESS YOU REALLY WANT TO KNOW THE TRUTH, I SUGGEST YOU DON'T ASK THAT QUESTION.
LISTEN, JR. WHEN YOU FINALLY MEET A GIRL, YOU'LL BE JUST AS DUMB ABOUT IT AS EVERY OTHER MAN ON EARTH. YOU'LL SEE HOW ALL PEOPLE JUST COME AND GO.
BUT THIS RING, SHE'LL NEVER TURN HER BACK ON YOU, AND YOU'LL ALWAYS RETURN TO HER.
REMEMBER THAT.

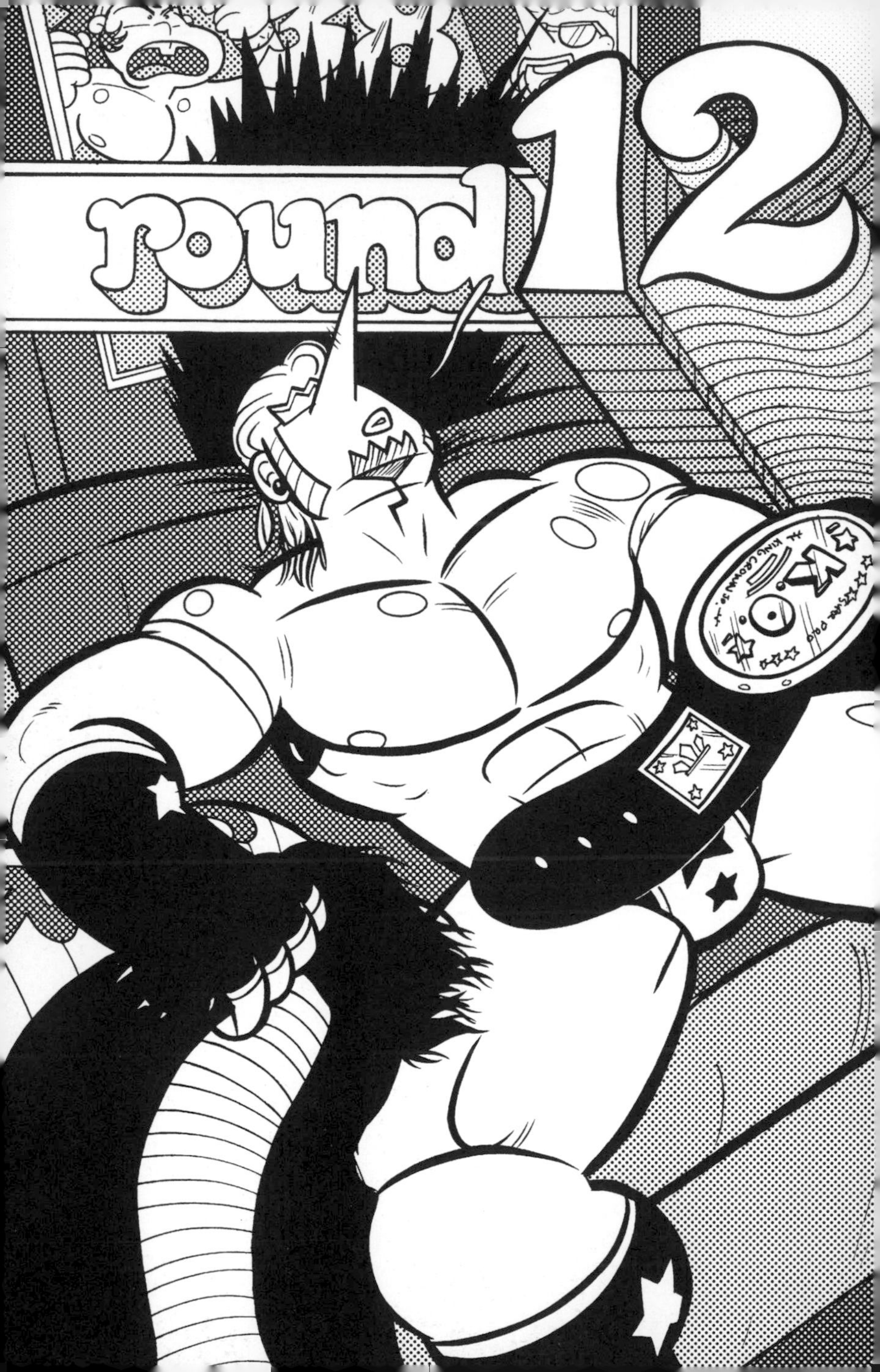
round 12

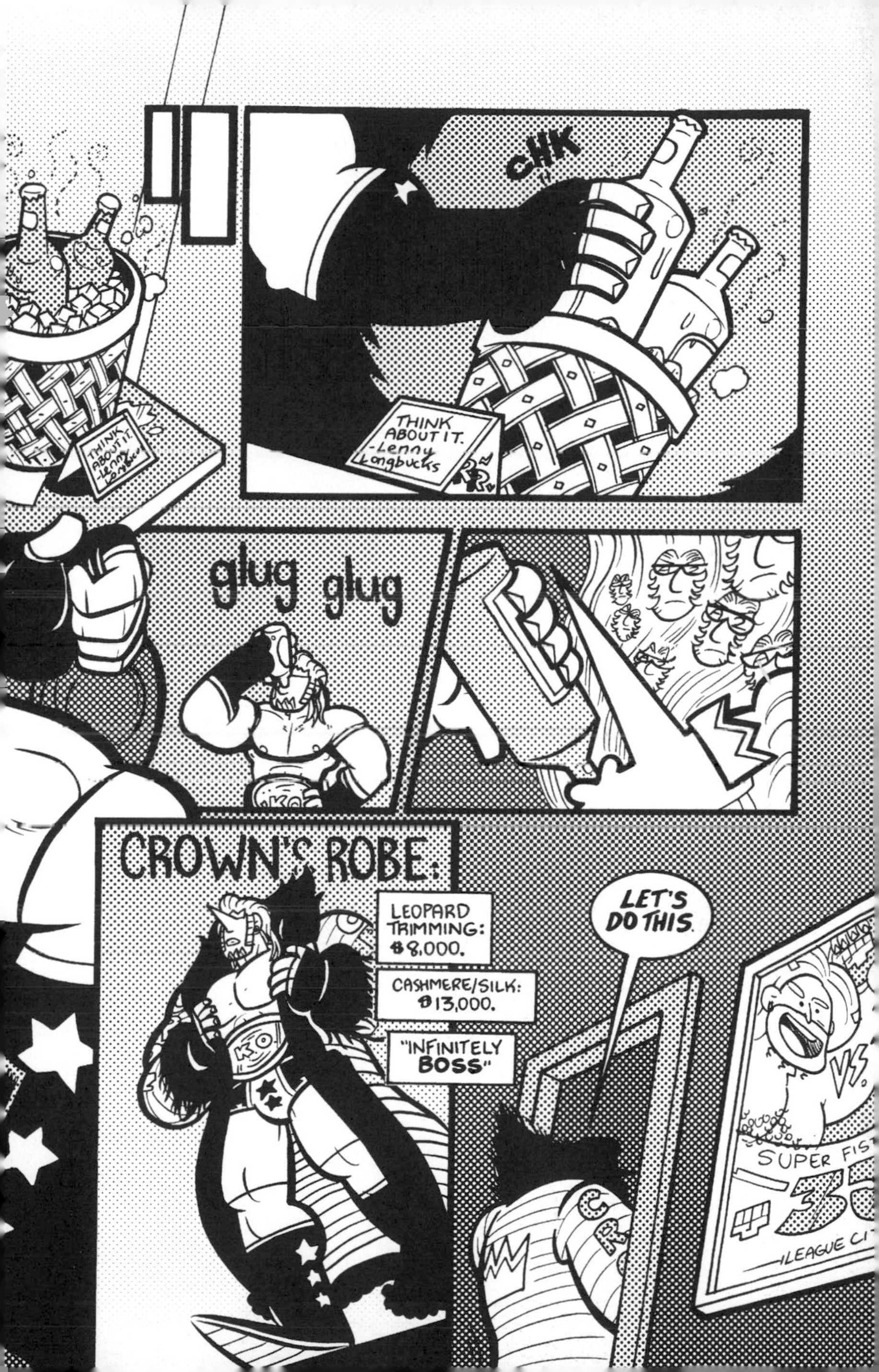
CHK
THINK ABOUT IT. -Lenny Longbucks
glug glug
CROWN'S ROBE:
LEOPARD TRIMMING: $8,000.
CASHMERE/SILK: $13,000.
"INFINITELY BOSS"
LET'S DO THIS.

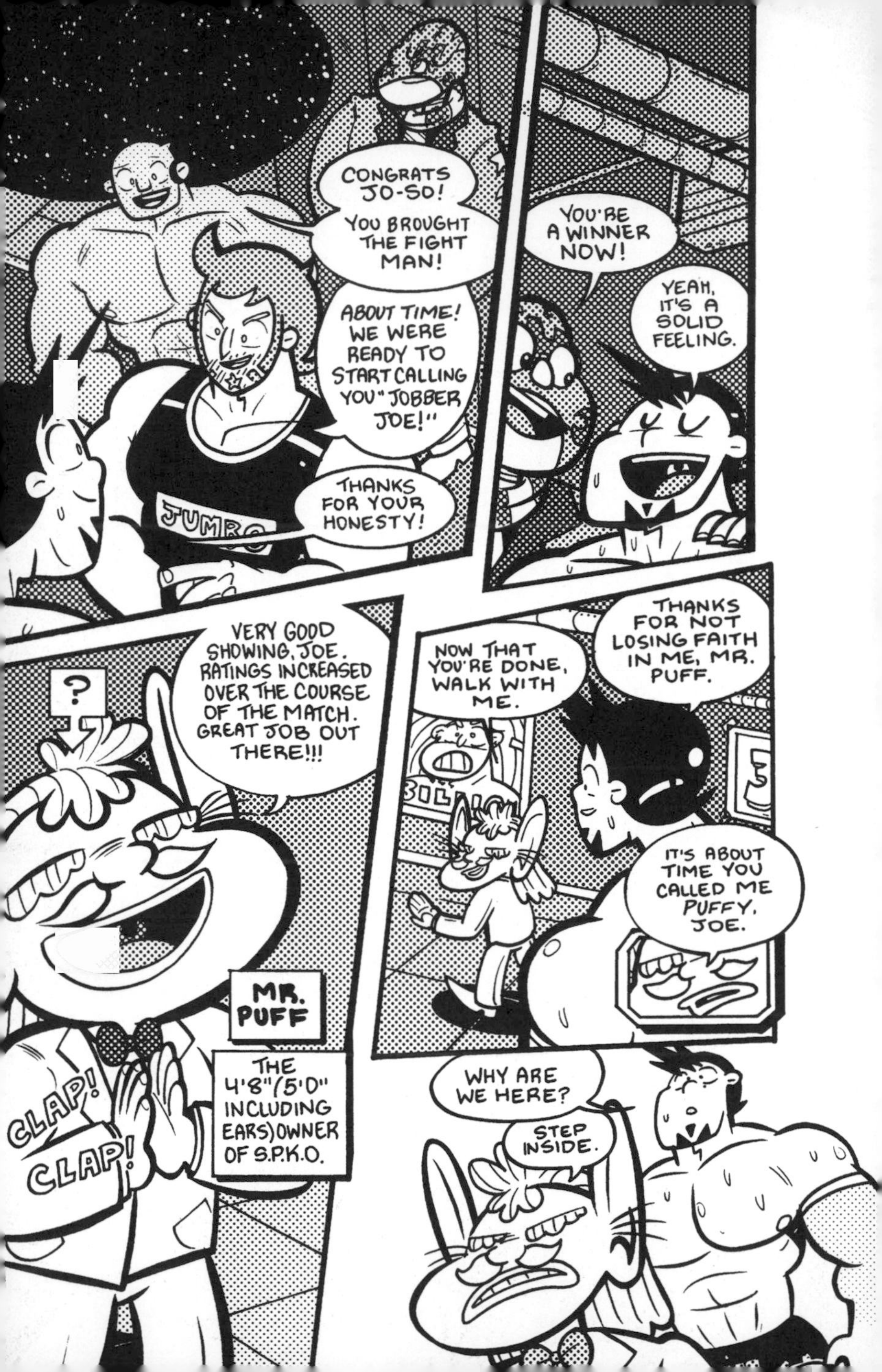
CONGRATS JO-SO!
YOU BROUGHT THE FIGHT MAN!
ABOUT TIME! WE WERE READY TO START CALLING YOU "JOBBER JOE!"
THANKS FOR YOUR HONESTY!
YOU'RE A WINNER NOW!
YEAH, IT'S A SOLID FEELING.
VERY GOOD SHOWING, JOE. RATINGS INCREASED OVER THE COURSE OF THE MATCH. GREAT JOB OUT THERE!!!
?
MR. PUFF
THE 4'8" (5'0" INCLUDING EARS) OWNER OF S.P.K.O.
CLAP!
CLAP!
NOW THAT YOU'RE DONE, WALK WITH ME.
THANKS FOR NOT LOSING FAITH IN ME, MR. PUFF.
IT'S ABOUT TIME YOU CALLED ME PUFFY, JOE.
WHY ARE WE HERE?
STEP INSIDE.

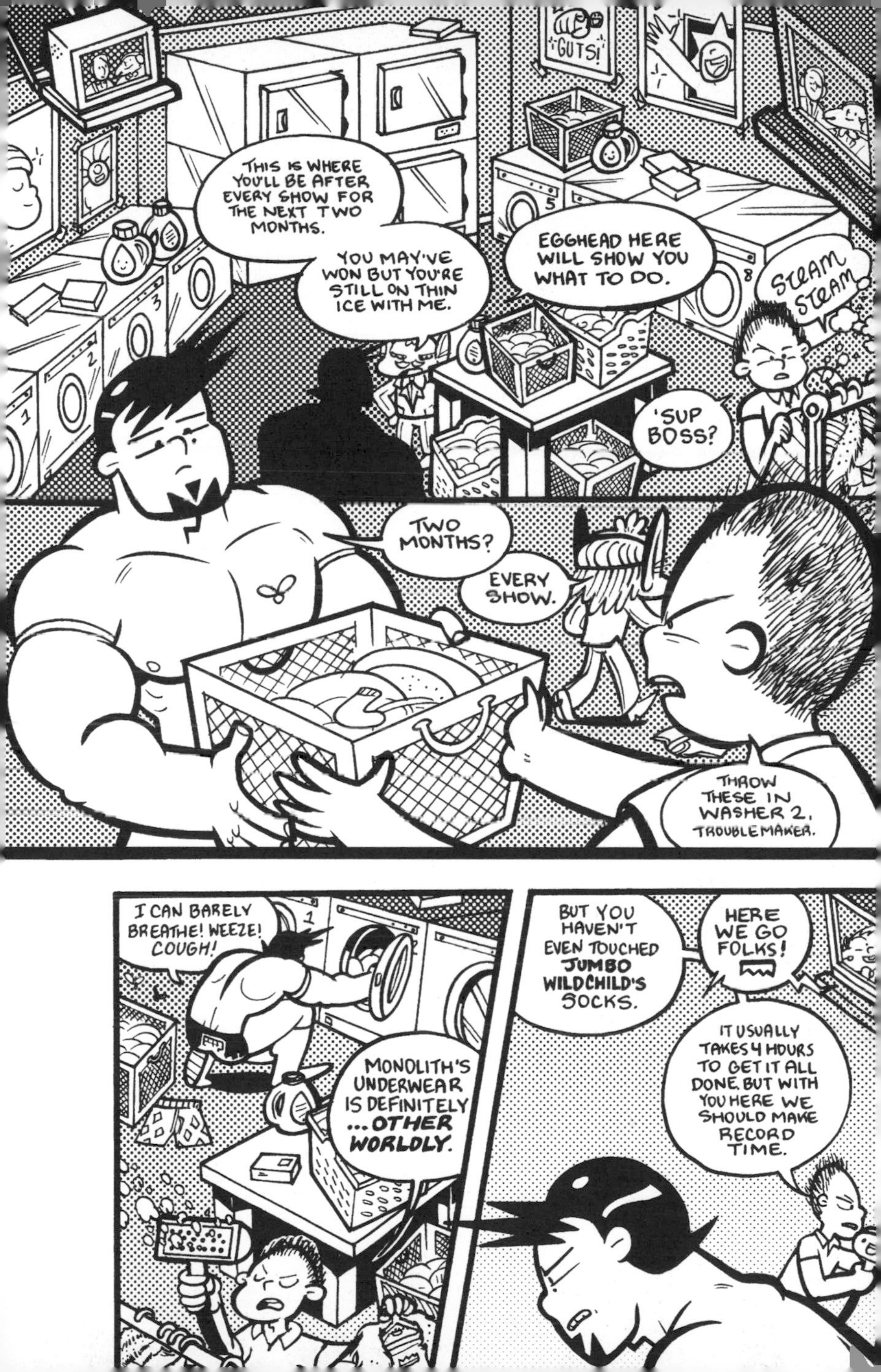
GUTS!
THIS IS WHERE YOU'LL BE AFTER EVERY SHOW FOR THE NEXT TWO MONTHS.
YOU MAY'VE WON BUT YOU'RE STILL ON THIN ICE WITH ME.
EGGHEAD HERE WILL SHOW YOU WHAT TO DO.
STEAM STEAM
'SUP BOSS?
TWO MONTHS?
EVERY SHOW.
THROW THESE IN WASHER 2, TROUBLEMAKER.
I CAN BARELY BREATHE! WEEZE! COUGH!
MONOLITH'S UNDERWEAR IS DEFINITELY ...OTHER WORLDLY.
BUT YOU HAVEN'T EVEN TOUCHED JUMBO WILDCHILD'S SOCKS.
HERE WE GO FOLKS!
IT USUALLY TAKES 4 HOURS TO GET IT ALL DONE, BUT WITH YOU HERE WE SHOULD MAKE RECORD TIME.

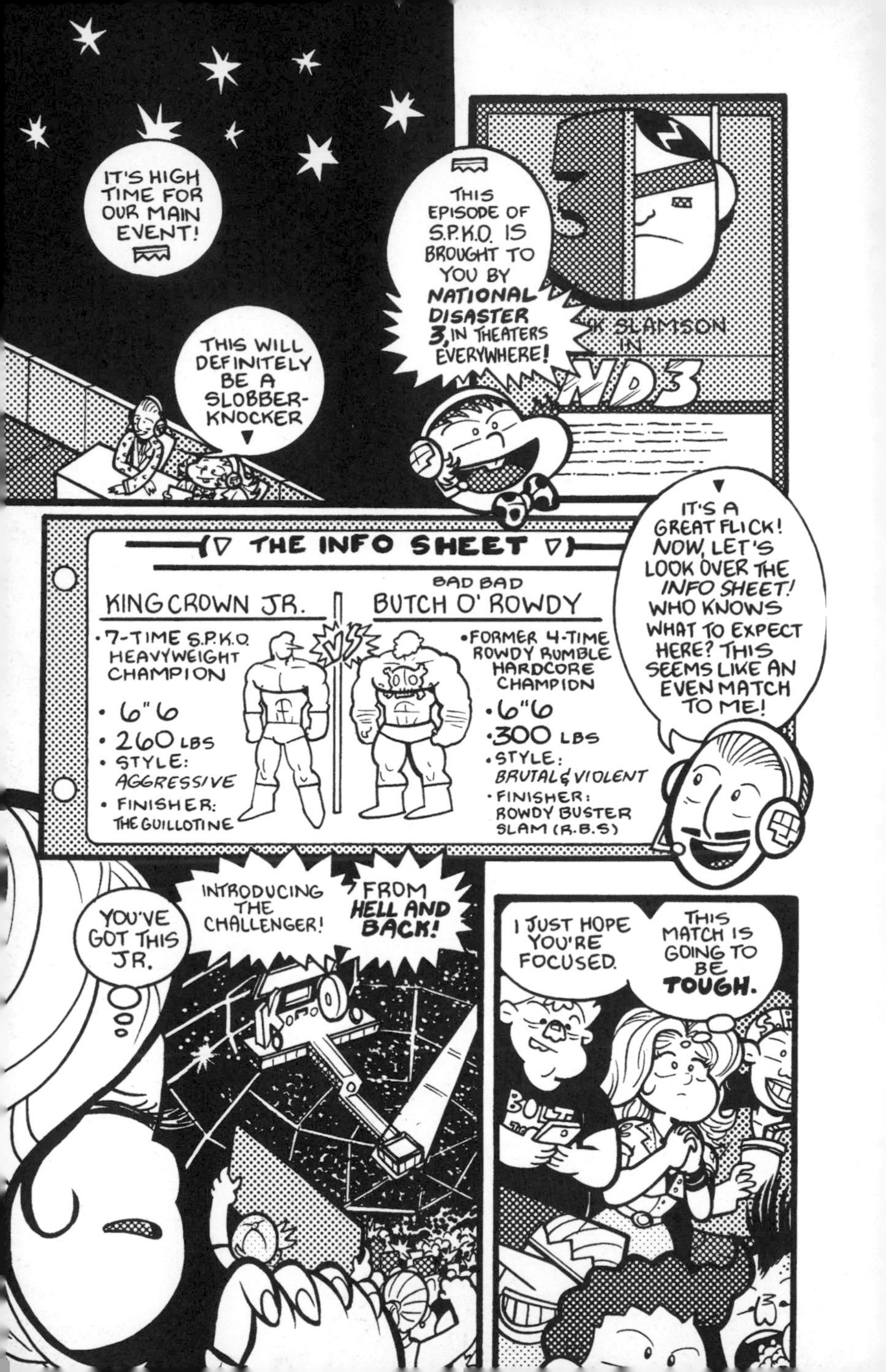
IT'S HIGH TIME FOR OUR MAIN EVENT!
THIS WILL DEFINITELY BE A SLOBBER-KNOCKER
THIS EPISODE OF S.P.K.O. IS BROUGHT TO YOU BY NATIONAL DISASTER 3, IN THEATERS EVERYWHERE!
K SLAMSON IN
ND3
THE INFO SHEET
KINGCROWN JR.
BAD BAD BUTCH O' ROWDY
• 7-TIME S.P.K.O. HEAVYWEIGHT CHAMPION
• 6"6
• 260 LBS
• STYLE: AGGRESSIVE
• FINISHER: THE GUILLOTINE
VS
• FORMER 4-TIME ROWDY RUMBLE HARDCORE CHAMPION
• 6"6
• 300 LBS
• STYLE: BRUTAL & VIOLENT
• FINISHER: ROWDY BUSTER SLAM (R.B.S)
IT'S A GREAT FLICK! NOW, LET'S LOOK OVER THE INFO SHEET! WHO KNOWS WHAT TO EXPECT HERE? THIS SEEMS LIKE AN EVEN MATCH TO ME!
YOU'VE GOT THIS JR.
INTRODUCING THE CHALLENGER!
FROM HELL AND BACK!
I JUST HOPE YOU'RE FOCUSED.
THIS MATCH IS GOING TO BE TOUGH.
BOLT

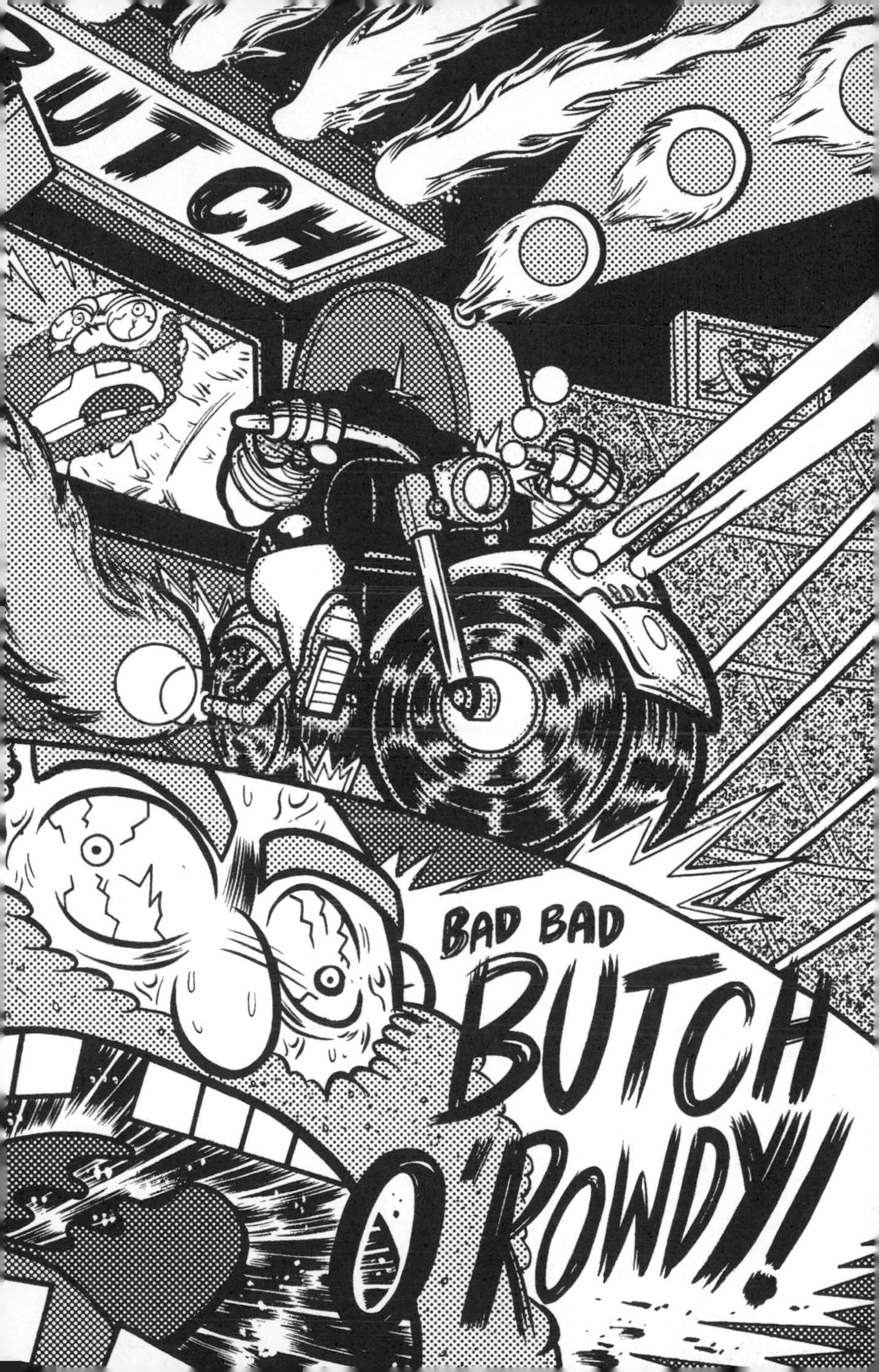
BAD BAD
BUTCH
O'ROWDY!

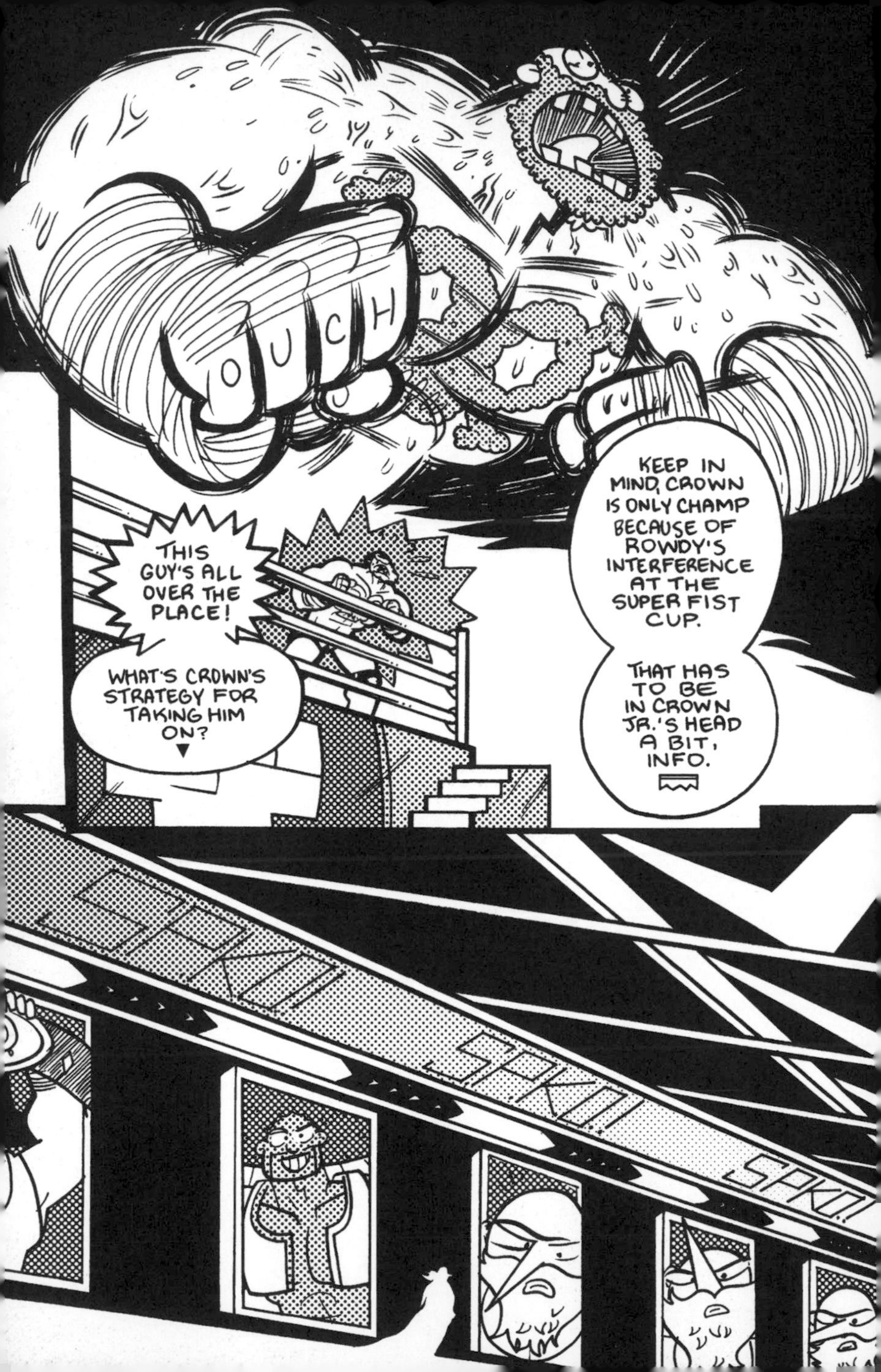
OUCH
THIS GUY'S ALL OVER THE PLACE!
WHAT'S CROWN'S STRATEGY FOR TAKING HIM ON?
KEEP IN MIND, CROWN IS ONLY CHAMP BECAUSE OF ROWDY'S INTERFERENCE AT THE SUPER FIST CUP.
THAT HAS TO BE IN CROWN JR.'S HEAD A BIT, INFO.
SPKO!!
SPKO!!
SPKO!!

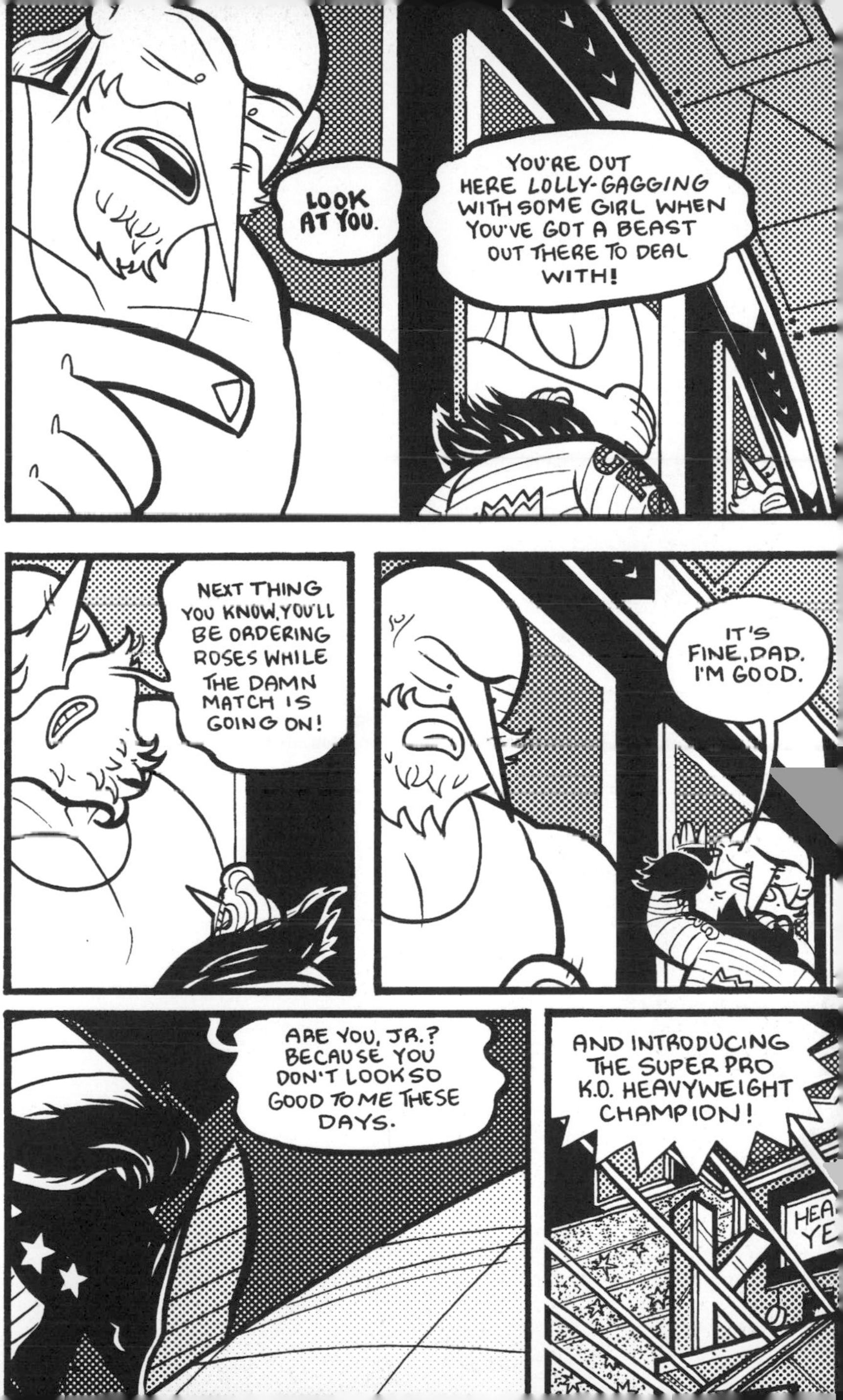
LOOK AT YOU.
YOU'RE OUT HERE LOLLY-GAGGING WITH SOME GIRL WHEN YOU'VE GOT A BEAST OUT THERE TO DEAL WITH!
NEXT THING YOU KNOW, YOU'LL BE ORDERING ROSES WHILE THE DAMN MATCH IS GOING ON!
IT'S FINE, DAD. I'M GOOD.
ARE YOU, JR.? BECAUSE YOU DON'T LOOK SO GOOD TO ME THESE DAYS.
AND INTRODUCING THE SUPER PRO K.O. HEAVYWEIGHT CHAMPION!

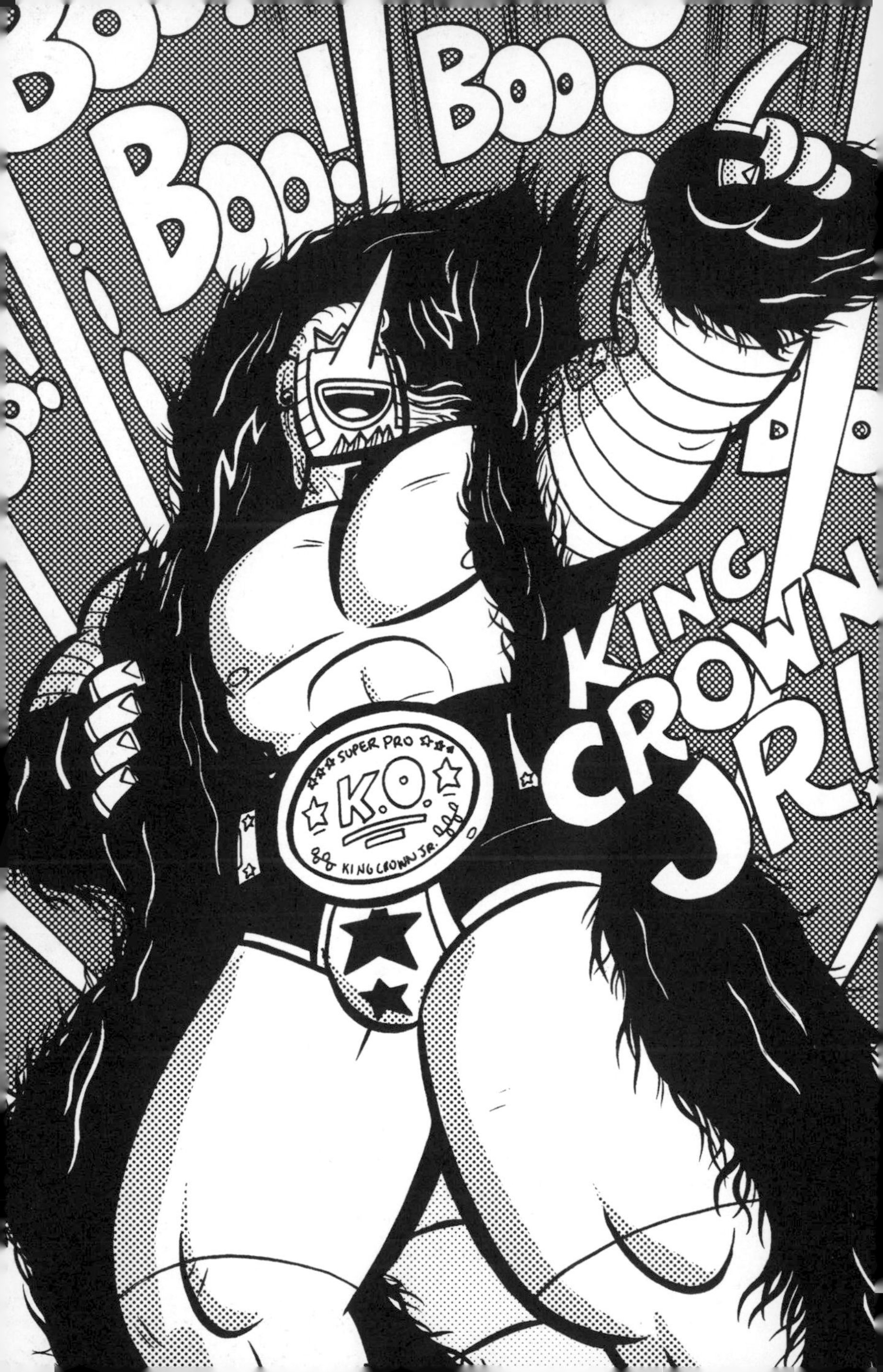
BOO!
BOO!!
BOO...
BOO!
KING CROWN JR!
SUPER PRO
K.O.
KING CROWN JR.

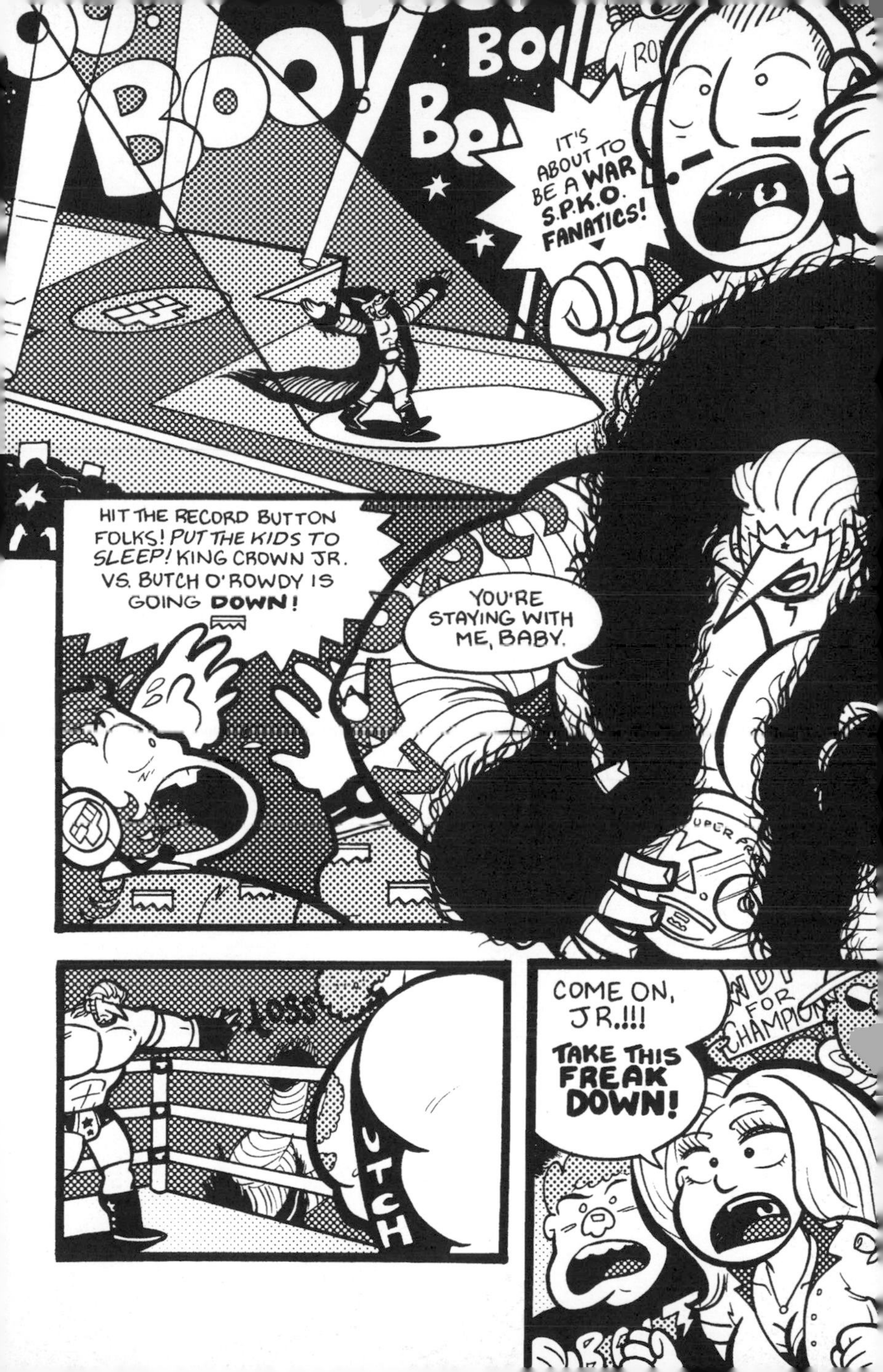
BOO!
IT'S ABOUT TO BE A WAR S.P.K.O. FANATICS!
HIT THE RECORD BUTTON FOLKS! PUT THE KIDS TO SLEEP! KING CROWN JR. VS. BUTCH O'ROWDY IS GOING DOWN!
YOU'RE STAYING WITH ME, BABY.
COME ON, JR.!!!
TAKE THIS FREAK DOWN!

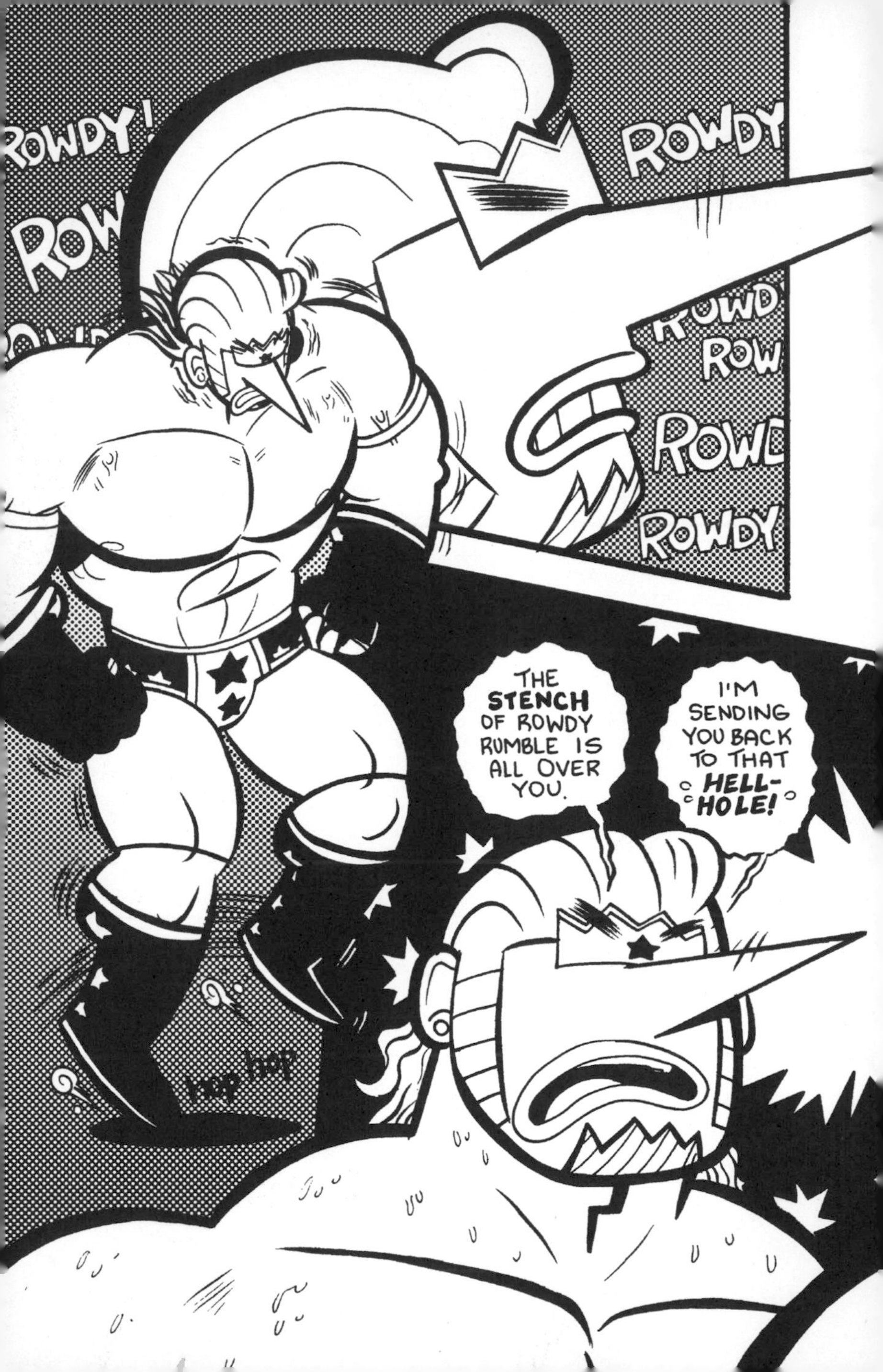
ROWDY!
ROW
ROWDY
ROWD
ROW
ROWD
ROWDY
THE **STENCH** OF ROWDY RUMBLE IS ALL OVER YOU.
I'M SENDING YOU BACK TO THAT ***HELL-HOLE!***
hop hop

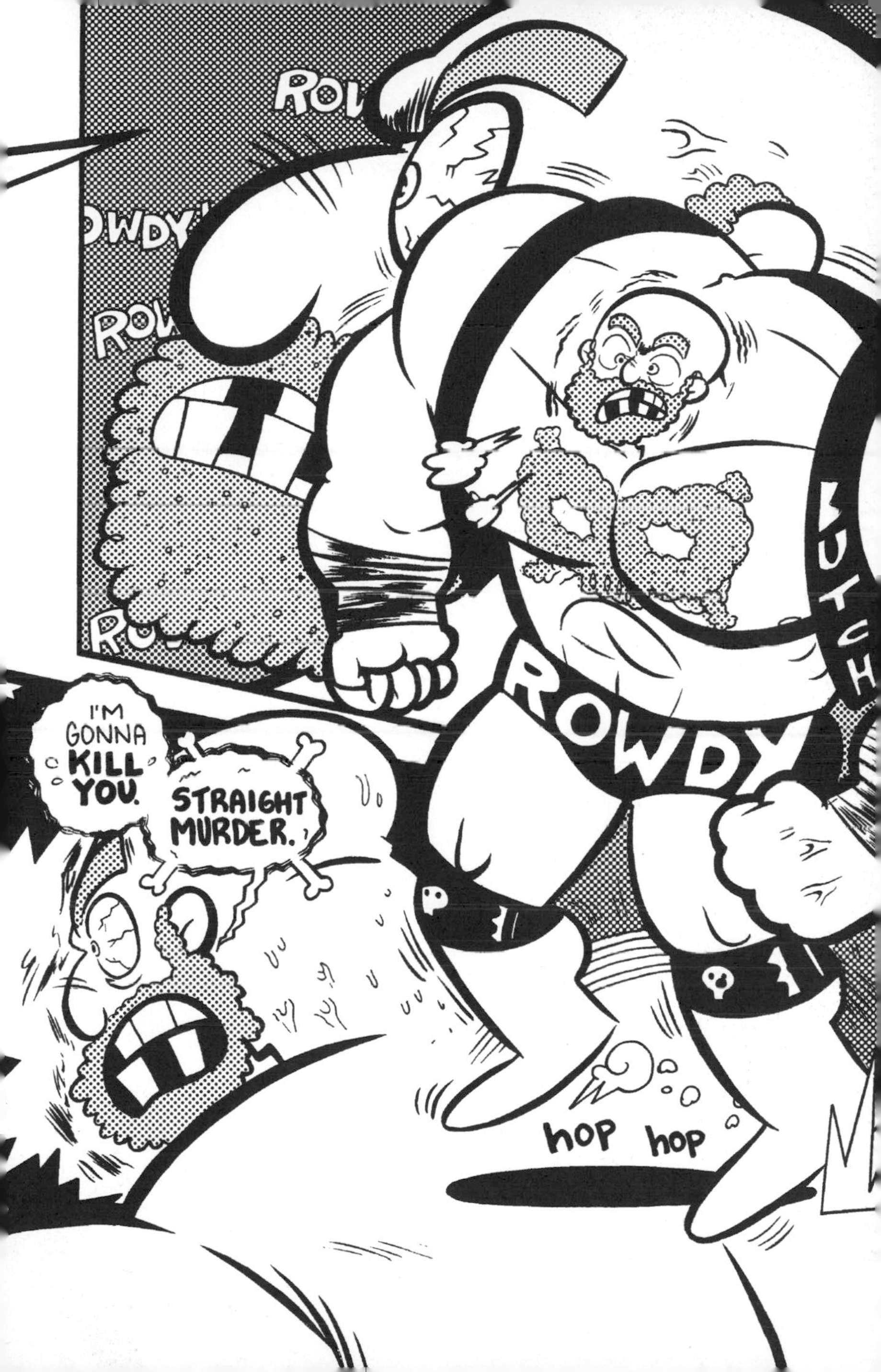
I'M GONNA KILL YOU.
STRAIGHT MURDER.
ROWDY
hop hop

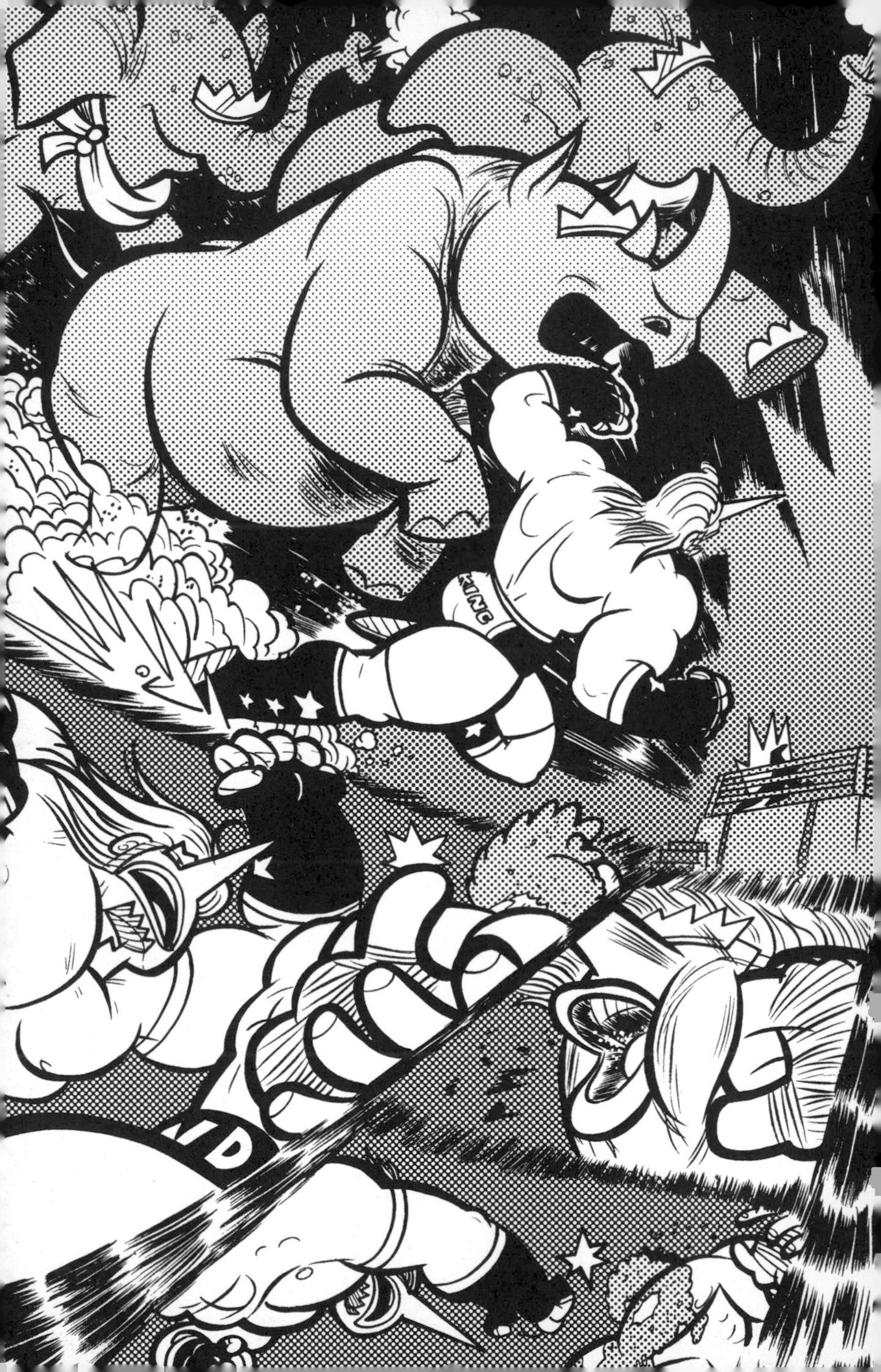

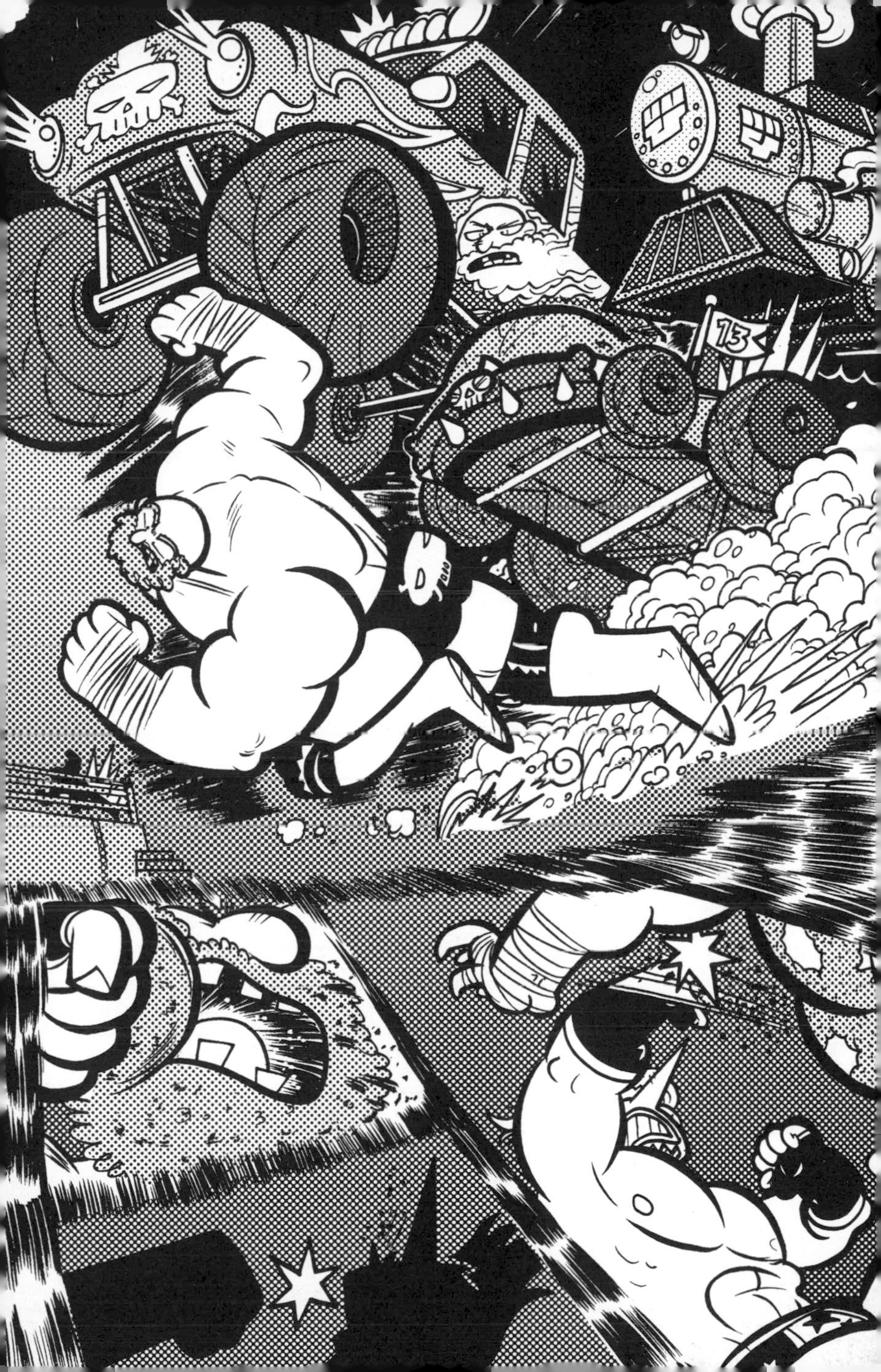
13

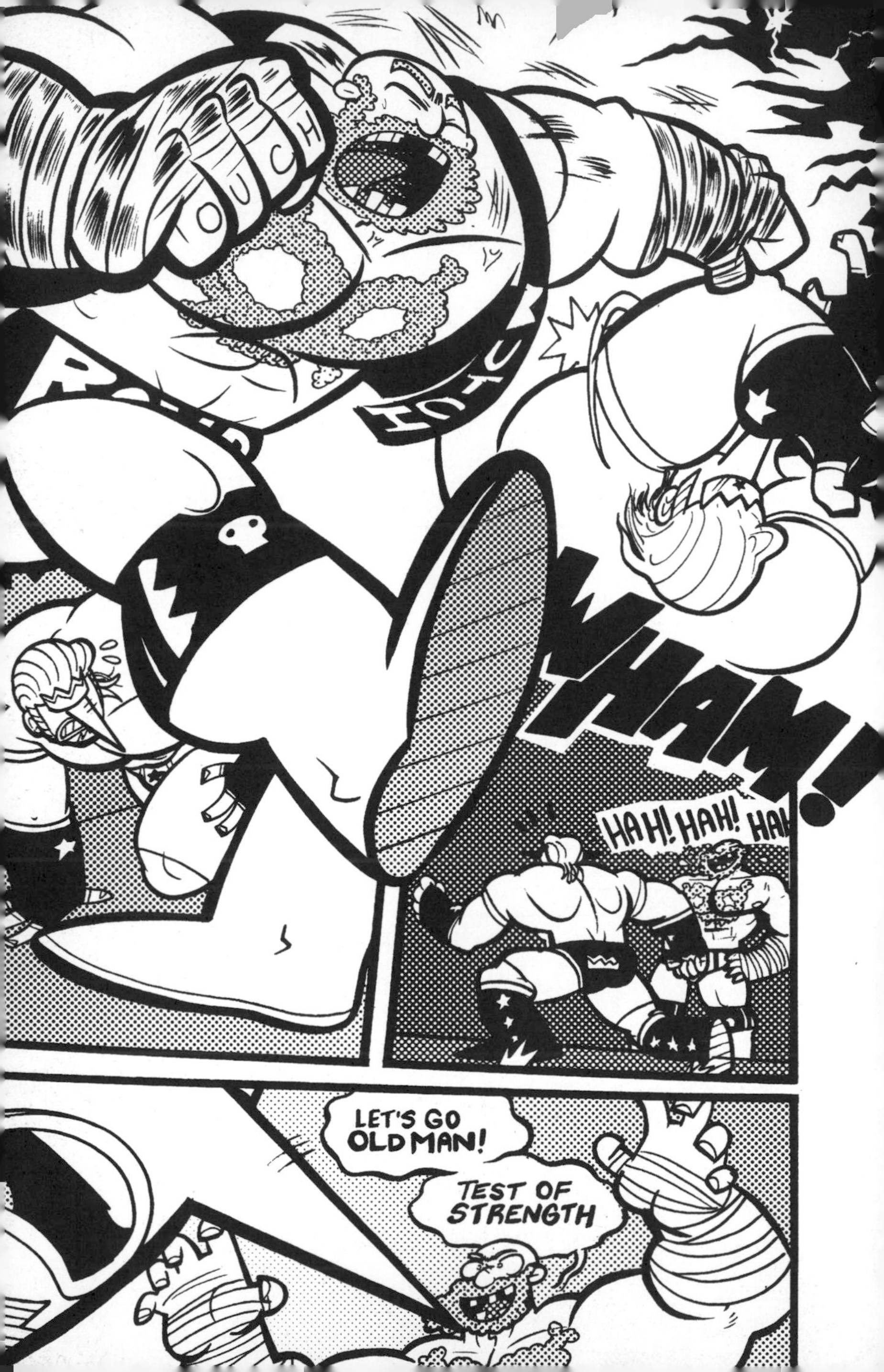

OUCH
TOUCH
WHAM!!
HAH! HAH! HAH
LET'S GO OLD MAN!
TEST OF STRENGTH

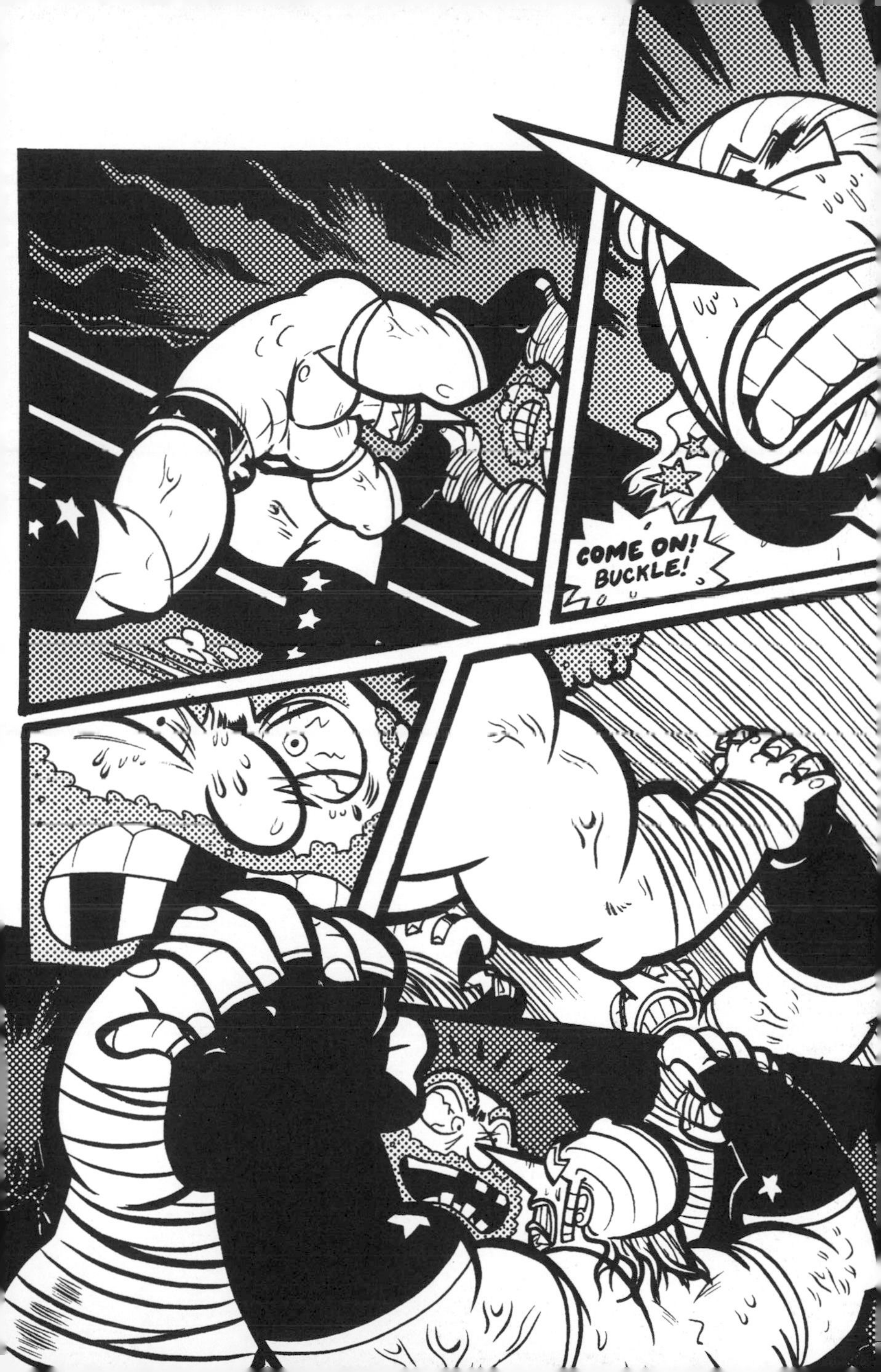
COME ON! BUCKLE!

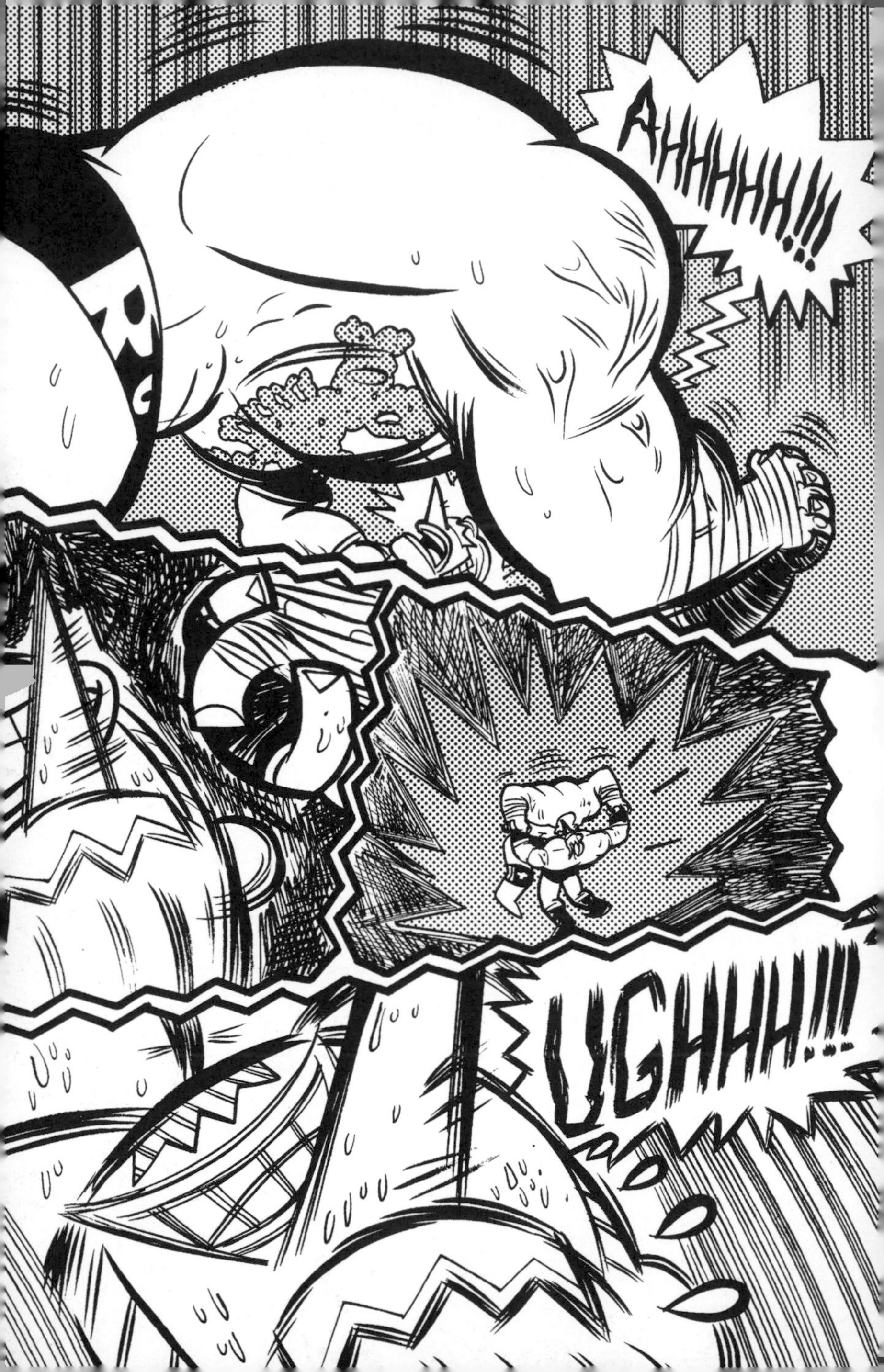
AHHHHH!!!!
UGHHH!!!

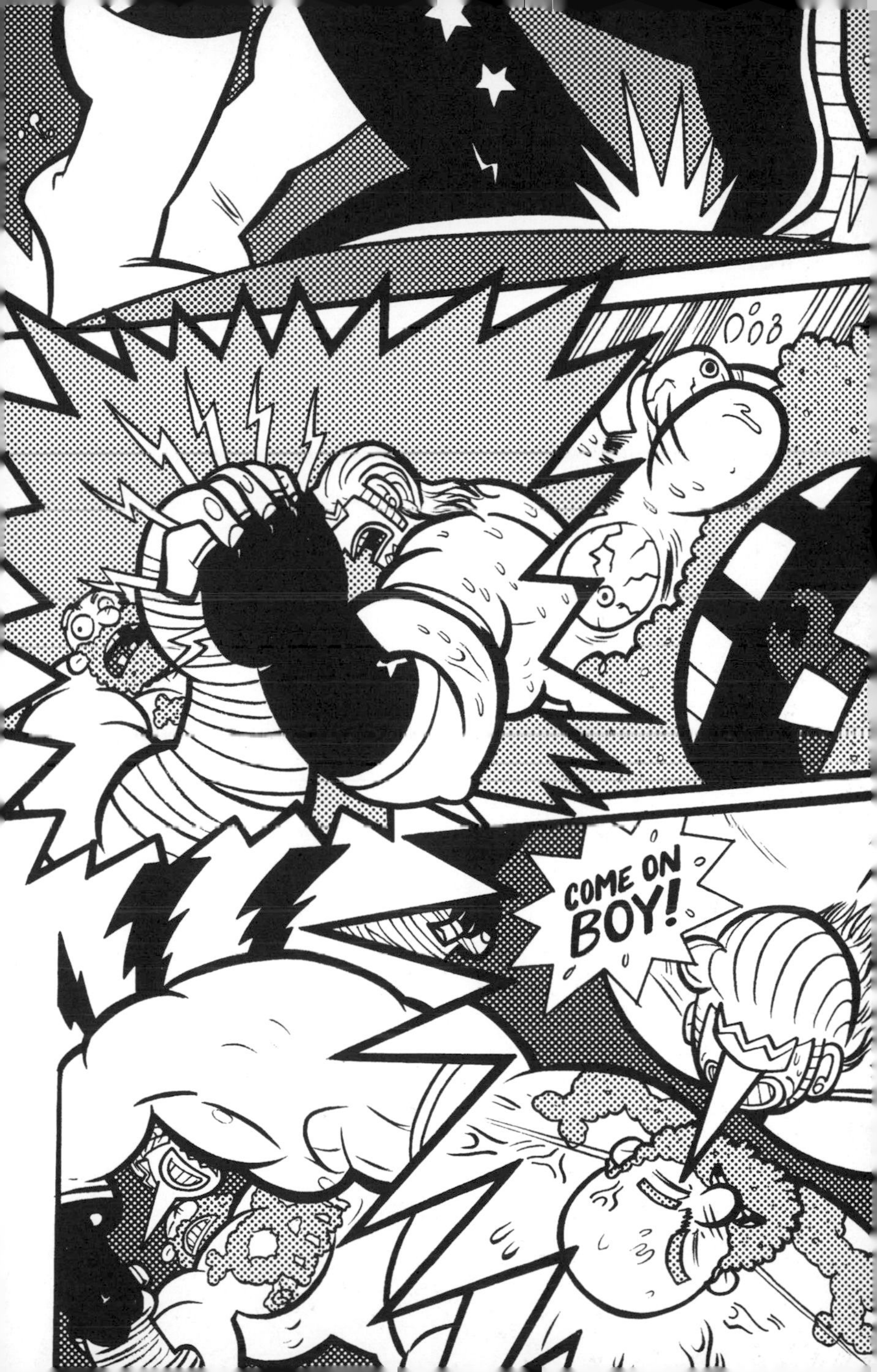
OOF
COME ON BOY!

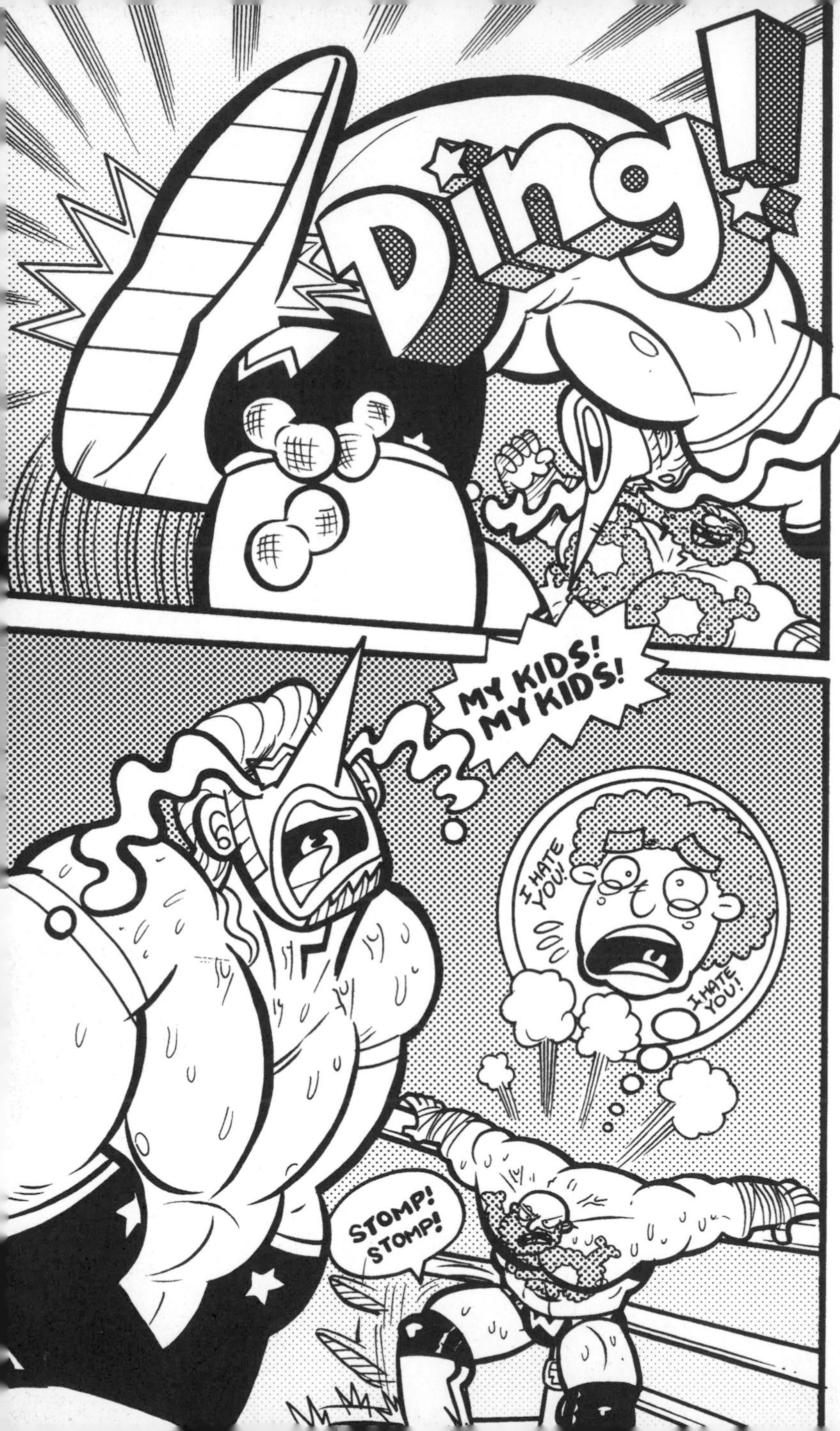
Ding!
MY KIDS! MY KIDS!
I HATE YOU!
I HATE YOU!
STOMP! STOMP!

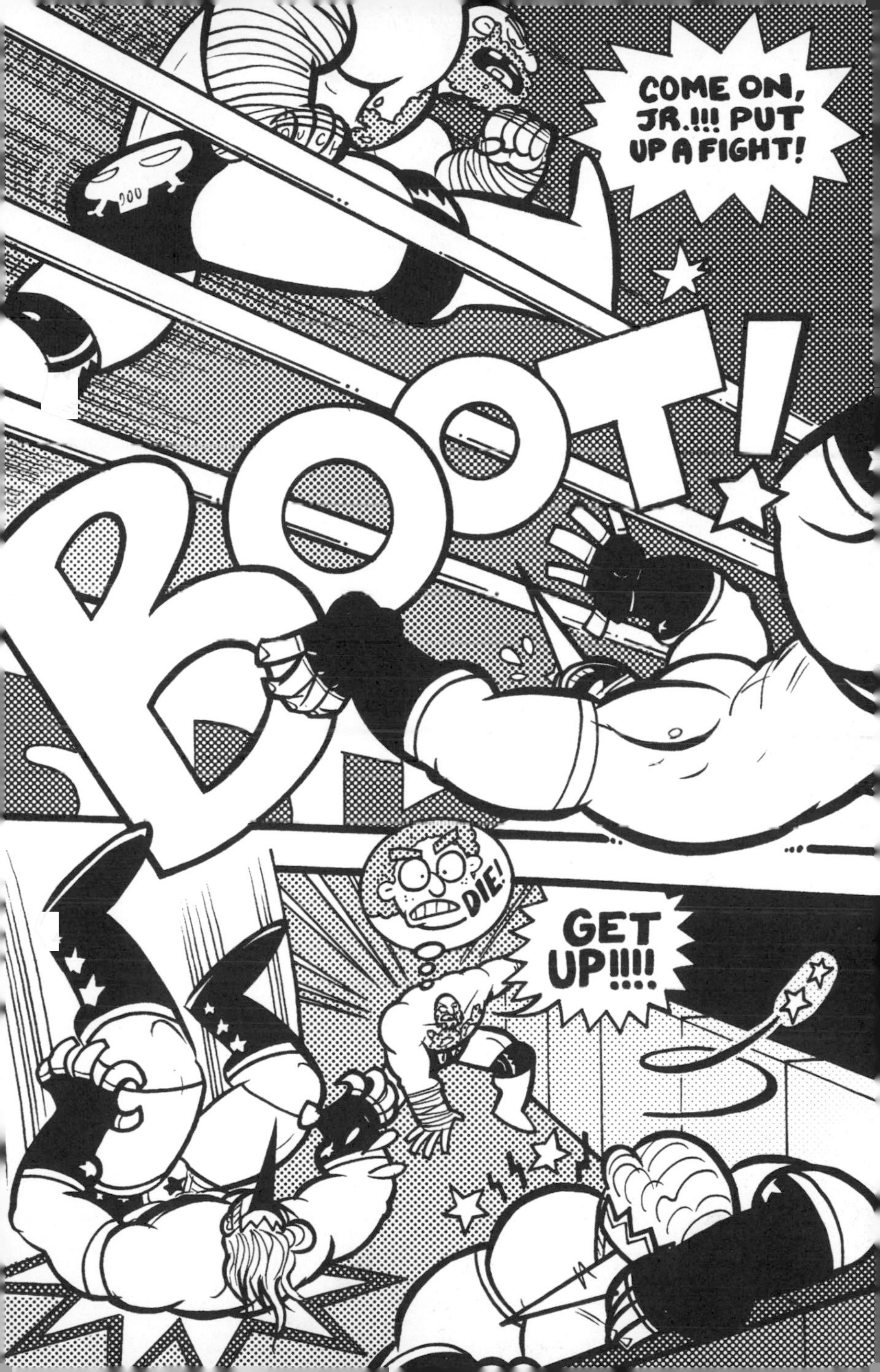
COME ON, JR.!!! PUT UP A FIGHT!
BOOT!
DIE!
GET UP!!!!

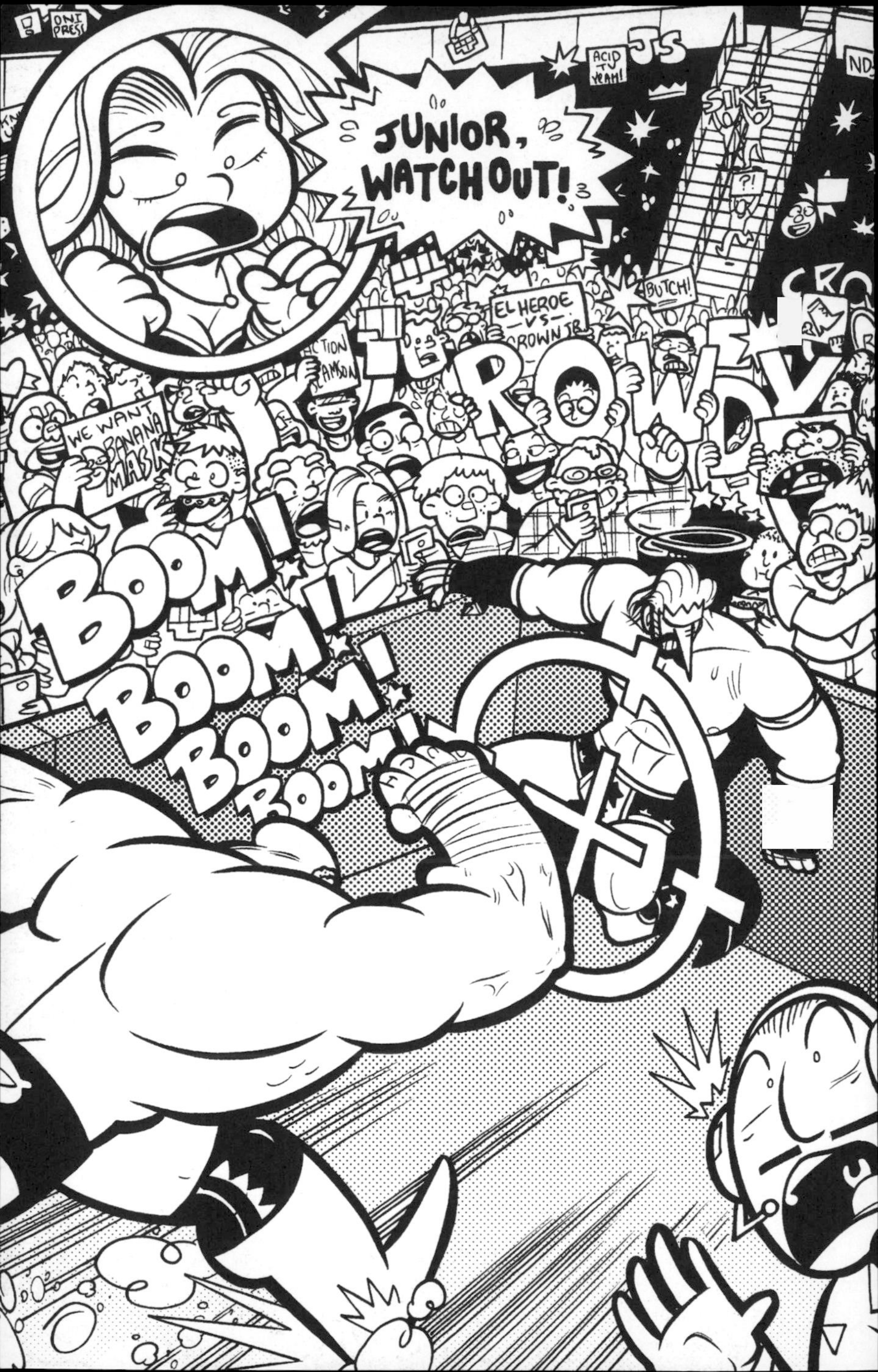
JUNIOR, WATCH OUT!
ONI PRESS
ACID TV TEAM!
BUTCH!
EL HEROE -VS- CROWN JR.
WE WANT BANANA MASK
ROWDY
BOOM!! BOOM! BOOM! BOOM!

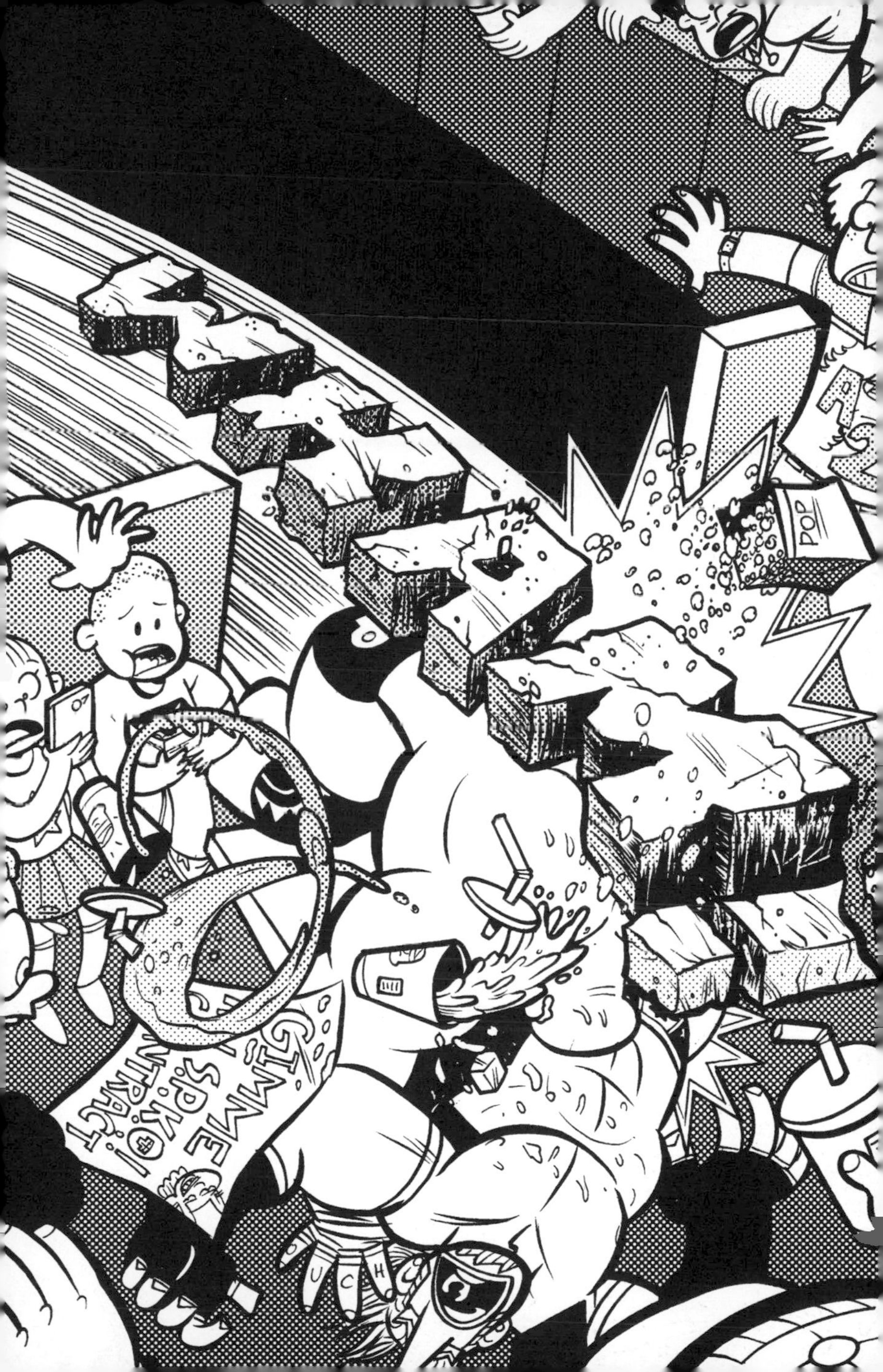
POP
GIMME SPIKO!
NTRACT
OUCH

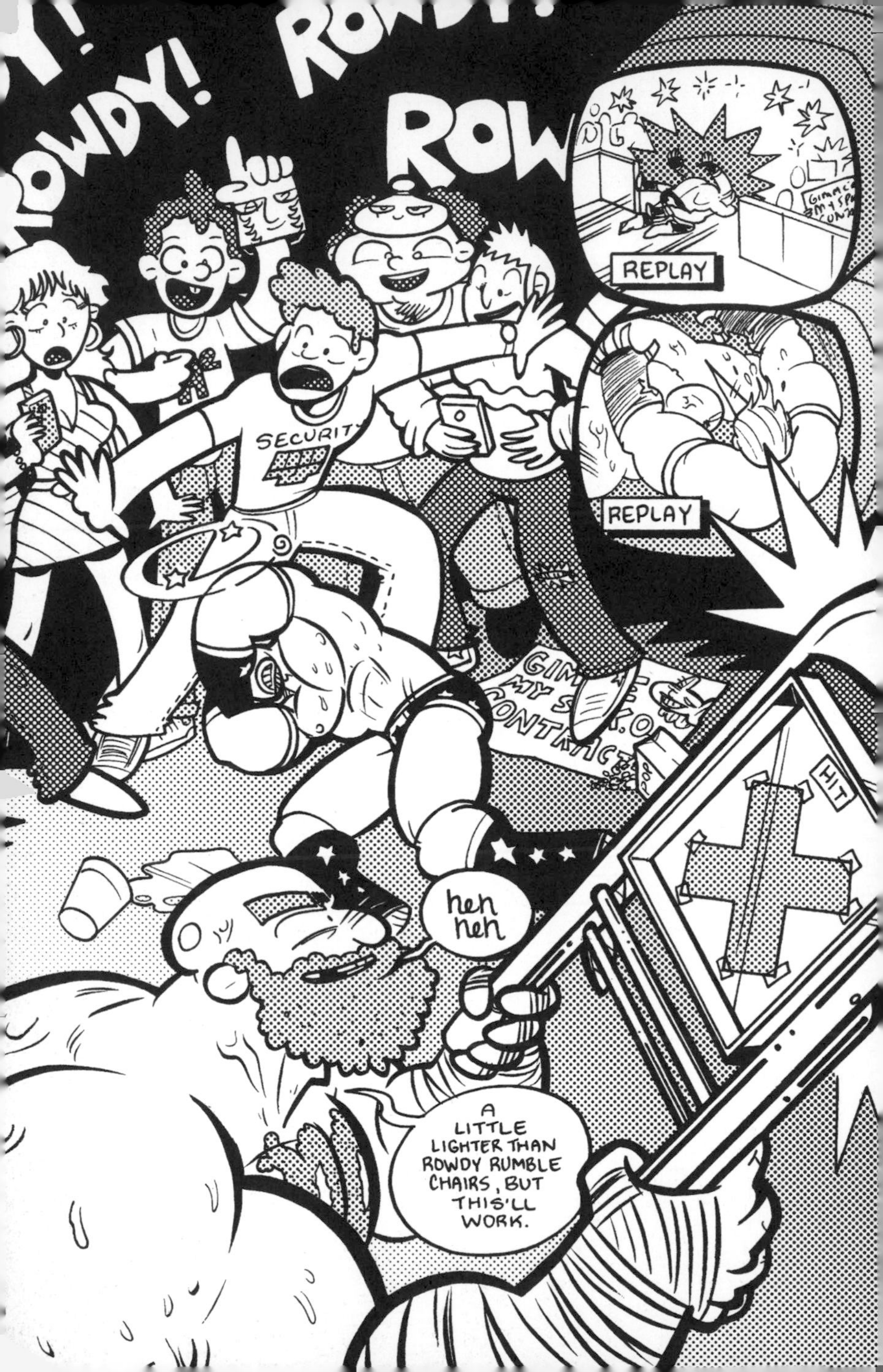
ROWDY!
ROW
REPLAY
SECURITY
REPLAY
HIT
heh neh
A LITTLE LIGHTER THAN ROWDY RUMBLE CHAIRS, BUT THIS'LL WORK.

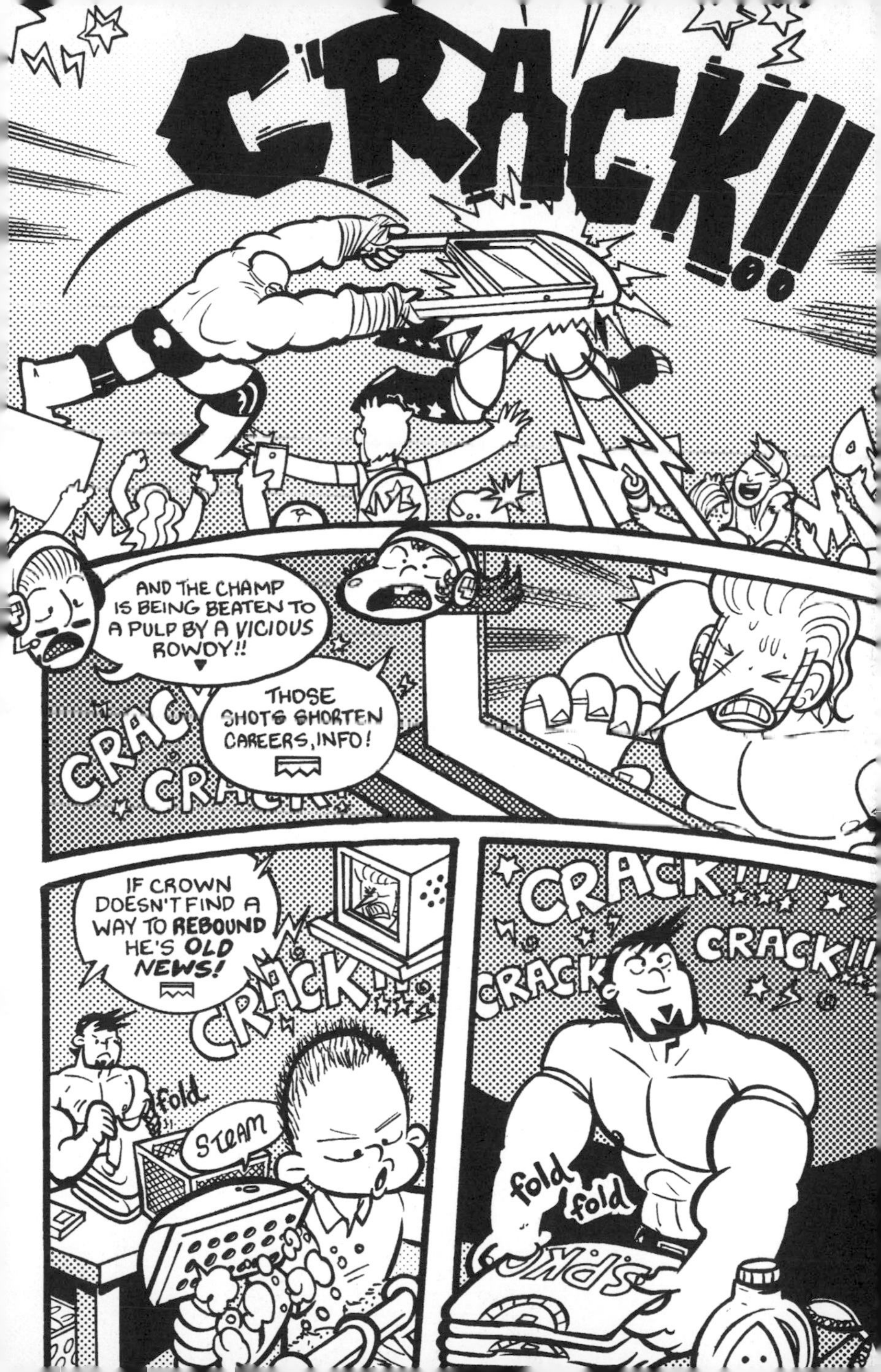
CRACK!!
AND THE CHAMP IS BEING BEATEN TO A PULP BY A VICIOUS ROWDY!!
THOSE SHOTS SHORTEN CAREERS, INFO!
IF CROWN DOESN'T FIND A WAY TO REBOUND HE'S OLD NEWS!
CRACK!!
fold
STEAM
CRACK!!!
CRACK
CRACK!!
fold
fold

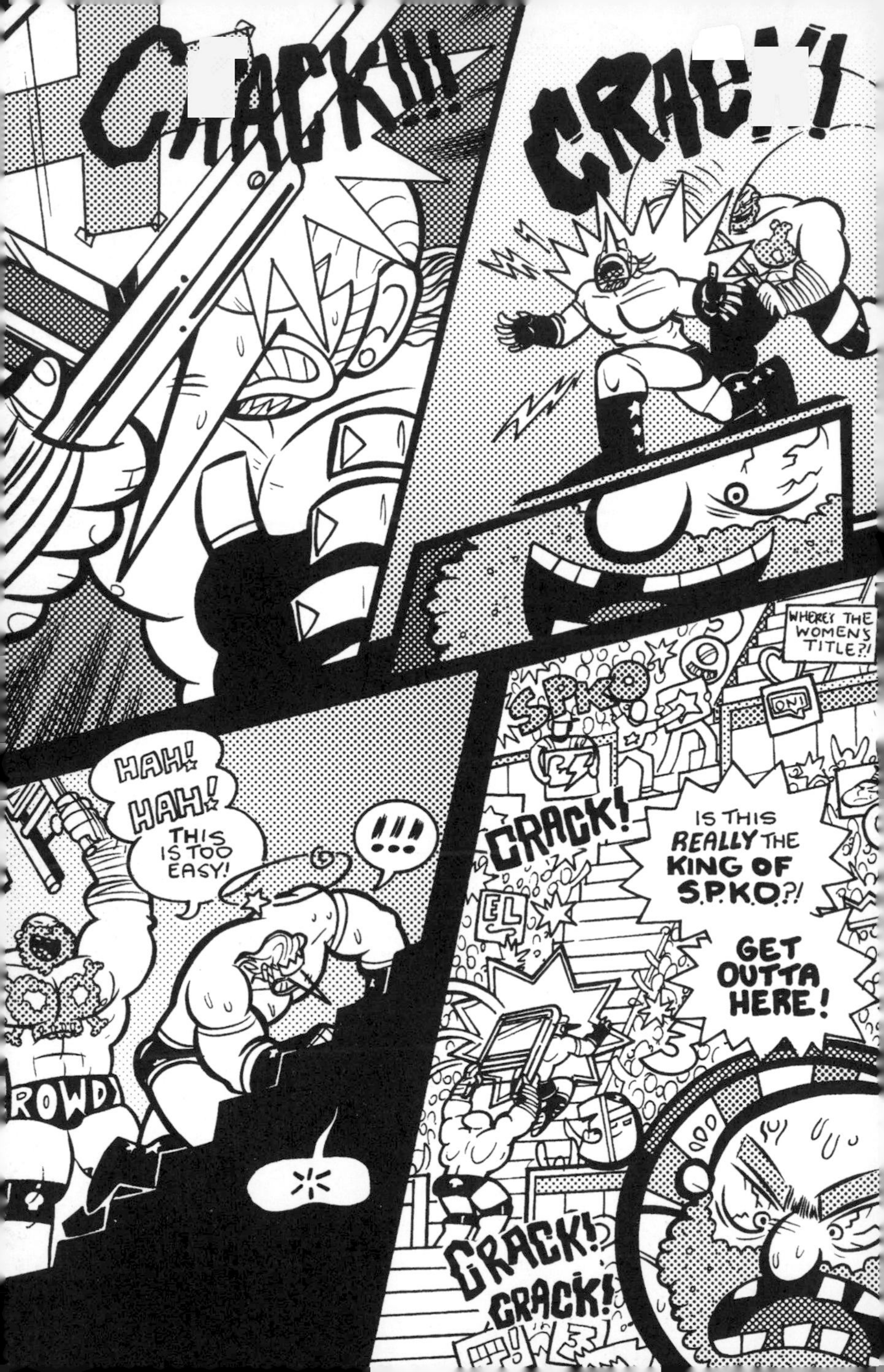
HAH! HAH! THIS IS TOO EASY!
!!!
WHERE'S THE WOMEN'S TITLE?!
SPKO
ON!
CRACK!
EL
IS THIS REALLY THE KING OF S.P.K.O?!
GET OUTTA HERE!
CRACK!
CRACK!

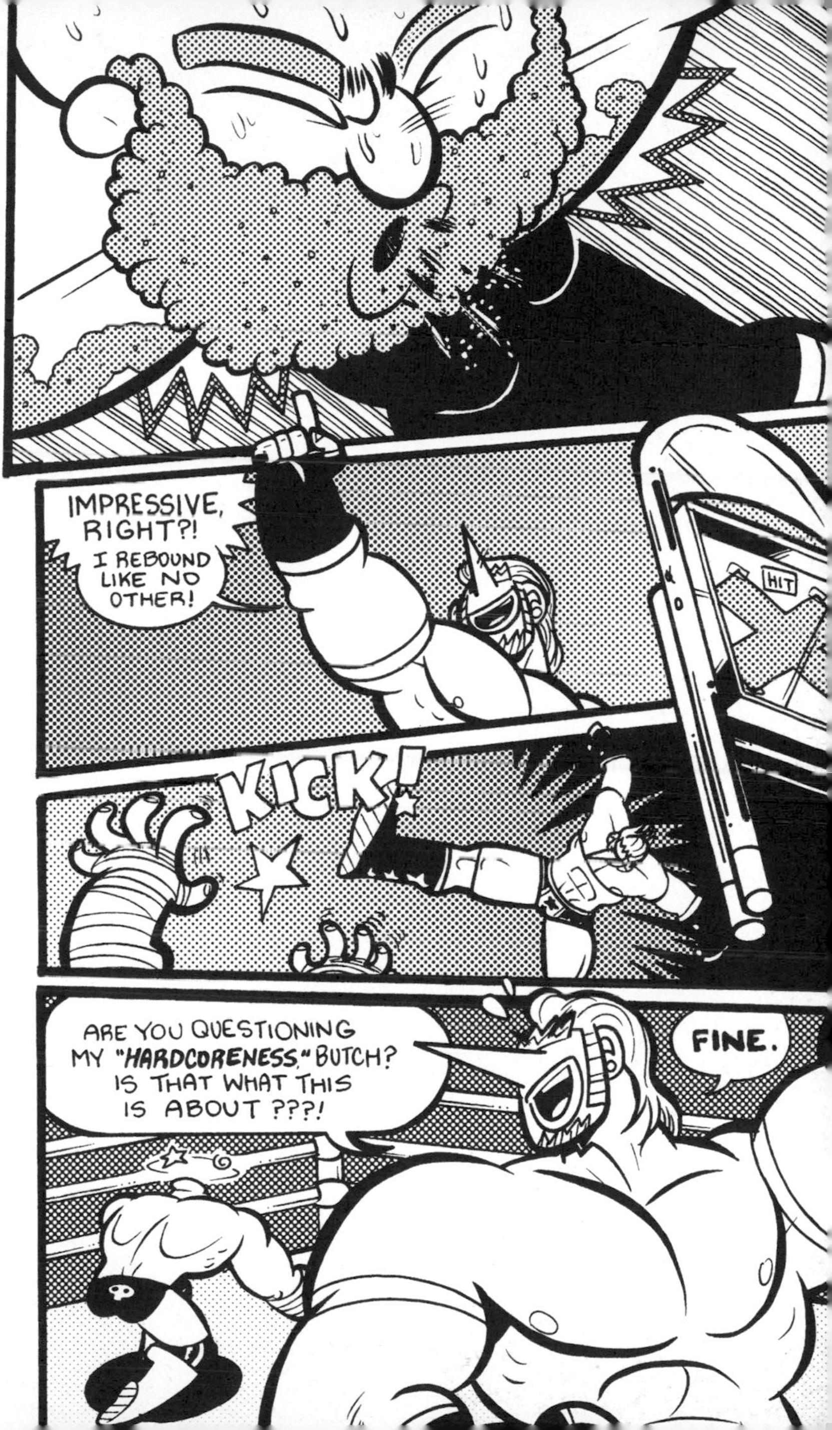
IMPRESSIVE, RIGHT?!
I REBOUND LIKE NO OTHER!
HIT
KICK!
ARE YOU QUESTIONING MY "HARDCORENESS," BUTCH? IS THAT WHAT THIS IS ABOUT ???!
FINE.

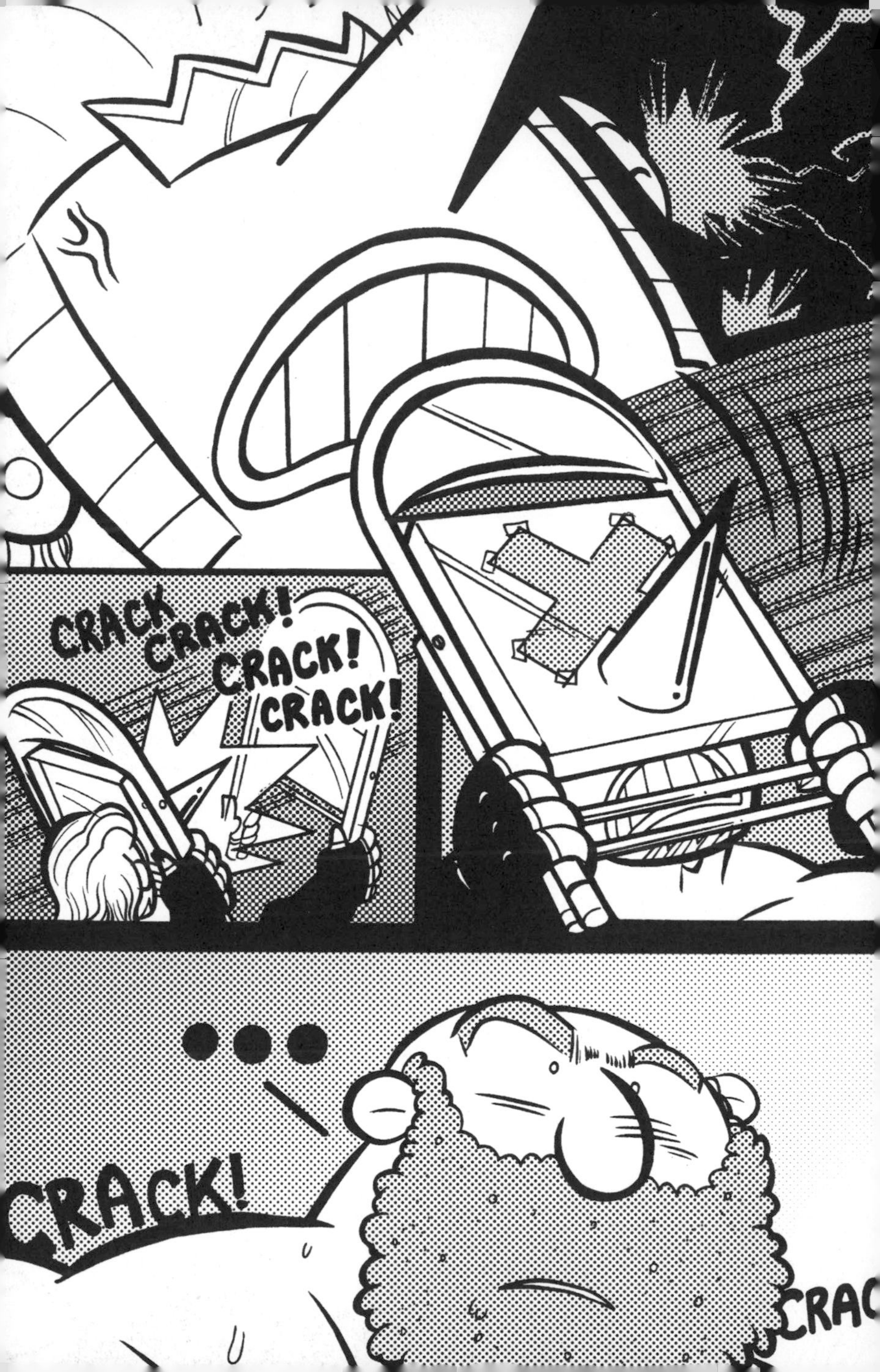
CRACK
CRACK!
CRACK!
CRACK!
•••
CRACK!
CRAC

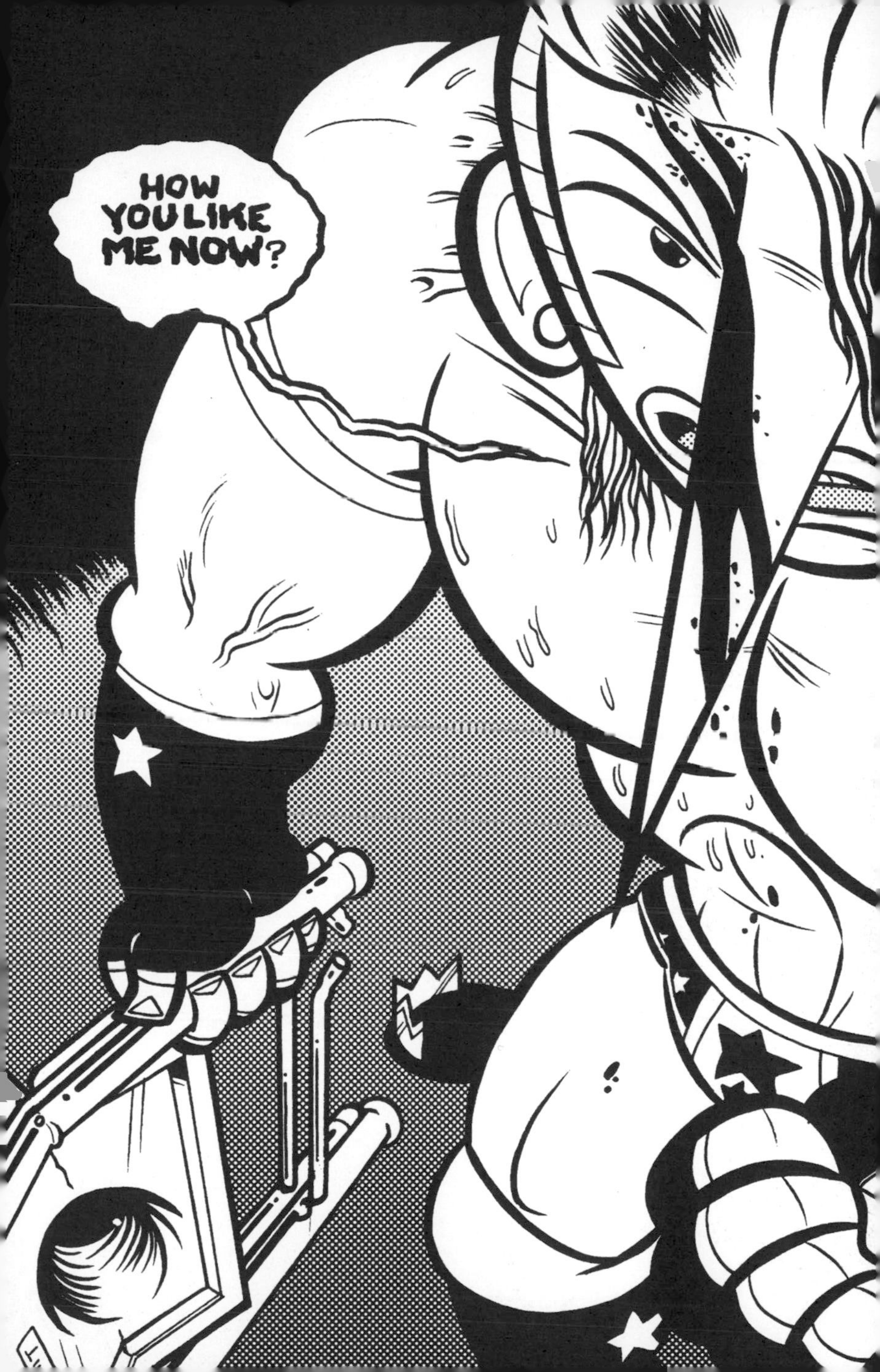
HOW YOU LIKE ME NOW?

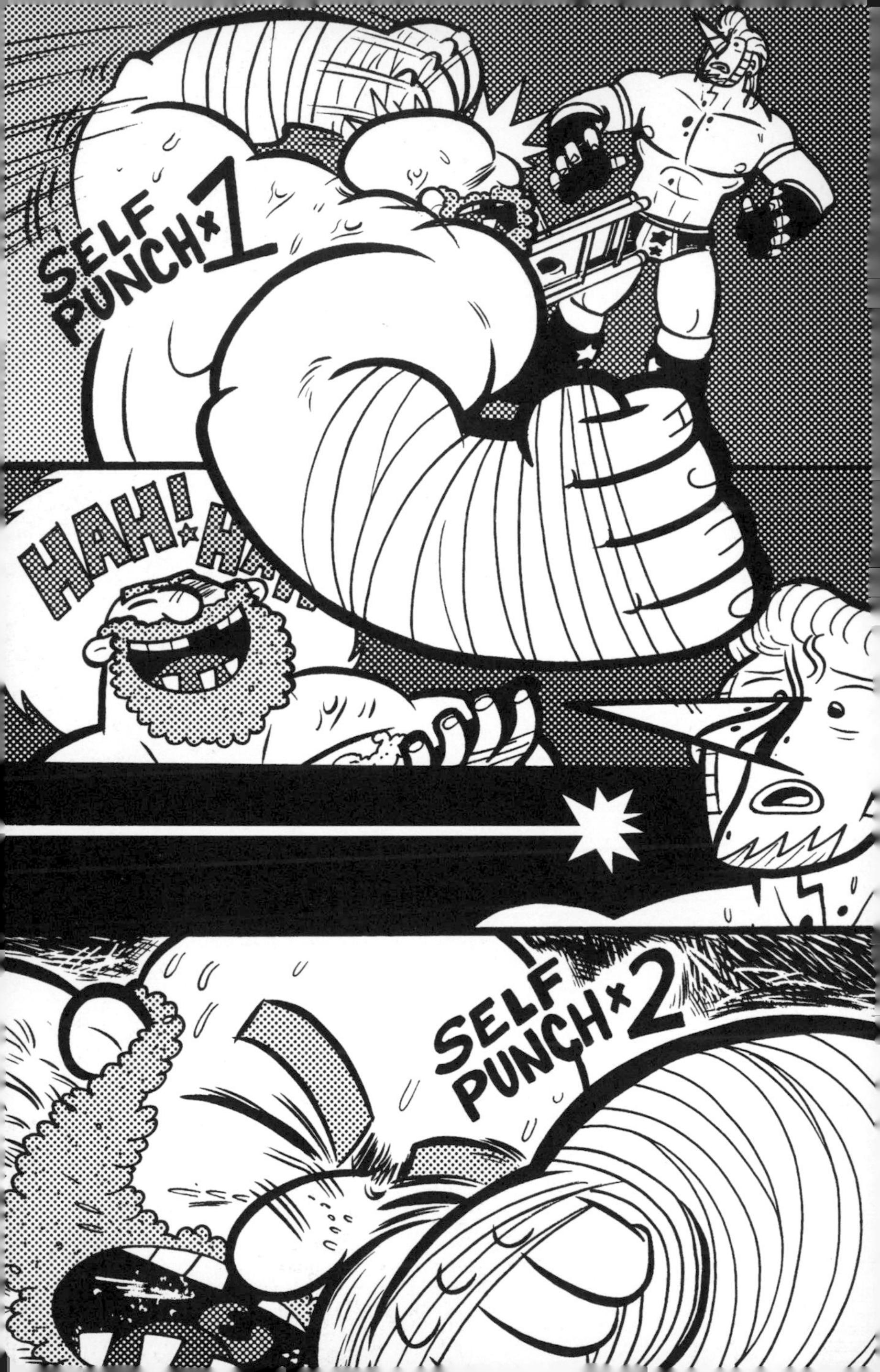
SELF PUNCH×1
HAH!★HAH
SELF PUNCH×2

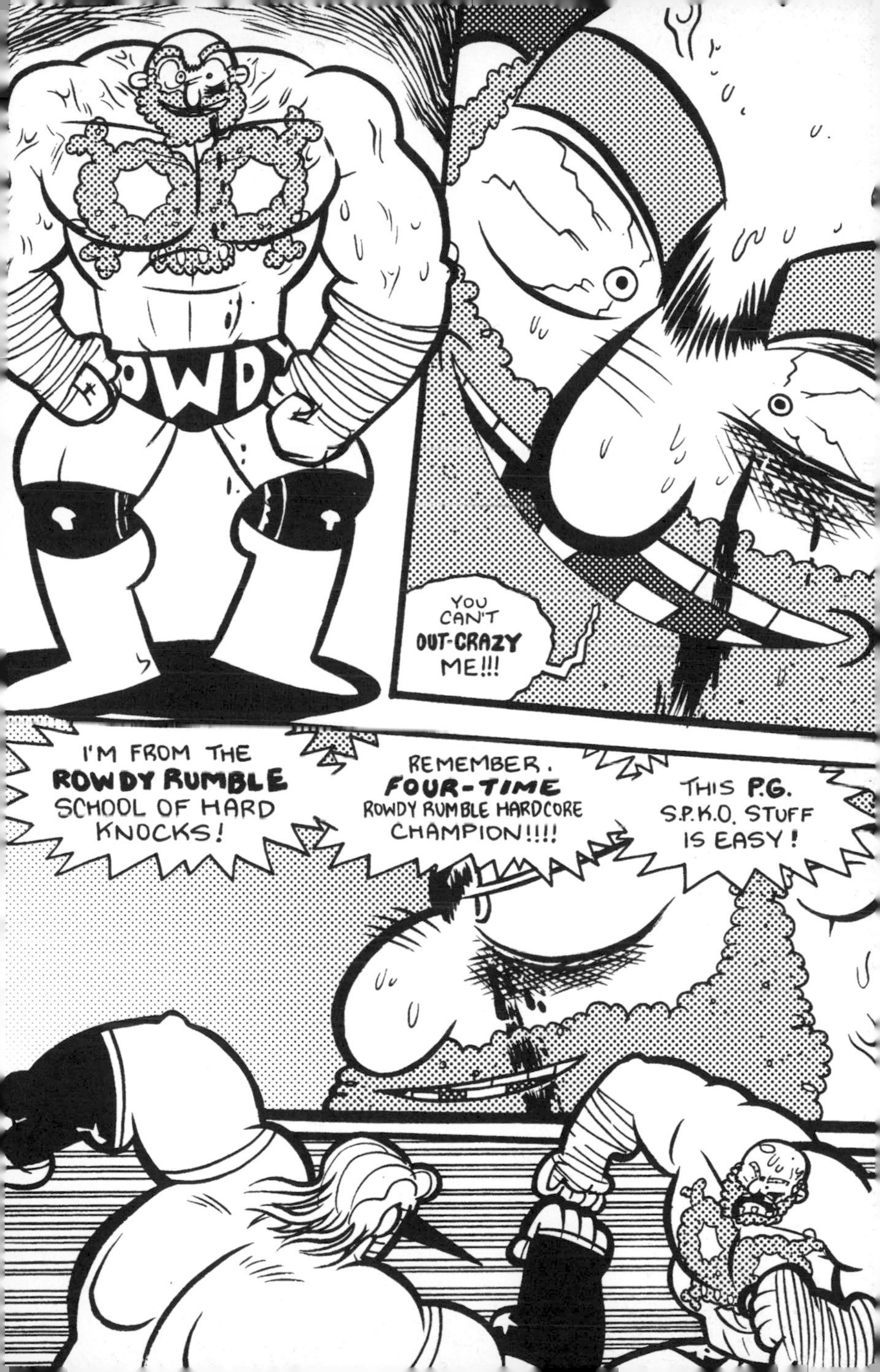
OWD
YOU CAN'T OUT-CRAZY ME!!!
I'M FROM THE ROWDY RUMBLE SCHOOL OF HARD KNOCKS!
REMEMBER. FOUR-TIME ROWDY RUMBLE HARDCORE CHAMPION!!!!
THIS P.G. S.P.K.O. STUFF IS EASY!

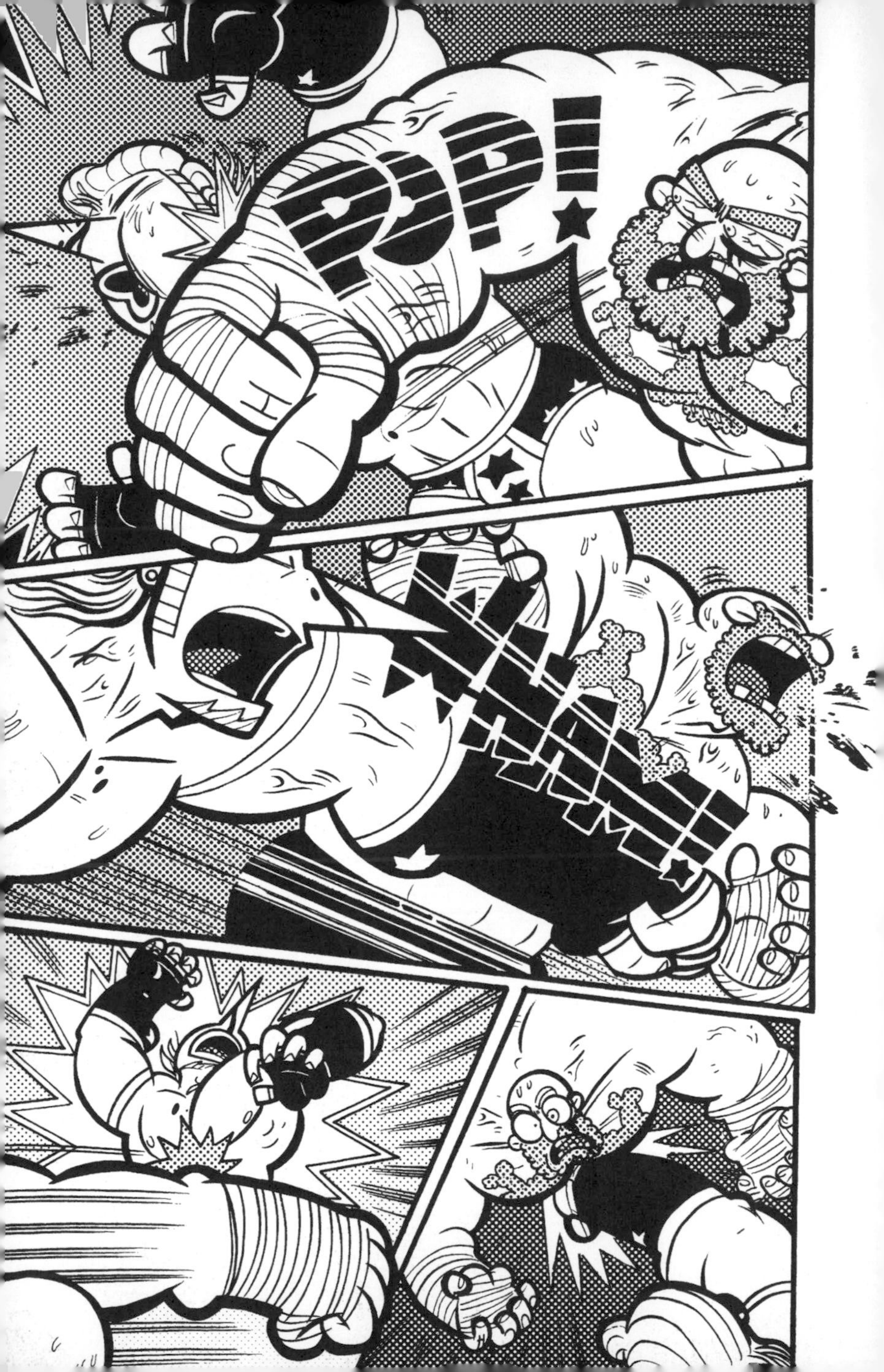
POP!

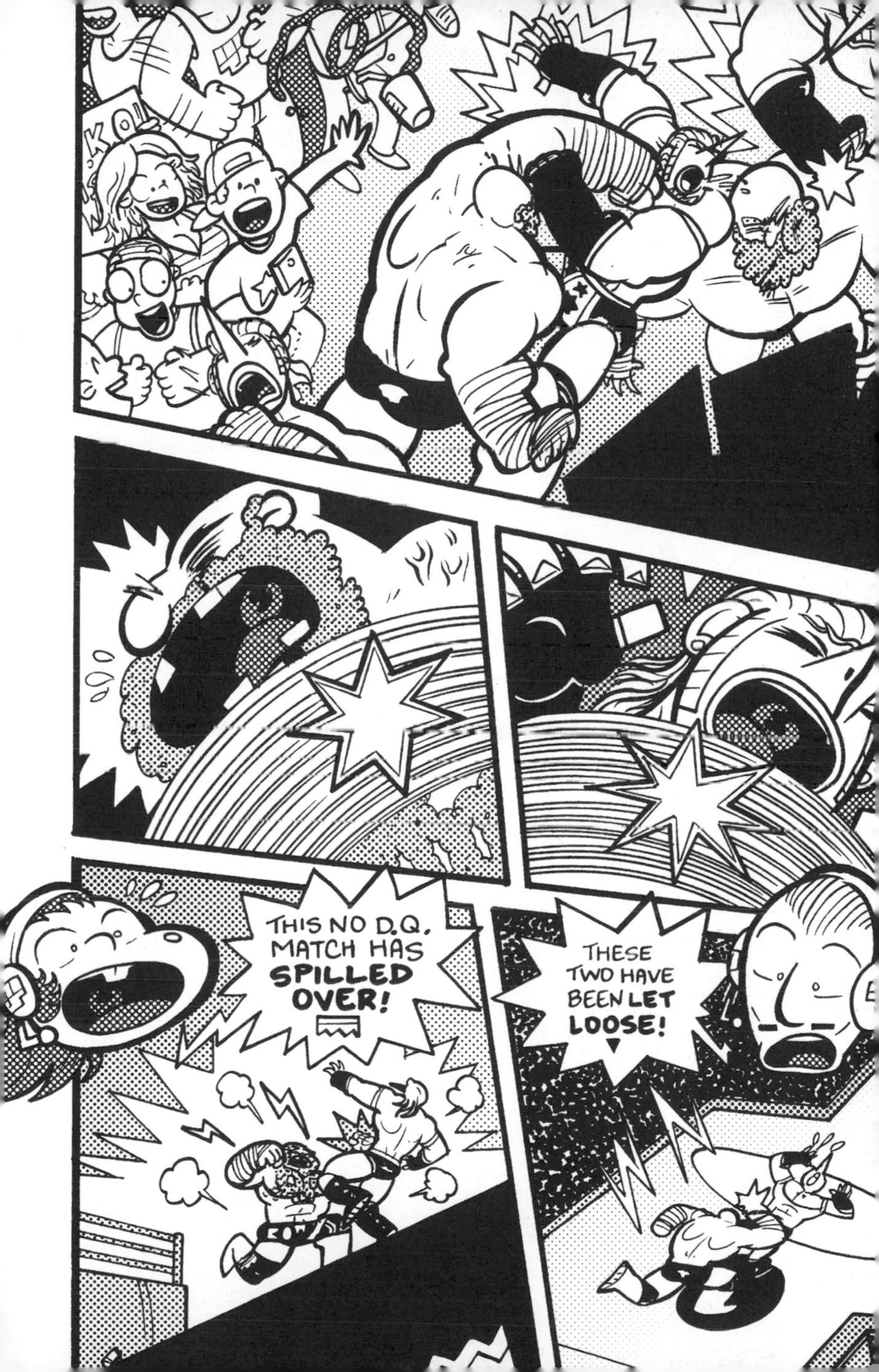
THIS NO D.Q. MATCH HAS **SPILLED OVER!**
THESE TWO HAVE BEEN **LET LOOSE!**

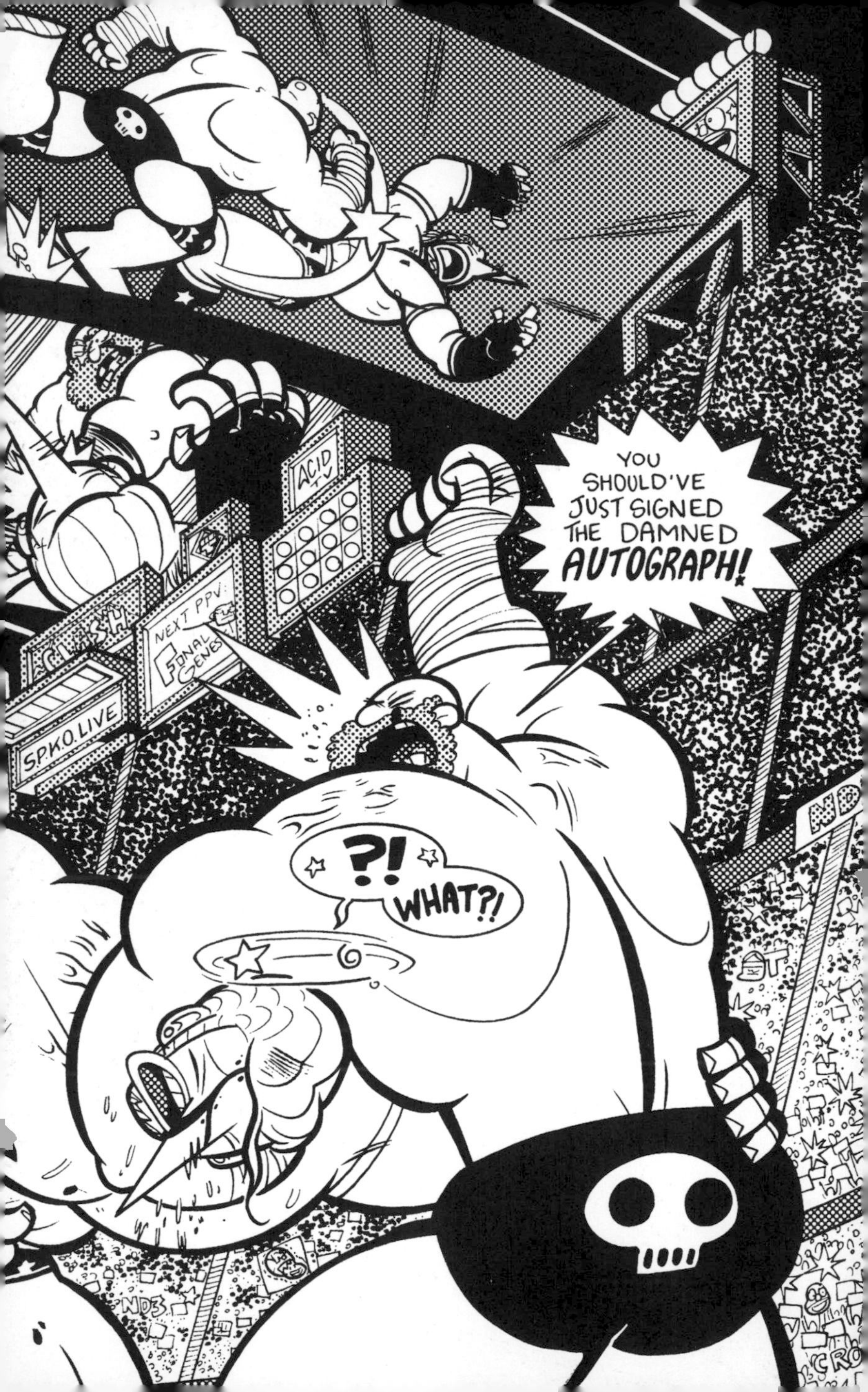
ACID TV
NEXT PPV: Fonal Genes
S.P.K.O. LIVE
YOU SHOULD'VE JUST SIGNED THE DAMNED AUTOGRAPH!
?!
WHAT?!

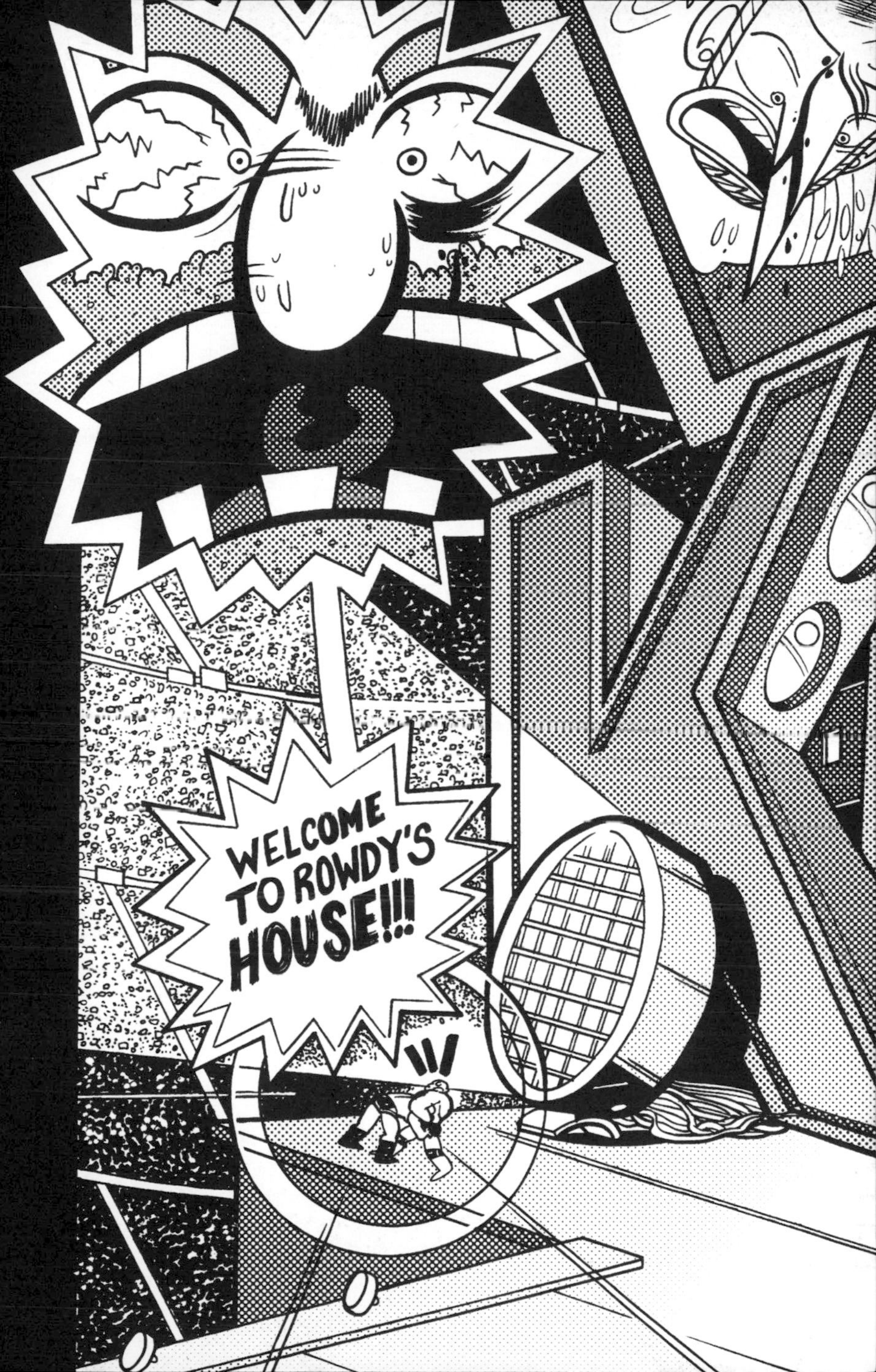
WELCOME TO ROWDY'S HOUSE!!!

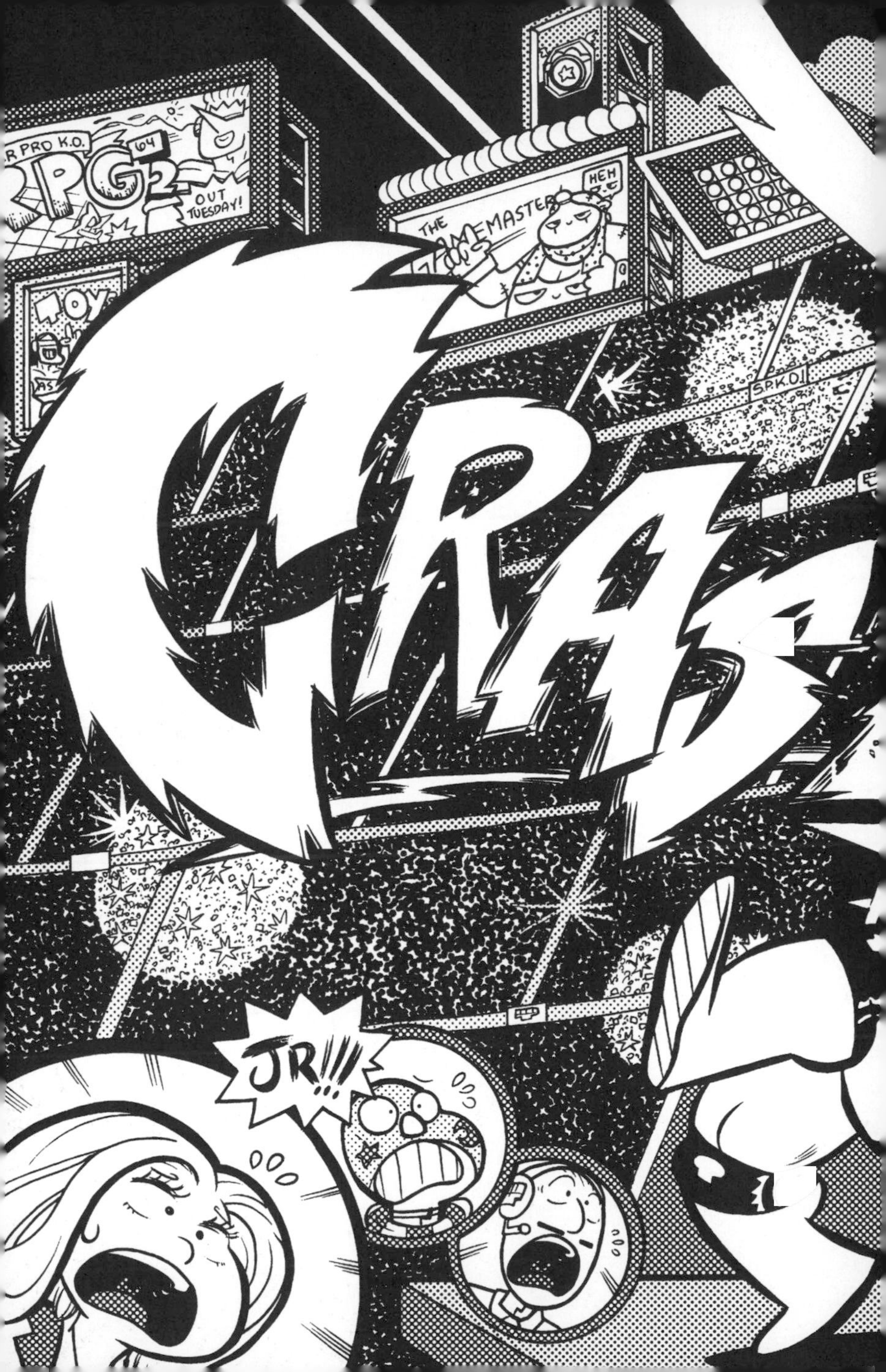
PRO K.O.
PG2
'64
OUT TUESDAY!
THE
MASTER
HEH
S.P.K.01
CRA
JR!!!

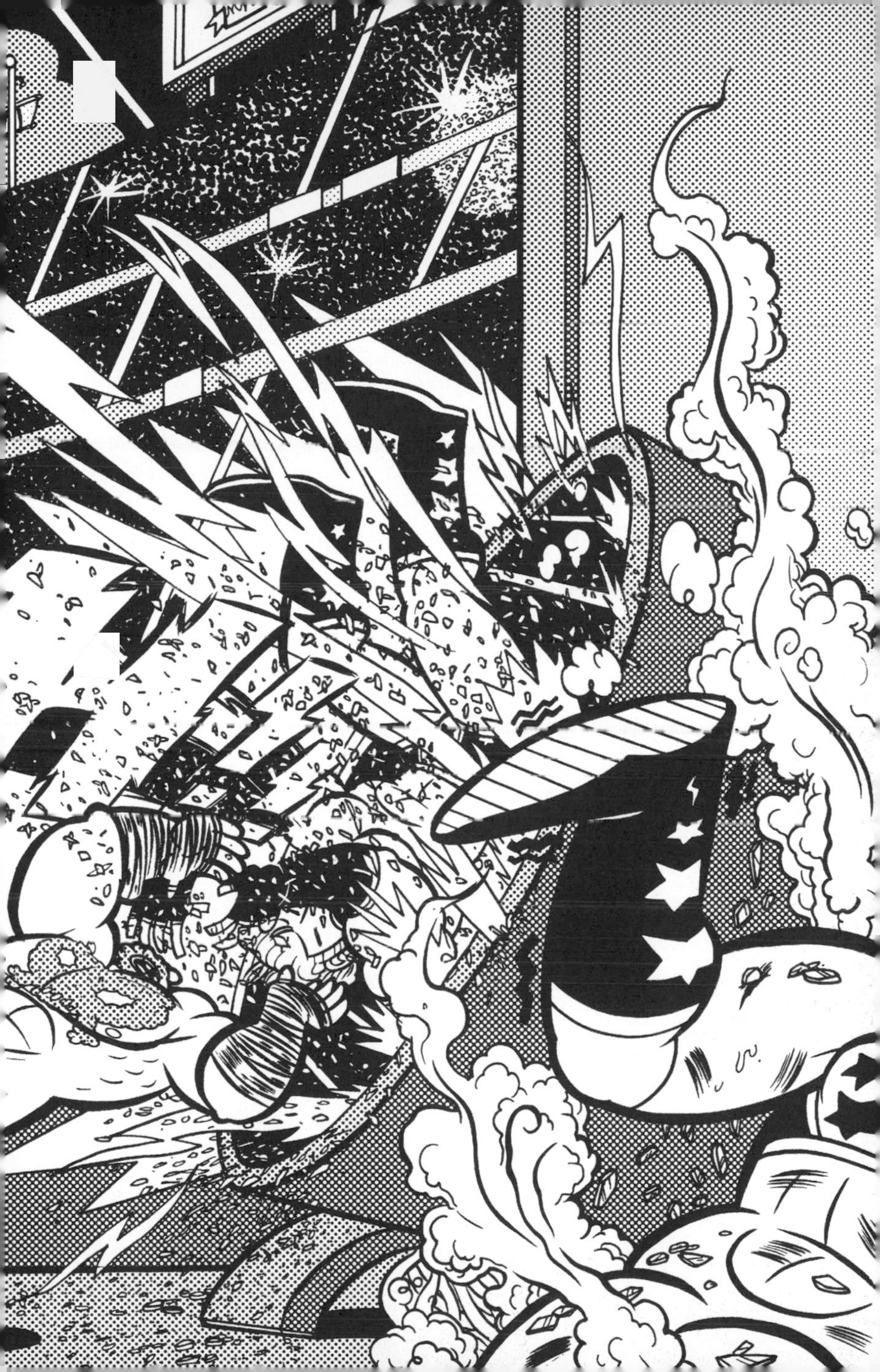

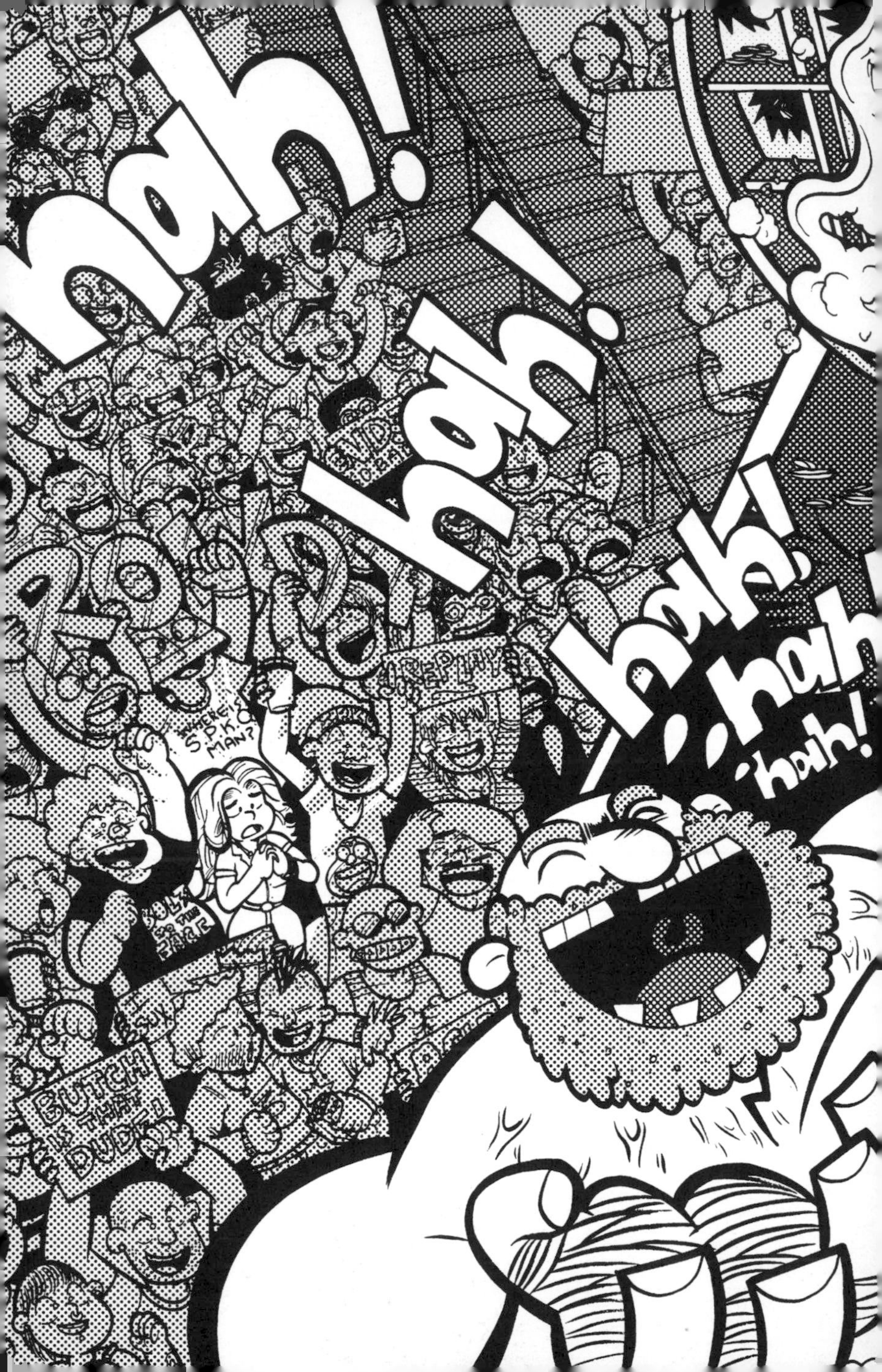
hah!
hah!
hah!
hah!
hah!
hah!
WHERE'S S.P.K. MAN?
REPLAYS
BUTCH IS THAT DUDE

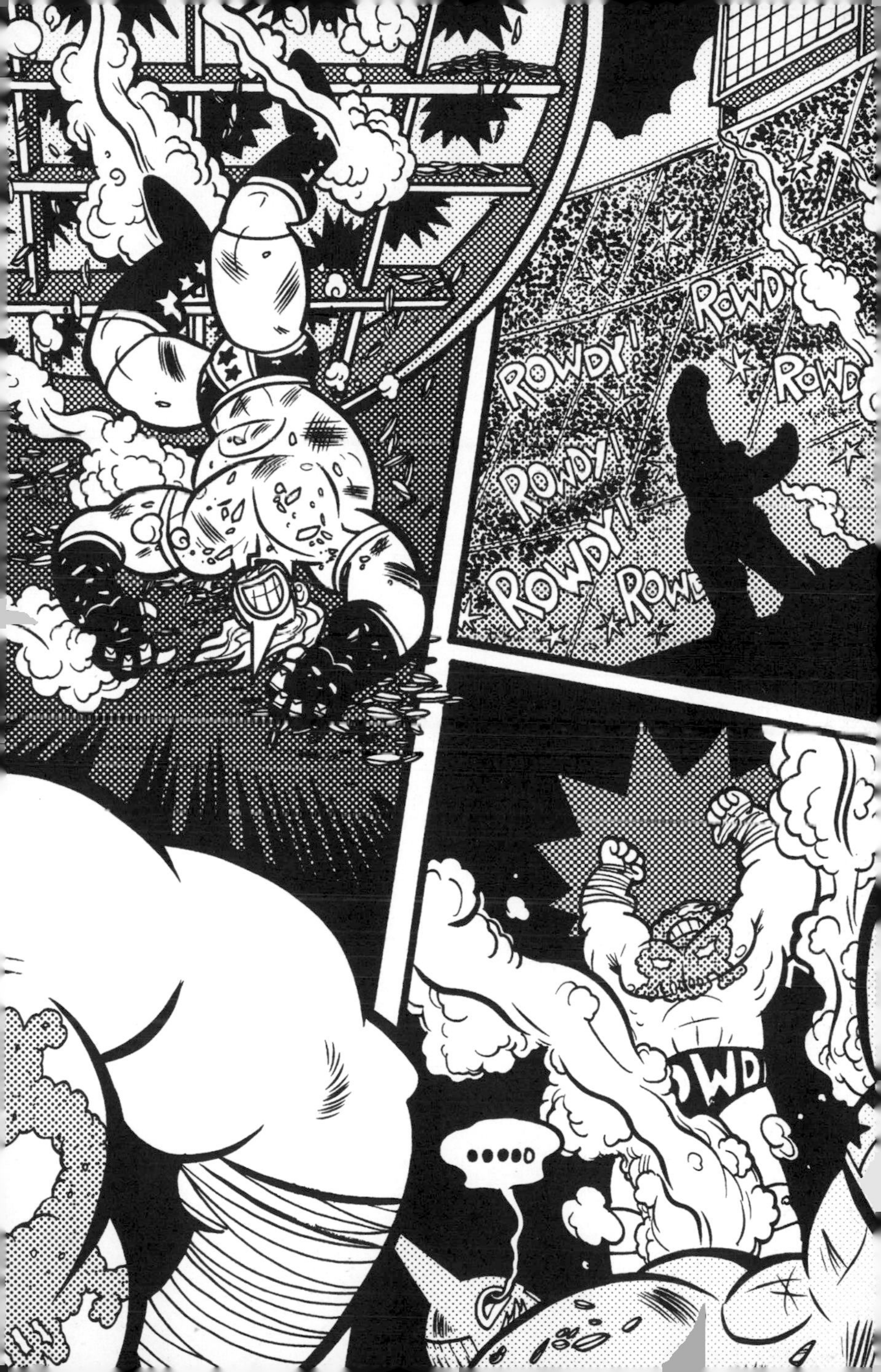
ROWDY!
ROWD
ROWDY!
ROWD
ROWDY!
ROWDY!
ROWDY!
ROWD

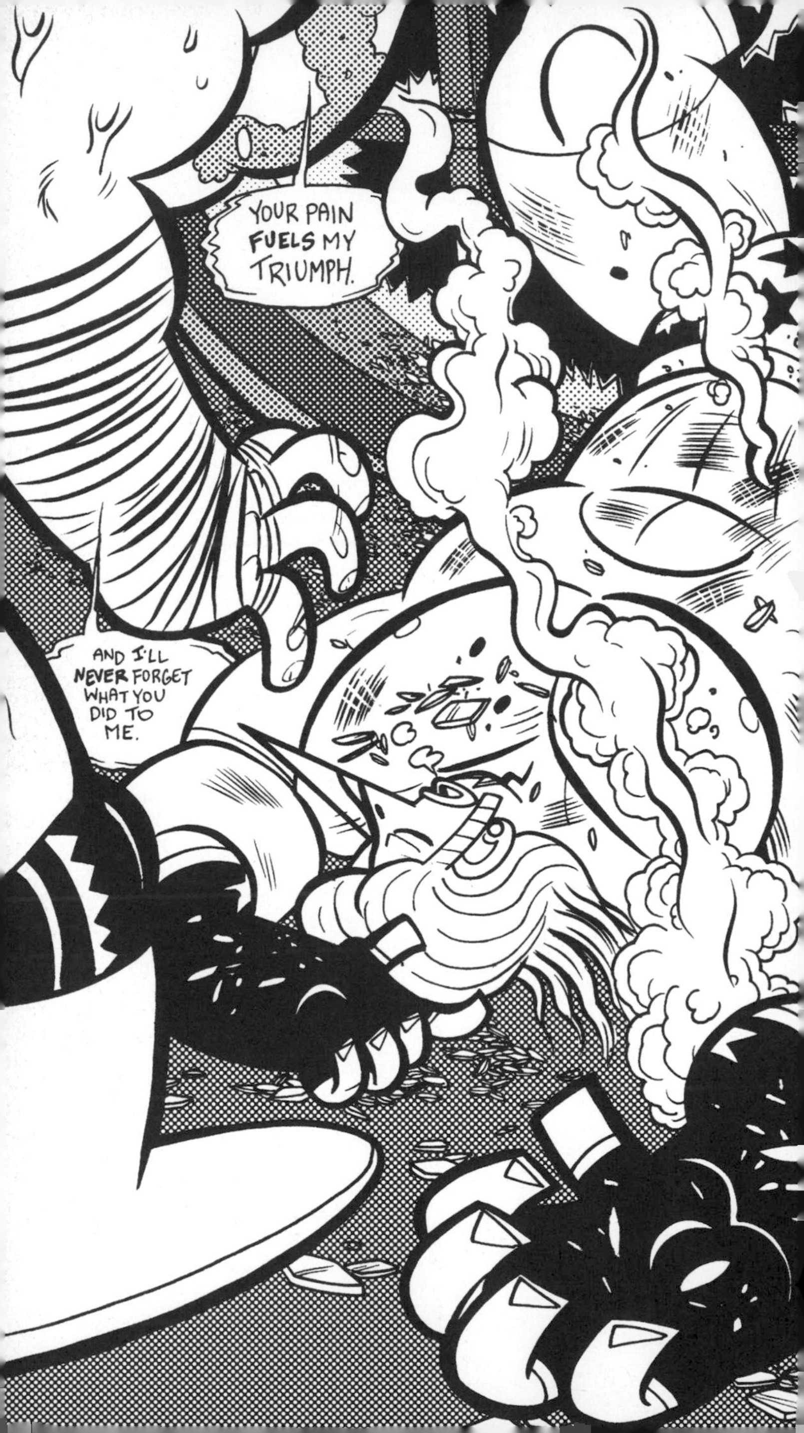
YOUR PAIN FUELS MY TRIUMPH.
AND I'LL NEVER FORGET WHAT YOU DID TO ME.

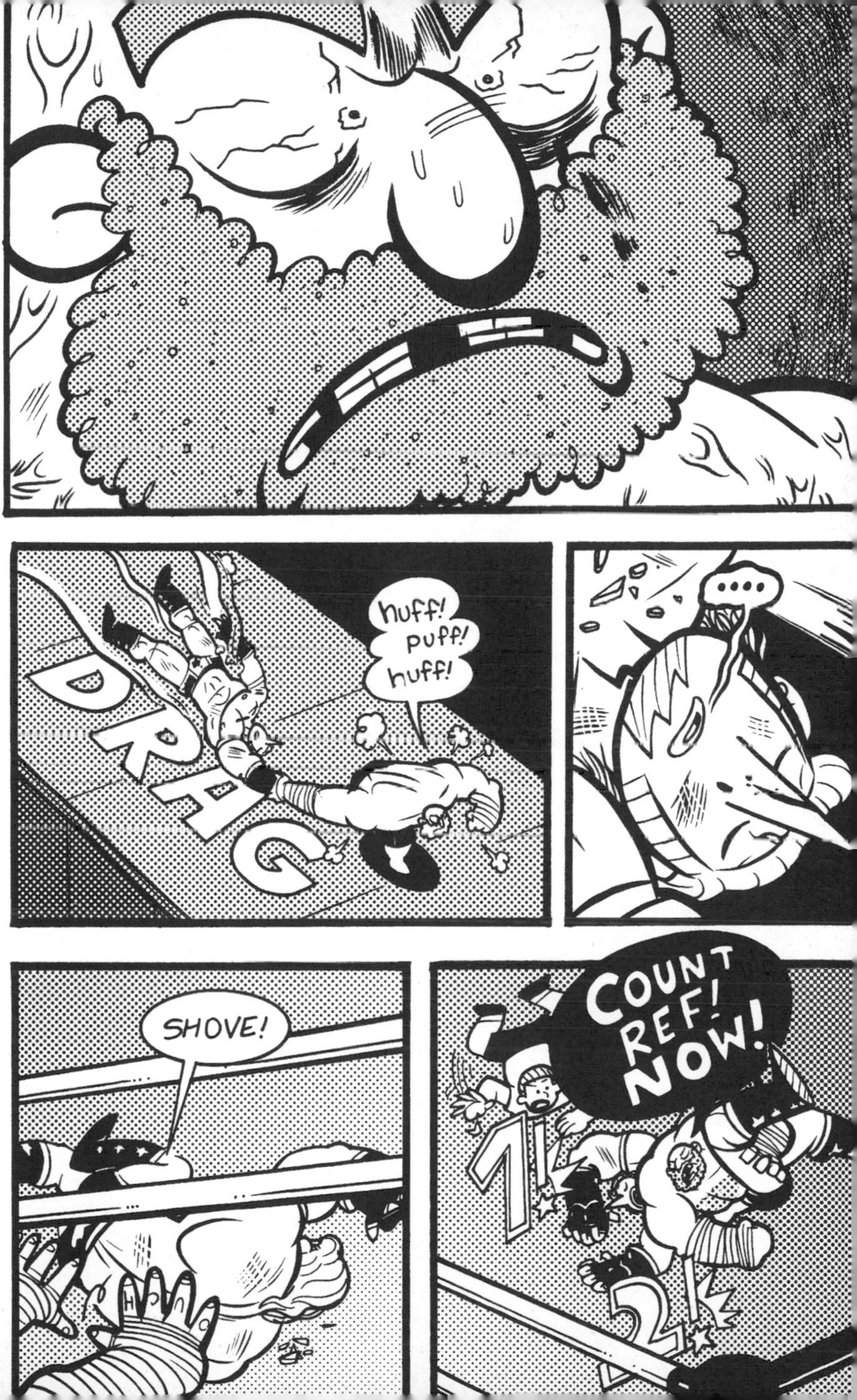
DRAG
huff! puff! huff!
....
SHOVE!
COUNT REF! NOW!
1
2

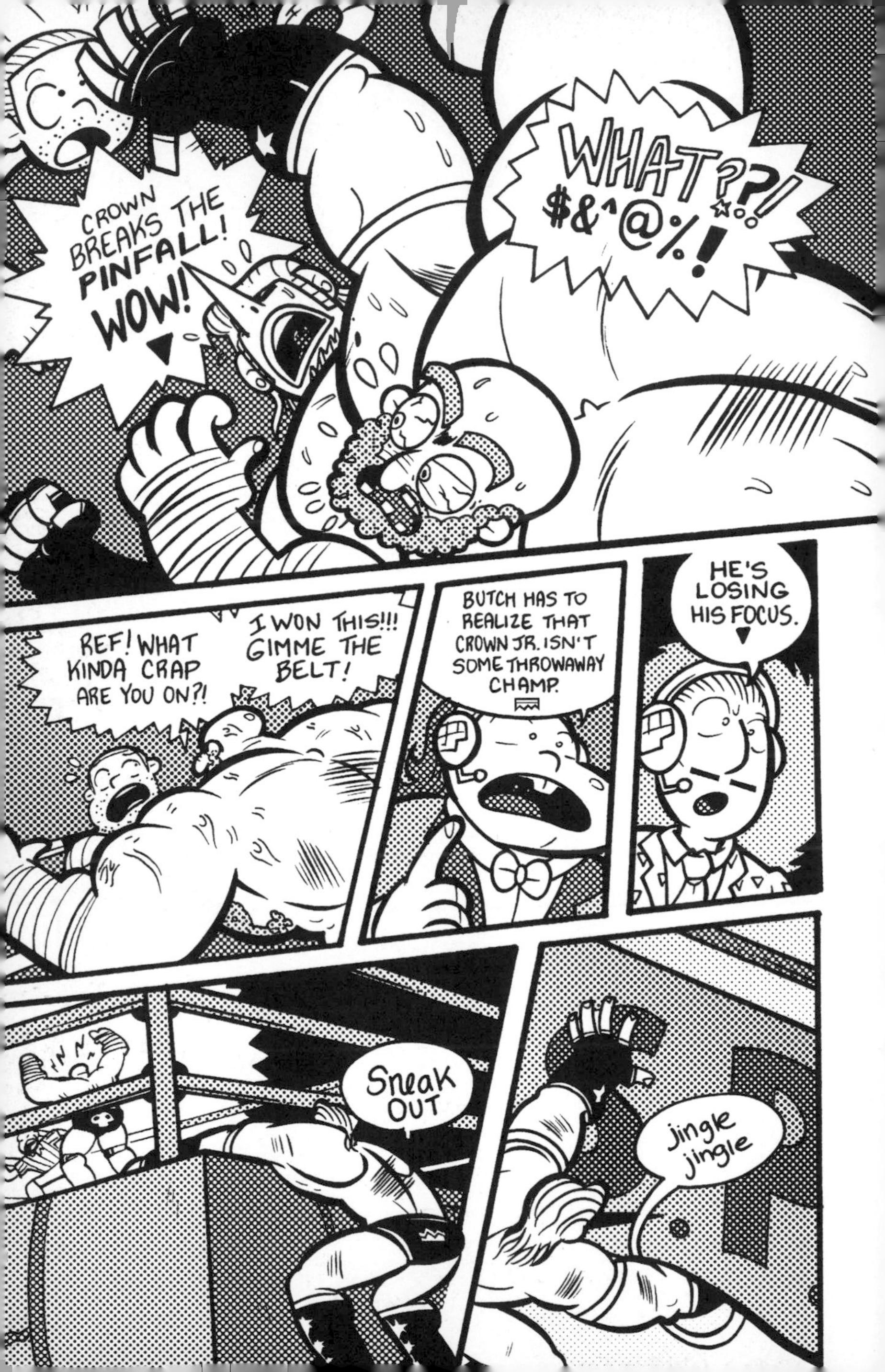

CROWN BREAKS THE PINFALL! WOW!
WHAT??! $&^@%!
REF! WHAT KINDA CRAP ARE YOU ON?!
I WON THIS!!! GIMME THE BELT!
BUTCH HAS TO REALIZE THAT CROWN JR. ISN'T SOME THROWAWAY CHAMP.
HE'S LOSING HIS FOCUS.
Sneak OUT
jingle jingle

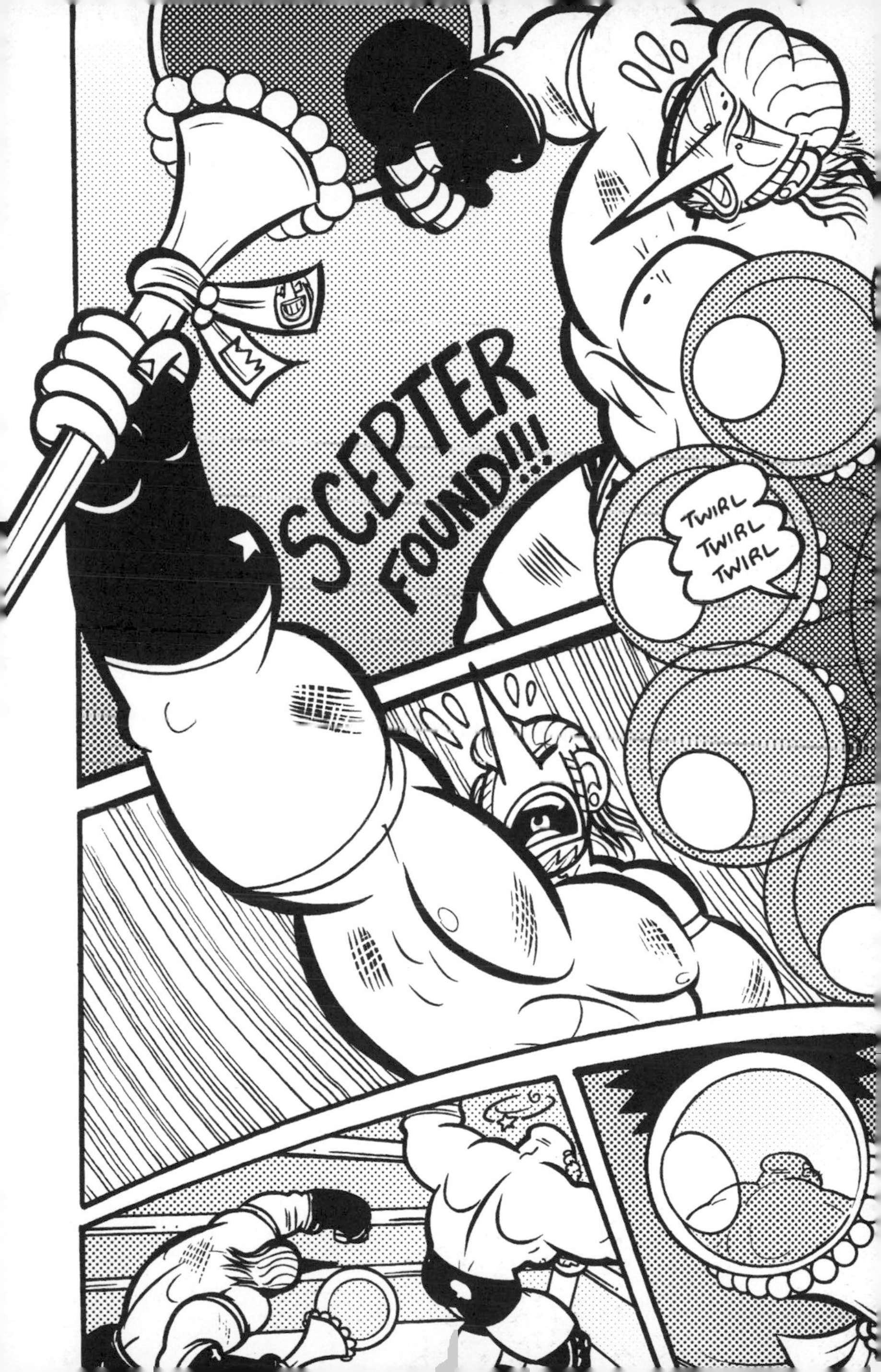
SCEPTER FOUND!!!
TWIRL TWIRL TWIRL

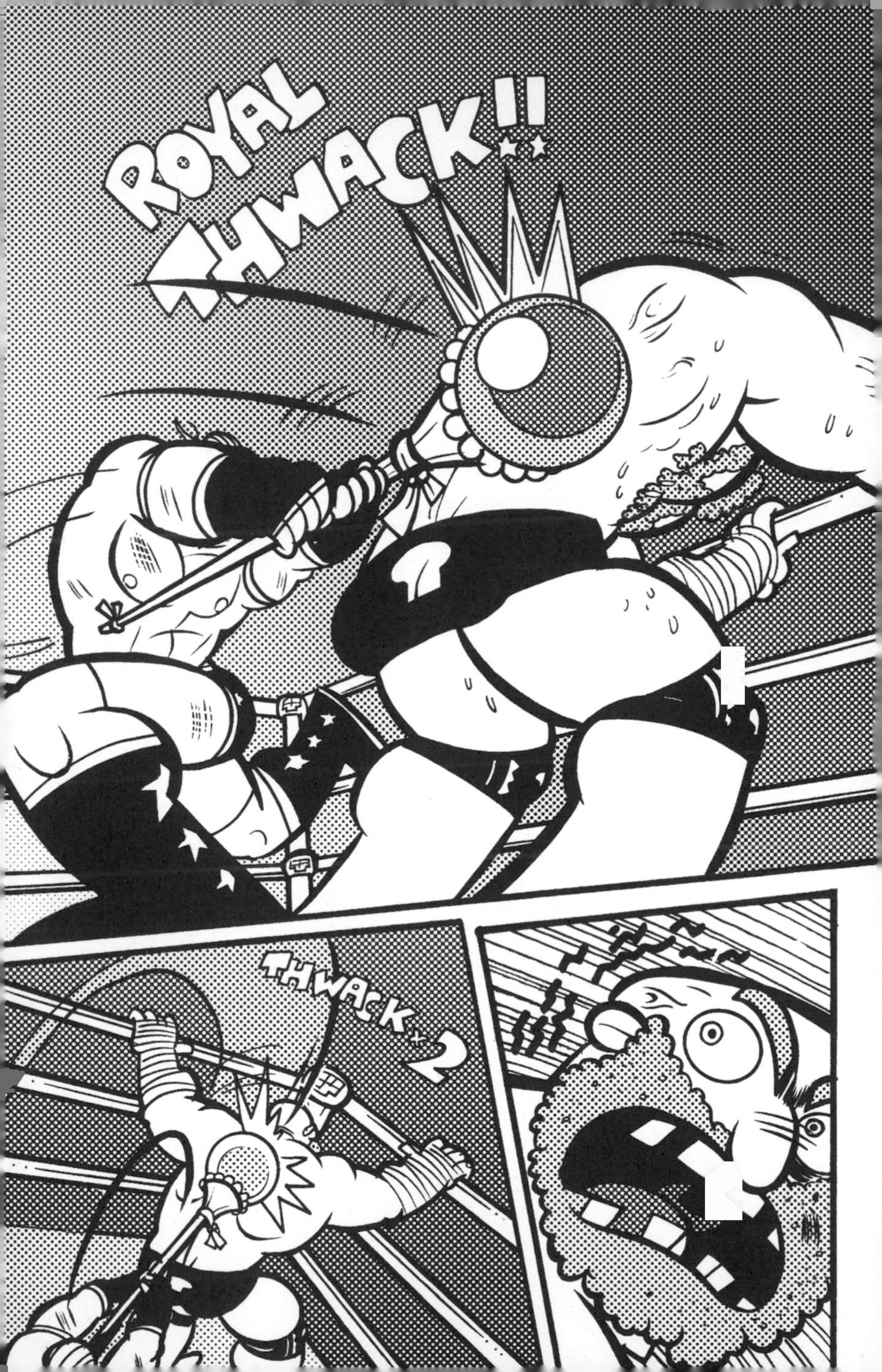
ROYAL THWACK!!
THWACK x 2

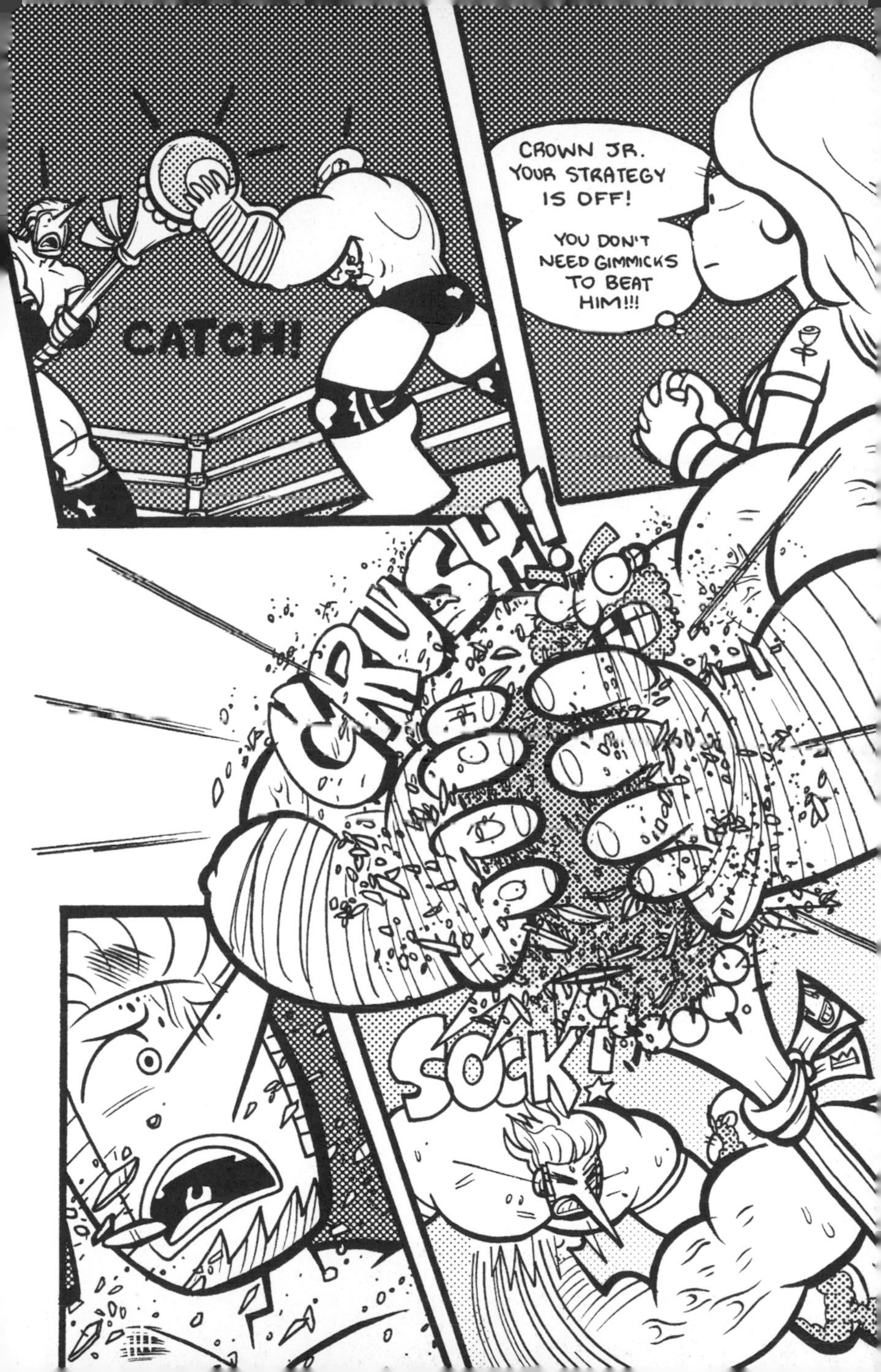
CATCH!
CROWN JR. YOUR STRATEGY IS OFF!
YOU DON'T NEED GIMMICKS TO BEAT HIM!!!
CRUSH!
SOCK!

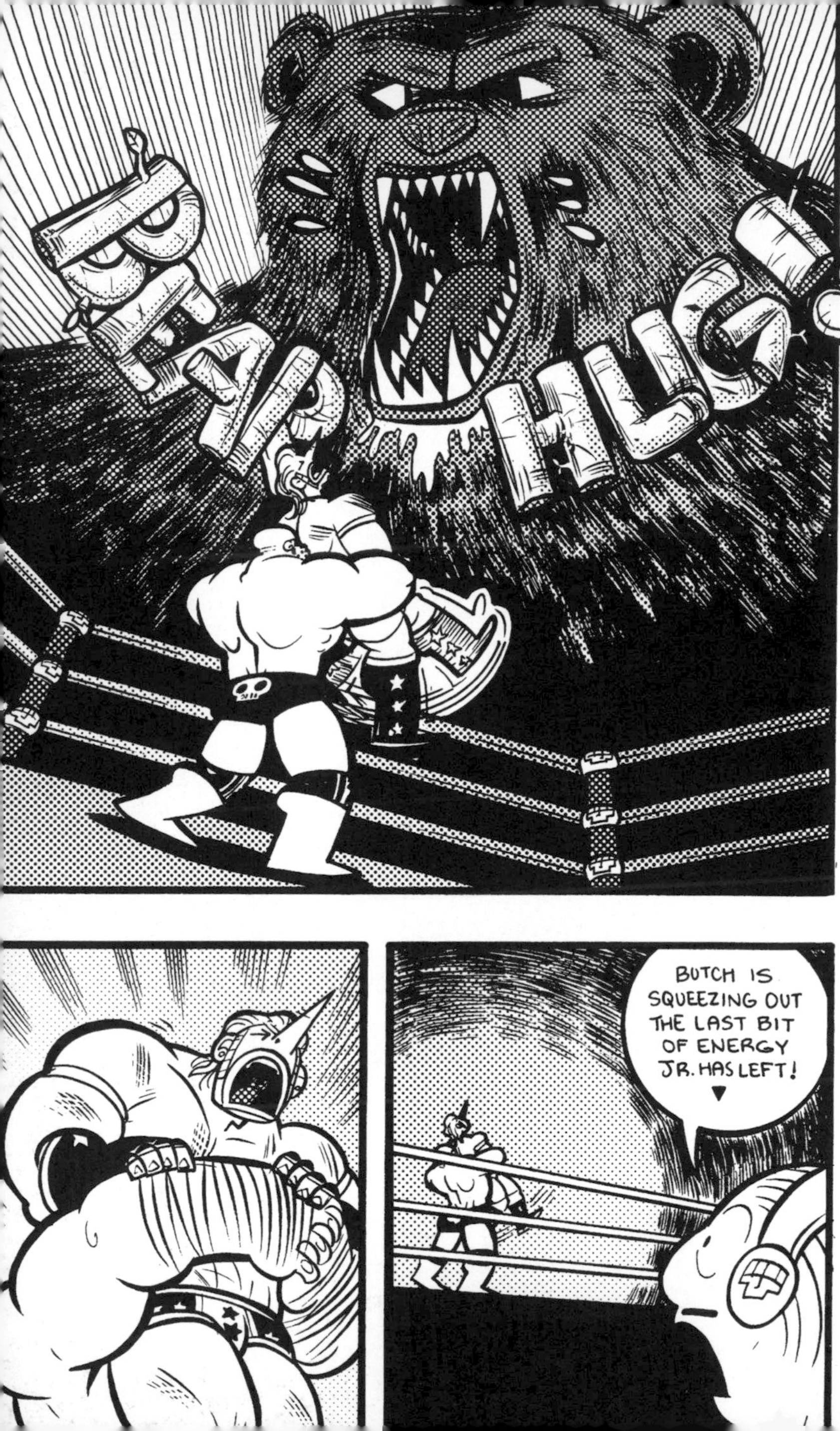
BEAR HUG!
BUTCH IS SQUEEZING OUT THE LAST BIT OF ENERGY JR. HAS LEFT!

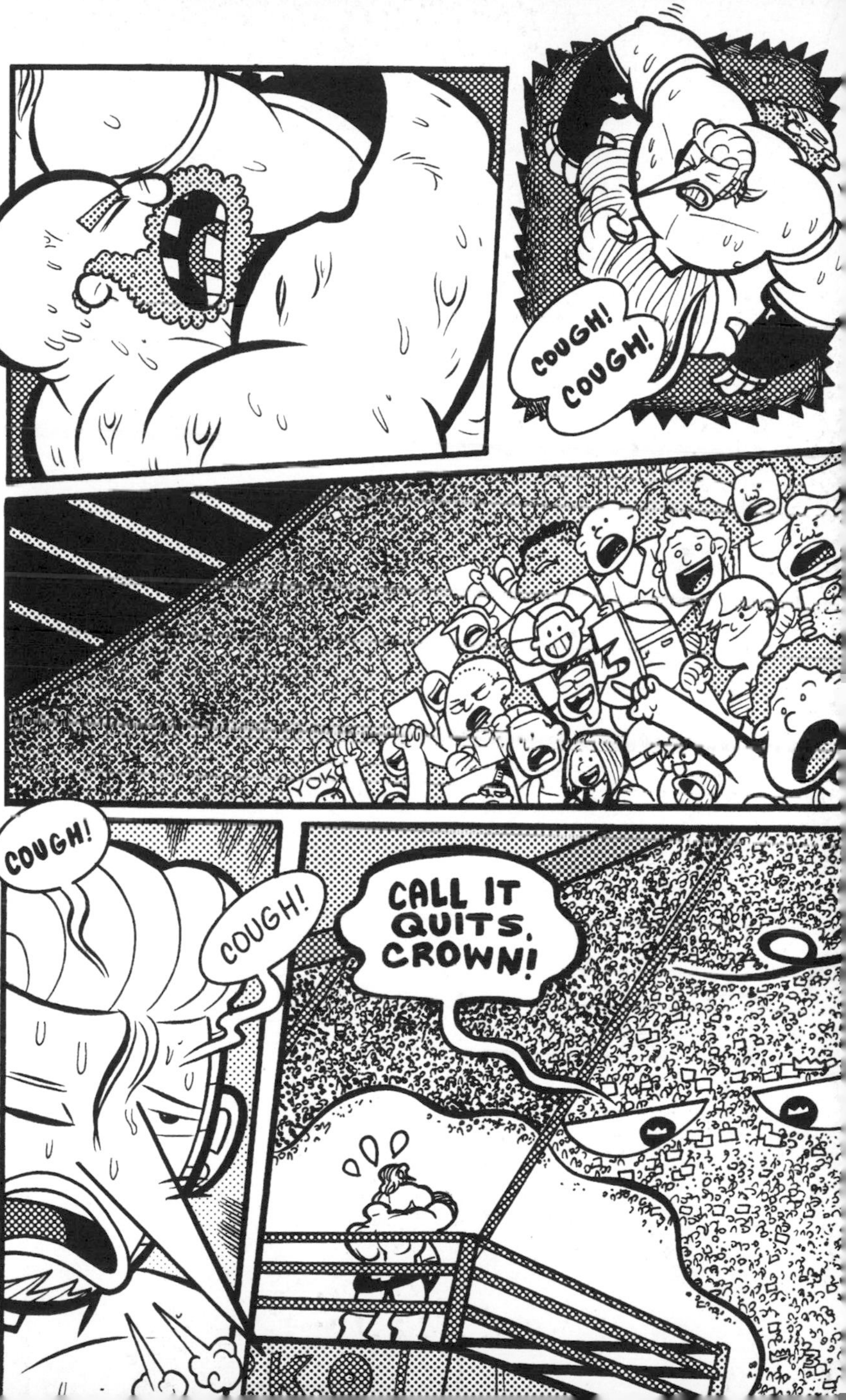
COUGH! COUGH!
COUGH!
COUGH!
CALL IT QUITS, CROWN!

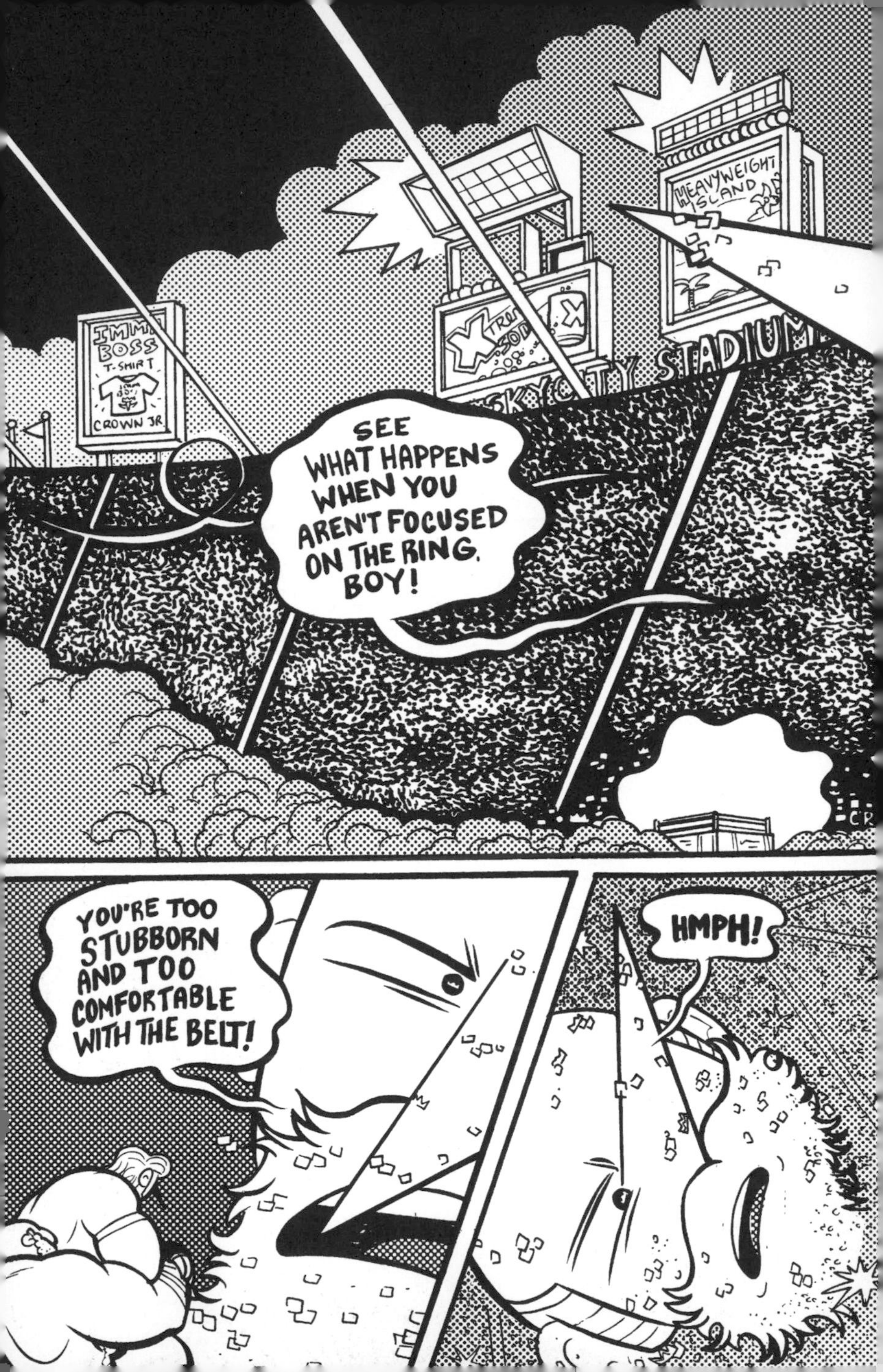
BOSS
T-SHIRT
CROWN JR
HEAVYWEIGHT ISLAND
STADIUM
SEE WHAT HAPPENS WHEN YOU AREN'T FOCUSED ON THE RING, BOY!
YOU'RE TOO STUBBORN AND TOO COMFORTABLE WITH THE BELT!
HMPH!

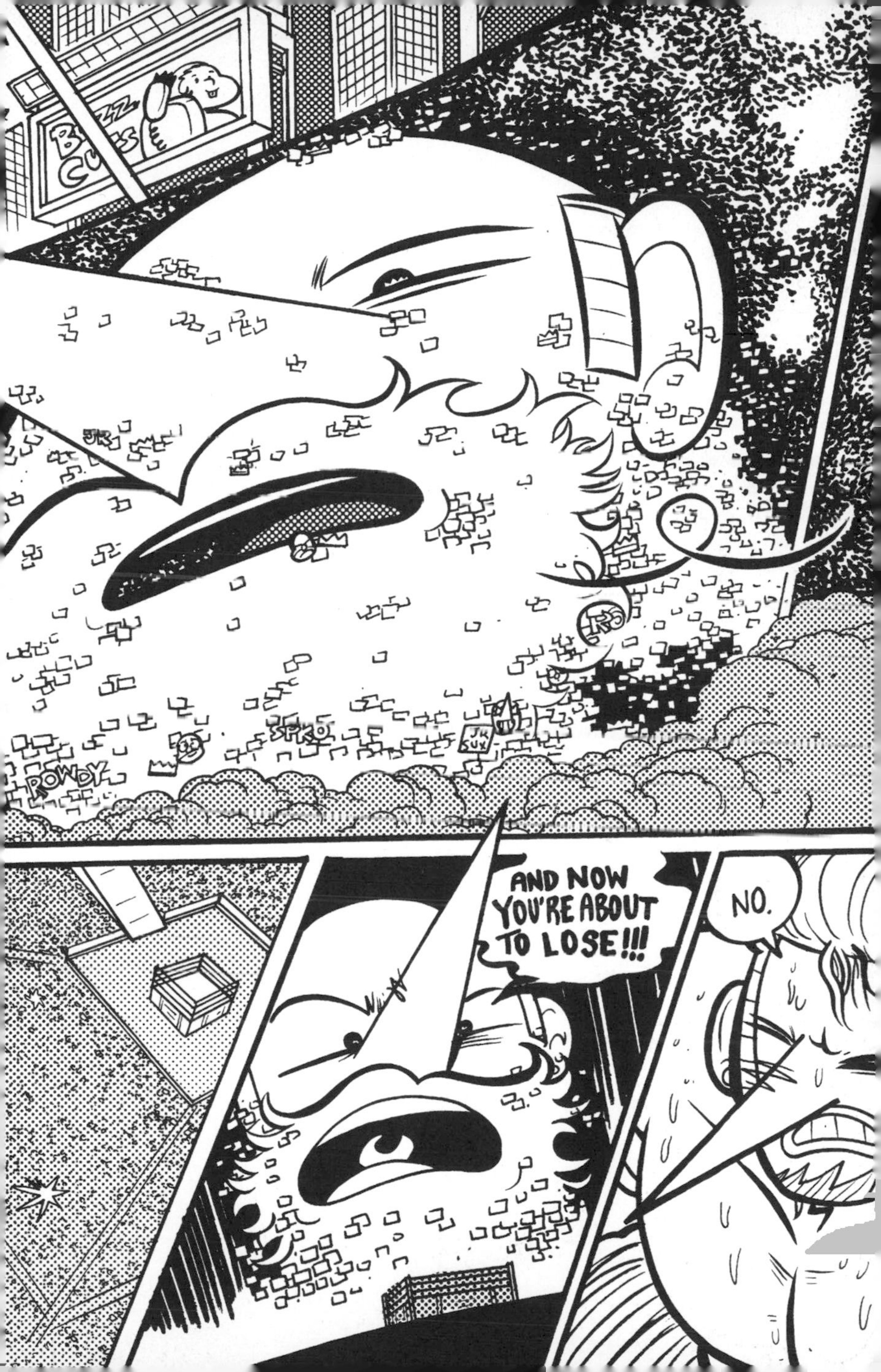
BUZZ CUTS
ROWDY
SPKO!
JK SUX
AND NOW YOU'RE ABOUT TO LOSE!!!
NO.

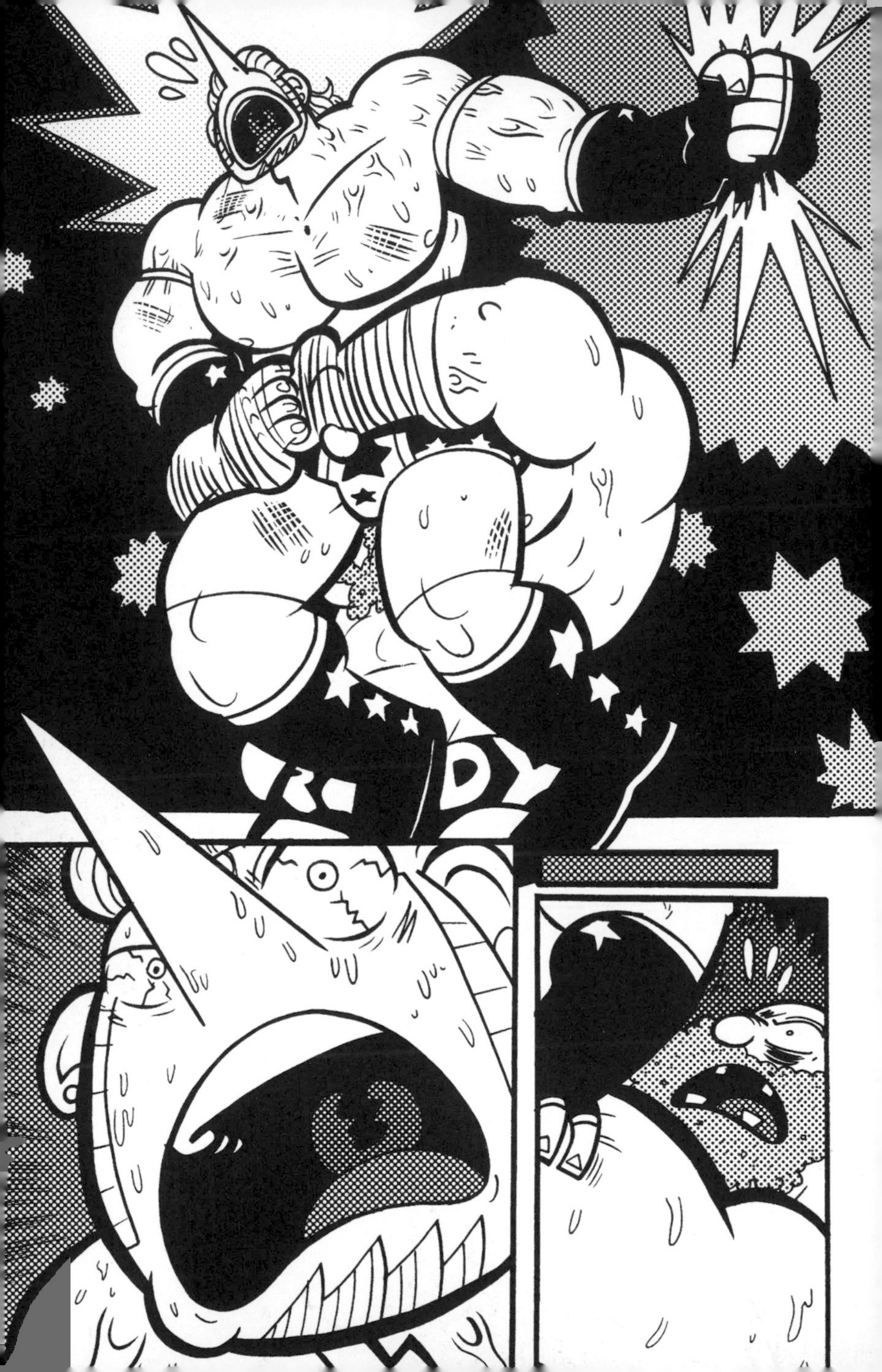

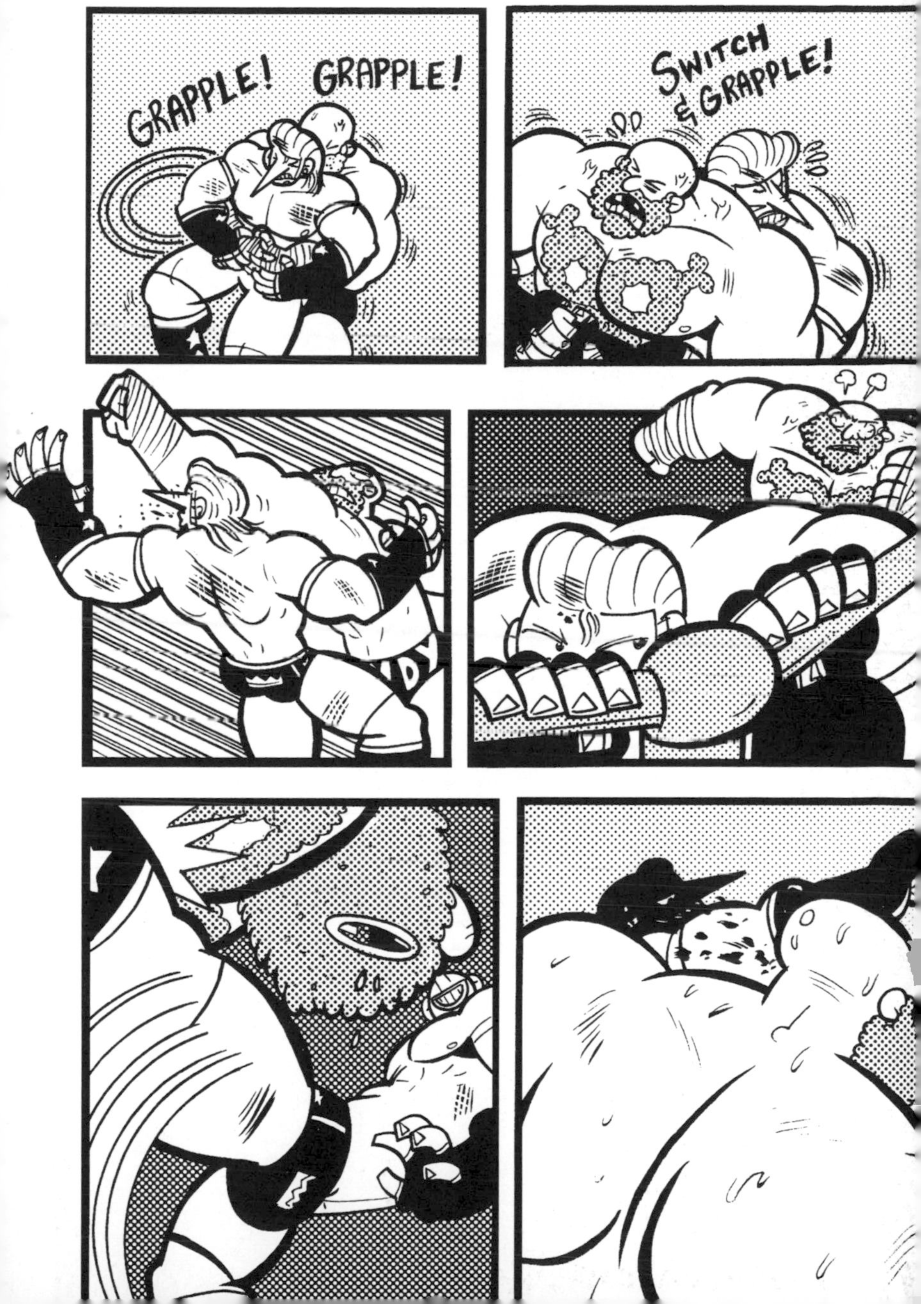
GRAPPLE! GRAPPLE!
SWITCH & GRAPPLE!

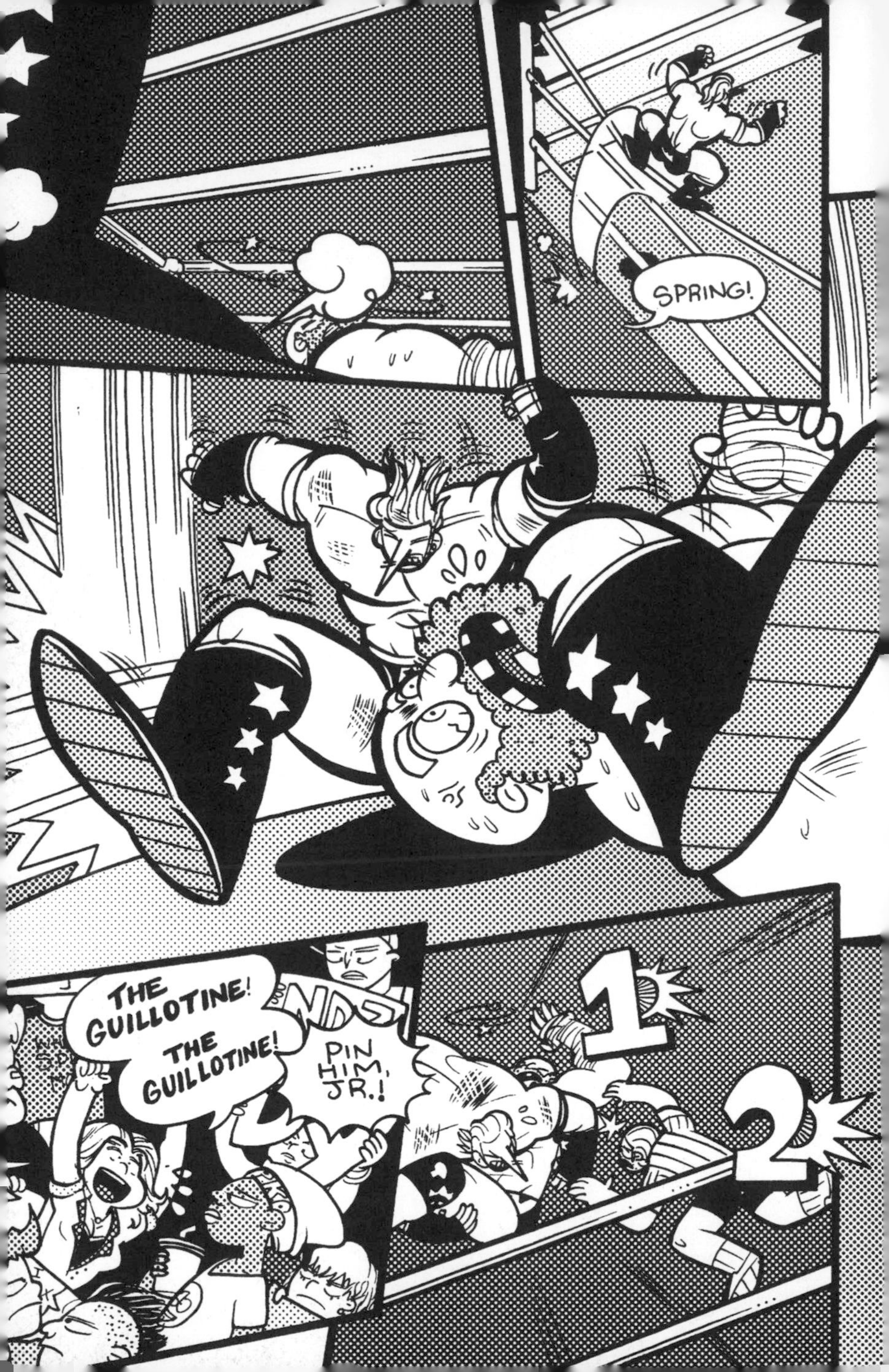
SPRING!
THE GUILLOTINE!
THE GUILLOTINE!
PIN HIM, JR.!
1
2

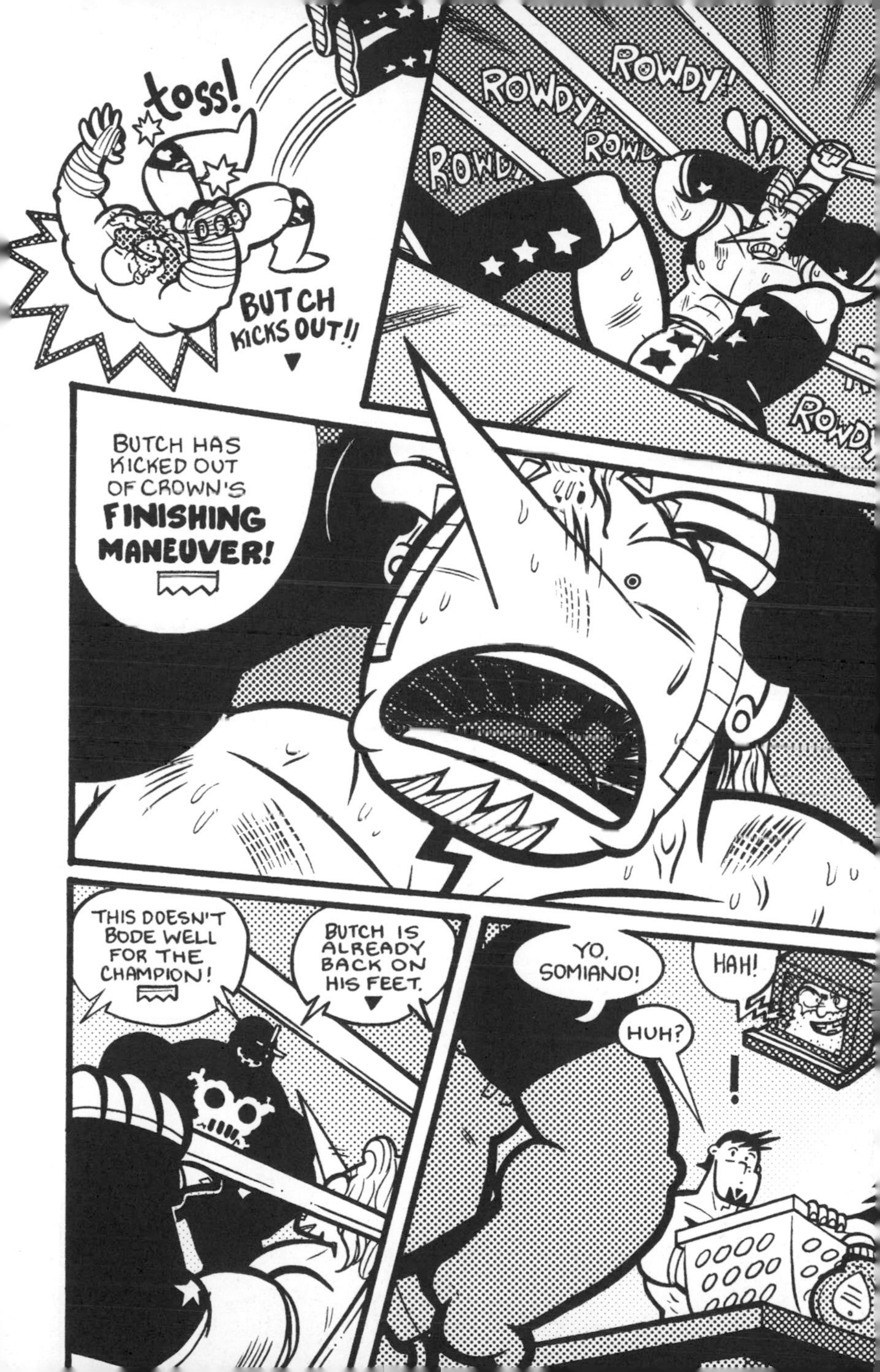
toss!
BUTCH KICKS OUT!!
ROWDY!
ROWDY!
ROWDY!
ROWDY!
BUTCH HAS KICKED OUT OF CROWN'S **FINISHING MANEUVER!**
THIS DOESN'T BODE WELL FOR THE CHAMPION!
BUTCH IS ALREADY BACK ON HIS FEET.
YO, SOMIANO!
HAH!
HUH?
!

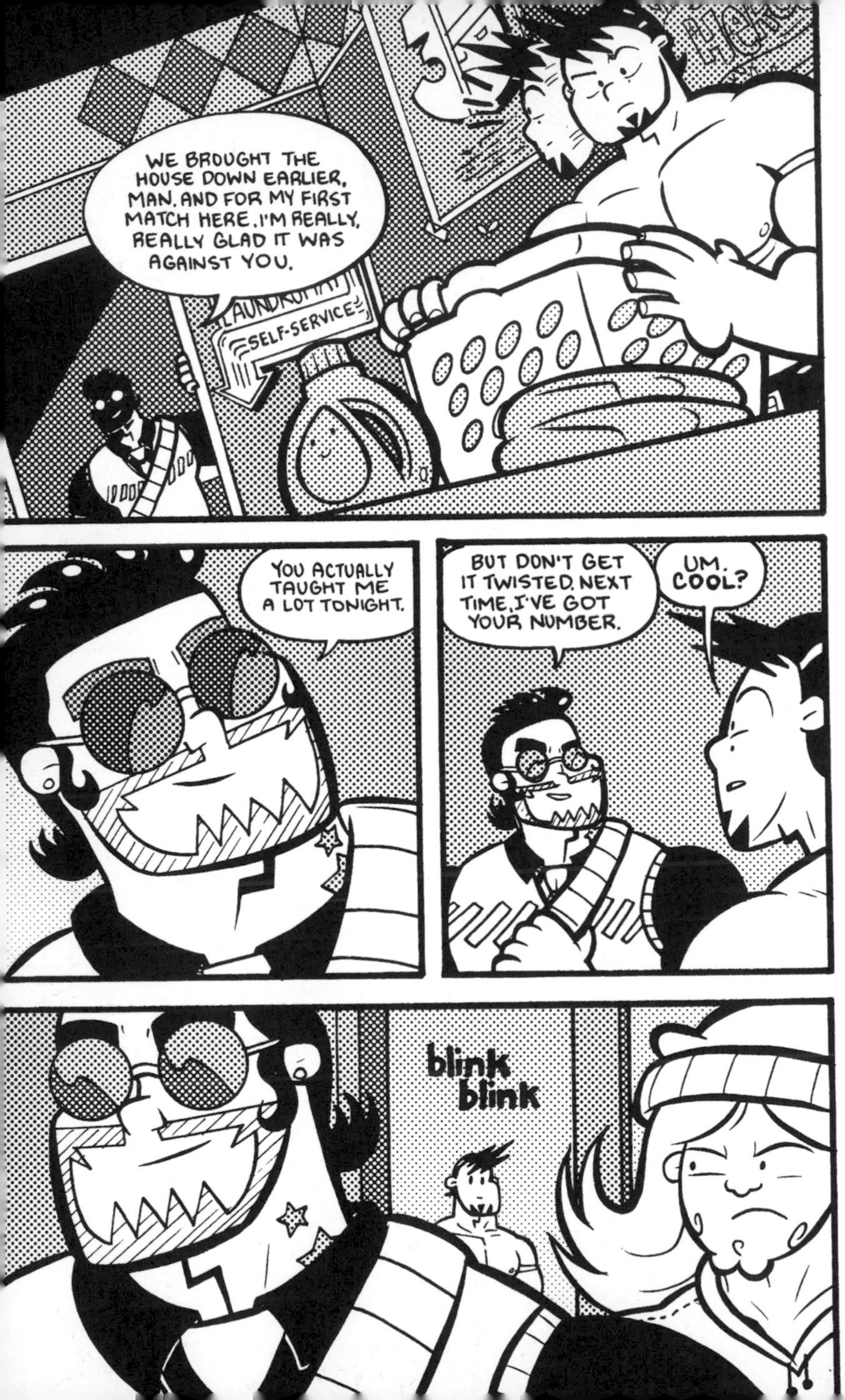
LAUNDROMAT
SELF-SERVICE
WE BROUGHT THE HOUSE DOWN EARLIER, MAN. AND FOR MY FIRST MATCH HERE, I'M REALLY, REALLY GLAD IT WAS AGAINST YOU.
YOU ACTUALLY TAUGHT ME A LOT TONIGHT.
BUT DON'T GET IT TWISTED. NEXT TIME, I'VE GOT YOUR NUMBER.
UM. COOL?
blink
blink

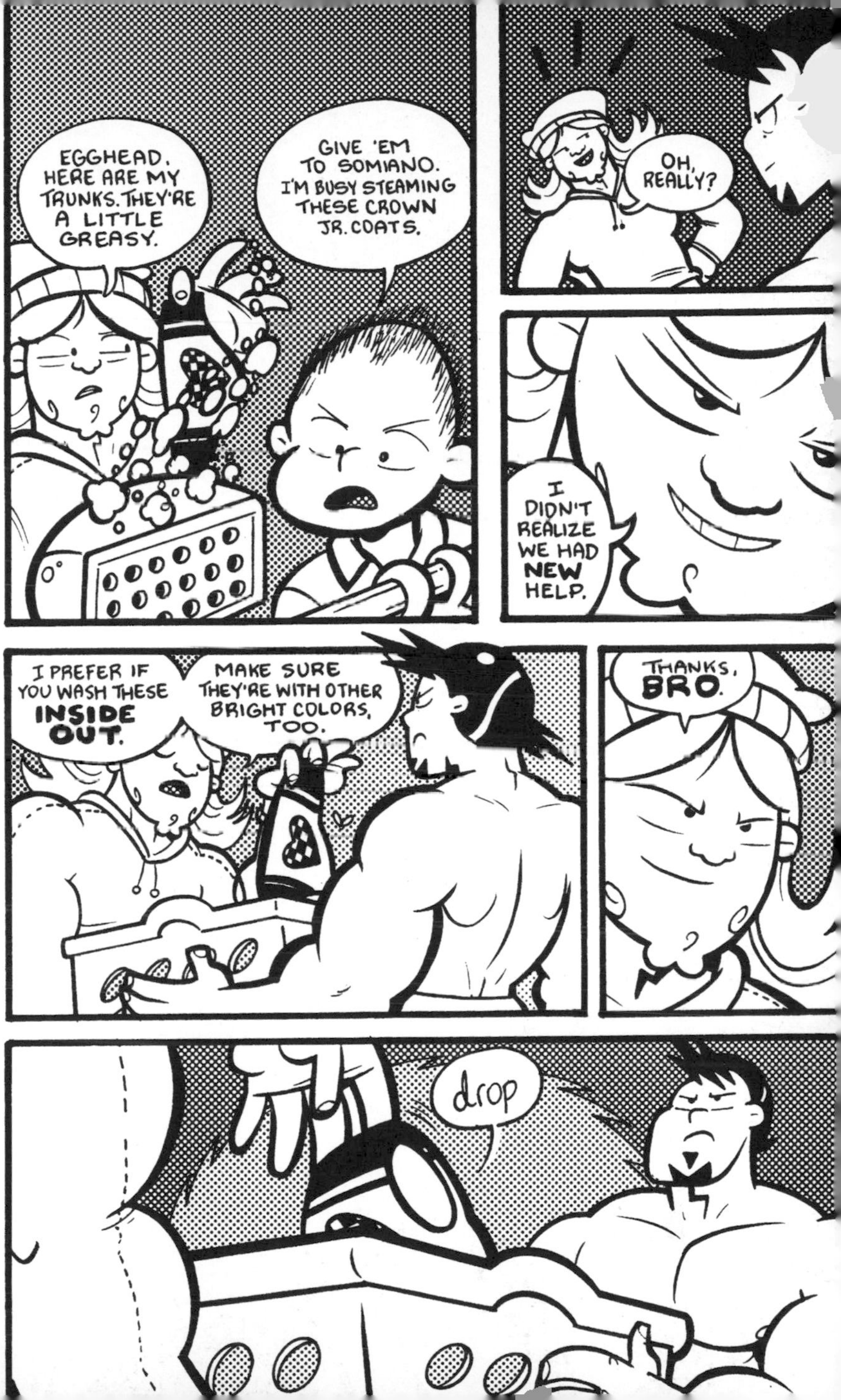
EGGHEAD. HERE ARE MY TRUNKS. THEY'RE A LITTLE GREASY.
GIVE 'EM TO SOMIANO. I'M BUSY STEAMING THESE CROWN JR. COATS.
OH, REALLY?
I DIDN'T REALIZE WE HAD NEW HELP.
I PREFER IF YOU WASH THESE INSIDE OUT.
MAKE SURE THEY'RE WITH OTHER BRIGHT COLORS, TOO.
THANKS, BRO.
drop

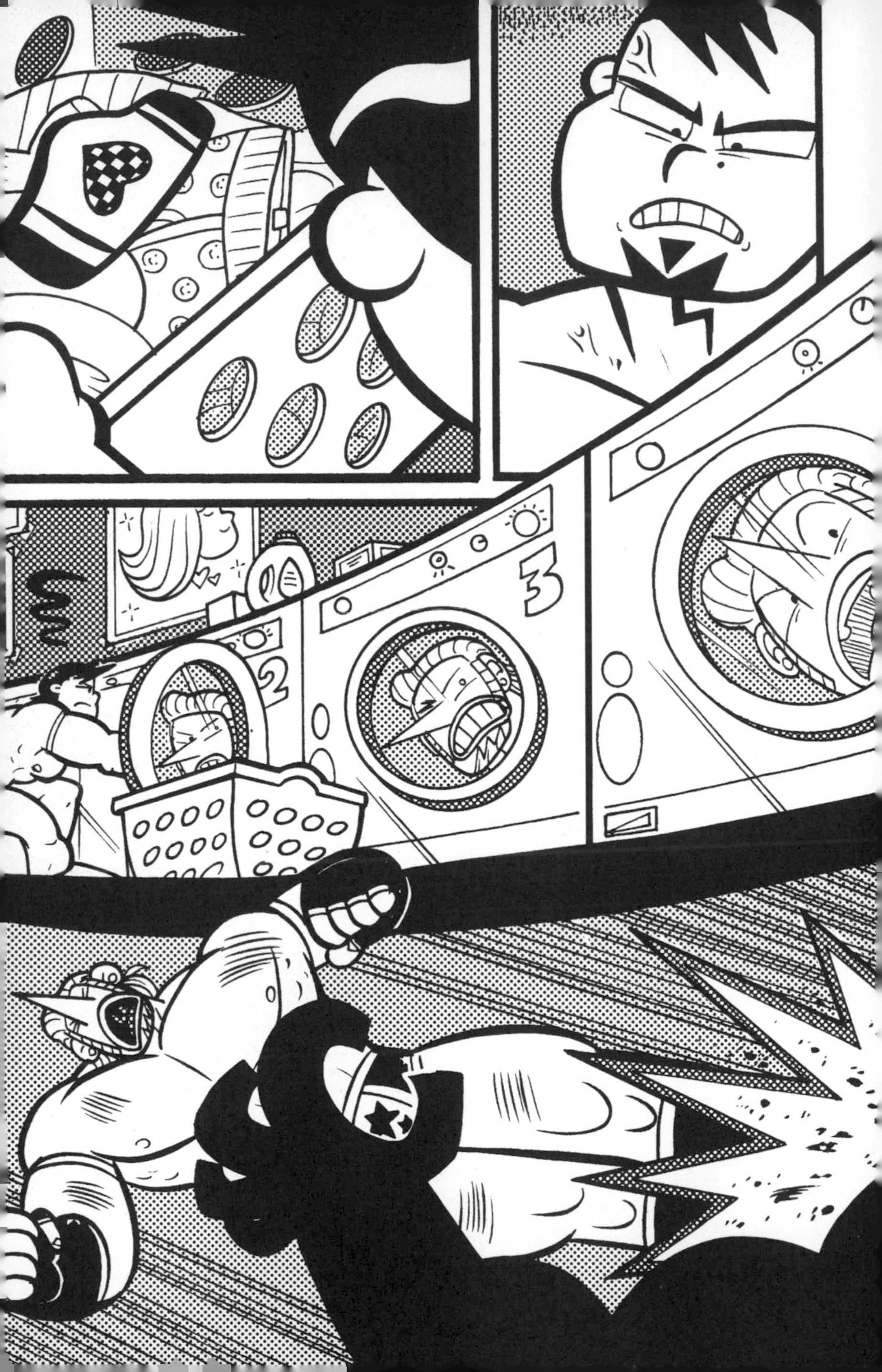
2
3

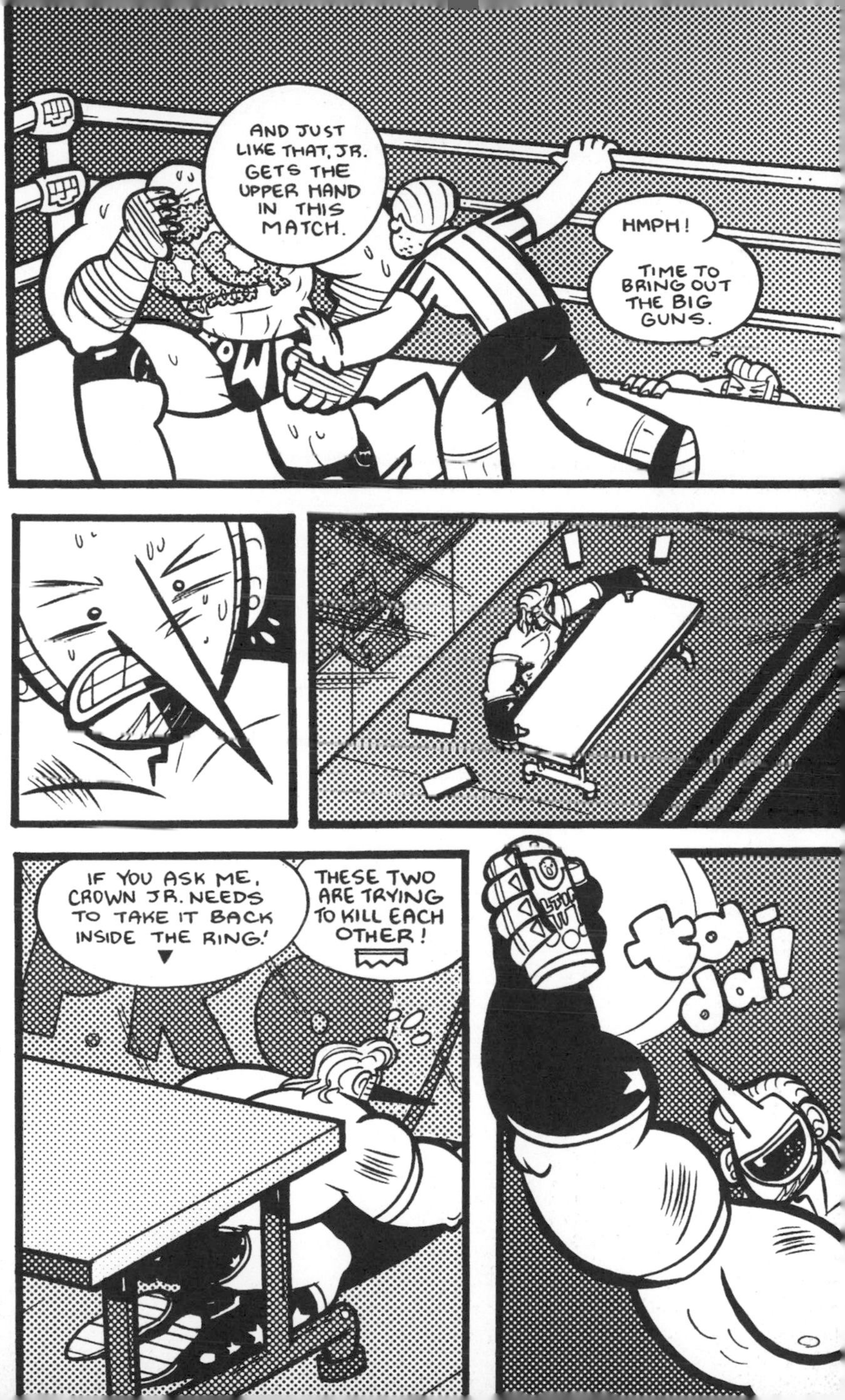
AND JUST LIKE THAT, JR. GETS THE UPPER HAND IN THIS MATCH.
HMPH!
TIME TO BRING OUT THE BIG GUNS.
IF YOU ASK ME, CROWN JR. NEEDS TO TAKE IT BACK INSIDE THE RING!
THESE TWO ARE TRYING TO KILL EACH OTHER!
ta-da!

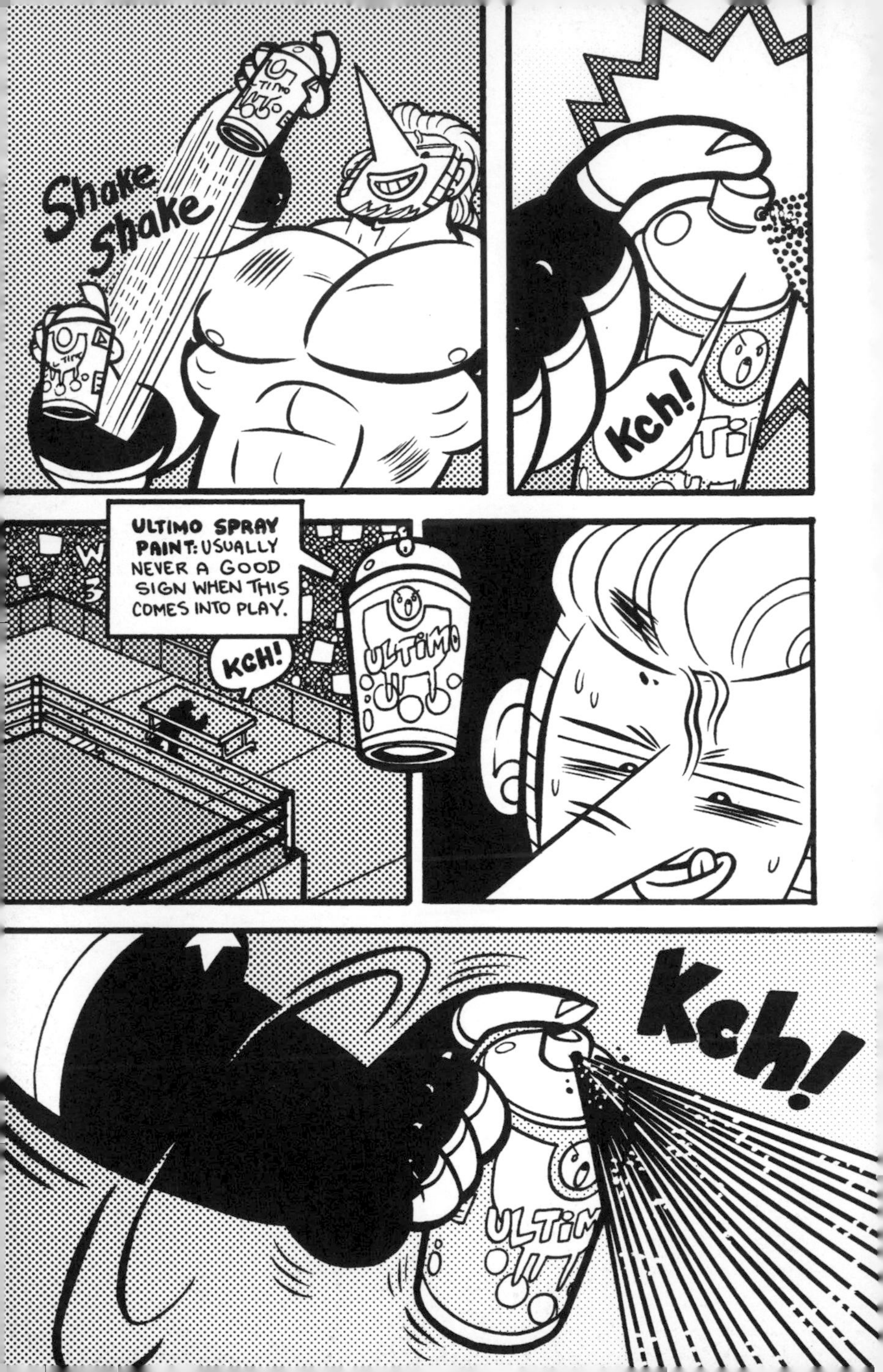

Shake Shake
Kch!
ULTIMO SPRAY PAINT: USUALLY NEVER A GOOD SIGN WHEN THIS COMES INTO PLAY.
KCH!
ULTIMO
Kch!

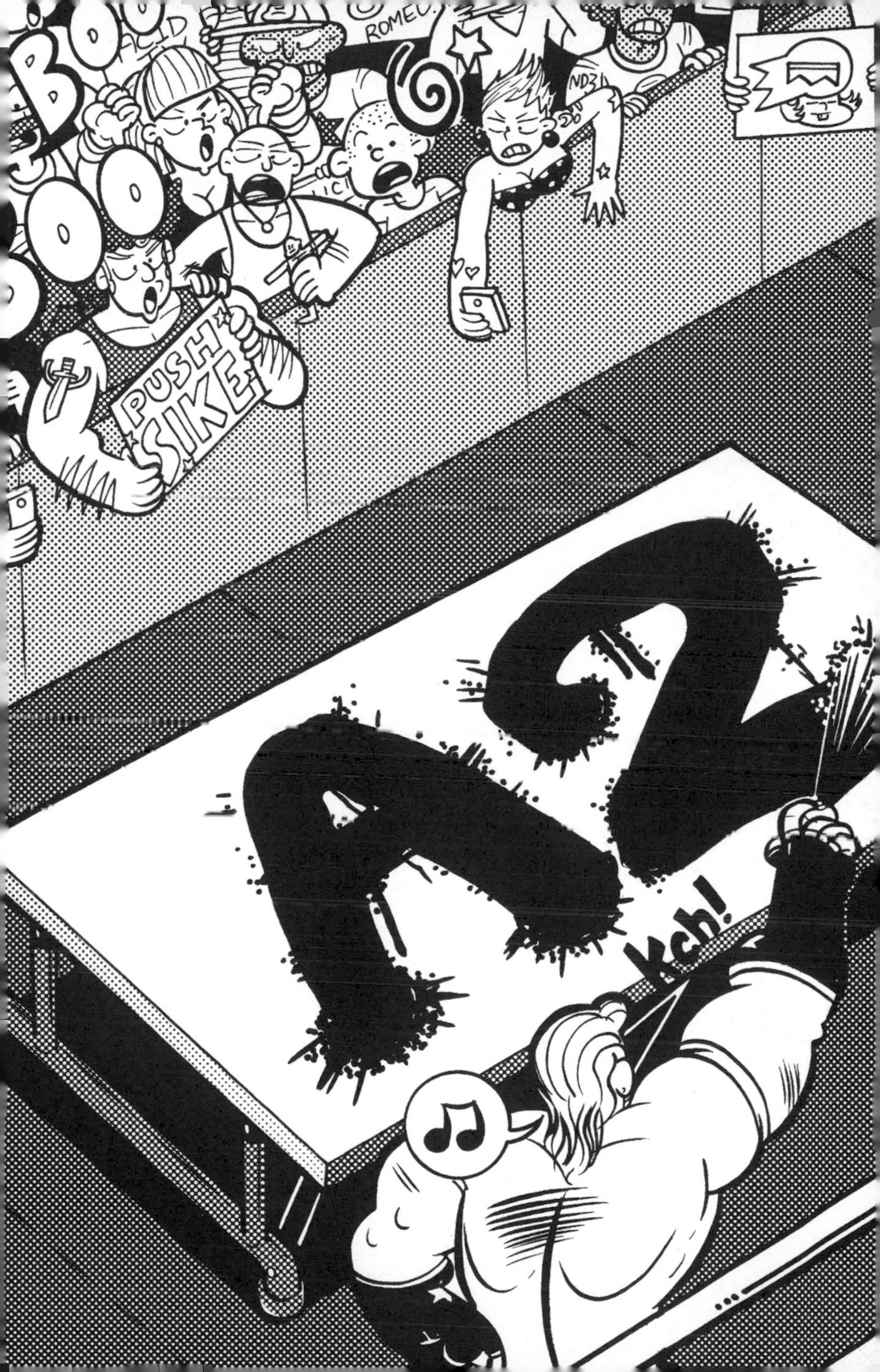
PUSH SIKE
Kch!

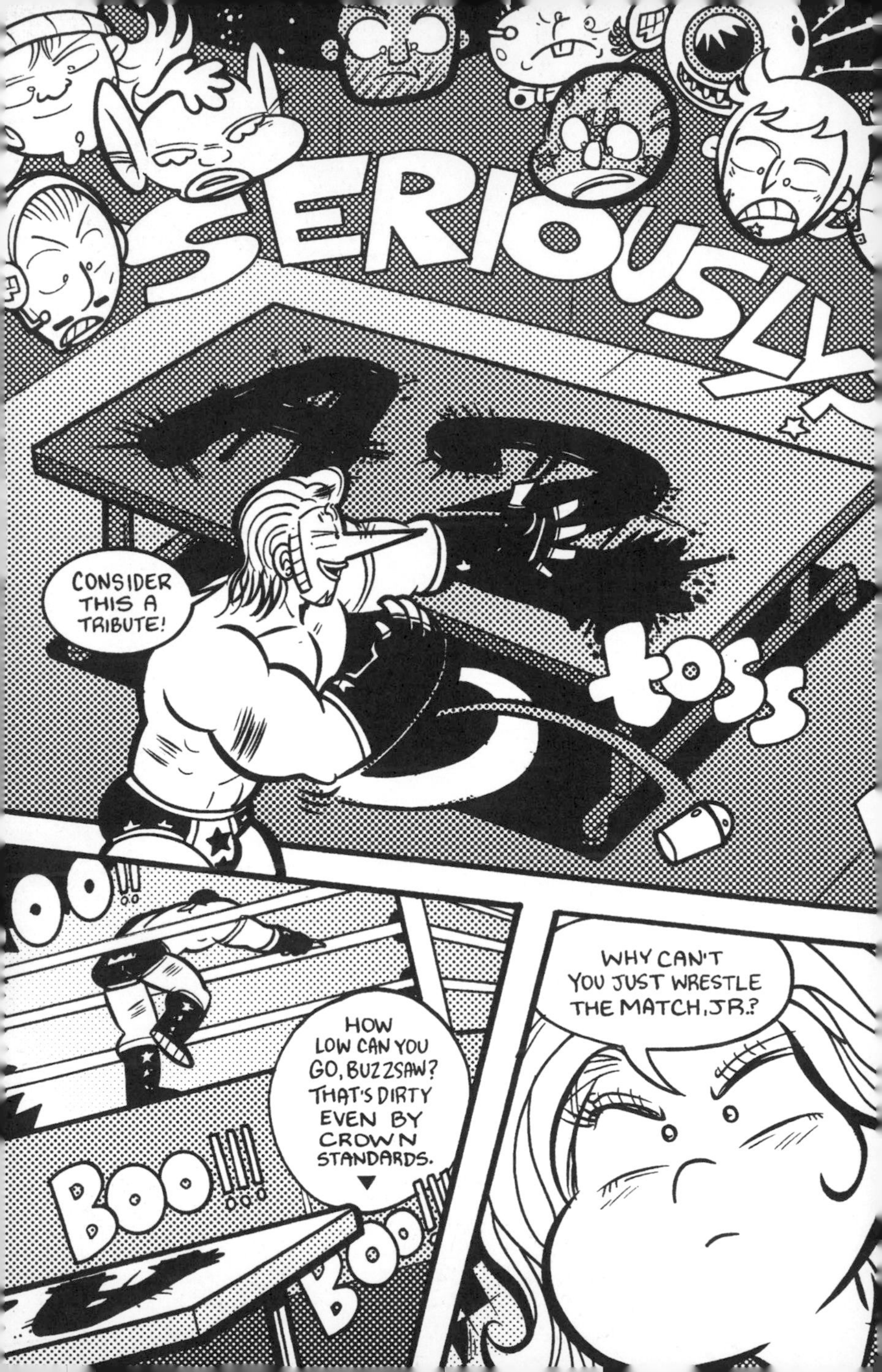
SERIOUSLY
CONSIDER THIS A TRIBUTE!
toss
BOO!!!
BOO!!!
HOW LOW CAN YOU GO, BUZZSAW? THAT'S DIRTY EVEN BY CROWN STANDARDS.
BOO!!!
WHY CAN'T YOU JUST WRESTLE THE MATCH, JR.?

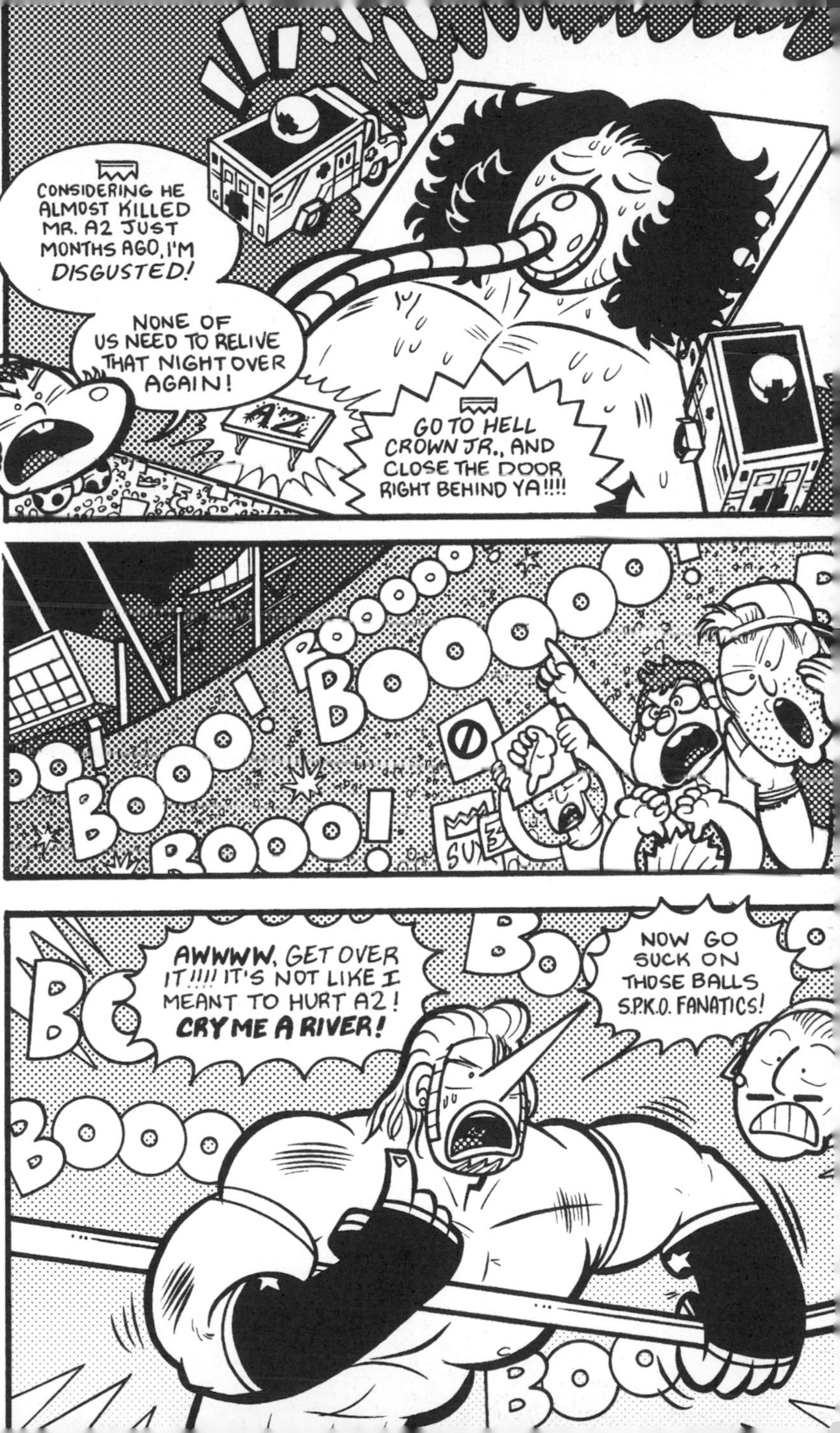
CONSIDERING HE ALMOST KILLED MR. A2 JUST MONTHS AGO, I'M DISGUSTED!
NONE OF US NEED TO RELIVE THAT NIGHT OVER AGAIN!
A2
GO TO HELL CROWN JR., AND CLOSE THE DOOR RIGHT BEHIND YA!!!!
BOOOOOO! BOOOOOO! BOOOOOO! BOOO! BOOO!
AWWWW, GET OVER IT!!!! IT'S NOT LIKE I MEANT TO HURT A2! CRY ME A RIVER!
NOW GO SUCK ON THOSE BALLS S.P.K.O. FANATICS!
BOOO

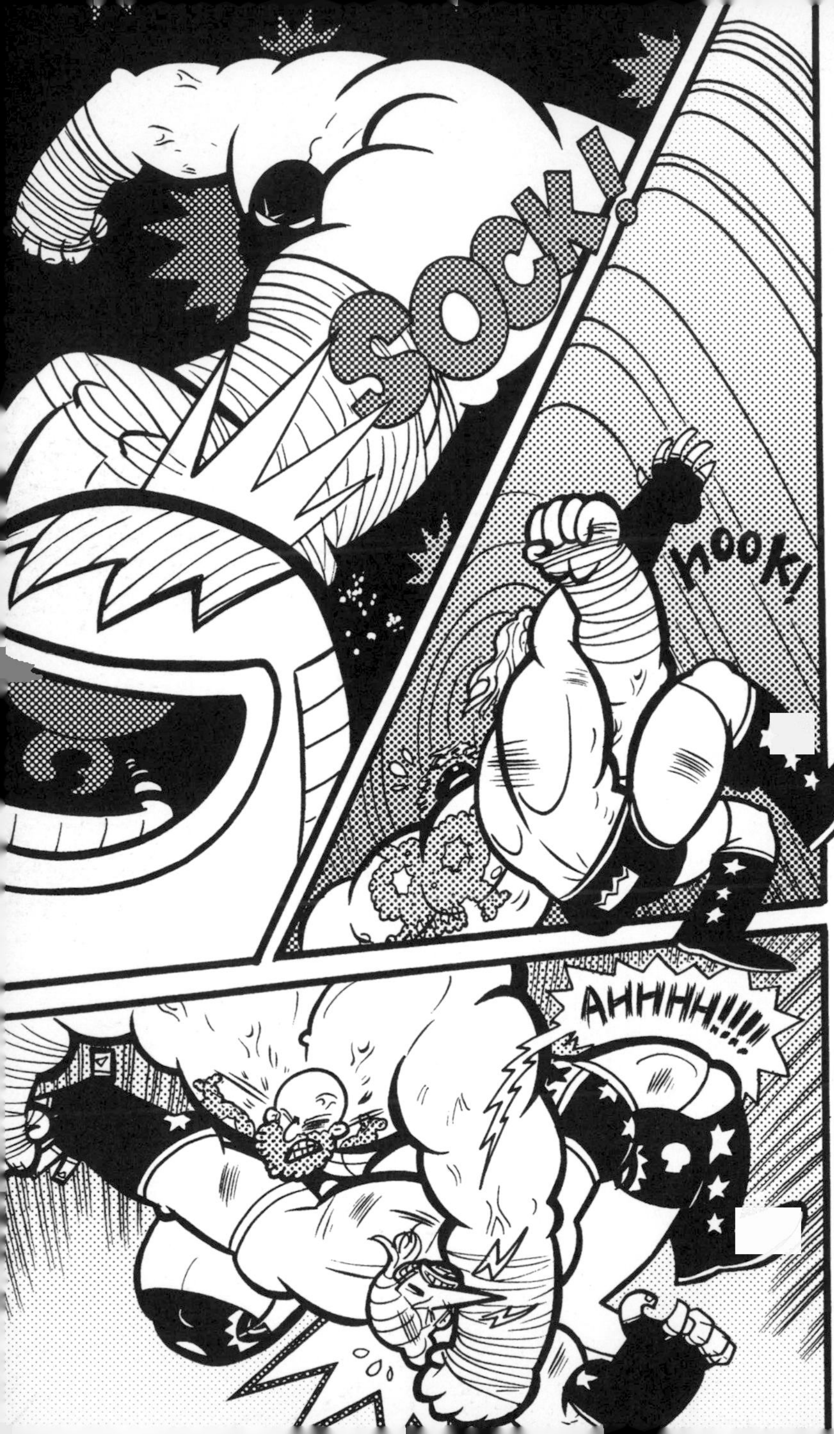
SOCK!
HOOK!
AHHHH!!!!

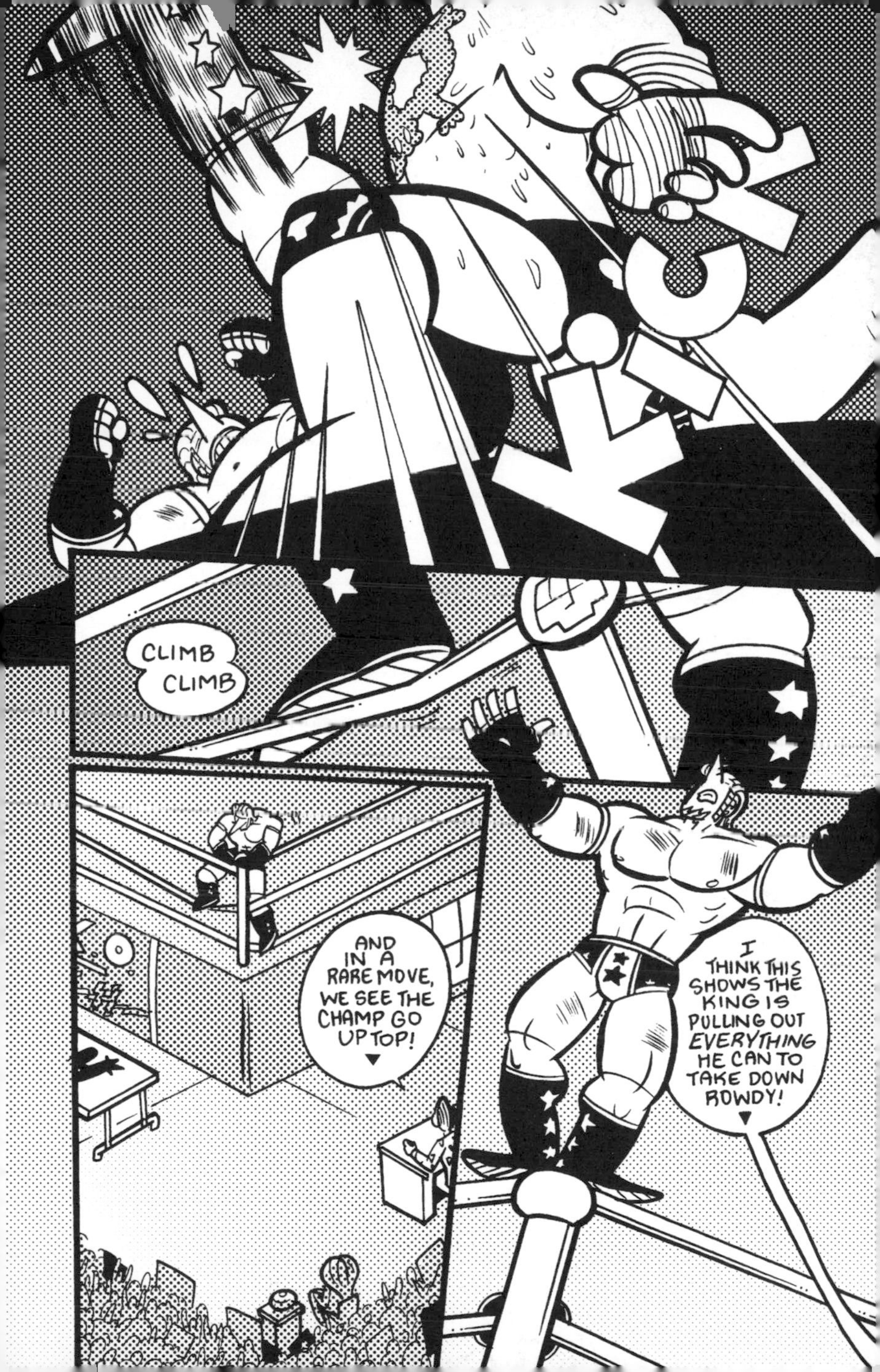
CLIMB CLIMB
AND IN A RARE MOVE, WE SEE THE CHAMP GO UP TOP!
I THINK THIS SHOWS THE KING IS PULLING OUT *EVERYTHING* HE CAN TO TAKE DOWN ROWDY!

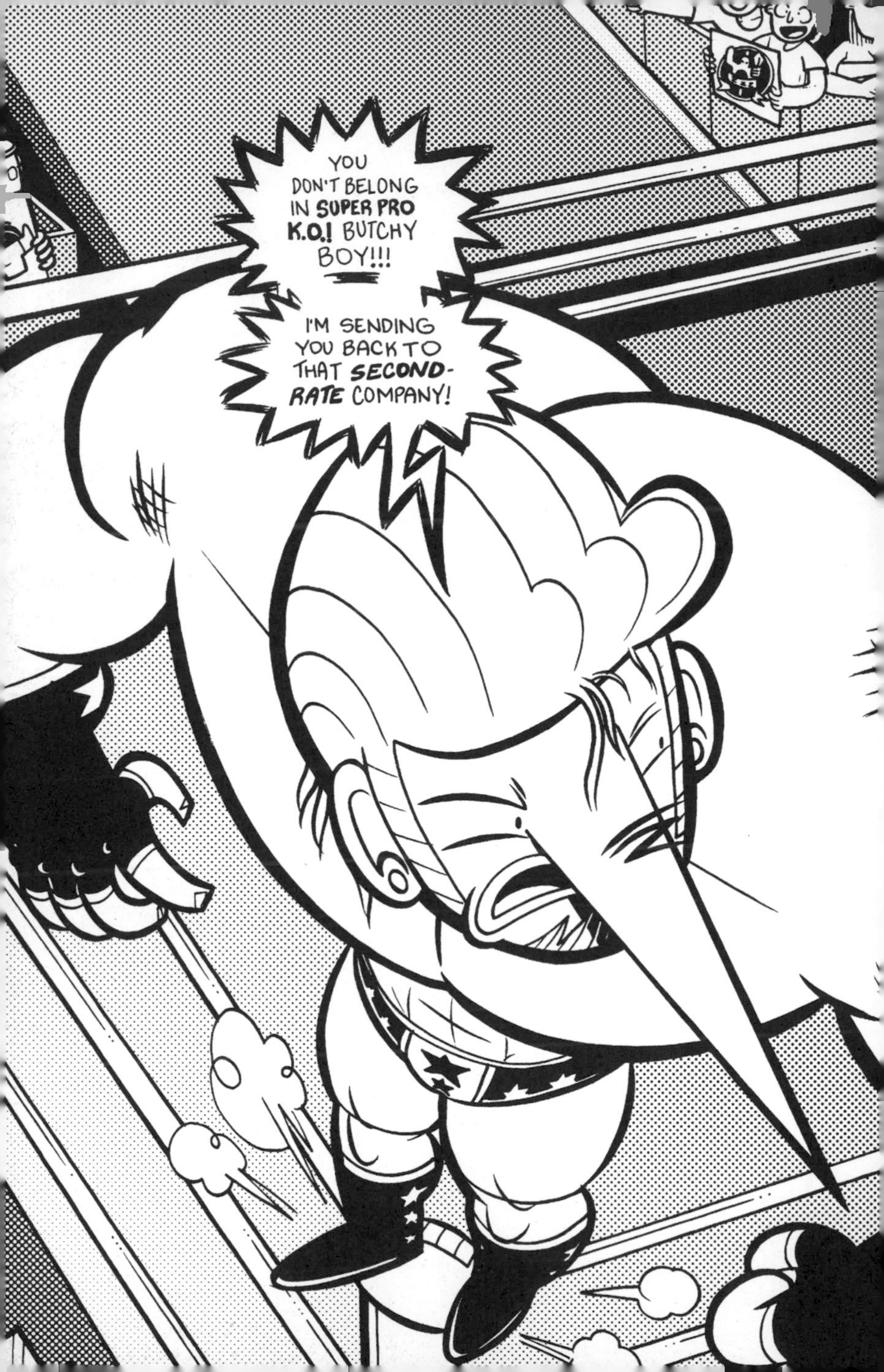
YOU DON'T BELONG IN SUPER PRO K.O.! BUTCHY BOY!!!
I'M SENDING YOU BACK TO THAT SECOND-RATE COMPANY!

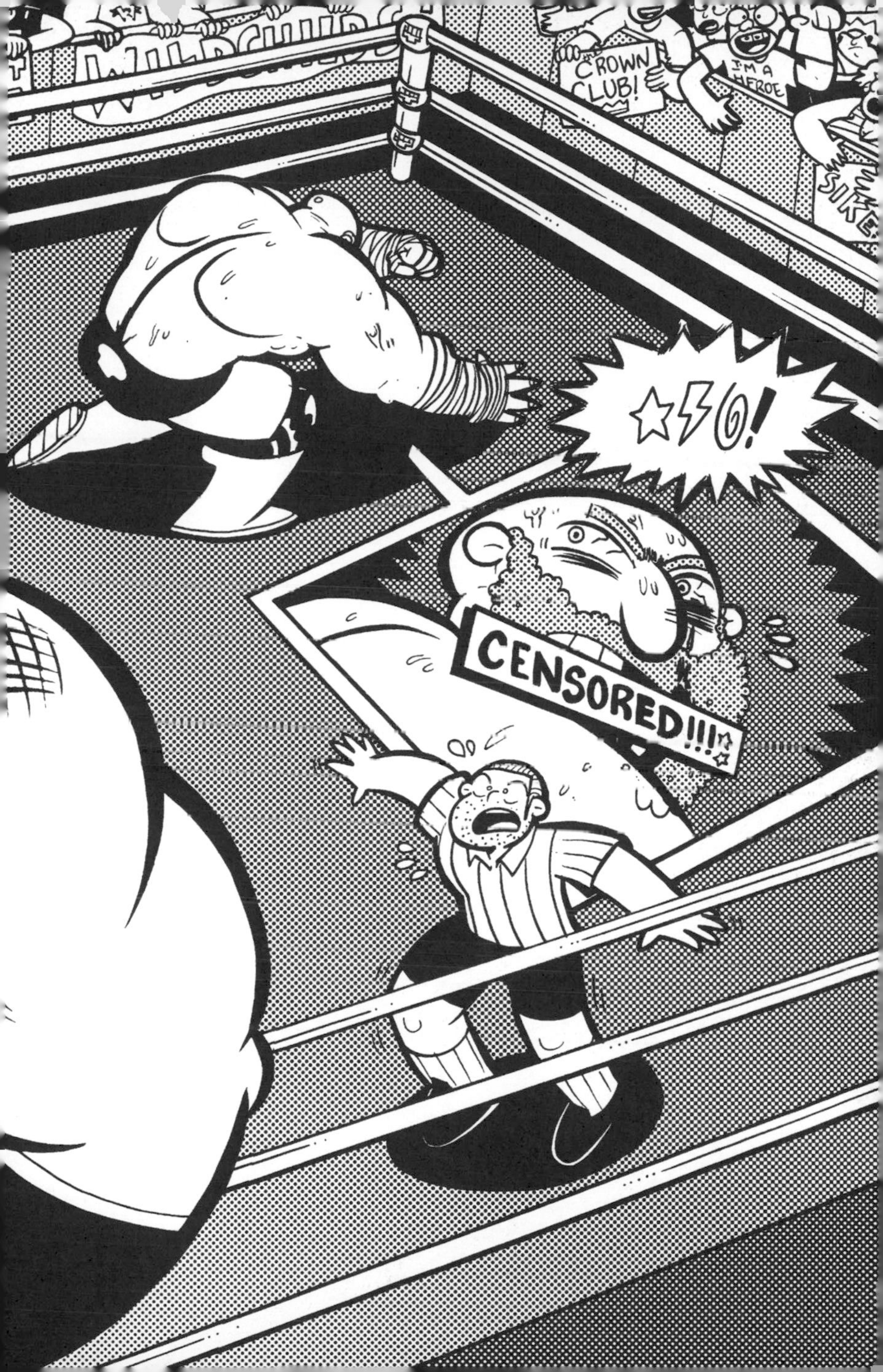
CROWN CLUB!
I'M A HEROE
SIKE
CENSORED!!!

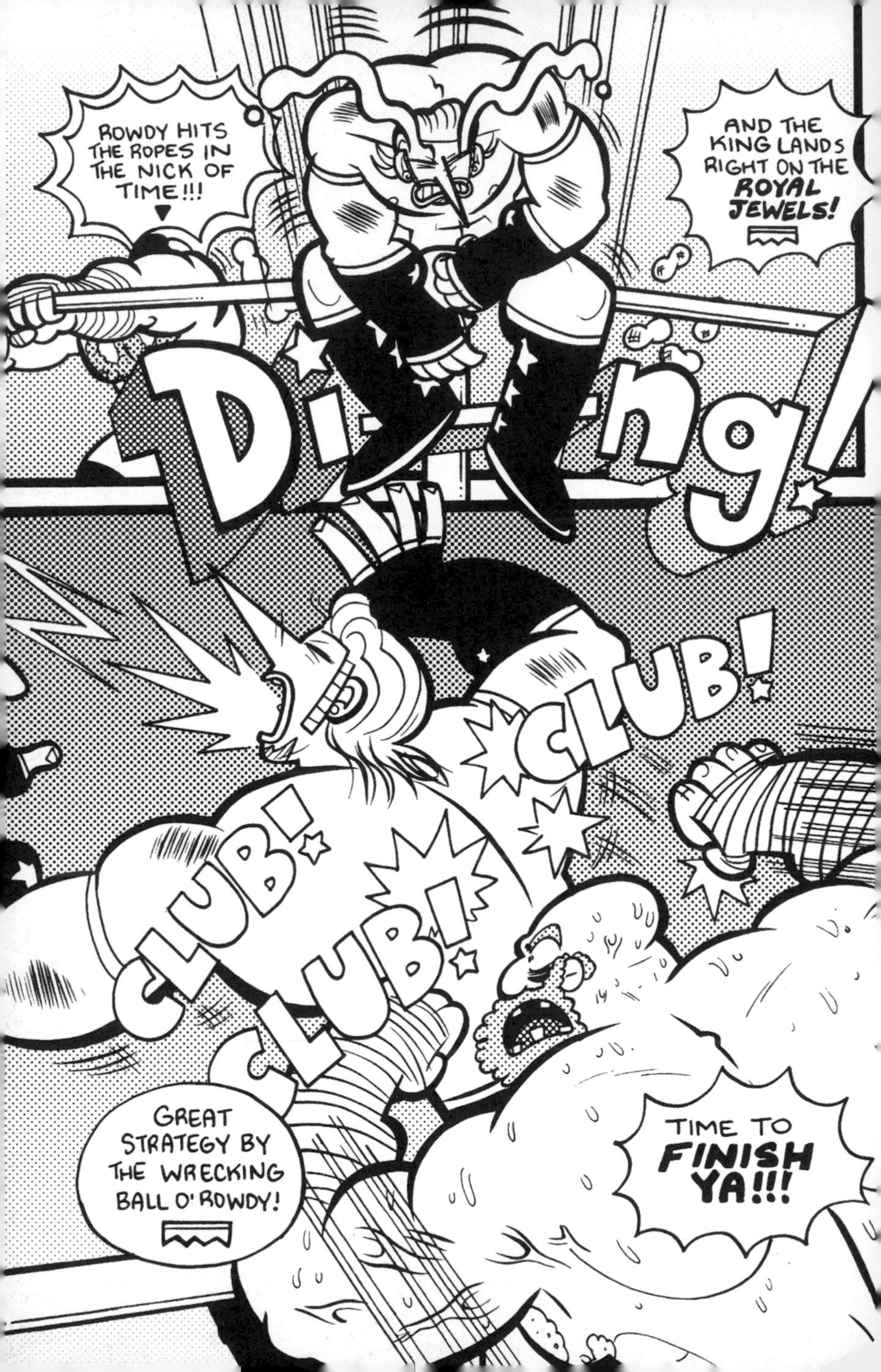
ROWDY HITS THE ROPES IN THE NICK OF TIME!!!
AND THE KING LANDS RIGHT ON THE ROYAL JEWELS!
CLUB!
CLUB!
CLUB!
GREAT STRATEGY BY THE WRECKING BALL O' ROWDY!
TIME TO FINISH YA!!!

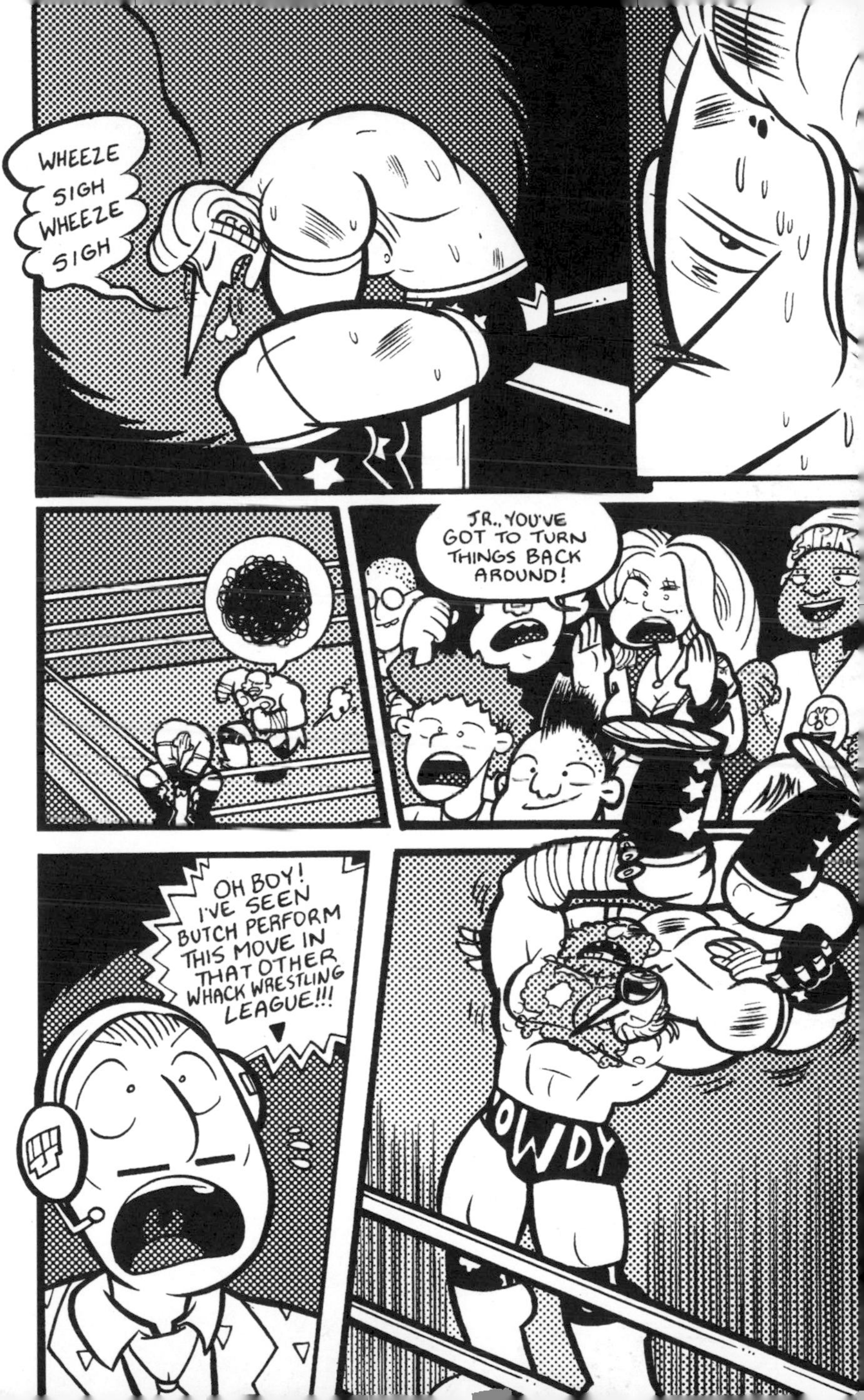
WHEEZE SIGH WHEEZE SIGH
JR., YOU'VE GOT TO TURN THINGS BACK AROUND!
OH BOY! I'VE SEEN BUTCH PERFORM THIS MOVE IN THAT OTHER WHACK WRESTLING LEAGUE!!!
OWDY

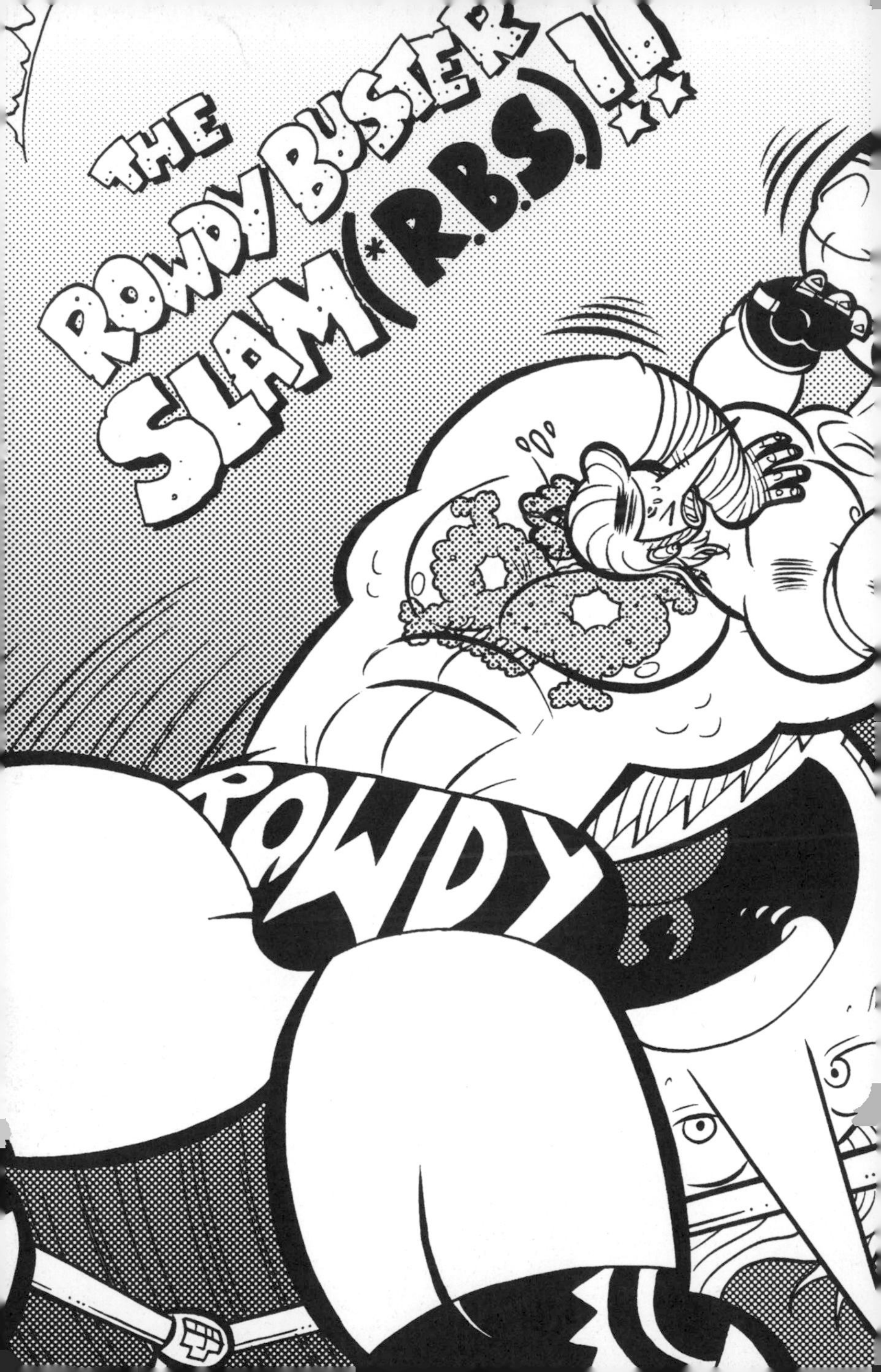
THE ROWDY BUSTER SLAM (*R.B.S.)!!
ROWDY

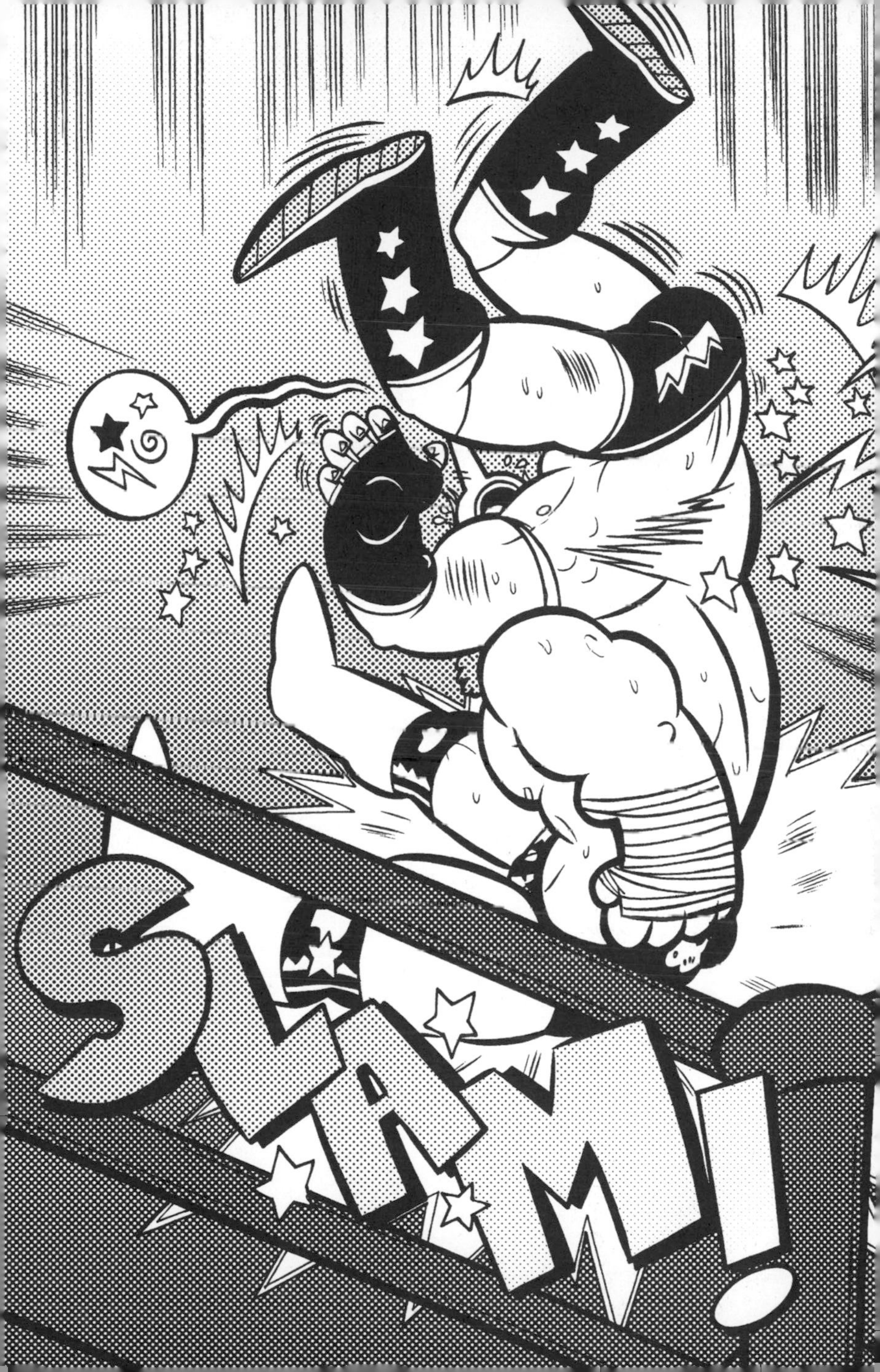
SLAM!

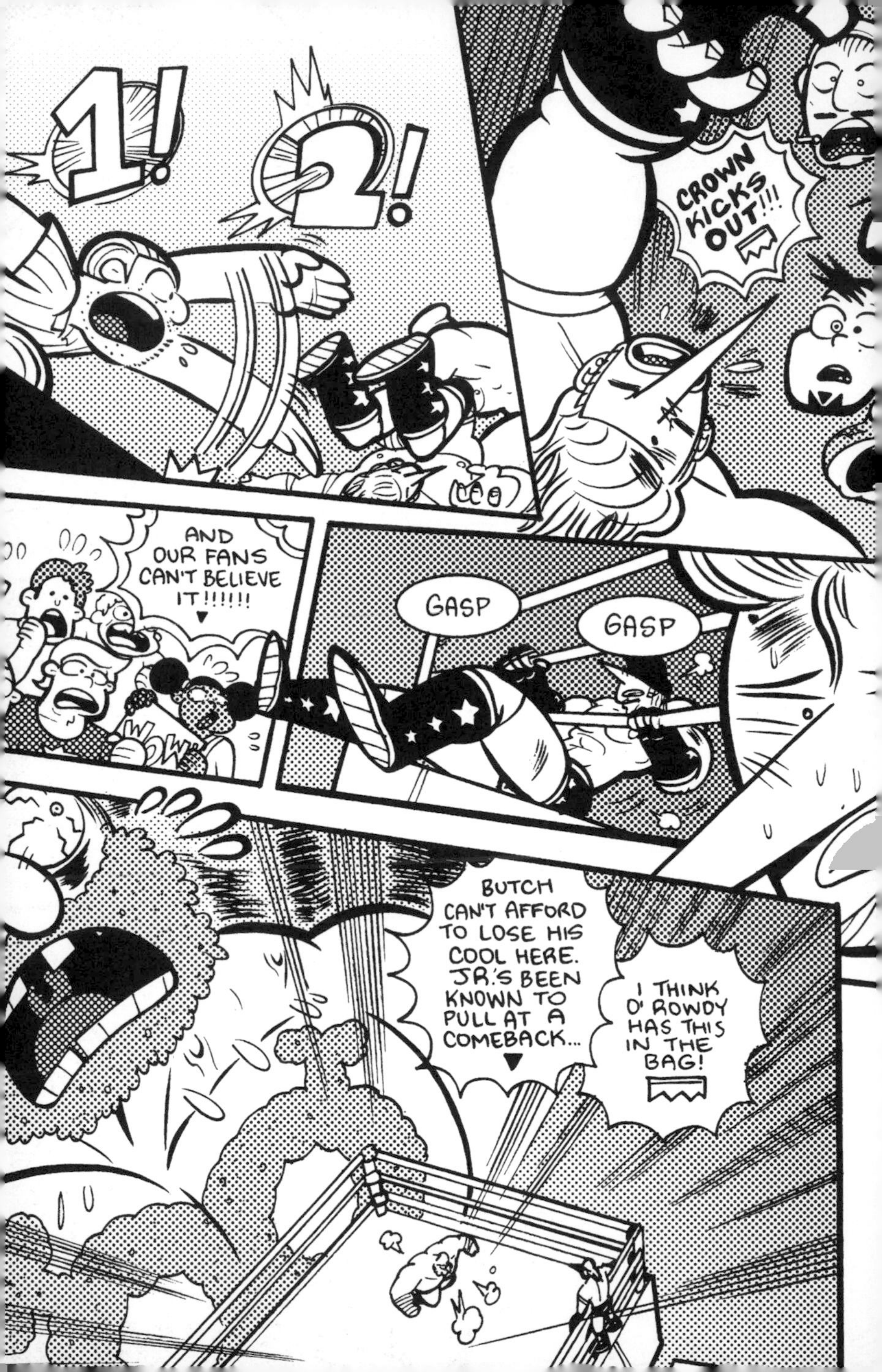
1!
2!
CROWN KICKS OUT!!!
AND OUR FANS CAN'T BELIEVE IT!!!!!!
WOW
GASP
GASP
BUTCH CAN'T AFFORD TO LOSE HIS COOL HERE. JR.'S BEEN KNOWN TO PULL AT A COMEBACK...
I THINK O' ROWDY HAS THIS IN THE BAG!

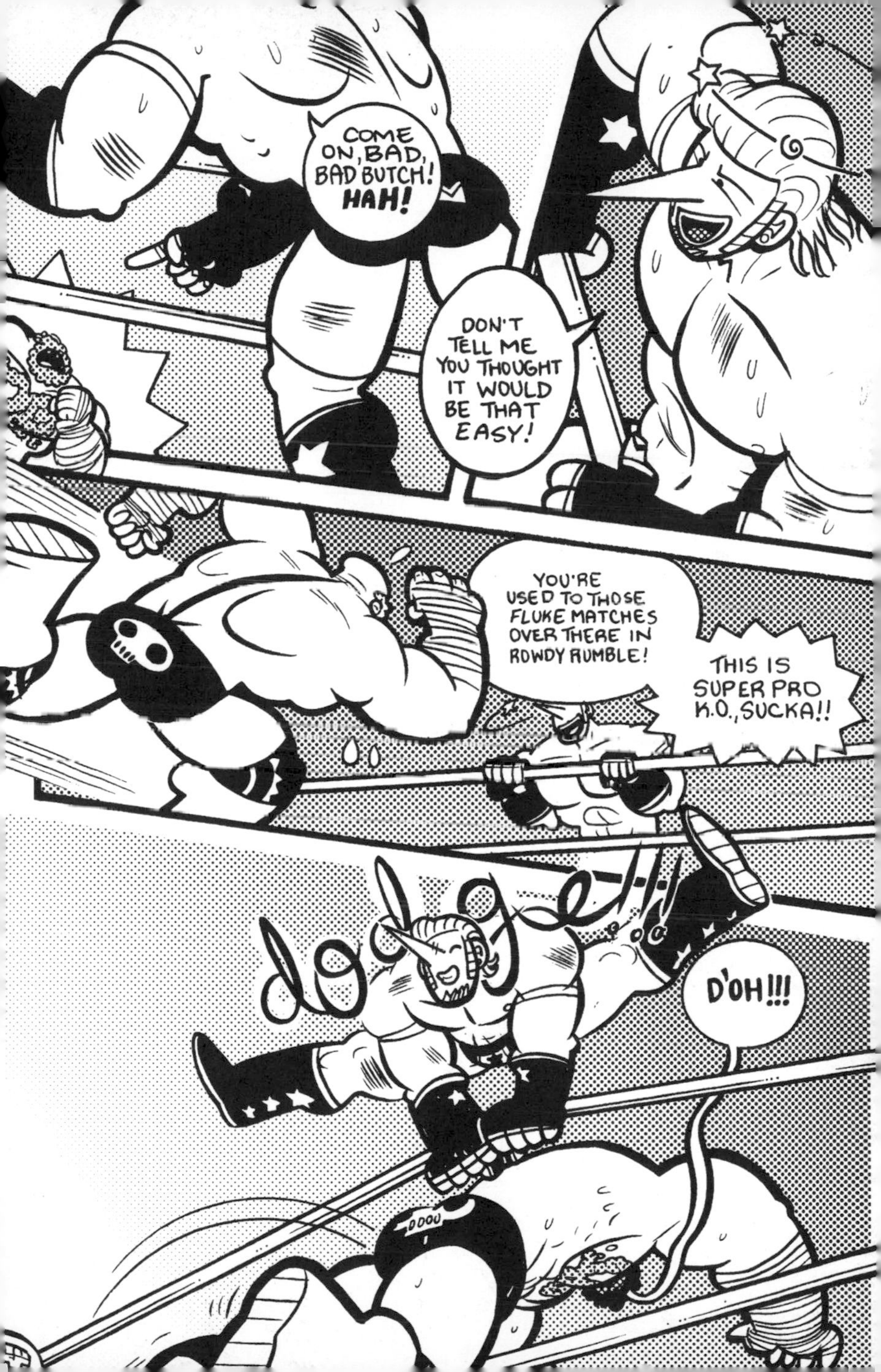
COME ON, BAD, BAD BUTCH! HAH!
DON'T TELL ME YOU THOUGHT IT WOULD BE THAT EASY!
YOU'RE USED TO THOSE FLUKE MATCHES OVER THERE IN ROWDY RUMBLE!
THIS IS SUPER PRO K.O., SUCKA!!
doogel!
D'OH!!!

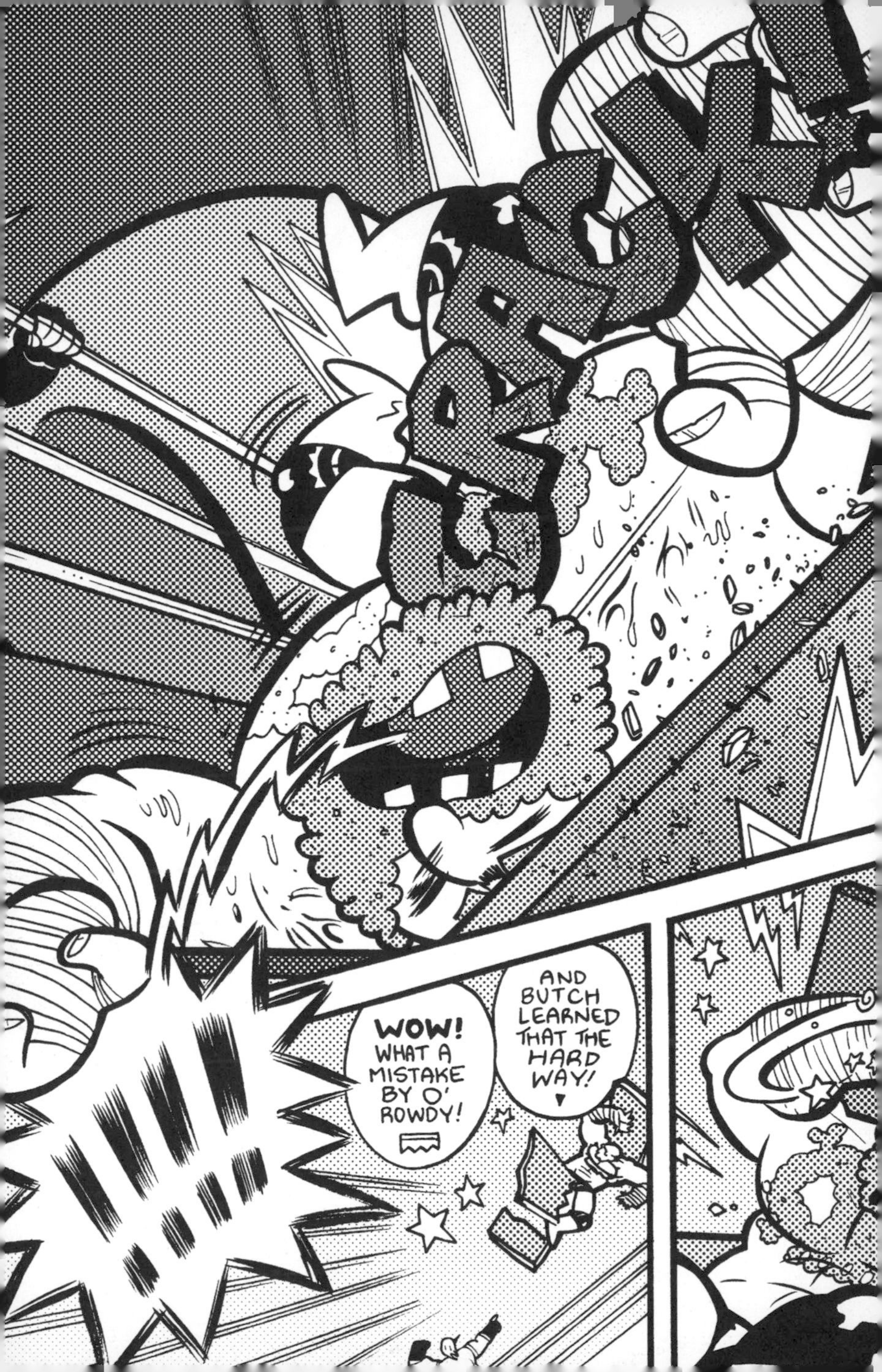
WOW! WHAT A MISTAKE BY O' ROWDY!
AND BUTCH LEARNED THAT THE HARD WAY!

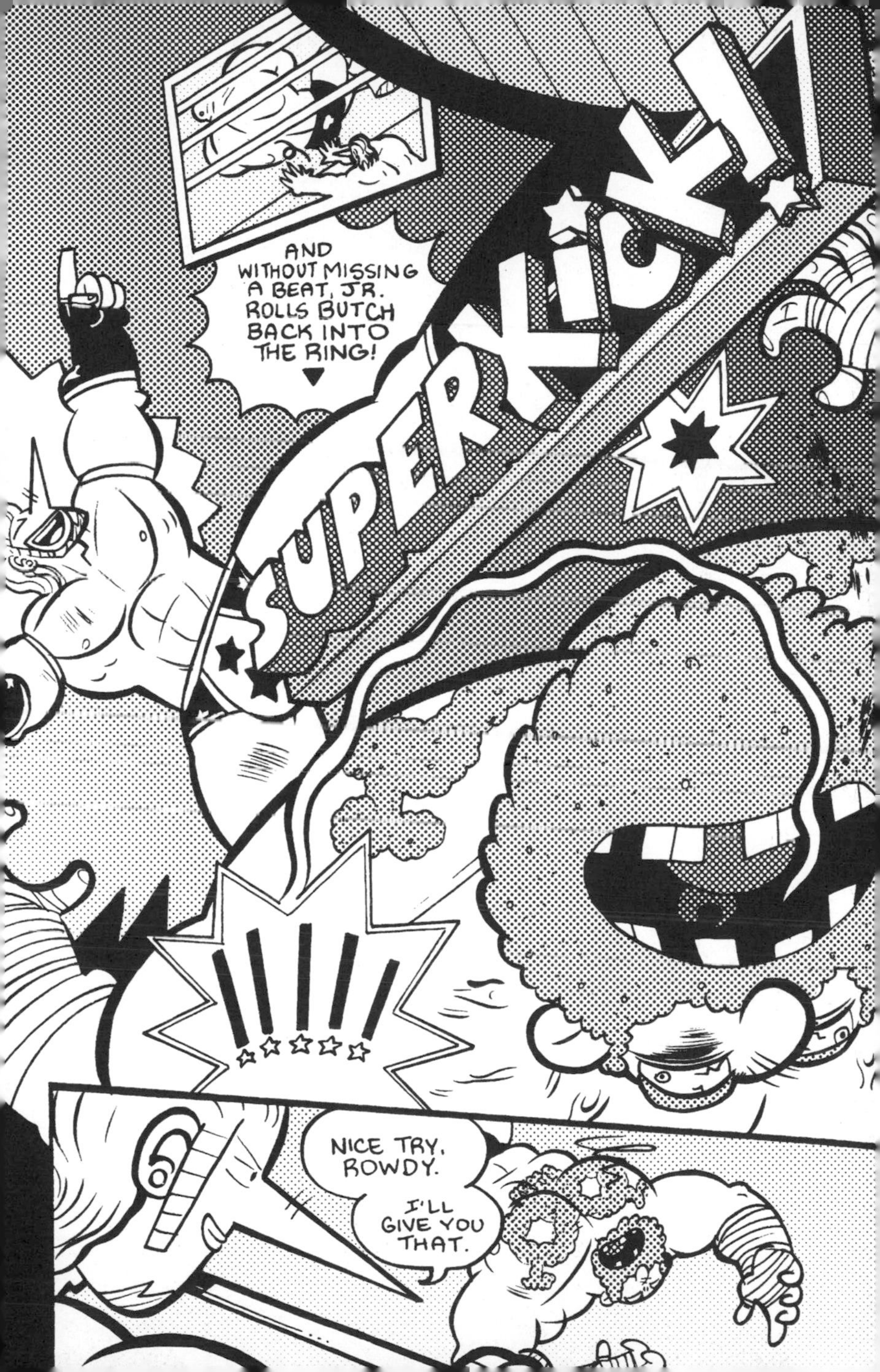
AND WITHOUT MISSING A BEAT, JR. ROLLS BUTCH BACK INTO THE RING!
SUPERKICK!
NICE TRY, ROWDY.
I'LL GIVE YOU THAT.

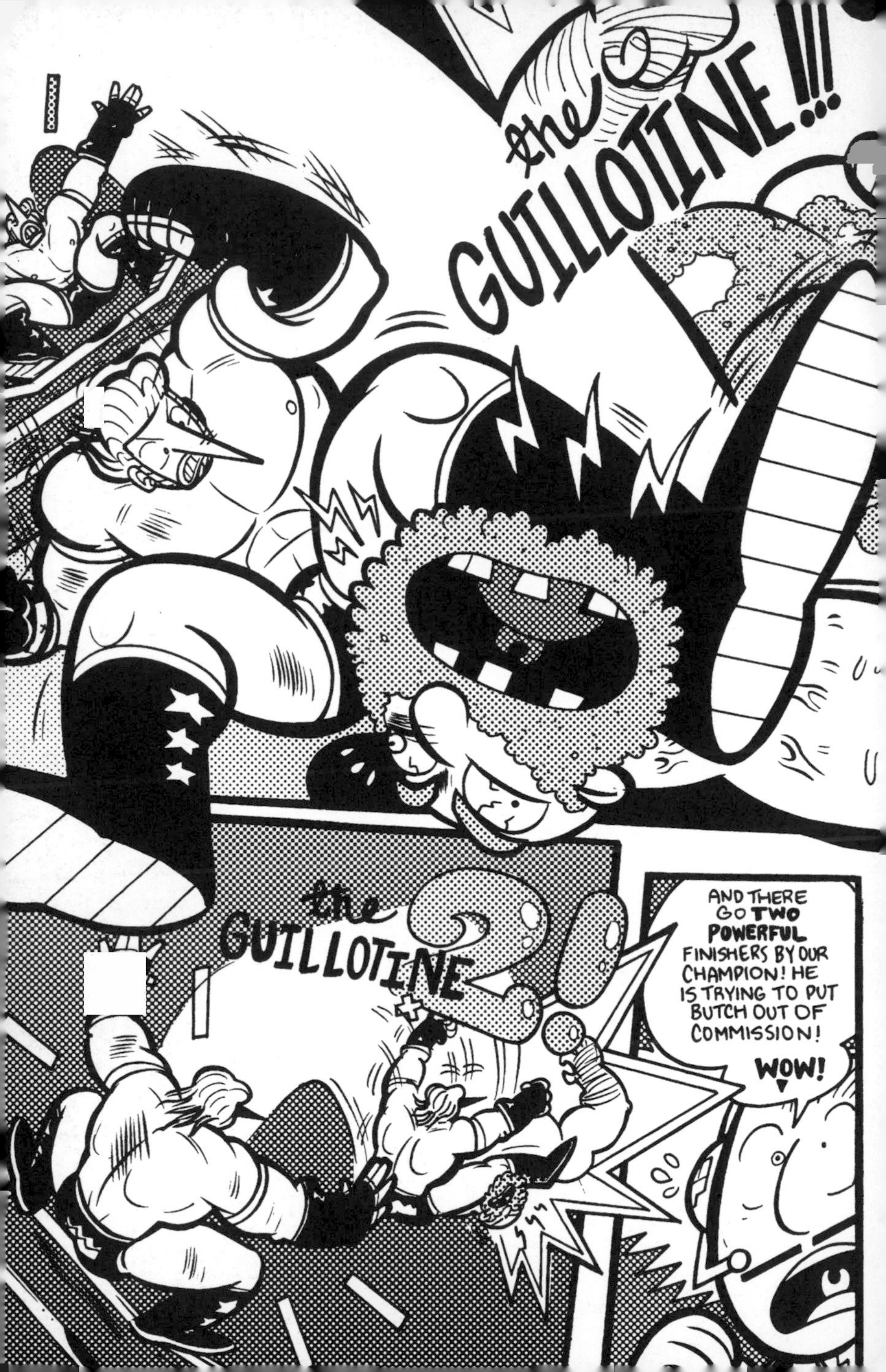
the GUILLOTINE!!!
the GUILLOTINE
AND THERE GO **TWO POWERFUL** FINISHERS BY OUR CHAMPION! HE IS TRYING TO PUT BUTCH OUT OF COMMISSION!
WOW!

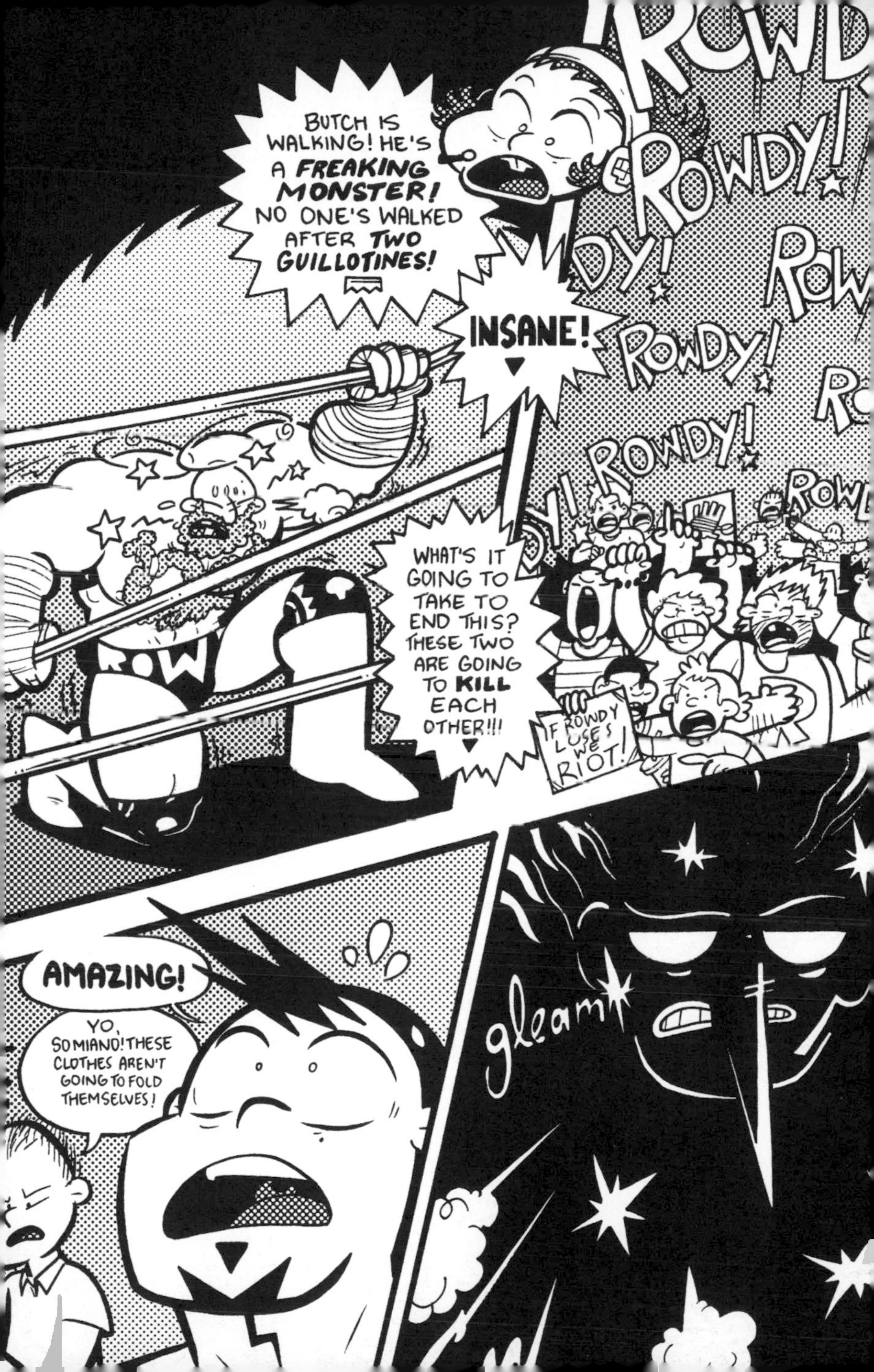

ROWDY!
BUTCH IS WALKING! HE'S A **FREAKING MONSTER!** NO ONE'S WALKED AFTER **TWO GUILLOTINES!**
ROWDY!
ROWDY!
ROWDY!
INSANE!
ROWDY!
ROWDY!
WHAT'S IT GOING TO TAKE TO END THIS? THESE TWO ARE GOING TO **KILL** EACH OTHER!!!
IF ROWDY LOSES WE RIOT!
ROW
AMAZING!
YO, SOMIANO! THESE CLOTHES AREN'T GOING TO FOLD THEMSELVES!
gleam

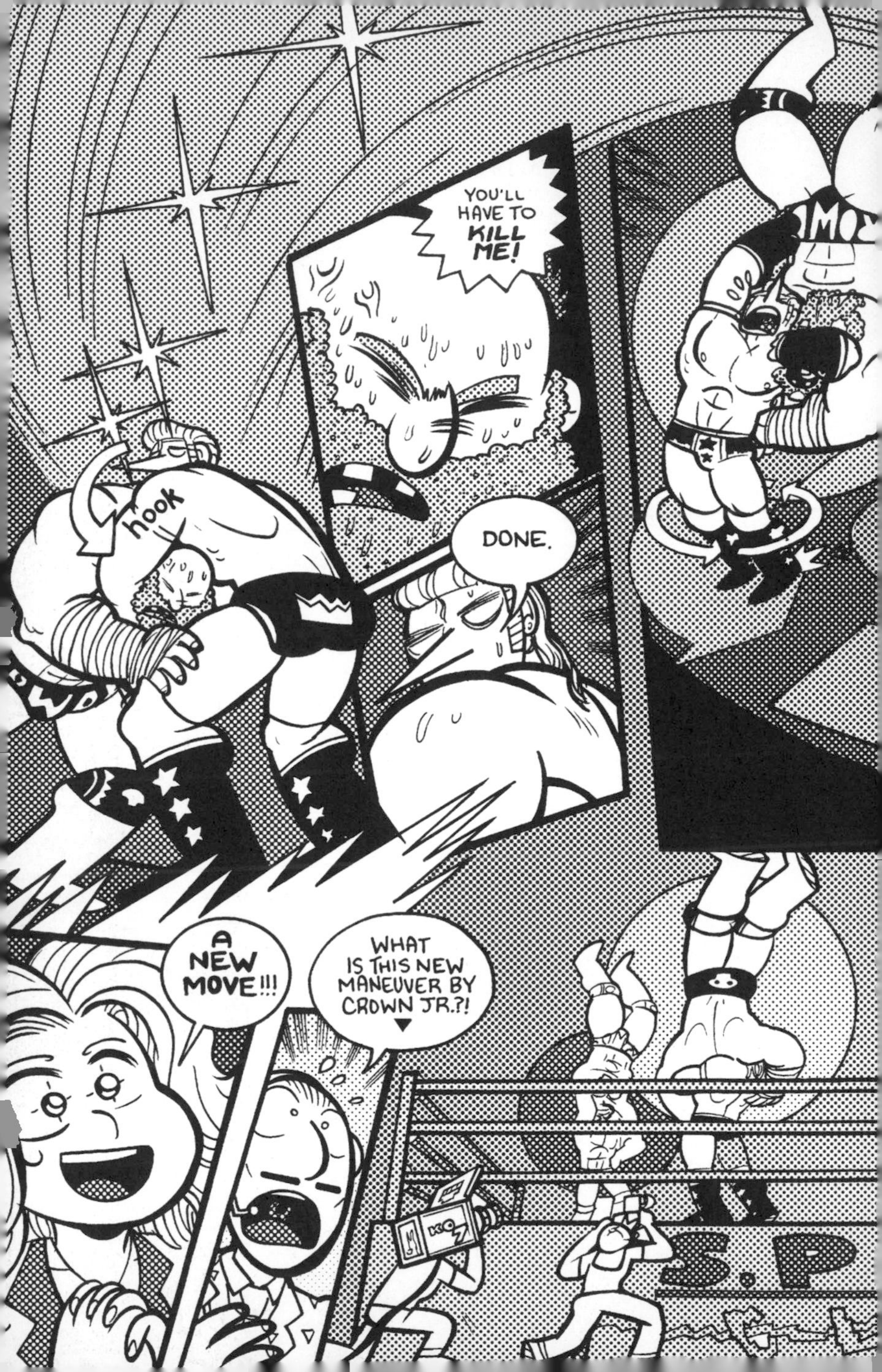
hook
YOU'LL HAVE TO KILL ME!
DONE.
A NEW MOVE!!!
WHAT IS THIS NEW MANEUVER BY CROWN JR.?!

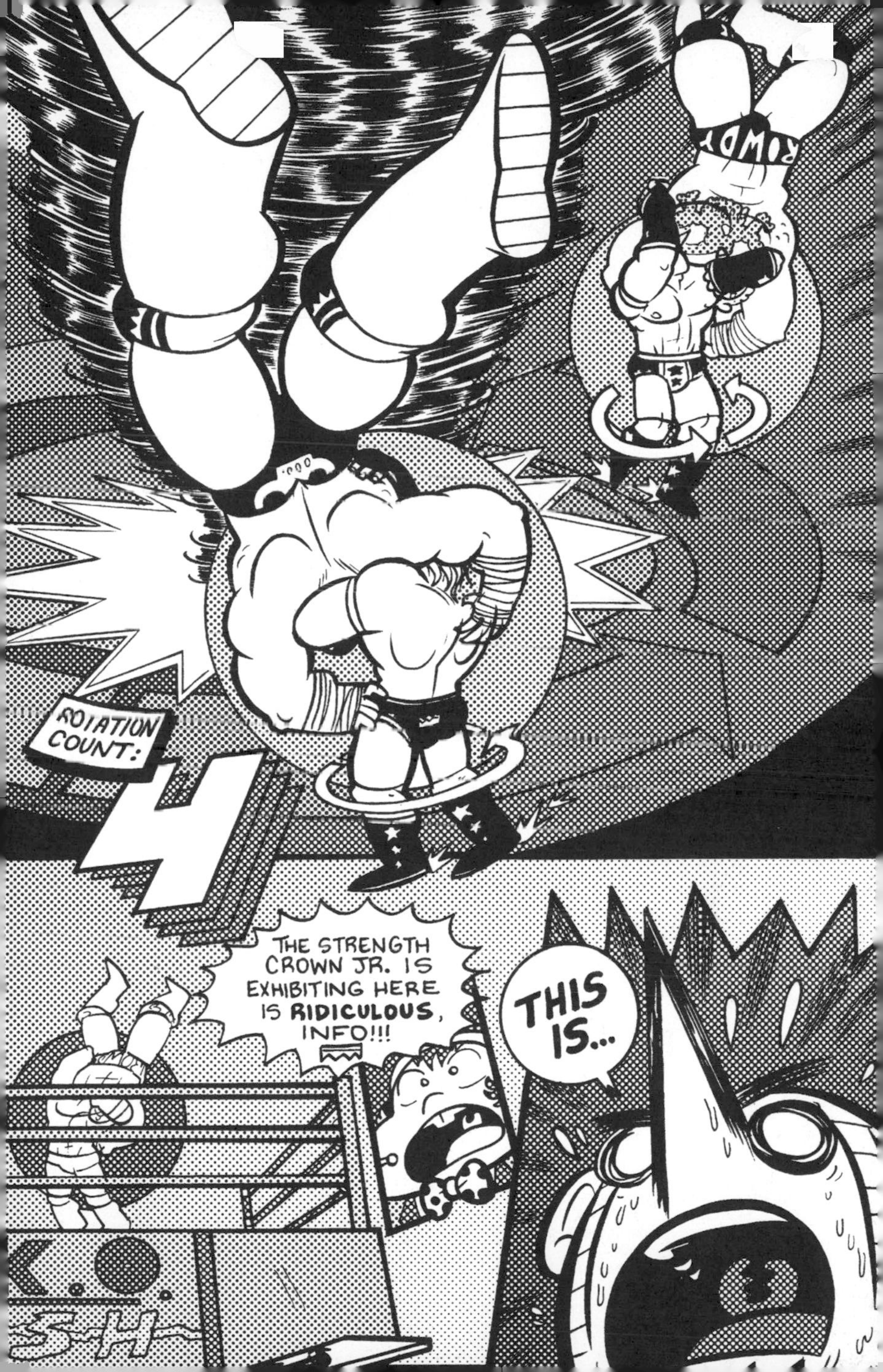
ROWDY
ROTATION COUNT:
4
THE STRENGTH CROWN JR. IS EXHIBITING HERE IS **RIDICULOUS**, INFO!!!
THIS IS...

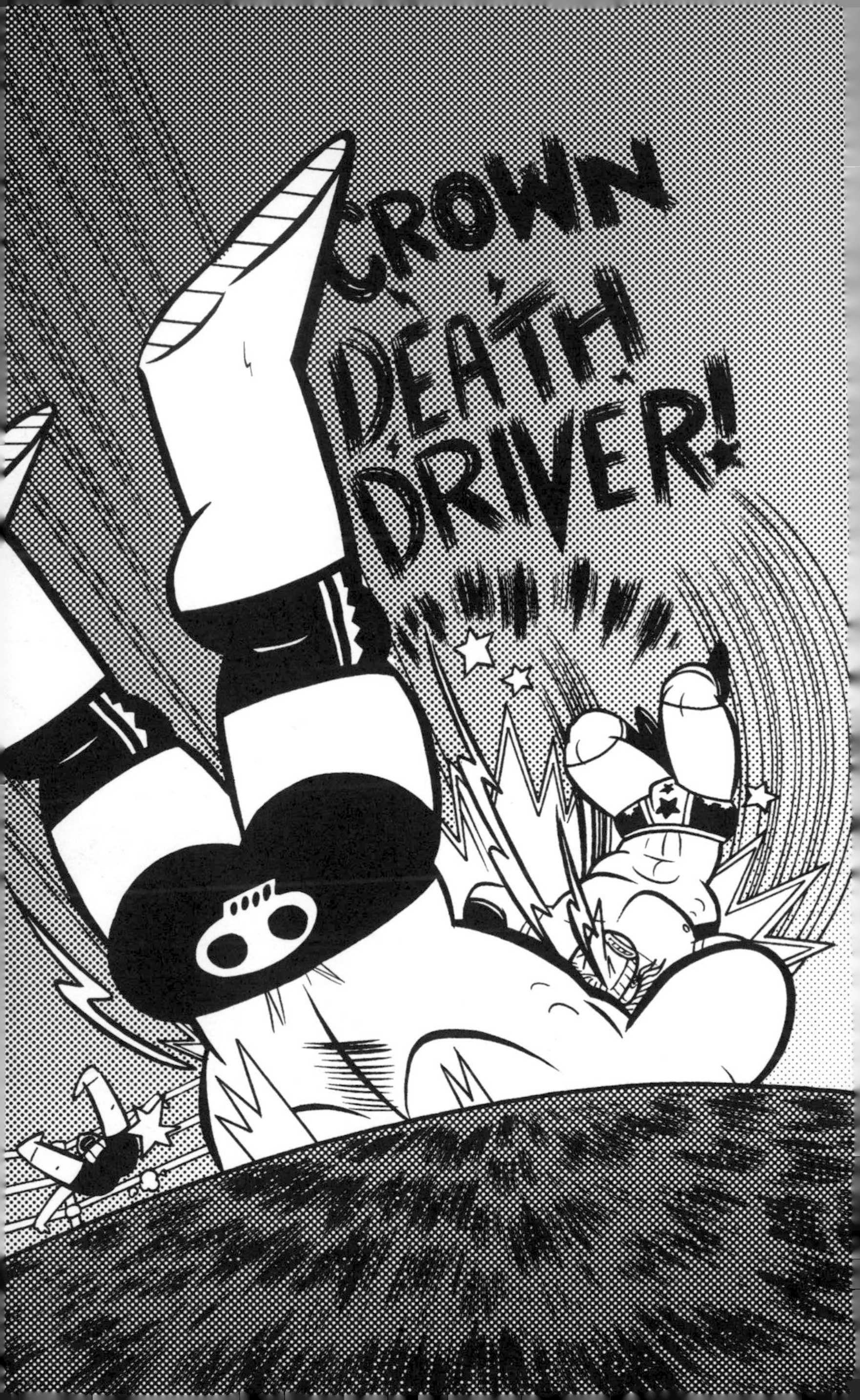
CROWN DEATH DRIVER!

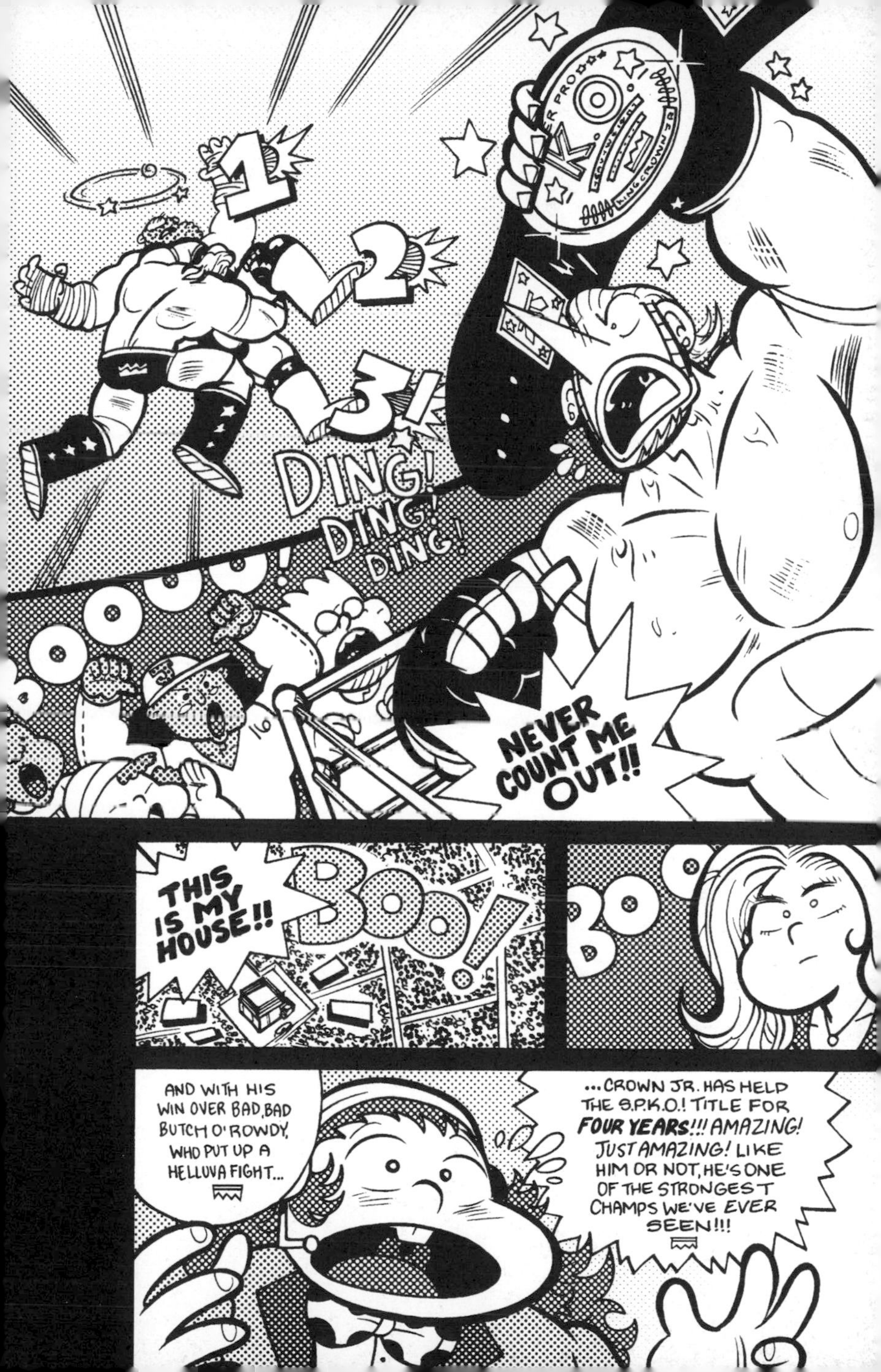
1
2
3!
DING! DING! DING!
BOOOOO!
NEVER COUNT ME OUT!!
THIS IS MY HOUSE!!
BOOO!
BOO
AND WITH HIS WIN OVER BAD, BAD BUTCH O'ROWDY, WHO PUT UP A HELLUVA FIGHT...
...CROWN JR. HAS HELD THE S.P.K.O.! TITLE FOR FOUR YEARS!!! AMAZING! JUST AMAZING! LIKE HIM OR NOT, HE'S ONE OF THE STRONGEST CHAMPS WE'VE EVER SEEN!!!

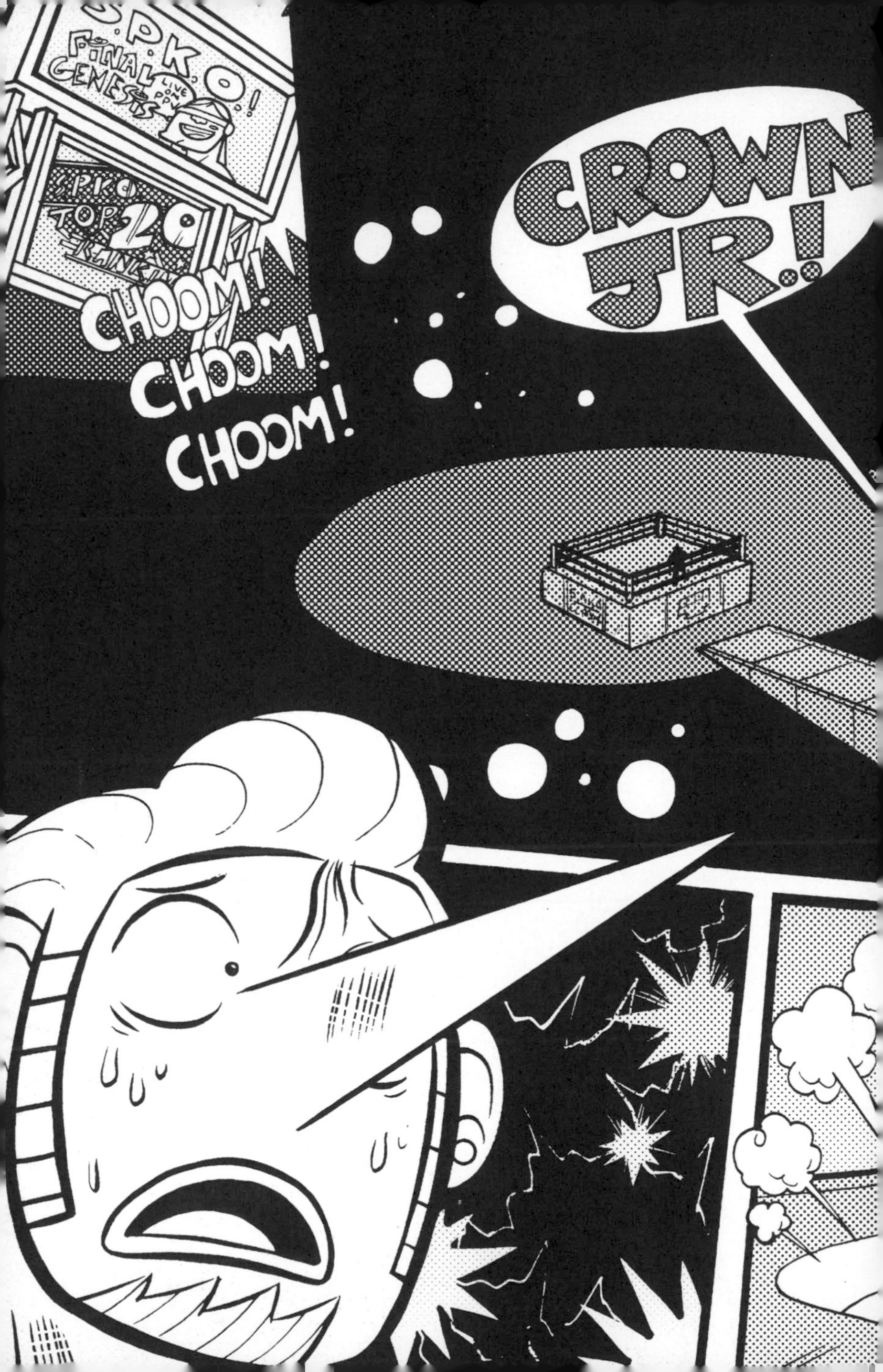
S.P.K.O.!
FINAL GENESIS
LIVE ON PPV
SPKO TOP 20
CHOOM! CHOOM! CHOOM!
CROWN JR.!

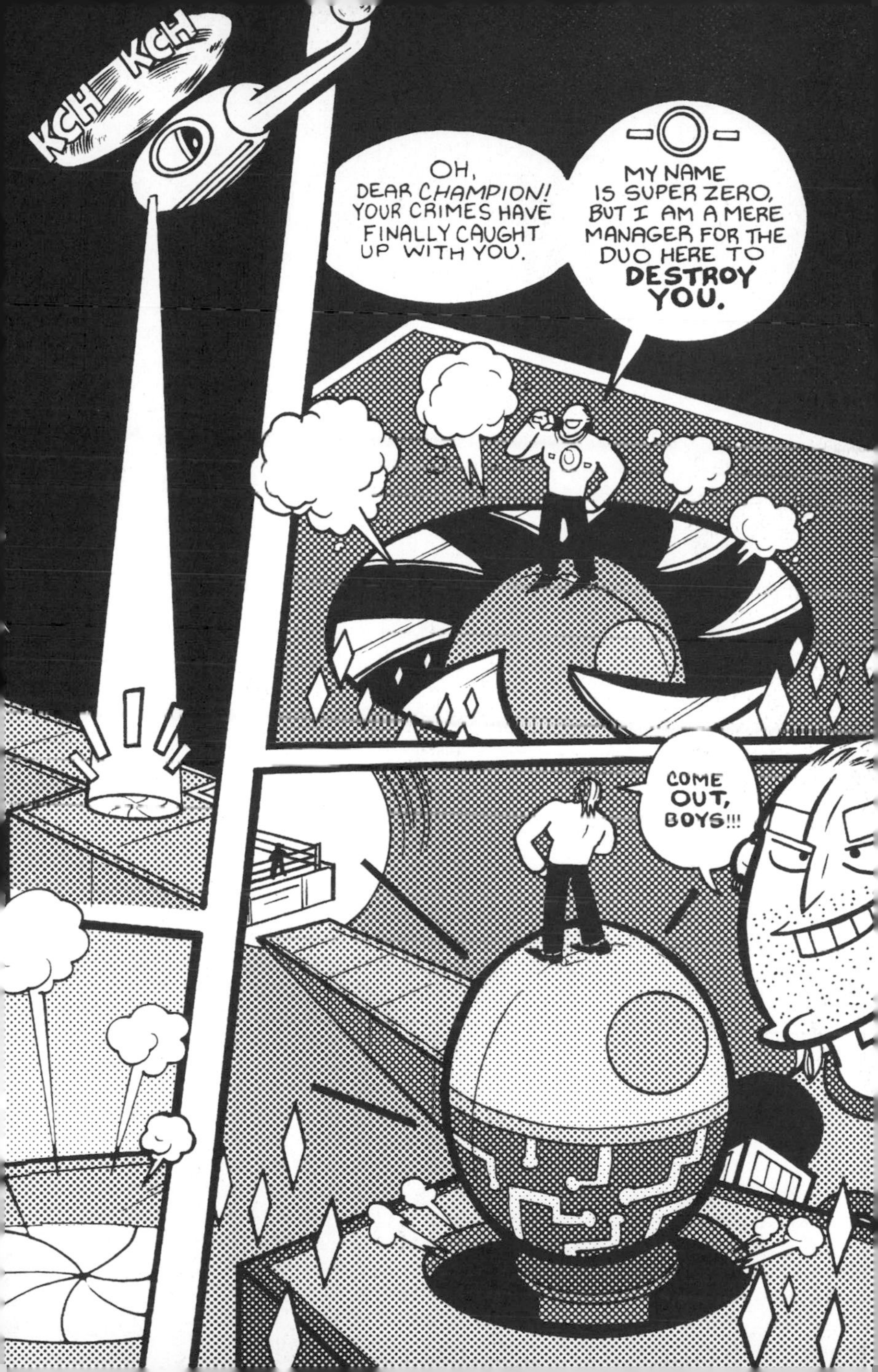
KCH KCH
OH, DEAR CHAMPION! YOUR CRIMES HAVE FINALLY CAUGHT UP WITH YOU.
MY NAME IS SUPER ZERO, BUT I AM A MERE MANAGER FOR THE DUO HERE TO DESTROY YOU.
COME OUT, BOYS!!!

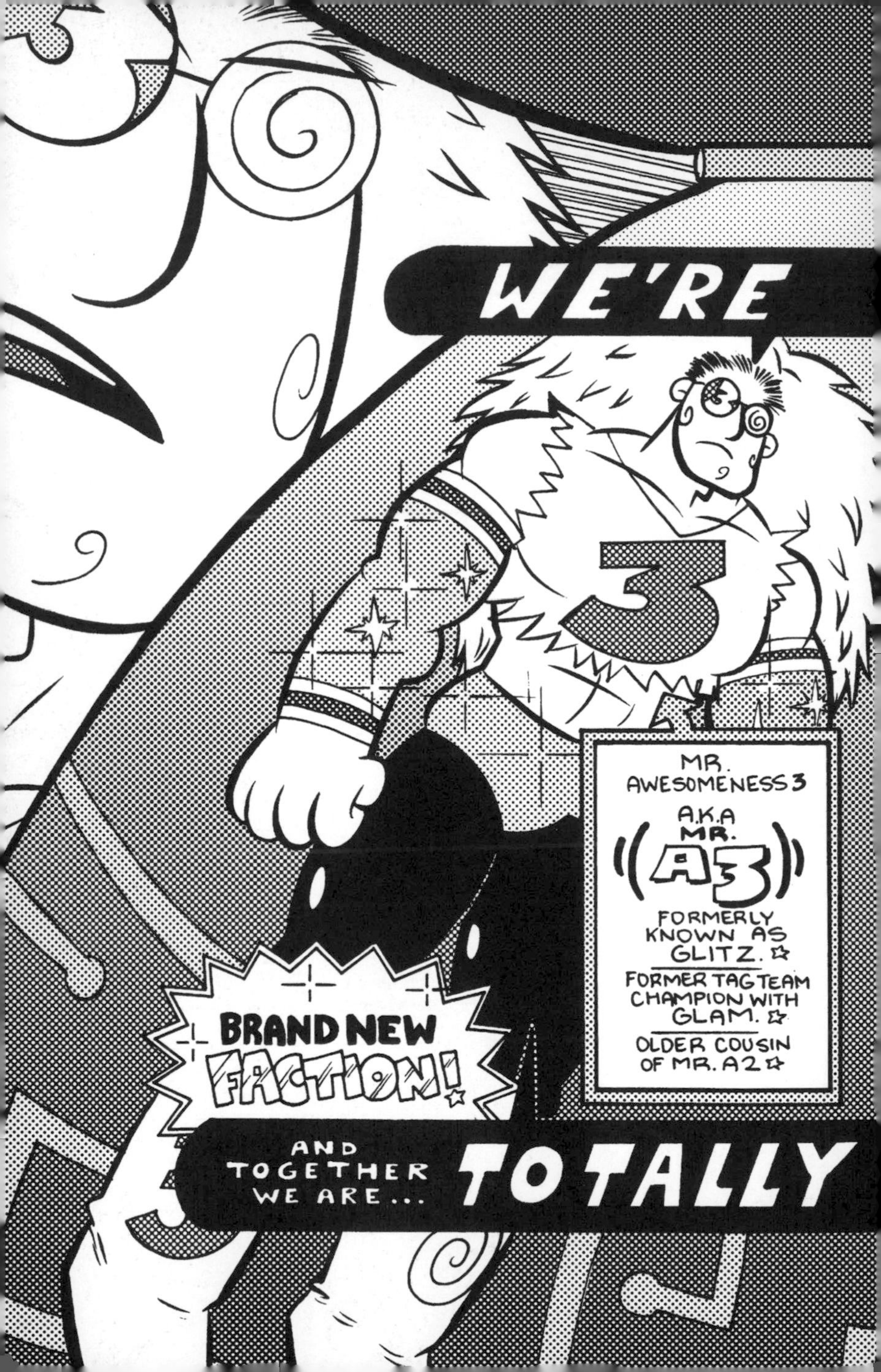
WE'RE
MR. AWESOMENESS 3
A.K.A MR. A3
FORMERLY KNOWN AS GLITZ.
FORMER TAG TEAM CHAMPION WITH GLAM.
OLDER COUSIN OF MR. A2
BRAND NEW FACTION!
AND TOGETHER WE ARE... TOTALLY

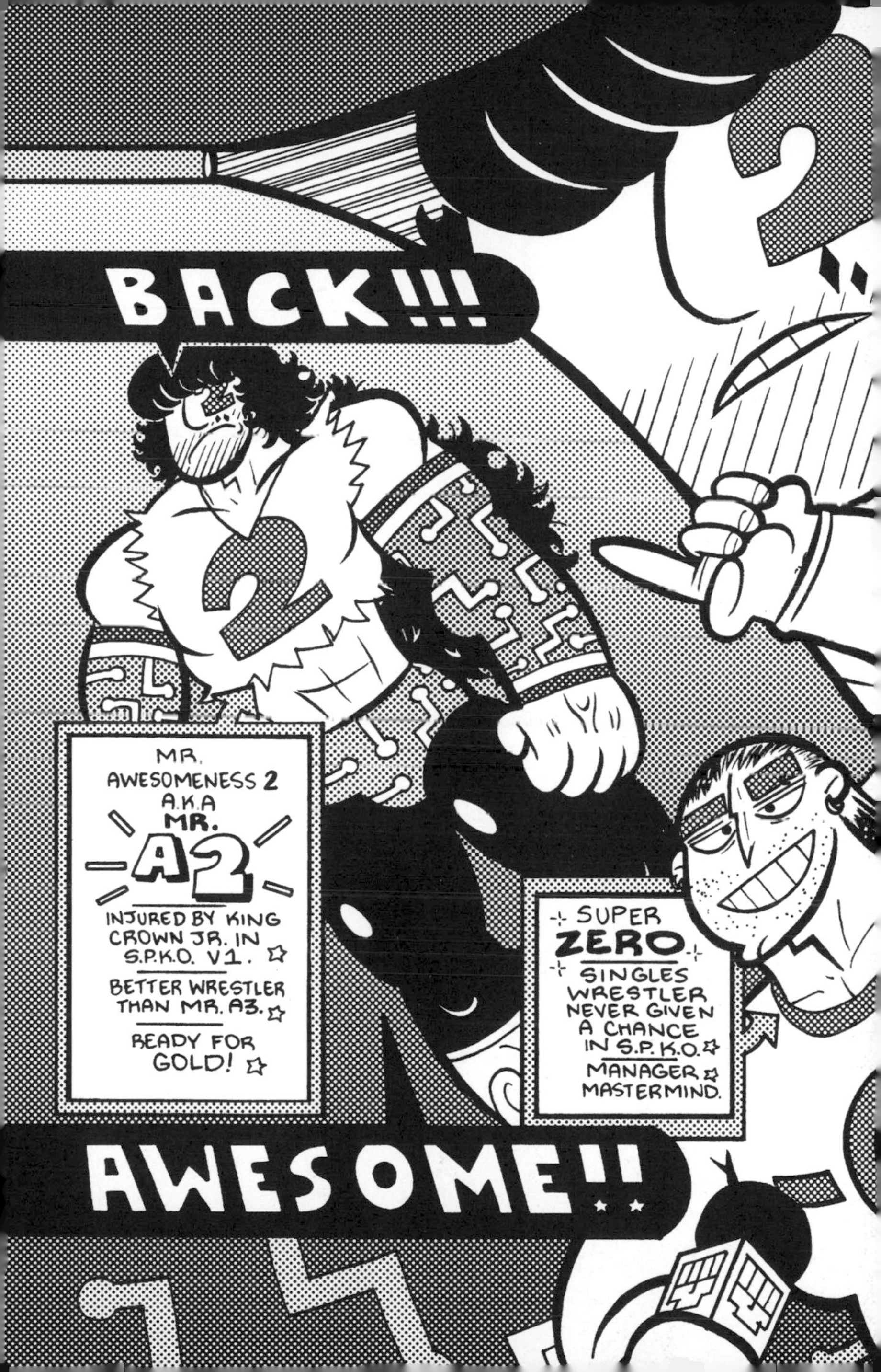

BACK!!!
MR. AWESOMENESS 2 A.K.A MR. A2
INJURED BY KING CROWN JR. IN S.P.K.O. V1.
BETTER WRESTLER THAN MR. A3.
READY FOR GOLD!
SUPER ZERO
SINGLES WRESTLER NEVER GIVEN A CHANCE IN S.P.K.O.
MANAGER MASTERMIND.
AWESOME!!

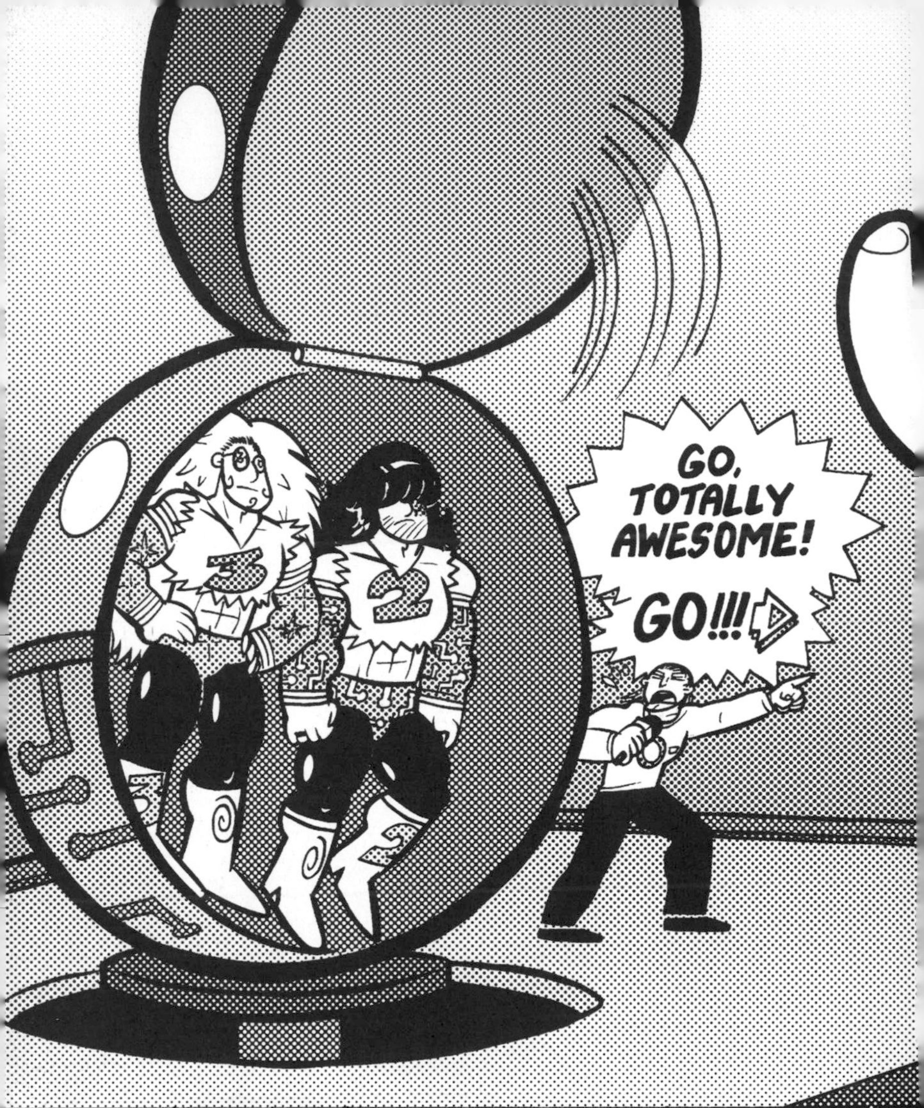
GO, TOTALLY AWESOME!
GO!!!
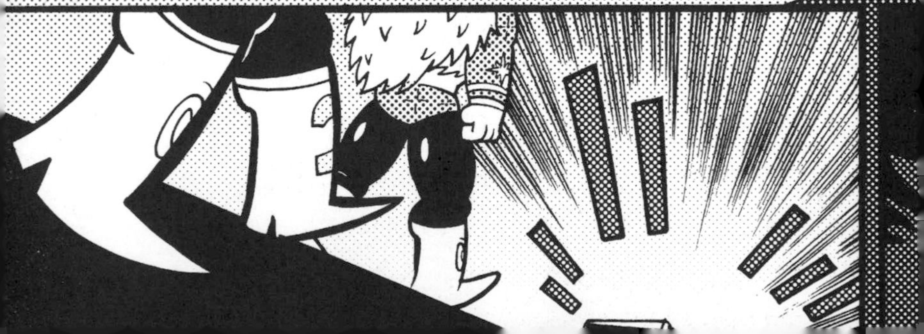

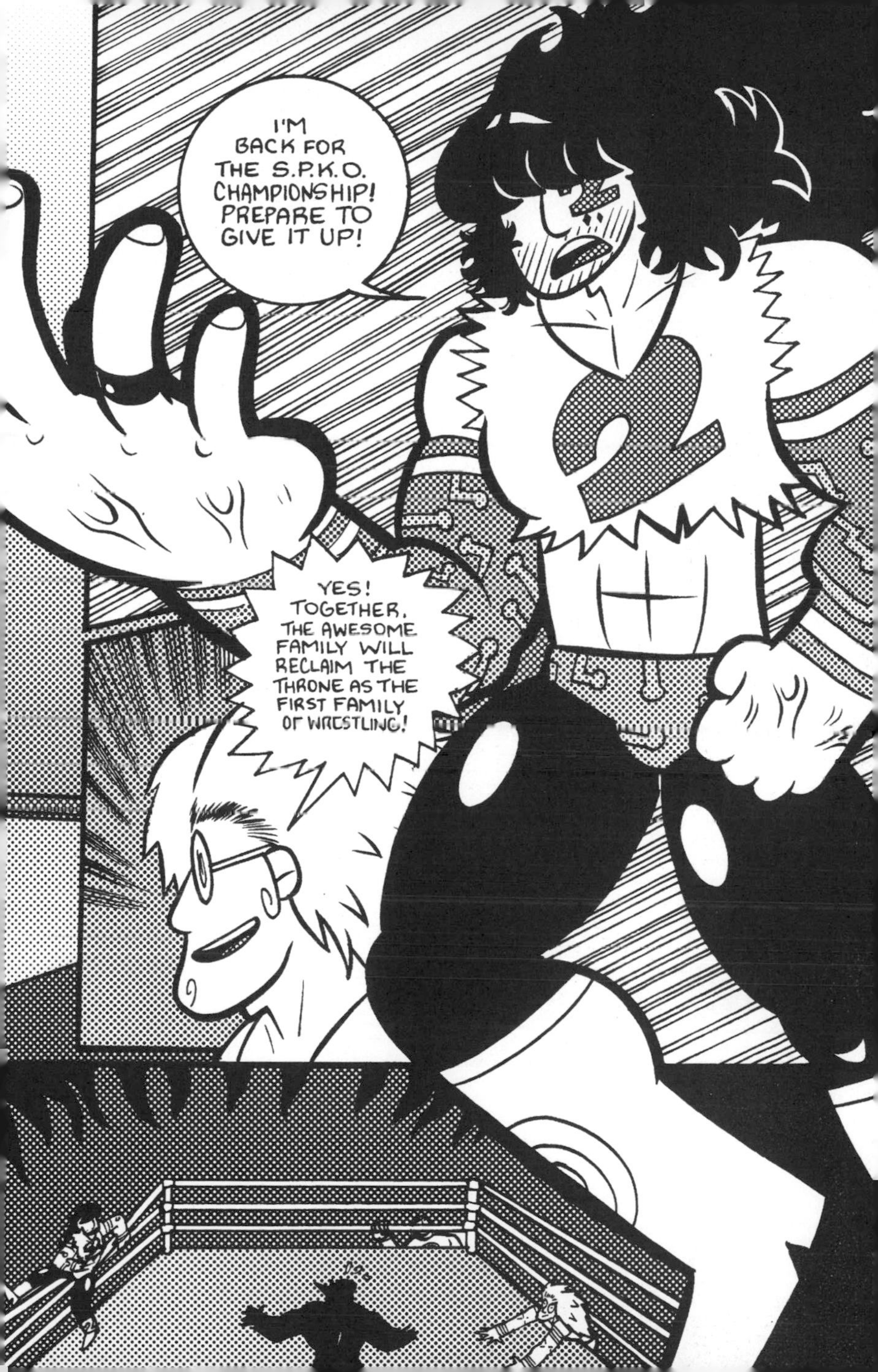
I'M BACK FOR THE S.P.K.O. CHAMPIONSHIP! PREPARE TO GIVE IT UP!
YES! TOGETHER, THE AWESOME FAMILY WILL RECLAIM THE THRONE AS THE FIRST FAMILY OF WRESTLING!

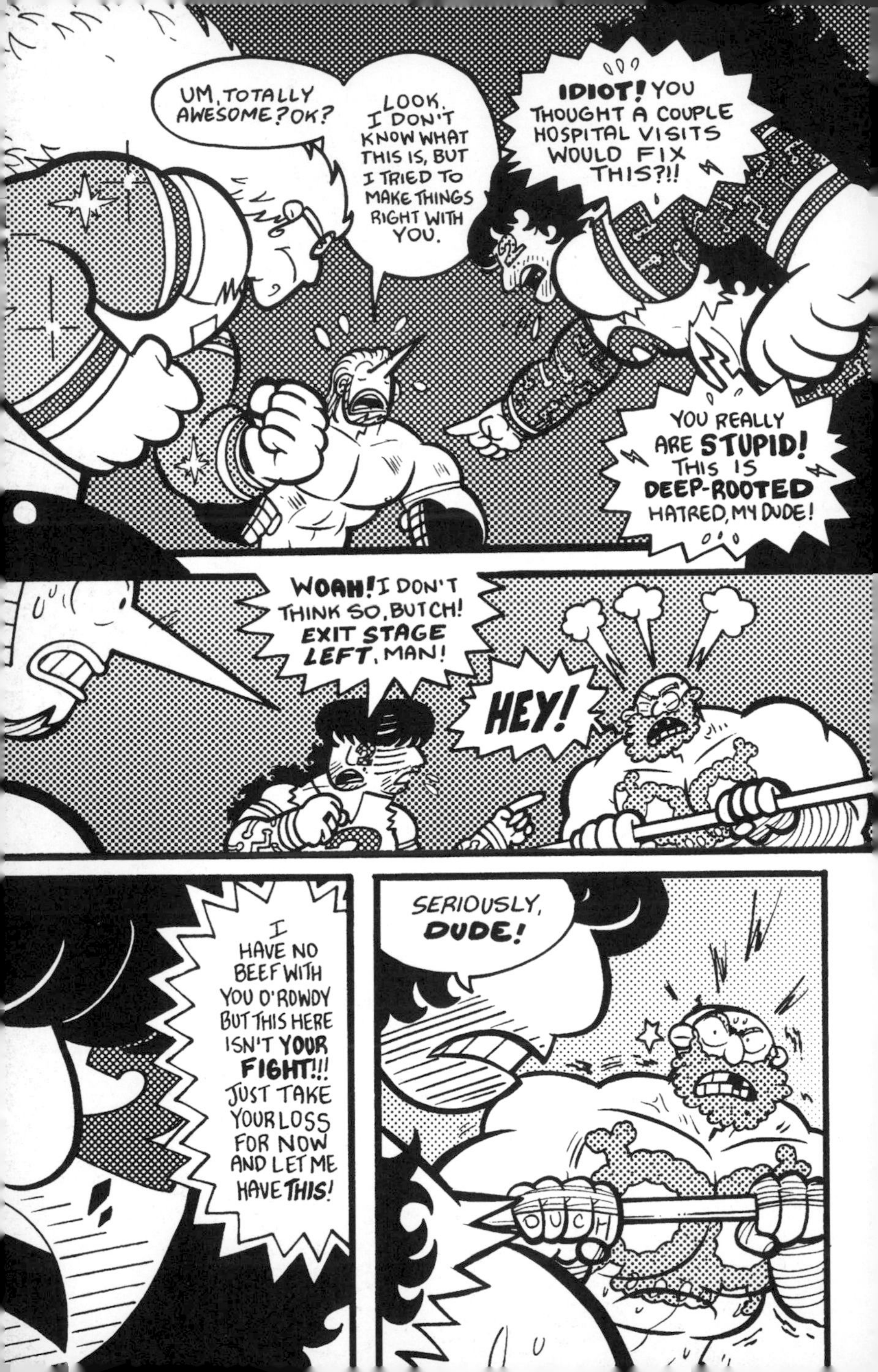
UM, TOTALLY AWESOME? OK?
LOOK. I DON'T KNOW WHAT THIS IS, BUT I TRIED TO MAKE THINGS RIGHT WITH YOU.
IDIOT! YOU THOUGHT A COUPLE HOSPITAL VISITS WOULD FIX THIS?!!
YOU REALLY ARE STUPID! THIS IS DEEP-ROOTED HATRED, MY DUDE!
WOAH! I DON'T THINK SO, BUTCH! EXIT STAGE LEFT, MAN!
HEY!
I HAVE NO BEEF WITH YOU O'ROWDY BUT THIS HERE ISN'T YOUR FIGHT!!! JUST TAKE YOUR LOSS FOR NOW AND LET ME HAVE THIS!
SERIOUSLY, DUDE!
OUCH

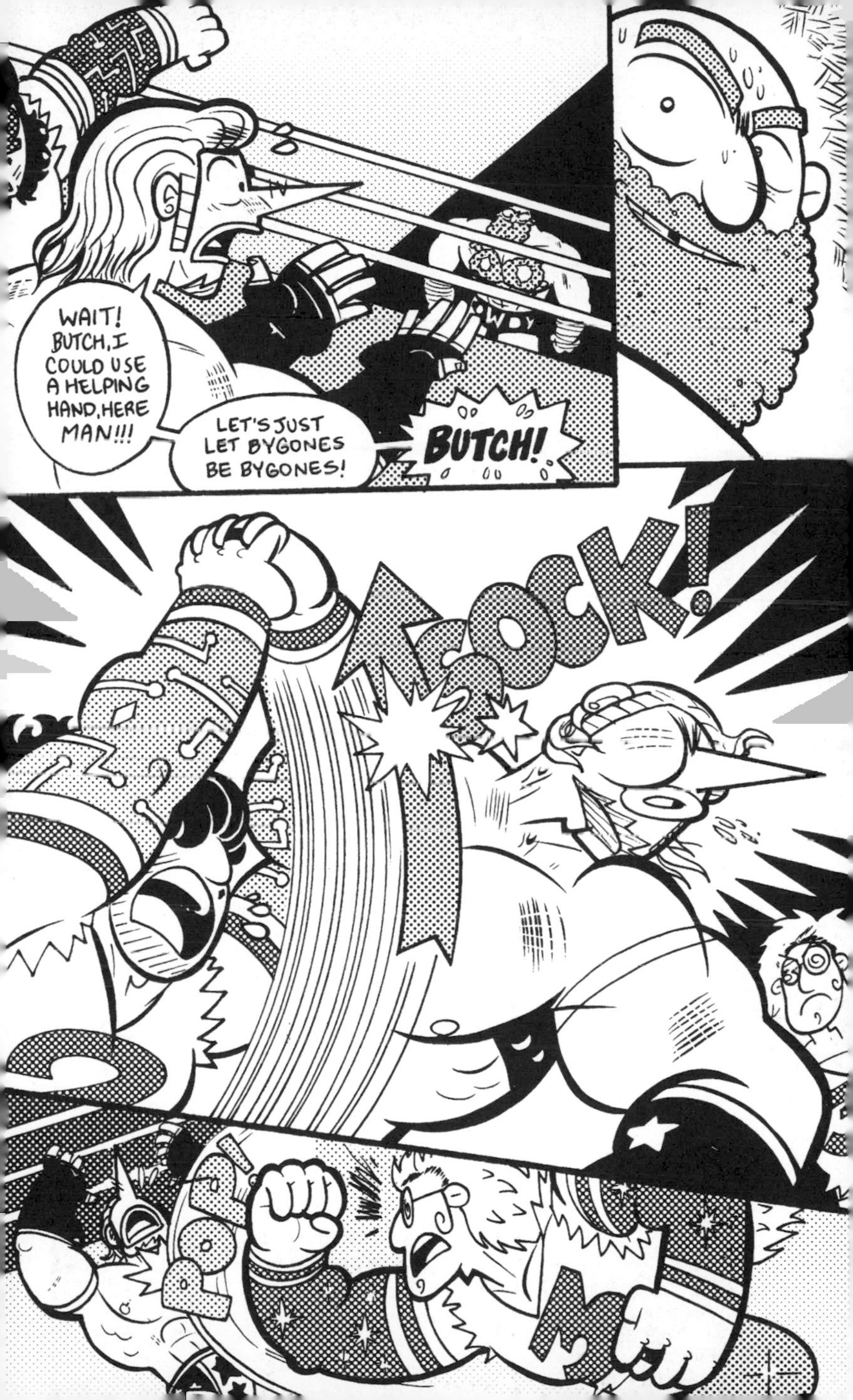
WAIT! BUTCH, I COULD USE A HELPING HAND, HERE MAN!!!
LET'S JUST LET BYGONES BE BYGONES!
BUTCH!
SOCK!

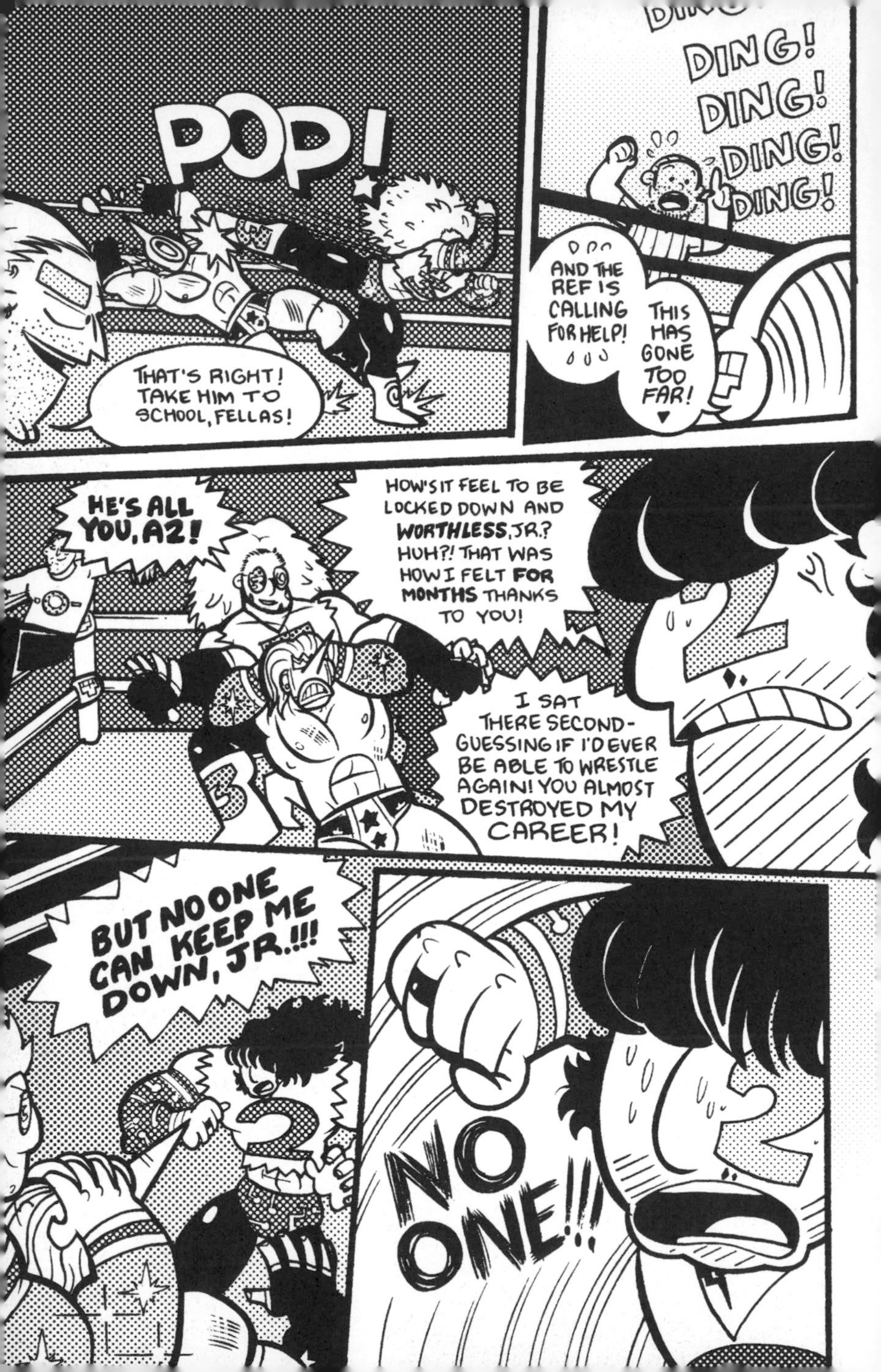
POP!
THAT'S RIGHT! TAKE HIM TO SCHOOL, FELLAS!
DING! DING! DING! DING!
AND THE REF IS CALLING FOR HELP!
THIS HAS GONE TOO FAR!
HE'S ALL YOU, AZ!
HOW'S IT FEEL TO BE LOCKED DOWN AND WORTHLESS, JR.? HUH?! THAT WAS HOW I FELT FOR MONTHS THANKS TO YOU!
I SAT THERE SECOND-GUESSING IF I'D EVER BE ABLE TO WRESTLE AGAIN! YOU ALMOST DESTROYED MY CAREER!
BUT NO ONE CAN KEEP ME DOWN, JR.!!!
NO ONE!!!

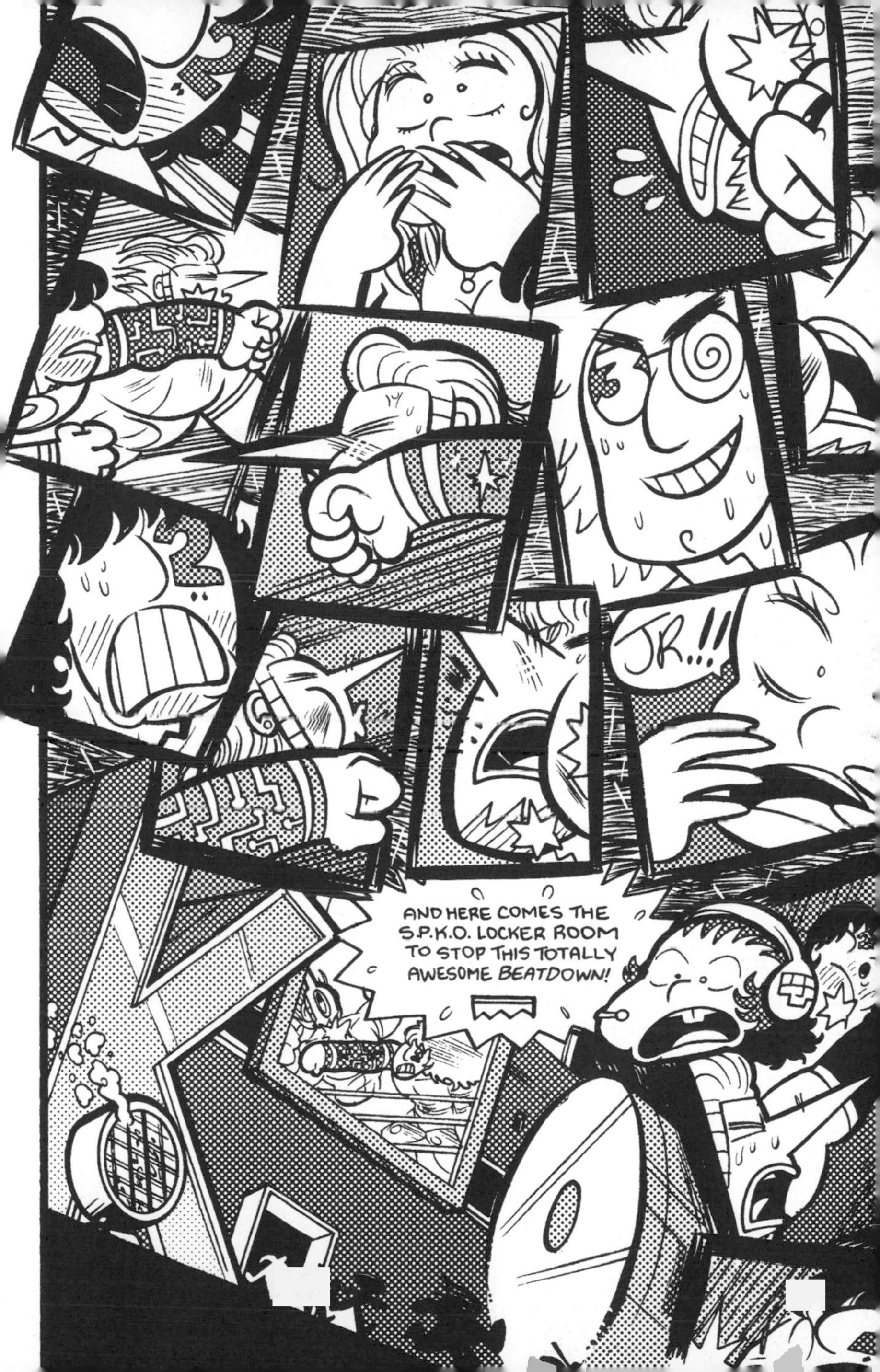

JR..!!
AND HERE COMES THE S.P.K.O. LOCKER ROOM TO STOP THIS TOTALLY AWESOME *BEATDOWN!*

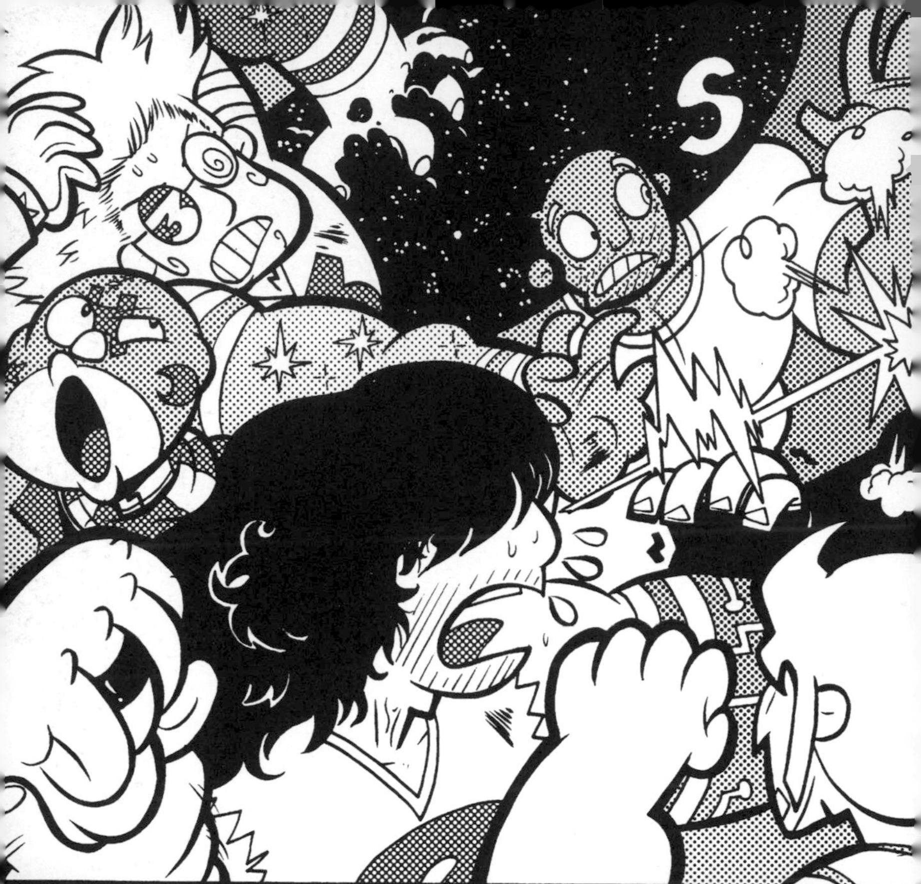

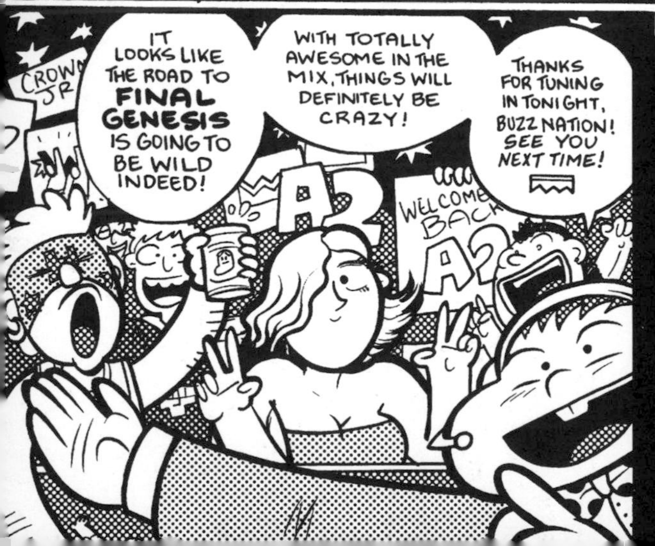

IT LOOKS LIKE THE ROAD TO **FINAL GENESIS** IS GOING TO BE WILD INDEED!
WITH TOTALLY AWESOME IN THE MIX, THINGS WILL DEFINITELY BE CRAZY!
THANKS FOR TUNING IN TONIGHT, BUZZ NATION! SEE YOU NEXT TIME!
WELCOME BACK A2

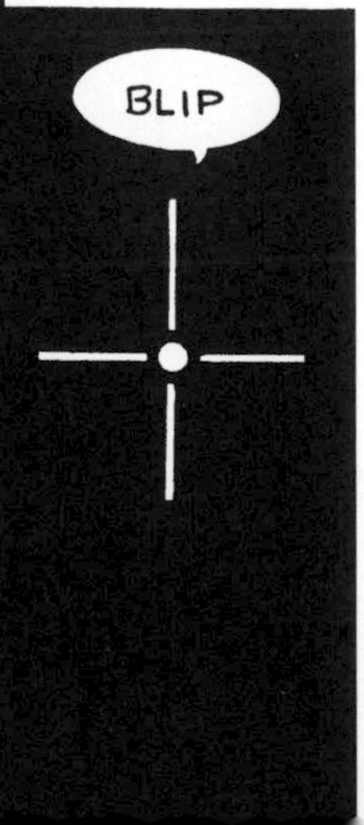

BLIP

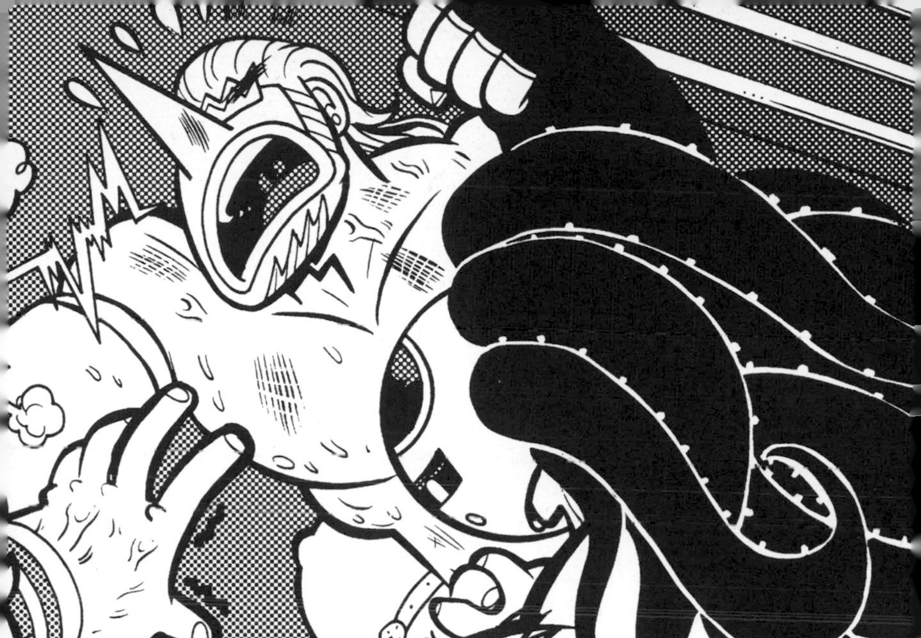
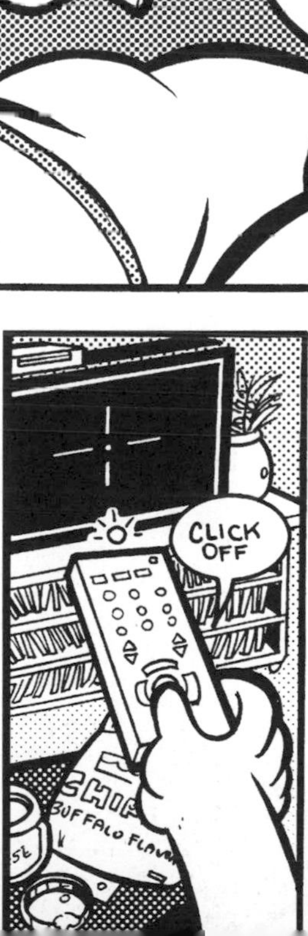
CLICK OFF
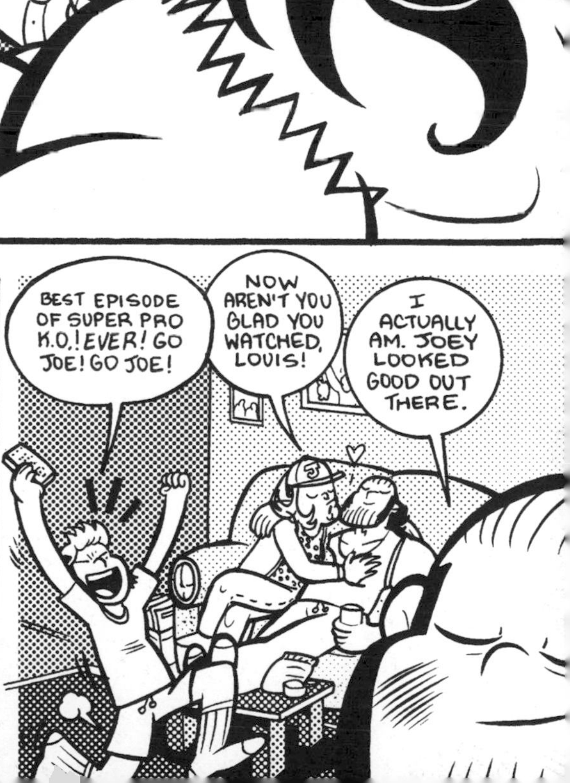
BEST EPISODE OF SUPER PRO K.O.! EVER! GO JOE! GO JOE!
NOW AREN'T YOU GLAD YOU WATCHED, LOUIS!
I ACTUALLY AM. JOEY LOOKED GOOD OUT THERE.

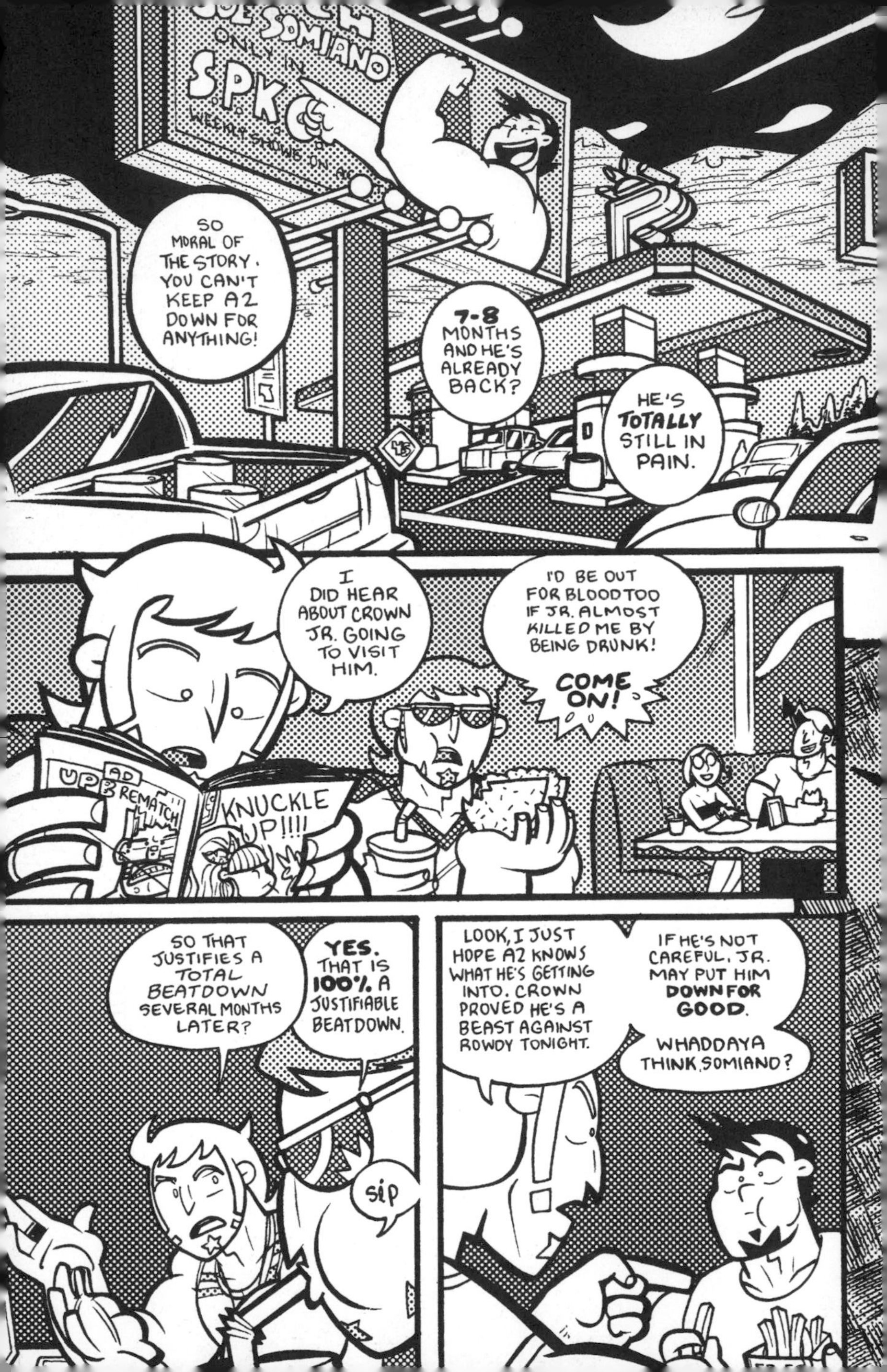
JOE SOMIANO
ONLY IN
SPK
WEEKLY SHOWS ON
SO MORAL OF THE STORY. YOU CAN'T KEEP A2 DOWN FOR ANYTHING!
7-8 MONTHS AND HE'S ALREADY BACK?
HE'S TOTALLY STILL IN PAIN.
I DID HEAR ABOUT CROWN JR. GOING TO VISIT HIM.
I'D BE OUT FOR BLOOD TOO IF JR. ALMOST KILLED ME BY BEING DRUNK!
COME ON!
AD
UP
REMATCH
KNUCKLE UP!!!!
SO THAT JUSTIFIES A TOTAL BEATDOWN SEVERAL MONTHS LATER?
YES. THAT IS 100%. A JUSTIFIABLE BEATDOWN.
SIP
LOOK, I JUST HOPE A2 KNOWS WHAT HE'S GETTING INTO. CROWN PROVED HE'S A BEAST AGAINST ROWDY TONIGHT.
IF HE'S NOT CAREFUL, JR. MAY PUT HIM DOWN FOR GOOD.
WHADDAYA THINK, SOMIANO?

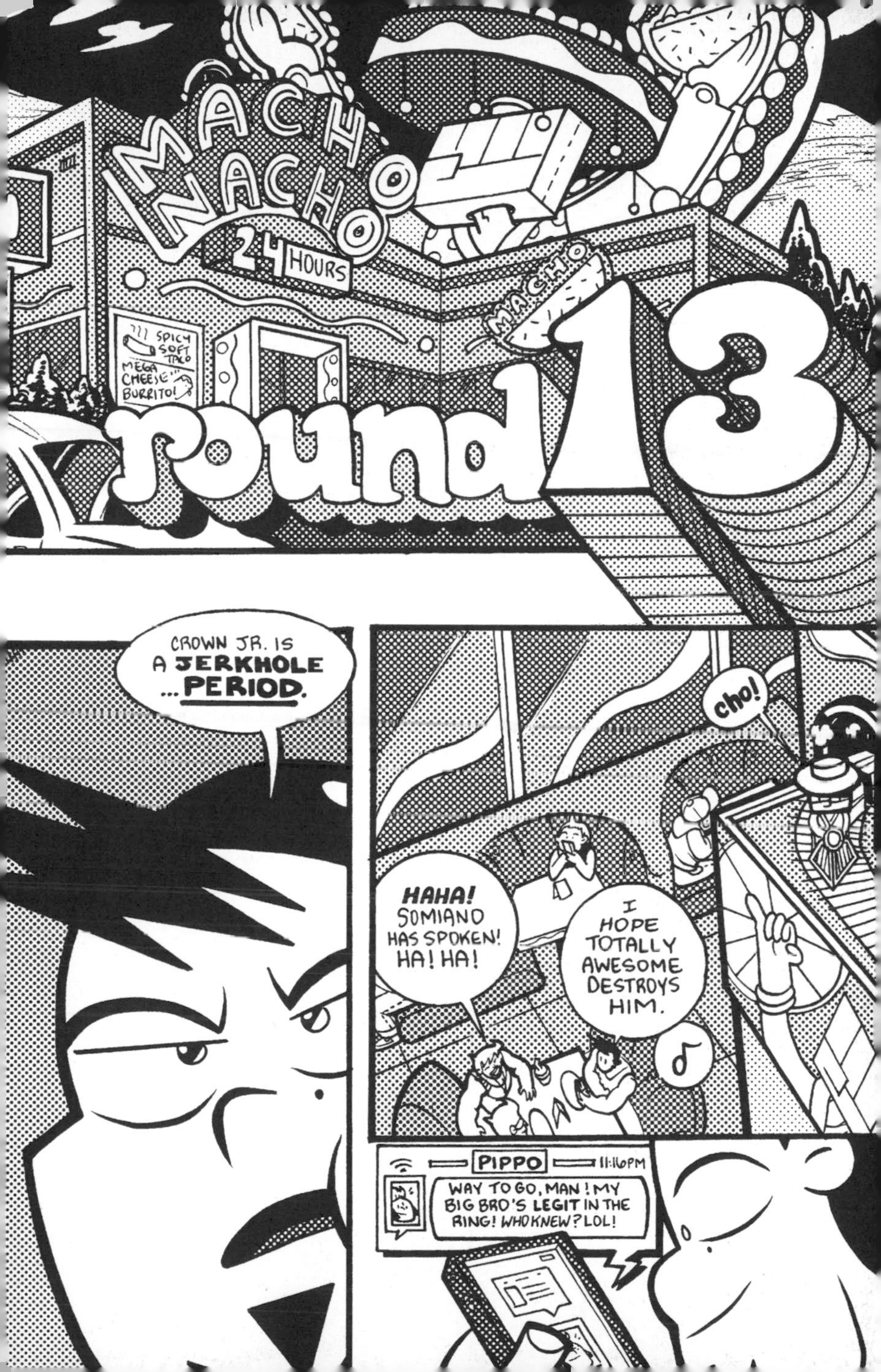
MACHO NACHO
24 HOURS
SPICY SOFT TACO
MEGA CHEESE BURRITO!
MACHO
round 13
CROWN JR. IS A JERKHOLE ...PERIOD.
cho!
HAHA! SOMIANO HAS SPOKEN! HA! HA!
I HOPE TOTALLY AWESOME DESTROYS HIM.
PIPPO 11:16PM
WAY TO GO, MAN! MY BIG BRO'S LEGIT IN THE RING! WHO KNEW? LOL!

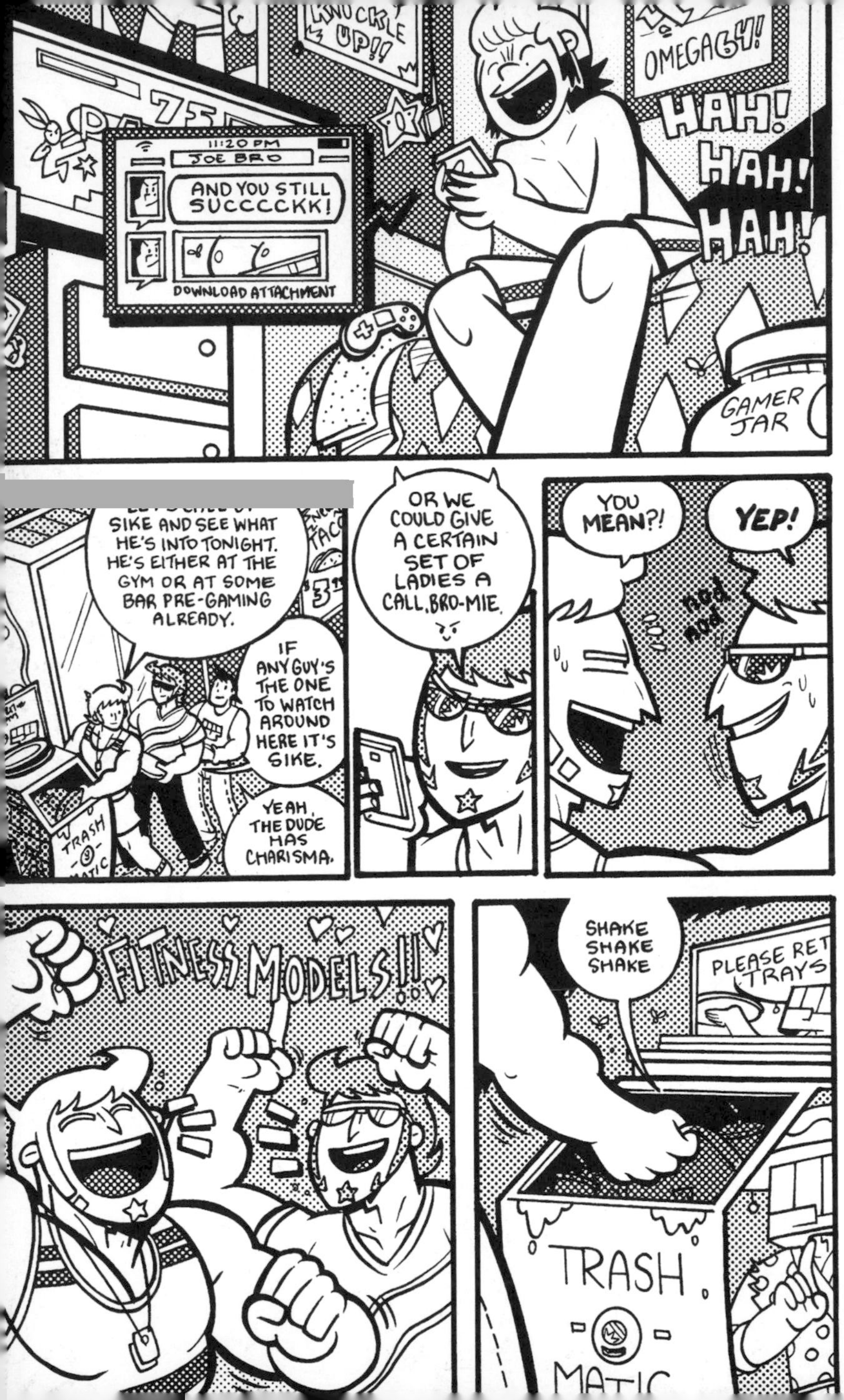

KNUCKLE UP!!
OMEGA64!
11:20 PM
JOE BRO
AND YOU STILL SUCCCCKK!
DOWNLOAD ATTACHMENT
HAH! HAH! HAH!
GAMER JAR
SIKE AND SEE WHAT HE'S INTO TONIGHT. HE'S EITHER AT THE GYM OR AT SOME BAR PRE-GAMING ALREADY.
TACO
IF ANY GUY'S THE ONE TO WATCH AROUND HERE IT'S SIKE.
YEAH, THE DUDE HAS CHARISMA.
TRASH-O-MATIC
OR WE COULD GIVE A CERTAIN SET OF LADIES A CALL, BRO-MIE.
YOU MEAN?!
YEP!
nod nod
FITNESS MODELS!!
SHAKE SHAKE SHAKE
PLEASE RET TRAYS
TRASH -O- MATIC

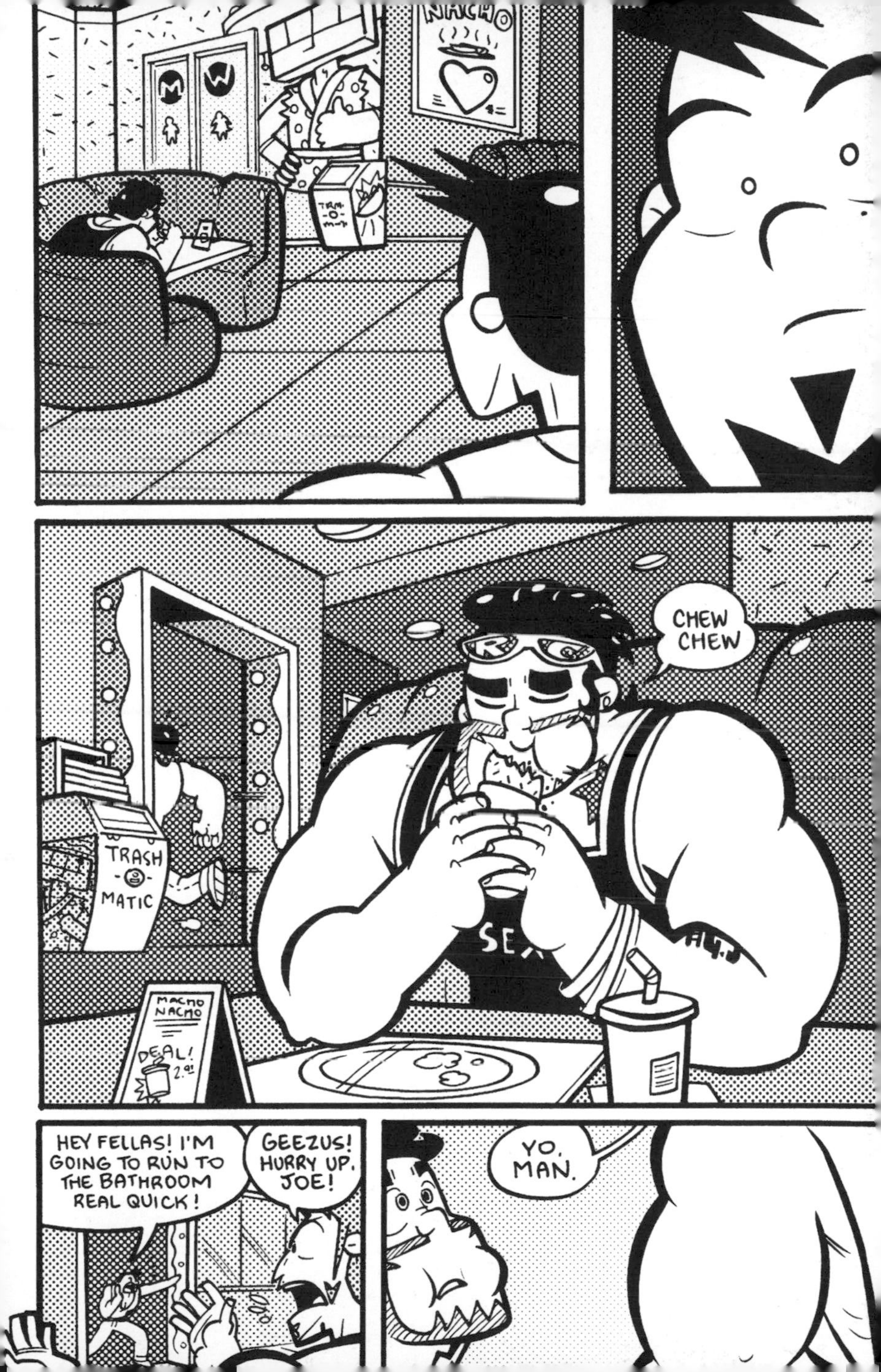
NACHO
CHEW CHEW
TRASH -O- MATIC
MACHO NACHO DEAL!
HEY FELLAS! I'M GOING TO RUN TO THE BATHROOM REAL QUICK!
GEEZUS! HURRY UP, JOE!
YO, MAN.

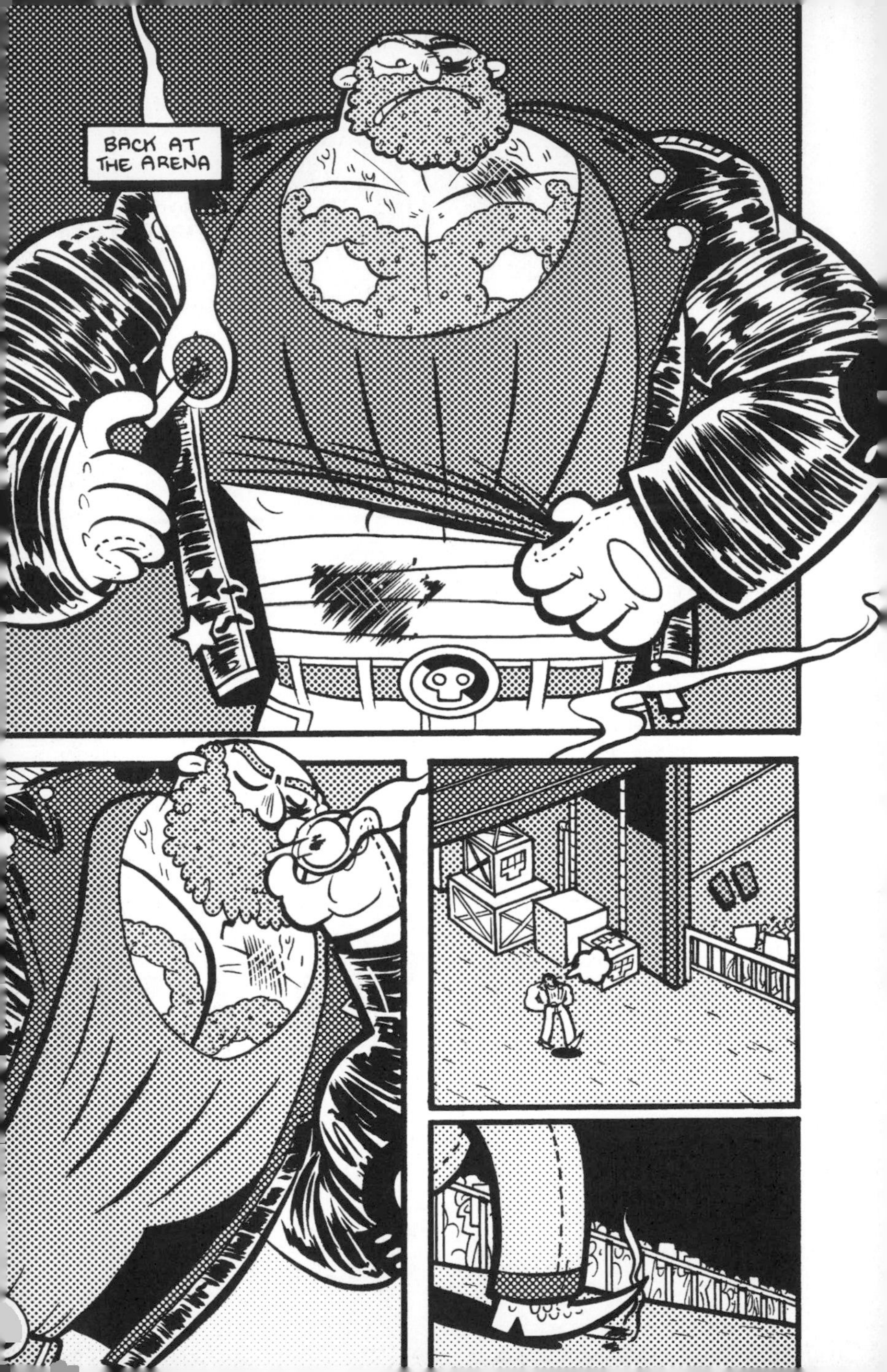
BACK AT THE ARENA

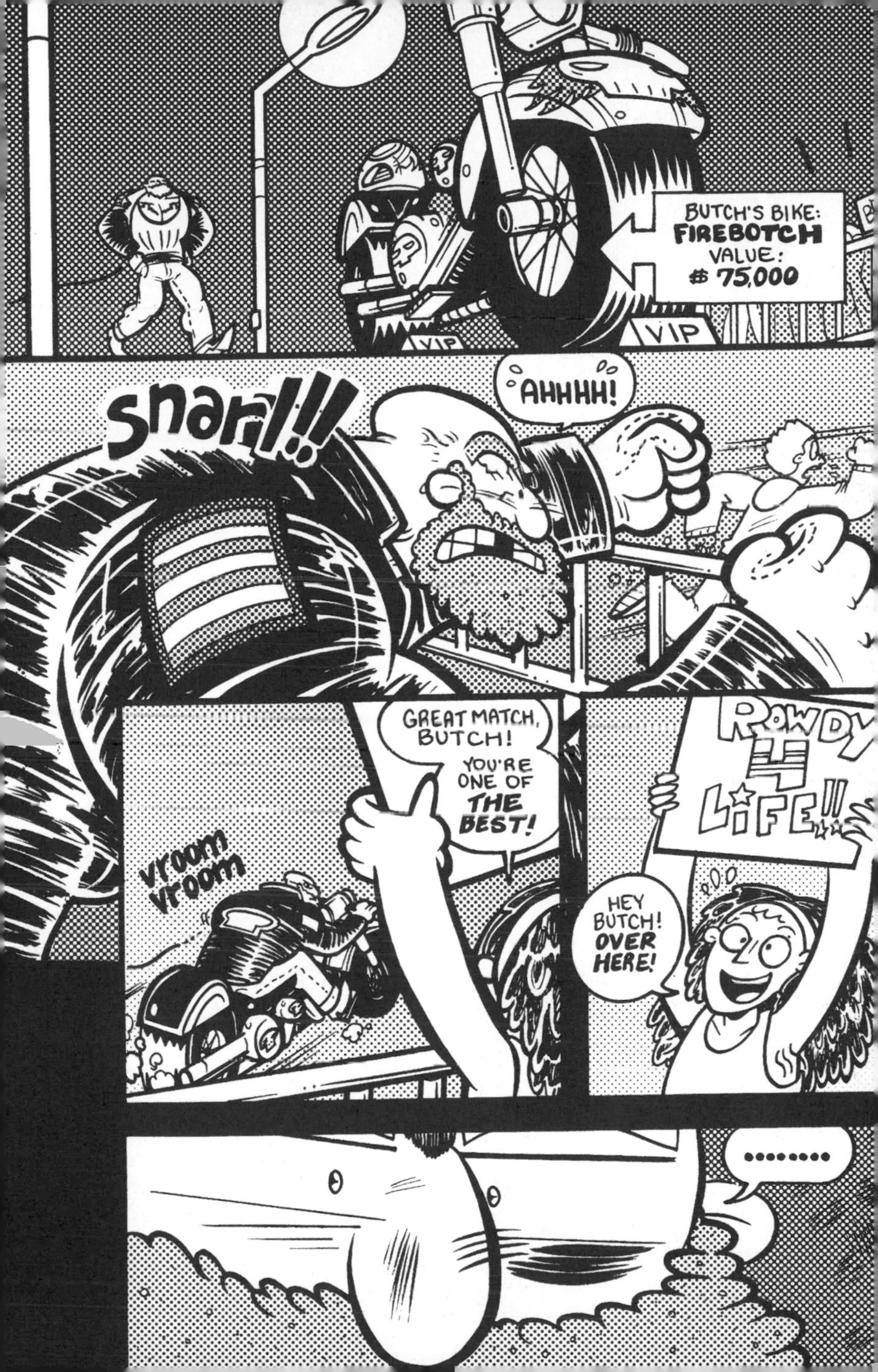
BUTCH'S BIKE:
FIREBOTCH
VALUE:
$ 75,000
VIP
VIP
SNARL!!!
AHHHH!
GREAT MATCH, BUTCH!
YOU'RE ONE OF THE BEST!
vroom vroom
ROWDY 4 LIFE!!
HEY BUTCH! OVER HERE!
....

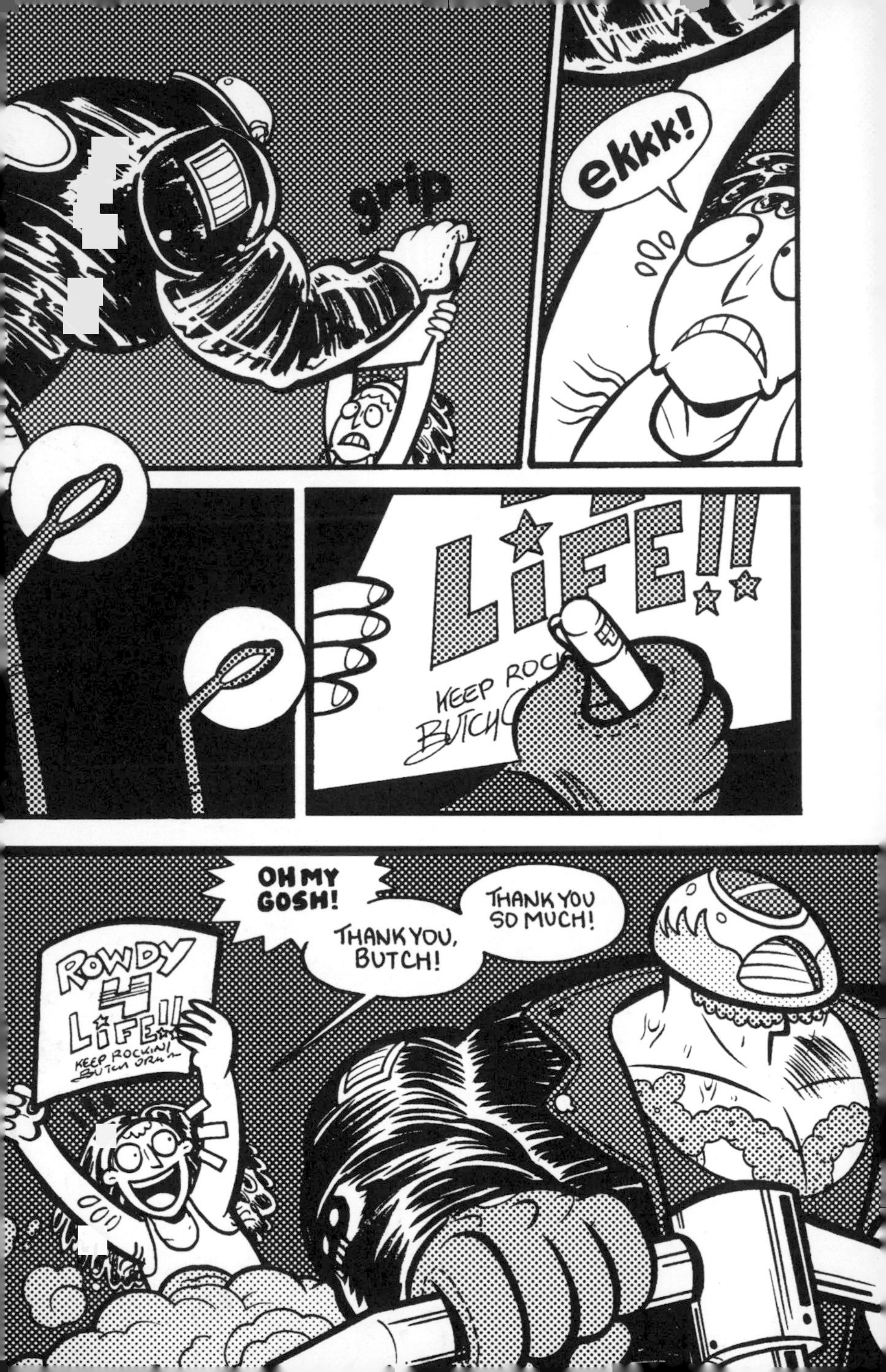
grip
ekkk!
LiFE!!
KEEP ROC
ROWDY 4 LIFE!!
KEEP ROCKIN!
OH MY GOSH!
THANK YOU, BUTCH!
THANK YOU SO MUCH!

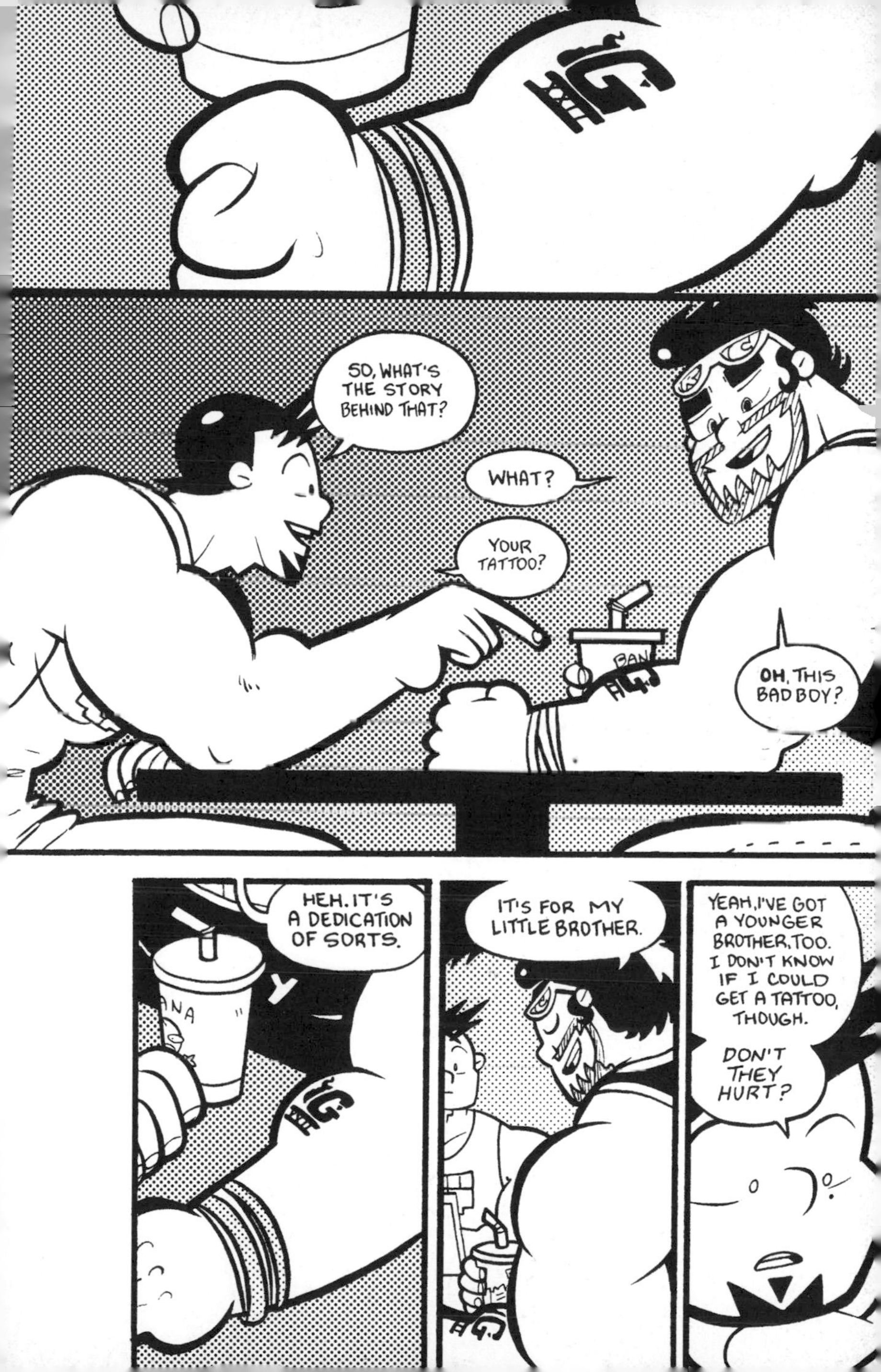
HG
SO, WHAT'S THE STORY BEHIND THAT?
WHAT?
YOUR TATTOO?
OH, THIS BAD BOY?
HEH. IT'S A DEDICATION OF SORTS.
IT'S FOR MY LITTLE BROTHER.
YEAH, I'VE GOT A YOUNGER BROTHER, TOO. I DON'T KNOW IF I COULD GET A TATTOO, THOUGH.
DON'T THEY HURT?

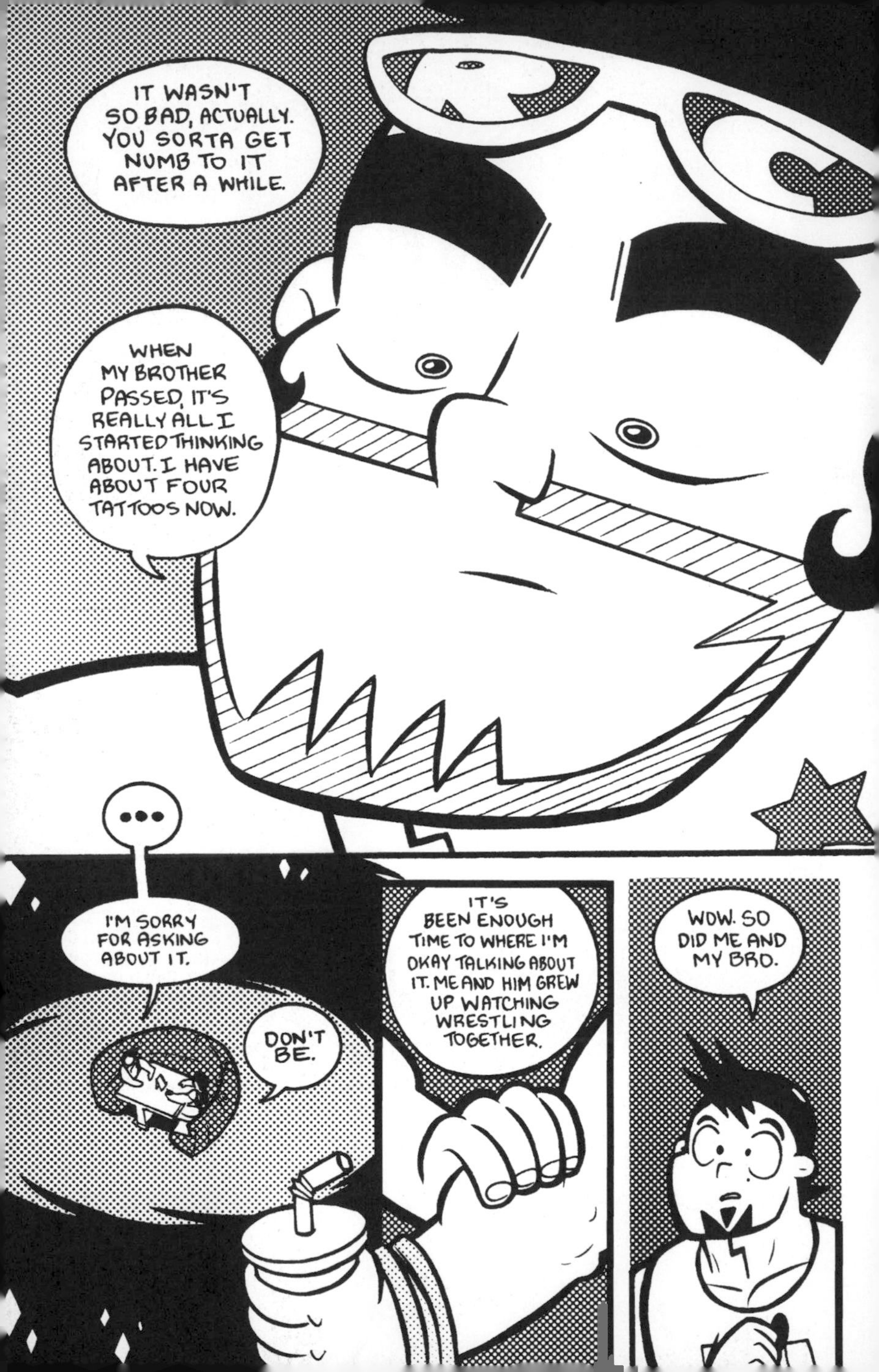
IT WASN'T SO BAD, ACTUALLY. YOU SORTA GET NUMB TO IT AFTER A WHILE.
WHEN MY BROTHER PASSED, IT'S REALLY ALL I STARTED THINKING ABOUT. I HAVE ABOUT FOUR TATTOOS NOW.
...
I'M SORRY FOR ASKING ABOUT IT.
DON'T BE.
IT'S BEEN ENOUGH TIME TO WHERE I'M OKAY TALKING ABOUT IT. ME AND HIM GREW UP WATCHING WRESTLING TOGETHER.
WOW. SO DID ME AND MY BRO.

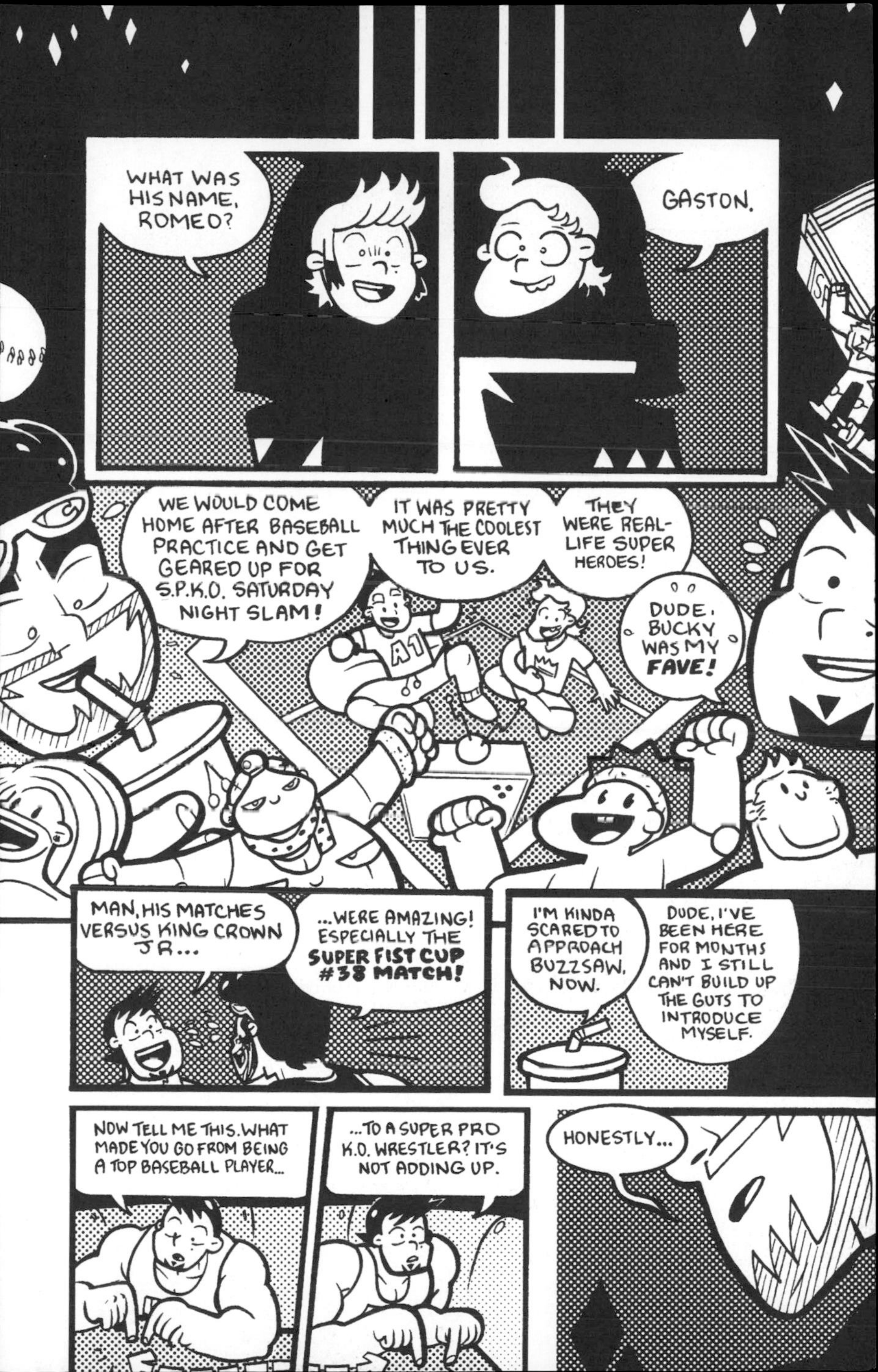

WHAT WAS HIS NAME, ROMEO?
GASTON.
WE WOULD COME HOME AFTER BASEBALL PRACTICE AND GET GEARED UP FOR S.P.K.O. SATURDAY NIGHT SLAM!
IT WAS PRETTY MUCH THE COOLEST THING EVER TO US.
THEY WERE REAL-LIFE SUPER HEROES!
DUDE, BUCKY WAS MY **FAVE!**
MAN, HIS MATCHES VERSUS KING CROWN JR...
...WERE AMAZING! ESPECIALLY THE **SUPER FIST CUP #38 MATCH!**
I'M KINDA SCARED TO APPROACH BUZZSAW, NOW.
DUDE, I'VE BEEN HERE FOR MONTHS AND I STILL CAN'T BUILD UP THE GUTS TO INTRODUCE MYSELF.
NOW TELL ME THIS. WHAT MADE YOU GO FROM BEING A TOP BASEBALL PLAYER...
...TO A SUPER PRO K.O. WRESTLER? IT'S NOT ADDING UP.
HONESTLY...

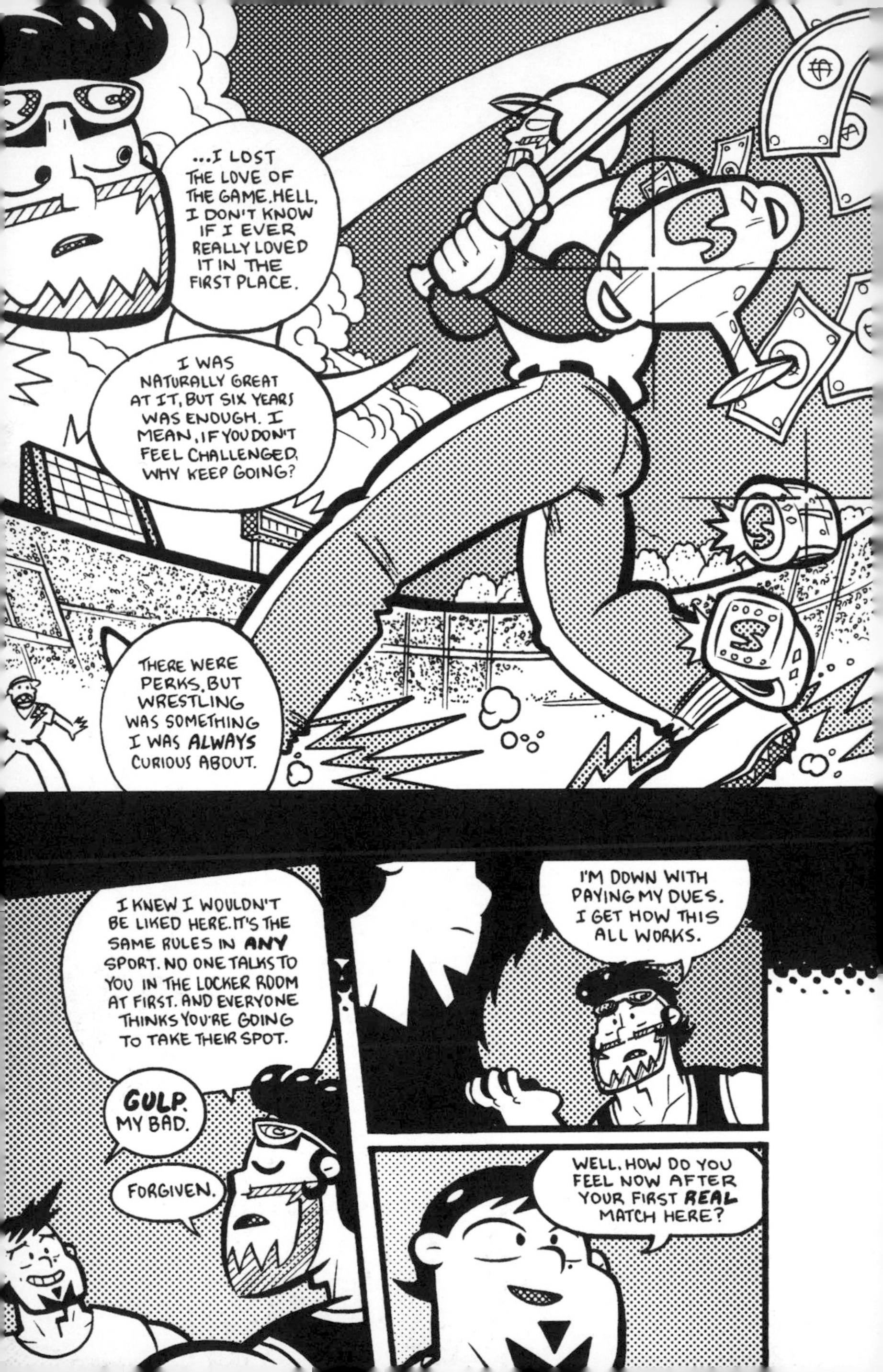

...I LOST THE LOVE OF THE GAME. HELL, I DON'T KNOW IF I EVER REALLY LOVED IT IN THE FIRST PLACE.
I WAS NATURALLY GREAT AT IT, BUT SIX YEARS WAS ENOUGH. I MEAN, IF YOU DON'T FEEL CHALLENGED, WHY KEEP GOING?
THERE WERE PERKS, BUT WRESTLING WAS SOMETHING I WAS **ALWAYS** CURIOUS ABOUT.
I KNEW I WOULDN'T BE LIKED HERE. IT'S THE SAME RULES IN **ANY** SPORT. NO ONE TALKS TO YOU IN THE LOCKER ROOM AT FIRST. AND EVERYONE THINKS YOU'RE GOING TO TAKE THEIR SPOT.
GULP. MY BAD.
FORGIVEN.
I'M DOWN WITH PAYING MY DUES. I GET HOW THIS ALL WORKS.
WELL, HOW DO YOU FEEL NOW AFTER YOUR FIRST **REAL** MATCH HERE?

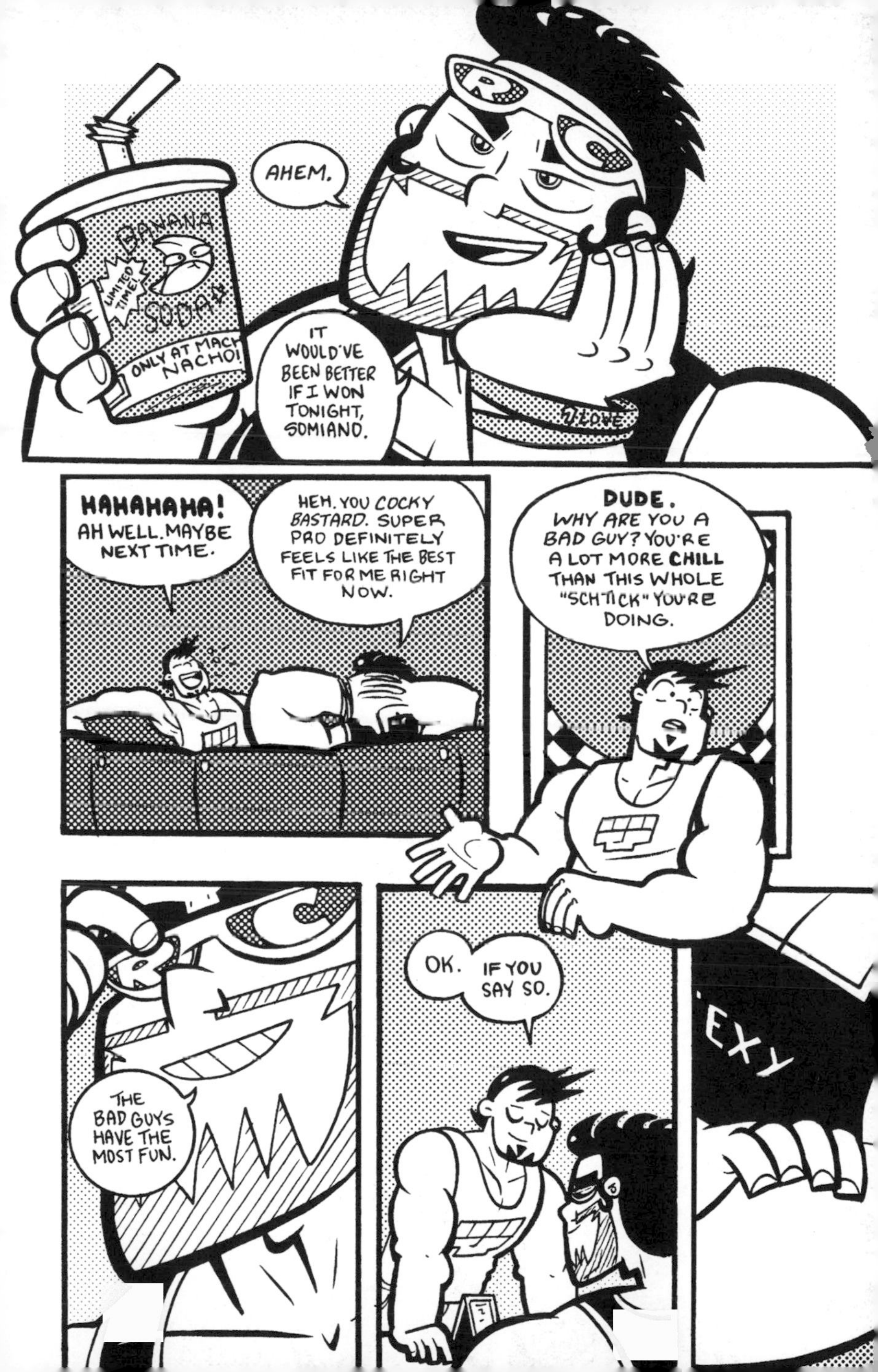
BANANA SODA
LIMITED TIME!
ONLY AT MACH NACHO!
AHEM.
IT WOULD'VE BEEN BETTER IF I WON TONIGHT, SOMIANO.
I LOVE
HAHAHAHA! AH WELL. MAYBE NEXT TIME.
HEH. YOU COCKY BASTARD. SUPER PRO DEFINITELY FEELS LIKE THE BEST FIT FOR ME RIGHT NOW.
DUDE. WHY ARE YOU A BAD GUY? YOU'RE A LOT MORE CHILL THAN THIS WHOLE "SCHTICK" YOU'RE DOING.
THE BAD GUYS HAVE THE MOST FUN.
OK.
IF YOU SAY SO.
EXY

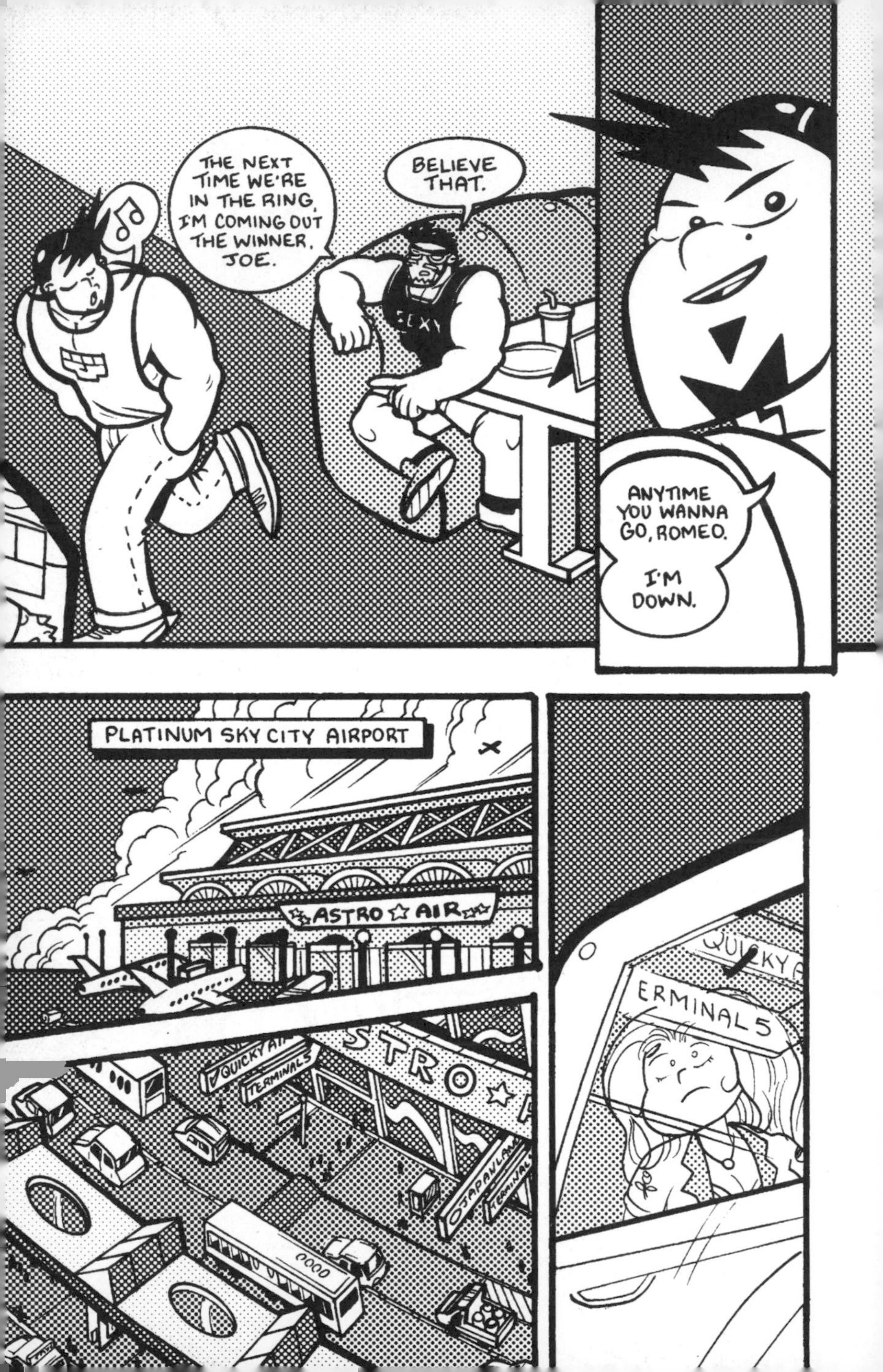
THE NEXT TIME WE'RE IN THE RING, I'M COMING OUT THE WINNER, JOE.
BELIEVE THAT.
ANYTIME YOU WANNA GO, ROMEO.
I'M DOWN.
PLATINUM SKY CITY AIRPORT
ASTRO ☆ AIR
TERMINALS

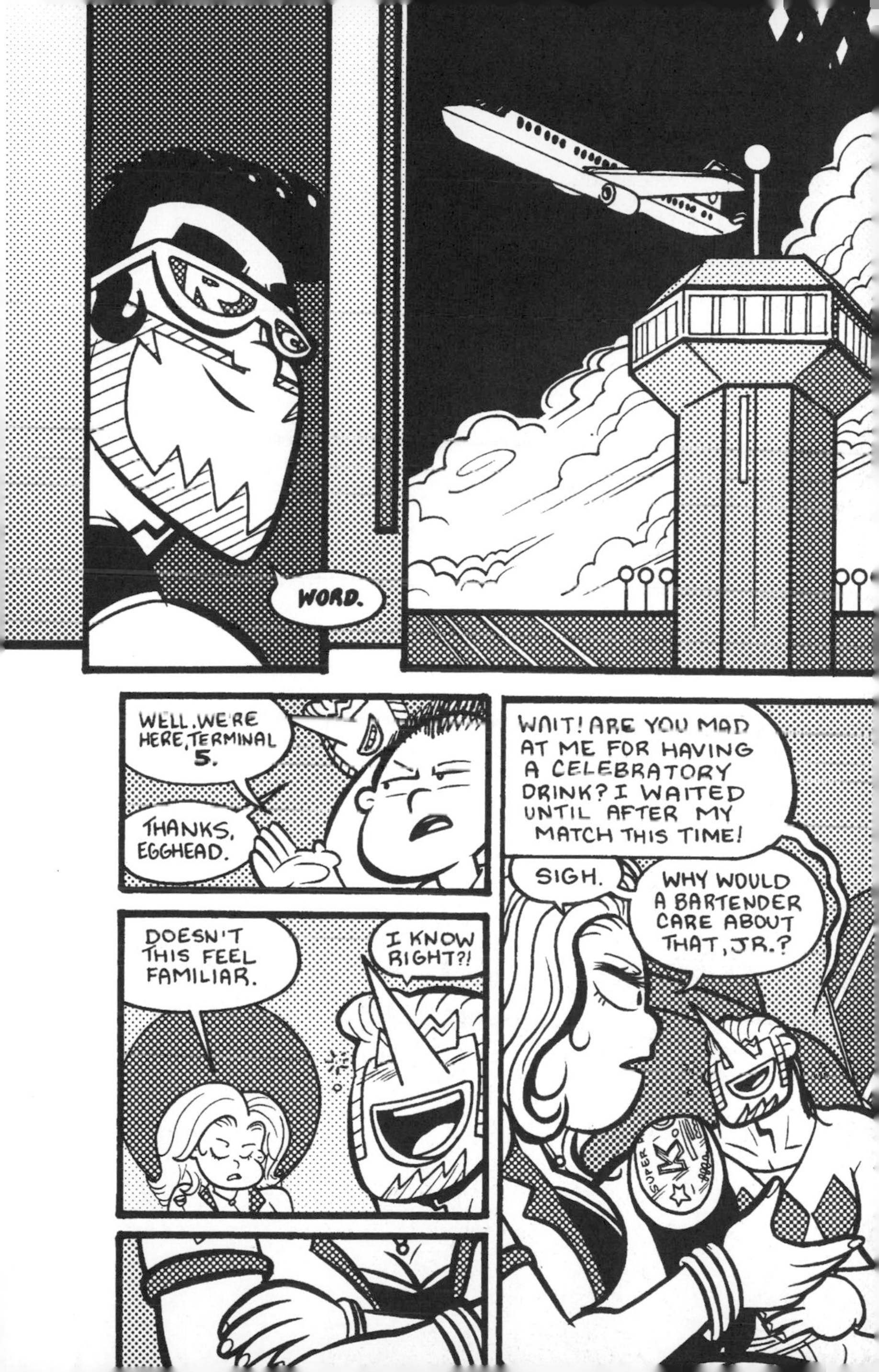
WORD.
WELL, WE'RE HERE, TERMINAL 5.
THANKS, EGGHEAD.
WAIT! ARE YOU MAD AT ME FOR HAVING A CELEBRATORY DRINK? I WAITED UNTIL AFTER MY MATCH THIS TIME!
SIGH.
WHY WOULD A BARTENDER CARE ABOUT THAT, JR.?
DOESN'T THIS FEEL FAMILIAR.
I KNOW RIGHT?!
SUPER

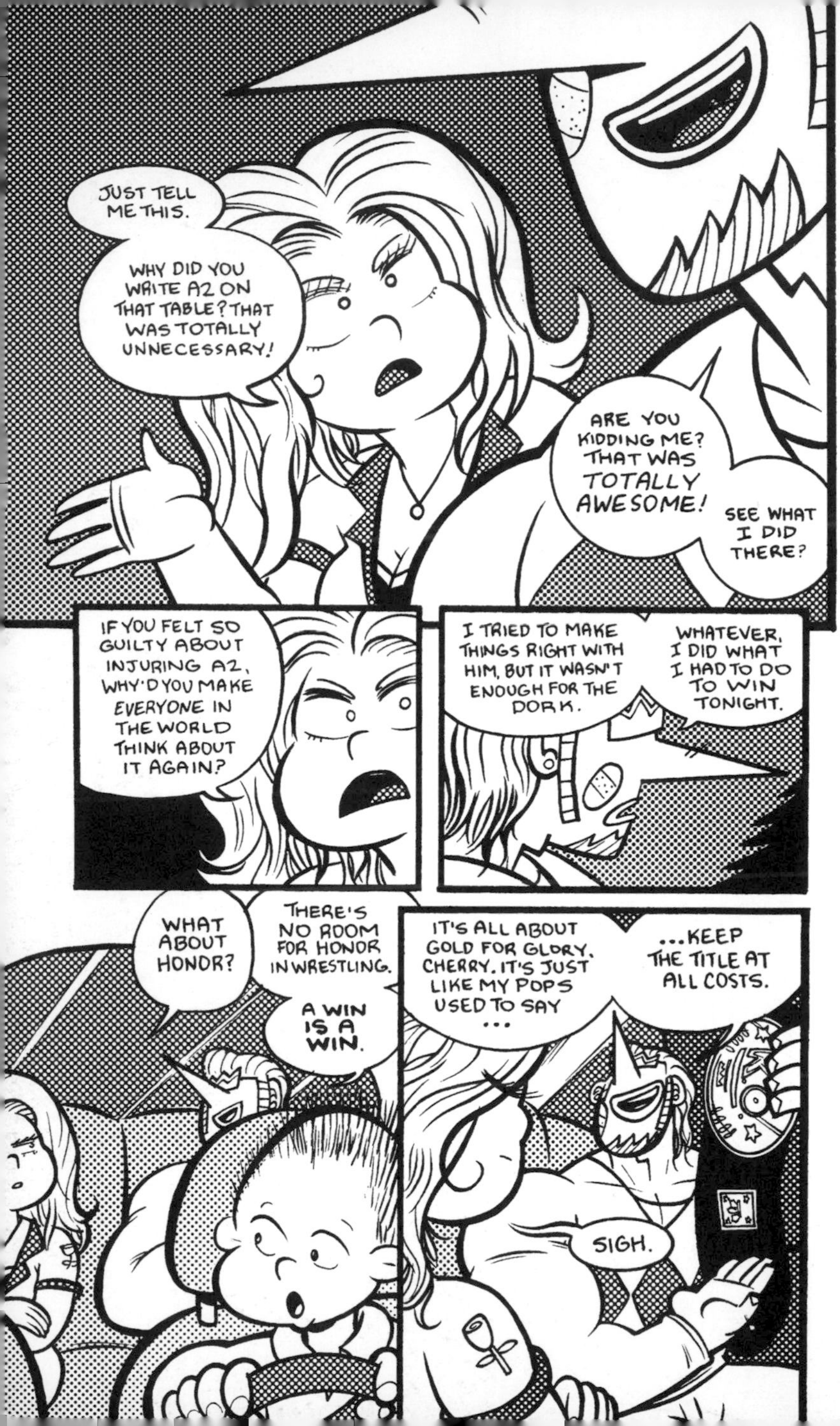
JUST TELL ME THIS.
WHY DID YOU WRITE A2 ON THAT TABLE? THAT WAS TOTALLY UNNECESSARY!
ARE YOU KIDDING ME? THAT WAS TOTALLY AWESOME!
SEE WHAT I DID THERE?
IF YOU FELT SO GUILTY ABOUT INJURING A2, WHY'D YOU MAKE EVERYONE IN THE WORLD THINK ABOUT IT AGAIN?
I TRIED TO MAKE THINGS RIGHT WITH HIM, BUT IT WASN'T ENOUGH FOR THE DORK.
WHATEVER. I DID WHAT I HAD TO DO TO WIN TONIGHT.
WHAT ABOUT HONOR?
THERE'S NO ROOM FOR HONOR IN WRESTLING.
A WIN IS A WIN.
IT'S ALL ABOUT GOLD FOR GLORY, CHERRY. IT'S JUST LIKE MY POPS USED TO SAY ...
...KEEP THE TITLE AT ALL COSTS.
SIGH.

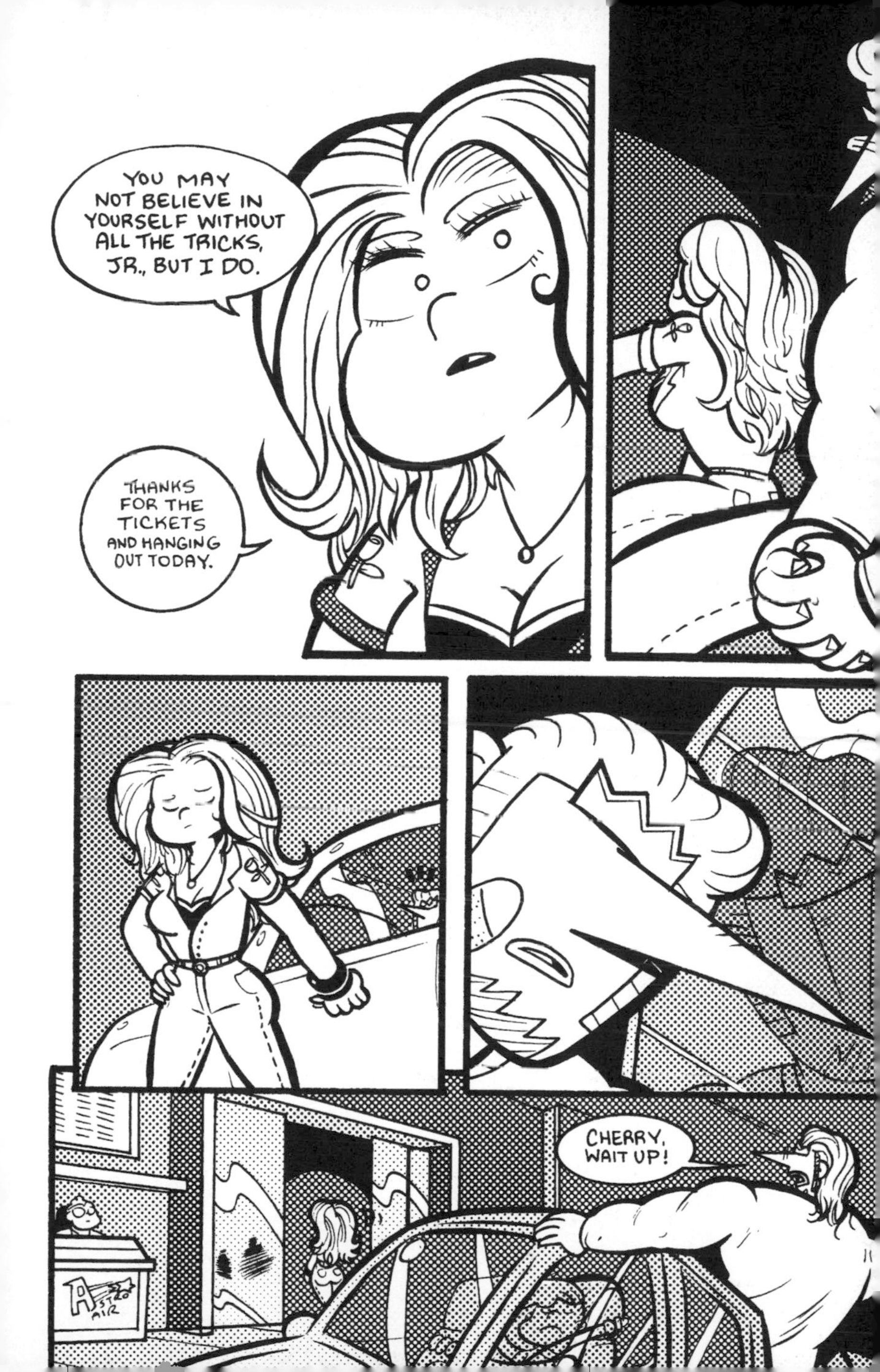
YOU MAY NOT BELIEVE IN YOURSELF WITHOUT ALL THE TRICKS, JR., BUT I DO.
THANKS FOR THE TICKETS AND HANGING OUT TODAY.
CHERRY, WAIT UP!
ASTRO AIR

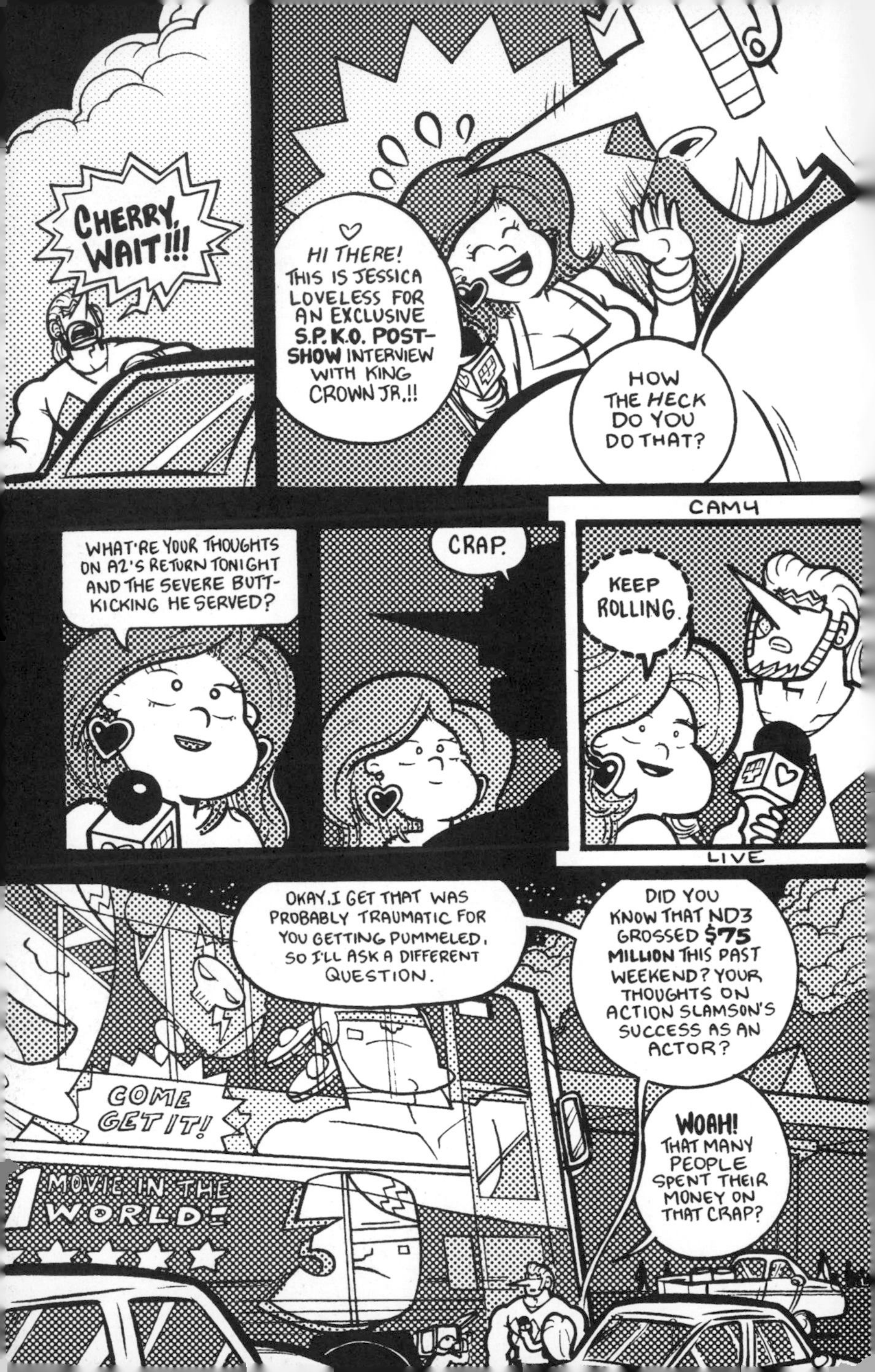

CHERRY, WAIT!!!
HI THERE! THIS IS JESSICA LOVELESS FOR AN EXCLUSIVE S.P.K.O. POST-SHOW INTERVIEW WITH KING CROWN JR.!!
HOW THE HECK DO YOU DO THAT?
WHAT'RE YOUR THOUGHTS ON A2'S RETURN TONIGHT AND THE SEVERE BUTT-KICKING HE SERVED?
CRAP.
CAM4
KEEP ROLLING.
LIVE
OKAY, I GET THAT WAS PROBABLY TRAUMATIC FOR YOU GETTING PUMMELED, SO I'LL ASK A DIFFERENT QUESTION.
DID YOU KNOW THAT ND3 GROSSED $75 MILLION THIS PAST WEEKEND? YOUR THOUGHTS ON ACTION SLAMSON'S SUCCESS AS AN ACTOR?
COME GET IT!
1 MOVIE IN THE WORLD!
WOAH! THAT MANY PEOPLE SPENT THEIR MONEY ON THAT CRAP?

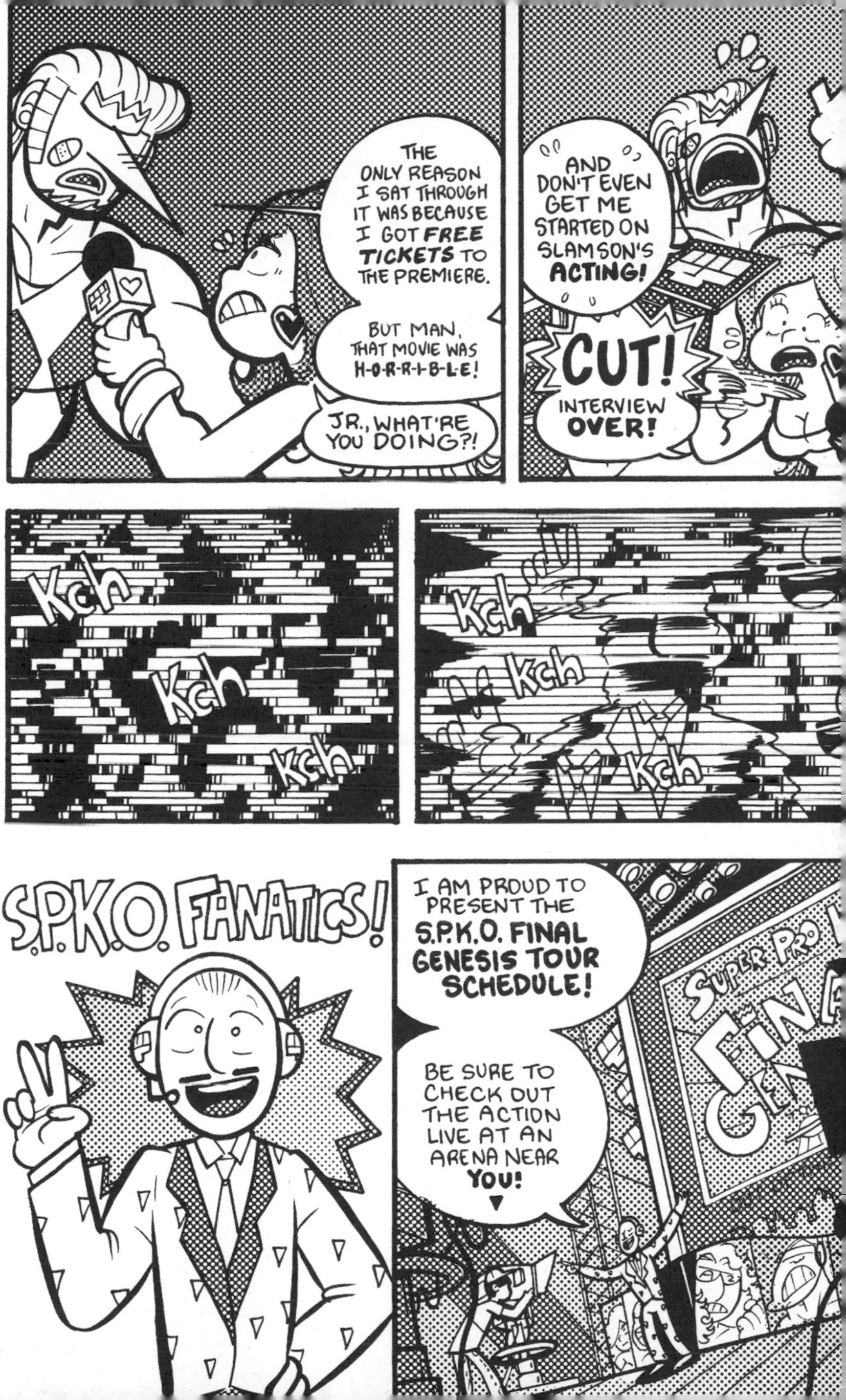
THE ONLY REASON I SAT THROUGH IT WAS BECAUSE I GOT FREE TICKETS TO THE PREMIERE.
BUT MAN, THAT MOVIE WAS H-O-R-R-I-B-L-E!
JR., WHAT'RE YOU DOING?!
AND DON'T EVEN GET ME STARTED ON SLAMSON'S ACTING!
CUT!
INTERVIEW OVER!
Kch
Kch
Kch
Kch
Kch
Kch
S.P.K.O. FANATICS!
I AM PROUD TO PRESENT THE S.P.K.O. FINAL GENESIS TOUR SCHEDULE!
BE SURE TO CHECK OUT THE ACTION LIVE AT AN ARENA NEAR YOU!
SUPER PRO

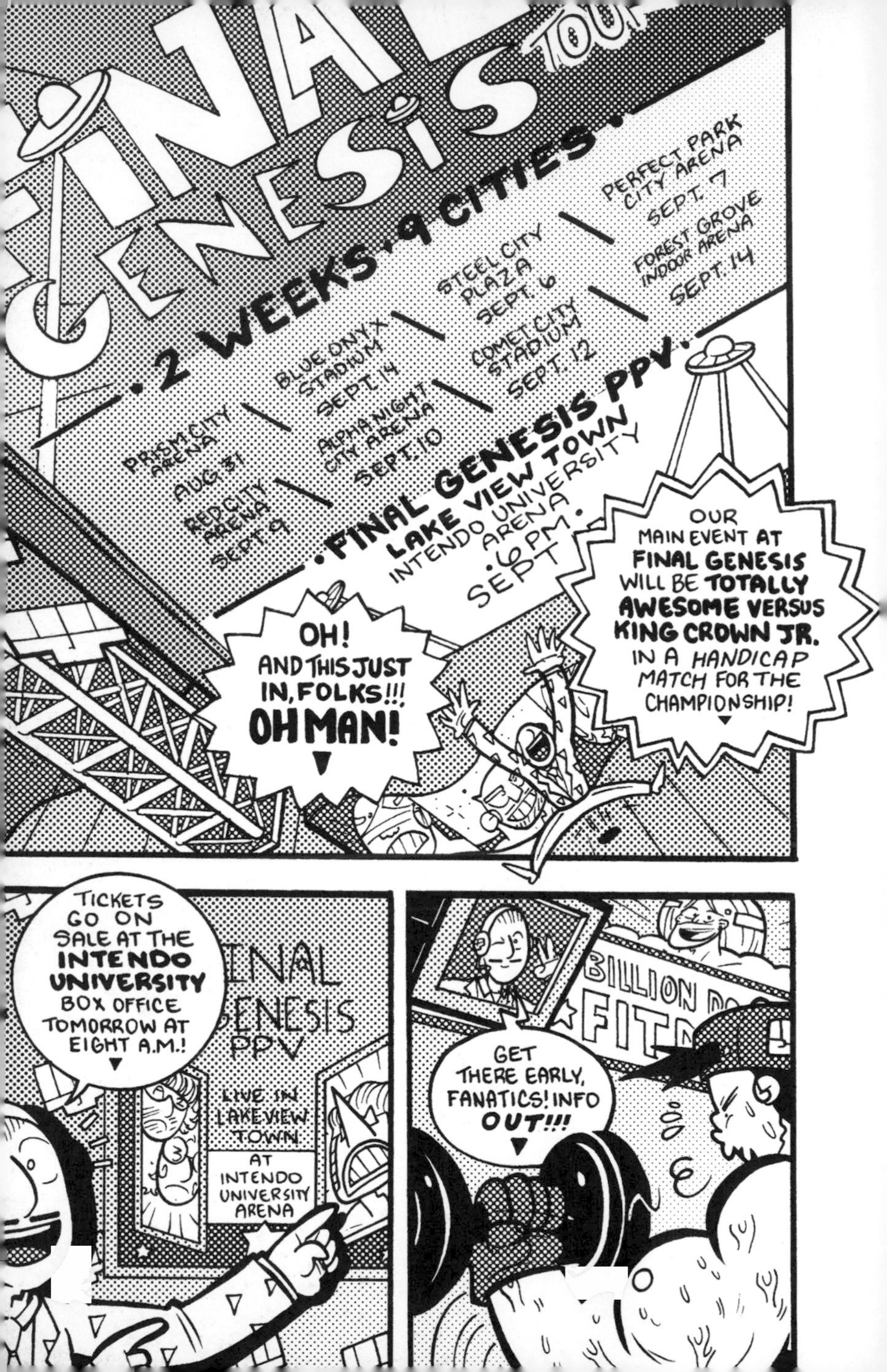
FINAL GENESIS TOUR
• 2 WEEKS • 9 CITIES •
PRISM CITY ARENA AUG. 31
RED CITY ARENA SEPT. 9
BLUE ONYX STADIUM SEPT. 14
ALPHA NIGHT CITY ARENA SEPT. 10
STEEL CITY PLAZA SEPT. 6
COMET CITY STADIUM SEPT. 12
PERFECT PARK CITY ARENA SEPT. 7
FOREST GROVE INDOOR ARENA SEPT. 14
• FINAL GENESIS PPV •
LAKE VIEW TOWN
INTENDO UNIVERSITY ARENA
• 6PM •
OH! AND THIS JUST IN, FOLKS!!! OH MAN!
OUR MAIN EVENT AT FINAL GENESIS WILL BE TOTALLY AWESOME VERSUS KING CROWN JR. IN A HANDICAP MATCH FOR THE CHAMPIONSHIP!
TICKETS GO ON SALE AT THE INTENDO UNIVERSITY BOX OFFICE TOMORROW AT EIGHT A.M.!
GENESIS PPV
LIVE IN LAKE VIEW TOWN
AT INTENDO UNIVERSITY ARENA
GET THERE EARLY, FANATICS! INFO OUT!!!

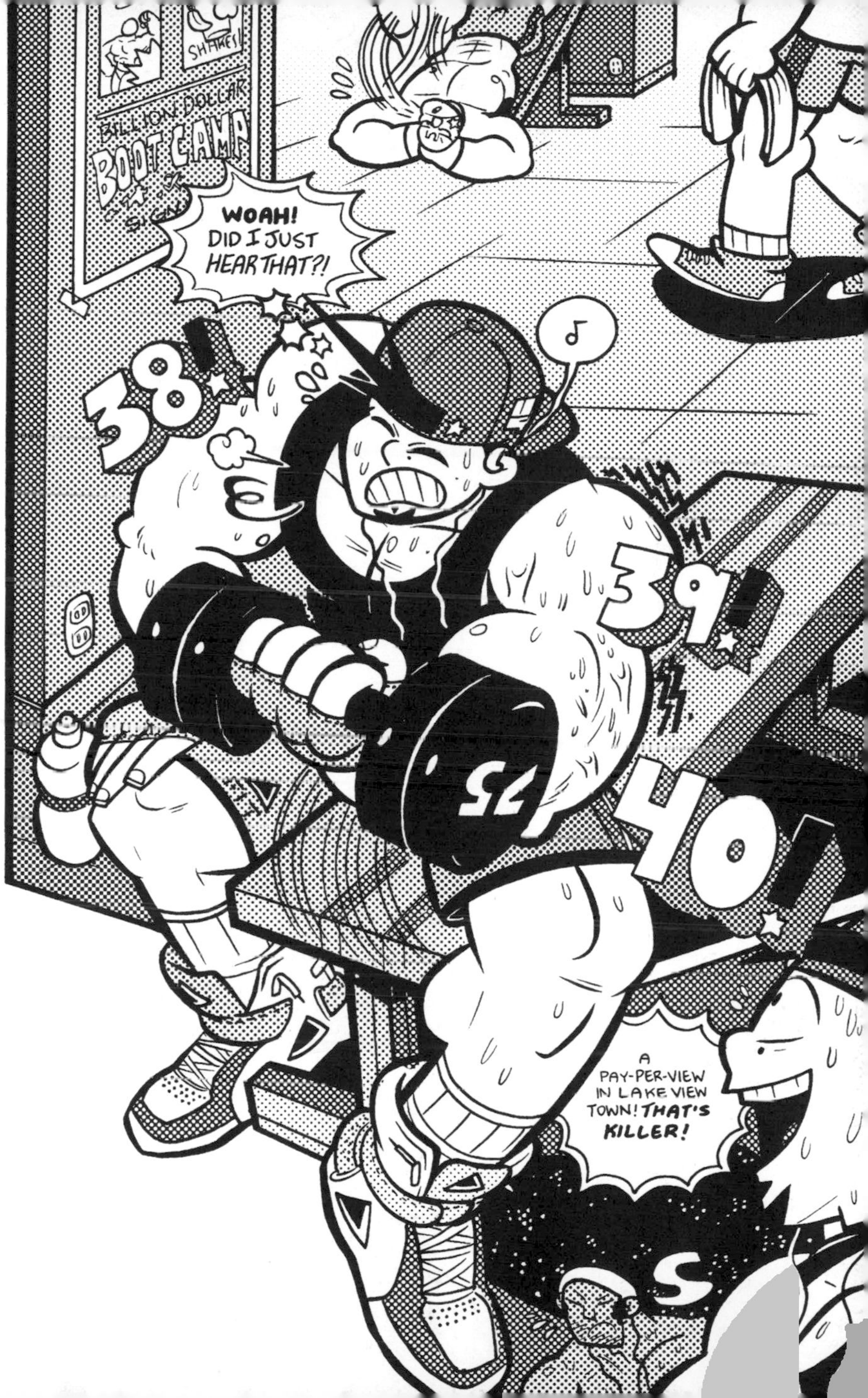
SHAKES!!
BILLION DOLLAR BOOT CAMP
WOAH! DID I JUST HEAR THAT?!
38!
39!
75
40!
A PAY-PER-VIEW IN LAKE VIEW TOWN! THAT'S KILLER!

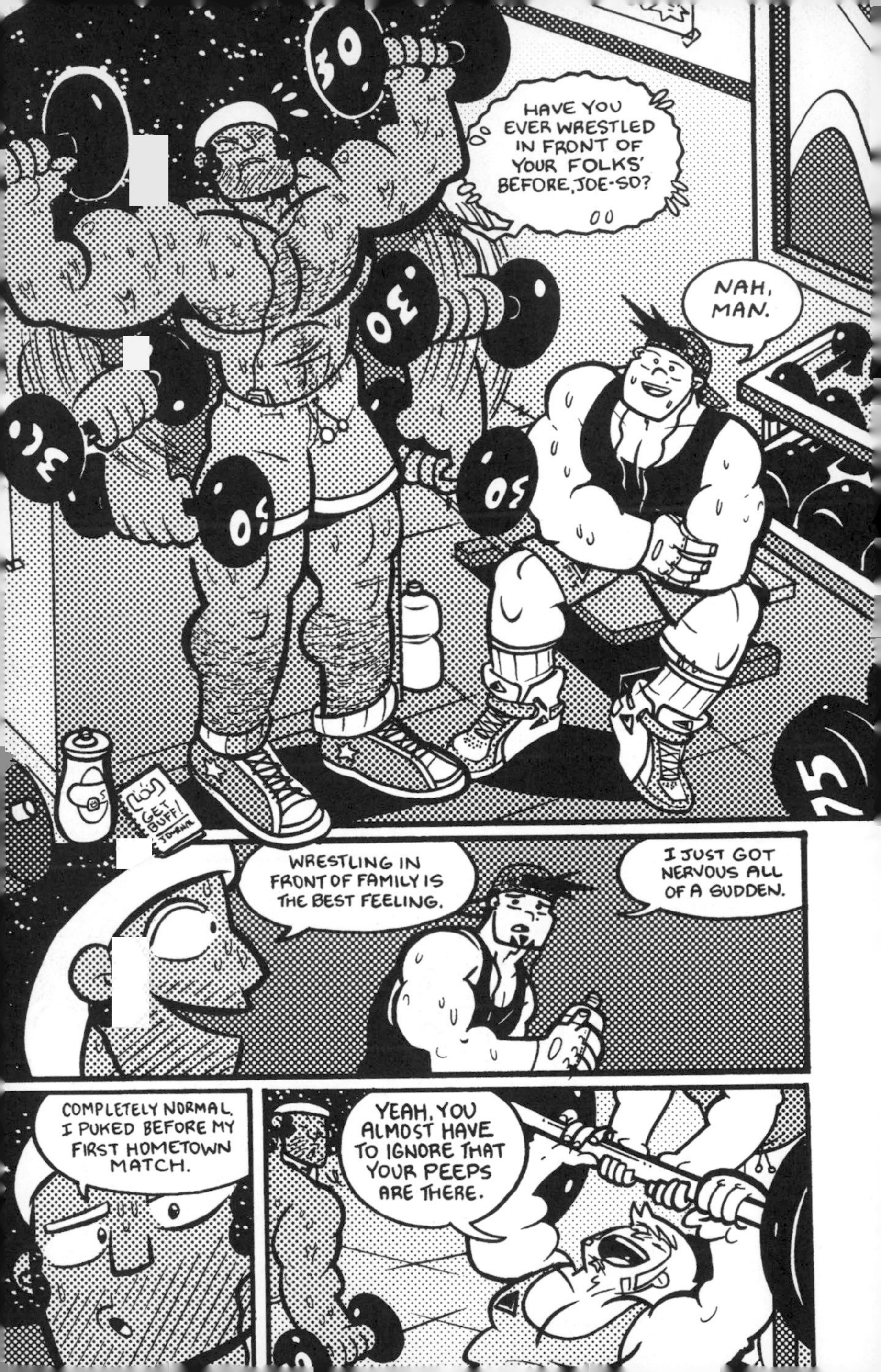
HAVE YOU EVER WRESTLED IN FRONT OF YOUR FOLKS' BEFORE, JOE-SO?
NAH, MAN.
GET BUFF!
WRESTLING IN FRONT OF FAMILY IS THE BEST FEELING.
I JUST GOT NERVOUS ALL OF A SUDDEN.
COMPLETELY NORMAL. I PUKED BEFORE MY FIRST HOMETOWN MATCH.
YEAH, YOU ALMOST HAVE TO IGNORE THAT YOUR PEEPS ARE THERE.

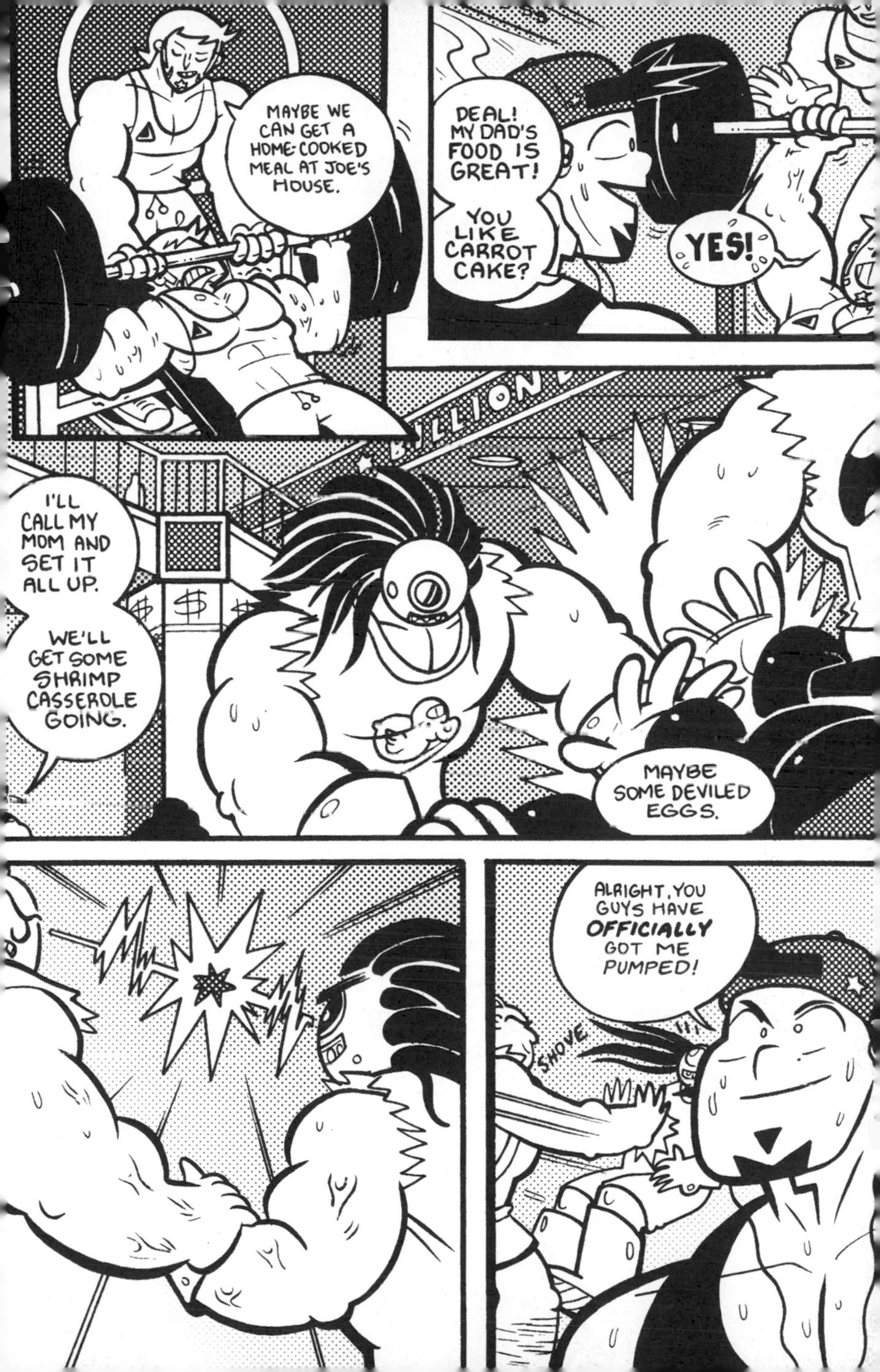
MAYBE WE CAN GET A HOME-COOKED MEAL AT JOE'S HOUSE.
DEAL! MY DAD'S FOOD IS GREAT!
YOU LIKE CARROT CAKE?
YES!
BILLION
I'LL CALL MY MOM AND SET IT ALL UP.
WE'LL GET SOME SHRIMP CASSEROLE GOING.
MAYBE SOME DEVILED EGGS.
ALRIGHT, YOU GUYS HAVE **OFFICIALLY** GOT ME PUMPED!
SHOVE

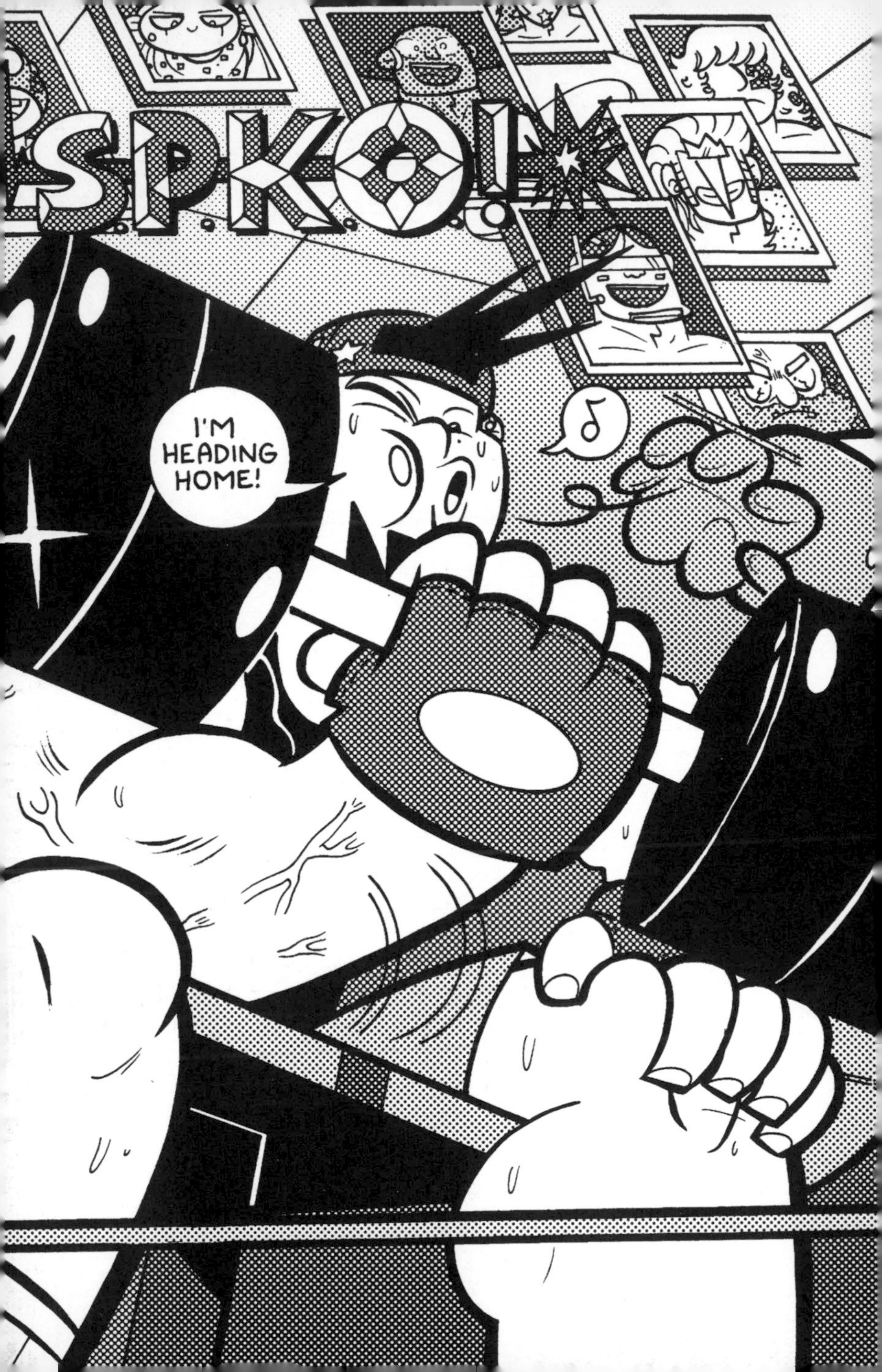
SPKO!
I'M HEADING HOME!

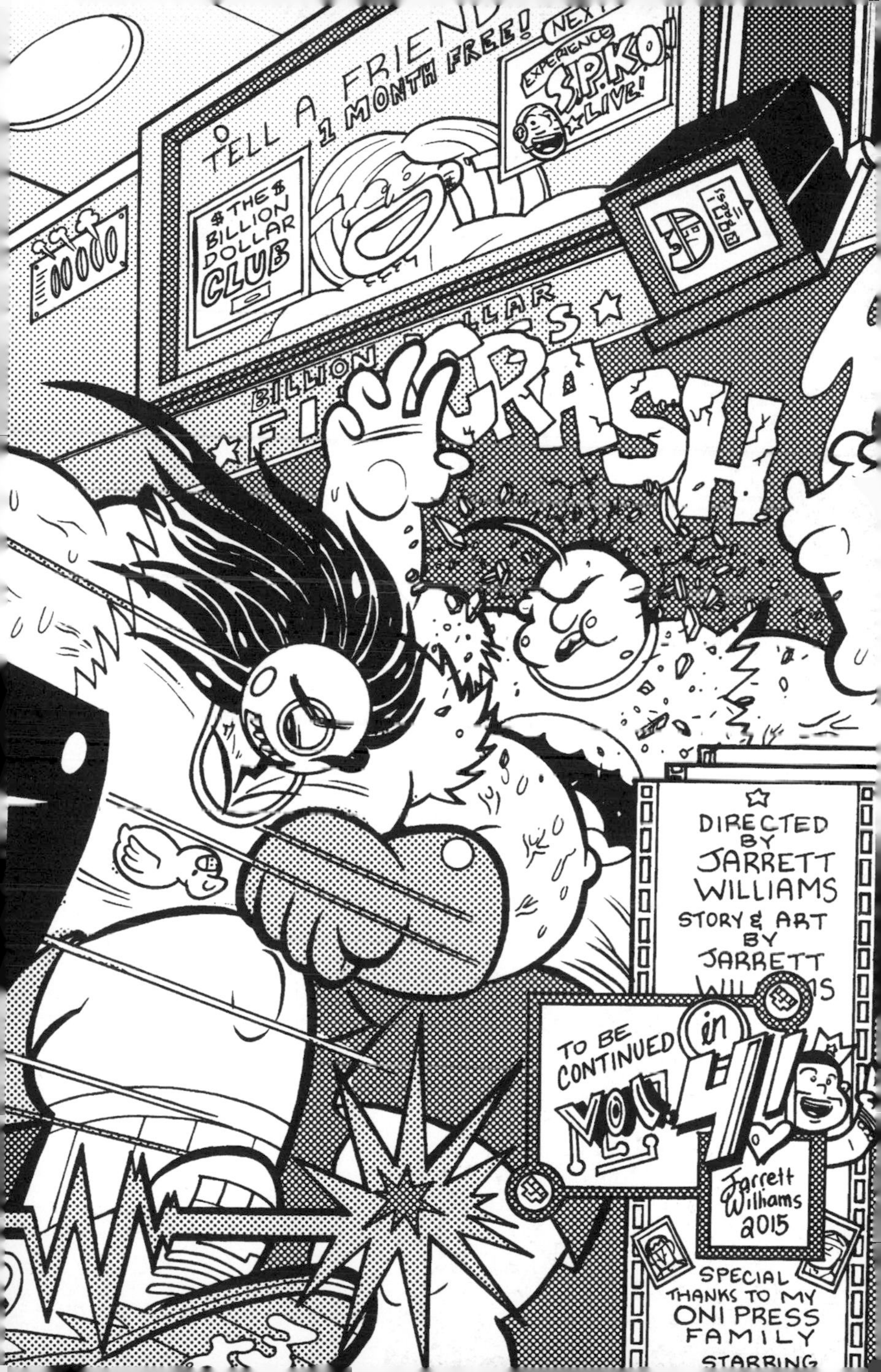
TELL A FRIEND
1 MONTH FREE!
NEXT
EXPERIENCE S.P.K.O.!! LIVE!
$ THE $ BILLION DOLLAR CLUB
BILLION DOLLAR
CRASH
DIRECTED BY JARRETT WILLIAMS
STORY & ART BY JARRETT WILLIAMS
TO BE CONTINUED in V.O.L. 4!
Jarrett Williams 2015
SPECIAL THANKS TO MY ONI PRESS FAMILY
STARRING

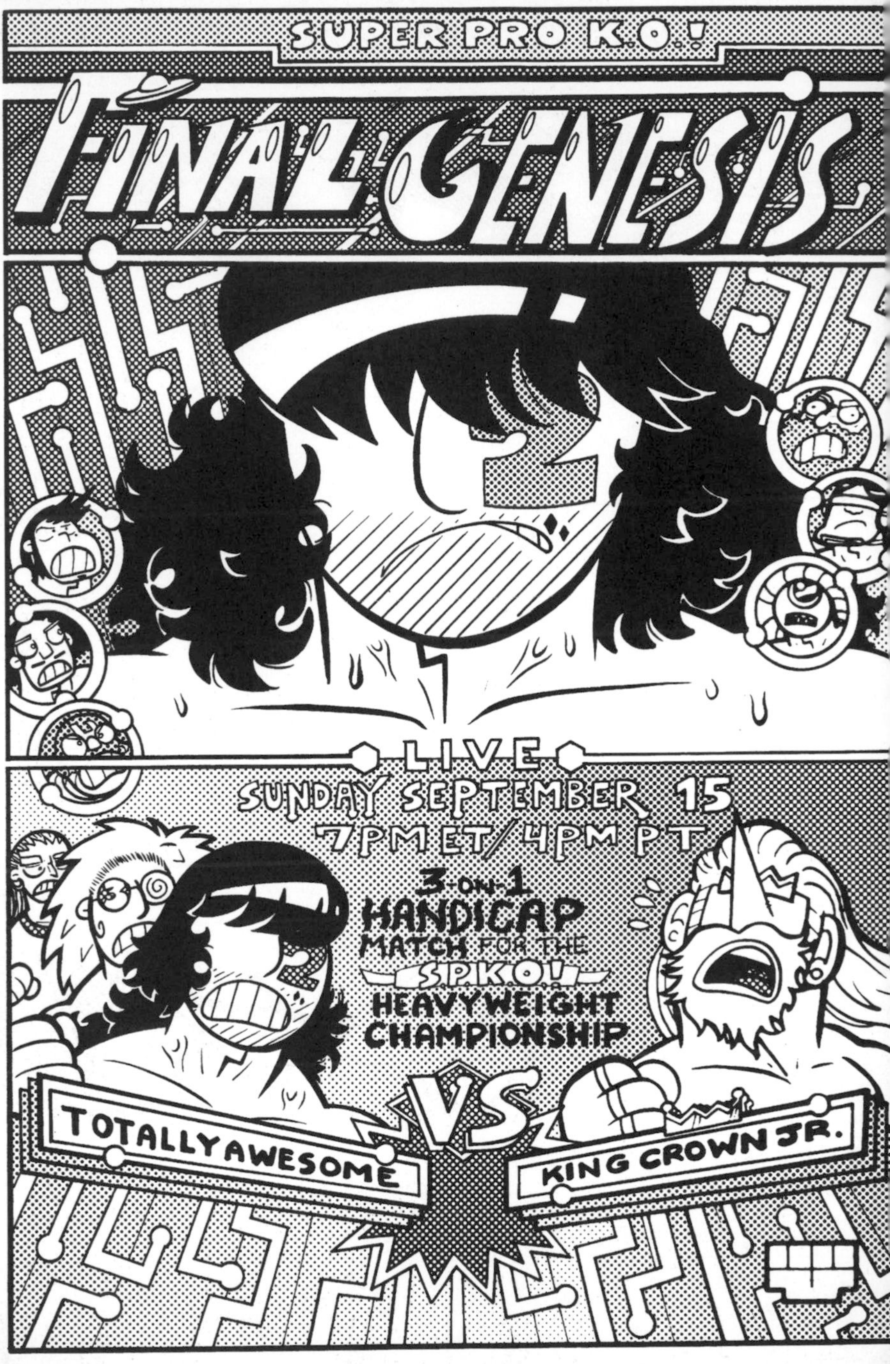
SUPER PRO K.O.!
FINAL GENESIS
LIVE
SUNDAY SEPTEMBER 15
7PM ET/4PM PT
3-ON-1
HANDICAP
MATCH FOR THE
S.P.K.O.!
HEAVYWEIGHT
CHAMPIONSHIP
TOTALLY AWESOME
VS
KING CROWN JR.

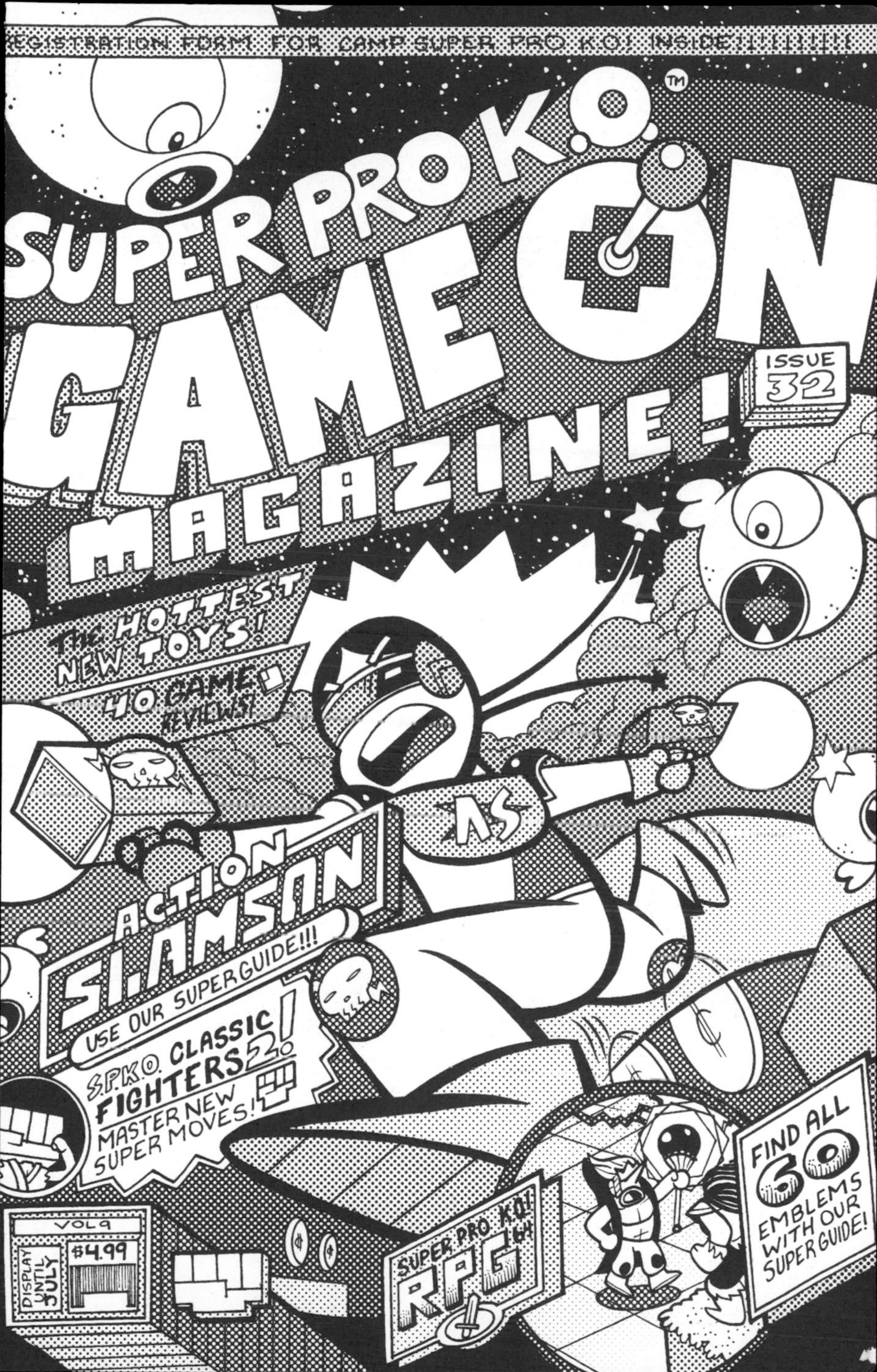

REGISTRATION FORM FOR CAMP SUPER PRO K.O! INSIDE!!!!!!!
SUPER PRO K.O.™
GAME ON MAGAZINE!
ISSUE 32
THE HOTTEST NEW TOYS!
40 GAME REVIEWS!
AS
ACTION SLAMSON
USE OUR SUPERGUIDE!!!
S.P.K.O. CLASSIC FIGHTERS 2!
MASTER NEW SUPER MOVES!
VOL 9
DISPLAY UNTIL JULY
$4.99
SUPER PRO K.O! RPG 64
FIND ALL 60 EMBLEMS WITH OUR SUPER GUIDE!

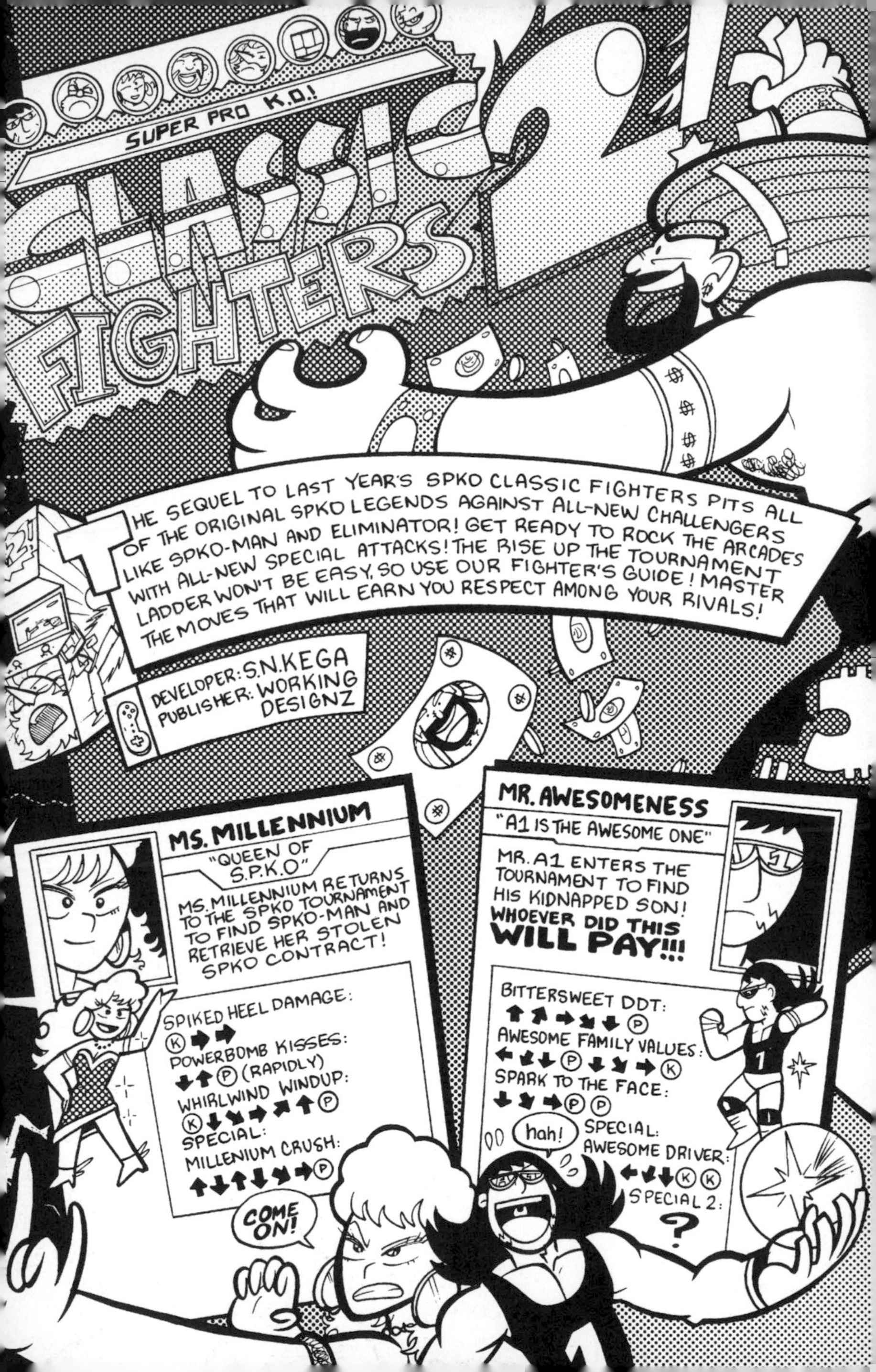
SUPER PRO K.O.!
CLASSIC FIGHTERS 2!
THE SEQUEL TO LAST YEAR'S SPKO CLASSIC FIGHTERS PITS ALL OF THE ORIGINAL SPKO LEGENDS AGAINST ALL-NEW CHALLENGERS LIKE SPKO-MAN AND ELIMINATOR! GET READY TO ROCK THE ARCADES WITH ALL-NEW SPECIAL ATTACKS! THE RISE UP THE TOURNAMENT LADDER WON'T BE EASY, SO USE OUR FIGHTER'S GUIDE! MASTER THE MOVES THAT WILL EARN YOU RESPECT AMONG YOUR RIVALS!
DEVELOPER: S.N.KEGA
PUBLISHER: WORKING DESIGNZ
MS. MILLENNIUM
"QUEEN OF S.P.K.O"
MS. MILLENNIUM RETURNS TO THE SPKO TOURNAMENT TO FIND SPKO-MAN AND RETRIEVE HER STOLEN SPKO CONTRACT!
SPIKED HEEL DAMAGE:
(K) → →
POWERBOMB KISSES:
↓ ↑ (P) (RAPIDLY)
WHIRLWIND WINDUP:
(K) ↓ ↘ → ↗ ↑ (P)
SPECIAL:
MILLENIUM CRUSH:
↑ ↓ ↑ ↓ ↘ → (P)
MR. AWESOMENESS
"A1 IS THE AWESOME ONE"
MR. A1 ENTERS THE TOURNAMENT TO FIND HIS KIDNAPPED SON! WHOEVER DID THIS WILL PAY!!!
BITTERSWEET DDT:
↑ ↗ → ↘ ↓ (P)
AWESOME FAMILY VALUES:
← ↙ ↓ (P) ↓ ↘ → (K)
SPARK TO THE FACE:
↓ ↘ → (P) (P)
SPECIAL:
AWESOME DRIVER:
← ↙ ↓ (K) (K)
SPECIAL 2:
?
hah!
COME ON!

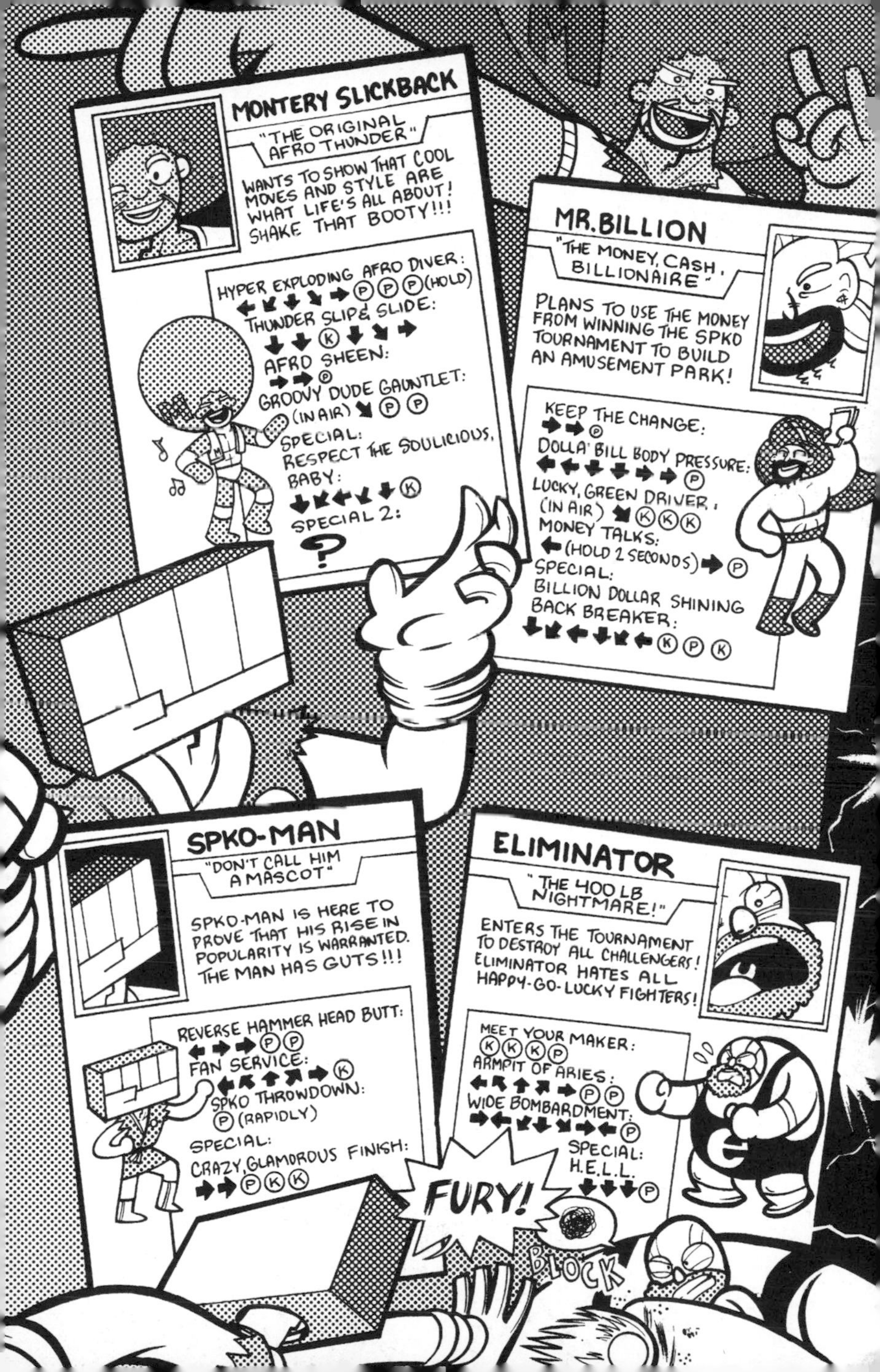
MONTERY SLICKBACK
"THE ORIGINAL AFRO THUNDER"
WANTS TO SHOW THAT COOL MOVES AND STYLE ARE WHAT LIFE'S ALL ABOUT! SHAKE THAT BOOTY!!!
HYPER EXPLODING AFRO DIVER:
(P)(P)(P)(HOLD)
THUNDER SLIP & SLIDE:
(K)
AFRO SHEEN:
(P)
GROOVY DUDE GAUNTLET:
(IN AIR) (P)(P)
SPECIAL:
RESPECT THE SOULICIOUS, BABY:
(K)
SPECIAL 2:
?
MR. BILLION
"THE MONEY, CASH, BILLIONAIRE"
PLANS TO USE THE MONEY FROM WINNING THE SPKO TOURNAMENT TO BUILD AN AMUSEMENT PARK!
KEEP THE CHANGE:
(P)
DOLLA' BILL BODY PRESSURE:
(P)
LUCKY, GREEN DRIVER:
(IN AIR) (K)(K)(K)
MONEY TALKS:
(HOLD 2 SECONDS) (P)
SPECIAL:
BILLION DOLLAR SHINING BACK BREAKER:
(K)(P)(K)
SPKO-MAN
"DON'T CALL HIM A MASCOT"
SPKO-MAN IS HERE TO PROVE THAT HIS RISE IN POPULARITY IS WARRANTED. THE MAN HAS GUTS!!!
REVERSE HAMMER HEAD BUTT:
(P)(P)
FAN SERVICE:
(K)
SPKO THROWDOWN:
(P) (RAPIDLY)
SPECIAL:
CRAZY, GLAMOROUS FINISH:
(P)(K)(K)
ELIMINATOR
"THE 400 LB NIGHTMARE!"
ENTERS THE TOURNAMENT TO DESTROY ALL CHALLENGERS! ELIMINATOR HATES ALL HAPPY-GO-LUCKY FIGHTERS!
MEET YOUR MAKER:
(K)(K)(K)(P)
ARMPIT OF ARIES:
(P)(P)
WIDE BOMBARDMENT:
(P)
SPECIAL:
H.E.L.L.
(P)
FURY!
BLOCK

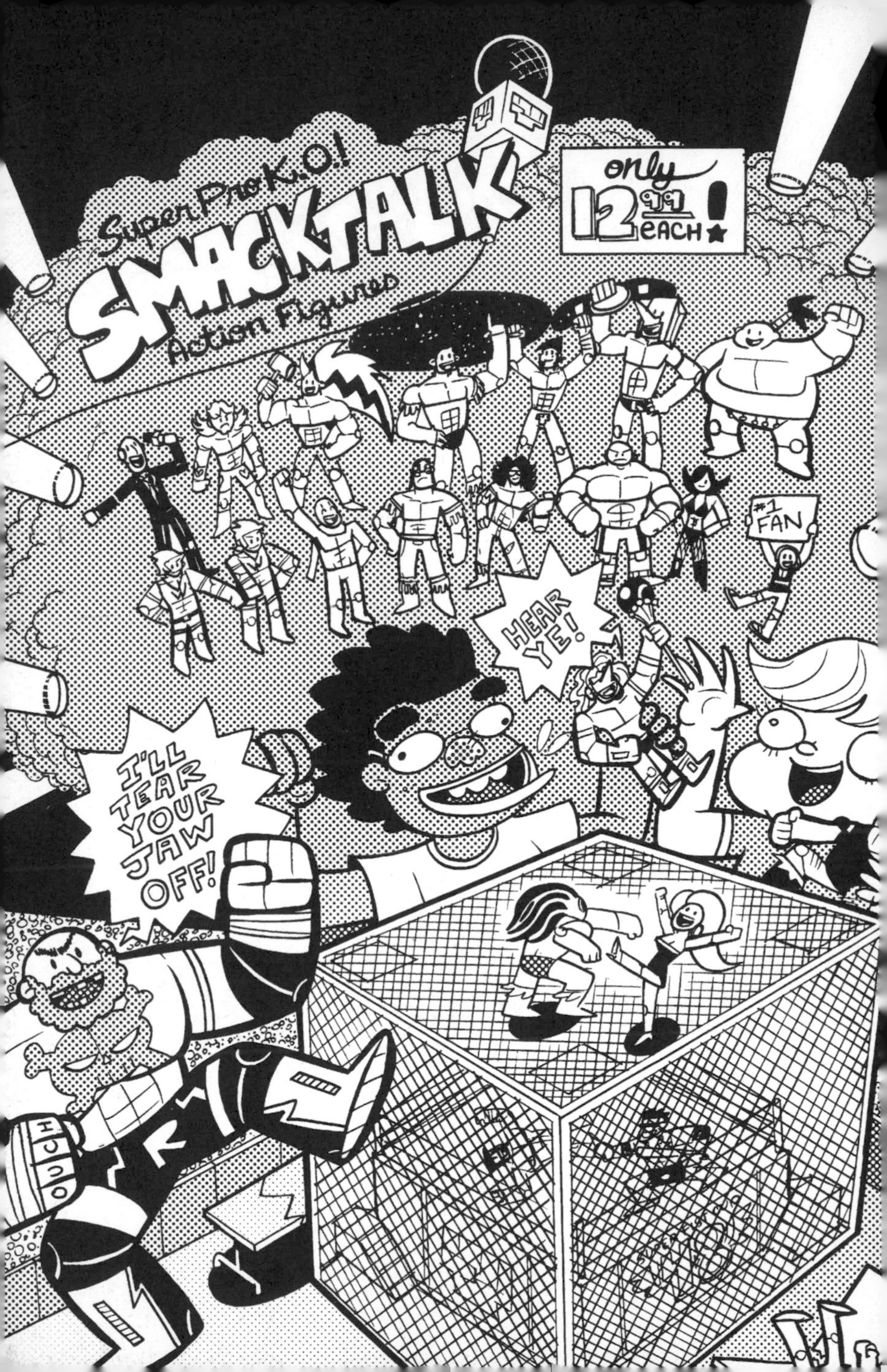

Super Pro K.O.!
SMACKTALK
Action Figures
only 12.99 EACH!
#1 FAN
HEAR YE!
I'LL TEAR YOUR JAW OFF!
OUCH

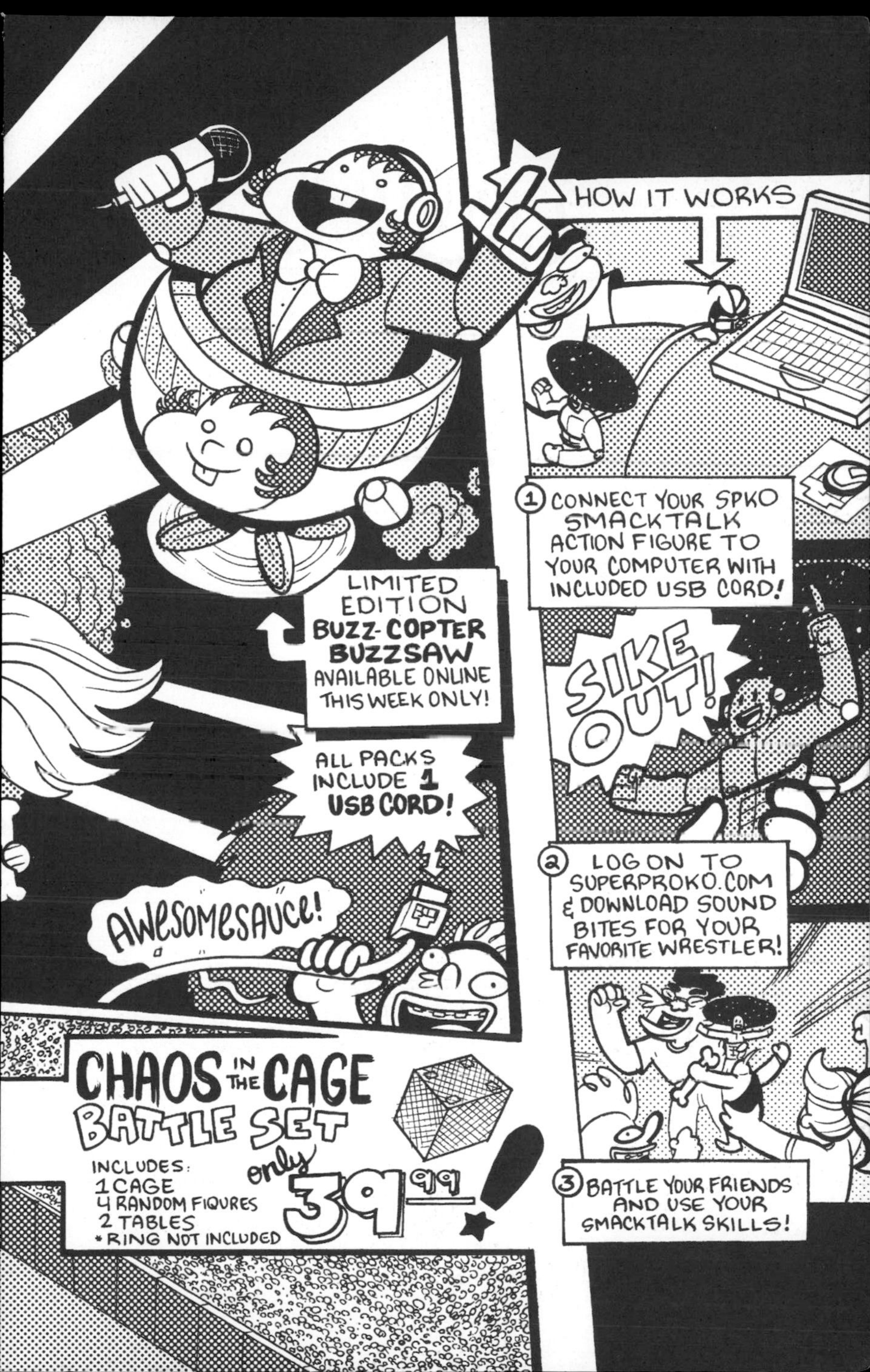
LIMITED EDITION BUZZ-COPTER BUZZSAW AVAILABLE ONLINE THIS WEEK ONLY!
ALL PACKS INCLUDE 1 USB CORD!
AWESOMESAUCE!
CHAOS IN THE CAGE BATTLE SET
INCLUDES:
1 CAGE
4 RANDOM FIGURES
2 TABLES
* RING NOT INCLUDED
only 39.99!
HOW IT WORKS
1 CONNECT YOUR SPKO SMACKTALK ACTION FIGURE TO YOUR COMPUTER WITH INCLUDED USB CORD!
SIKE OUT!
2 LOG ON TO SUPERPROKO.COM & DOWNLOAD SOUND BITES FOR YOUR FAVORITE WRESTLER!
3 BATTLE YOUR FRIENDS AND USE YOUR SMACKTALK SKILLS!

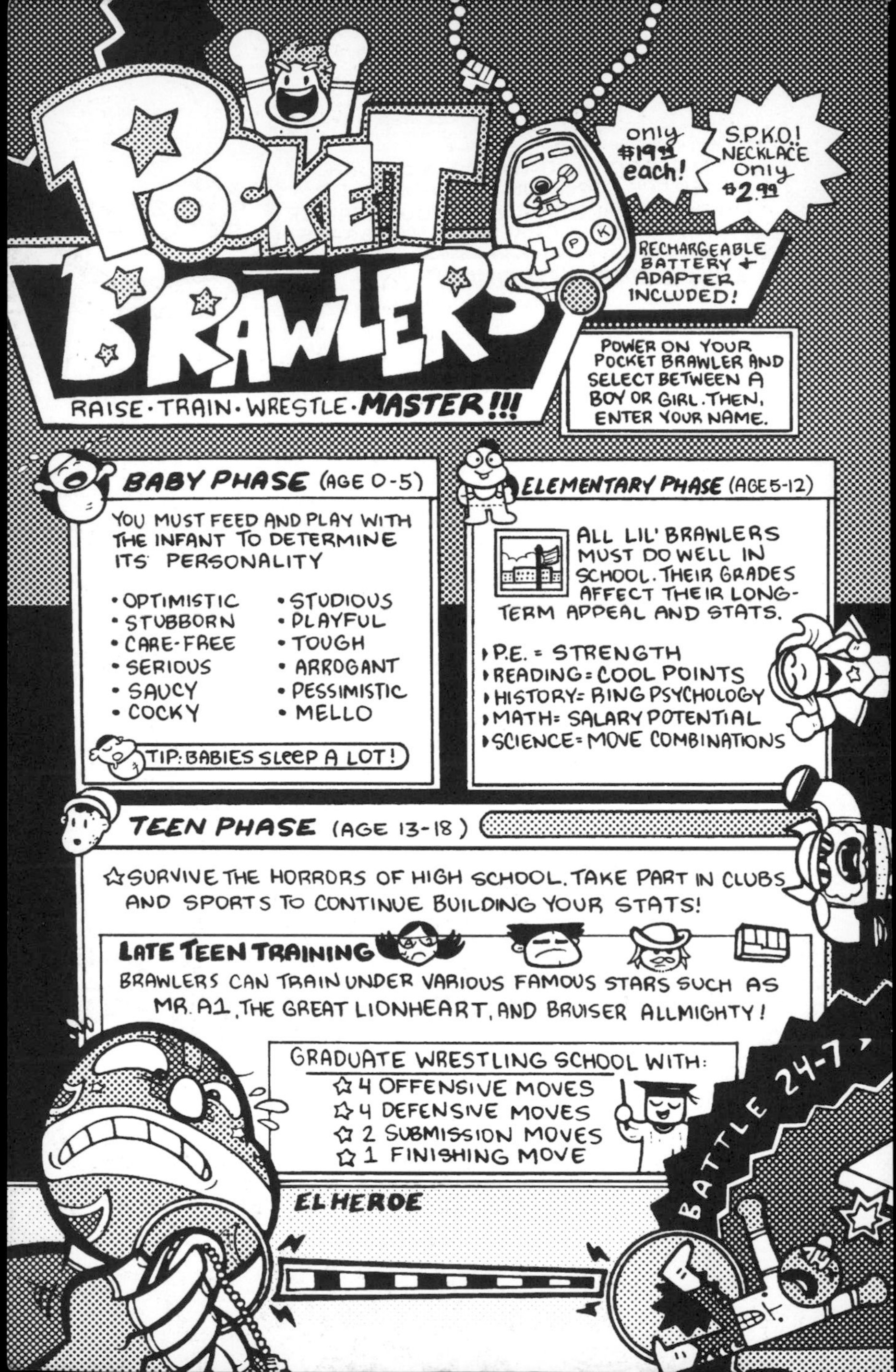
POCKET BRAWLERS
RAISE · TRAIN · WRESTLE · MASTER!!!
only $19.99 each!
S.P.K.O.! NECKLACE Only $2.99
P K
RECHARGEABLE BATTERY + ADAPTER INCLUDED!
POWER ON YOUR POCKET BRAWLER AND SELECT BETWEEN A BOY OR GIRL. THEN, ENTER YOUR NAME.
BABY PHASE (AGE 0-5)
YOU MUST FEED AND PLAY WITH THE INFANT TO DETERMINE ITS PERSONALITY
• OPTIMISTIC • STUBBORN • CARE-FREE • SERIOUS • SAUCY • COCKY
• STUDIOUS • PLAYFUL • TOUGH • ARROGANT • PESSIMISTIC • MELLO
TIP: BABIES SLEEP A LOT!
ELEMENTARY PHASE (AGE 5-12)
ALL LIL' BRAWLERS MUST DO WELL IN SCHOOL. THEIR GRADES AFFECT THEIR LONG-TERM APPEAL AND STATS.
P.E. = STRENGTH
READING = COOL POINTS
HISTORY = RING PSYCHOLOGY
MATH = SALARY POTENTIAL
SCIENCE = MOVE COMBINATIONS
TEEN PHASE (AGE 13-18)
SURVIVE THE HORRORS OF HIGH SCHOOL. TAKE PART IN CLUBS AND SPORTS TO CONTINUE BUILDING YOUR STATS!
LATE TEEN TRAINING
BRAWLERS CAN TRAIN UNDER VARIOUS FAMOUS STARS SUCH AS MR. A1, THE GREAT LIONHEART, AND BRUISER ALLMIGHTY!
GRADUATE WRESTLING SCHOOL WITH:
4 OFFENSIVE MOVES
4 DEFENSIVE MOVES
2 SUBMISSION MOVES
1 FINISHING MOVE
BATTLE 24-7
EL HEROE

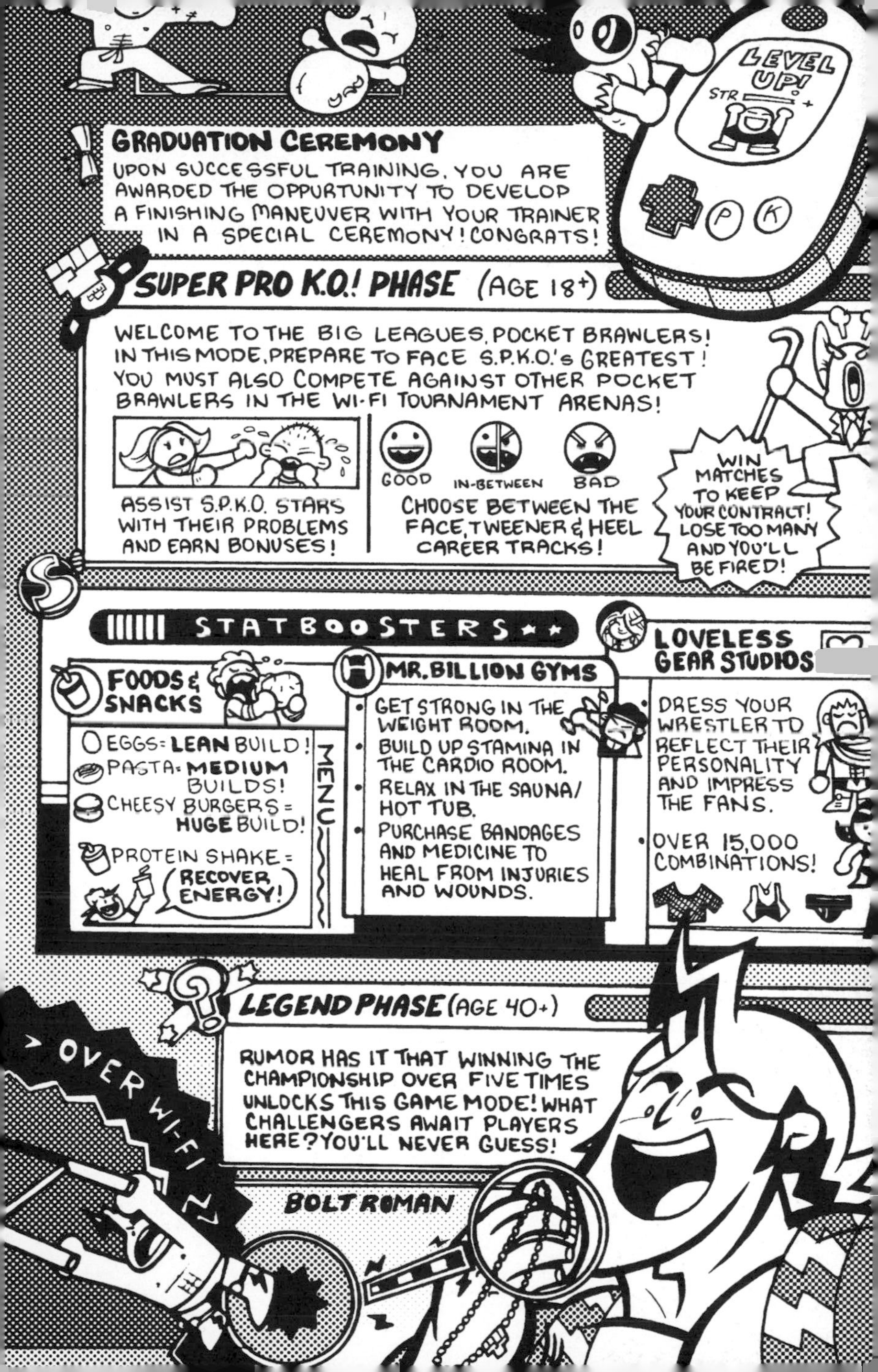

LEVEL UP!
STR
GRADUATION CEREMONY
UPON SUCCESSFUL TRAINING, YOU ARE AWARDED THE OPPURTUNITY TO DEVELOP A FINISHING MANEUVER WITH YOUR TRAINER IN A SPECIAL CEREMONY! CONGRATS!
P
K
SUPER PRO K.O.! PHASE (AGE 18+)
WELCOME TO THE BIG LEAGUES, POCKET BRAWLERS! IN THIS MODE, PREPARE TO FACE S.P.K.O.'s GREATEST! YOU MUST ALSO COMPETE AGAINST OTHER POCKET BRAWLERS IN THE WI-FI TOURNAMENT ARENAS!
ASSIST S.P.K.O. STARS WITH THEIR PROBLEMS AND EARN BONUSES!
GOOD
IN-BETWEEN
BAD
CHOOSE BETWEEN THE FACE, TWEENER & HEEL CAREER TRACKS!
WIN MATCHES TO KEEP YOUR CONTRACT! LOSE TOO MANY AND YOU'LL BE FIRED!
STATBOOSTERS
FOODS & SNACKS
EGGS = LEAN BUILD!
PASTA = MEDIUM BUILDS!
CHEESY BURGERS = HUGE BUILD!
PROTEIN SHAKE =
RECOVER ENERGY!
MENU
MR. BILLION GYMS
GET STRONG IN THE WEIGHT ROOM.
BUILD UP STAMINA IN THE CARDIO ROOM.
RELAX IN THE SAUNA/ HOT TUB.
PURCHASE BANDAGES AND MEDICINE TO HEAL FROM INJURIES AND WOUNDS.
LOVELESS GEAR STUDIOS
DRESS YOUR WRESTLER TO REFLECT THEIR PERSONALITY AND IMPRESS THE FANS.
OVER 15,000 COMBINATIONS!
LEGEND PHASE (AGE 40+)
RUMOR HAS IT THAT WINNING THE CHAMPIONSHIP OVER FIVE TIMES UNLOCKS THIS GAME MODE! WHAT CHALLENGERS AWAIT PLAYERS HERE? YOU'LL NEVER GUESS!
OVER WI-FI
BOLT ROMAN

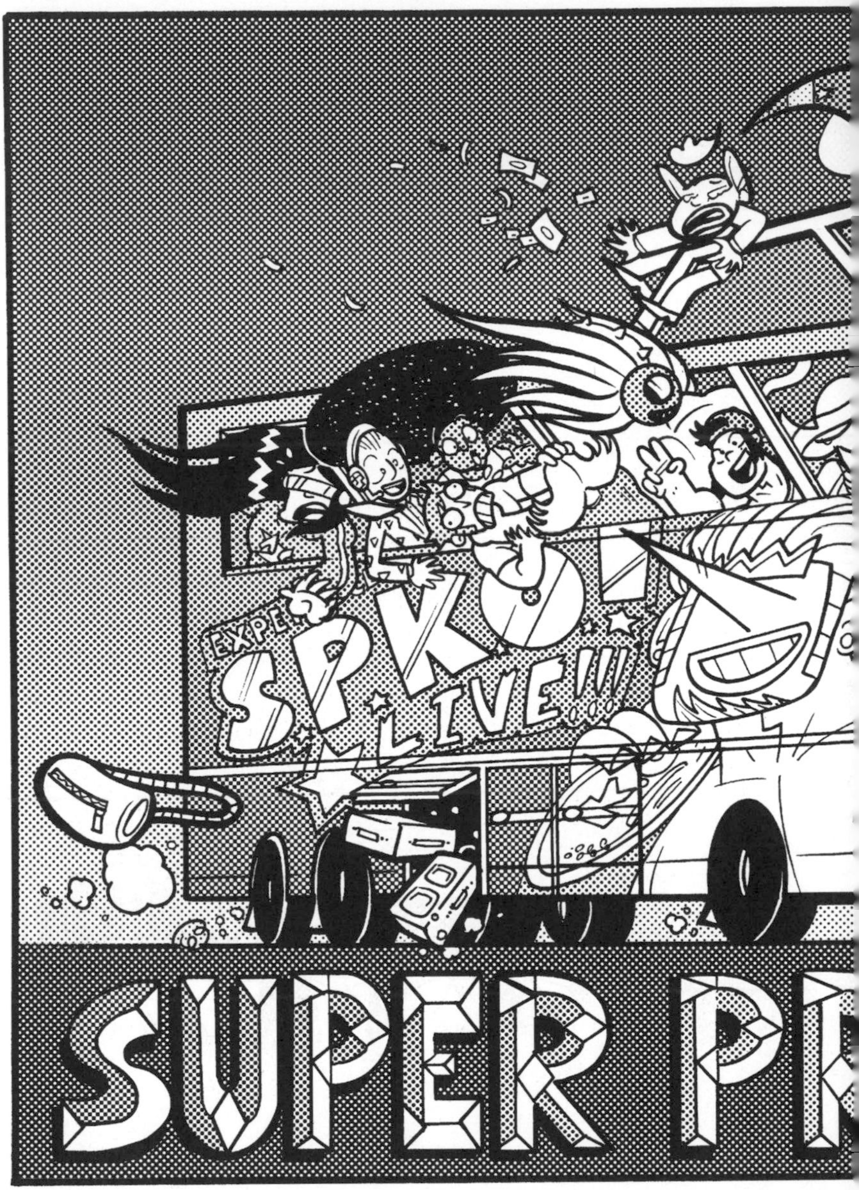
EXPE
SPK
LIVE!!!
SUPER PR

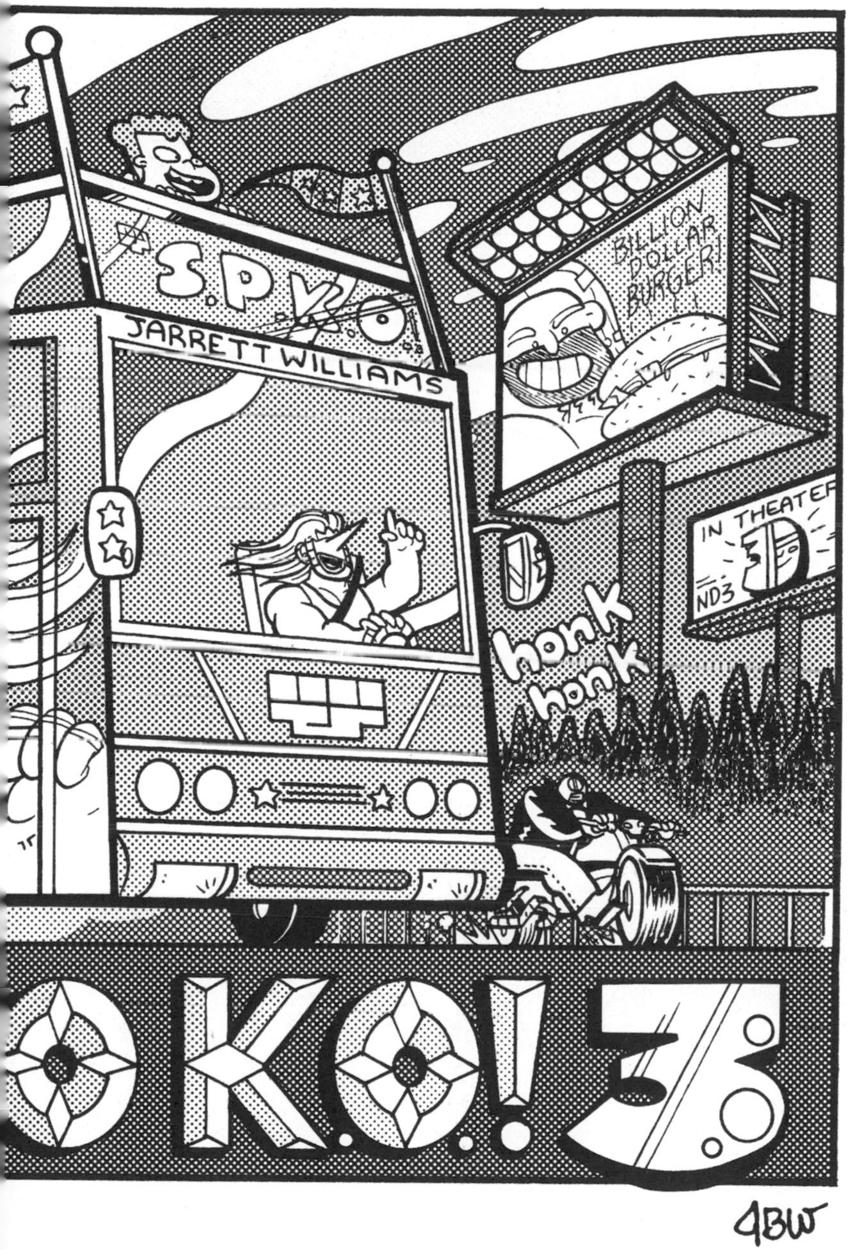
S.P.
JARRETT WILLIAMS
BILLION DOLLAR BURGER!
IN THEATER
ND3
honk honk
K.O.!
JBW

Published by

Oni Press, Inc.

publisher **Joe Nozemack** ★ editor in chief **James Lucas Jones**

v.p. of marketing & sales **Andrew McIntire** ★ director of sales **Cheyenne Allott**

publicity coordinator **Rachel Reed** ★ director of design & production **Troy Look**

graphic designer **Hilary Thompson** ★ digital art technician **Jared Jones**

managing editor **Ari Yarwood** ★ senior editor **Charlie Chu**

editor **Robin Herrera** ★ editorial assistant **Bess Pallares**

director of logistics **Brad Rooks** ★ logistics associate **Jung Lee**

superproko.squarespace.com ★ @jarrettwilliams

onipress.com ★ facebook.com/onipress ★ twitter.com/onipress
onipress.tumblr.com ★ instagram.com/onipress

This is the third story in the *Super Pro K.O.!* series!

ONI PRESS, INC.
1305 SE Martin Luther King Jr. Blvd.
Suite A
Portland, OR 97214
USA

First edition: June 2016

ISBN: 978-1-934964-97-2 ★ eISBN: 978-1-62010-040-0

Library of Congress Control Number: 2015959949

1 3 5 7 9 10 8 6 4 2

Printed in China.

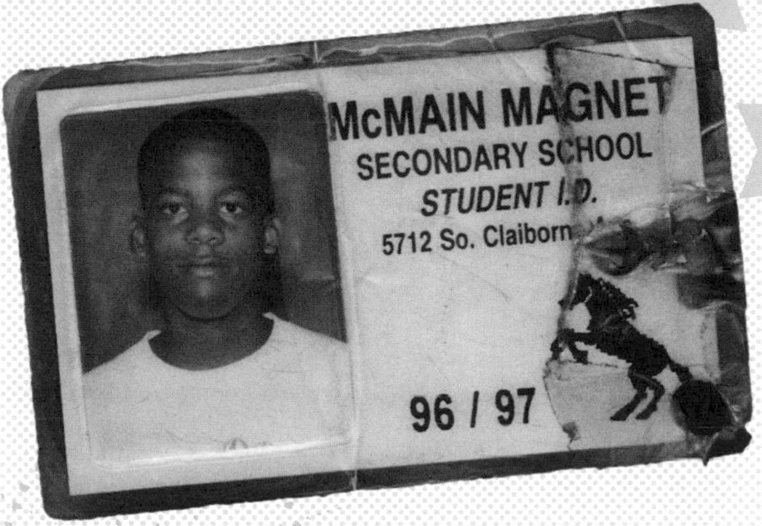
McMAIN MAGNET
SECONDARY SCHOOL
STUDENT I.D.
5712 So. Claiborn
96 / 97

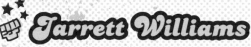

Jarrett Williams

was born in 1984 in New Orleans, Louisiana, where he was cornfed comics and all sorts of retro vibes. He spends his nights drawing and dancing all over the place. He currently resides in Savannah, Georgia, where he feels pretty good about life and what's up ahead.

superproko.squarespace.com / @jarrettwilliams

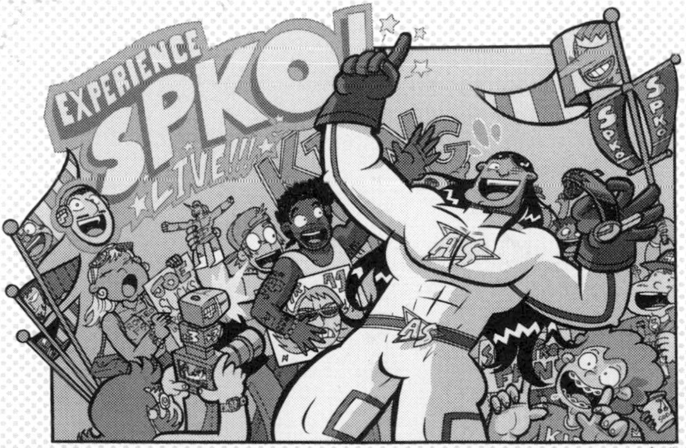
EXPERIENCE
SPKO!
LIVE!!!
SPKO
SPKO

Available Now!

Joe Somiano is late to his first match in Super Pro K.O., and has no clue what awaits him in the rowdy ring! A seasoned sumo wrestler, a jolly luchador, a flamboyant tag team, suspicious executives, and a drunken Heavyweight Champion all stand between him and the superstardom that is his destiny. If the huge egos, clothesline take-downs, and broken chairs across the head don't squash Joe's dreams, he may just come out on top. But if he's going to take home the champion's belt, he'll need to bring his best moves against the likes of S.P.K.O.! stars Tomahawk Slamson, Yoko No-No, Mr. Awesomeness 2, and many more in this grand slamma jamma event of a graphic novel!

. . . .

SUPER PRO K.O.
VOLUME ONE
By Jarrett Williams
256 pages, softcover, black and white interiors
$11.99 US
ISBN 978-1-934964-41-5

. . . .

IT'S TIME FOR THE MAIN EVENT! Be stupefied as King Crown Jr., Tomahawk Slamson, The Other, and the high-flying El Heroe face off in the STEEL CAGE! But where's Joe Somiano?! Didn't he set the world on fire with his ferocious tenacity and heart?!?! Not really. He's backstage like a chump, trying to figure out how to win the S.P.K.O. fans over. WHAT A LOSER! But wait! Who is Romeo Colossus?! Does that ex-baseball superstar really think he can just waltz into Super Pro K.O. and be the ultimate wrestling champion?!? Not if Joe can help it! Find out who goes the distance in this second volume of the high-flying, kick-dropping, piledriving, high-octane wrestling series, SUPER PRO K.O.!

. . . .

SUPER PRO K.O.
VOLUME TWO: CHAOS IN THE CAGE
By Jarrett Williams
176 pages, softcover, black and white interiors
$11.99 US
ISBN 978-1-934964-51-4

. . . .

For more information on these and other fine Oni Press comic books and graphic novels, visit www.onipress.com. To find a comic specialty store in your area, call 1-888-COMICBOOK or visit www.comicshops.us.